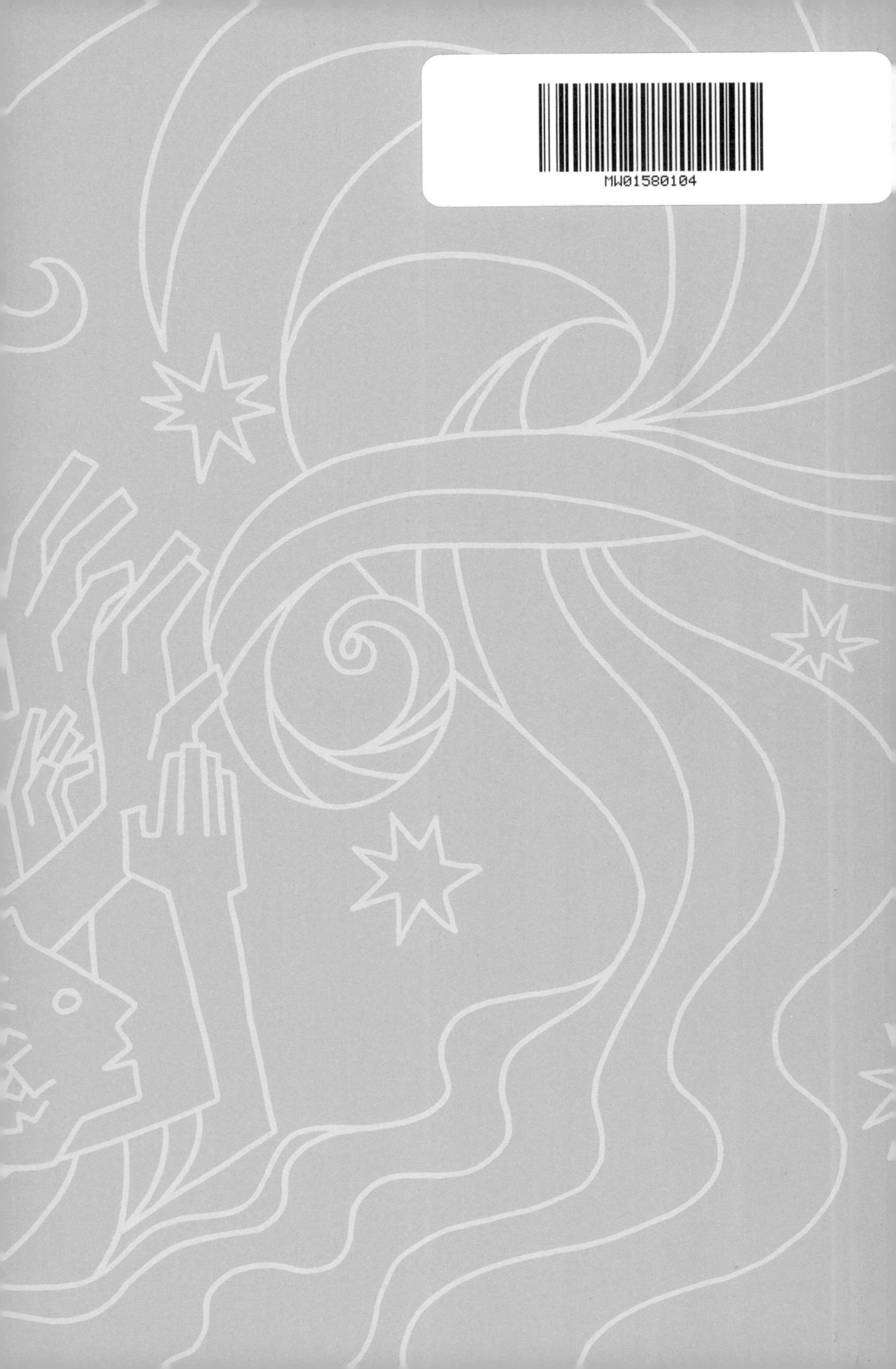

AMY KIM

THE REMA CHRONICLES

BOOK TWO

KINGDOM OF WATER

graphix
AN IMPRINT OF
SCHOLASTIC

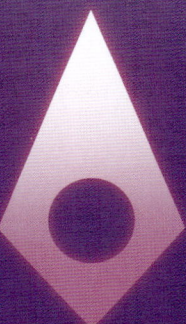

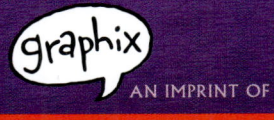

Copyright © 2025 by Amy Kim

All rights reserved. Published by Graphix, an imprint of Scholastic Inc., *Publishers since 1920*. SCHOLASTIC, GRAPHIX, and associated logos are trademarks and/or registered trademarks of Scholastic Inc.

The publisher does not have any control over and does not assume any responsibility for author or third-party websites or their content.

No part of this publication may be reproduced, stored in a retrieval system, or transmitted in any form or by any means, electronic, mechanical, photocopying, recording, or otherwise, or used to train any artificial intelligence technologies, without written permission of the publisher. For information regarding permission, write to Scholastic Inc., Attention: Permissions Department, 557 Broadway, New York, NY 10012.

This book is a work of fiction. Names, characters, places, and incidents are either the product of the author's imagination or are used fictitiously, and any resemblance to actual persons, living or dead, business establishments, events, or locales is entirely coincidental.

Library of Congress Control Number: 2024941464

ISBN 978-1-338-11518-5 (hardcover)
ISBN 978-1-338-11517-8 (paperback)

10 9 8 7 6 5 4 3 2 1   25 26 27 28 29

Printed in China   62
First edition, August 2025

Edited by Cassandra Pelham Fulton
Creative Director: Phil Falco
Publisher: David Saylor

PART I
THE LETTER

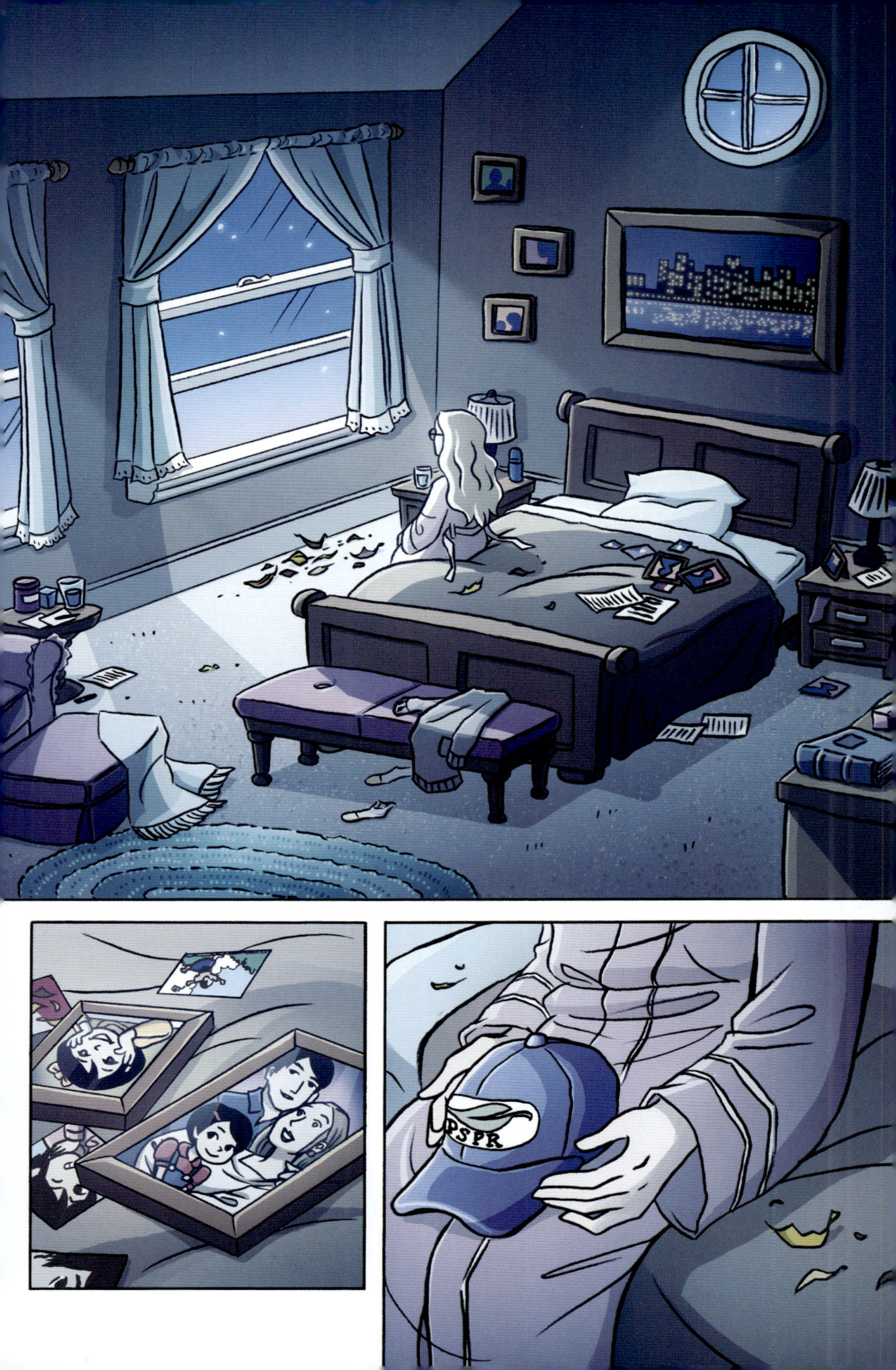
PSPR

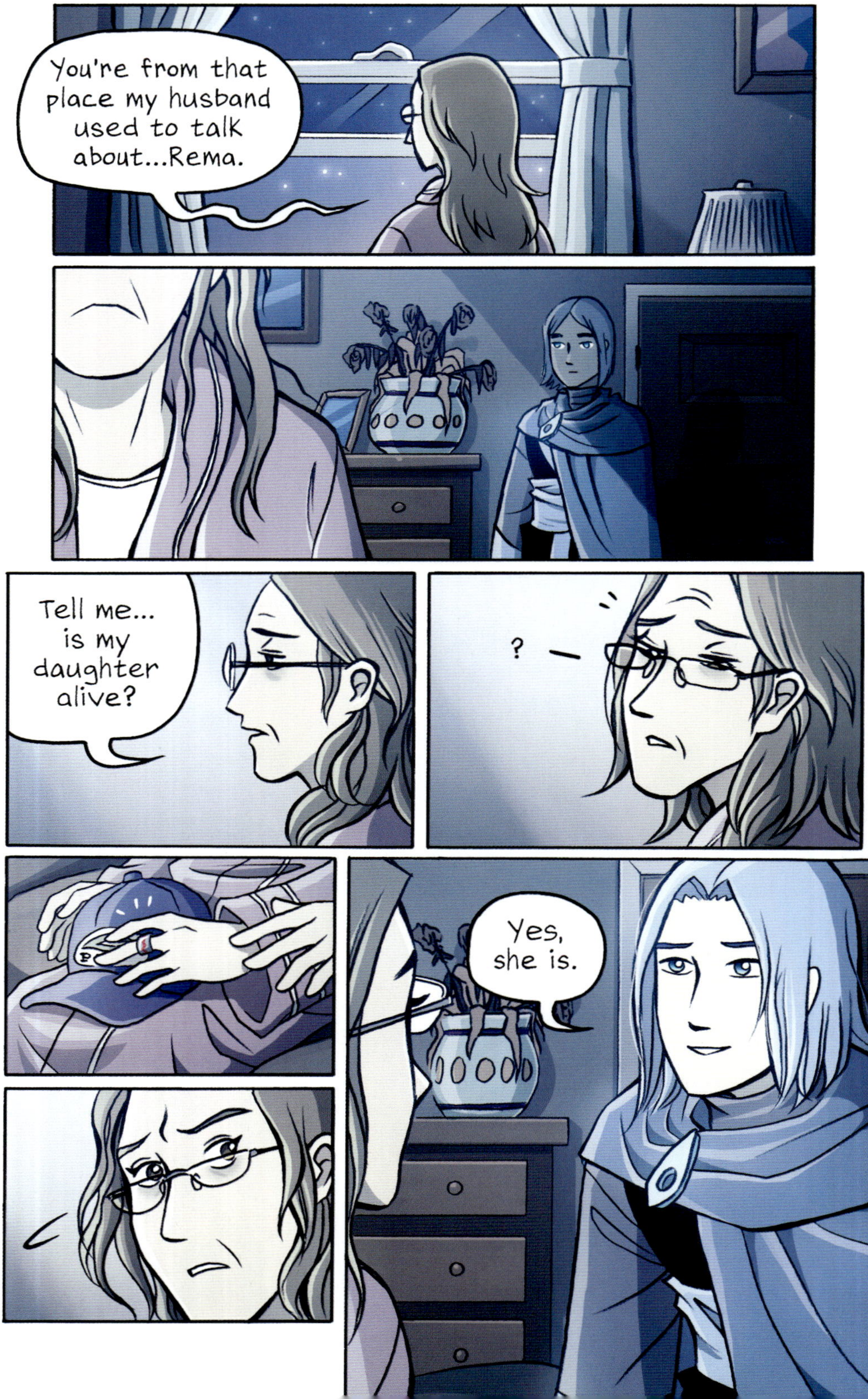
You're from that place my husband used to talk about...Rema.
Tell me... is my daughter alive?
?
Yes, she is.

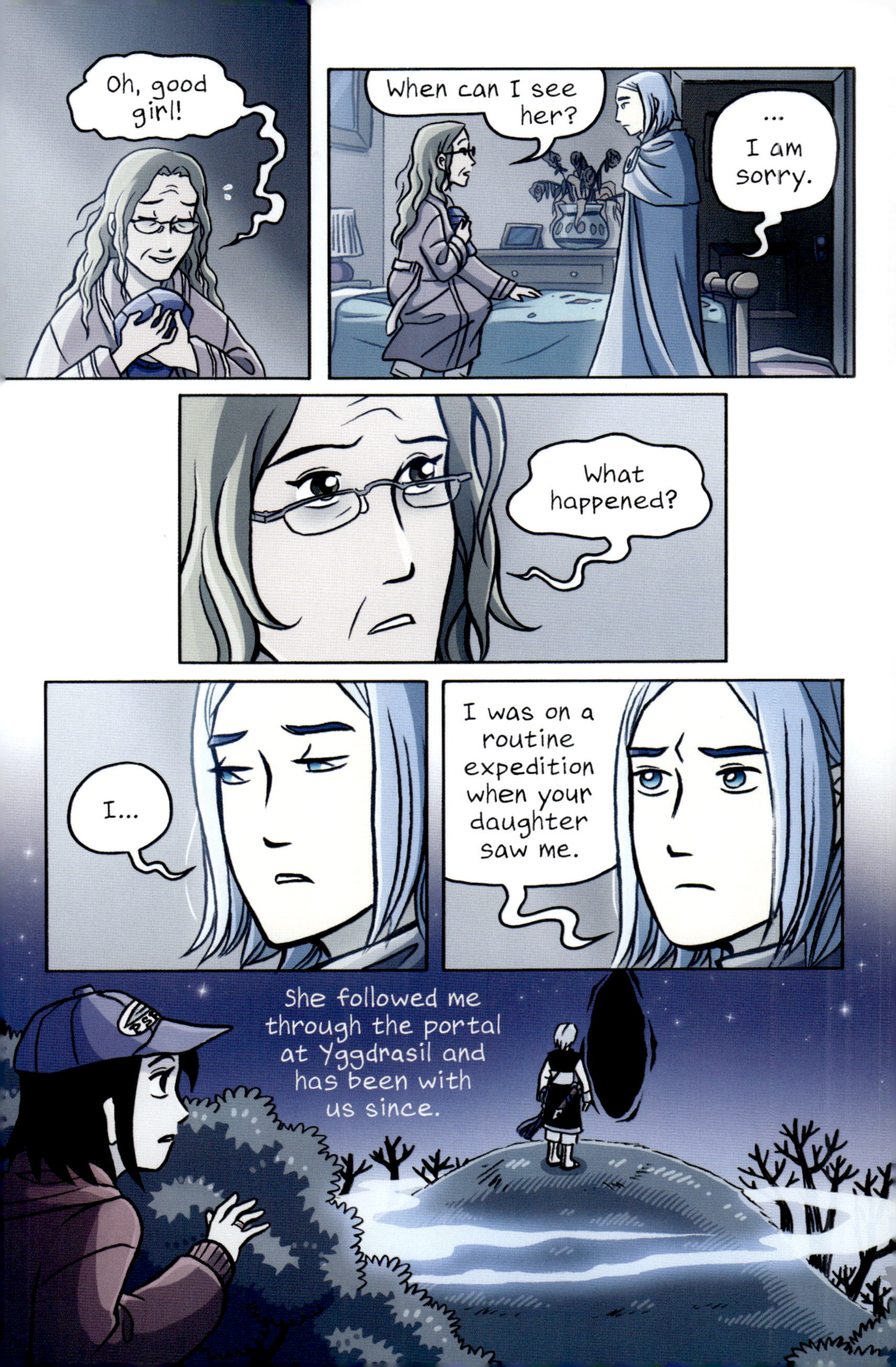
Oh, good girl!
When can I see her?
... I am sorry.
What happened?
I...
I was on a routine expedition when your daughter saw me.
She followed me through the portal at Yggdrasil and has been with us since.

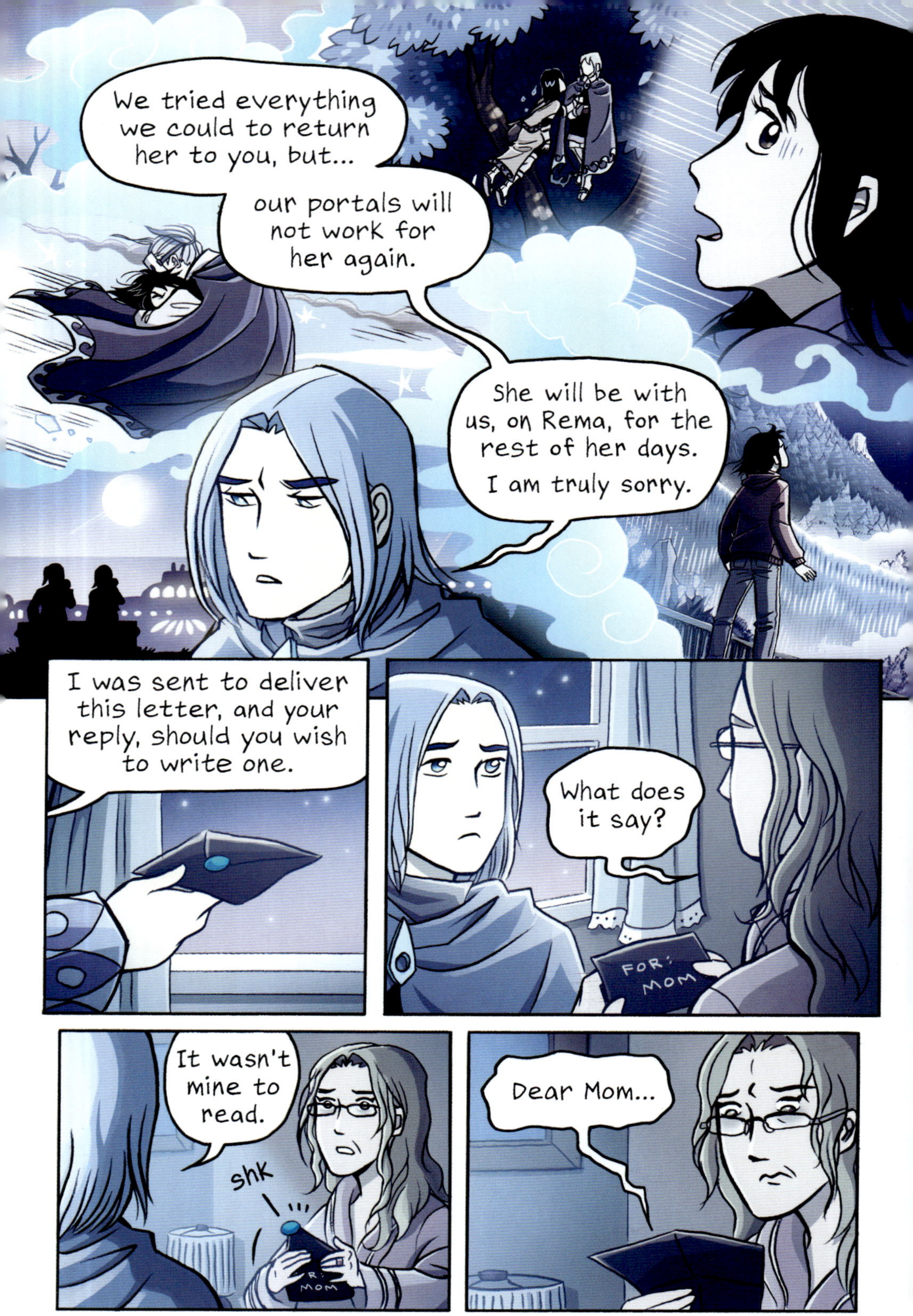
We tried everything we could to return her to you, but...
our portals will not work for her again.
She will be with us, on Rema, for the rest of her days.
I am truly sorry.
I was sent to deliver this letter, and your reply, should you wish to write one.
What does it say?
FOR: MOM
It wasn't mine to read.
shk
Dear Mom...

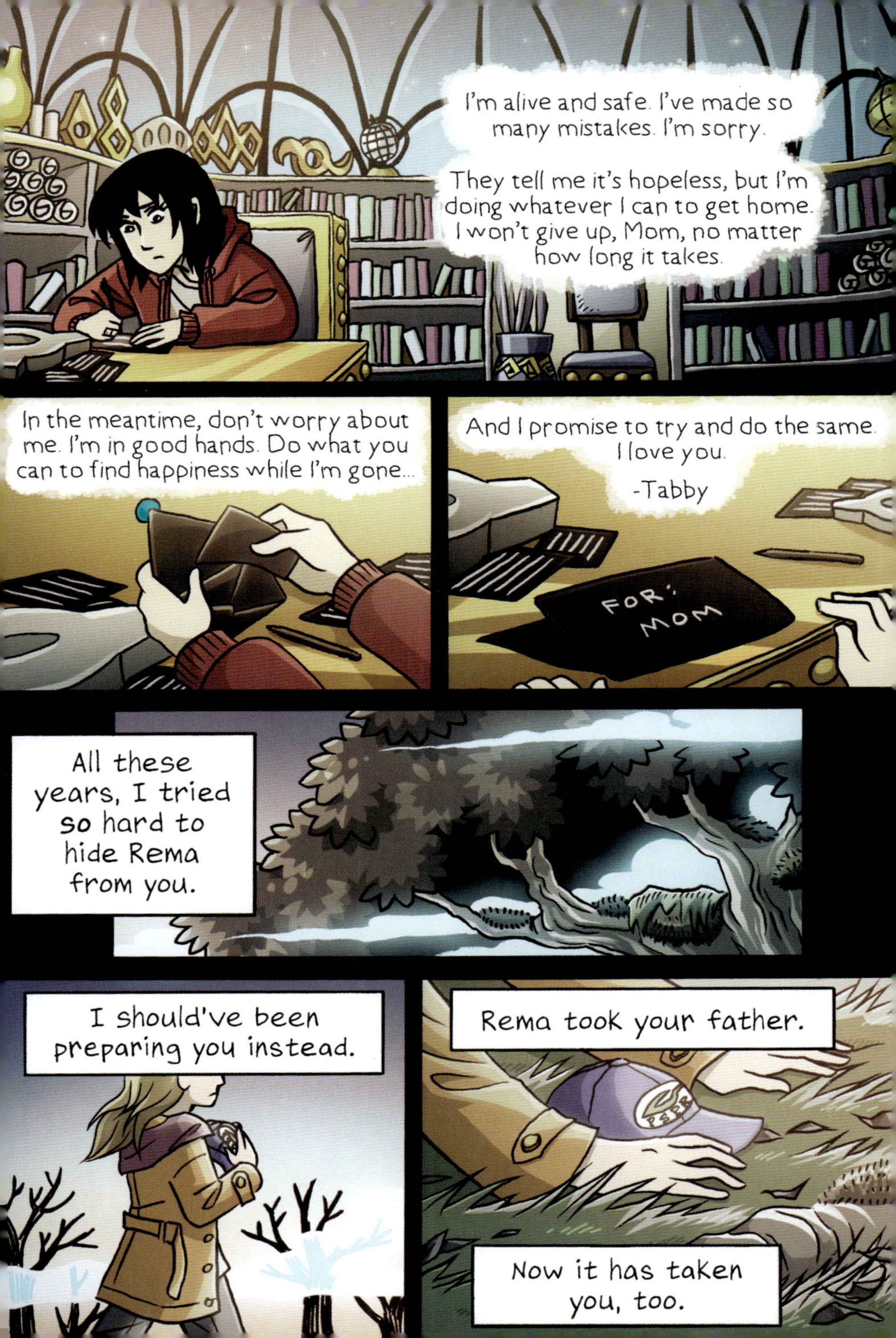
I'm alive and safe. I've made so many mistakes. I'm sorry.
They tell me it's hopeless, but I'm doing whatever I can to get home. I won't give up, Mom, no matter how long it takes.
In the meantime, don't worry about me. I'm in good hands. Do what you can to find happiness while I'm gone...
And I promise to try and do the same. I love you.
-Tabby
FOR: MOM
All these years, I tried so hard to hide Rema from you.
I should've been preparing you instead.
Rema took your father.
Now it has taken you, too.

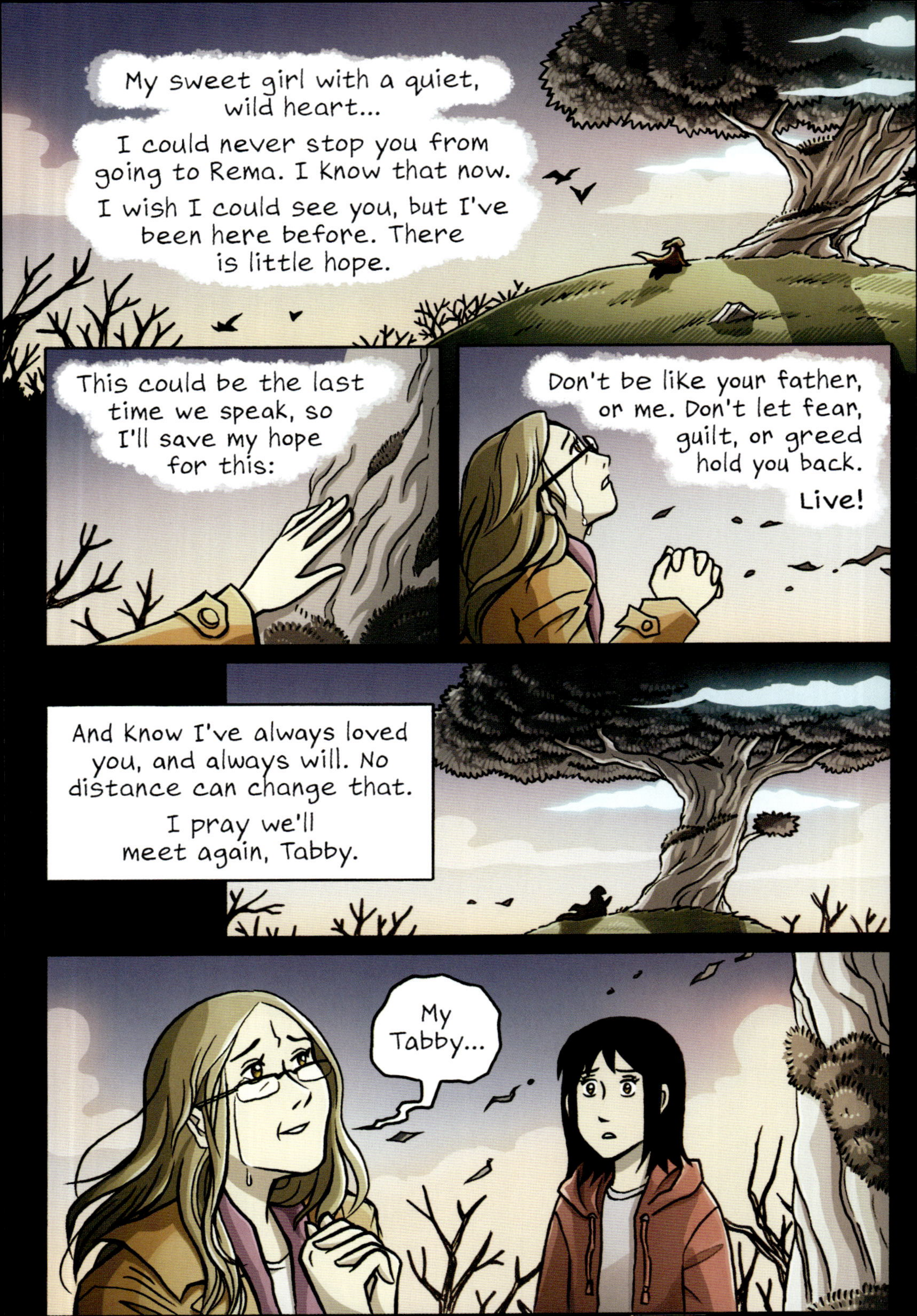
My sweet girl with a quiet, wild heart...
I could never stop you from going to Rema. I know that now.
I wish I could see you, but I've been here before. There is little hope.
This could be the last time we speak, so I'll save my hope for this:
Don't be like your father, or me. Don't let fear, guilt, or greed hold you back.
Live!
And know I've always loved you, and always will. No distance can change that.
I pray we'll meet again, Tabby.
My Tabby...

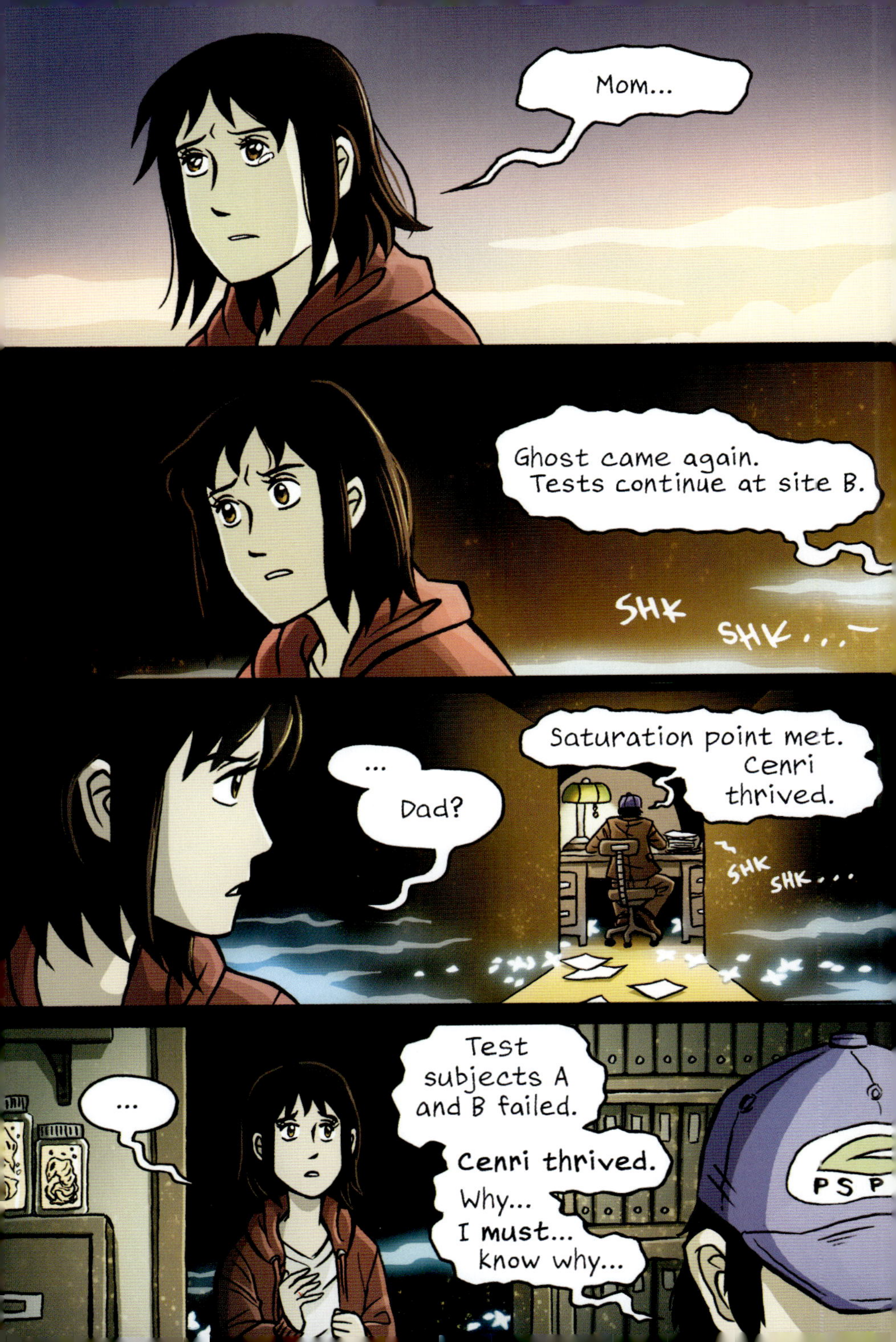
Mom...
Ghost came again. Tests continue at site B.
SHK
SHK...
...
Dad?
Saturation point met. Cenri thrived.
SHK
SHK...
...
Test subjects A and B failed.
Cenri thrived.
Why...
I must... know why...
PSP

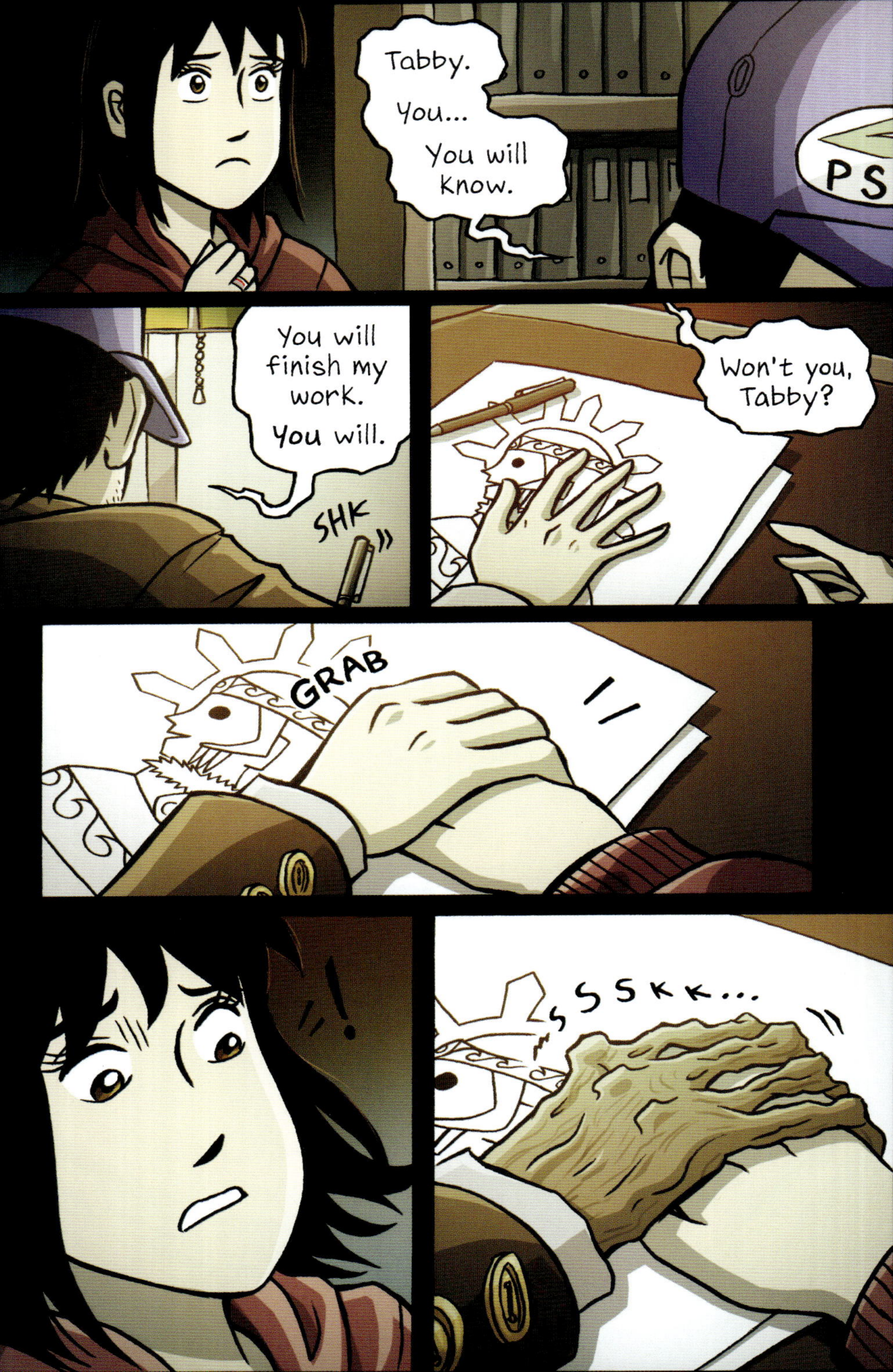
Tabby.
You...
You will know.
PS
You will finish my work.
You will.
SHK
Won't you, Tabby?
GRAB
!
SSSKK...

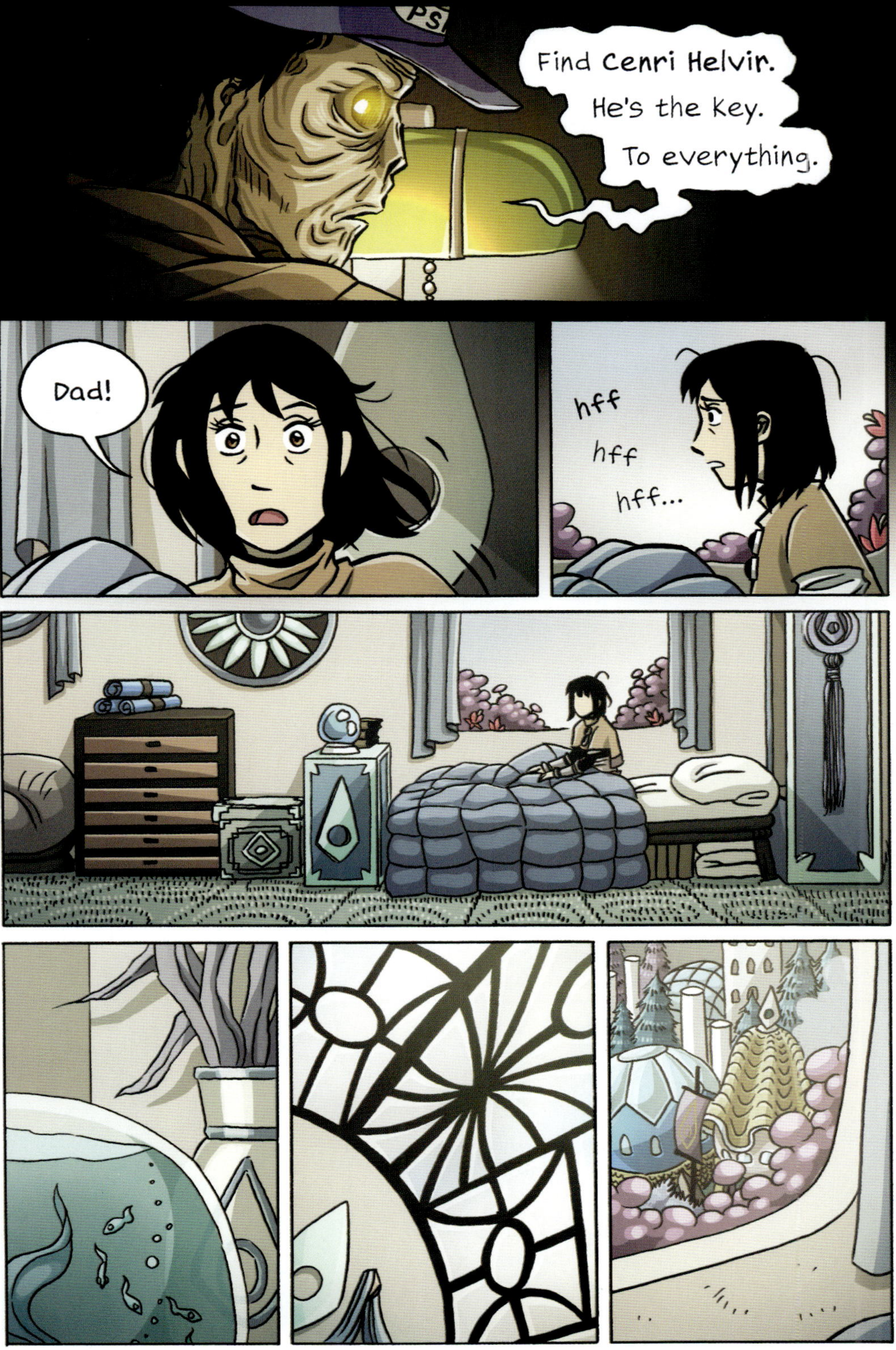
Find Cenri Helvir.
He's the Key.
To everything.
Dad!
hff
hff
hff...

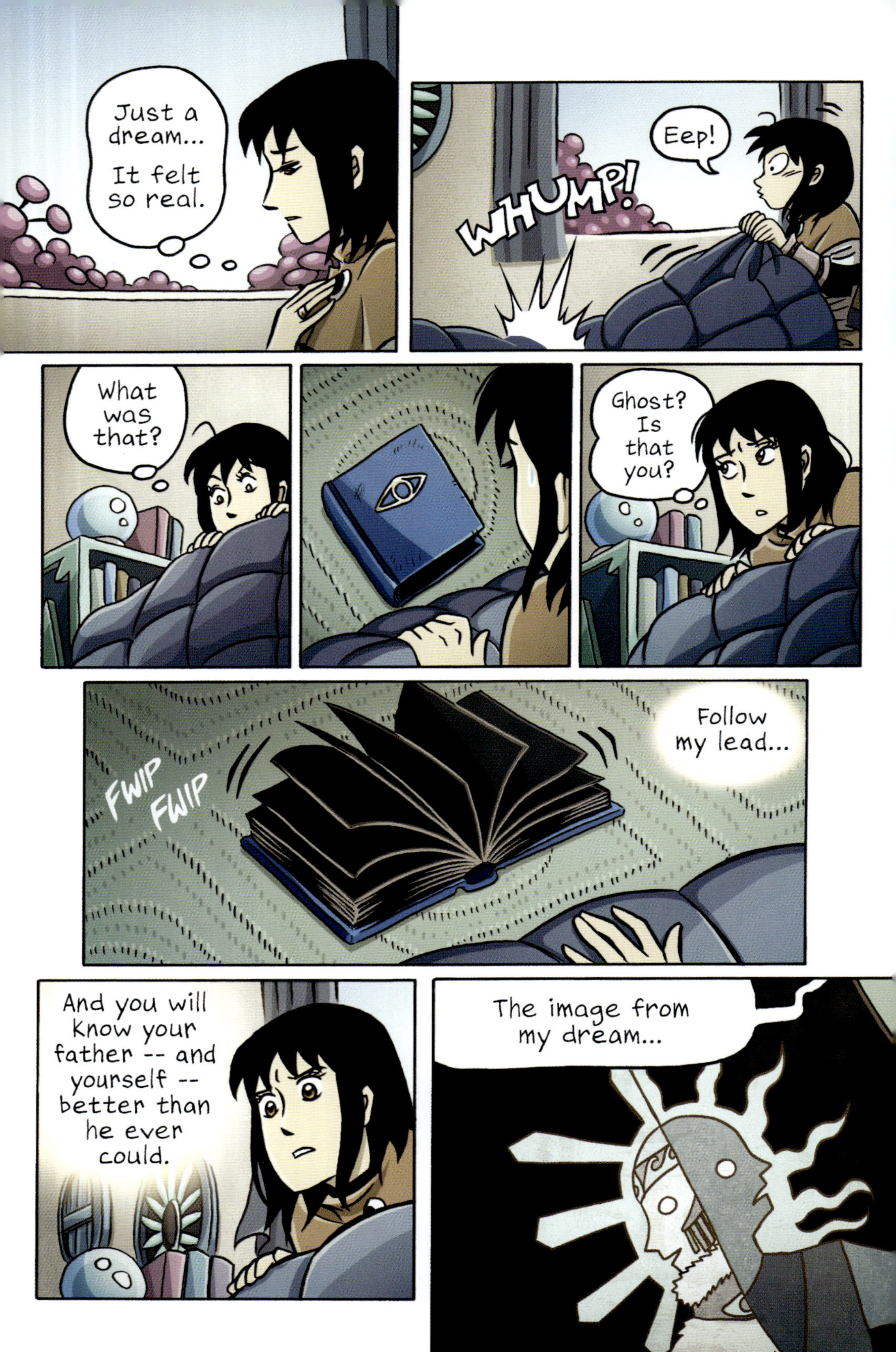

Just a dream...
It felt so real.
WHUMP!
Eep!
What was that?
Ghost? Is that you?
FWIP FWIP
Follow my lead...
And you will know your father -- and yourself -- better than he ever could.
The image from my dream...

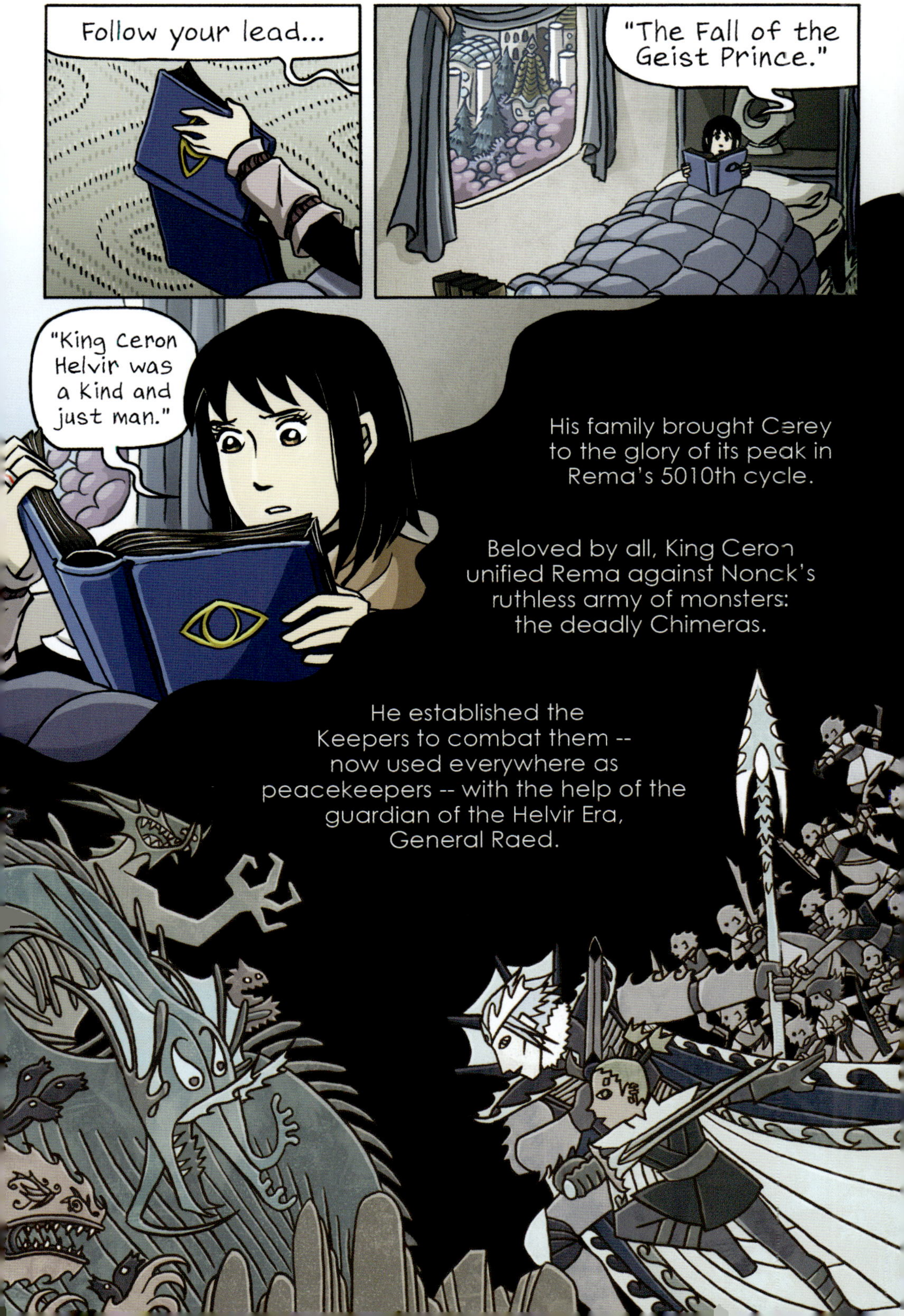
Follow your lead...
"The Fall of the Geist Prince."
"King Ceron Helvir was a kind and just man."
His family brought Cerey to the glory of its peak in Rema's 5010th cycle.
Beloved by all, King Ceron unified Rema against Nonck's ruthless army of monsters: the deadly Chimeras.
He established the Keepers to combat them -- now used everywhere as peacekeepers -- with the help of the guardian of the Helvir Era, General Raed.

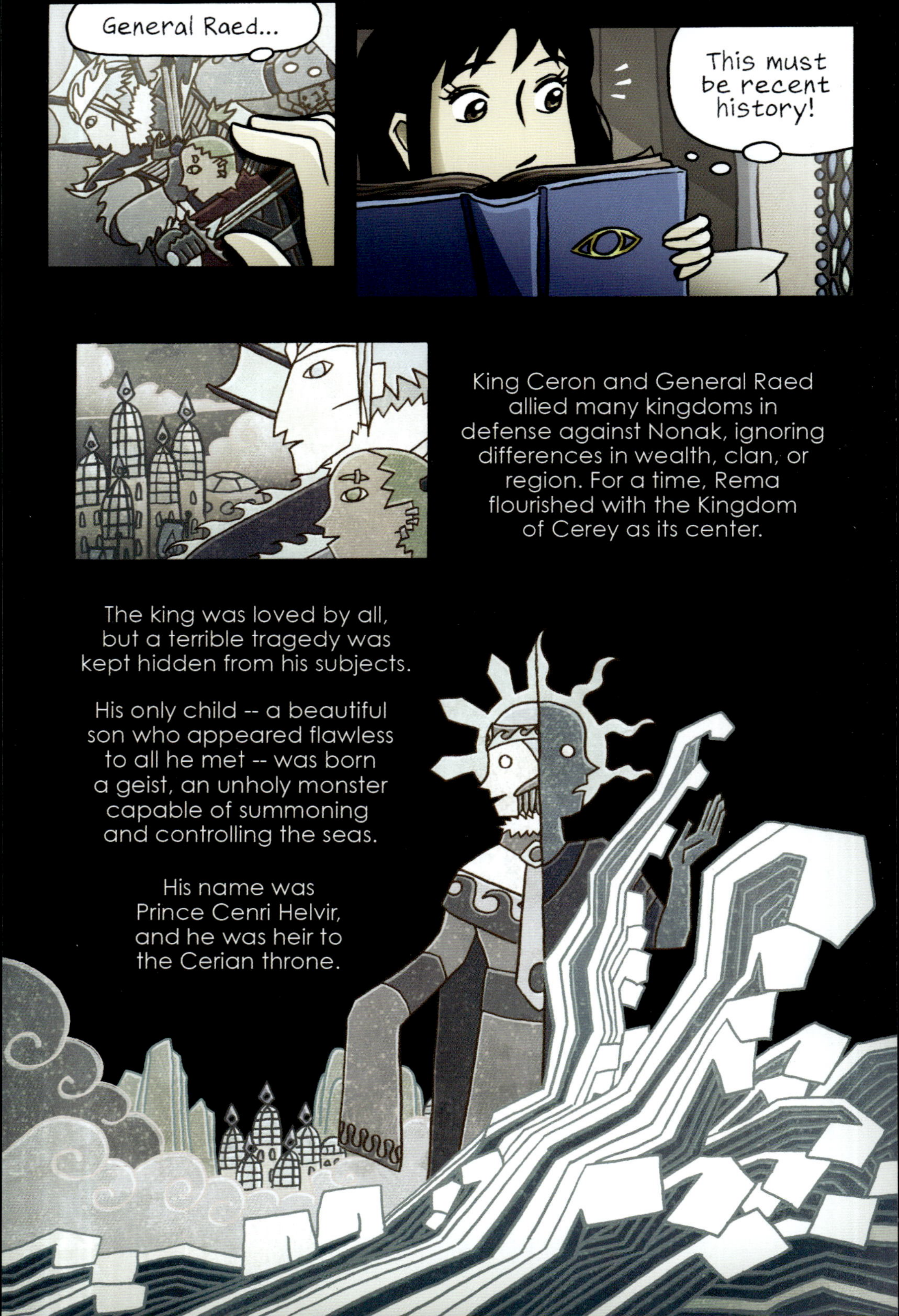
General Raed...
This must be recent history!
King Ceron and General Raed allied many kingdoms in defense against Nonak, ignoring differences in wealth, clan, or region. For a time, Rema flourished with the Kingdom of Cerey as its center.
The king was loved by all, but a terrible tragedy was kept hidden from his subjects.
His only child -- a beautiful son who appeared flawless to all he met -- was born a geist, an unholy monster capable of summoning and controlling the seas.
His name was Prince Cenri Helvir, and he was heir to the Cerian throne.

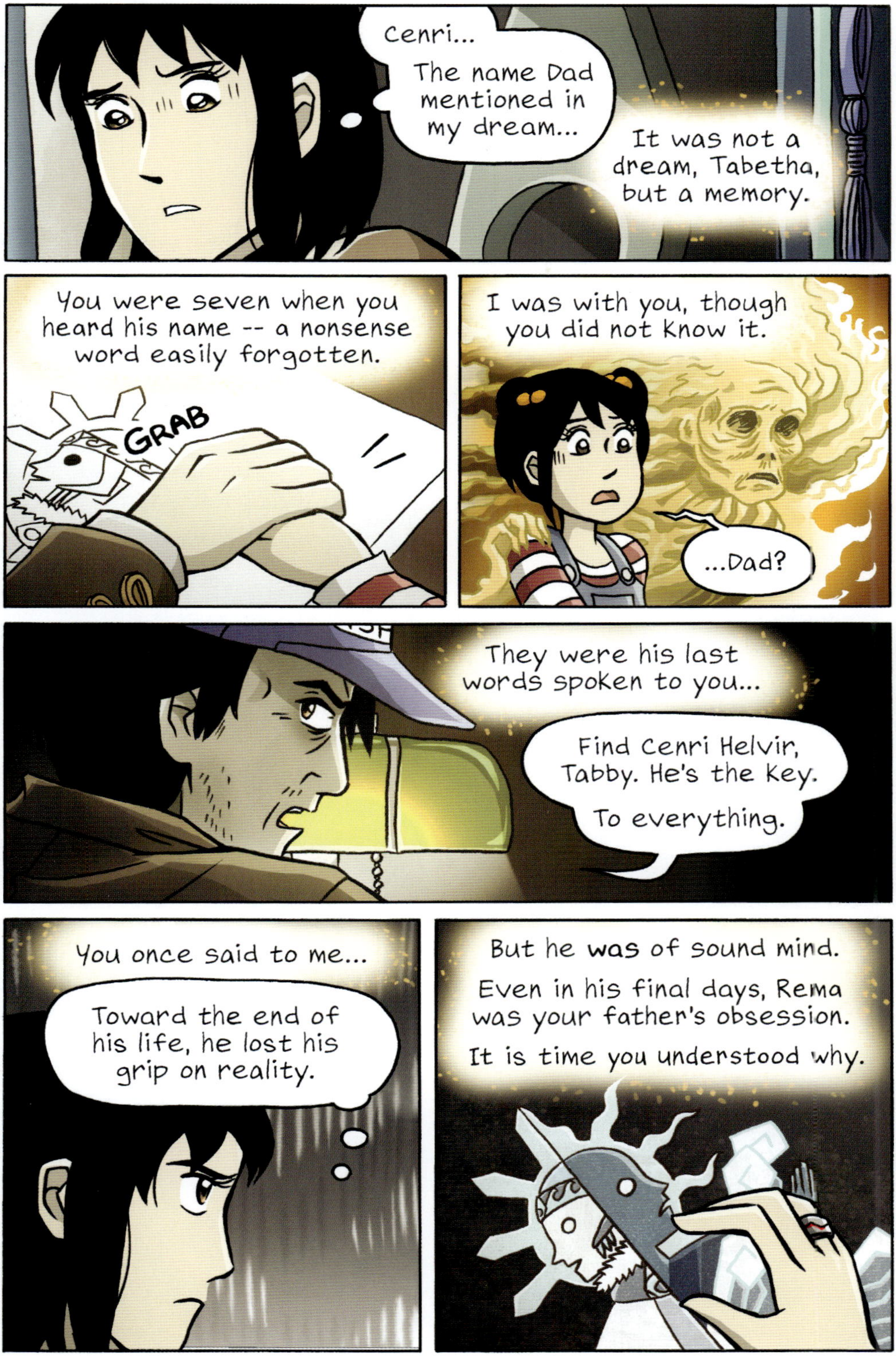
Cenri...
The name Dad mentioned in my dream...
It was not a dream, Tabetha, but a memory.
You were seven when you heard his name -- a nonsense word easily forgotten.
GRAB
I was with you, though you did not know it.
...Dad?
They were his last words spoken to you...
Find Cenri Helvir, Tabby. He's the key.
To everything.
You once said to me...
Toward the end of his life, he lost his grip on reality.
But he **was** of sound mind.
Even in his final days, Rema was your father's obsession.
It is time you understood why.

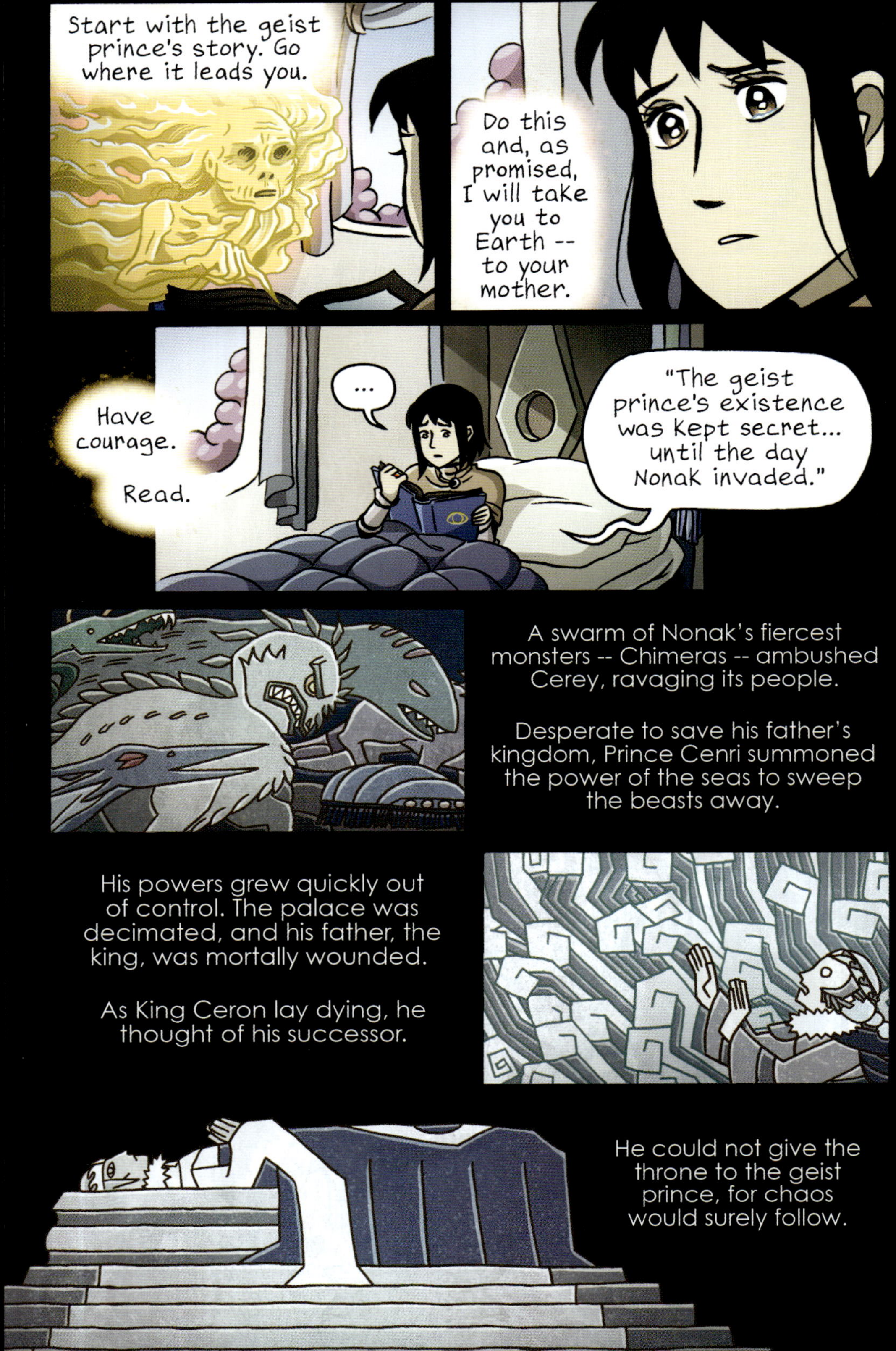
Start with the geist prince's story. Go where it leads you.
Do this and, as promised, I will take you to Earth -- to your mother.
Have courage.
Read.
...
"The geist prince's existence was kept secret... until the day Nonak invaded."
A swarm of Nonak's fiercest monsters -- Chimeras -- ambushed Cerey, ravaging its people.
Desperate to save his father's kingdom, Prince Cenri summoned the power of the seas to sweep the beasts away.
His powers grew quickly out of control. The palace was decimated, and his father, the king, was mortally wounded.
As King Ceron lay dying, he thought of his successor.
He could not give the throne to the geist prince, for chaos would surely follow.

"In my son's place, I shall appoint a council of trusted advisors," King Ceron declared. "Alongside the spiritual guidance of my sister, Priestess Hiida, the council will bring Cerey to a new age of peace."

To the geist prince, he instructed: "My beloved son -- when I fall, give my council your crown, my sister your blessing, and relinquish your power to rule this kingdom. If you truly love me, you will fullfill this, my final wish."

At spring's coming, King Ceron Helvir passed on to be with The Gods. The geist prince did as his father wished.

With his first and final act as monarch, the young prince passed the crown from the Helvir family to his father's council. From that day forth, the Kingom of Cerey became known as the City of Cerey.

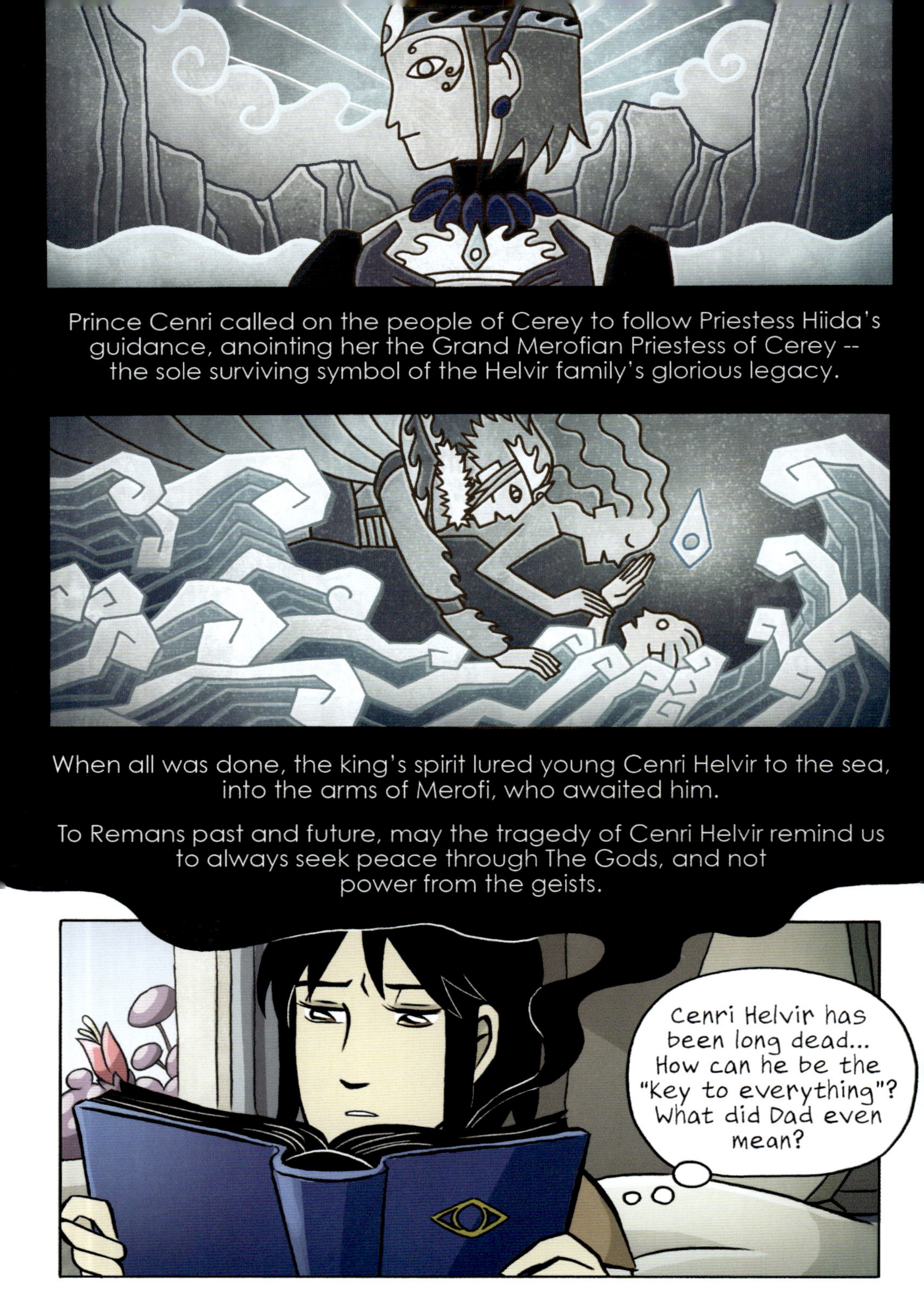
Prince Cenri called on the people of Cerey to follow Priestess Hiida's guidance, anointing her the Grand Merofian Priestess of Cerey -- the sole surviving symbol of the Helvir family's glorious legacy.
When all was done, the king's spirit lured young Cenri Helvir to the sea, into the arms of Merofi, who awaited him.
To Remans past and future, may the tragedy of Cenri Helvir remind us to always seek peace through The Gods, and not power from the geists.
Cenri Helvir has been long dead... How can he be the "key to everything"? What did Dad even mean?

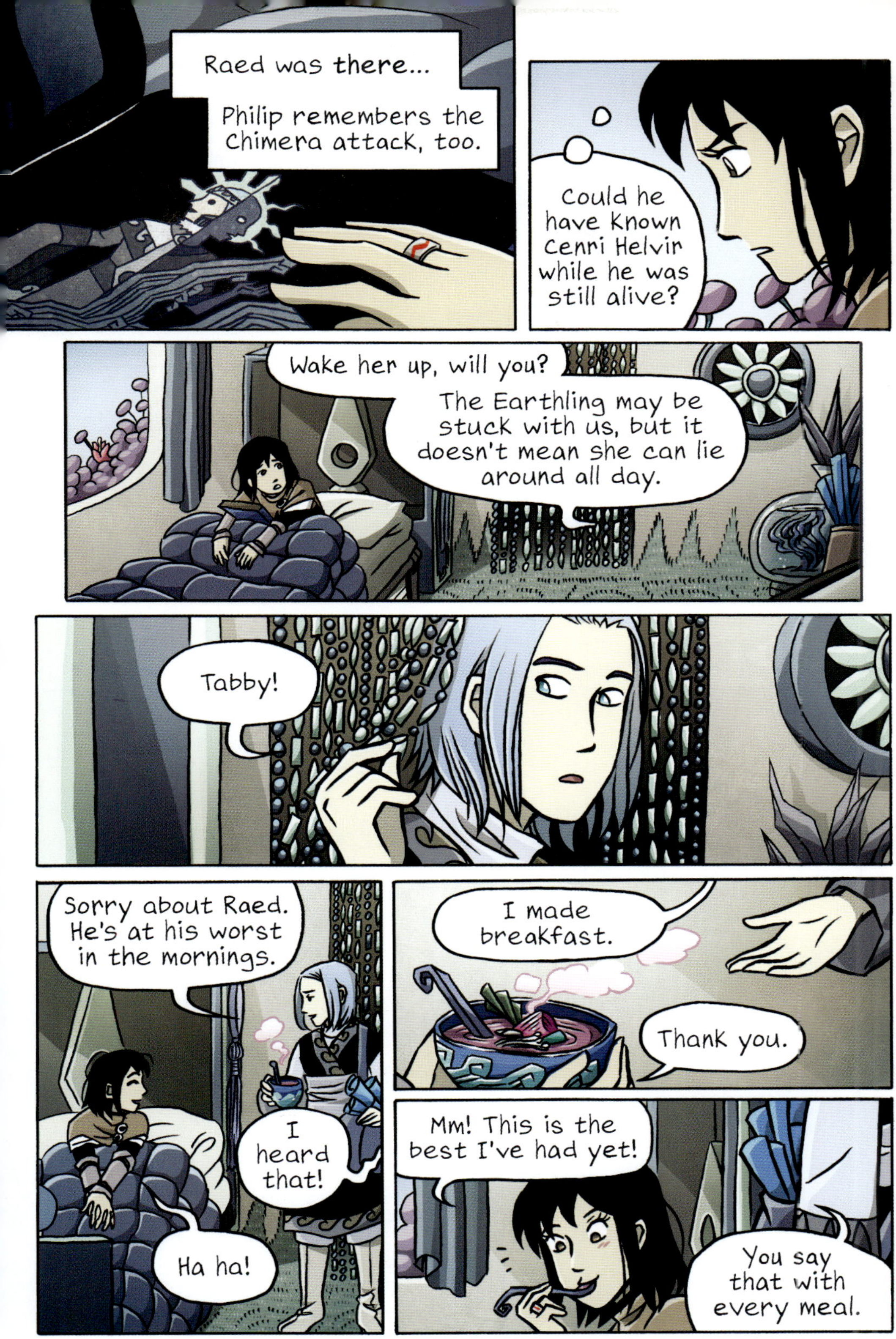
Raed was there...
Philip remembers the Chimera attack, too.
Could he have known Cenri Helvir while he was still alive?
Wake her up, will you?
The Earthling may be stuck with us, but it doesn't mean she can lie around all day.
Tabby!
Sorry about Raed. He's at his worst in the mornings.
I heard that!
Ha ha!
I made breakfast.
Thank you.
Mm! This is the best I've had yet!
You say that with every meal.

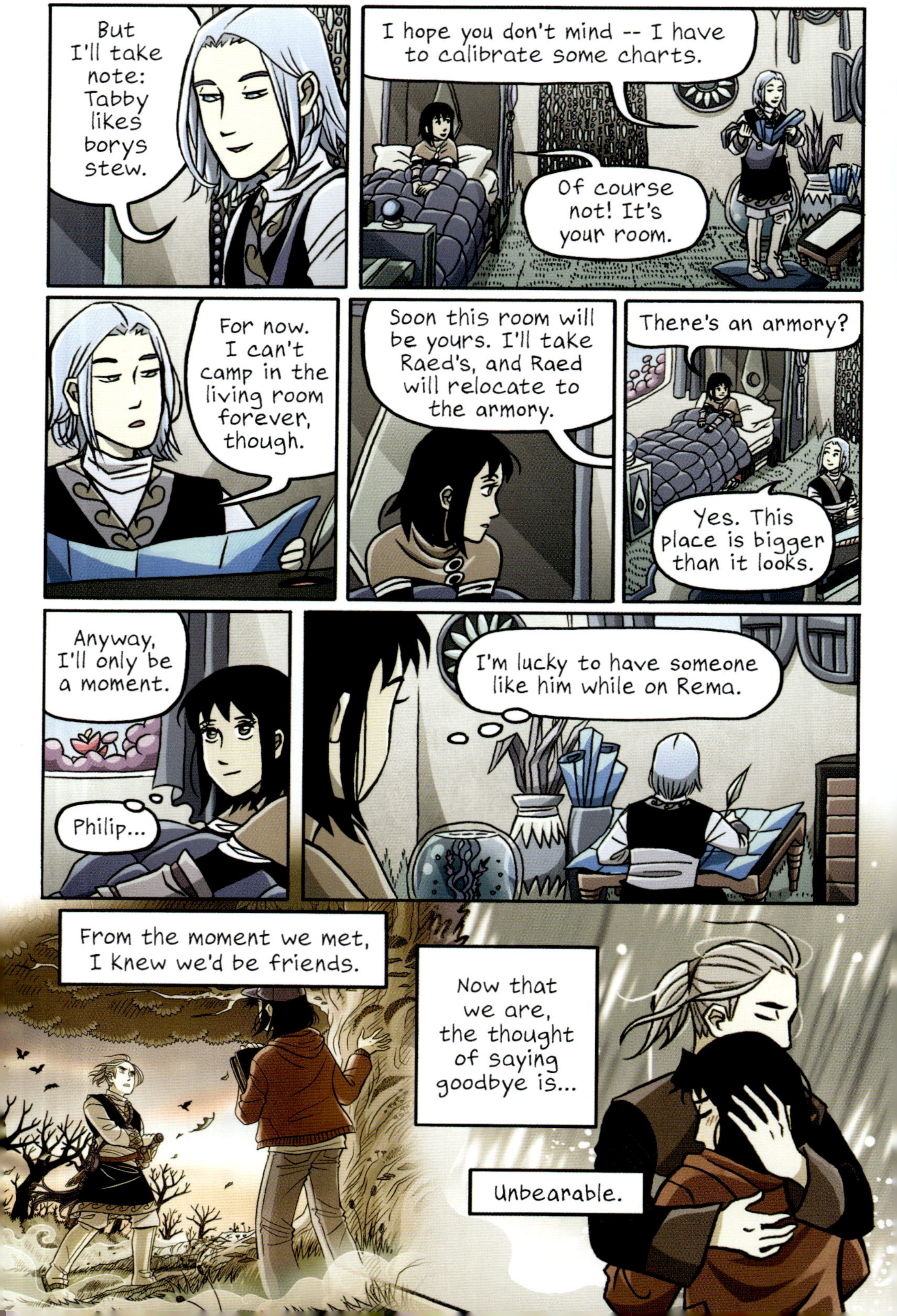

But I'll take note: Tabby likes borys stew.
I hope you don't mind -- I have to calibrate some charts.
Of course not! It's your room.
For now. I can't camp in the living room forever, though.
Soon this room will be yours. I'll take Raed's, and Raed will relocate to the armory.
There's an armory?
Yes. This place is bigger than it looks.
Anyway, I'll only be a moment.
Philip...
I'm lucky to have someone like him while on Rema.
From the moment we met, I knew we'd be friends.
Now that we are, the thought of saying goodbye is...
Unbearable.

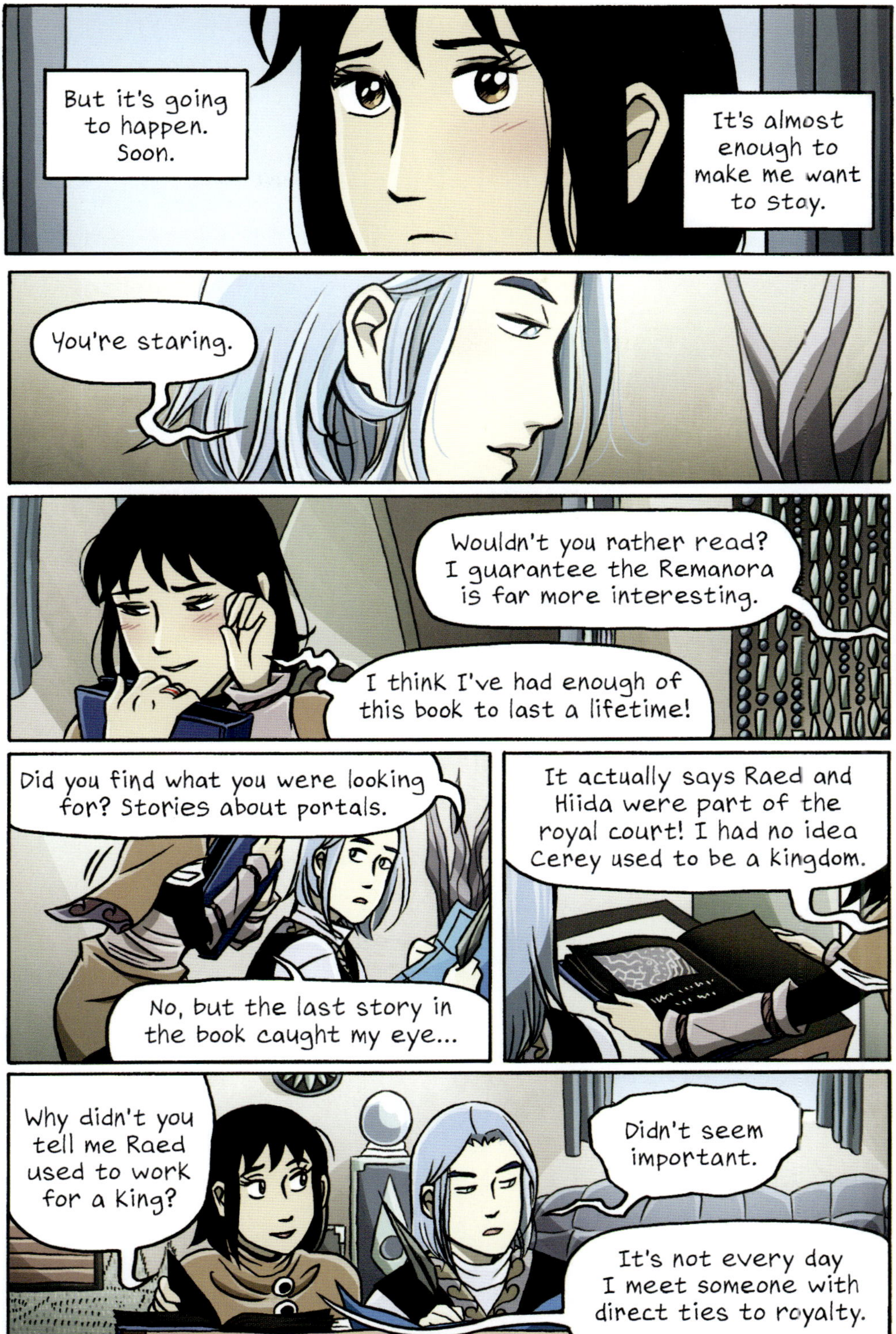
But it's going to happen. Soon.
It's almost enough to make me want to stay.
You're staring.
Wouldn't you rather read? I guarantee the Remanora is far more interesting.
I think I've had enough of this book to last a lifetime!
Did you find what you were looking for? Stories about portals.
No, but the last story in the book caught my eye...
It actually says Raed and Hiida were part of the royal court! I had no idea Cerey used to be a kingdom.
Why didn't you tell me Raed used to work for a king?
Didn't seem important.
It's not every day I meet someone with direct ties to royalty.

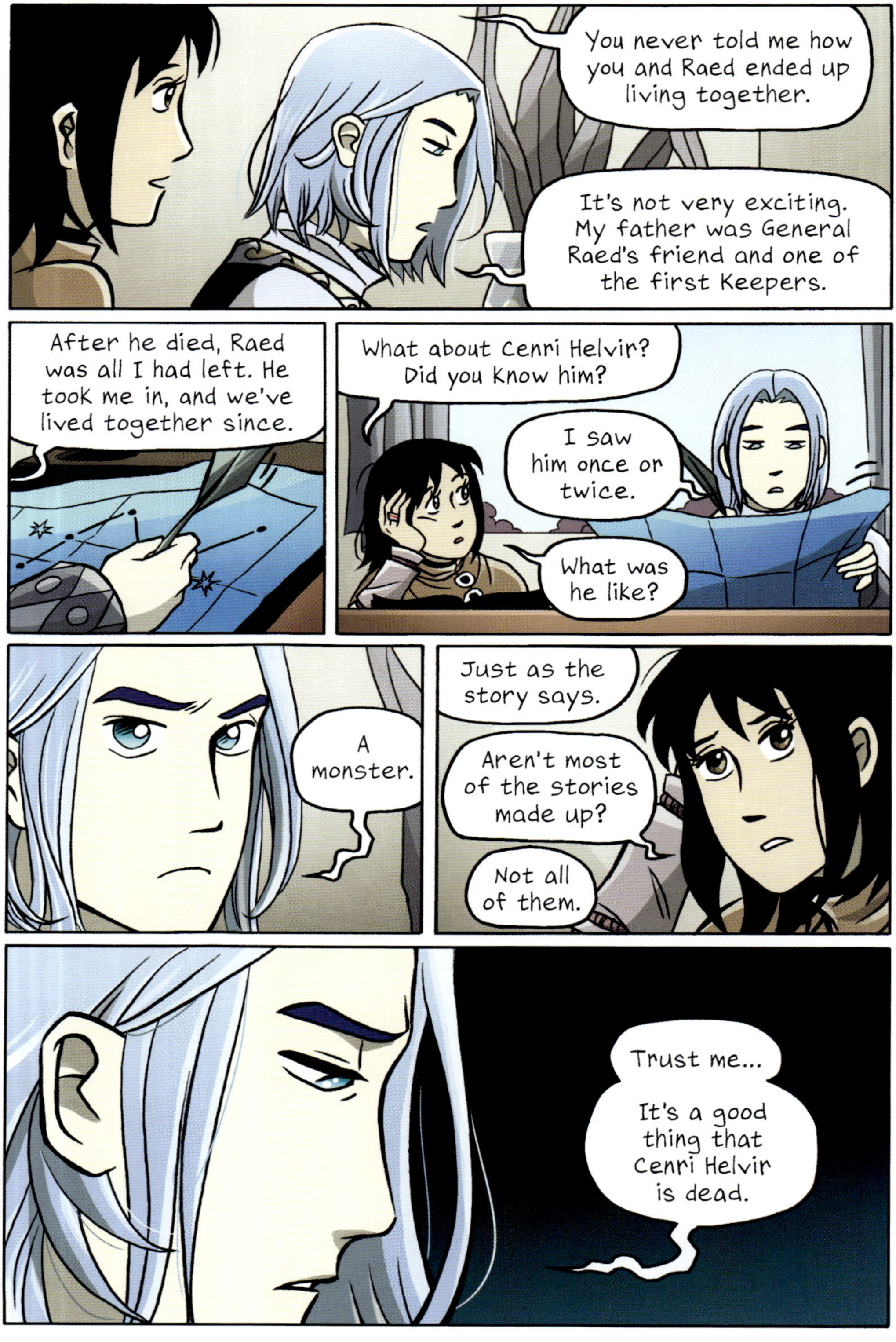
You never told me how you and Raed ended up living together.
It's not very exciting. My father was General Raed's friend and one of the first Keepers.
After he died, Raed was all I had left. He took me in, and we've lived together since.
What about Cenri Helvir? Did you know him?
I saw him once or twice.
What was he like?
A monster.
Just as the story says.
Aren't most of the stories made up?
Not all of them.
Trust me...
It's a good thing that Cenri Helvir is dead.

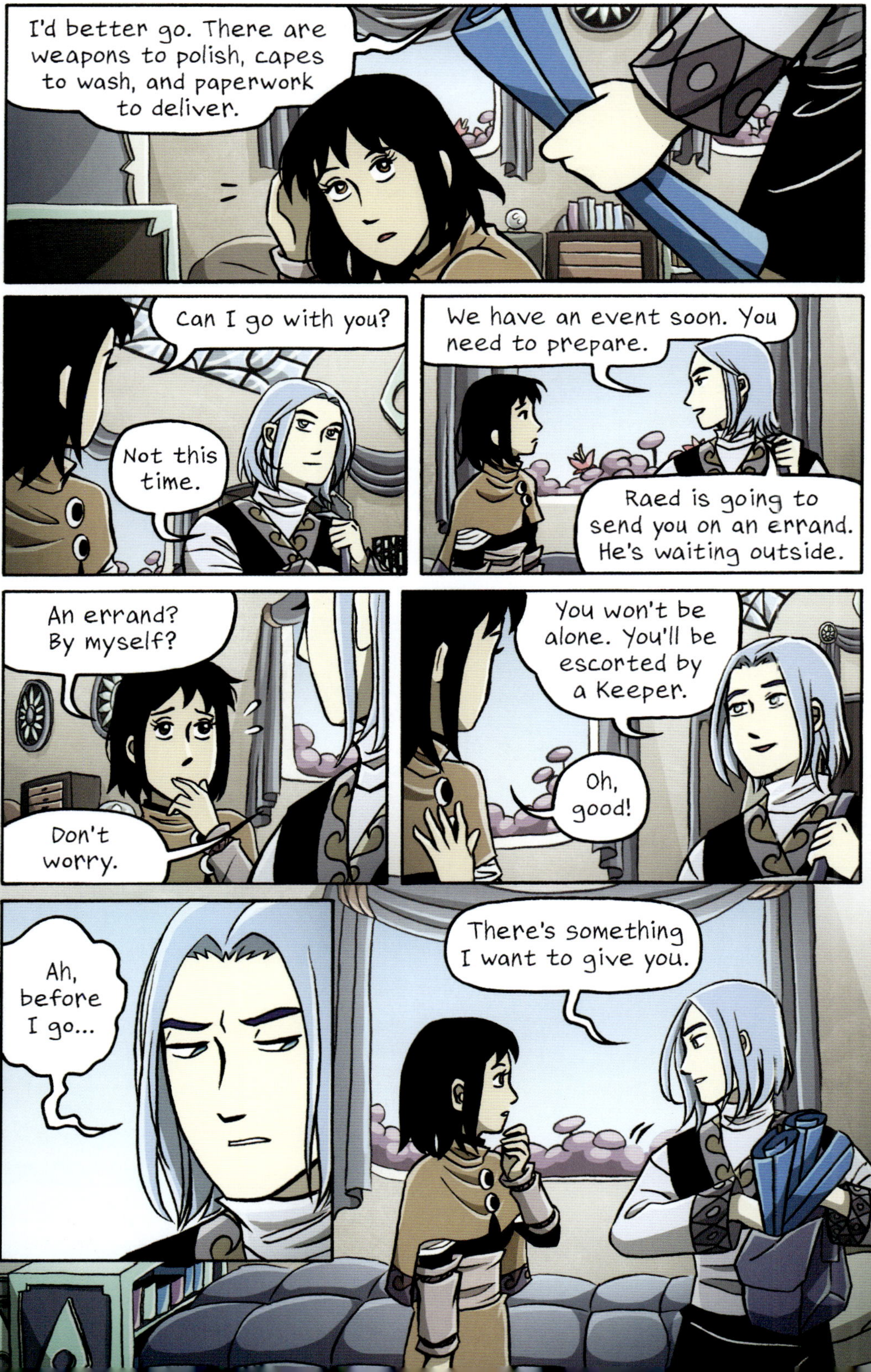
I'd better go. There are weapons to polish, capes to wash, and paperwork to deliver.
Can I go with you?
Not this time.
We have an event soon. You need to prepare.
Raed is going to send you on an errand. He's waiting outside.
An errand? By myself?
Don't worry.
You won't be alone. You'll be escorted by a Keeper.
Oh, good!
Ah, before I go...
There's something I want to give you.

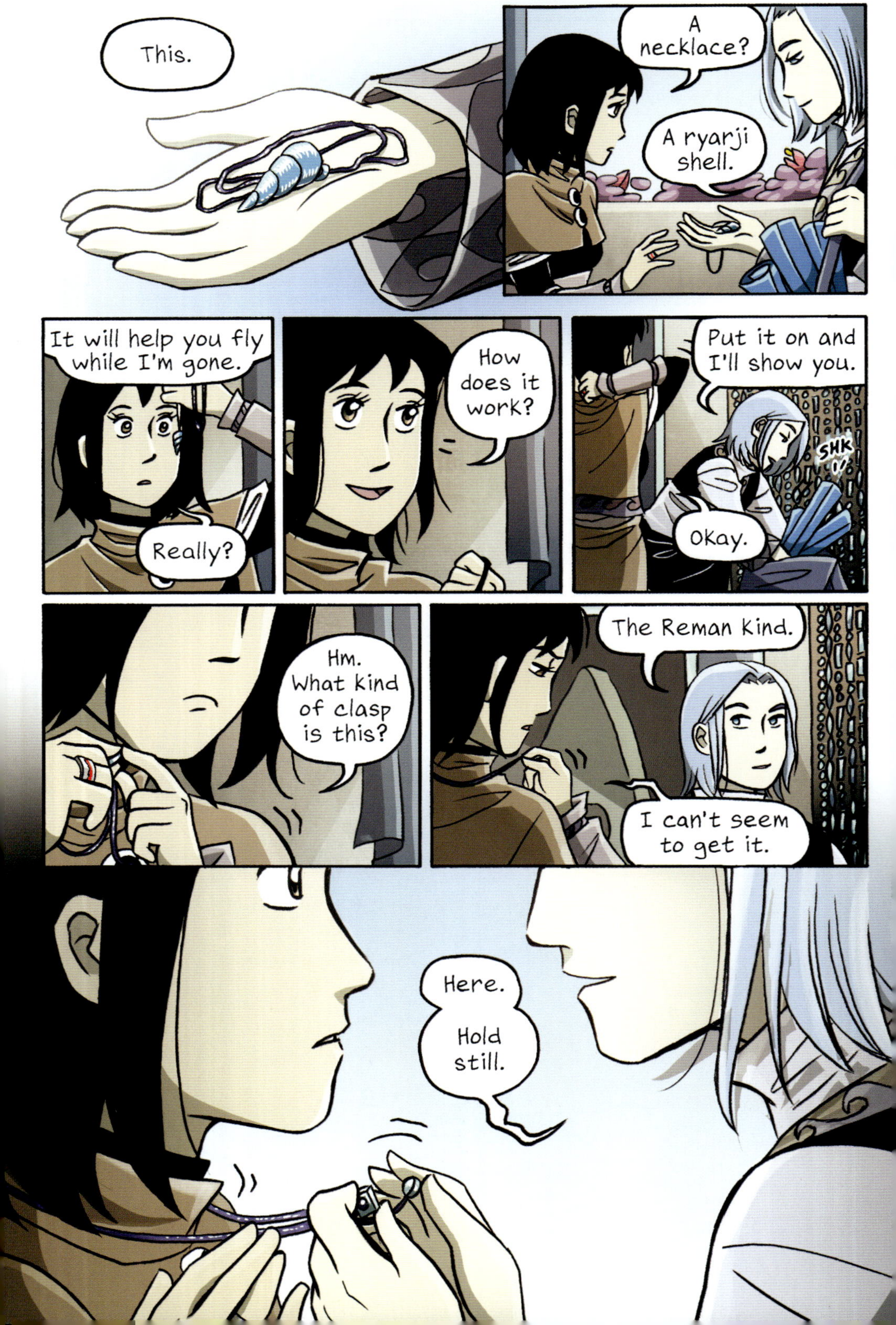
This.
A necklace?
A ryarji shell.
It will help you fly while I'm gone.
Really?
How does it work?
Put it on and I'll show you.
SHK
Okay.
Hm. What kind of clasp is this?
The Reman kind.
I can't seem to get it.
Here.
Hold still.

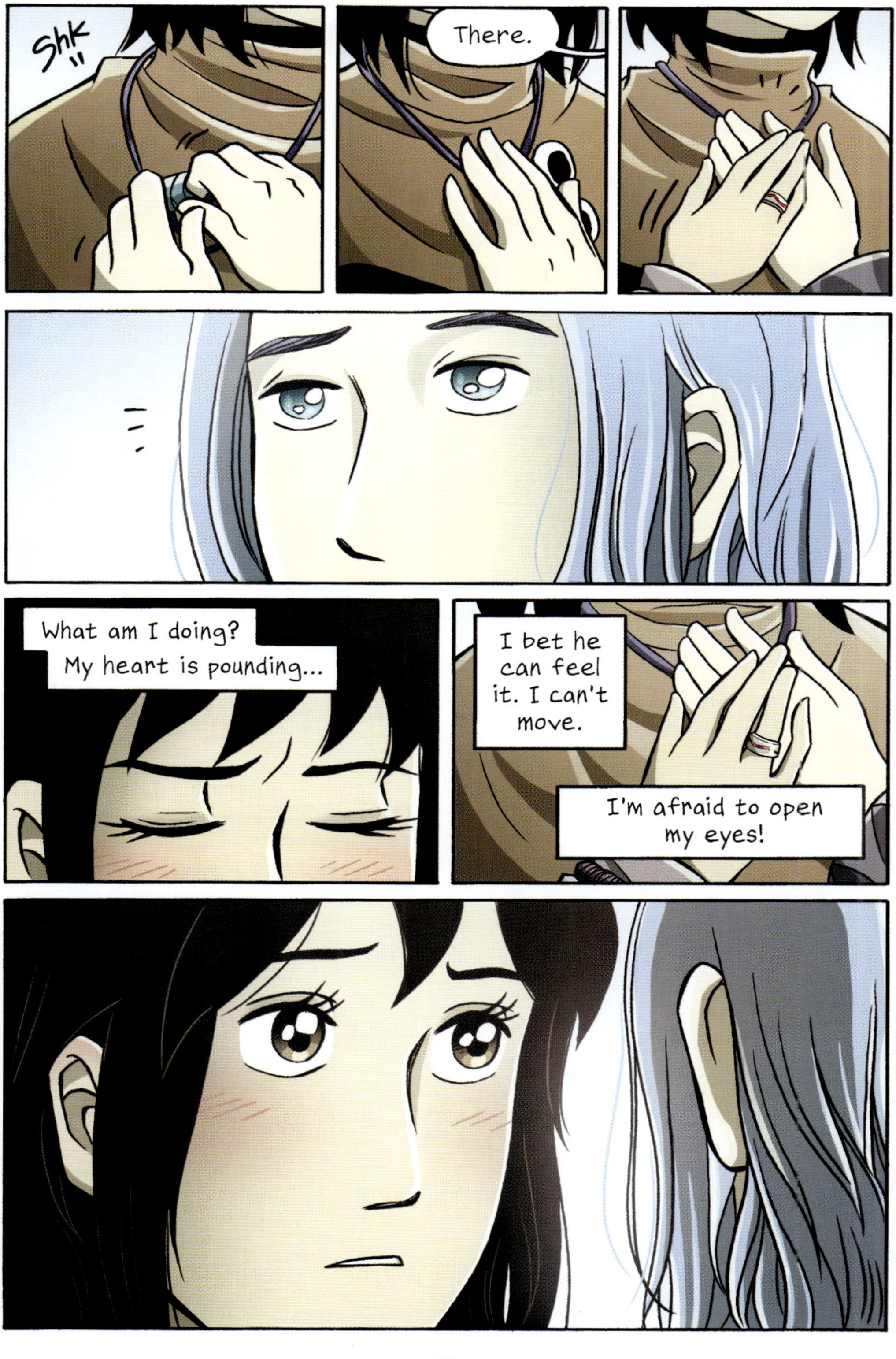
SHK
There.
What am I doing?
My heart is pounding...
I bet he can feel it. I can't move.
I'm afraid to open my eyes!

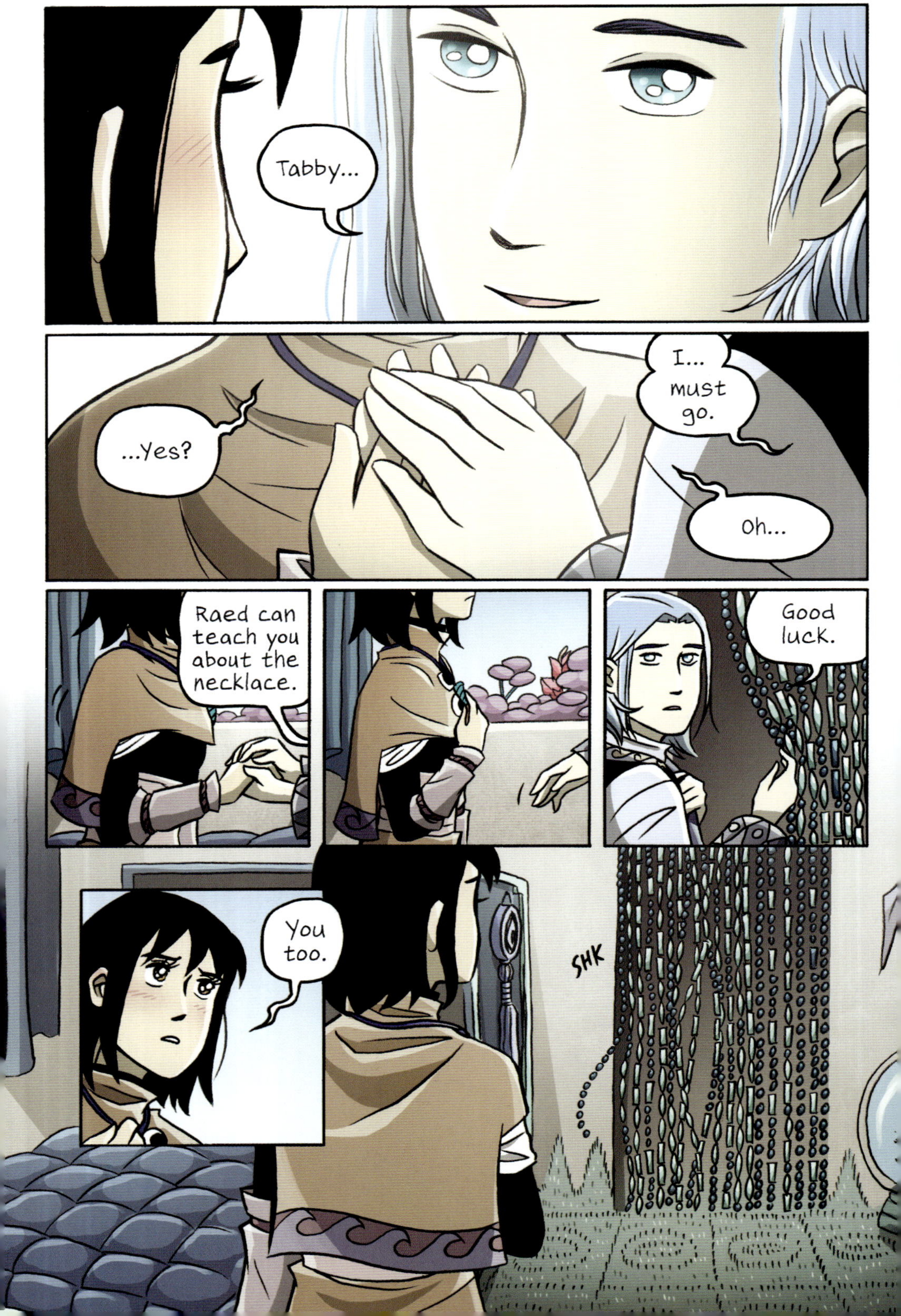
Tabby...
...Yes?
I... must go.
Oh...
Raed can teach you about the necklace.
Good luck.
You too.
SHK

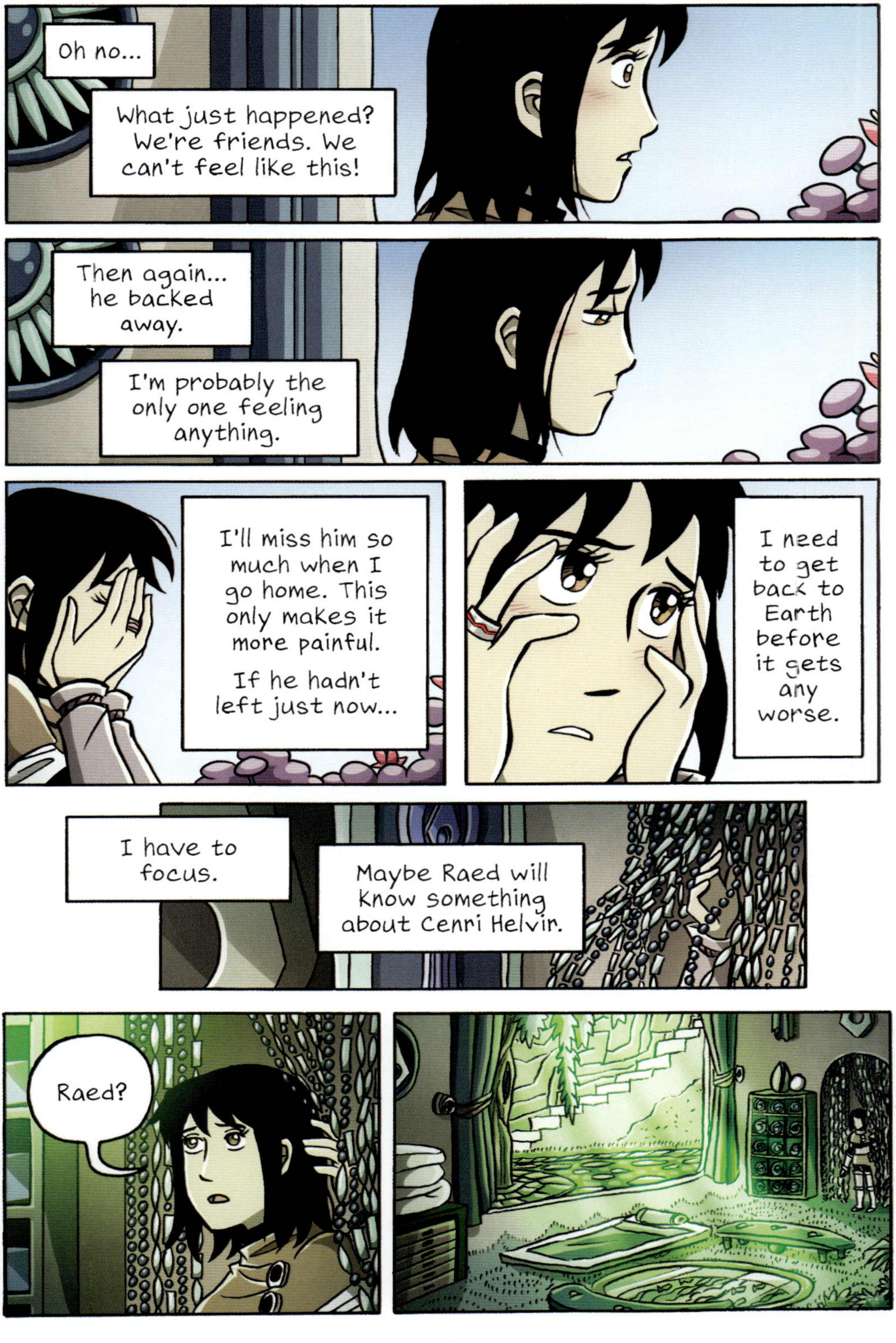
Oh no...
What just happened? We're friends. We can't feel like this!
Then again... he backed away.
I'm probably the only one feeling anything.
I'll miss him so much when I go home. This only makes it more painful.
If he hadn't left just now...
I need to get back to Earth before it gets any worse.
I have to focus.
Maybe Raed will know something about Cenri Helvir.
Raed?

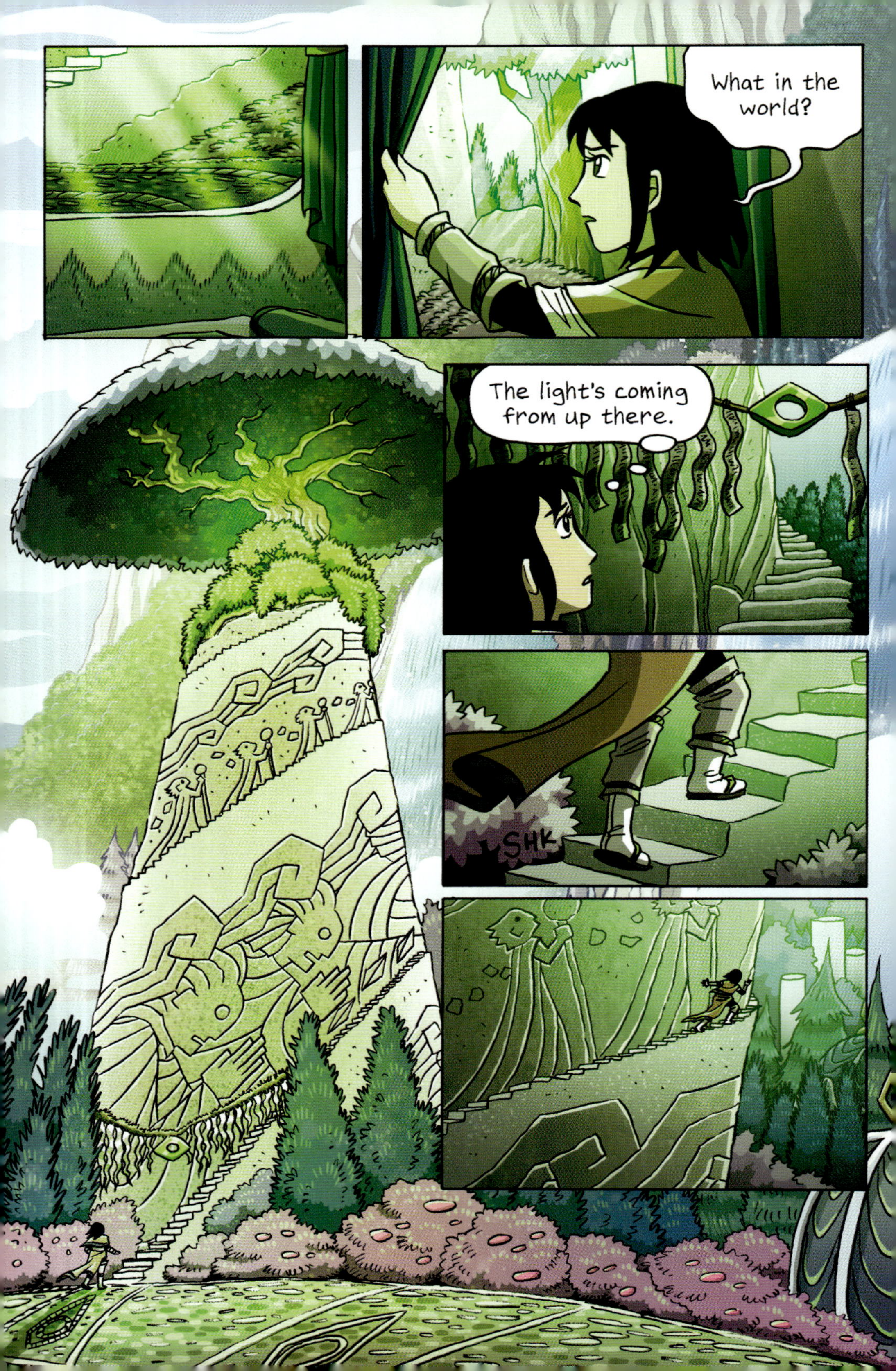
What in the world?
The light's coming from up there.
SHK

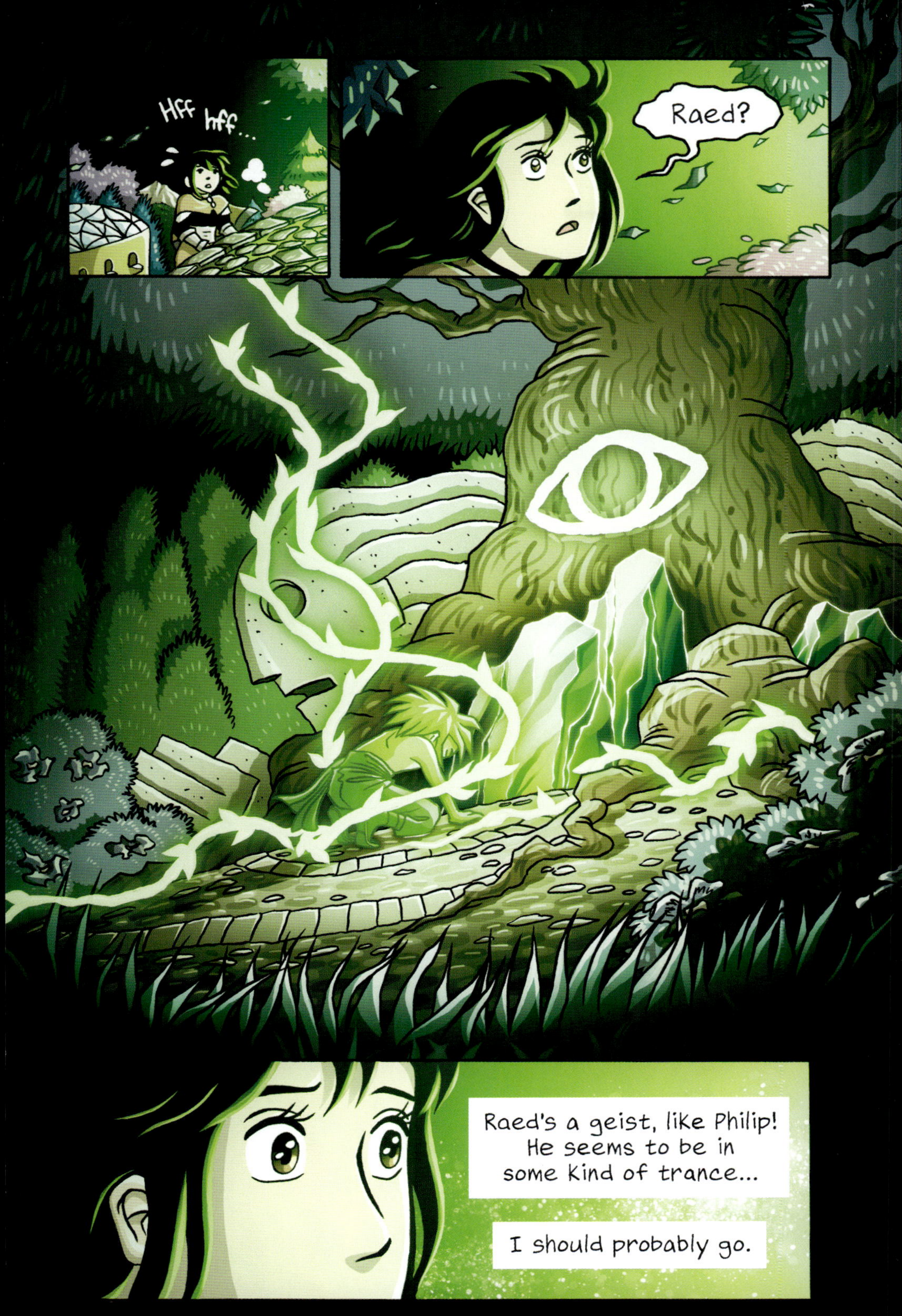
Hff hff...
Raed?
Raed's a geist, like Philip! He seems to be in some kind of trance...
I should probably go.

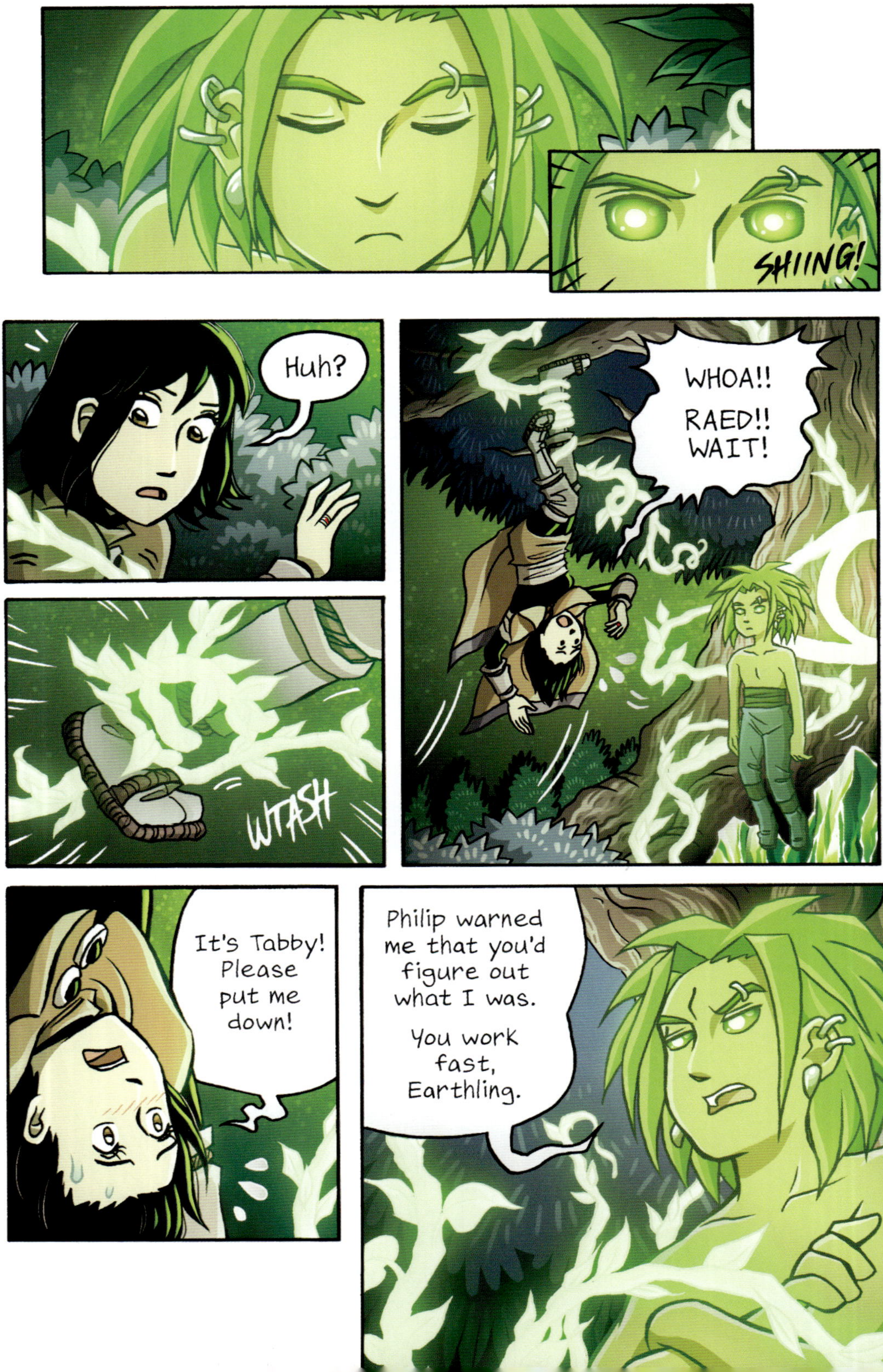
SHIING!
Huh?
WHOA!! RAED!! WAIT!
WTASH
It's Tabby! Please put me down!
Philip warned me that you'd figure out what I was.
You work fast, Earthling.

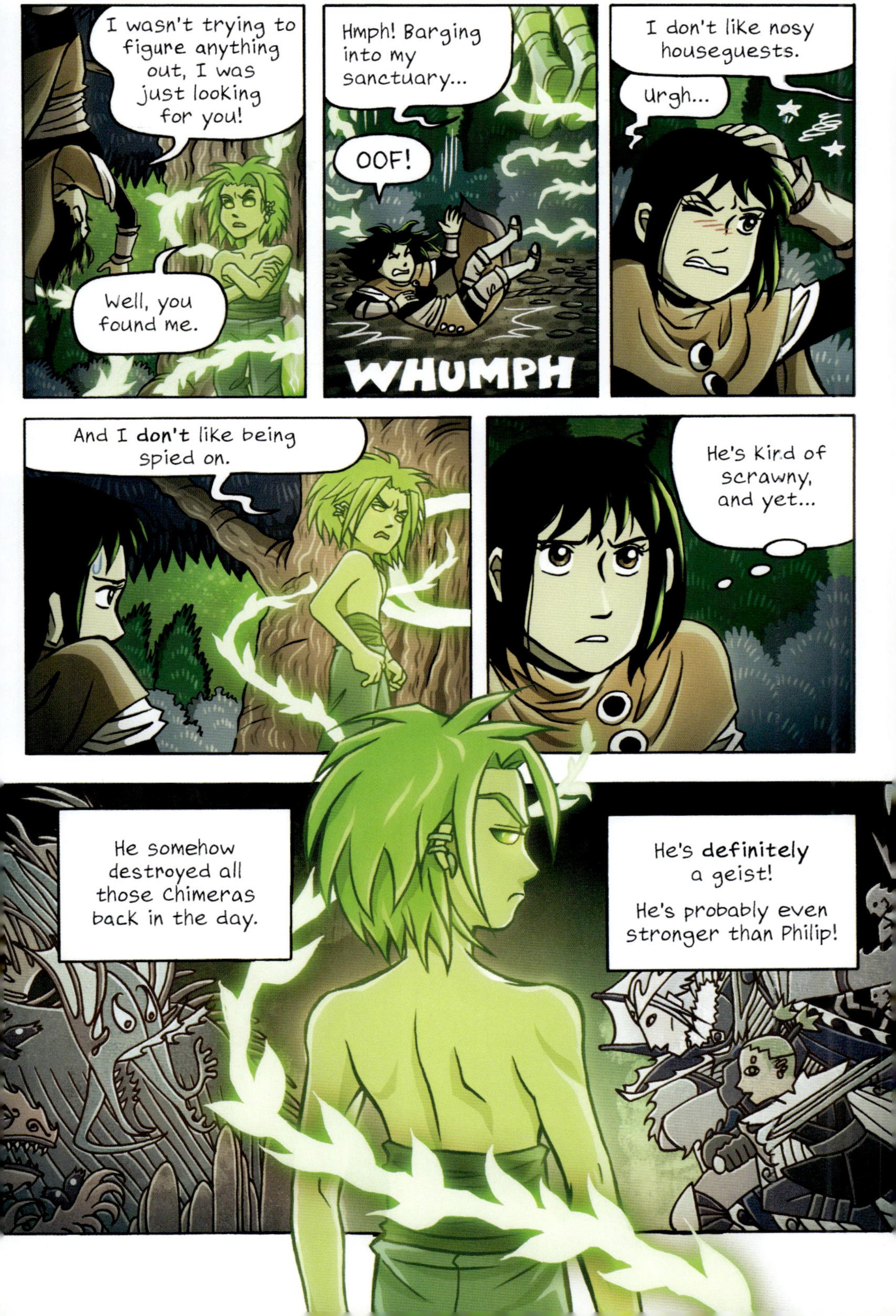
I wasn't trying to figure anything out, I was just looking for you!
Well, you found me.
Hmph! Barging into my sanctuary...
OOF!
WHUMPH
I don't like nosy houseguests.
Urgh...
And I **don't** like being spied on.
He's kind of scrawny, and yet...
He somehow destroyed all those Chimeras back in the day.
He's **definitely** a geist!
He's probably even stronger than Philip!

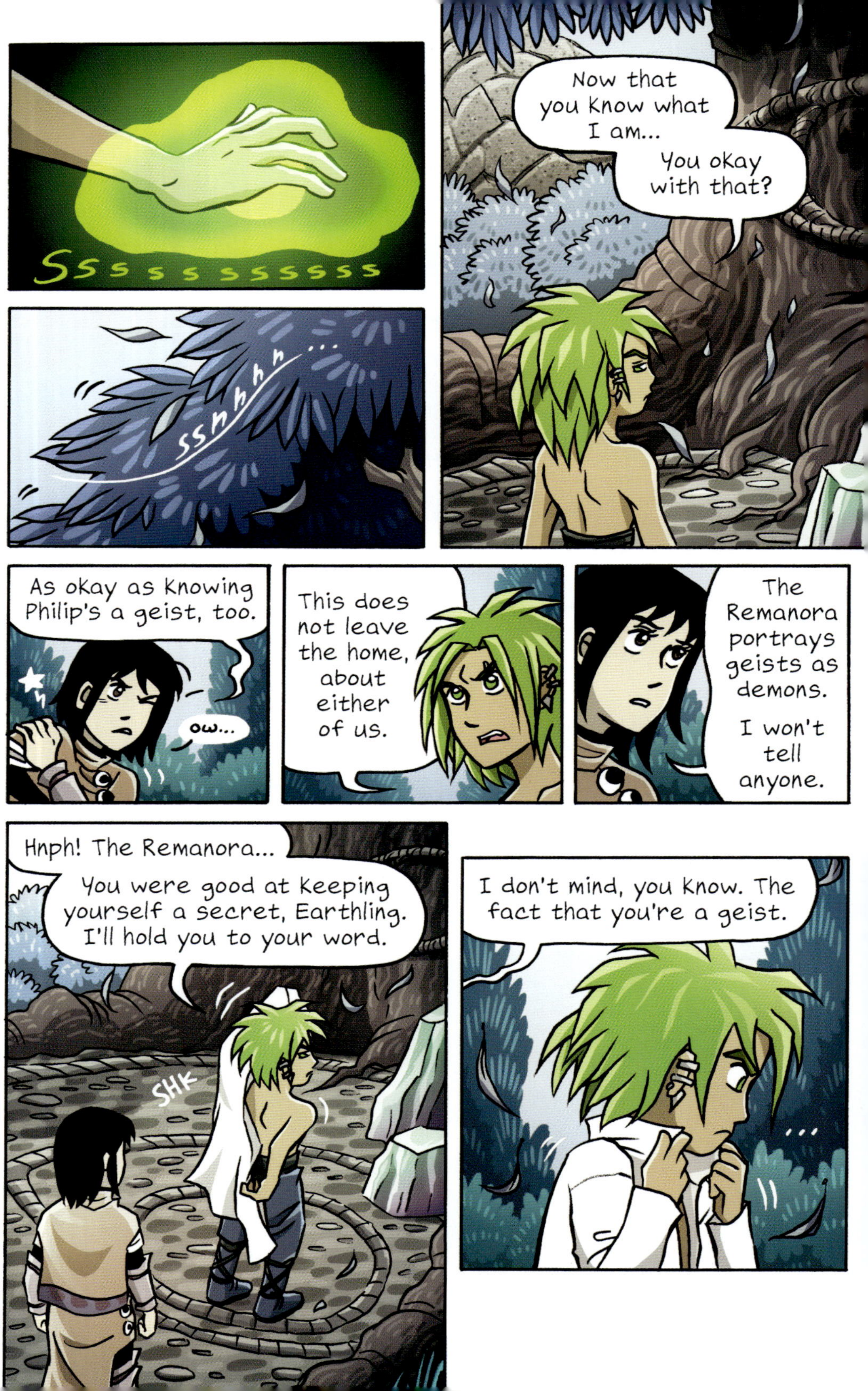
Ssssssssssss
sshhhh...
Now that you know what I am...
You okay with that?
As okay as knowing Philip's a geist, too.
ow...
This does not leave the home, about either of us.
The Remanora portrays geists as demons.
I won't tell anyone.
Hnph! The Remanora...
You were good at keeping yourself a secret, Earthling. I'll hold you to your word.
SHK
I don't mind, you know. The fact that you're a geist.
...

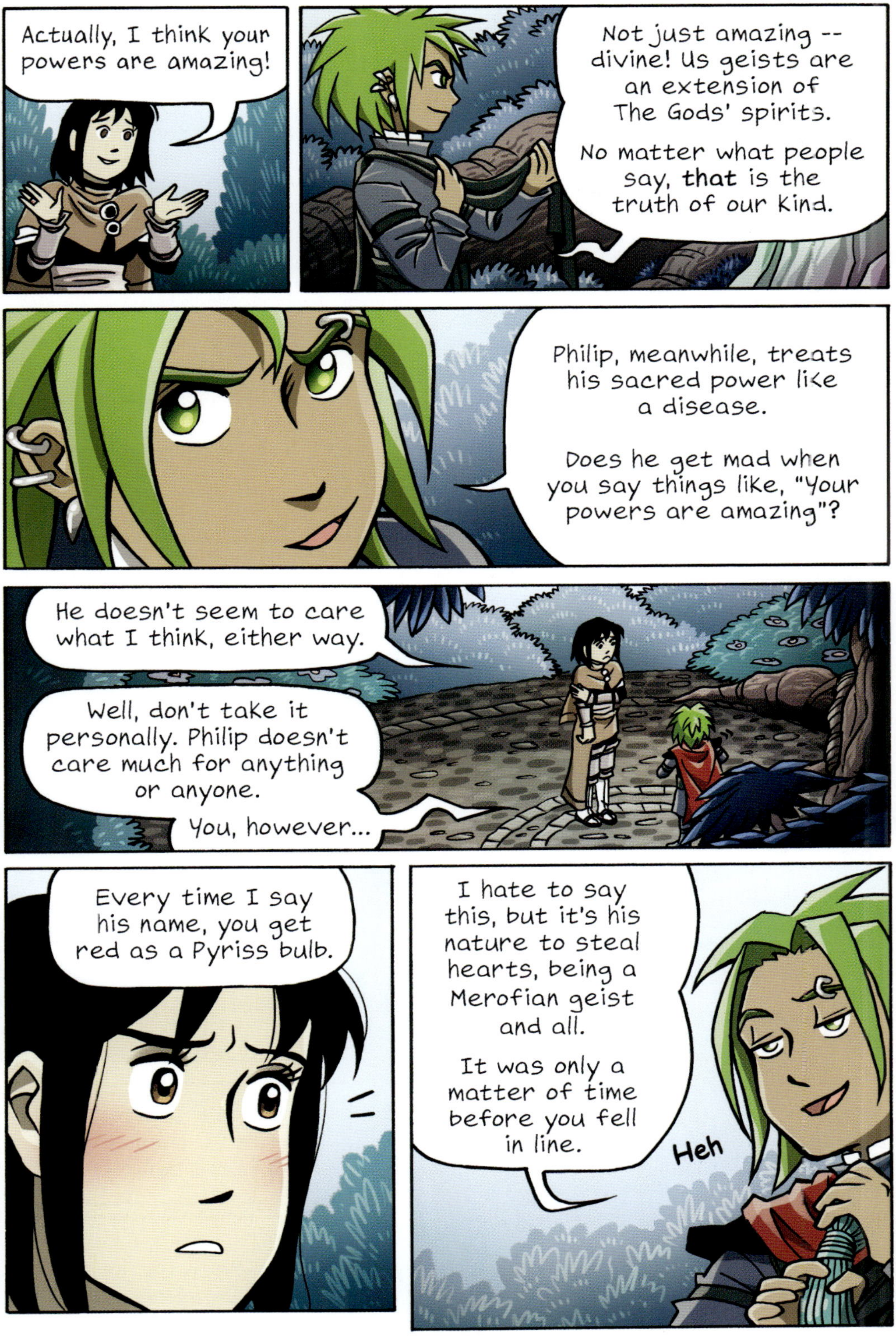

Actually, I think your powers are amazing!
Not just amazing -- divine! Us geists are an extension of The Gods' spirits.
No matter what people say, **that** is the truth of our Kind.
Philip, meanwhile, treats his sacred power like a disease.
Does he get mad when you say things like, "Your powers are amazing"?
He doesn't seem to care what I think, either way.
Well, don't take it personally. Philip doesn't care much for anything or anyone.
You, however...
Every time I say his name, you get red as a Pyriss bulb.
I hate to say this, but it's his nature to steal hearts, being a Merofian geist and all.
It was only a matter of time before you fell in line.
Heh

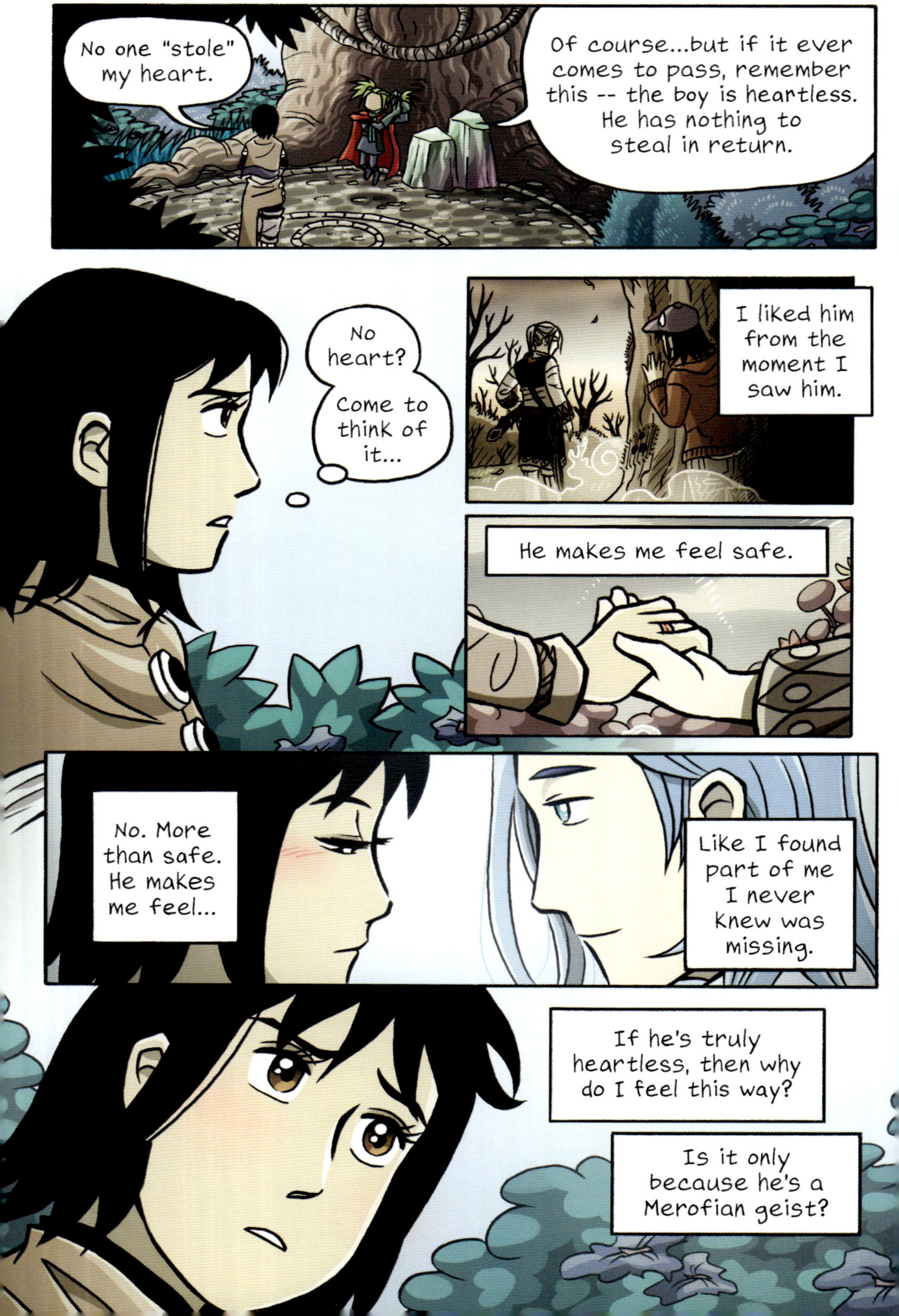
No one "stole" my heart.
Of course...but if it ever comes to pass, remember this -- the boy is heartless. He has nothing to steal in return.
No heart? Come to think of it...
I liked him from the moment I saw him.
He makes me feel safe.
No. More than safe. He makes me feel...
Like I found part of me I never knew was missing.
If he's truly heartless, then why do I feel this way?
Is it only because he's a Merofian geist?

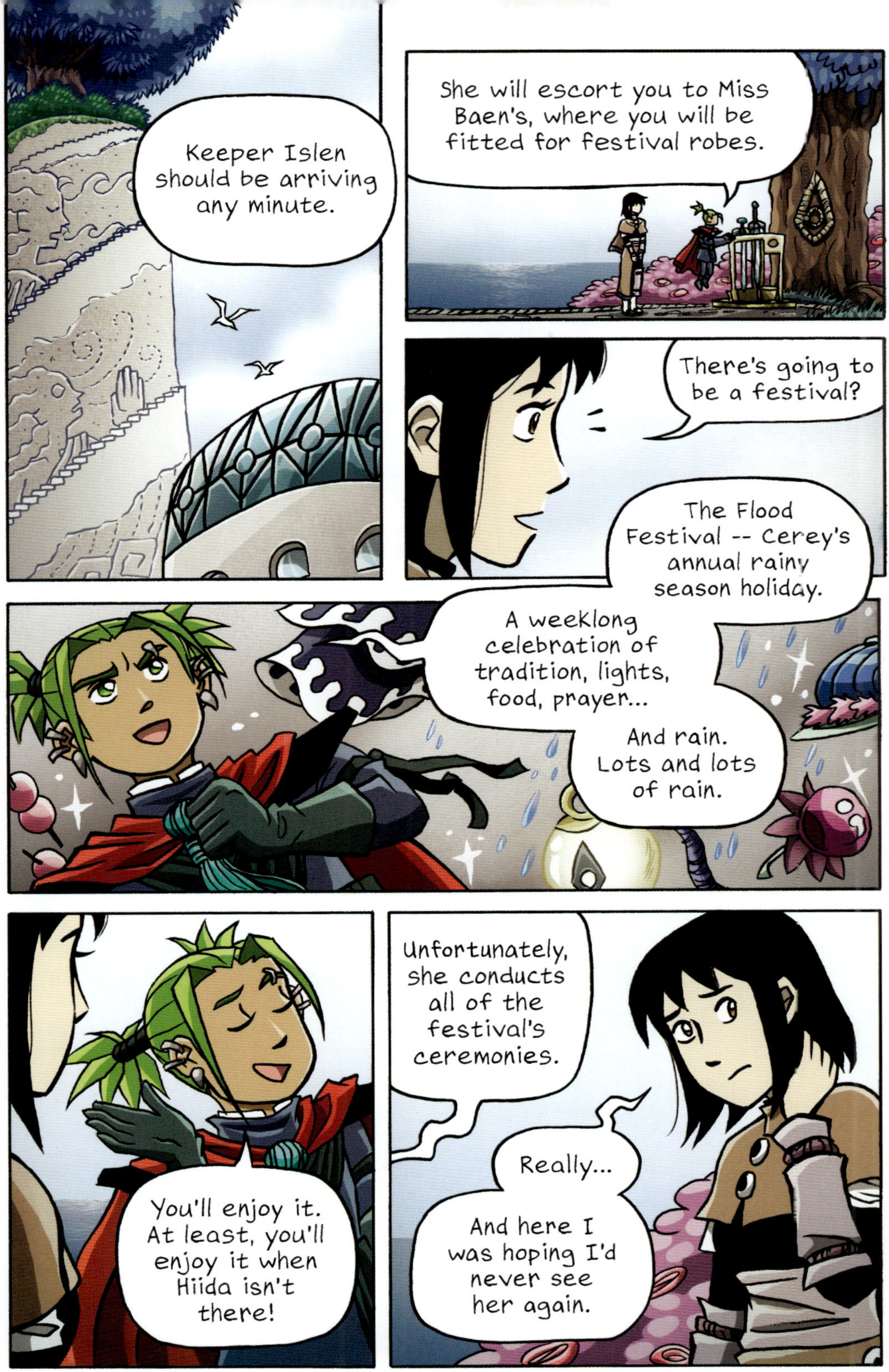
Keeper Islen should be arriving any minute.
She will escort you to Miss Baen's, where you will be fitted for festival robes.
There's going to be a festival?
The Flood Festival -- Cerey's annual rainy season holiday.
A weeklong celebration of tradition, lights, food, prayer...
And rain. Lots and lots of rain.
You'll enjoy it. At least, you'll enjoy it when Hiida isn't there!
Unfortunately, she conducts all of the festival's ceremonies.
Really...
And here I was hoping I'd never see her again.

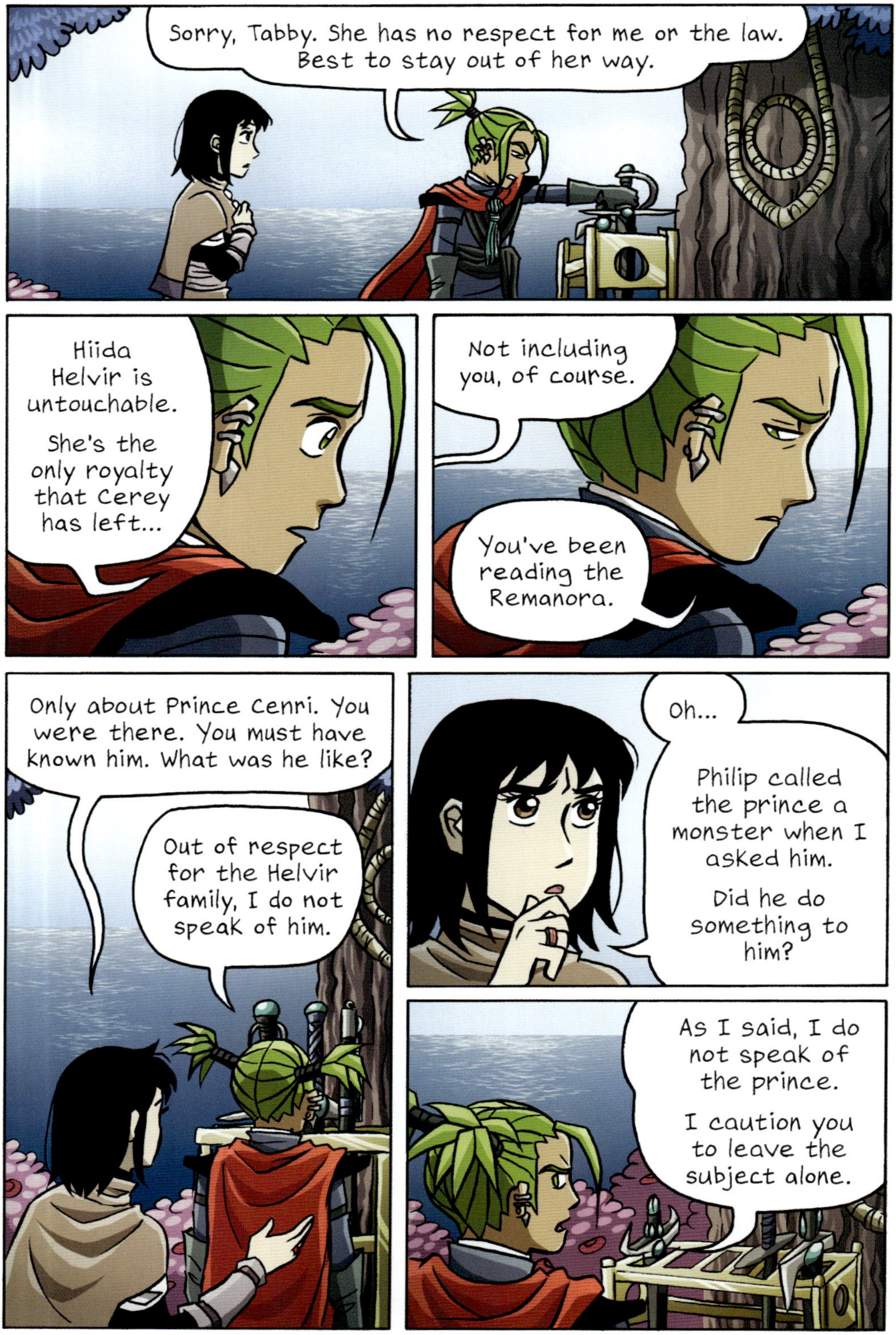
Sorry, Tabby. She has no respect for me or the law. Best to stay out of her way.
Hiida Helvir is untouchable.
She's the only royalty that Cerey has left...
Not including you, of course.
You've been reading the Remanora.
Only about Prince Cenri. You were there. You must have known him. What was he like?
Out of respect for the Helvir family, I do not speak of him.
Oh...
Philip called the prince a monster when I asked him.
Did he do something to him?
As I said, I do not speak of the prince.
I caution you to leave the subject alone.

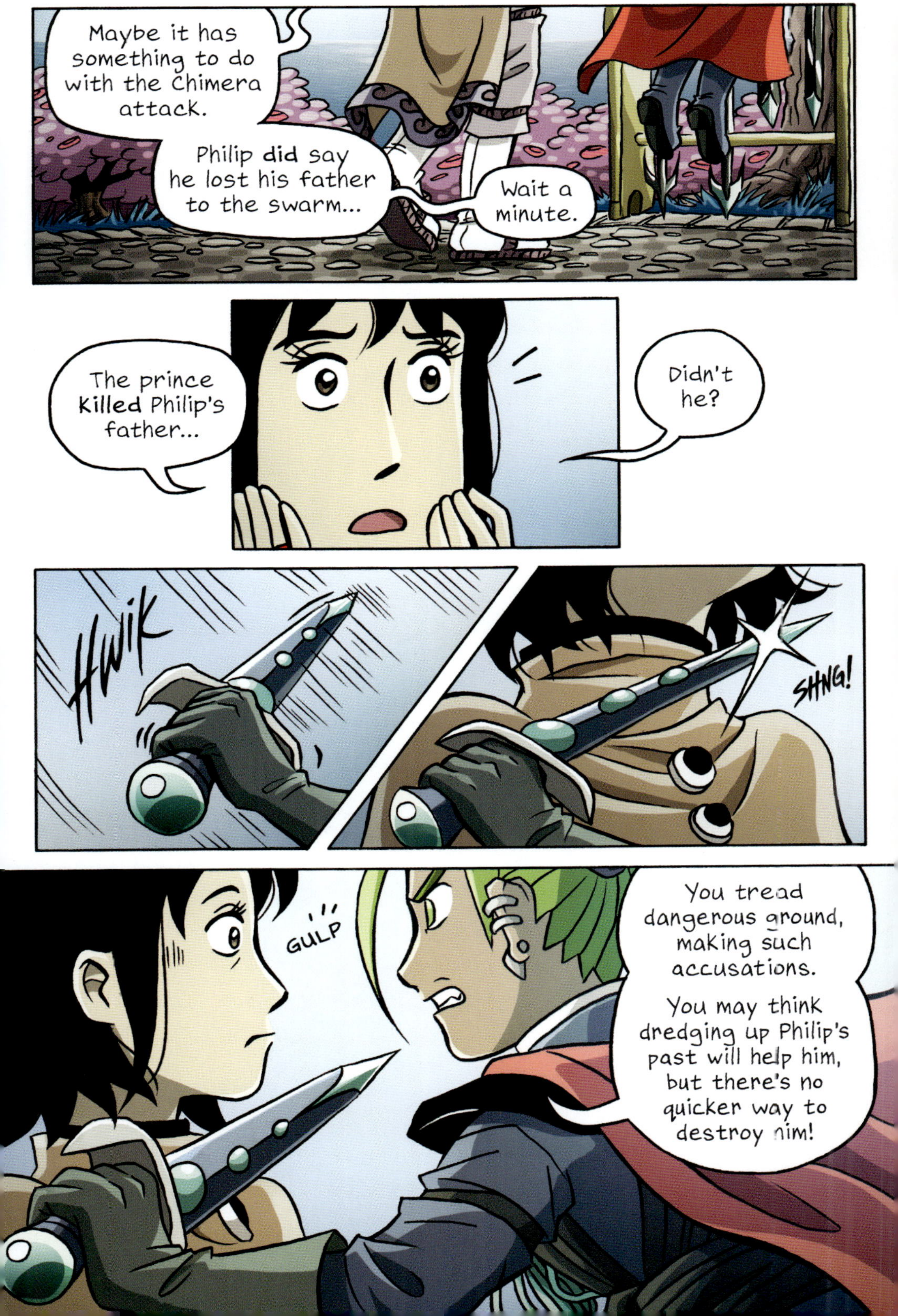

Maybe it has something to do with the Chimera attack.
Philip **did** say he lost his father to the swarm...
Wait a minute.
The prince **killed** Philip's father...
Didn't he?
HWIK
SHNG!
GULP
You tread dangerous ground, making such accusations.
You may think dredging up Philip's past will help him, but there's no quicker way to destroy him!

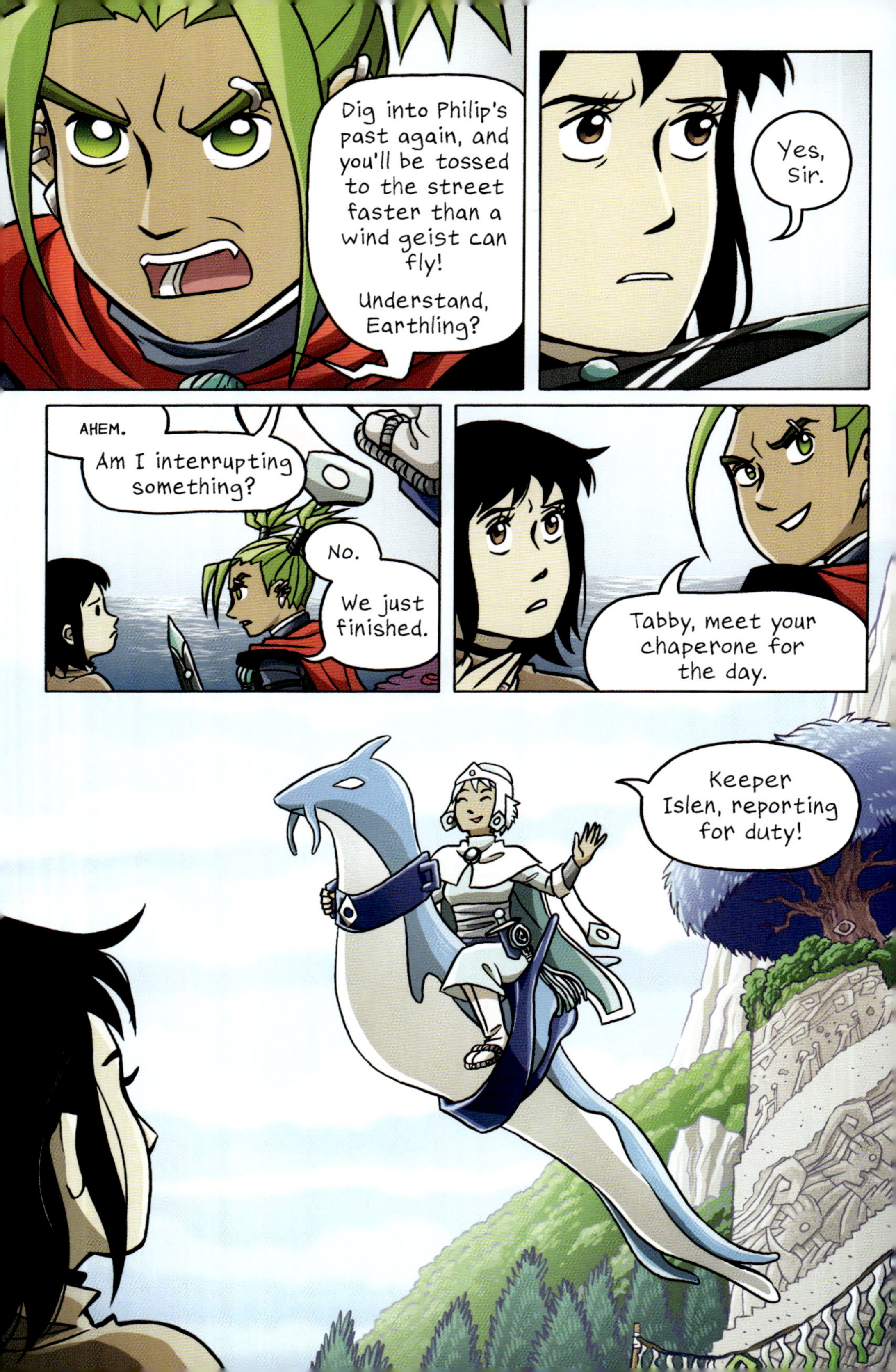

Dig into Philip's past again, and you'll be tossed to the street faster than a wind geist can fly!
Understand, Earthling?
Yes, Sir.
AHEM.
Am I interrupting something?
No.
We just finished.
Tabby, meet your chaperone for the day.
Keeper Islen, reporting for duty!

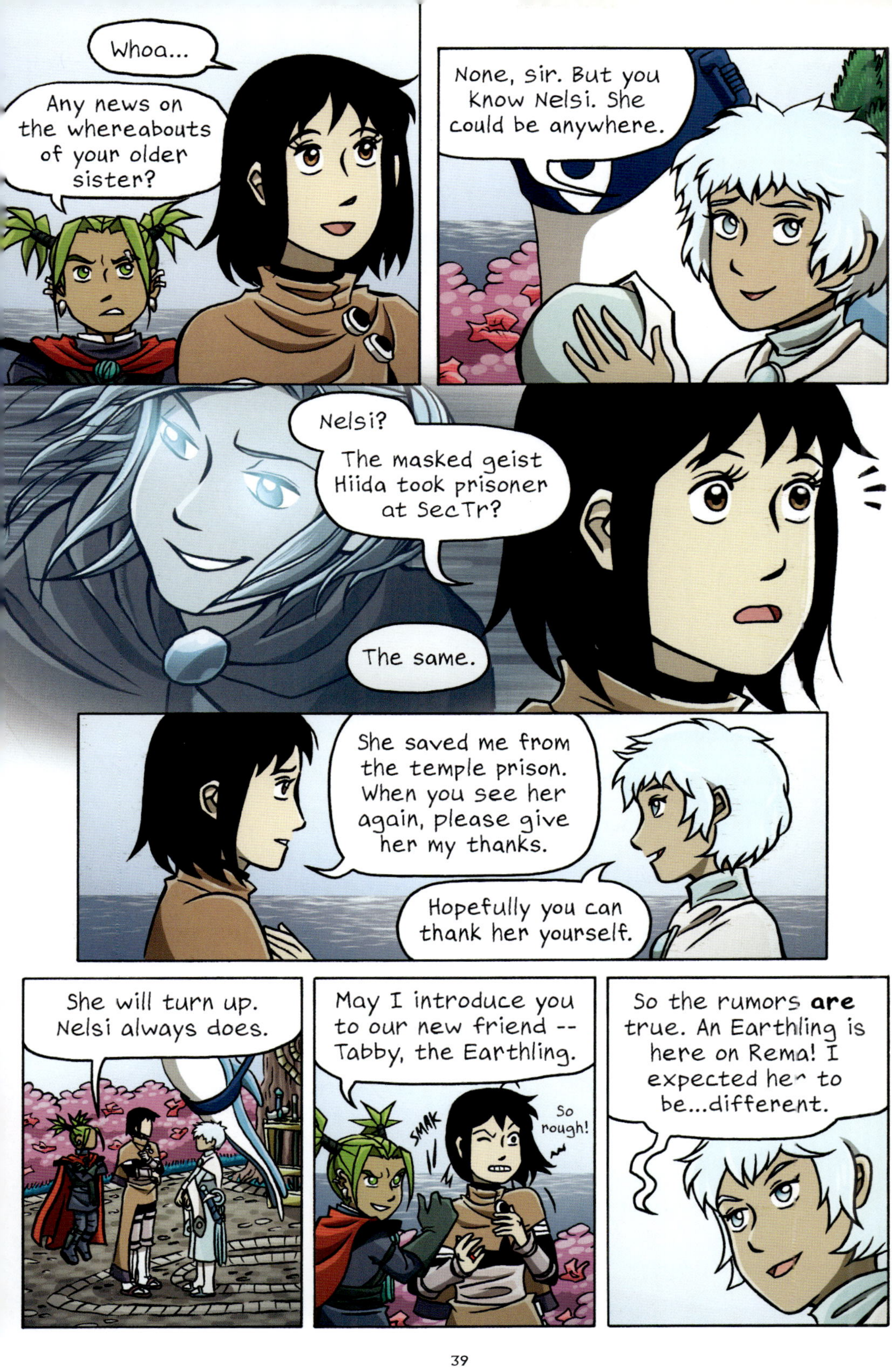
Whoa...
Any news on the whereabouts of your older sister?
None, sir. But you know Nelsi. She could be anywhere.
Nelsi?
The masked geist Hiida took prisoner at SecTr?
The same.
She saved me from the temple prison. When you see her again, please give her my thanks.
Hopefully you can thank her yourself.
She will turn up. Nelsi always does.
May I introduce you to our new friend -- Tabby, the Earthling.
SMAK
So rough!
So the rumors **are** true. An Earthling is here on Rema! I expected her to be...different.

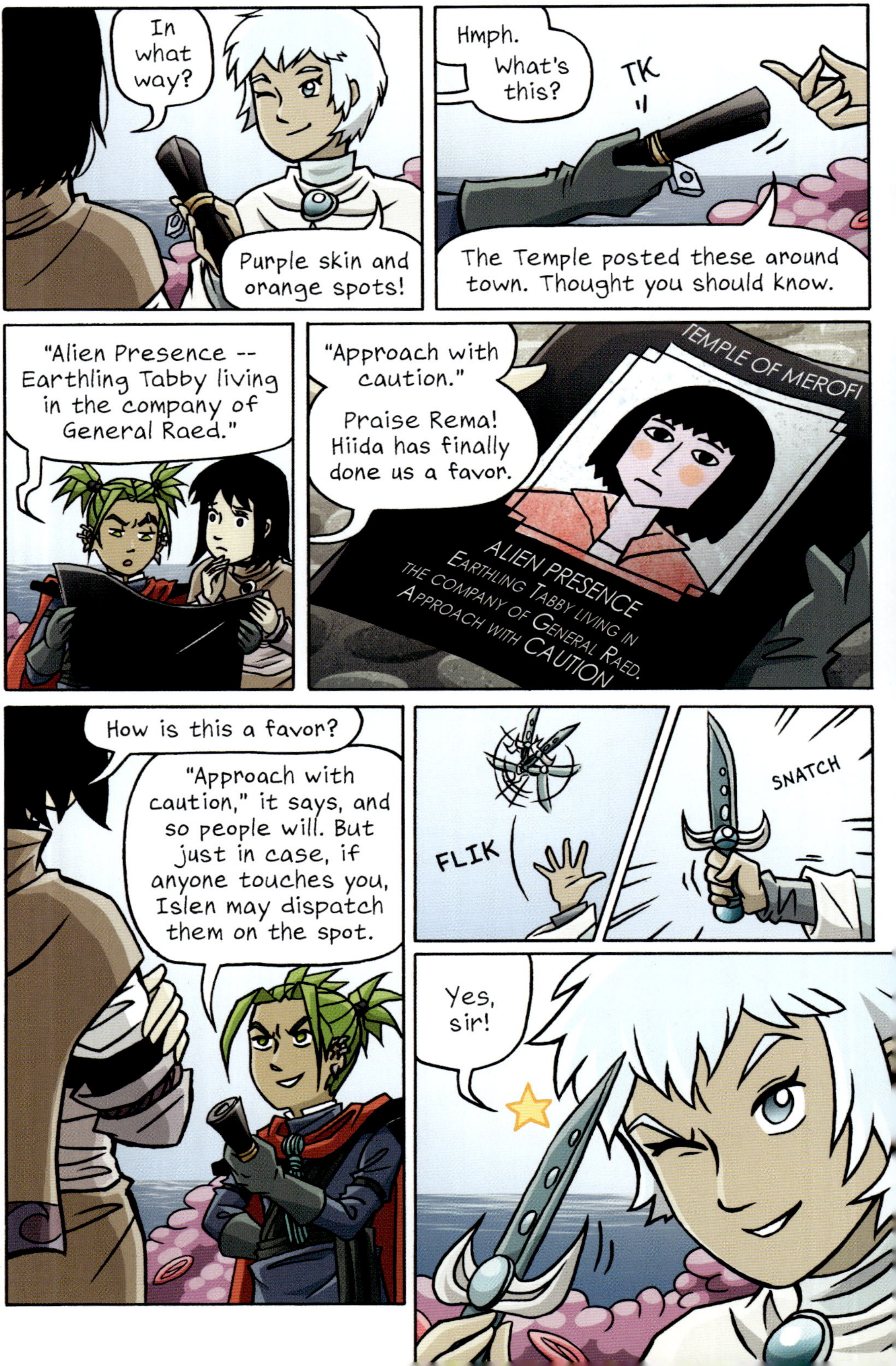
In what way?
Purple skin and orange spots!
Hmph. What's this?
TK
The Temple posted these around town. Thought you should know.
"Alien Presence -- Earthling Tabby living in the company of General Raed."
"Approach with caution."
Praise Rema! Hiida has finally done us a favor.
TEMPLE OF MEROFI
ALIEN PRESENCE
EARTHLING TABBY LIVING IN THE COMPANY OF GENERAL RAED.
APPROACH WITH CAUTION
How is this a favor?
"Approach with caution," it says, and so people will. But just in case, if anyone touches you, Islen may dispatch them on the spot.
FLIK
SNATCH
Yes, sir!

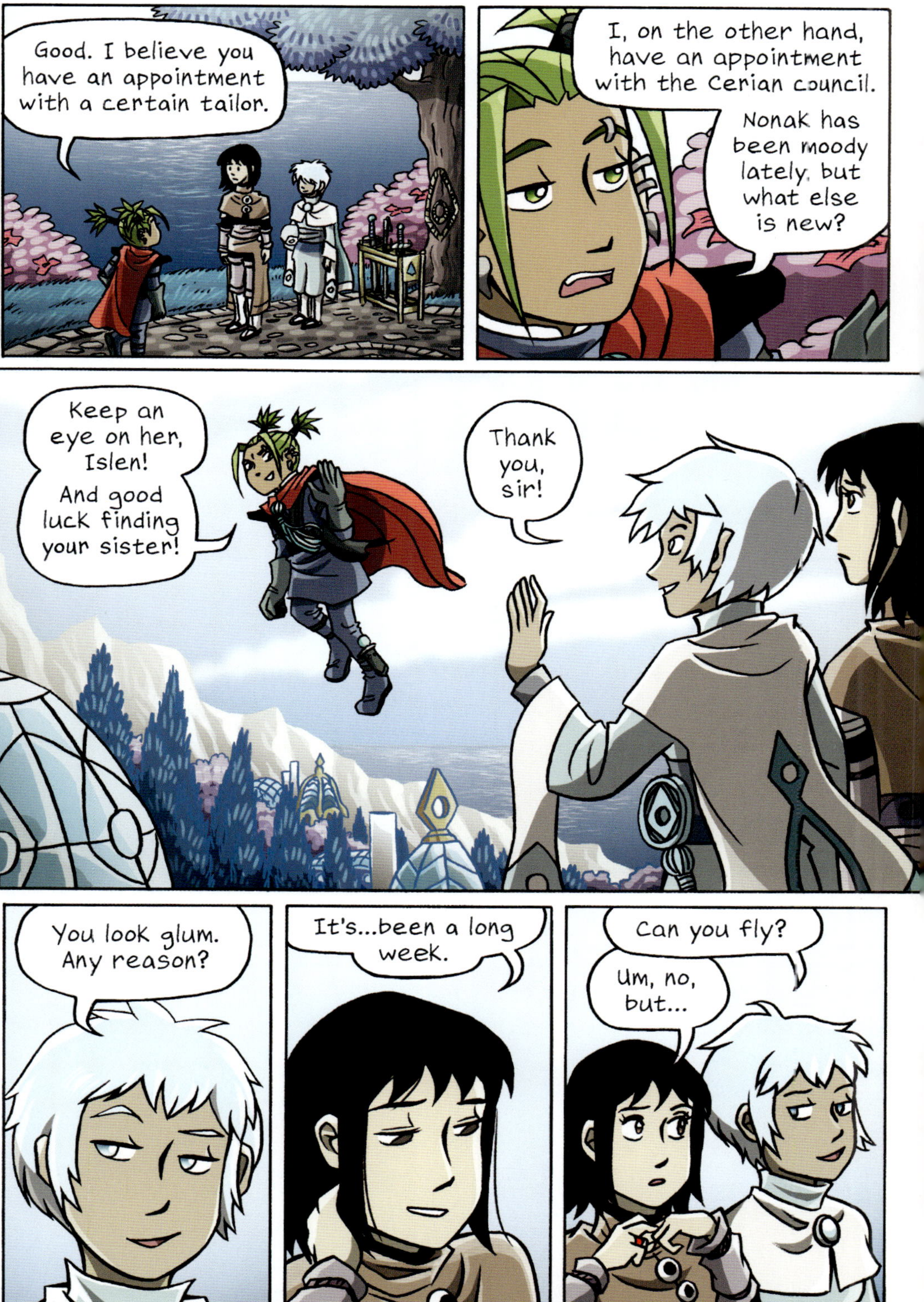
Good. I believe you have an appointment with a certain tailor.
I, on the other hand, have an appointment with the Cerian council.
Nonak has been moody lately, but what else is new?
Keep an eye on her, Islen!
And good luck finding your sister!
Thank you, sir!
You look glum. Any reason?
It's...been a long week.
Can you fly?
Um, no, but...

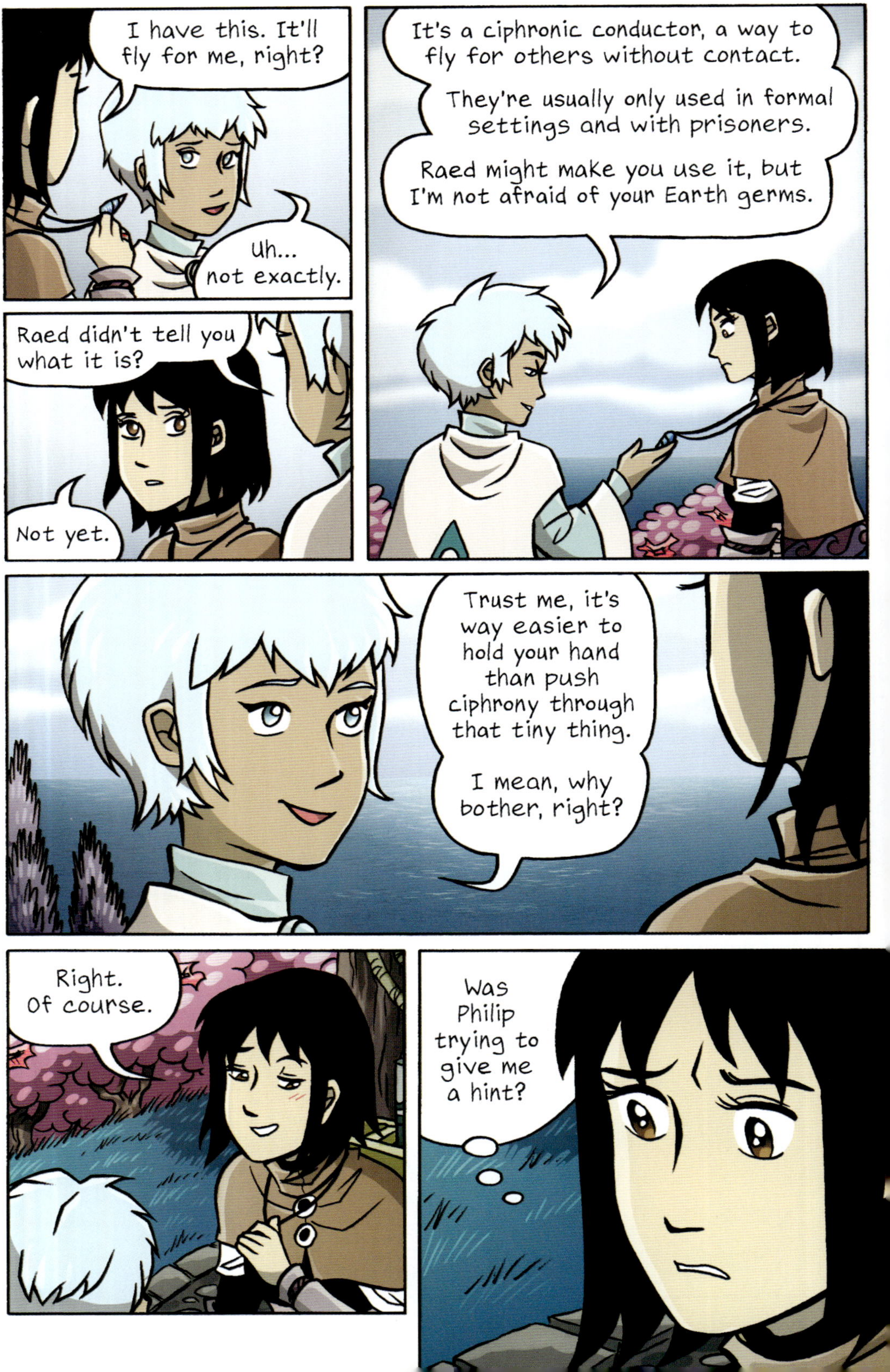
I have this. It'll fly for me, right?
Uh... not exactly.
It's a ciphronic conductor, a way to fly for others without contact.
They're usually only used in formal settings and with prisoners.
Raed might make you use it, but I'm not afraid of your Earth germs.
Raed didn't tell you what it is?
Not yet.
Trust me, it's way easier to hold your hand than push ciphrony through that tiny thing.
I mean, why bother, right?
Right. Of course.
Was Philip trying to give me a hint?

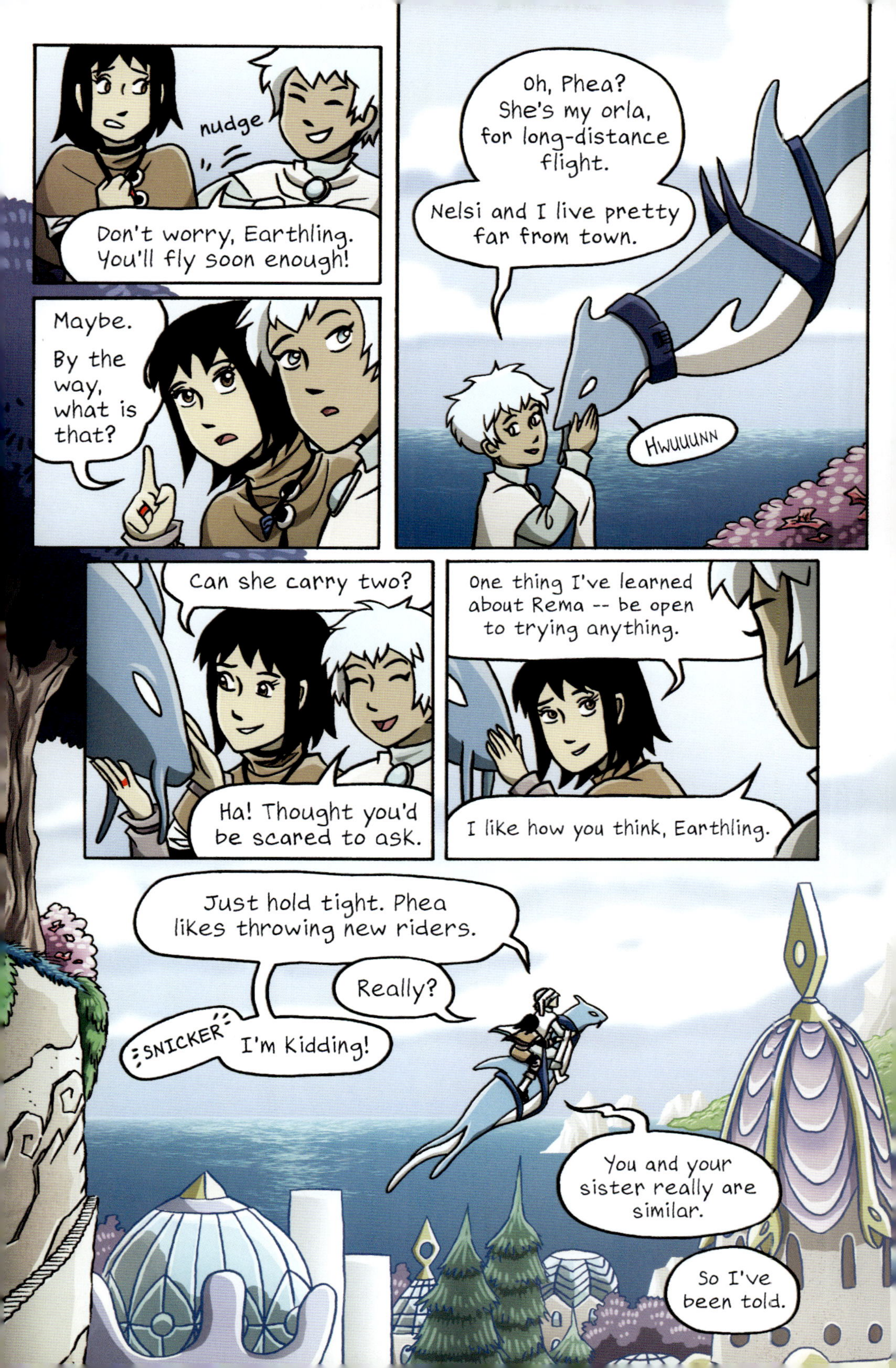
nudge
Don't worry, Earthling. You'll fly soon enough!
Maybe.
By the way, what is that?
Oh, Phea? She's my orla, for long-distance flight.
Nelsi and I live pretty far from town.
HWUUUNN
Can she carry two?
Ha! Thought you'd be scared to ask.
One thing I've learned about Rema -- be open to trying anything.
I like how you think, Earthling.
Just hold tight. Phea likes throwing new riders.
Really?
I'm kidding!
SNICKER
You and your sister really are similar.
So I've been told.

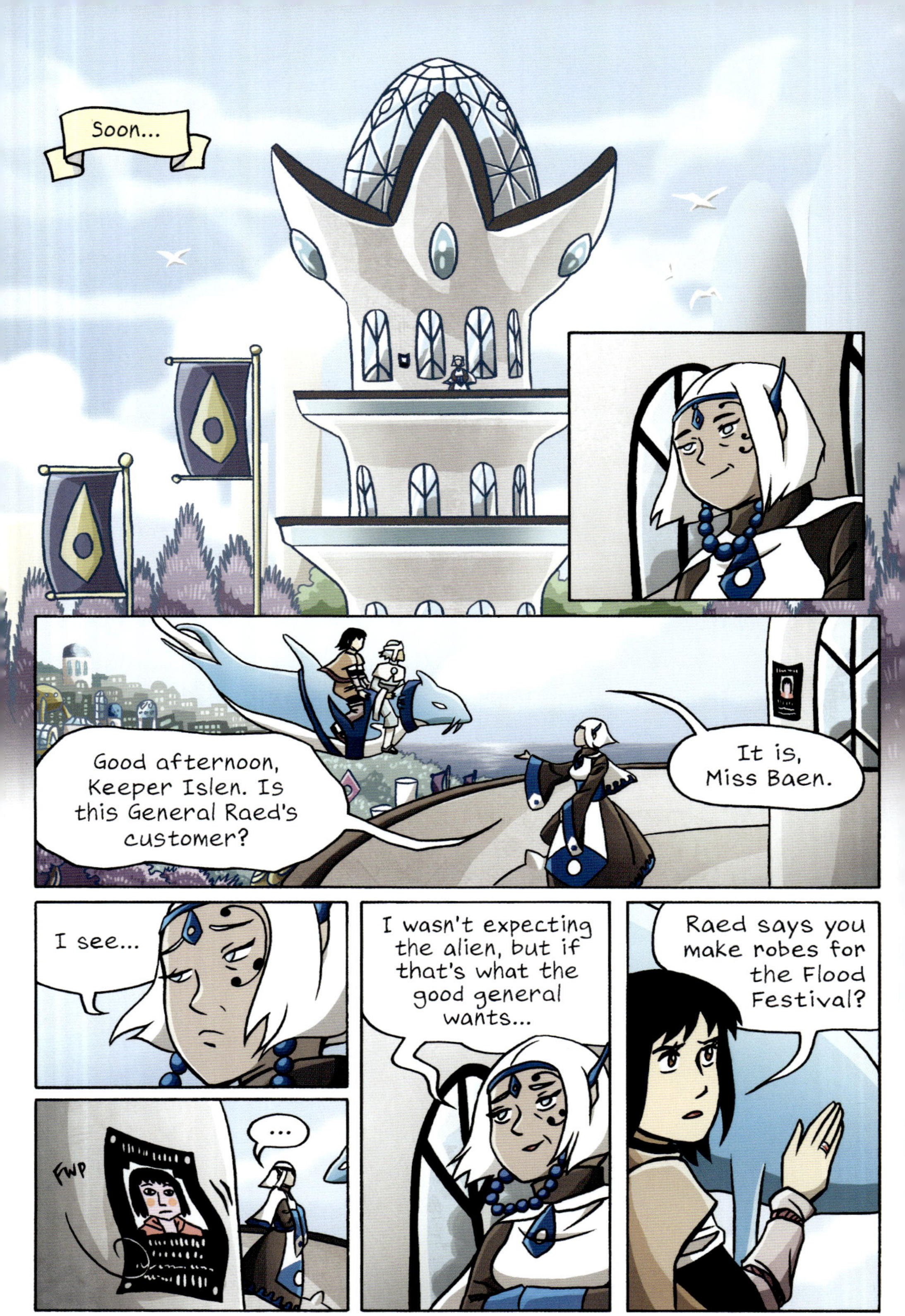
Soon...
Good afternoon, Keeper Islen. Is this General Raed's customer?
It is, Miss Baen.
I see...
I wasn't expecting the alien, but if that's what the good general wants...
Raed says you make robes for the Flood Festival?
FWP
...

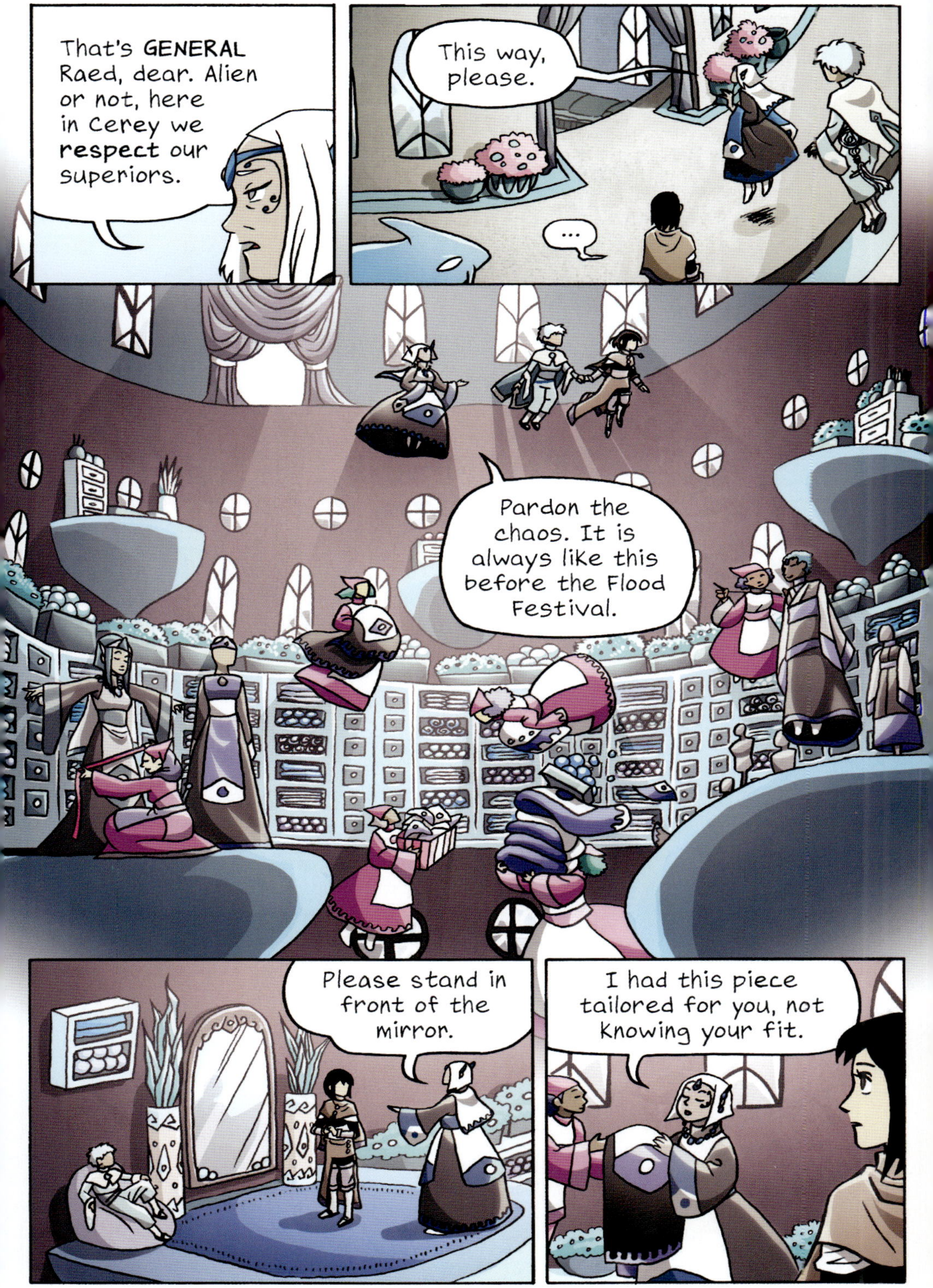
That's GENERAL Raed, dear. Alien or not, here in Cerey we respect our superiors.
This way, please.
...
Pardon the chaos. It is always like this before the Flood Festival.
Please stand in front of the mirror.
I had this piece tailored for you, not knowing your fit.

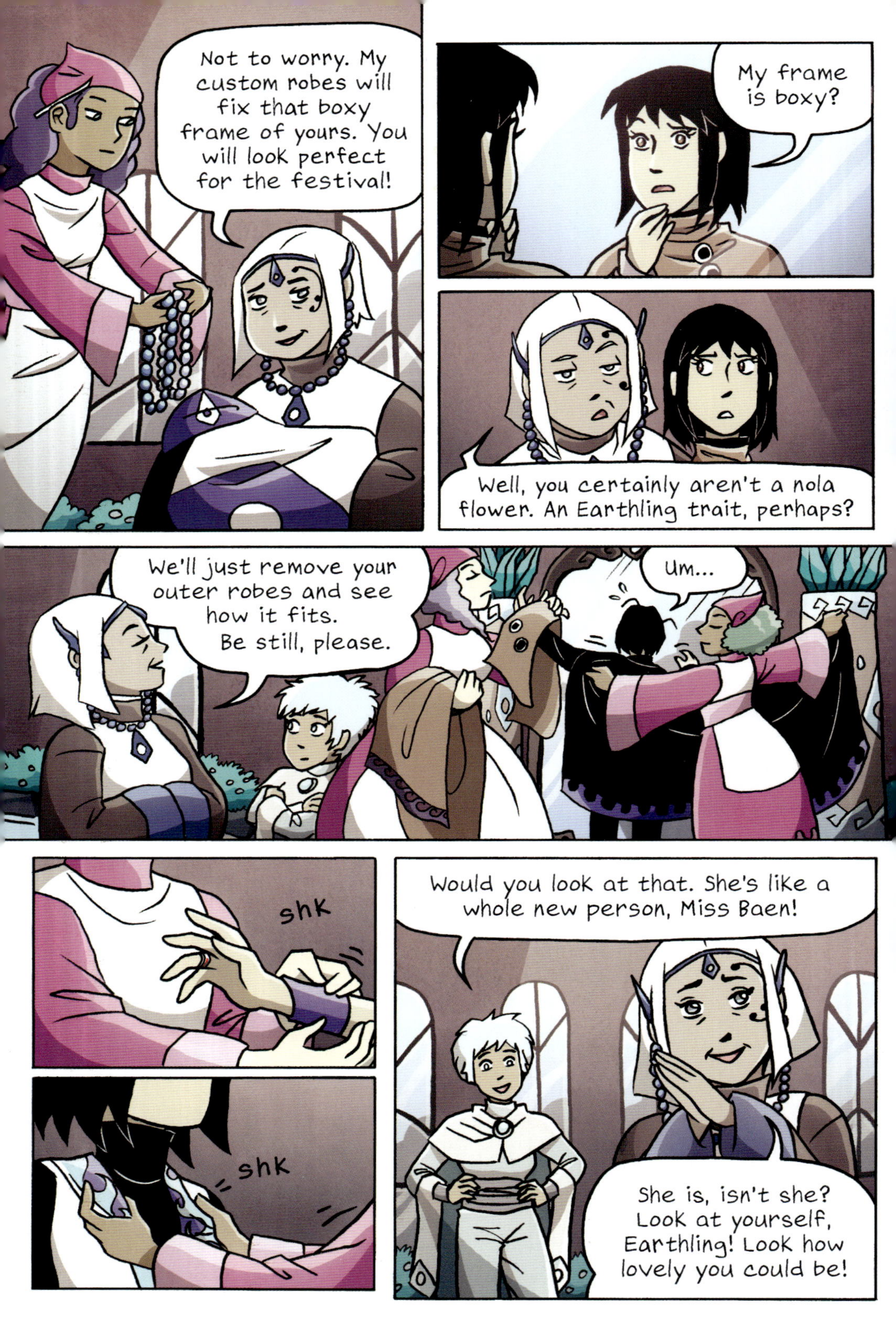
Not to worry. My custom robes will fix that boxy frame of yours. You will look perfect for the festival!
My frame is boxy?
Well, you certainly aren't a nola flower. An Earthling trait, perhaps?
We'll just remove your outer robes and see how it fits. Be still, please.
Um...
shk
shk
Would you look at that. She's like a whole new person, Miss Baen!
She is, isn't she? Look at yourself, Earthling! Look how lovely you could be!

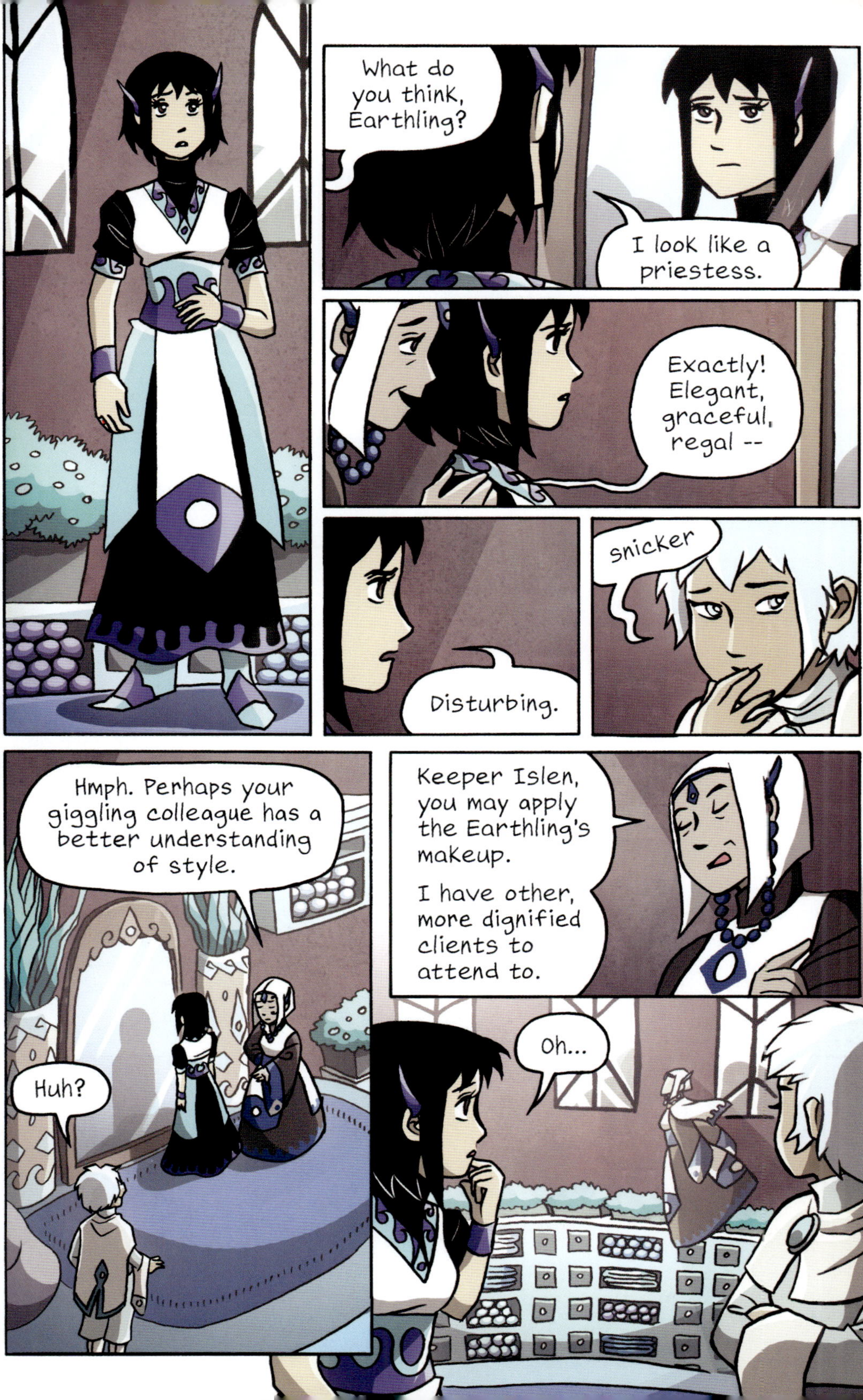
What do you think, Earthling?
I look like a priestess.
Exactly! Elegant, graceful, regal --
Disturbing.
snicker
Hmph. Perhaps your giggling colleague has a better understanding of style.
Huh?
Keeper Islen, you may apply the Earthling's makeup.
I have other, more dignified clients to attend to.
Oh...

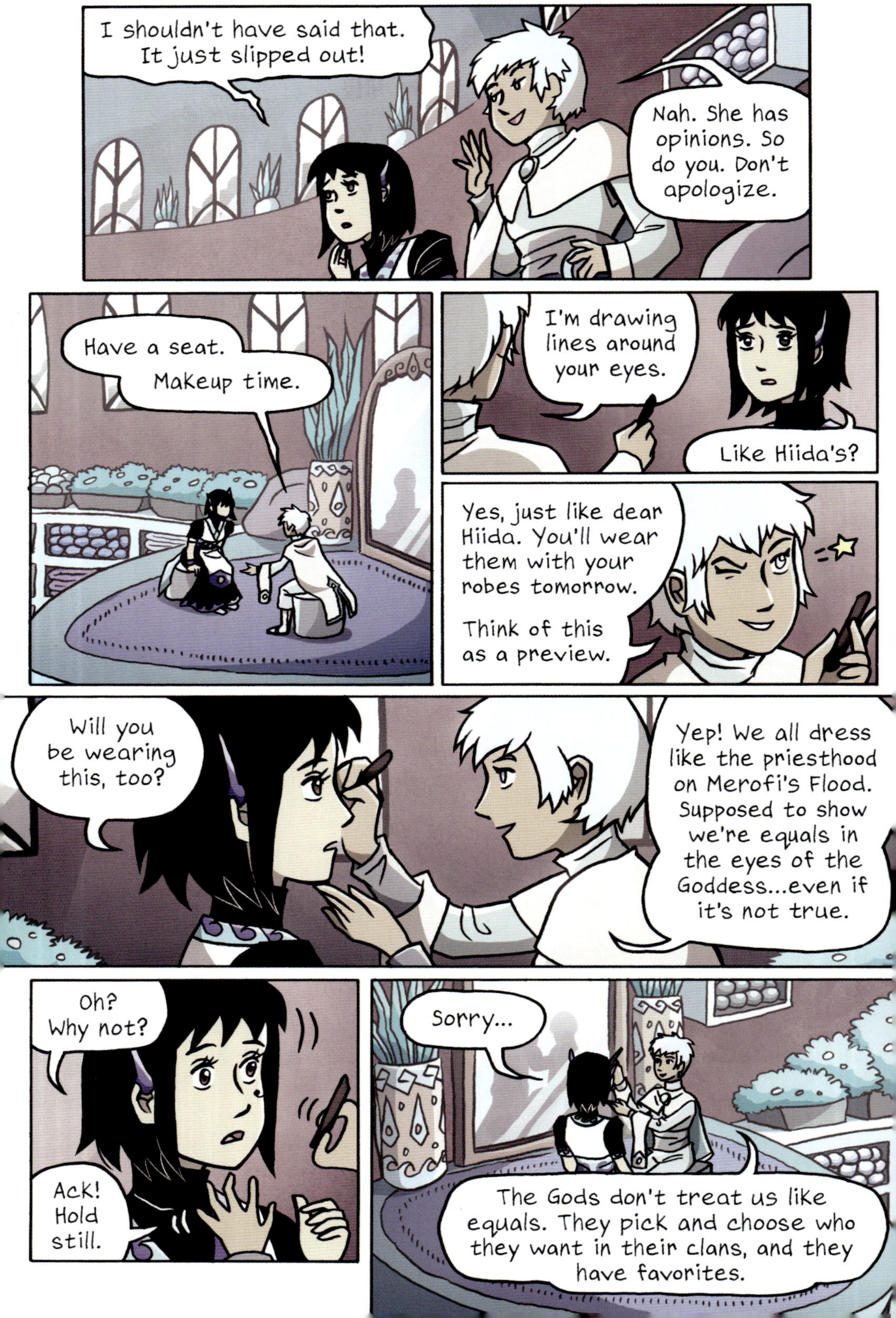
I shouldn't have said that. It just slipped out!
Nah. She has opinions. So do you. Don't apologize.
Have a seat.
Makeup time.
I'm drawing lines around your eyes.
Like Hiida's?
Yes, just like dear Hiida. You'll wear them with your robes tomorrow.
Think of this as a preview.
Will you be wearing this, too?
Yep! We all dress like the priesthood on Merofi's Flood. Supposed to show we're equals in the eyes of the Goddess...even if it's not true.
Oh? Why not?
Ack! Hold still.
Sorry...
The Gods don't treat us like equals. They pick and choose who they want in their clans, and they have favorites.

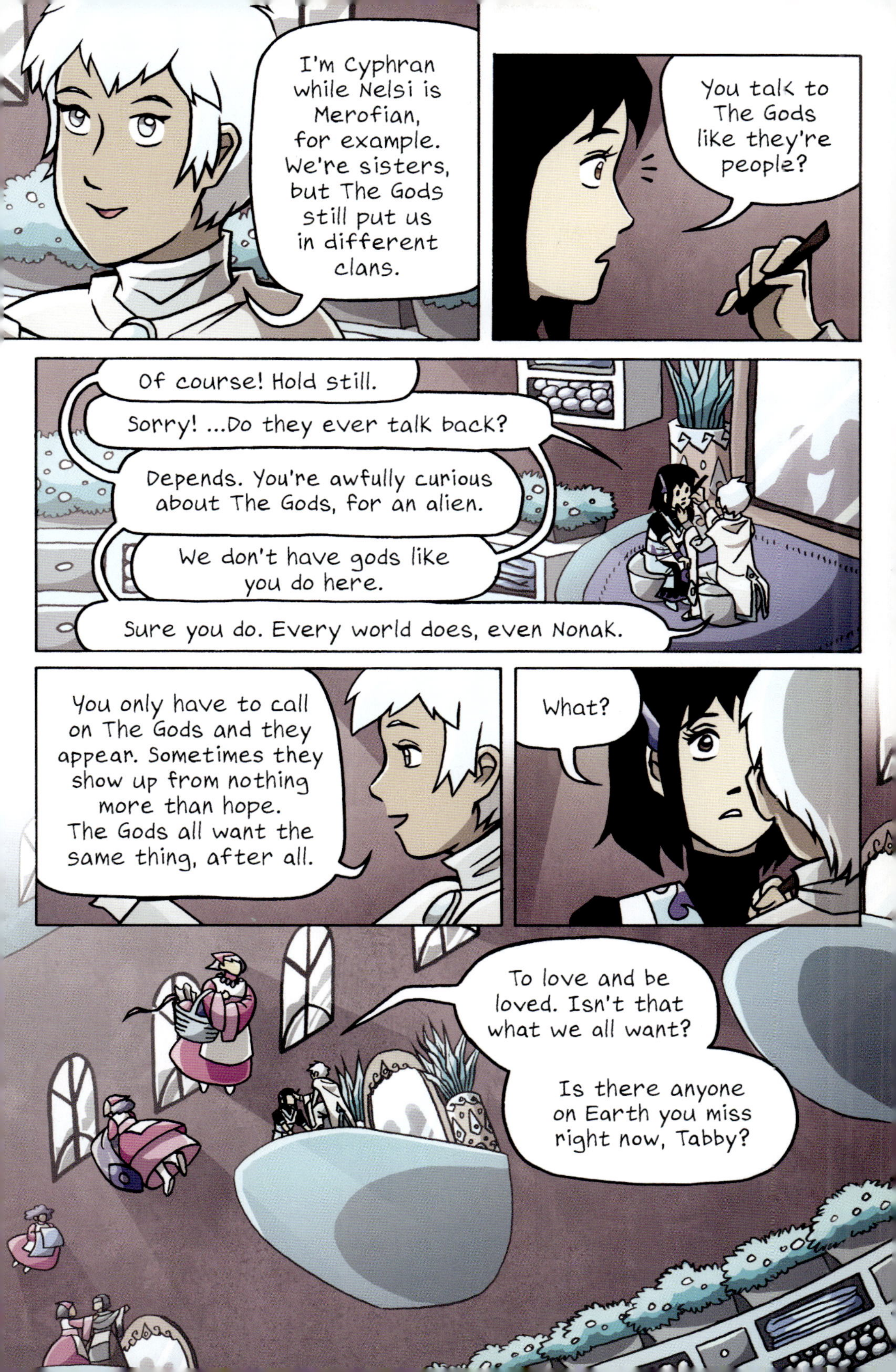
I'm Cyphran while Nelsi is Merofian, for example. We're sisters, but The Gods still put us in different clans.
You talk to The Gods like they're people?
Of course! Hold still.
Sorry! ...Do they ever talk back?
Depends. You're awfully curious about The Gods, for an alien.
We don't have gods like you do here.
Sure you do. Every world does, even Nonak.
You only have to call on The Gods and they appear. Sometimes they show up from nothing more than hope. The Gods all want the same thing, after all.
What?
To love and be loved. Isn't that what we all want?
Is there anyone on Earth you miss right now, Tabby?

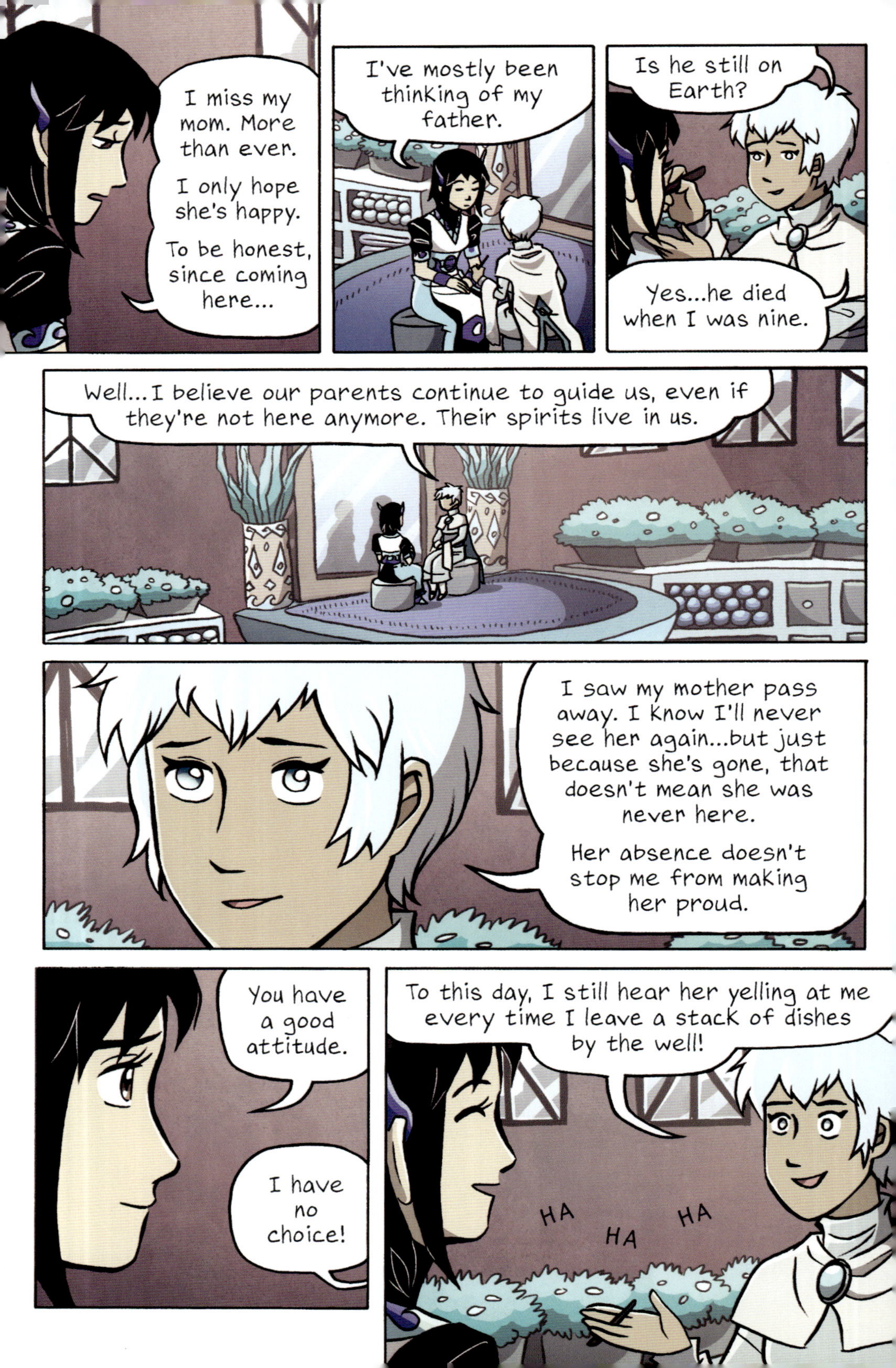
I miss my mom. More than ever.
I only hope she's happy.
To be honest, since coming here...
I've mostly been thinking of my father.
Is he still on Earth?
Yes...he died when I was nine.
Well...I believe our parents continue to guide us, even if they're not here anymore. Their spirits live in us.
I saw my mother pass away. I know I'll never see her again...but just because she's gone, that doesn't mean she was never here.
Her absence doesn't stop me from making her proud.
You have a good attitude.
I have no choice!
To this day, I still hear her yelling at me every time I leave a stack of dishes by the well!
HA
HA
HA

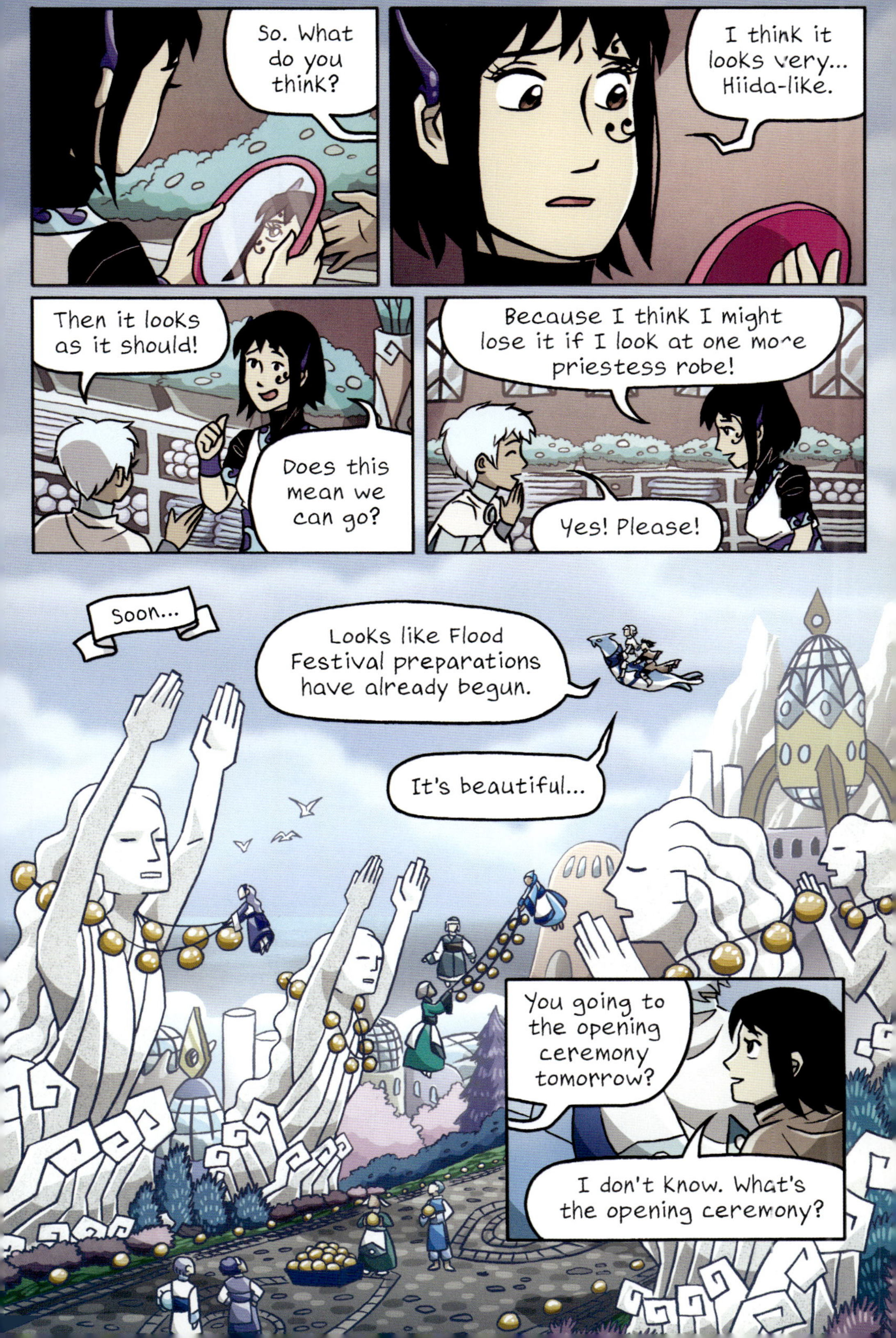
So. What do you think?
I think it looks very... Hiida-like.
Then it looks as it should!
Does this mean we can go?
Because I think I might lose it if I look at one more priestess robe!
Yes! Please!
Soon...
Looks like Flood Festival preparations have already begun.
It's beautiful...
You going to the opening ceremony tomorrow?
I don't know. What's the opening ceremony?

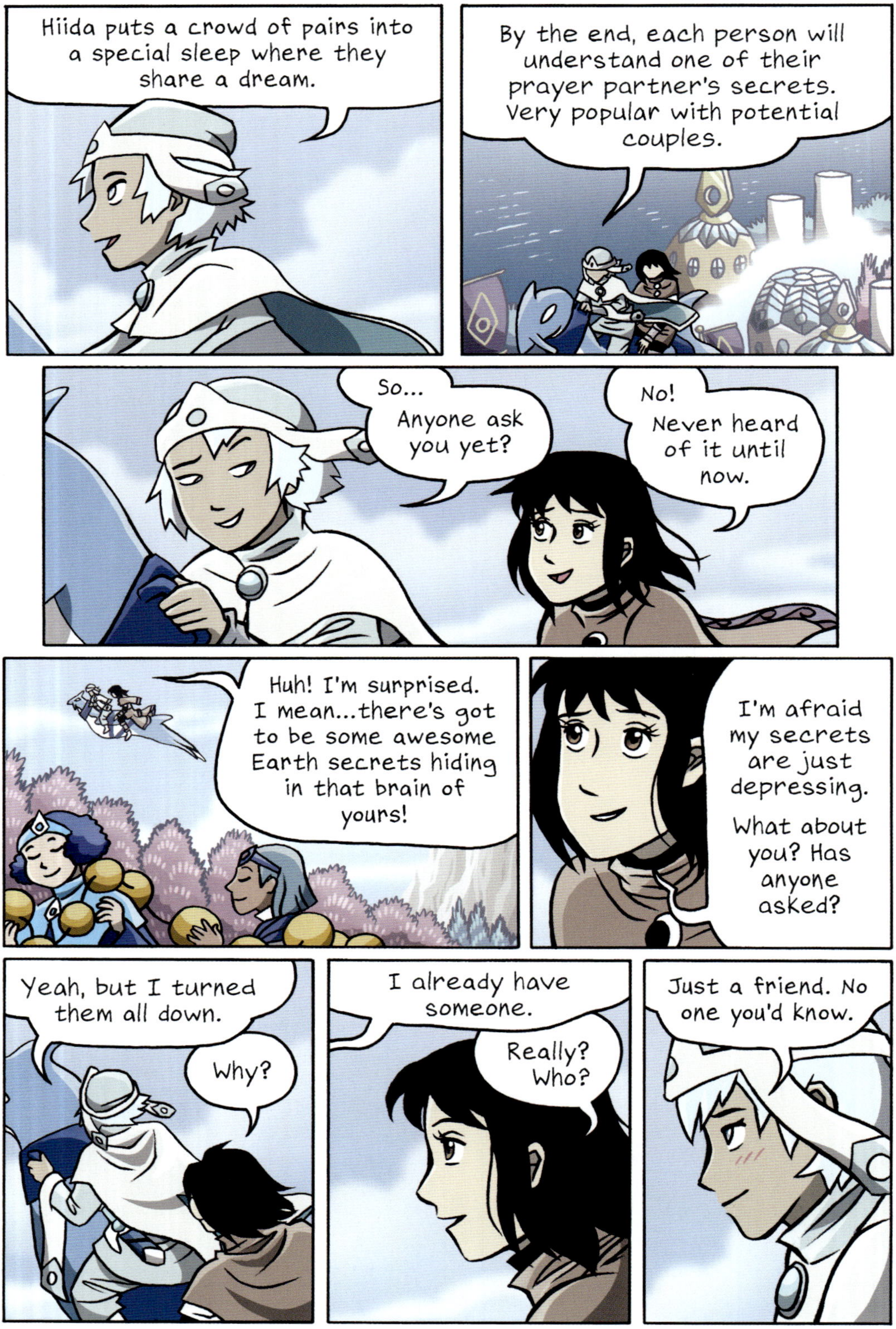
Hiida puts a crowd of pairs into a special sleep where they share a dream.
By the end, each person will understand one of their prayer partner's secrets. Very popular with potential couples.
So... Anyone ask you yet?
No! Never heard of it until now.
Huh! I'm surprised. I mean...there's got to be some awesome Earth secrets hiding in that brain of yours!
I'm afraid my secrets are just depressing.
What about you? Has anyone asked?
Yeah, but I turned them all down.
Why?
I already have someone.
Really? Who?
Just a friend. No one you'd know.

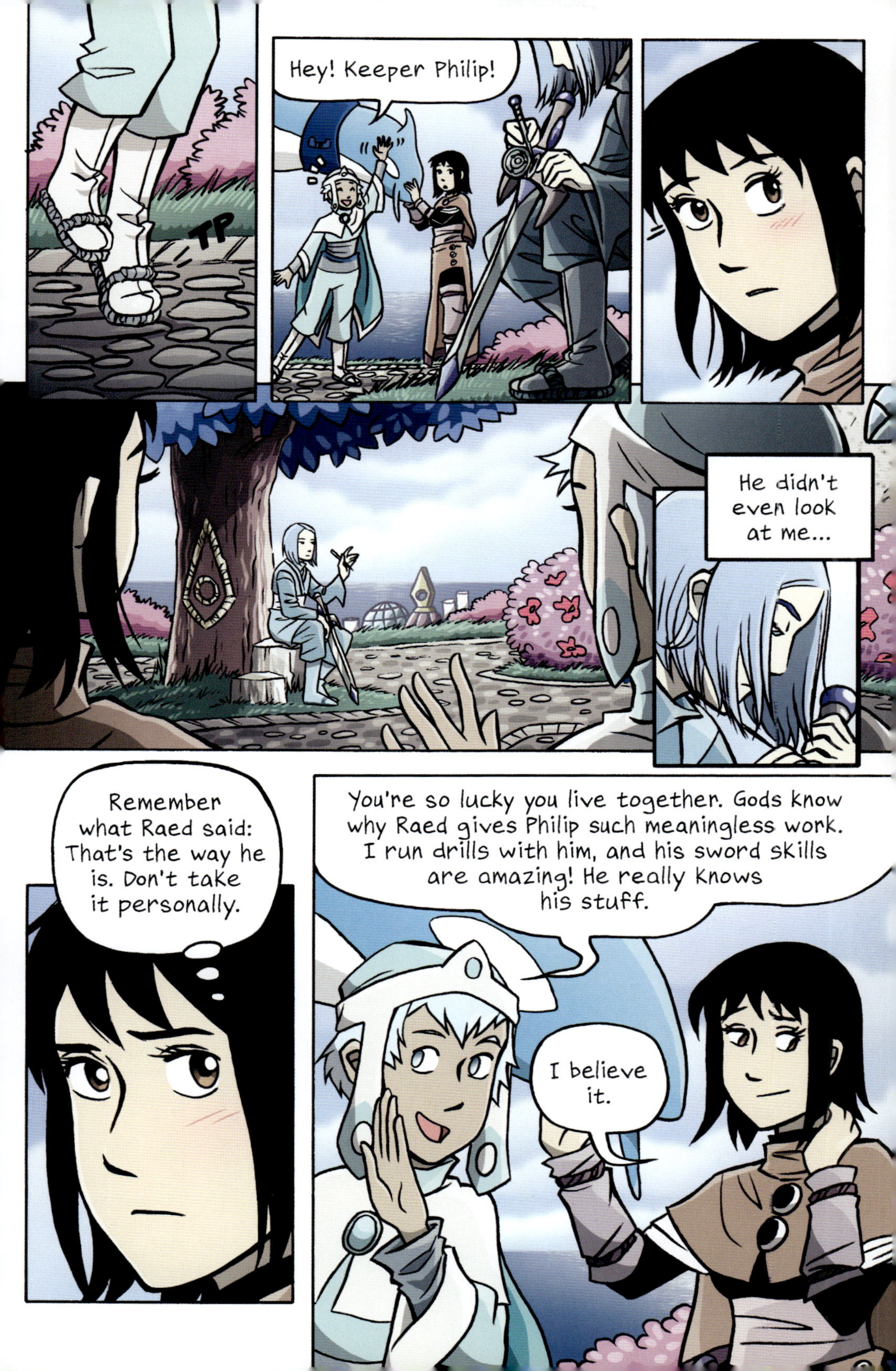
TP
Hey! Keeper Philip!
He didn't even look at me...
Remember what Raed said: That's the way he is. Don't take it personally.
You're so lucky you live together. Gods know why Raed gives Philip such meaningless work. I run drills with him, and his sword skills are amazing! He really knows his stuff.
I believe it.

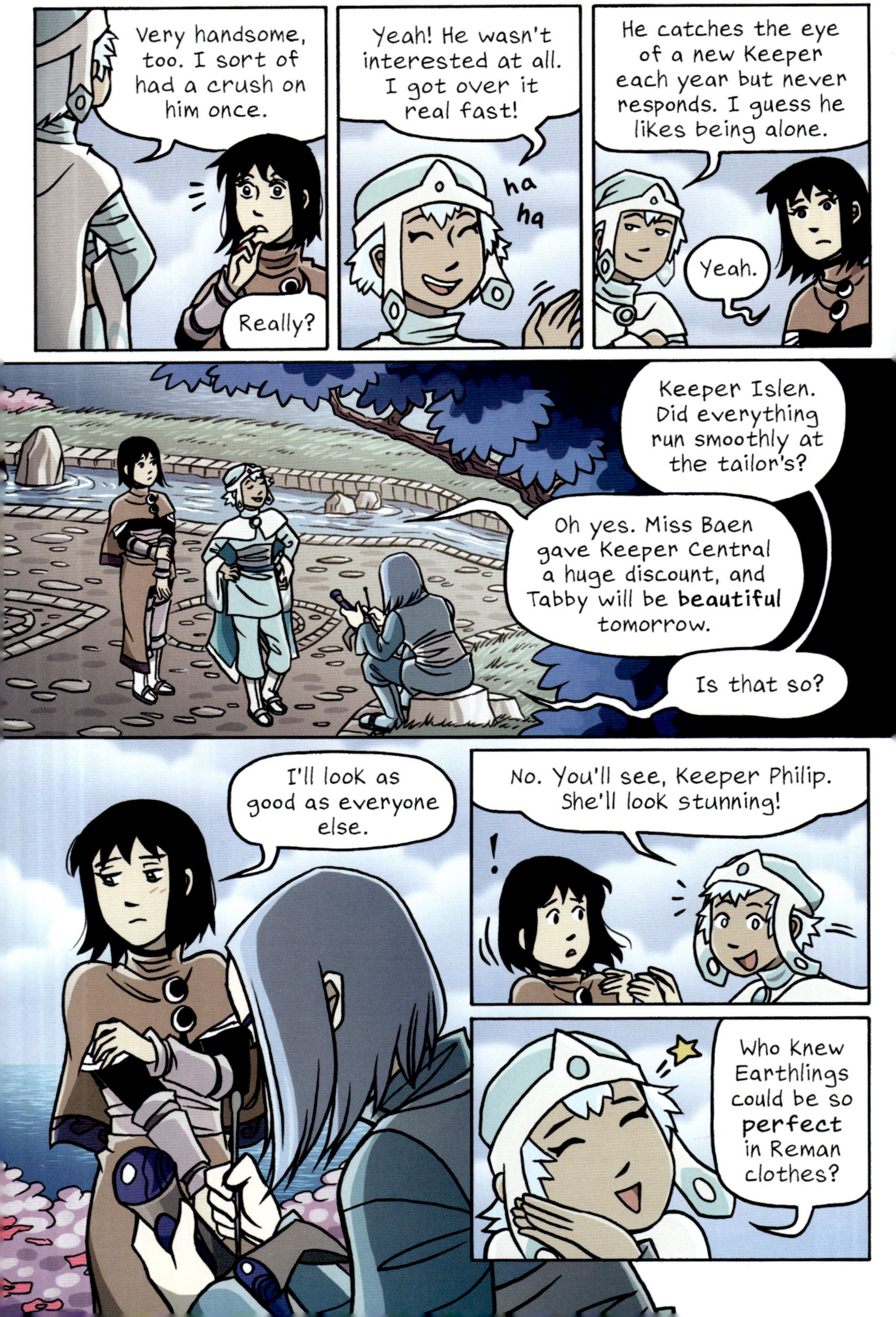
Very handsome, too. I sort of had a crush on him once.
Really?
Yeah! He wasn't interested at all. I got over it real fast!
ha ha
He catches the eye of a new Keeper each year but never responds. I guess he likes being alone.
Yeah.
Keeper Islen. Did everything run smoothly at the tailor's?
Oh yes. Miss Baen gave Keeper Central a huge discount, and Tabby will be **beautiful** tomorrow.
Is that so?
I'll look as good as everyone else.
No. You'll see, Keeper Philip. She'll look stunning!
!
Who knew Earthlings could be so **perfect** in Reman clothes?

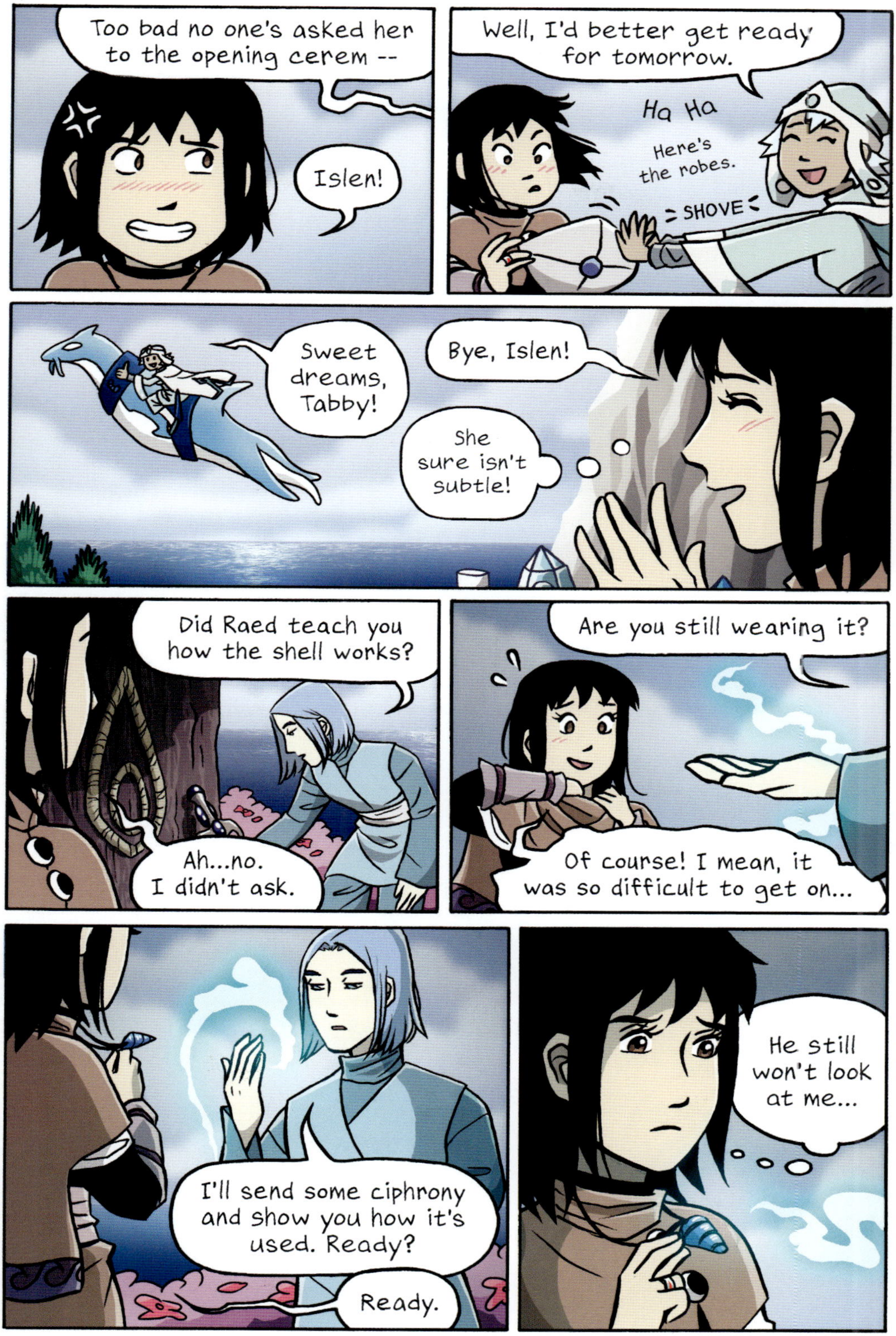
Too bad no one's asked her to the opening cerem --
Islen!
Well, I'd better get ready for tomorrow.
Ha Ha
Here's the robes.
SHOVE
Sweet dreams, Tabby!
Bye, Islen!
She sure isn't subtle!
Did Raed teach you how the shell works?
Ah...no. I didn't ask.
Are you still wearing it?
Of course! I mean, it was so difficult to get on...
I'll send some ciphrony and show you how it's used. Ready?
Ready.
He still won't look at me...

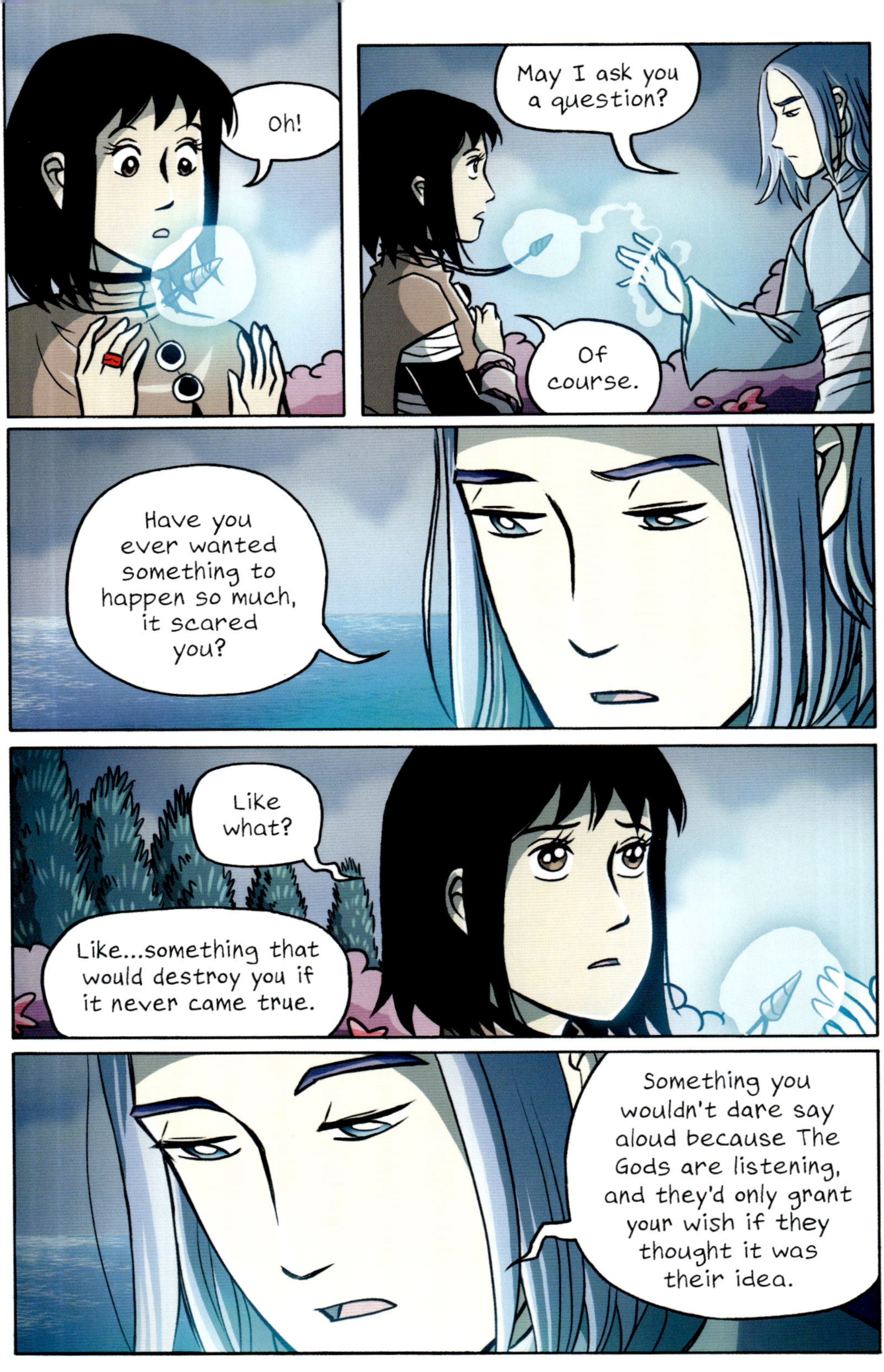
Oh!
May I ask you a question?
Of course.
Have you ever wanted something to happen so much, it scared you?
Like what?
Like...something that would destroy you if it never came true.
Something you wouldn't dare say aloud because The Gods are listening, and they'd only grant your wish if they thought it was their idea.

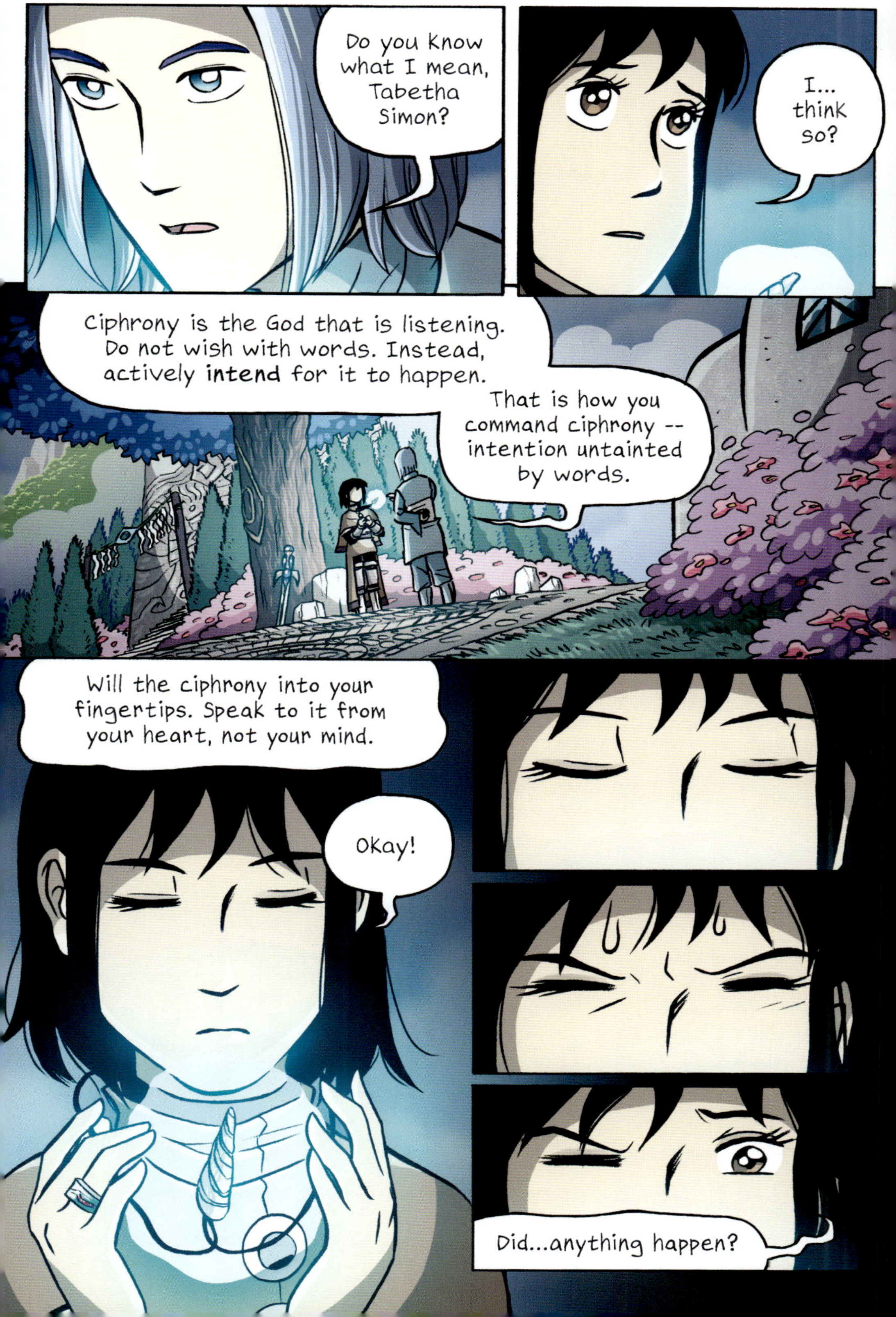
Do you know what I mean, Tabetha Simon?
I... think so?
Ciphrony is the God that is listening. Do not wish with words. Instead, actively **intend** for it to happen.
That is how you command ciphrony -- intention untainted by words.
Will the ciphrony into your fingertips. Speak to it from your heart, not your mind.
Okay!
Did...anything happen?

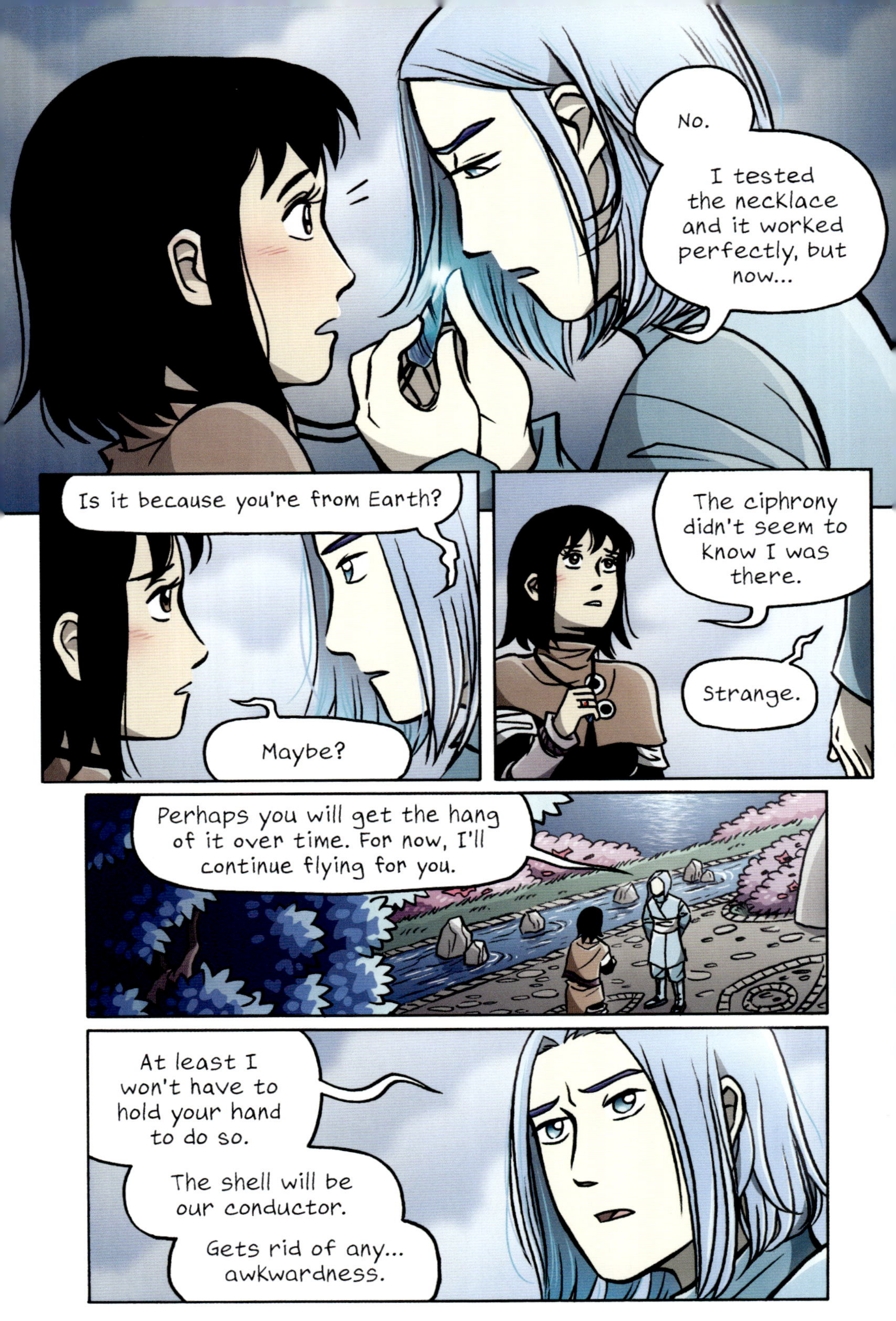
No.
I tested the necklace and it worked perfectly, but now...
Is it because you're from Earth?
Maybe?
The ciphrony didn't seem to know I was there.
Strange.
Perhaps you will get the hang of it over time. For now, I'll continue flying for you.
At least I won't have to hold your hand to do so.
The shell will be our conductor.
Gets rid of any... awkwardness.

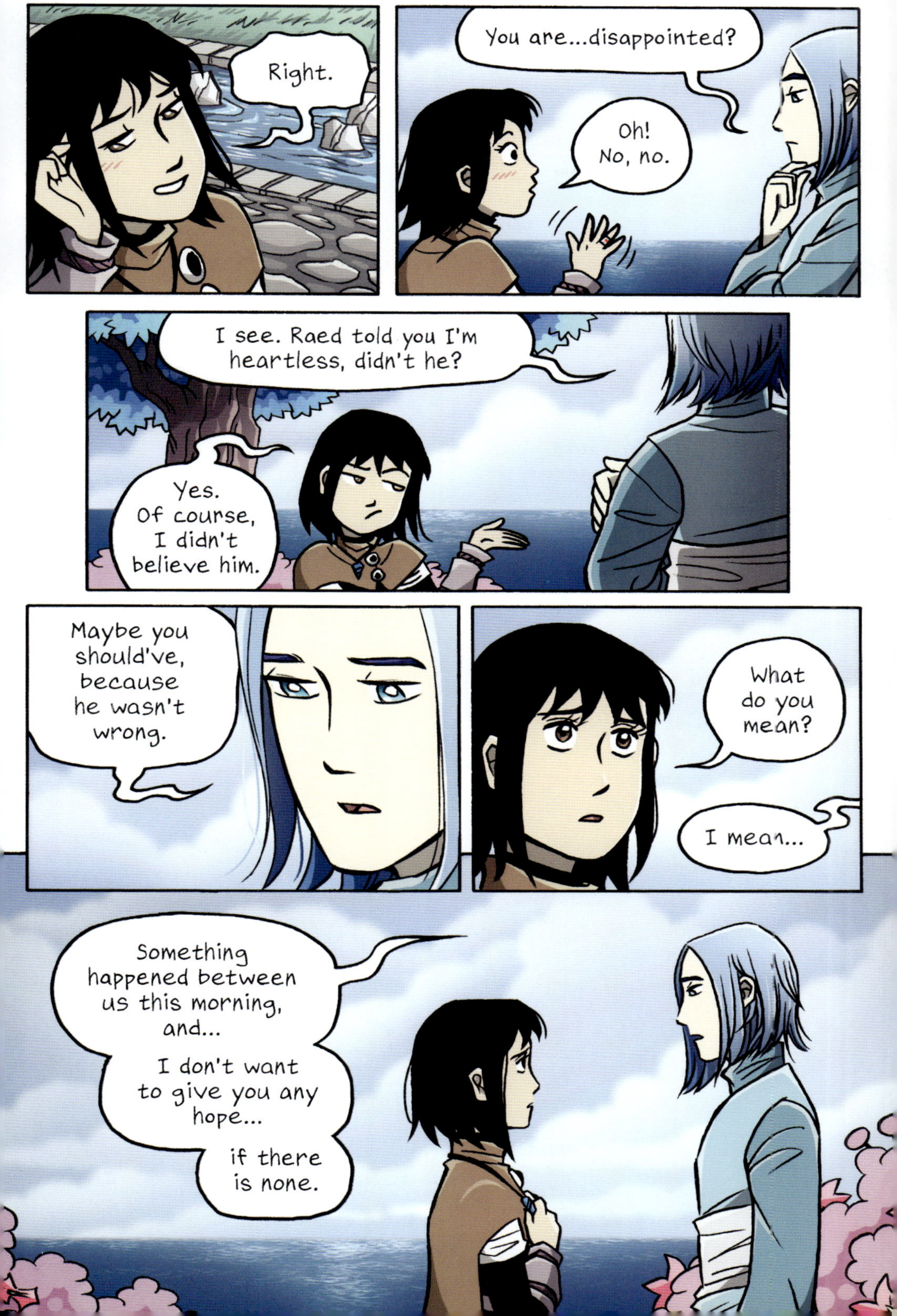

Right.
You are...disappointed?
Oh! No, no.
I see. Raed told you I'm heartless, didn't he?
Yes. Of course, I didn't believe him.
Maybe you should've, because he wasn't wrong.
What do you mean?
I mean...
Something happened between us this morning, and...
I don't want to give you any hope...
if there is none.

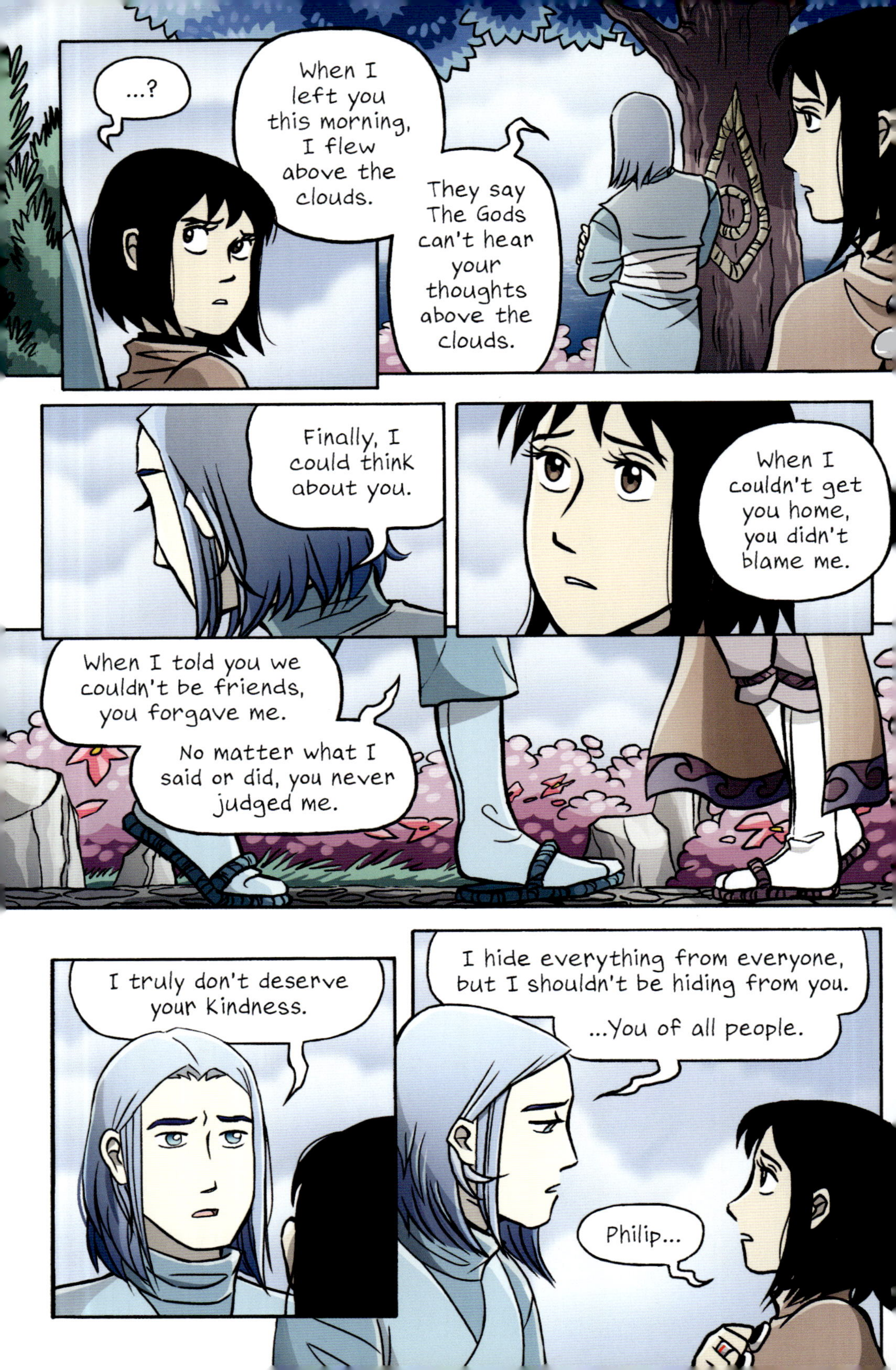
...?
When I left you this morning, I flew above the clouds.
They say The Gods can't hear your thoughts above the clouds.
Finally, I could think about you.
When I couldn't get you home, you didn't blame me.
When I told you we couldn't be friends, you forgave me.
No matter what I said or did, you never judged me.
I truly don't deserve your kindness.
I hide everything from everyone, but I shouldn't be hiding from you.
...You of all people.
Philip...

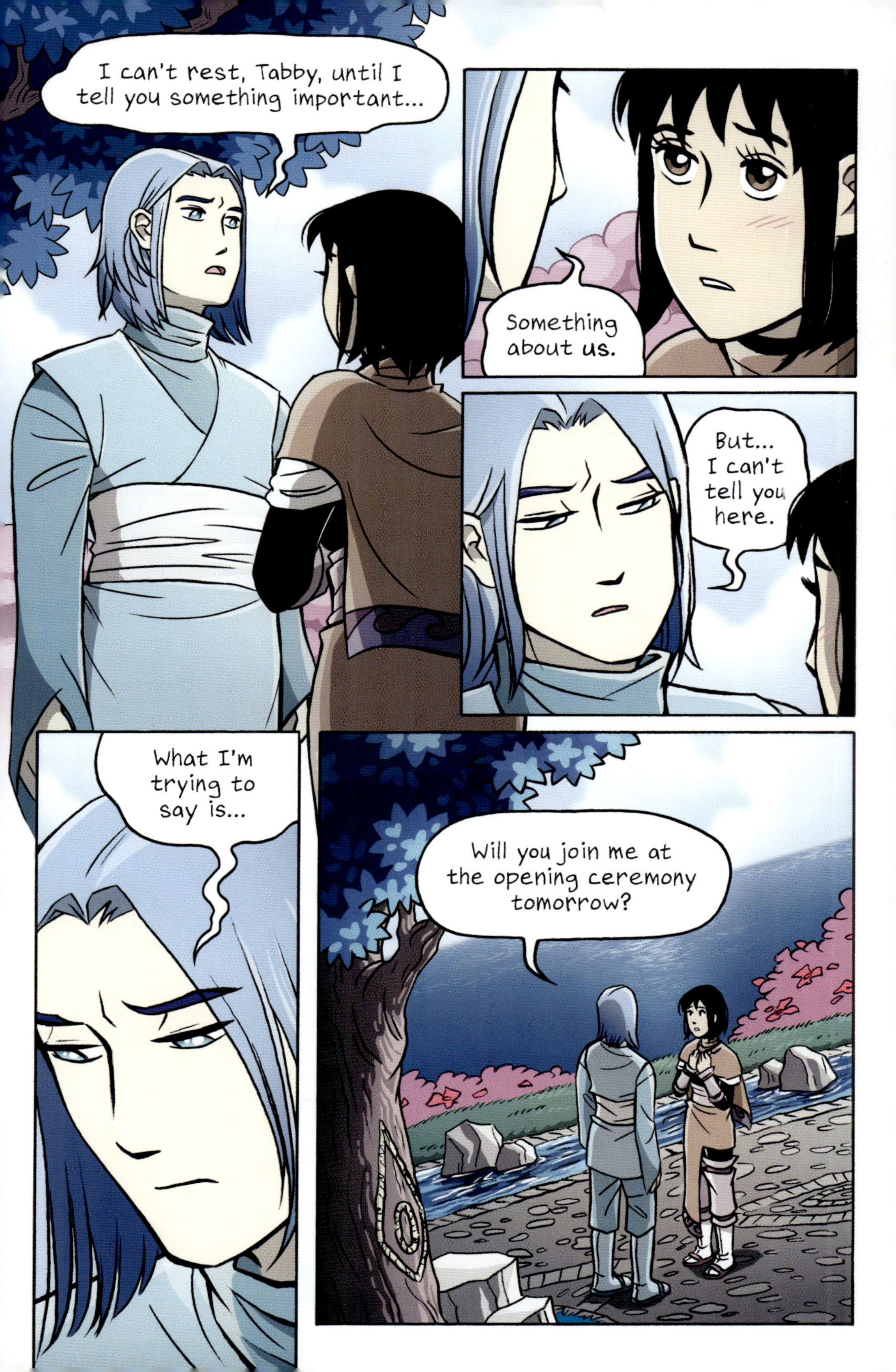
I can't rest, Tabby, until I tell you something important...
Something about us.
But... I can't tell you here.
What I'm trying to say is...
Will you join me at the opening ceremony tomorrow?

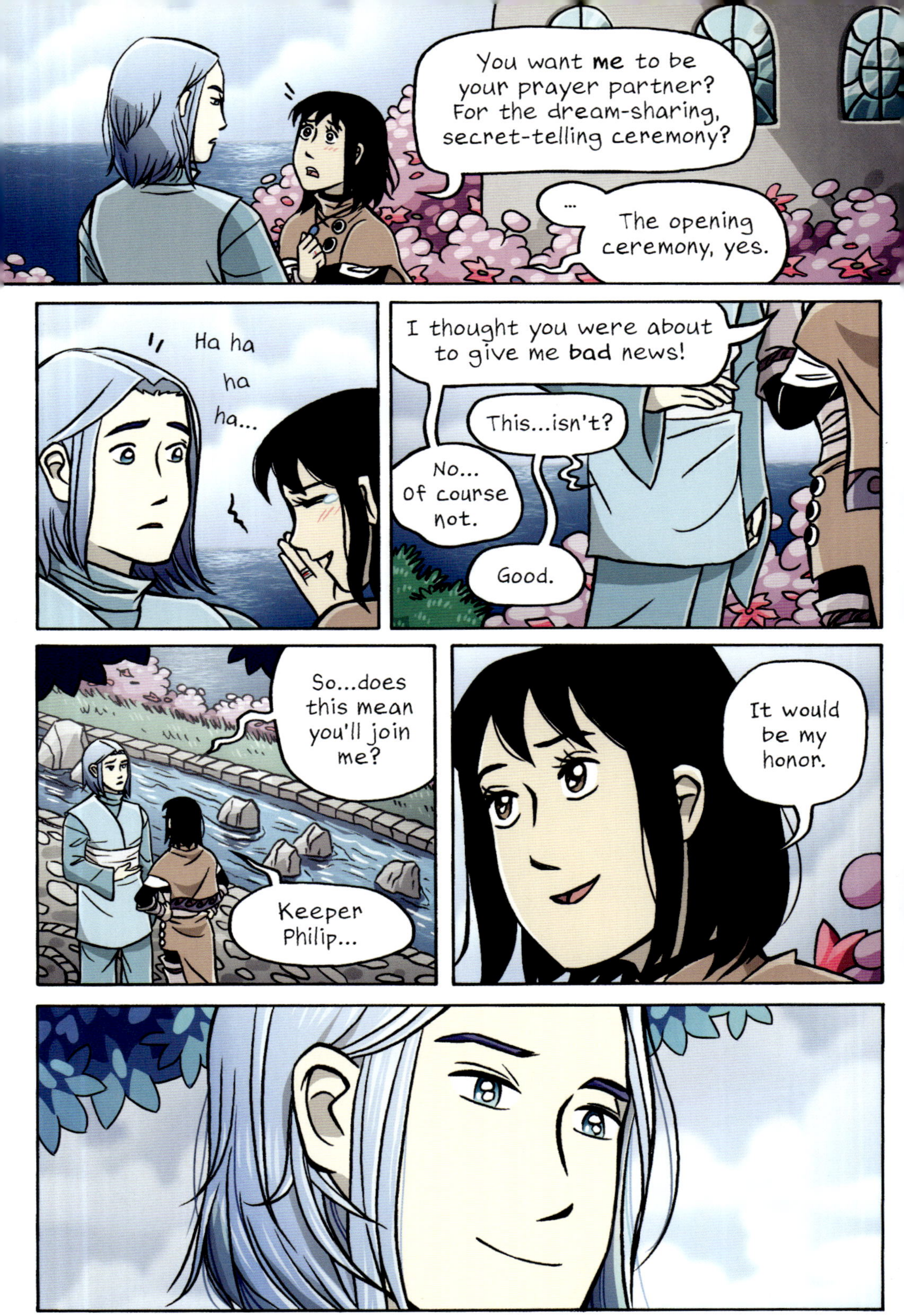
You want **me** to be your prayer partner? For the dream-sharing, secret-telling ceremony?
... The opening ceremony, yes.
Ha ha ha ha...
I thought you were about to give me **bad** news!
This...isn't?
No... Of course not.
Good.
So...does this mean you'll join me?
Keeper Philip...
It would be my honor.

PART II
MEROFI'S FLOOD

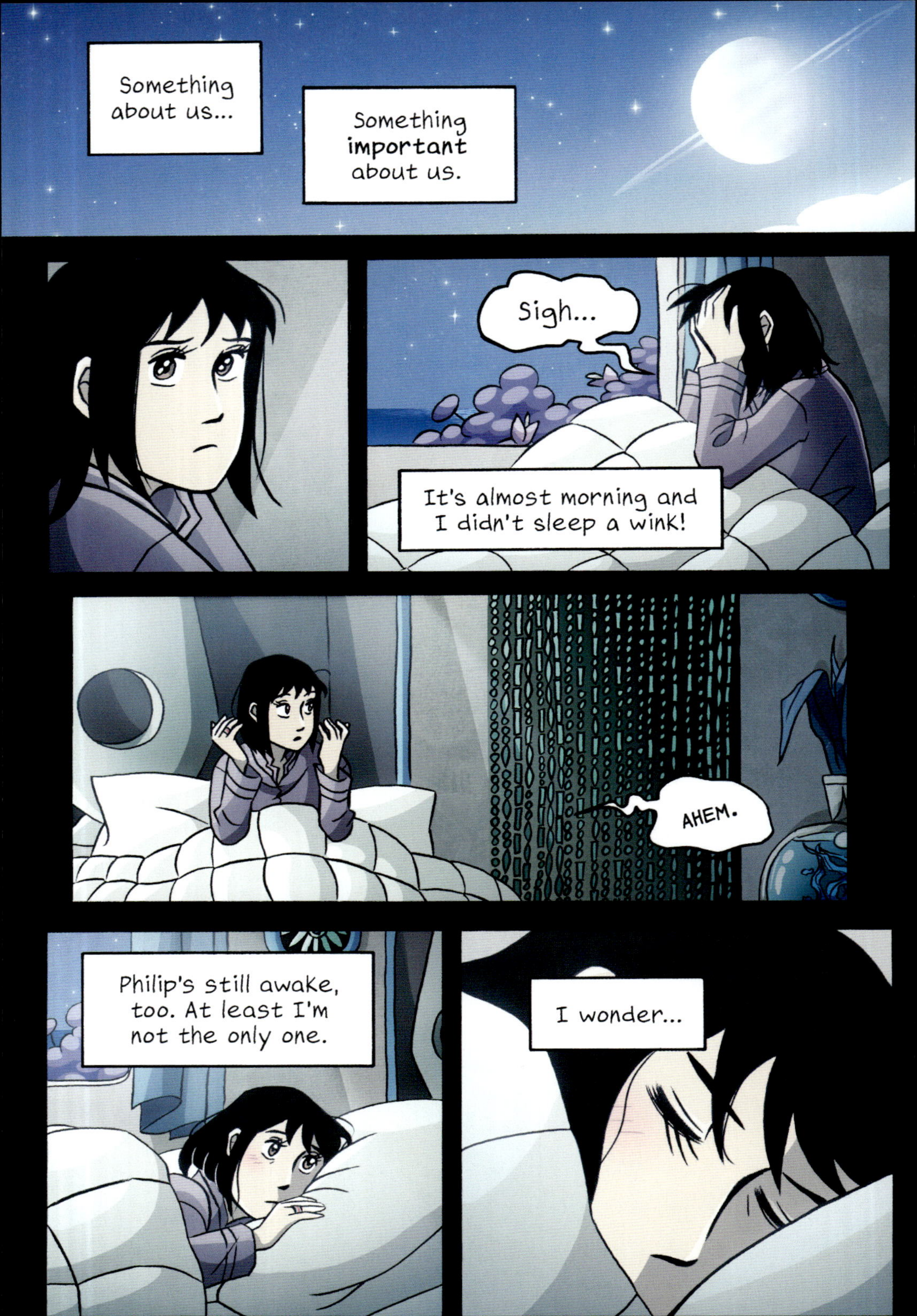
Something about us...
Something **important** about us.
Sigh...
It's almost morning and I didn't sleep a wink!
AHEM.
Philip's still awake, too. At least I'm not the only one.
I wonder...

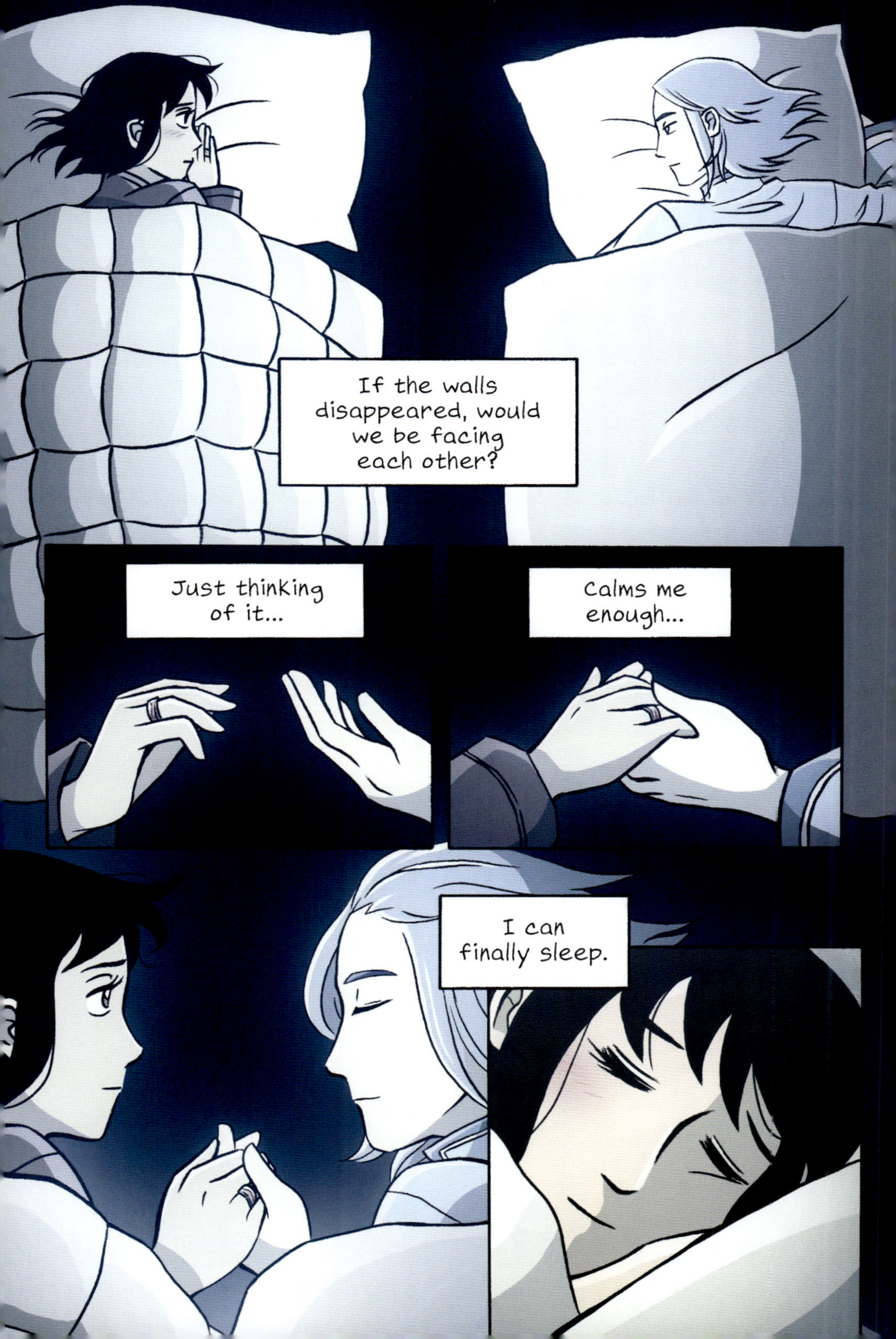

If the walls disappeared, would we be facing each other?
Just thinking of it...
Calms me enough...
I can finally sleep.

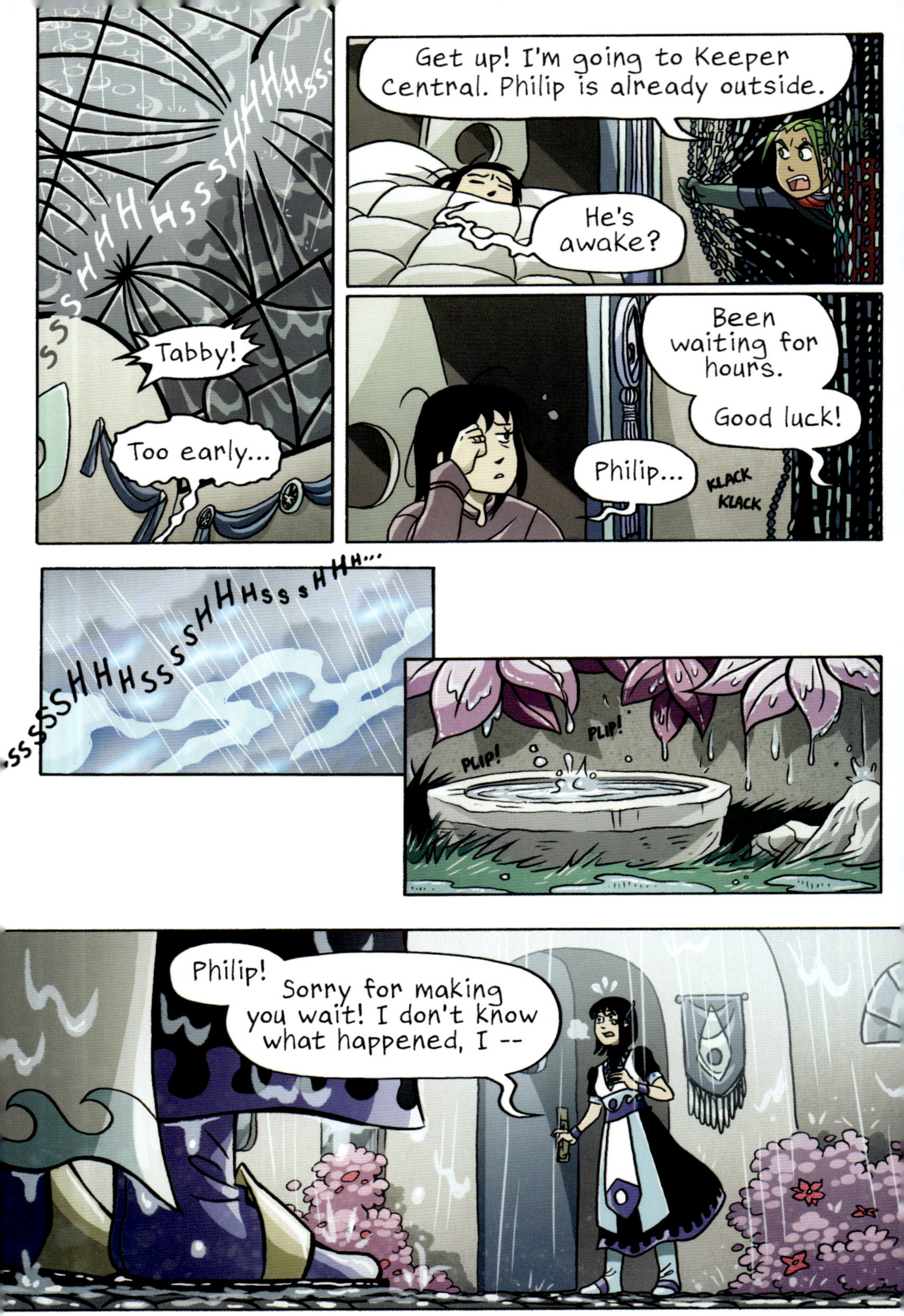

SSSHHHssSHHHHssS
Tabby!
Too early...
Get up! I'm going to Keeper Central. Philip is already outside.
He's awake?
Been waiting for hours.
Good luck!
Philip...
KLACK
KLACK
SSSSHHHsssSHHHsssHHH...
PLIP!
PLIP!
Philip!
Sorry for making you wait! I don't know what happened, I --

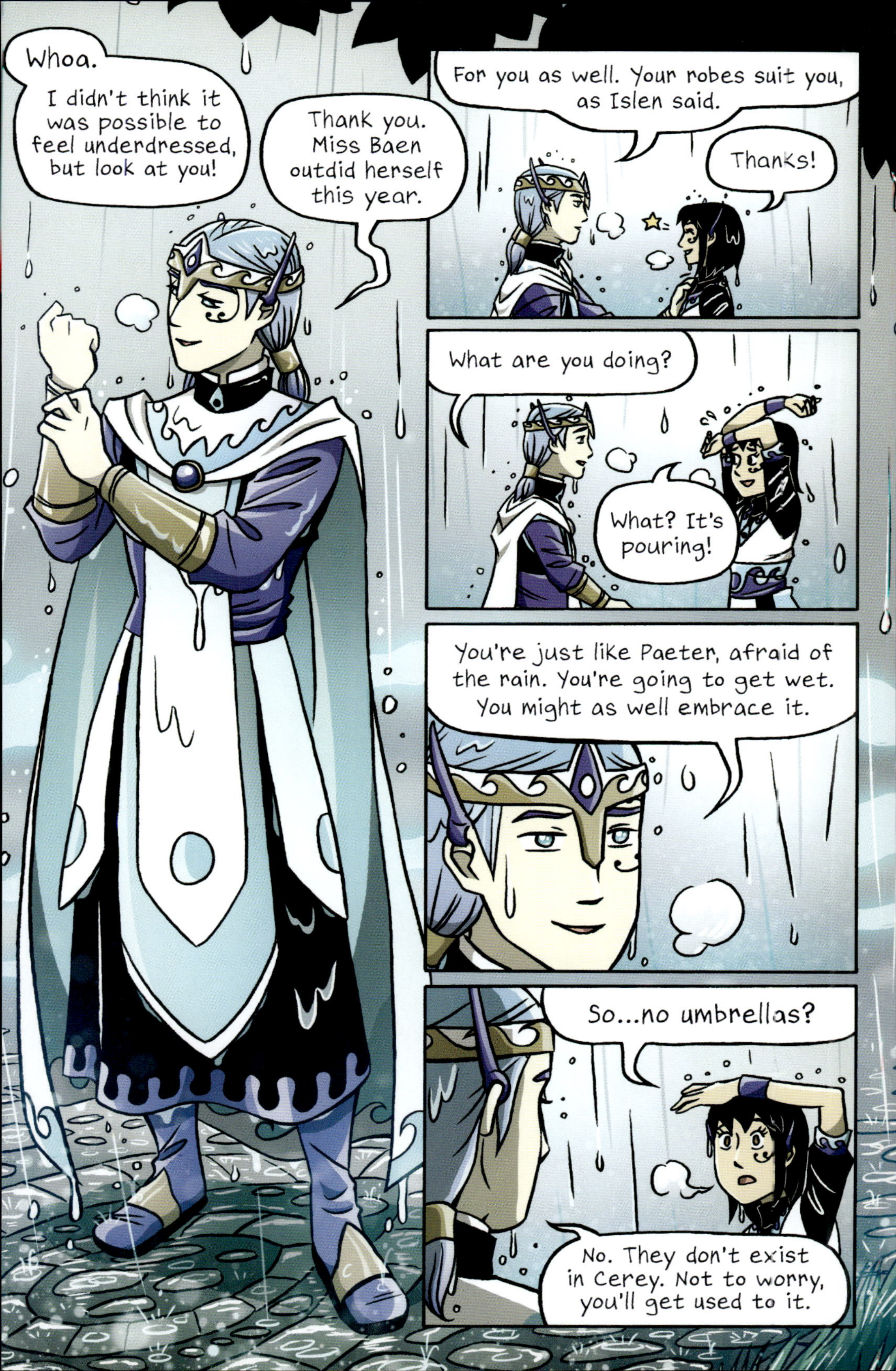
Whoa.
I didn't think it was possible to feel underdressed, but look at you!
Thank you. Miss Baen outdid herself this year.
For you as well. Your robes suit you, as Islen said.
Thanks!
What are you doing?
What? It's pouring!
You're just like Paeter, afraid of the rain. You're going to get wet. You might as well embrace it.
So...no umbrellas?
No. They don't exist in Cerey. Not to worry, you'll get used to it.

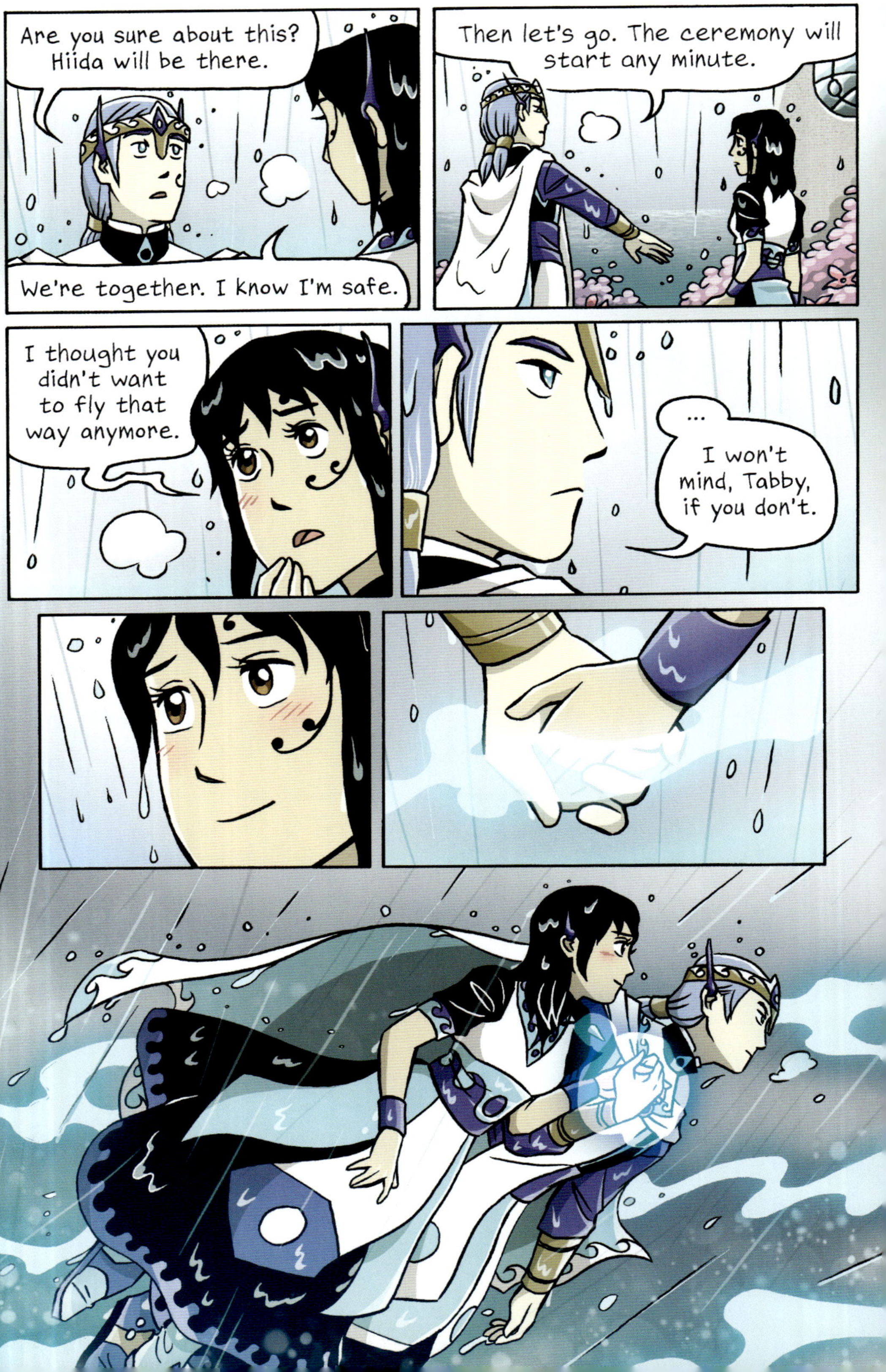

Are you sure about this? Hiida will be there.
We're together. I know I'm safe.
Then let's go. The ceremony will start any minute.
I thought you didn't want to fly that way anymore.
...
I won't mind, Tabby, if you don't.

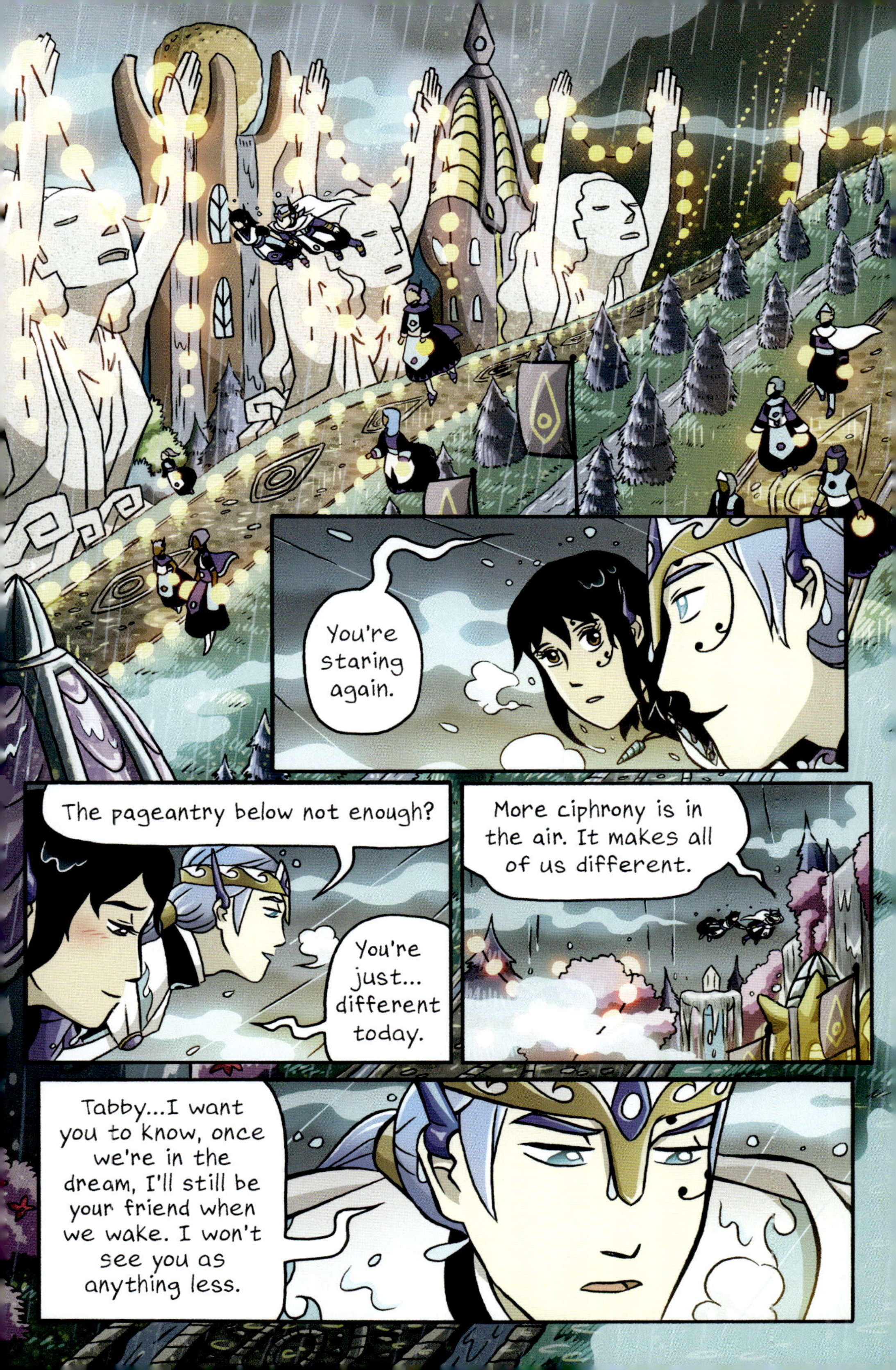
You're staring again.
The pageantry below not enough?
You're just... different today.
More ciphrony is in the air. It makes all of us different.
Tabby...I want you to know, once we're in the dream, I'll still be your friend when we wake. I won't see you as anything less.

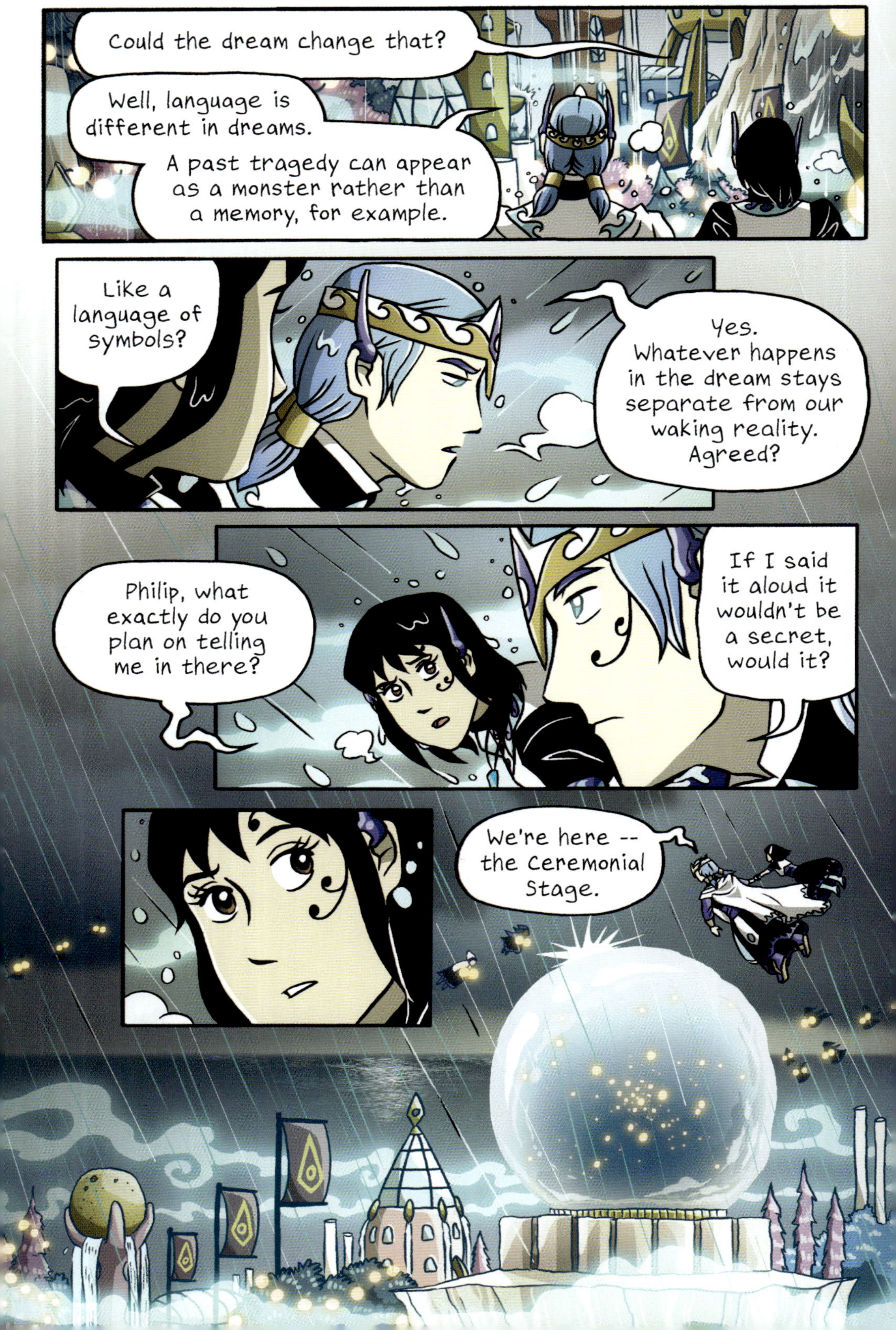
Could the dream change that?
Well, language is different in dreams.
A past tragedy can appear as a monster rather than a memory, for example.
Like a language of symbols?
Yes. Whatever happens in the dream stays separate from our waking reality. Agreed?
Philip, what exactly do you plan on telling me in there?
If I said it aloud it wouldn't be a secret, would it?
We're here -- the Ceremonial Stage.

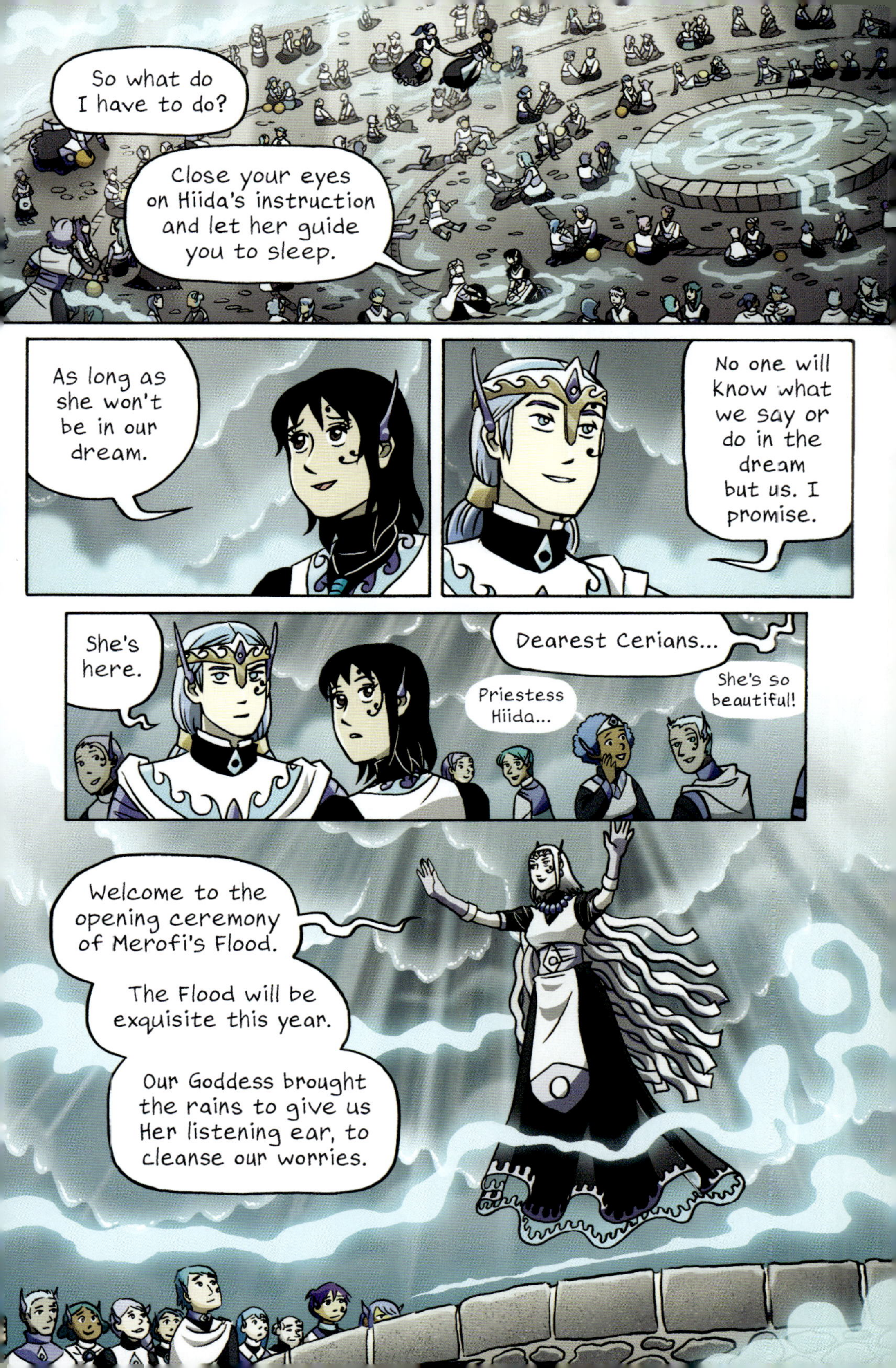
So what do I have to do?
Close your eyes on Hiida's instruction and let her guide you to sleep.
As long as she won't be in our dream.
No one will know what we say or do in the dream but us. I promise.
She's here.
Dearest Cerians...
Priestess Hiida...
She's so beautiful!
Welcome to the opening ceremony of Merofi's Flood.
The Flood will be exquisite this year.
Our Goddess brought the rains to give us Her listening ear, to cleanse our worries.

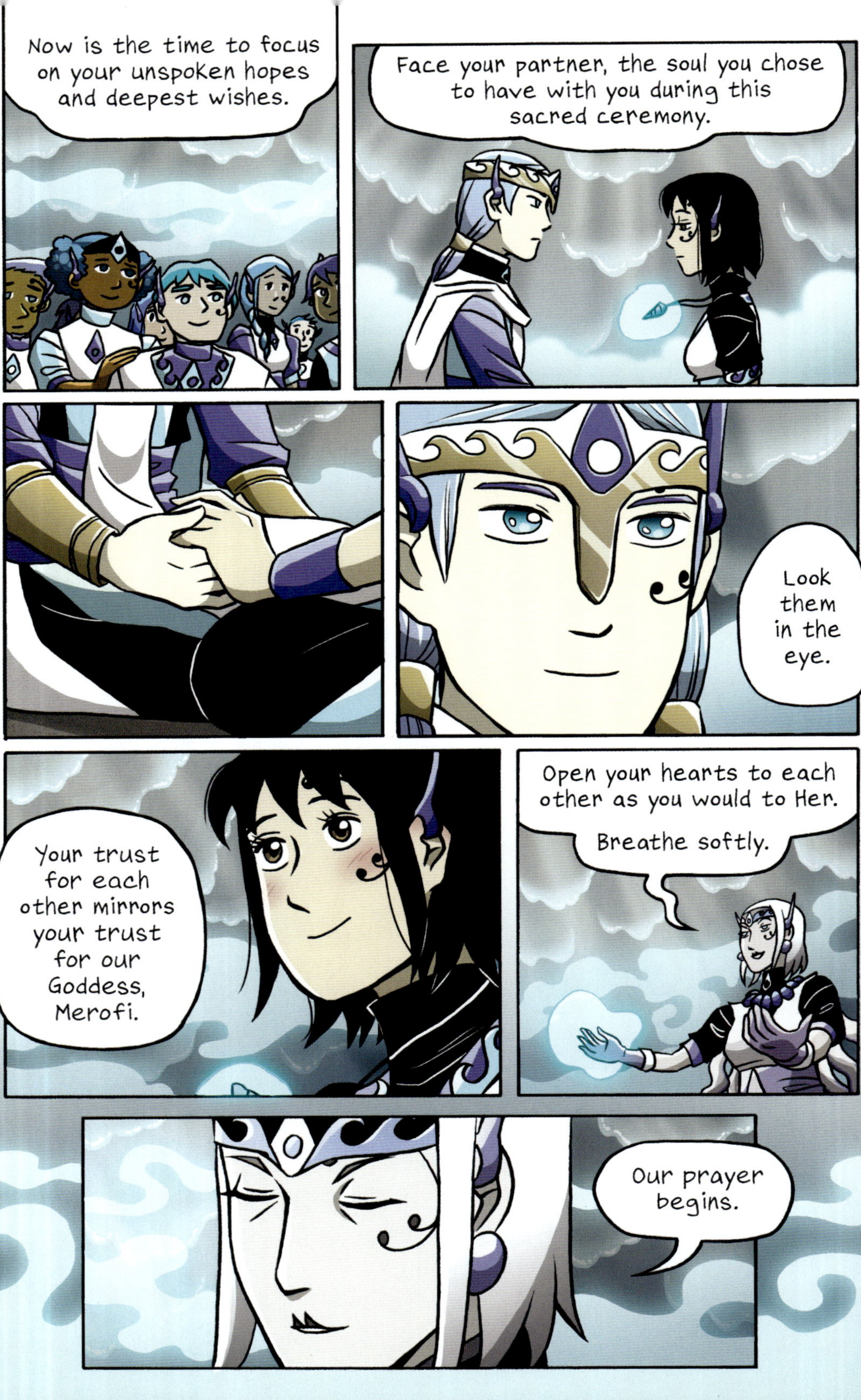
Now is the time to focus on your unspoken hopes and deepest wishes.
Face your partner, the soul you chose to have with you during this sacred ceremony.
Look them in the eye.
Your trust for each other mirrors your trust for our Goddess, Merofi.
Open your hearts to each other as you would to Her.
Breathe softly.
Our prayer begins.

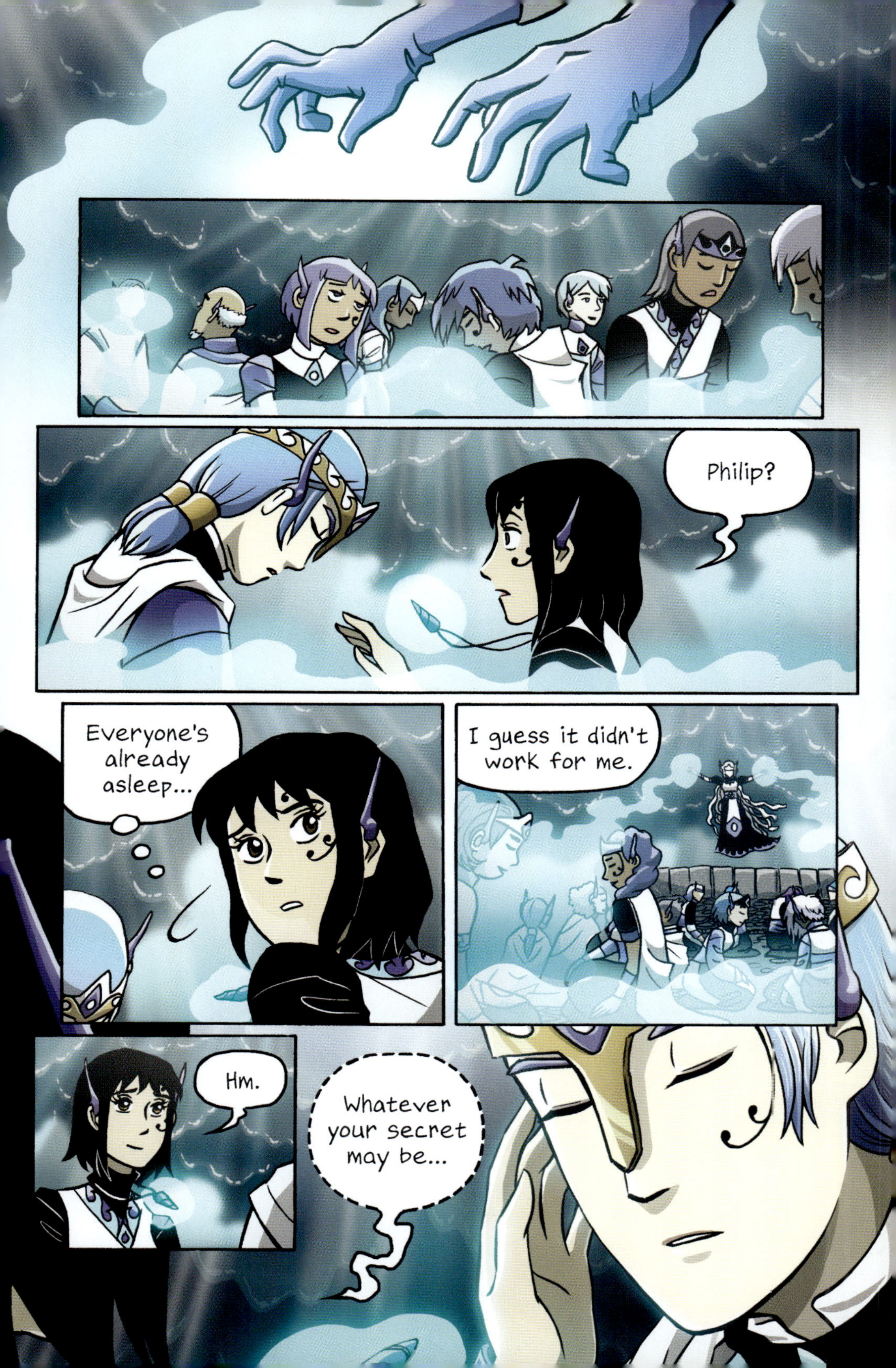
Philip?
Everyone's already asleep...
I guess it didn't work for me.
Hm.
Whatever your secret may be...

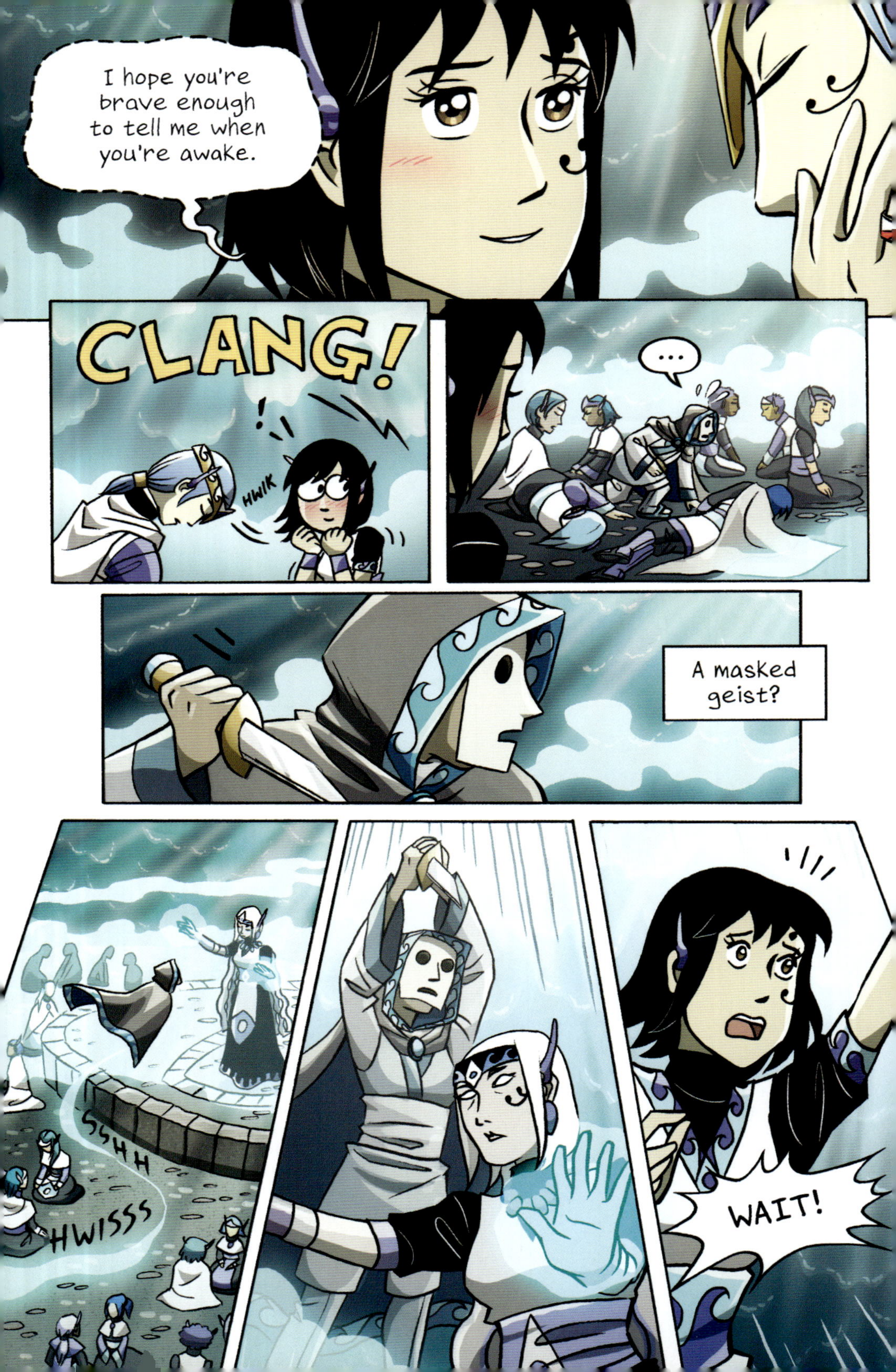
I hope you're brave enough to tell me when you're awake.
CLANG!
HWIK
...
A masked geist?
SSHH
HWISSS
WAIT!

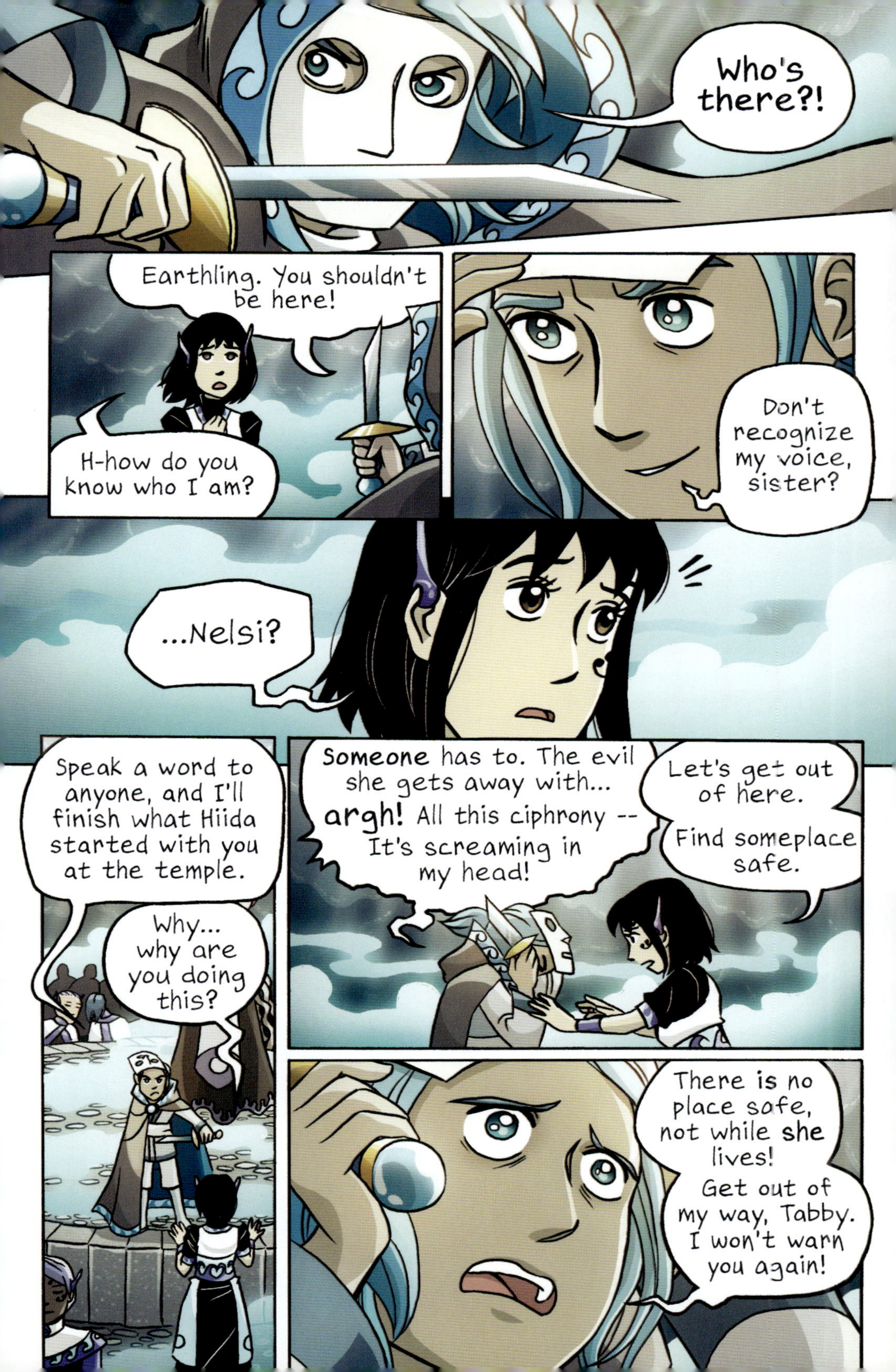
Who's there?!
Earthling. You shouldn't be here!
H-how do you know who I am?
Don't recognize my voice, sister?
...Nelsi?
Speak a word to anyone, and I'll finish what Hiida started with you at the temple.
Why... why are you doing this?
Someone has to. The evil she gets away with... argh! All this ciphrony -- It's screaming in my head!
Let's get out of here.
Find someplace safe.
There is no place safe, not while she lives!
Get out of my way, Tabby. I won't warn you again!

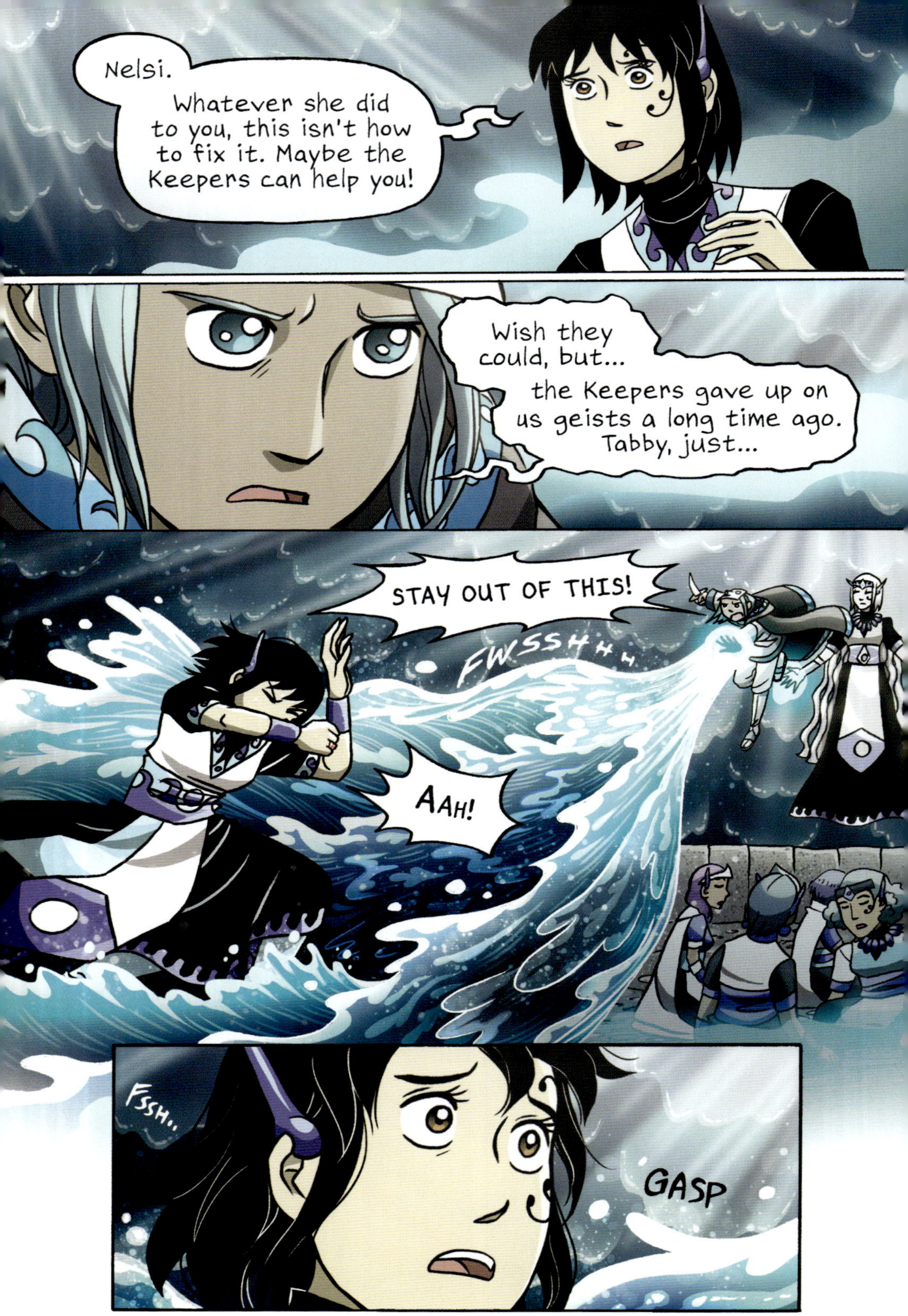
Nelsi.
Whatever she did to you, this isn't how to fix it. Maybe the Keepers can help you!
Wish they could, but...
the Keepers gave up on us geists a long time ago. Tabby, just...
STAY OUT OF THIS!
FWSSHHH
AAH!
FSSH..
GASP

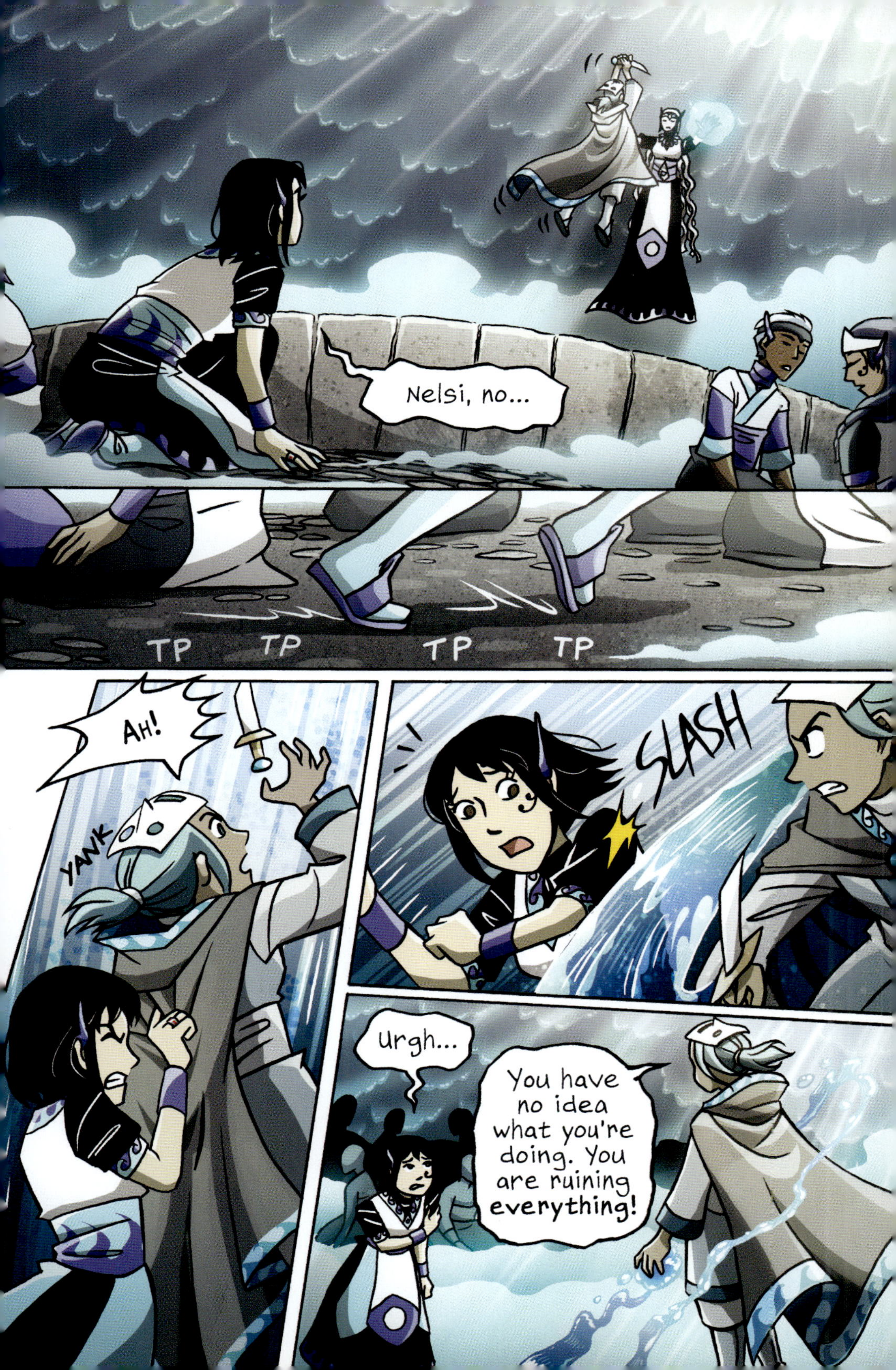
Nelsi, no...
TP TP TP TP
AH!
YANK
SLASH
Urgh...
You have no idea what you're doing. You are ruining **everything**!

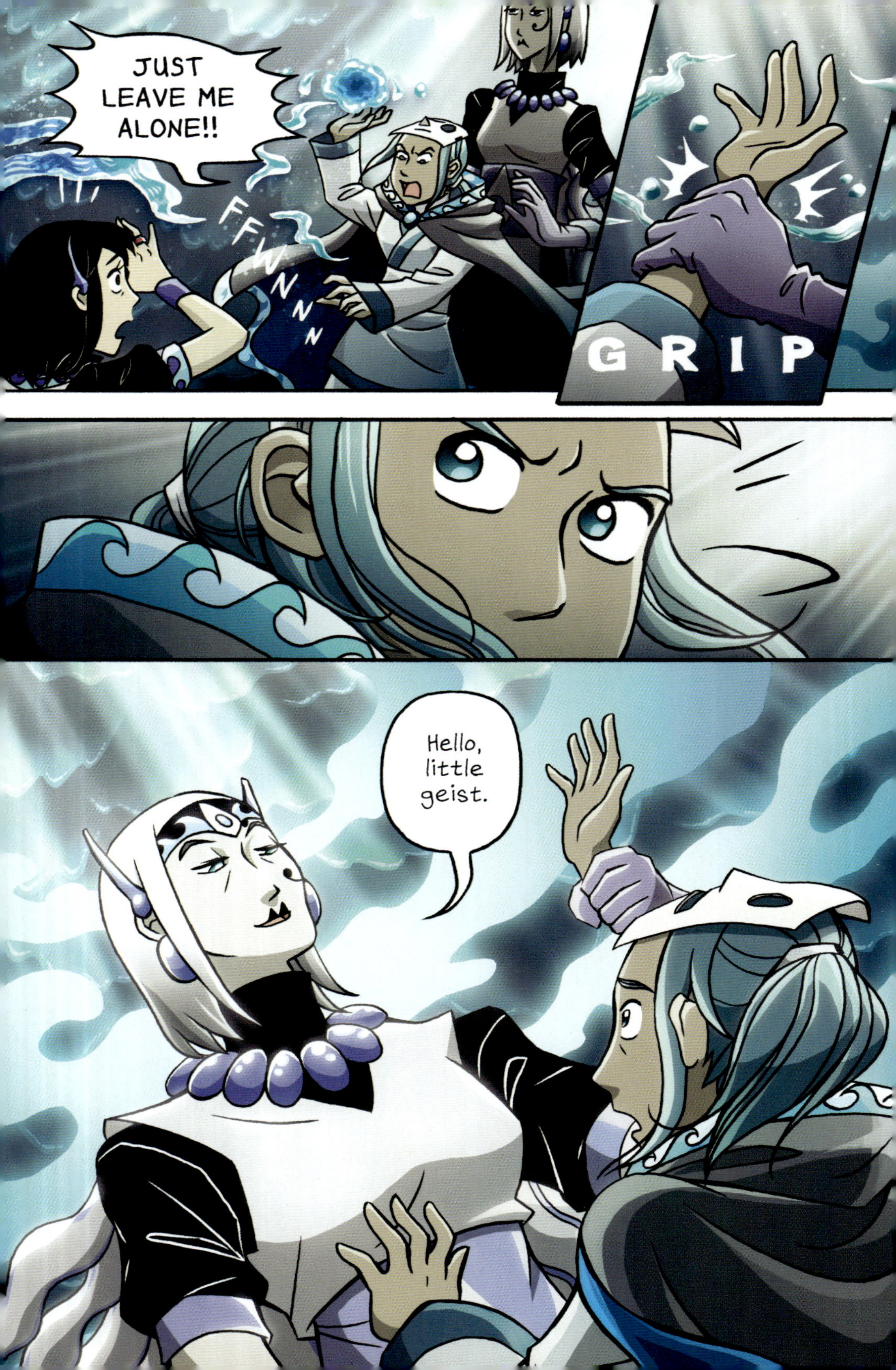
JUST LEAVE ME ALONE!!
FFWNNN
GRIP
Hello, little geist.

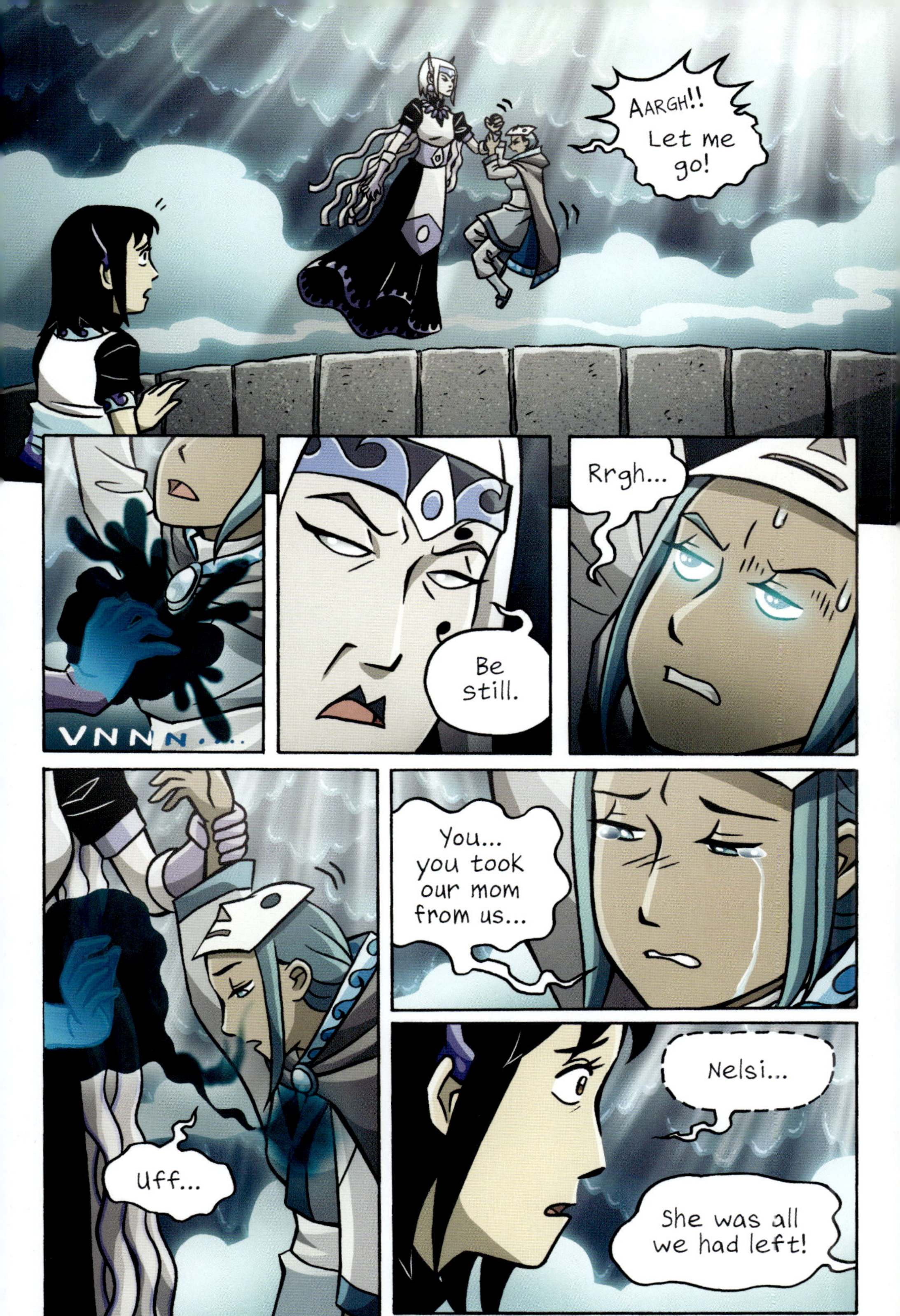
AARGH!! Let me go!
VNNN....
Be still.
Rrgh...
Uff...
You... you took our mom from us...
Nelsi...
She was all we had left!

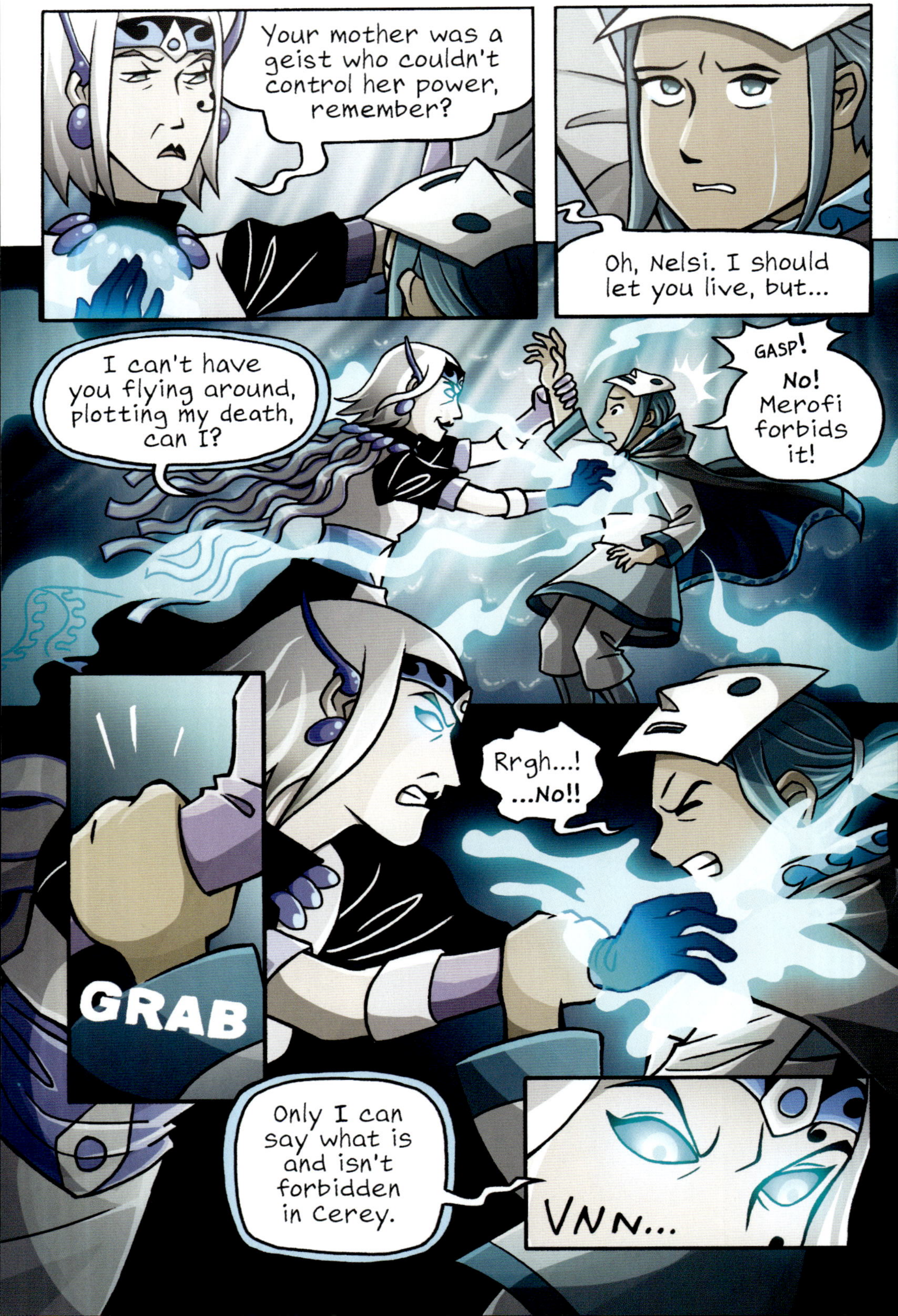
Your mother was a geist who couldn't control her power, remember?
Oh, Nelsi. I should let you live, but...
I can't have you flying around, plotting my death, can I?
GASP! No! Merofi forbids it!
GRAB
Rrgh...! ...No!!
Only I can say what is and isn't forbidden in Cerey.
VNN...

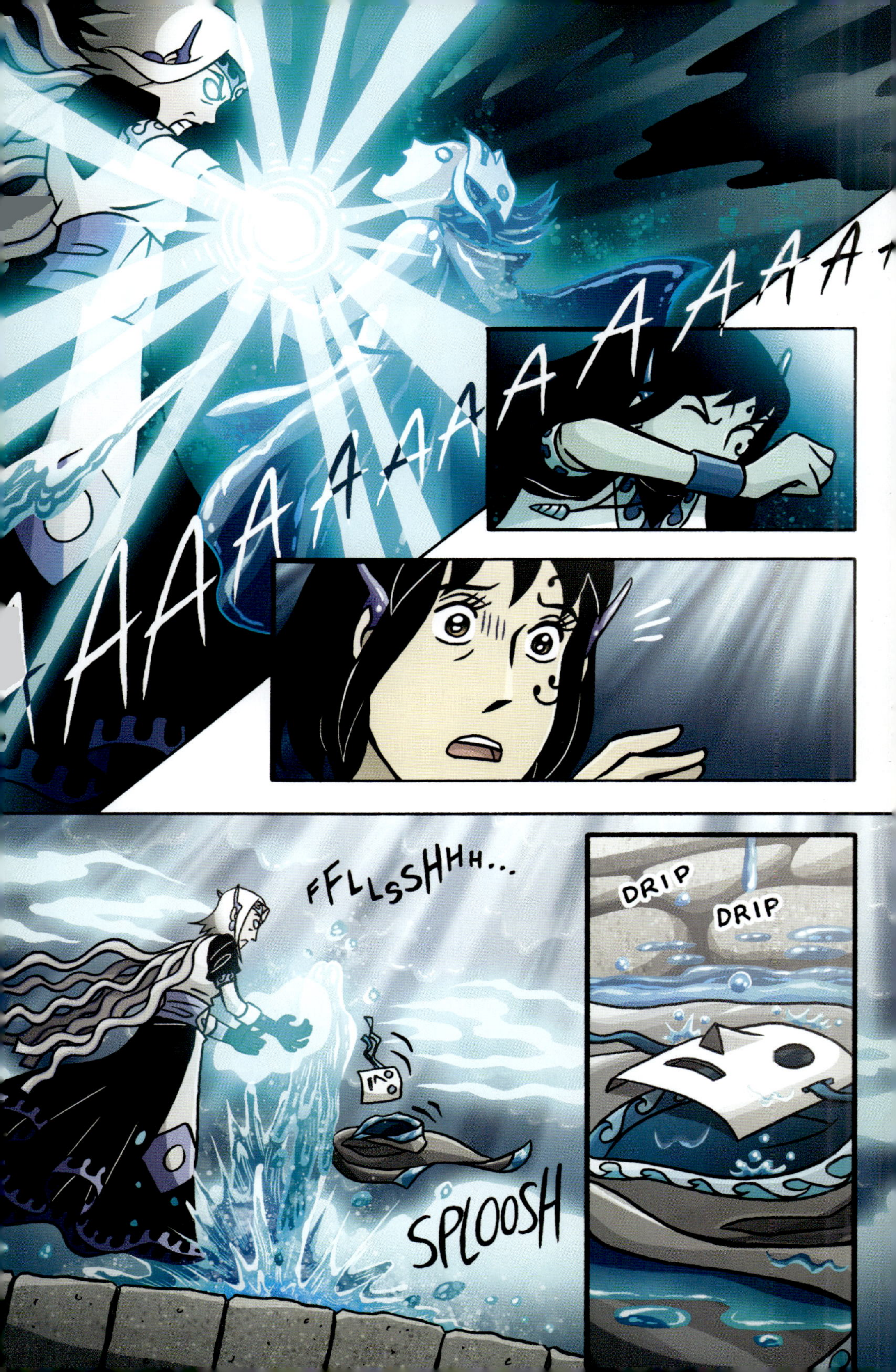
AAAAAAAAAAAAAA
FFLLSSHHH...
SPLOOSH
DRIP
DRIP

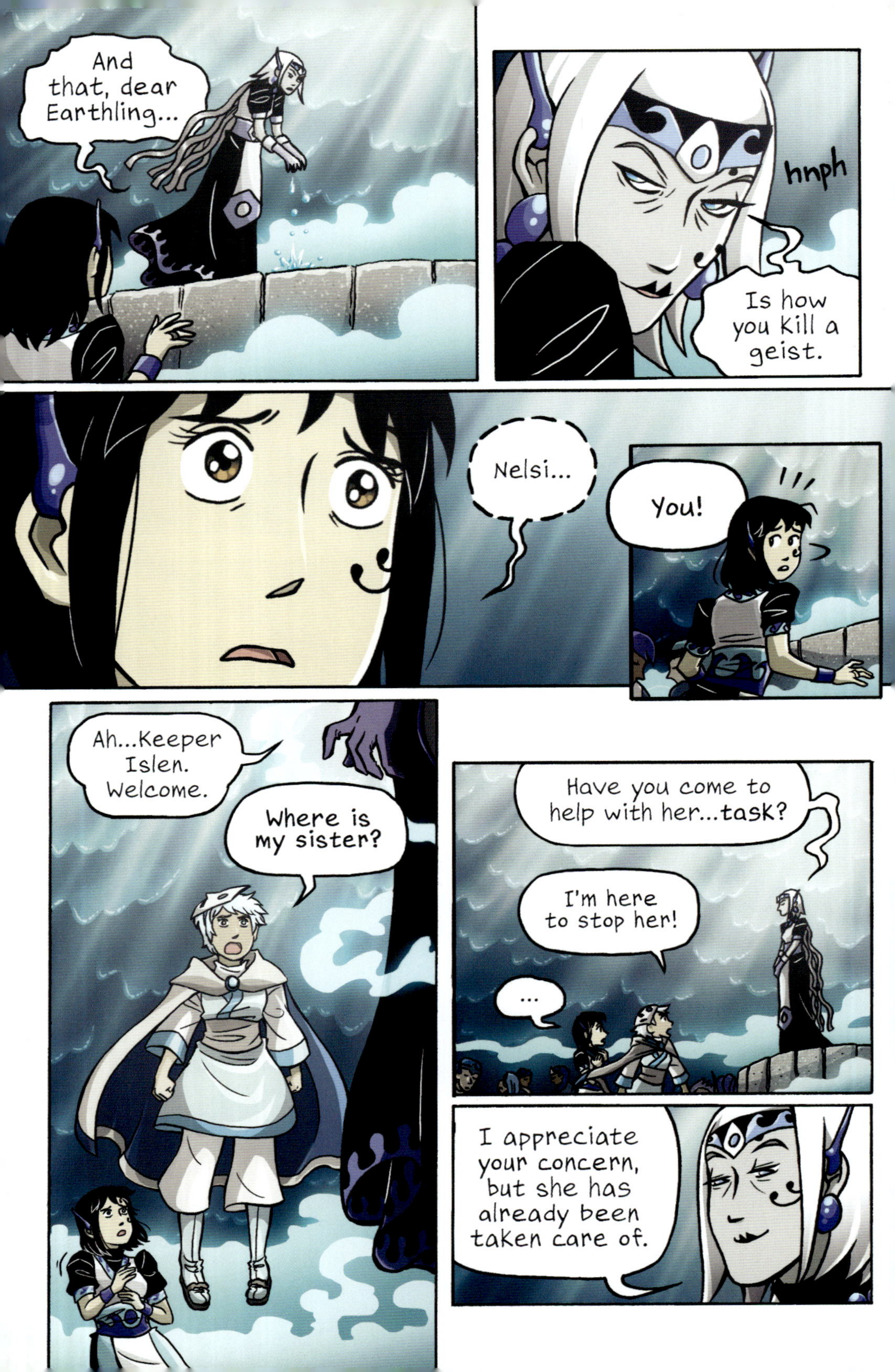
And that, dear Earthling...
hnph
Is how you kill a geist.
Nelsi...
You!
Ah...Keeper Islen. Welcome.
Where is my sister?
Have you come to help with her...task?
I'm here to stop her!
...
I appreciate your concern, but she has already been taken care of.

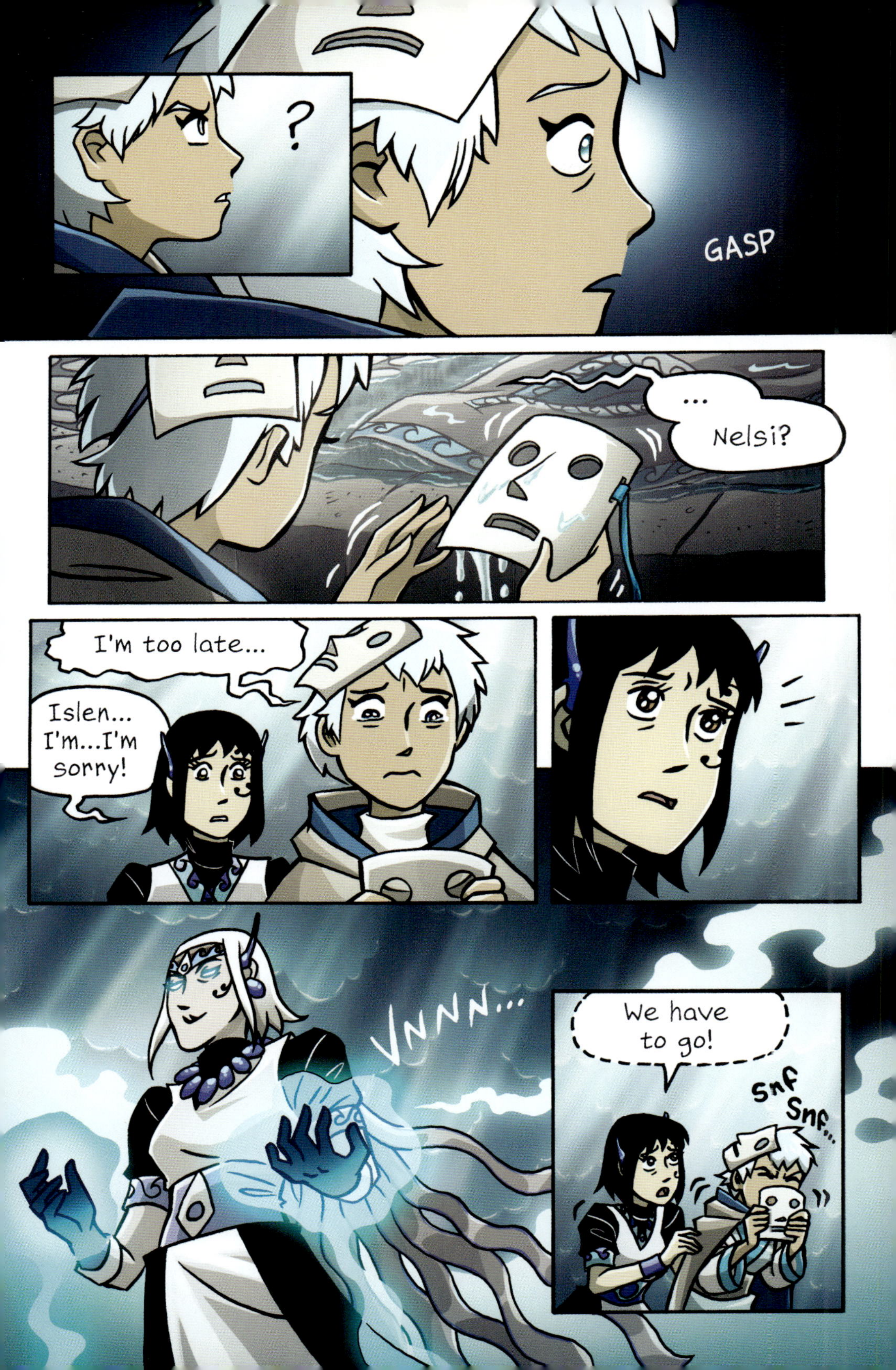
?
GASP
... Nelsi?
I'm too late...
Islen... I'm...I'm sorry!
VNNN...
We have to go!
Snf Snf...

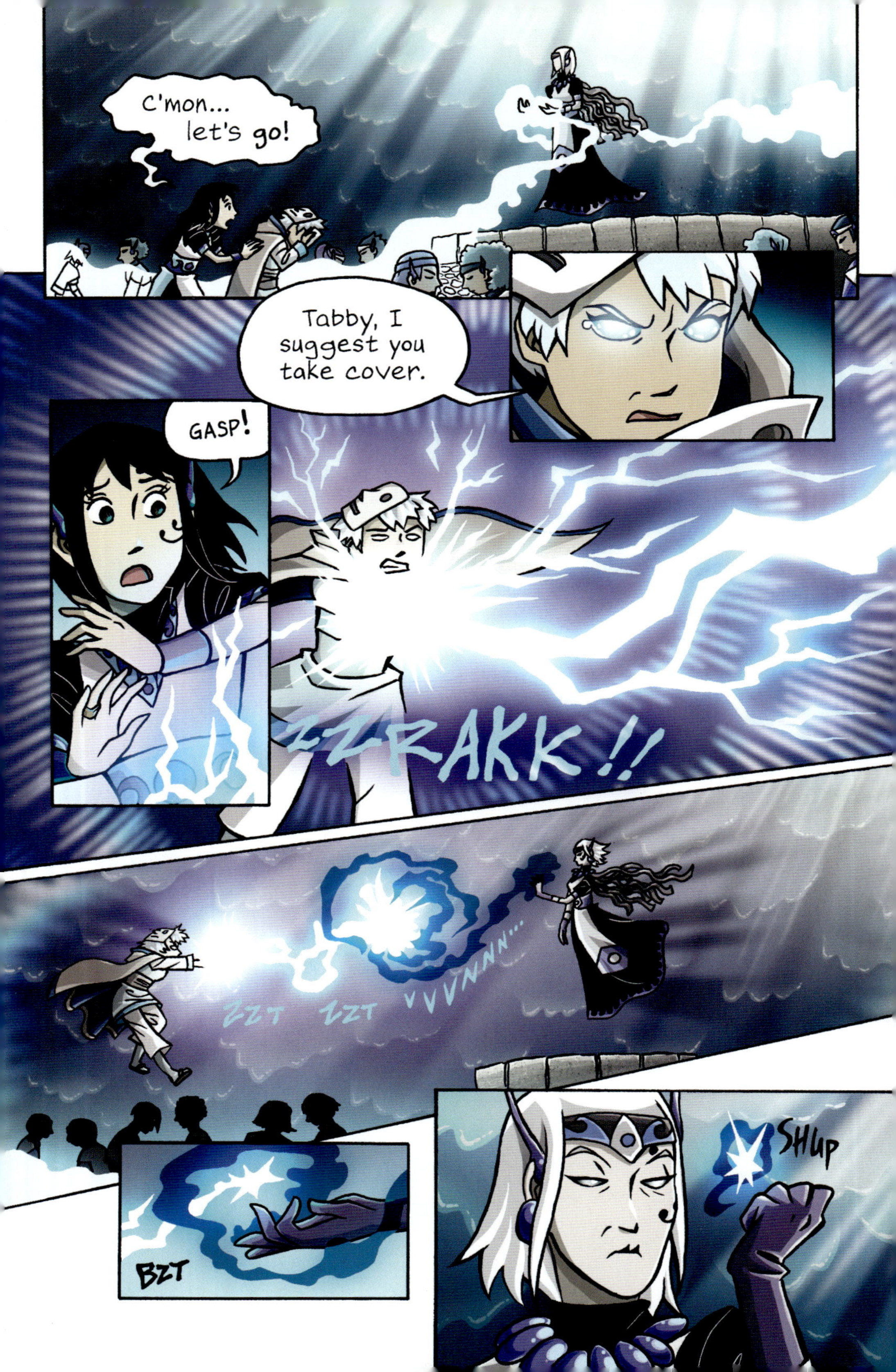
C'mon... let's go!
Tabby, I suggest you take cover.
GASP!
ZZRAKK!!
ZZT ZZT VVVNNN...
BZT
SHUP

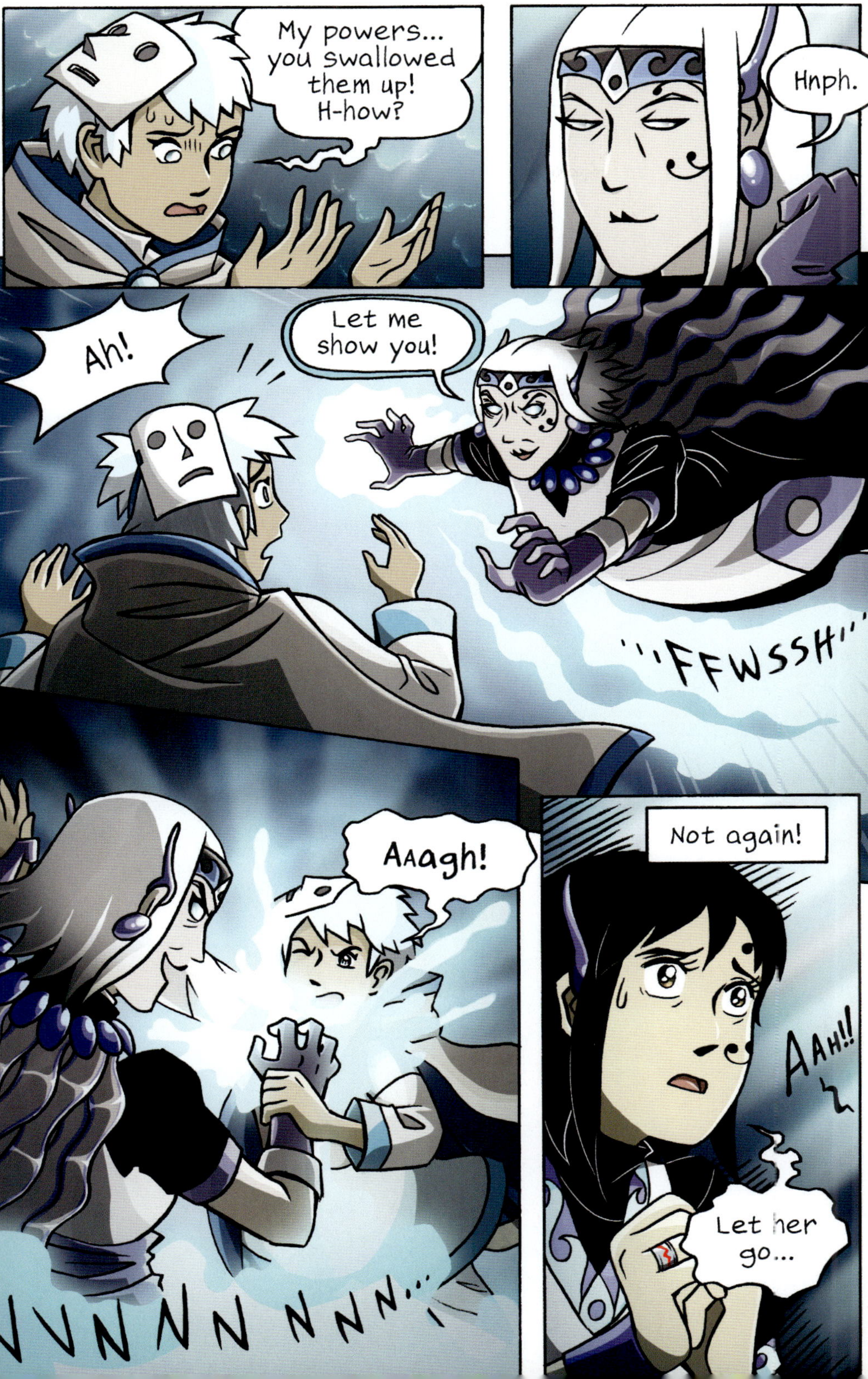

My powers... you swallowed them up! H-how?
Hnph.
Ah!
Let me show you!
FFWSSH
Aaagh!
VVVNNN NNN...
Not again!
AAH!!
Let her go...

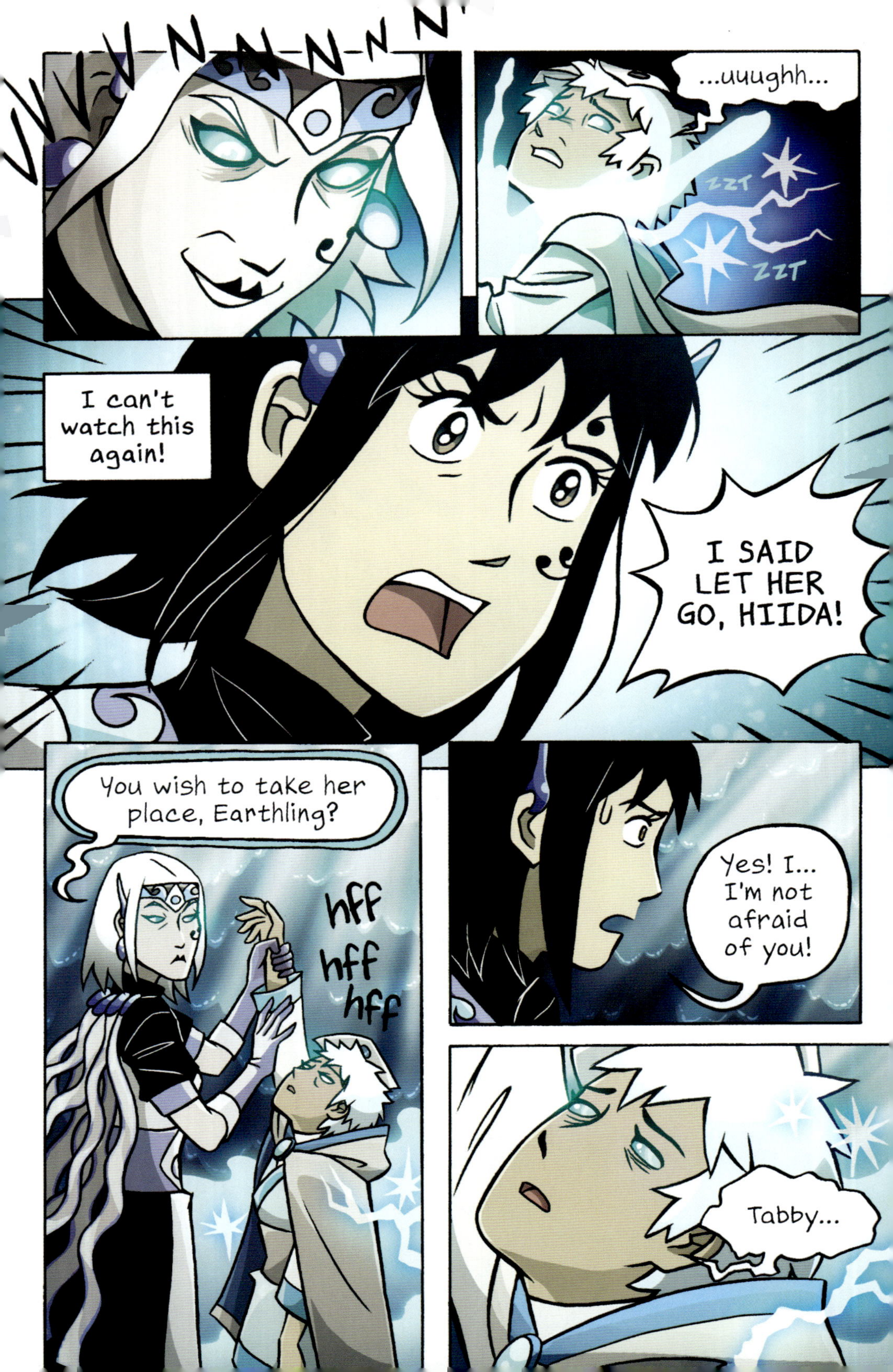
VVVVNNNNNNN
...uuughh...
ZZT
ZZT
I can't watch this again!
I SAID LET HER GO, HIIDA!
You wish to take her place, Earthling?
hff
hff
hff
Yes! I... I'm not afraid of you!
Tabby...

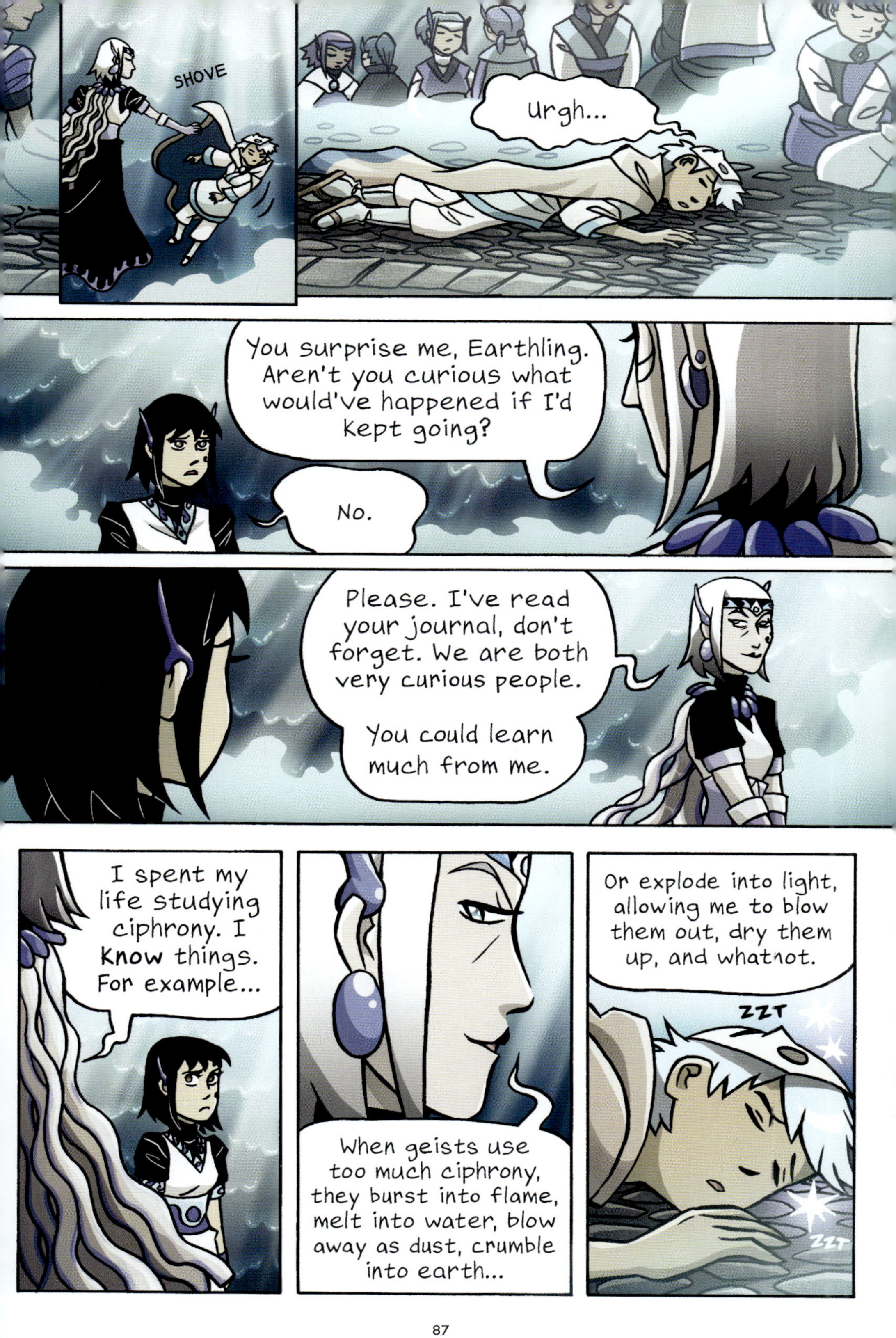
SHOVE
Urgh...
You surprise me, Earthling. Aren't you curious what would've happened if I'd kept going?
No.
Please. I've read your journal, don't forget. We are both very curious people.
You could learn much from me.
I spent my life studying ciphrony. I **know** things. For example...
When geists use too much ciphrony, they burst into flame, melt into water, blow away as dust, crumble into earth...
Or explode into light, allowing me to blow them out, dry them up, and whatnot.
ZZT
ZZT

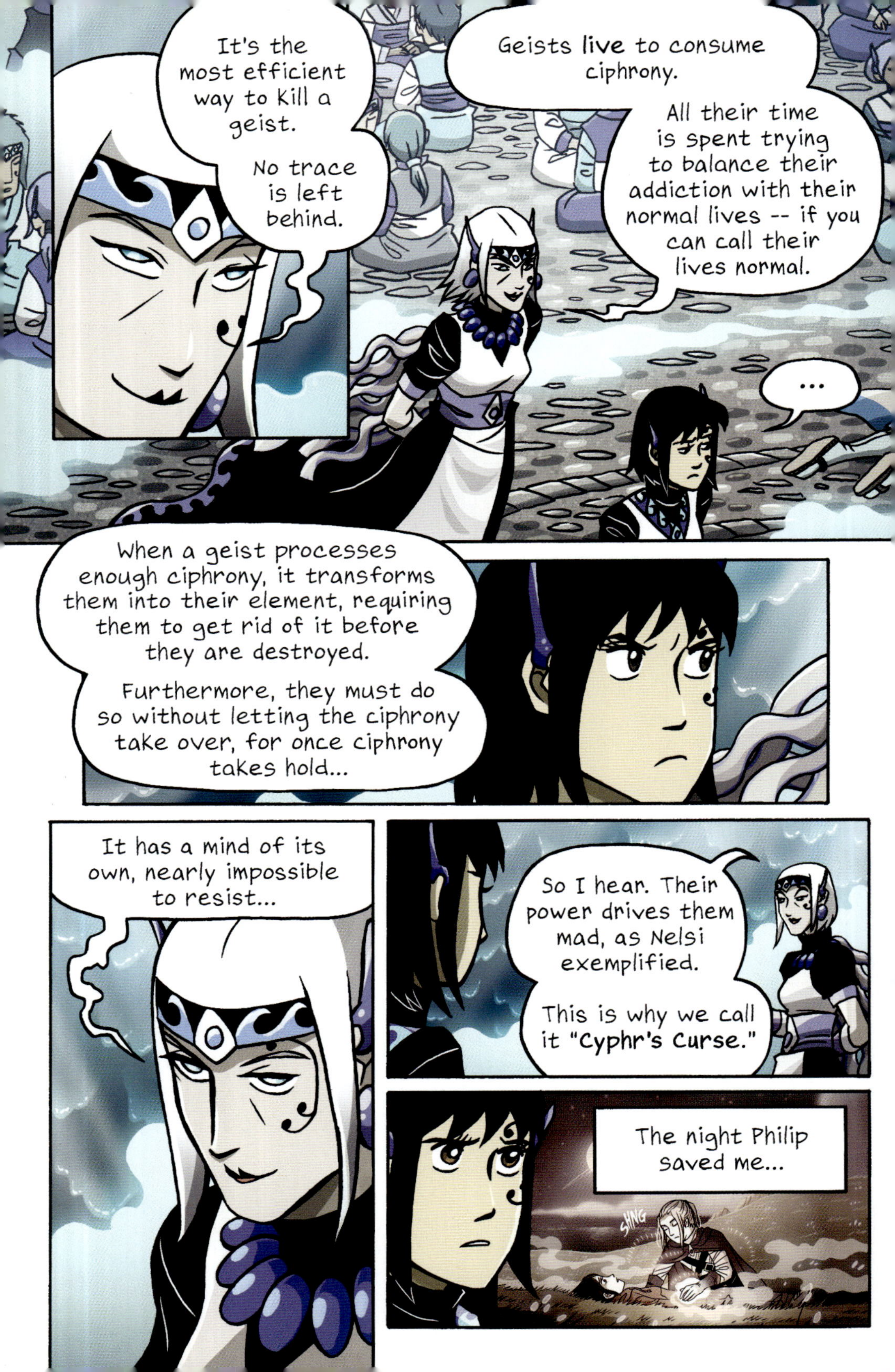

It's the most efficient way to kill a geist.
No trace is left behind.
Geists live to consume ciphrony.
All their time is spent trying to balance their addiction with their normal lives -- if you can call their lives normal.
...
When a geist processes enough ciphrony, it transforms them into their element, requiring them to get rid of it before they are destroyed.
Furthermore, they must do so without letting the ciphrony take over, for once ciphrony takes hold...
It has a mind of its own, nearly impossible to resist...
So I hear. Their power drives them mad, as Nelsi exemplified.
This is why we call it "Cyphr's Curse."
The night Philip saved me...
SHING

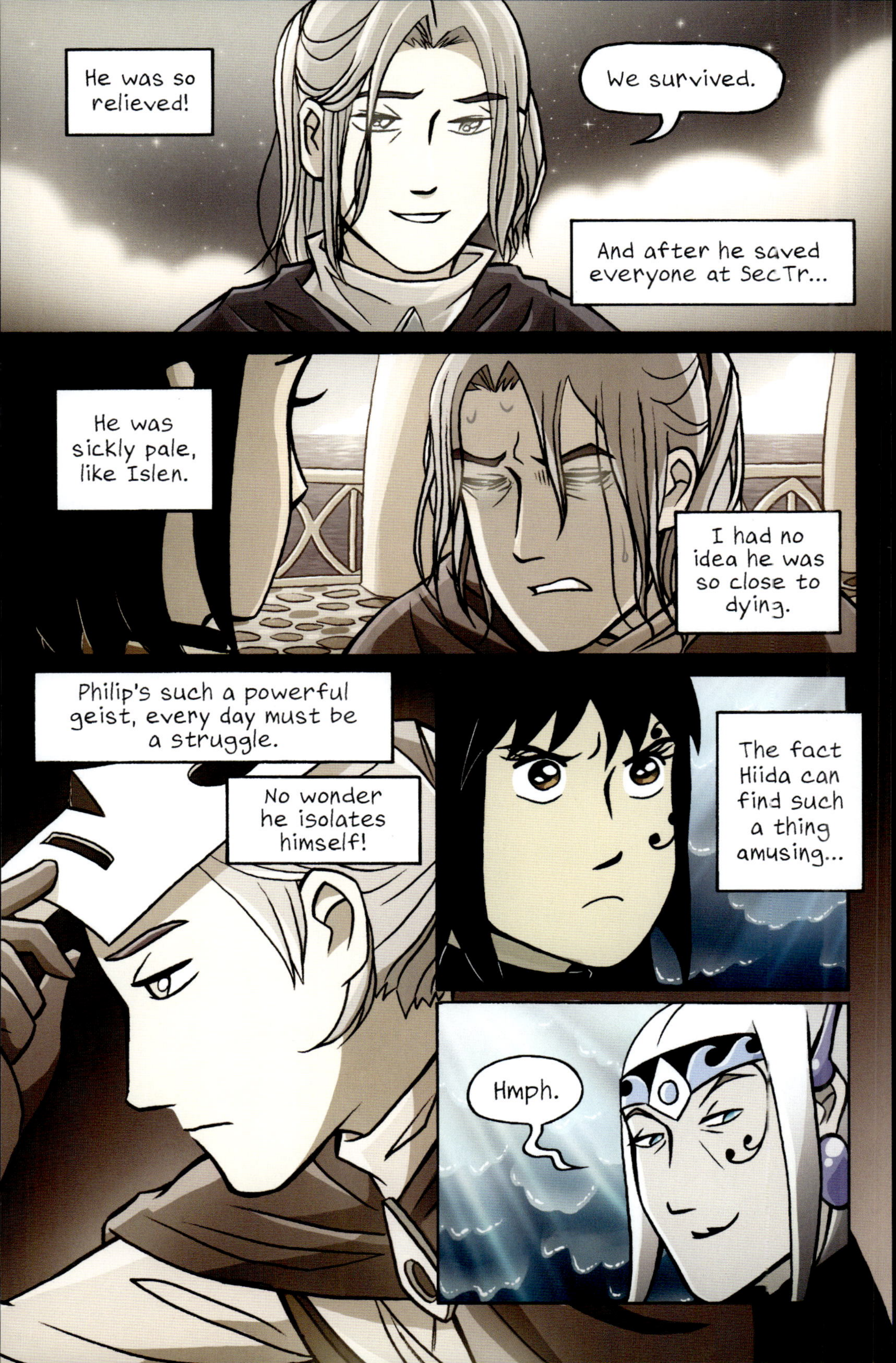
He was so relieved!
We survived.
And after he saved everyone at SecTr...
He was sickly pale, like Islen.
I had no idea he was so close to dying.
Philip's such a powerful geist, every day must be a struggle.
No wonder he isolates himself!
The fact Hiida can find such a thing amusing...
Hmph.

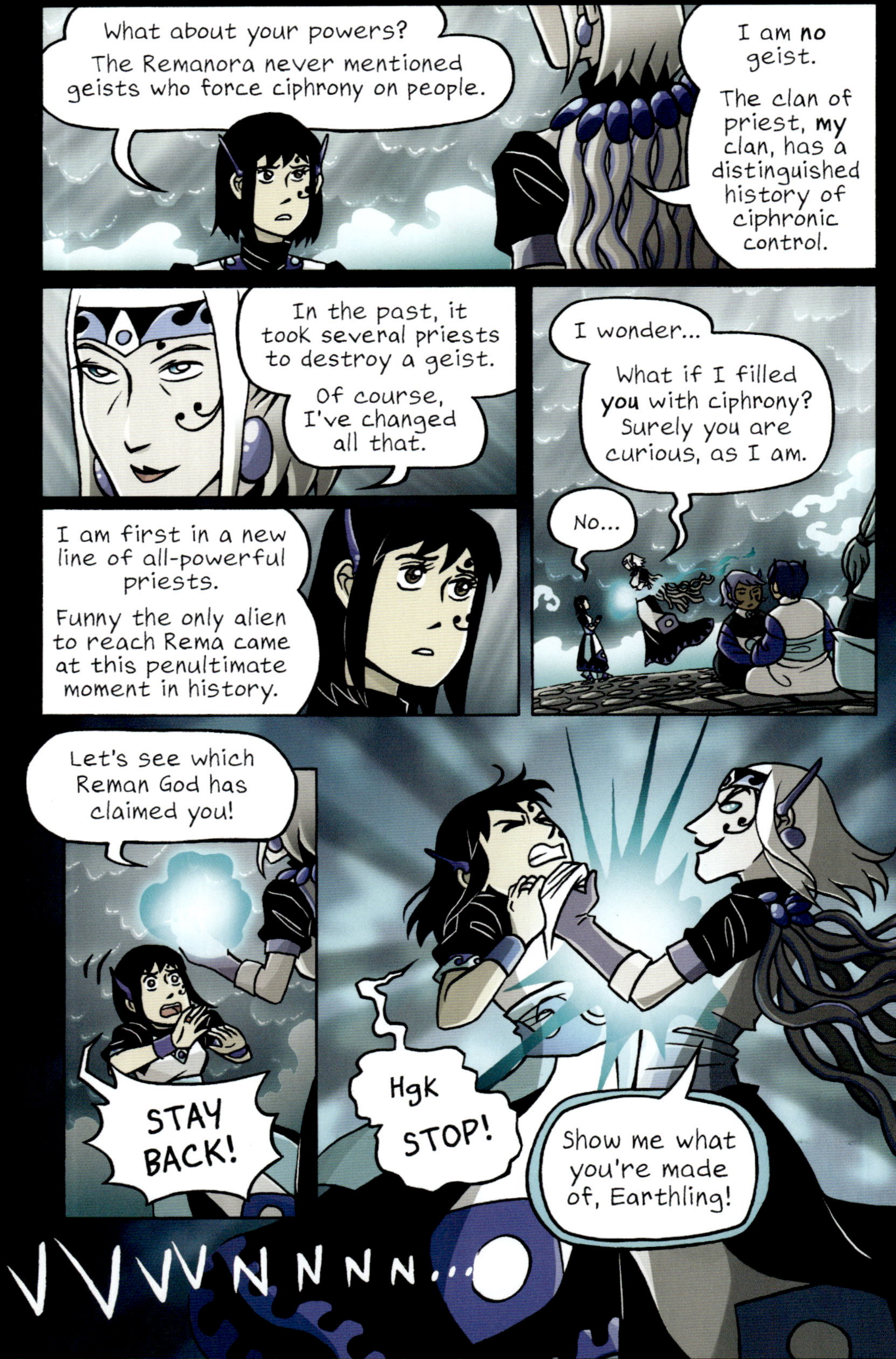
What about your powers?
The Remanora never mentioned geists who force ciphrony on people.
I am **no** geist.
The clan of priest, **my** clan, has a distinguished history of ciphronic control.
In the past, it took several priests to destroy a geist.
Of course, I've changed all that.
I wonder...
What if I filled **you** with ciphrony? Surely you are curious, as I am.
I am first in a new line of all-powerful priests.
Funny the only alien to reach Rema came at this penultimate moment in history.
No...
Let's see which Reman God has claimed you!
STAY BACK!
Hgk
STOP!
Show me what you're made of, Earthling!
VVVVNNNN...

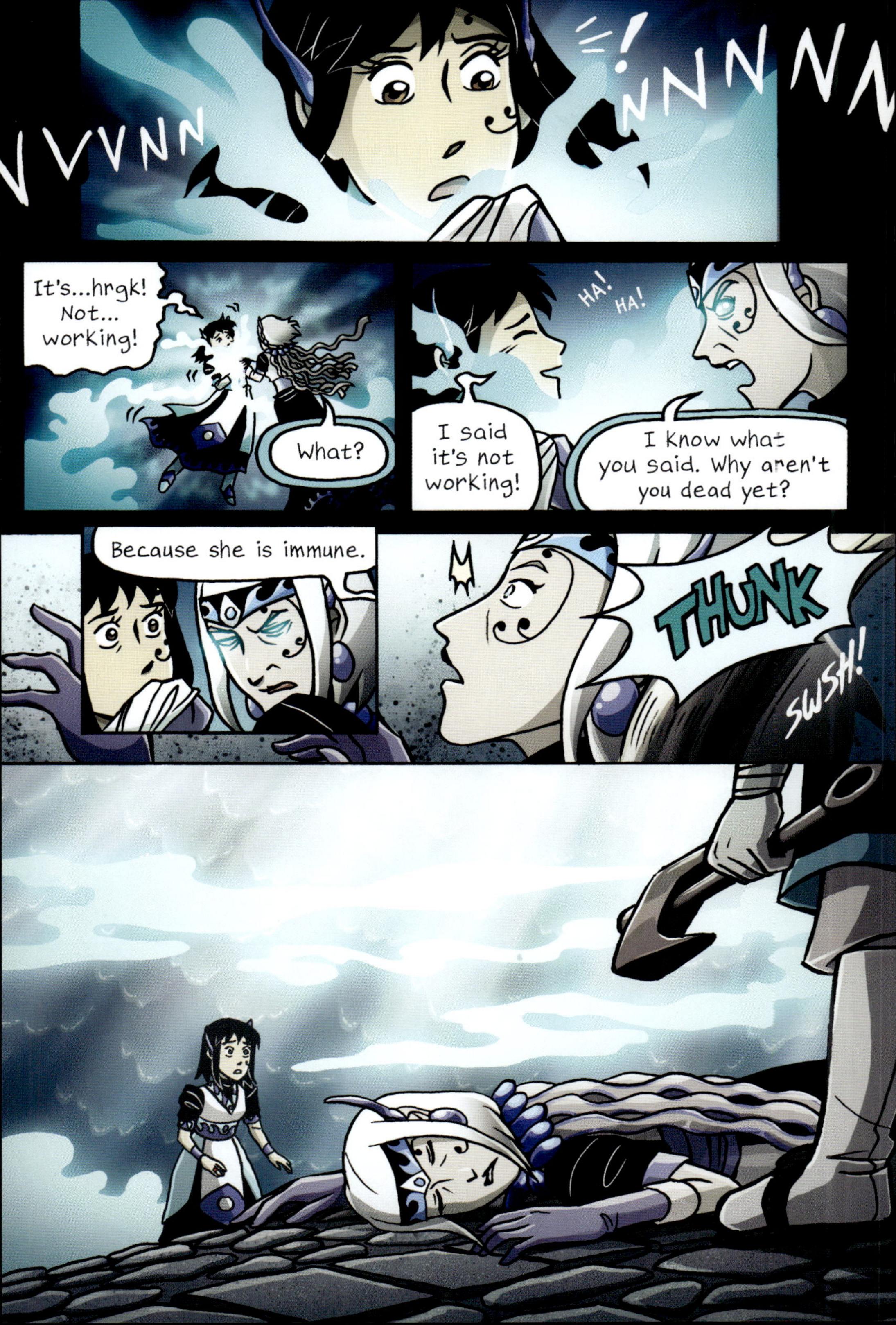

VVVNN
!
NNNNN
It's...hrgk! Not... working!
What?
HA! HA!
I said it's not working!
I know what you said. Why aren't you dead yet?
Because she is immune.
THUNK
SWSH!

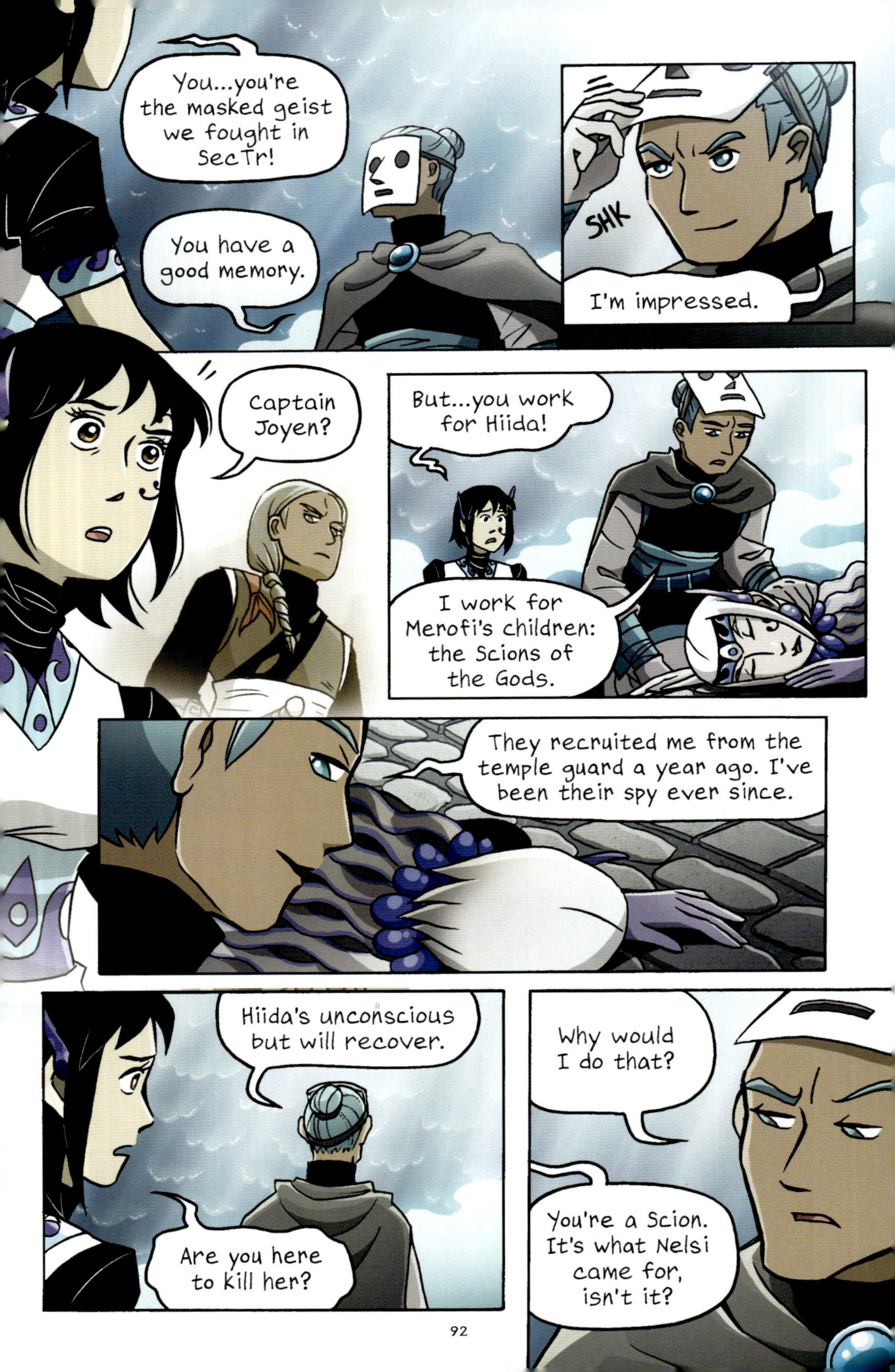
You...you're the masked geist we fought in SecTr!
You have a good memory.
SHK
I'm impressed.
Captain Joyen?
But...you work for Hiida!
I work for Merofi's children: the Scions of the Gods.
They recruited me from the temple guard a year ago. I've been their spy ever since.
Hiida's unconscious but will recover.
Are you here to kill her?
Why would I do that?
You're a Scion. It's what Nelsi came for, isn't it?

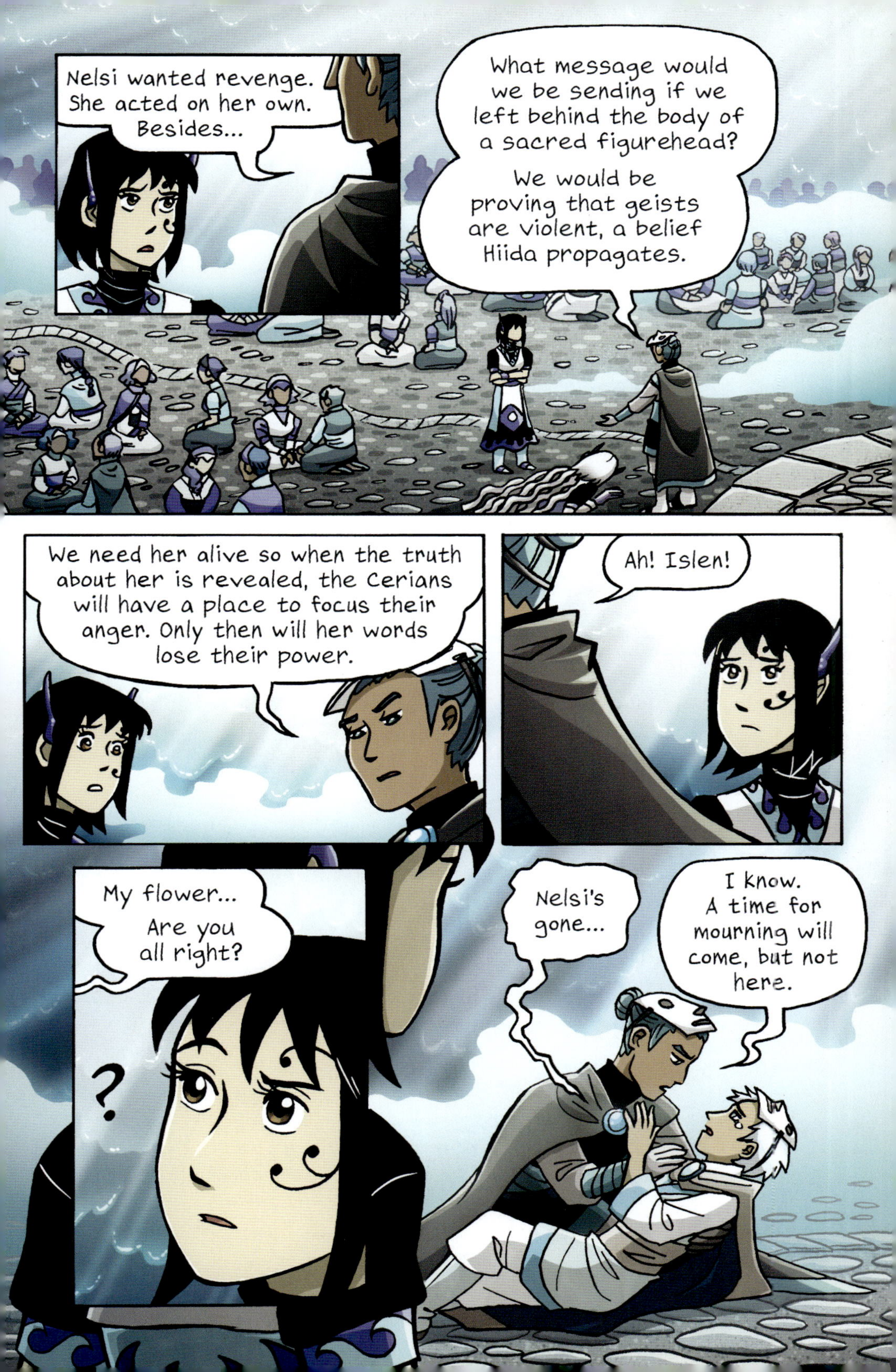

Nelsi wanted revenge. She acted on her own. Besides...
What message would we be sending if we left behind the body of a sacred figurehead?
We would be proving that geists are violent, a belief Hiida propagates.
We need her alive so when the truth about her is revealed, the Cerians will have a place to focus their anger. Only then will her words lose their power.
Ah! Islen!
My flower... Are you all right?
?
Nelsi's gone...
I know. A time for mourning will come, but not here.

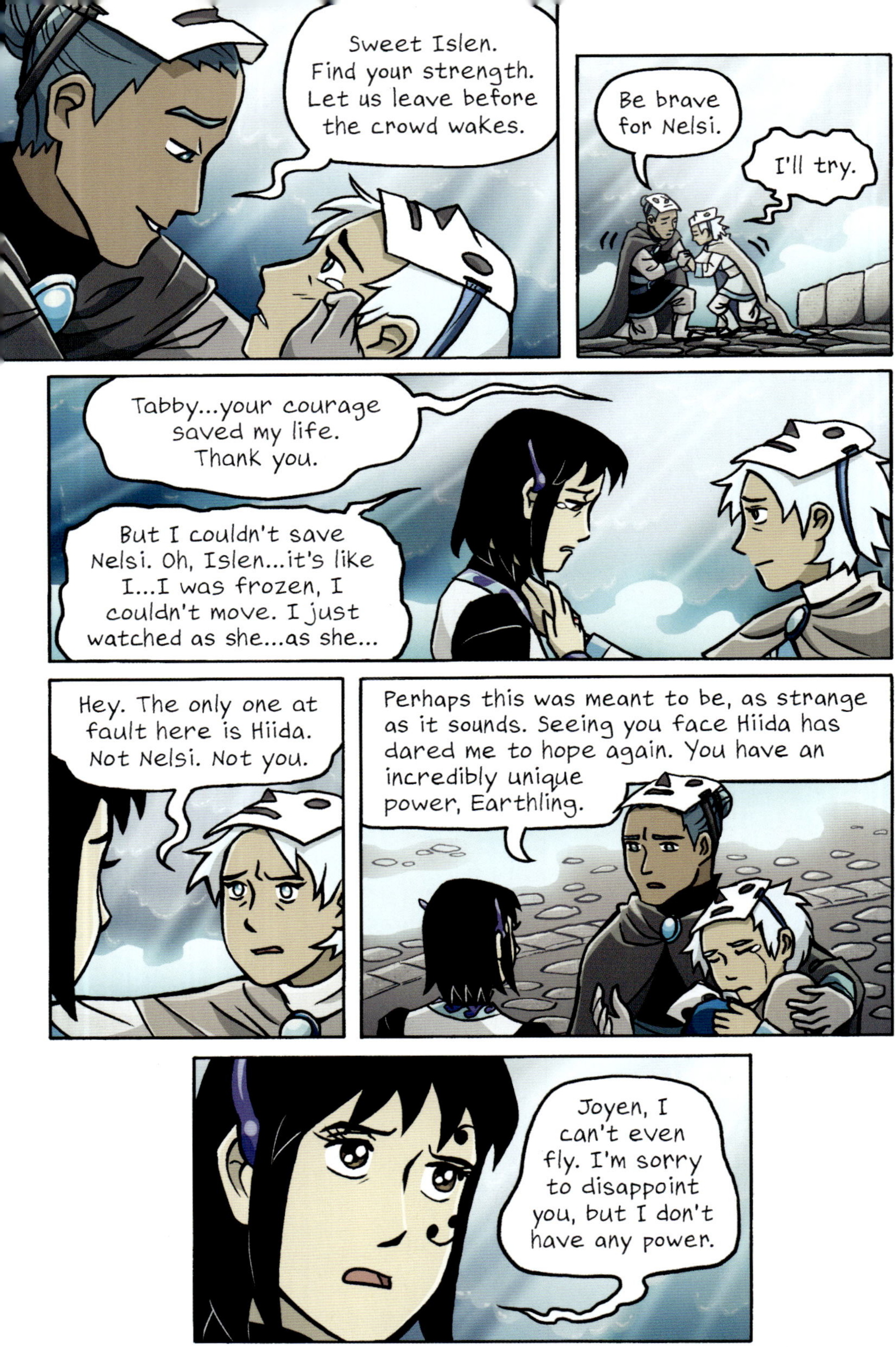
Sweet Islen. Find your strength. Let us leave before the crowd wakes.
Be brave for Nelsi.
I'll try.
Tabby...your courage saved my life. Thank you.
But I couldn't save Nelsi. Oh, Islen...it's like I...I was frozen, I couldn't move. I just watched as she...as she...
Hey. The only one at fault here is Hiida. Not Nelsi. Not you.
Perhaps this was meant to be, as strange as it sounds. Seeing you face Hiida has dared me to hope again. You have an incredibly unique power, Earthling.
Joyen, I can't even fly. I'm sorry to disappoint you, but I don't have any power.

But you do. Ciphrony distorts everything it touches -- plants, animals, and people.
You wade through it as if it were nothing!
Your immunity is a miracle sent to us from The Gods. The Scions need you.
For what?
To make an example of Priestess Hiida.
Do you know of the geist prince?
Cenri Helvir!
Yes...tragic, beloved Prince Cenri Helvir.
Everything you read about him in the Remanora was a lie. Priestess Hiida wrote those passages to hide the truth.
What truth?
That she killed the prince -- her own nephew -- just to stay in power.
You know Hiida is capable of it. Rema does not.

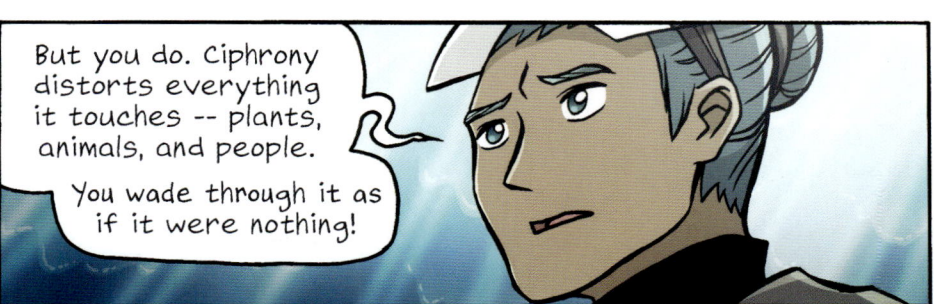

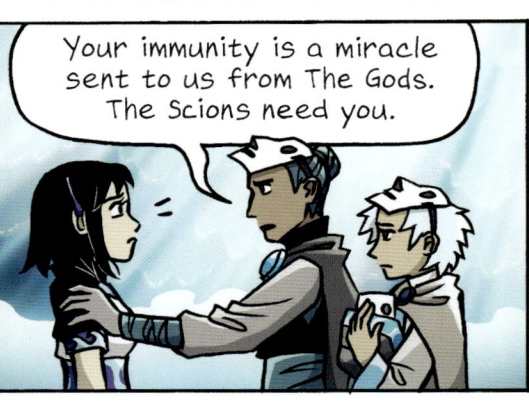

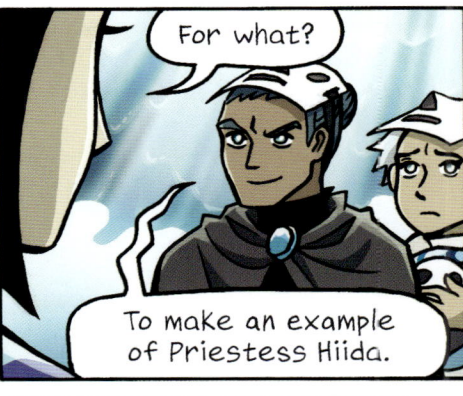

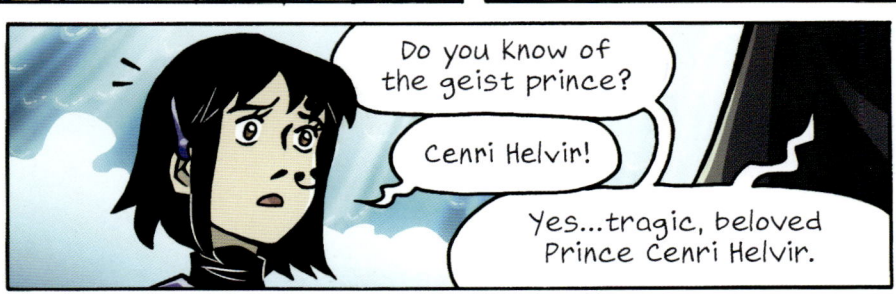

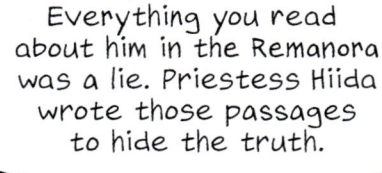

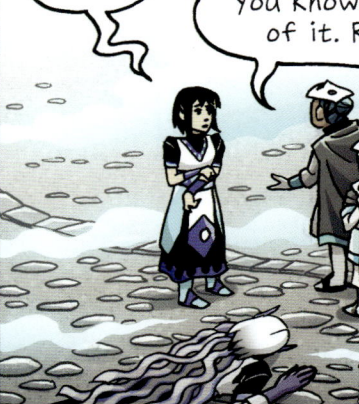

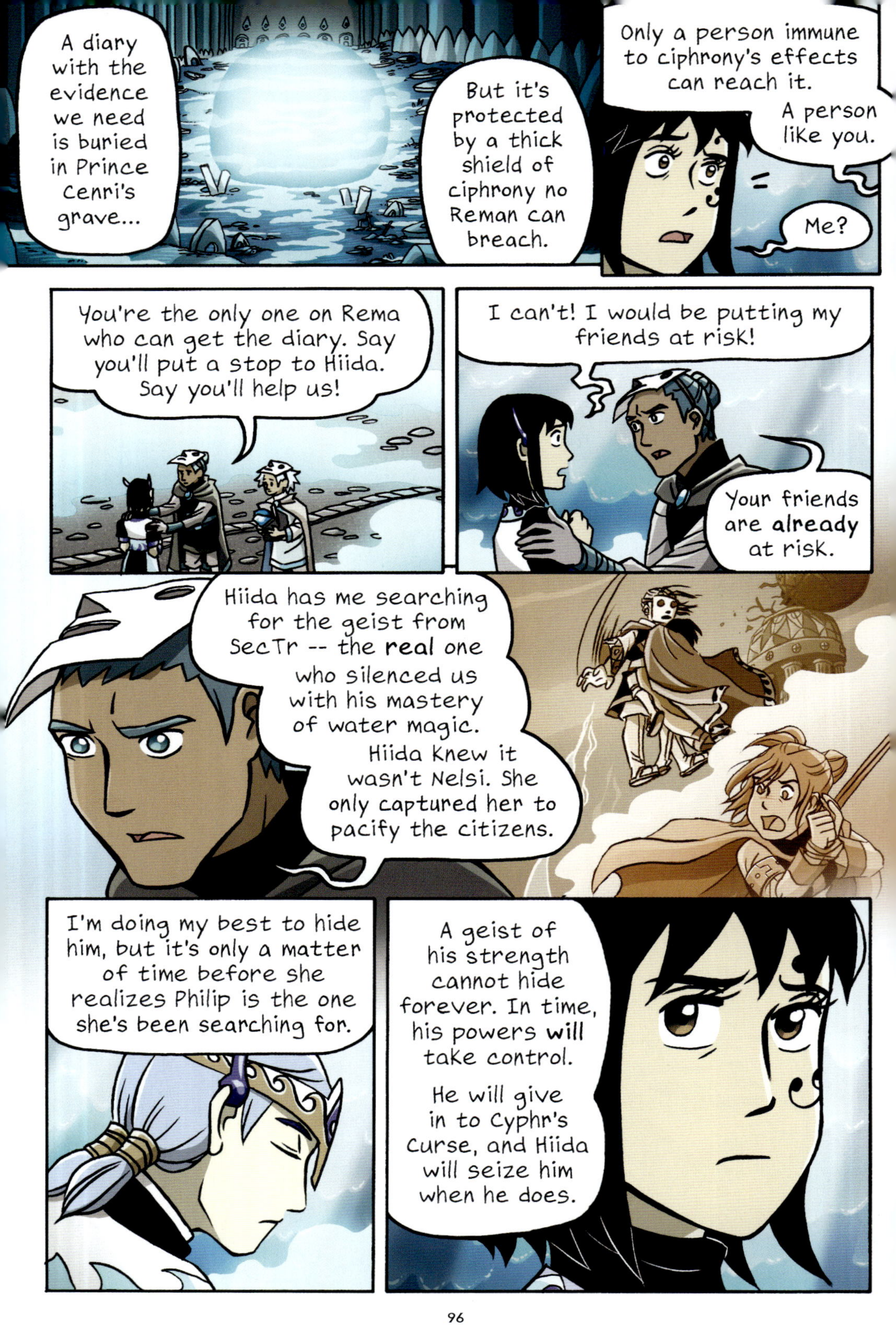
A diary with the evidence we need is buried in Prince Cenri's grave...
But it's protected by a thick shield of ciphrony no Reman can breach.
Only a person immune to ciphrony's effects can reach it.
A person like you.
Me?
You're the only one on Rema who can get the diary. Say you'll put a stop to Hiida. Say you'll help us!
I can't! I would be putting my friends at risk!
Your friends are **already** at risk.
Hiida has me searching for the geist from SecTr -- the **real** one who silenced us with his mastery of water magic.
Hiida knew it wasn't Nelsi. She only captured her to pacify the citizens.
I'm doing my best to hide him, but it's only a matter of time before she realizes Philip is the one she's been searching for.
A geist of his strength cannot hide forever. In time, his powers **will** take control.
He will give in to Cyphr's Curse, and Hiida will seize him when he does.

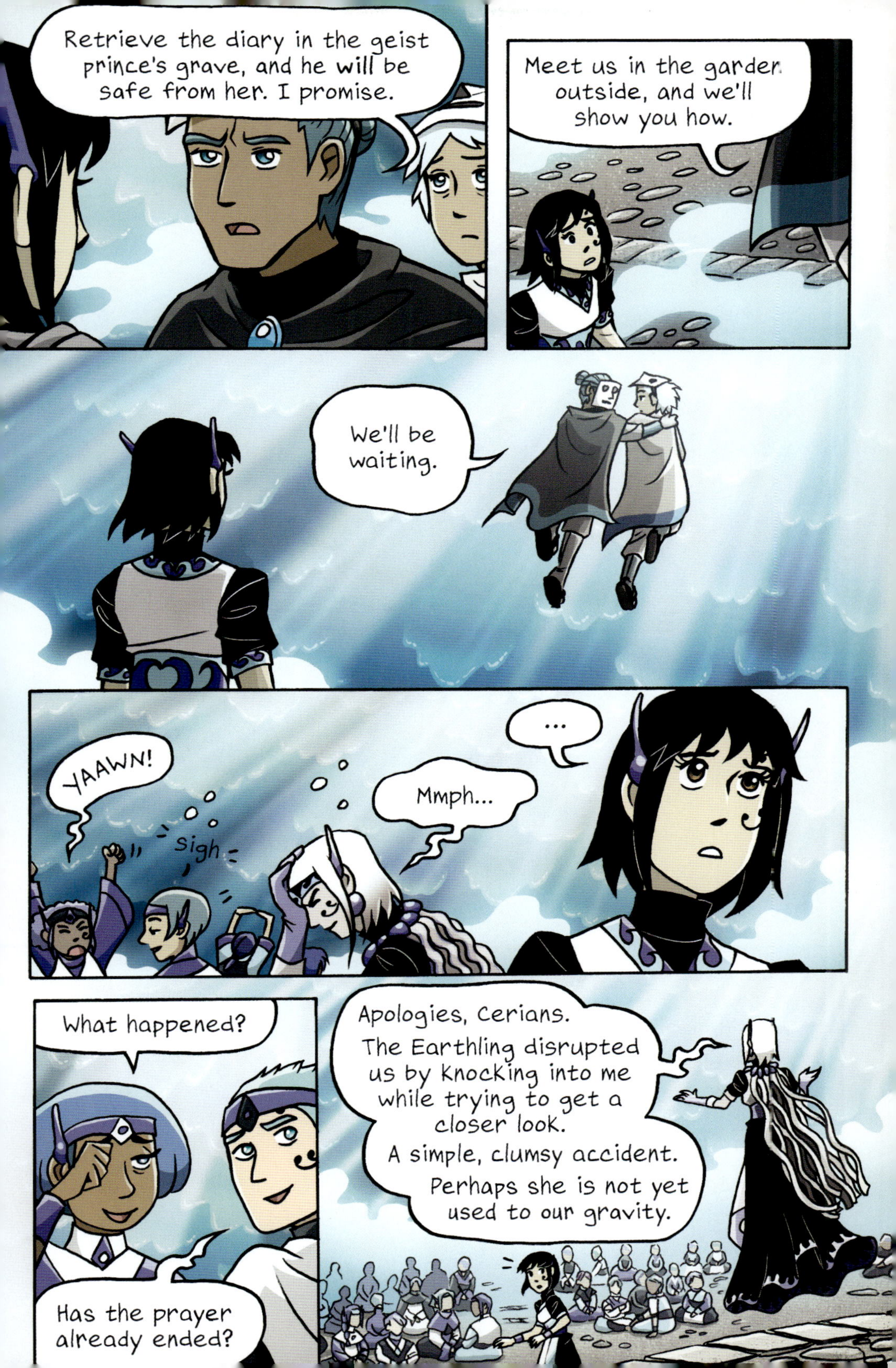

Retrieve the diary in the geist prince's grave, and he will be safe from her. I promise.
Meet us in the garden outside, and we'll show you how.
We'll be waiting.
YAAWN!
sigh
Mmph...
...
What happened?
Has the prayer already ended?
Apologies, Cerians.
The Earthling disrupted us by knocking into me while trying to get a closer look.
A simple, clumsy accident.
Perhaps she is not yet used to our gravity.

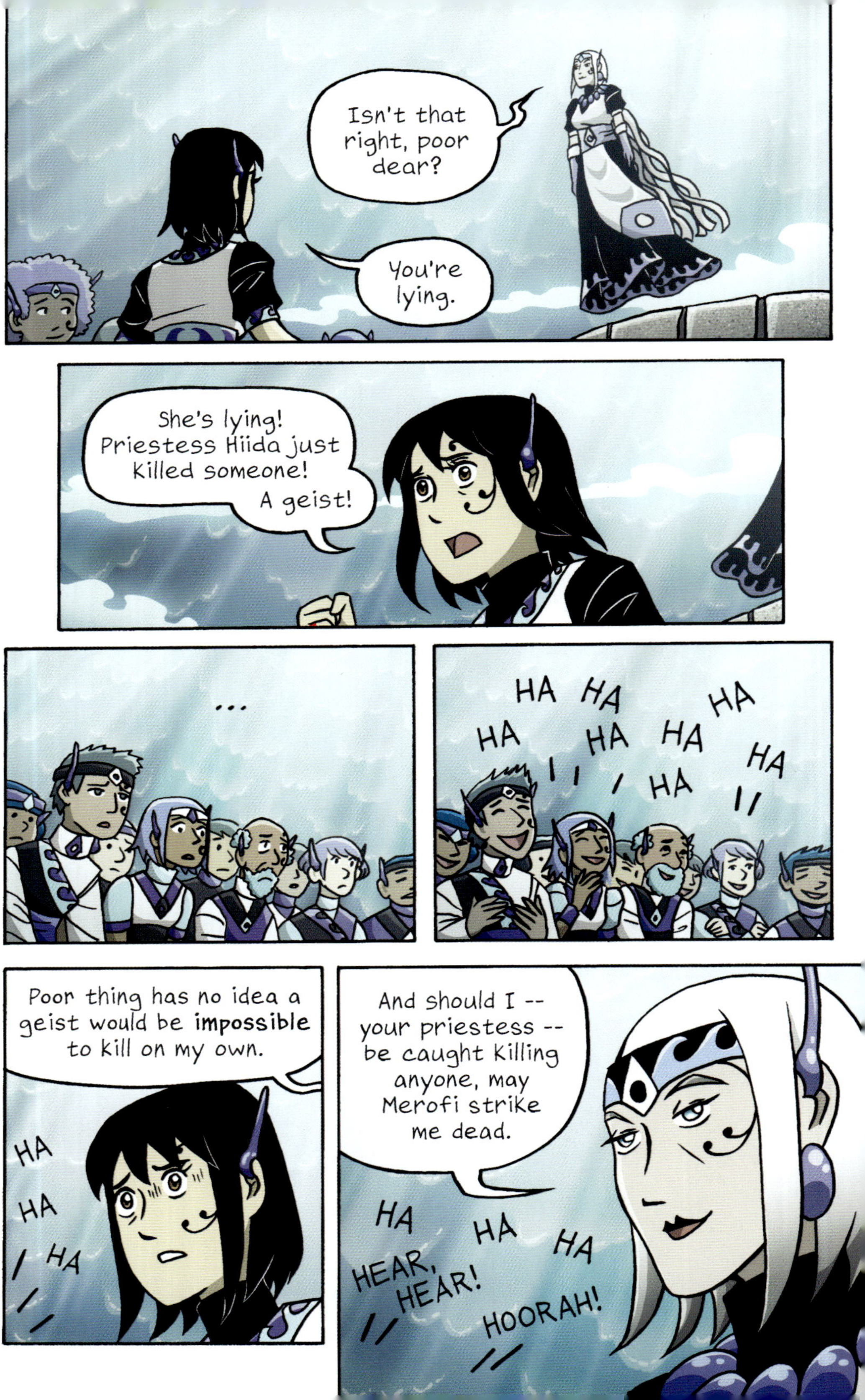

Isn't that right, poor dear?
You're lying.
She's lying! Priestess Hiida just Killed someone! A geist!
...
HA HA HA HA HA HA HA HA HA
Poor thing has no idea a geist would be **impossible** to kill on my own.
HA HA HA
And should I -- your priestess -- be caught Killing anyone, may Merofi strike me dead.
HA HA HA
HEAR, HEAR!
HOORAH!

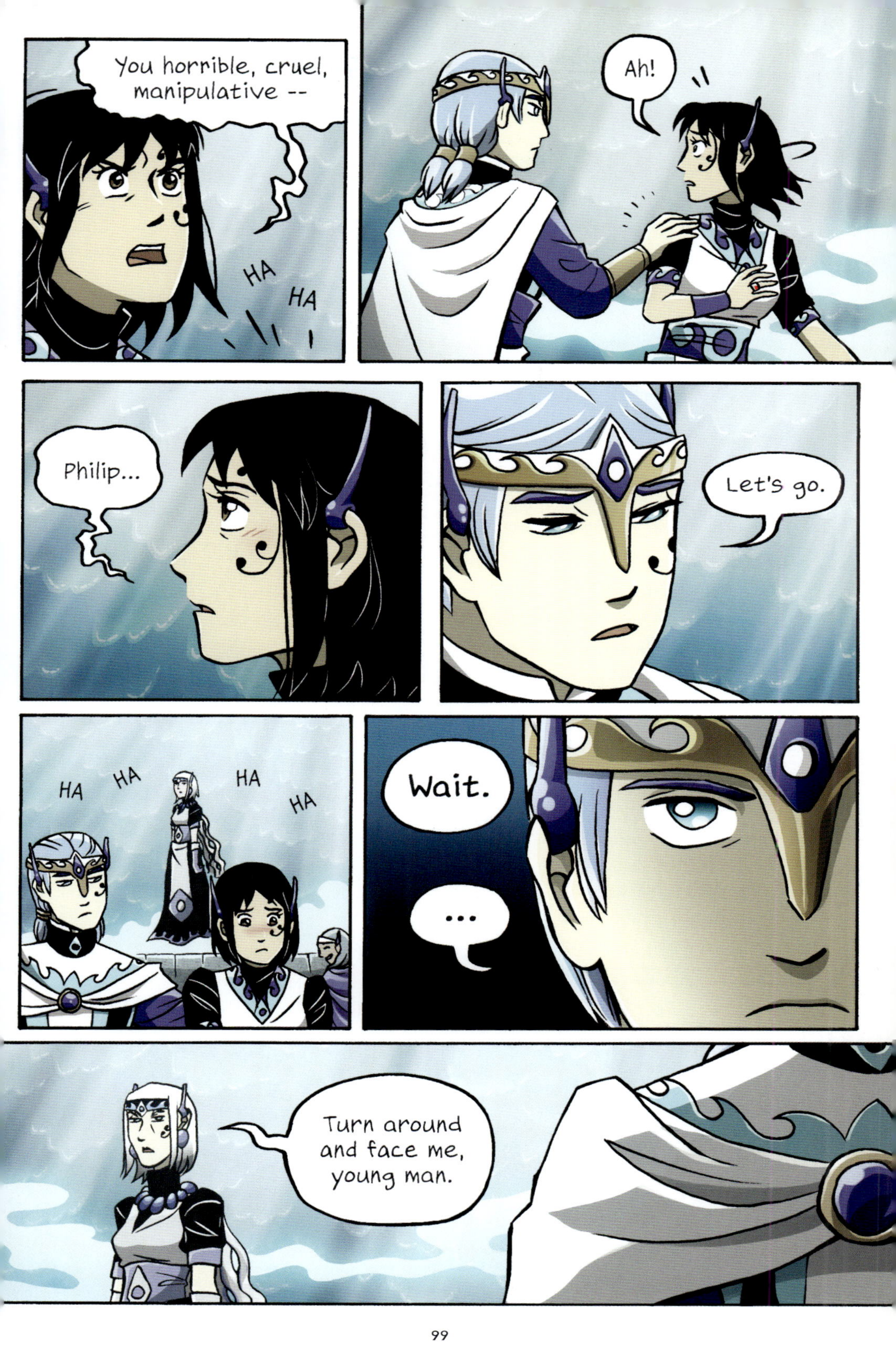
You horrible, cruel, manipulative --
HA
HA
Ah!
Philip...
Let's go.
HA
HA
HA
HA
Wait.
...
Turn around and face me, young man.

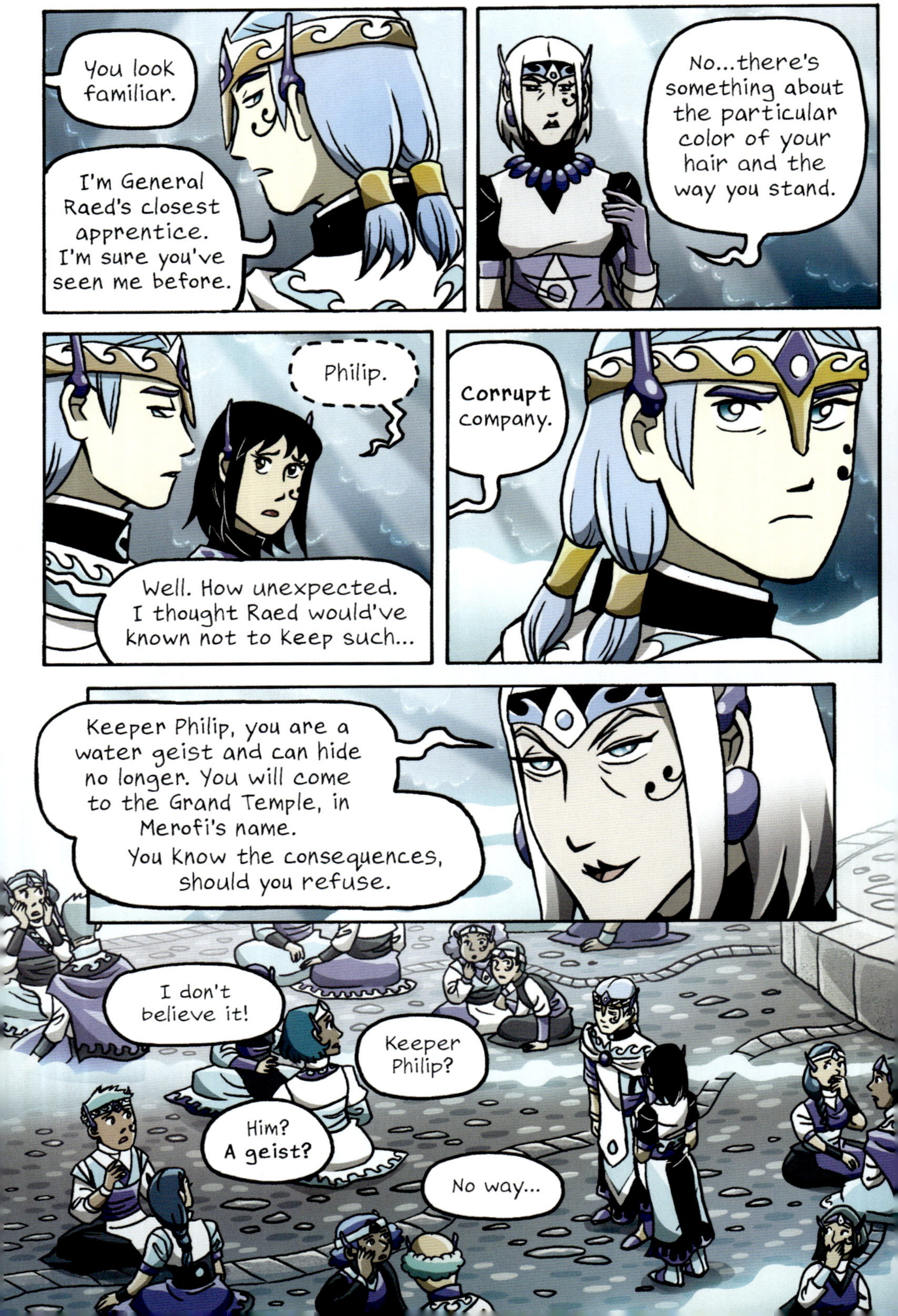
You look familiar.
I'm General Raed's closest apprentice. I'm sure you've seen me before.
No...there's something about the particular color of your hair and the way you stand.
Philip.
Well. How unexpected. I thought Raed would've known not to keep such...
Corrupt company.
Keeper Philip, you are a water geist and can hide no longer. You will come to the Grand Temple, in Merofi's name.
You know the consequences, should you refuse.
I don't believe it!
Keeper Philip?
Him? A geist?
No way...

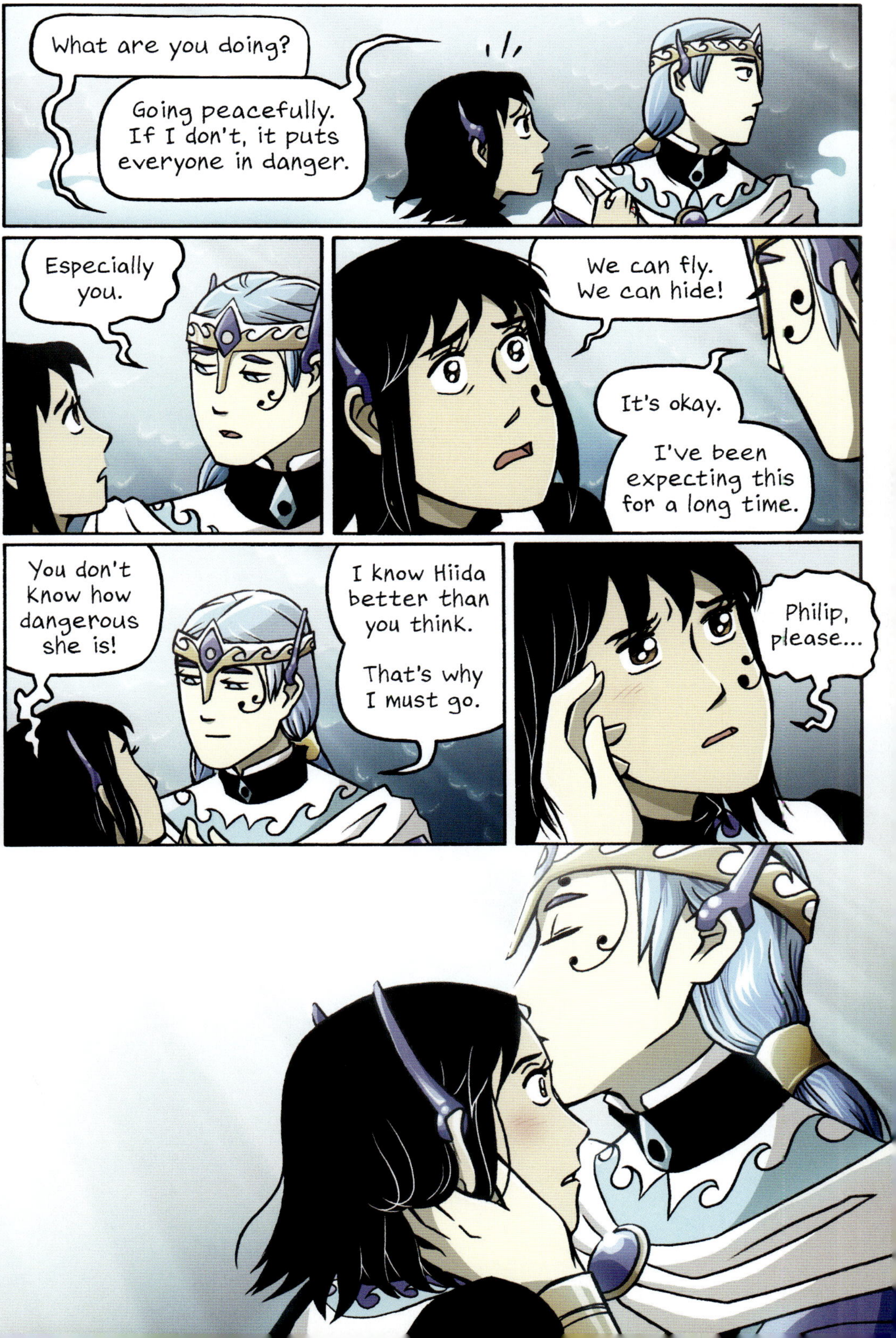
What are you doing?
Going peacefully. If I don't, it puts everyone in danger.
Especially you.
We can fly. We can hide!
It's okay.
I've been expecting this for a long time.
You don't know how dangerous she is!
I know Hiida better than you think.
That's why I must go.
Philip, please...

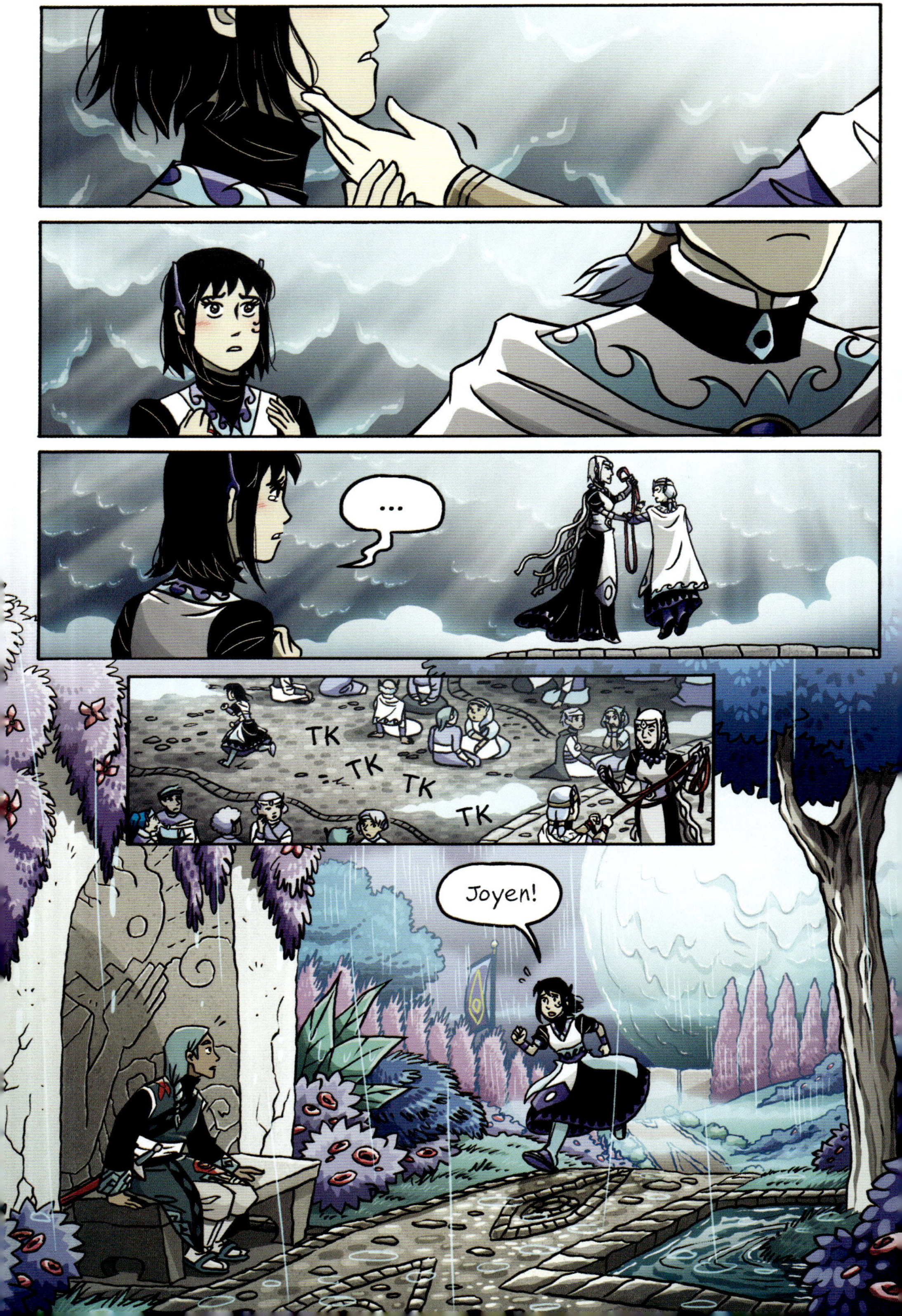
...
TK
TK
TK
TK
Joyen!

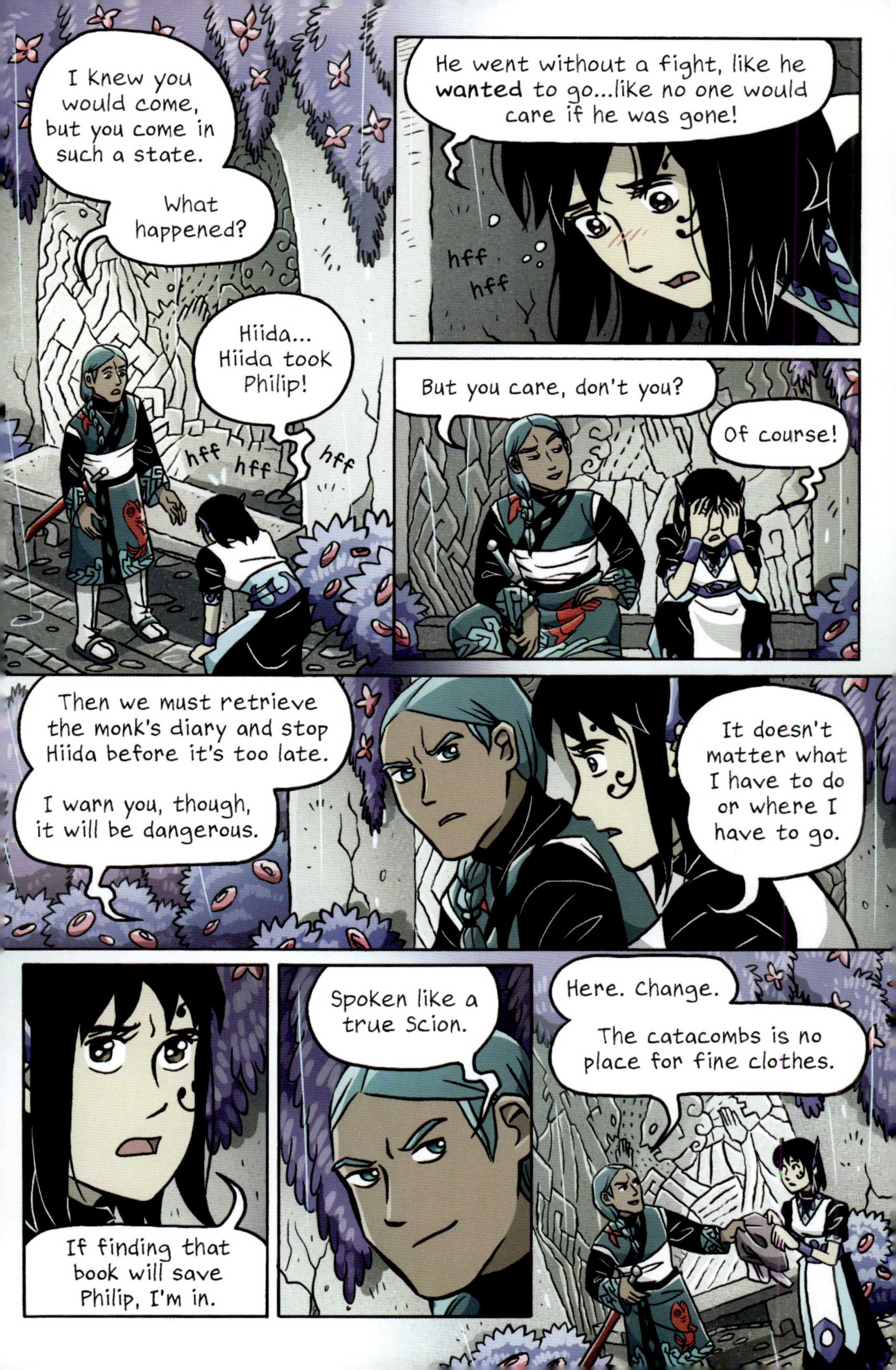
I knew you would come, but you come in such a state.
What happened?
He went without a fight, like he **wanted** to go...like no one would care if he was gone!
hff
hff
Hiida... Hiida took Philip!
hff
hff
hff
But you care, don't you?
Of course!
Then we must retrieve the monk's diary and stop Hiida before it's too late.
I warn you, though, it will be dangerous.
It doesn't matter what I have to do or where I have to go.
If finding that book will save Philip, I'm in.
Spoken like a true Scion.
Here. Change.
The catacombs is no place for fine clothes.

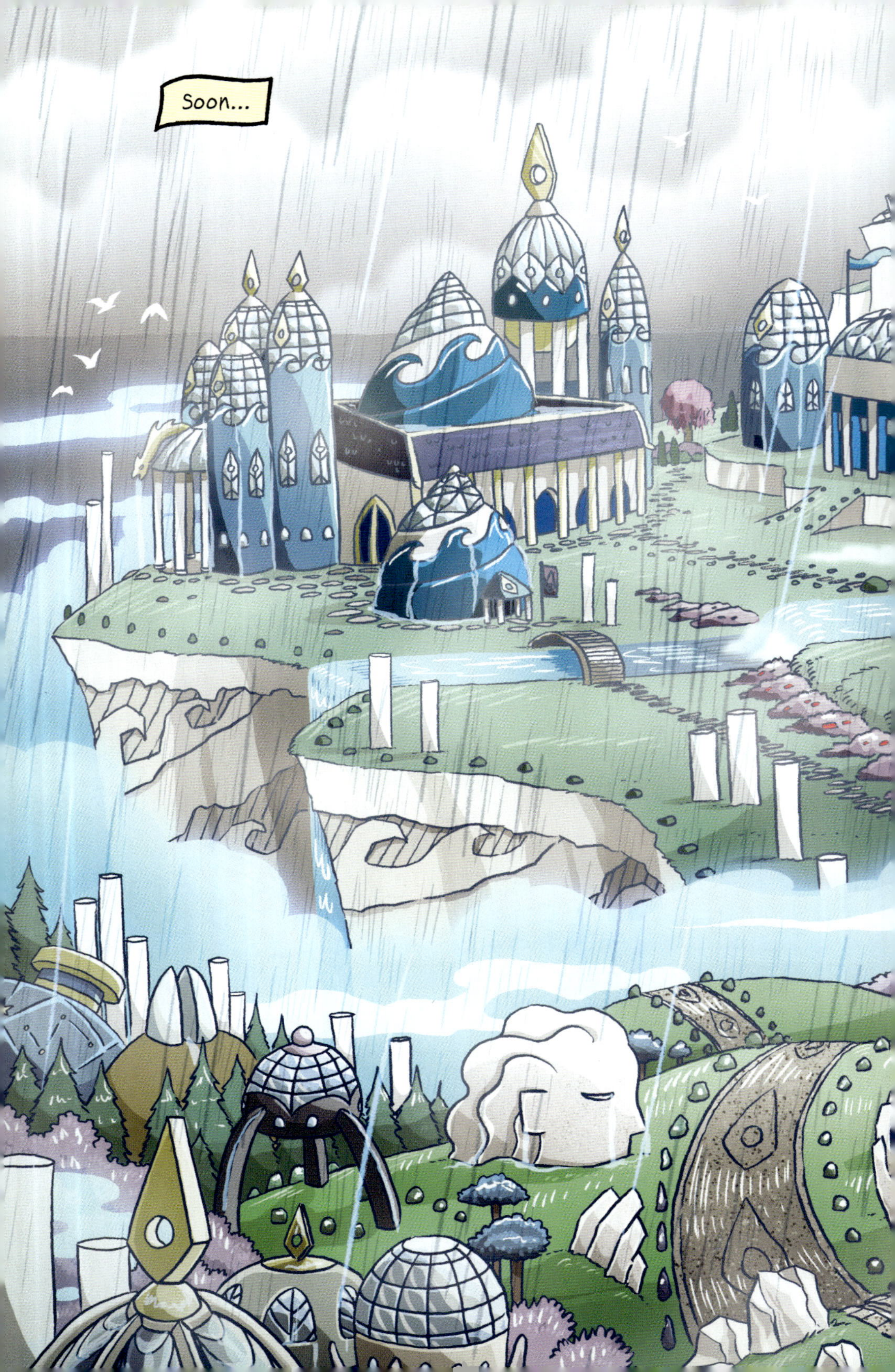
Soon...

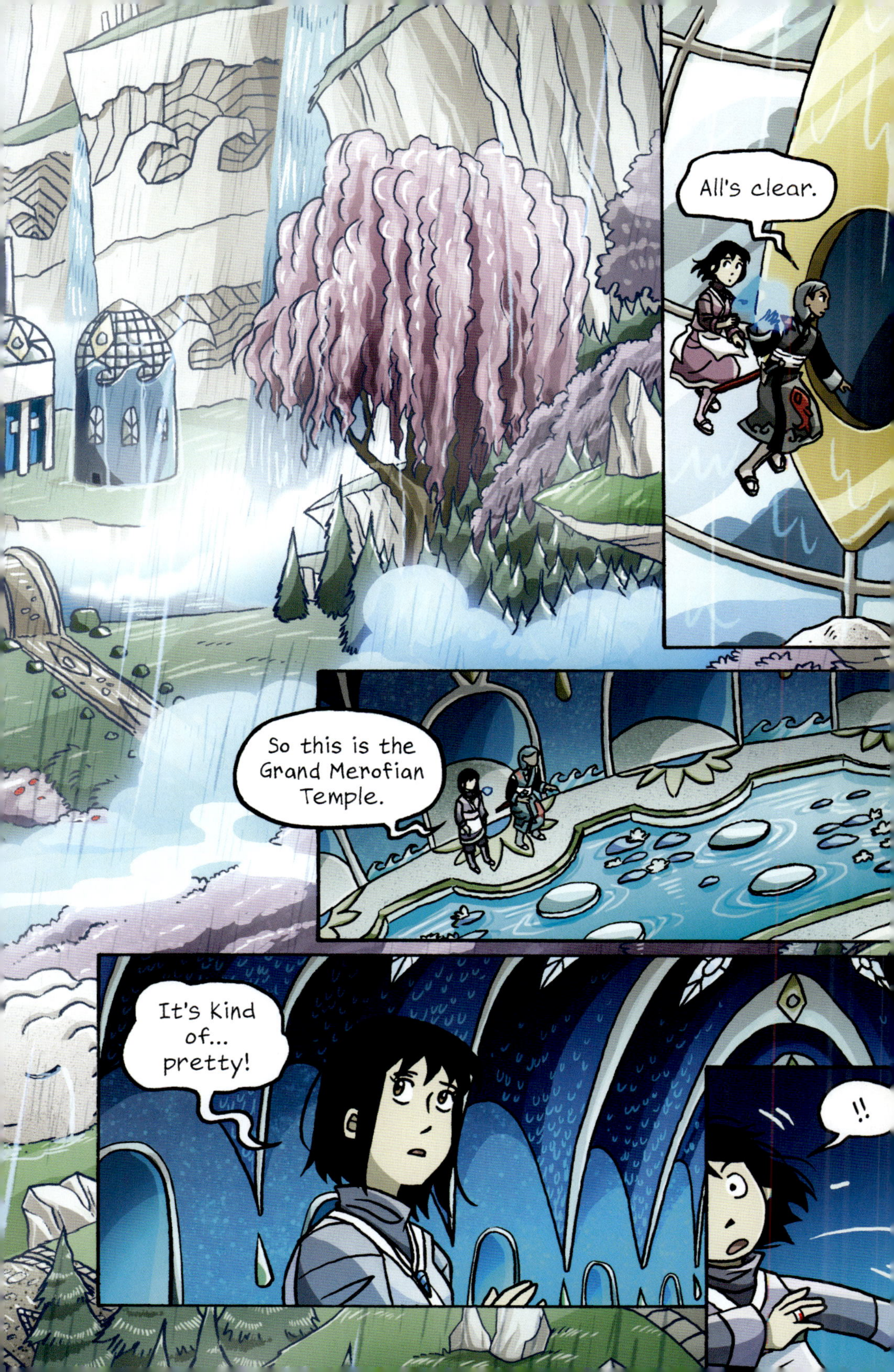
All's clear.
So this is the Grand Merofian Temple.
It's kind of... pretty!
!!

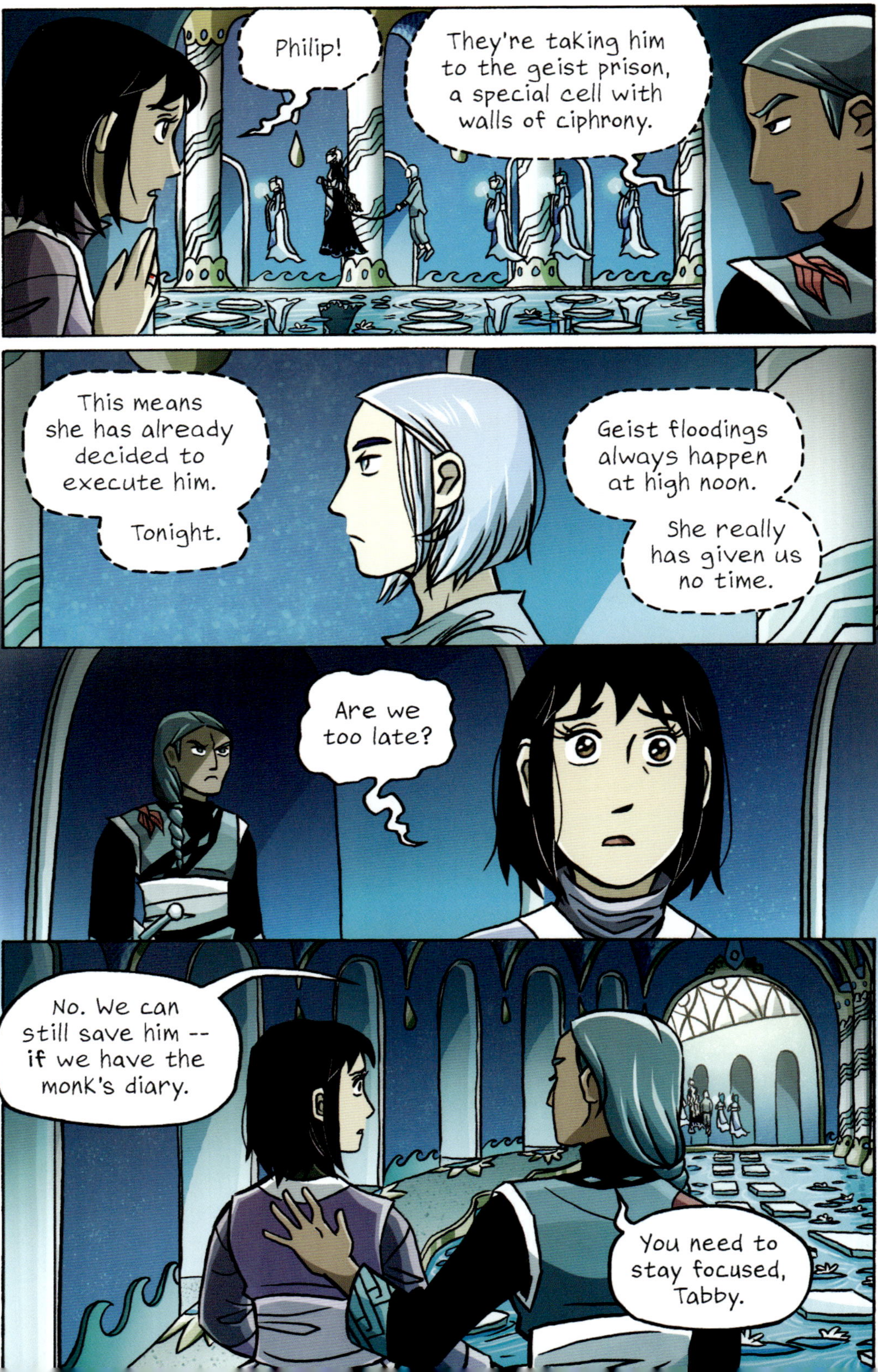
Philip!
They're taking him to the geist prison, a special cell with walls of ciphrony.
This means she has already decided to execute him.
Tonight.
Geist floodings always happen at high noon.
She really has given us no time.
Are we too late?
No. We can still save him -- if we have the monk's diary.
You need to stay focused, Tabby.

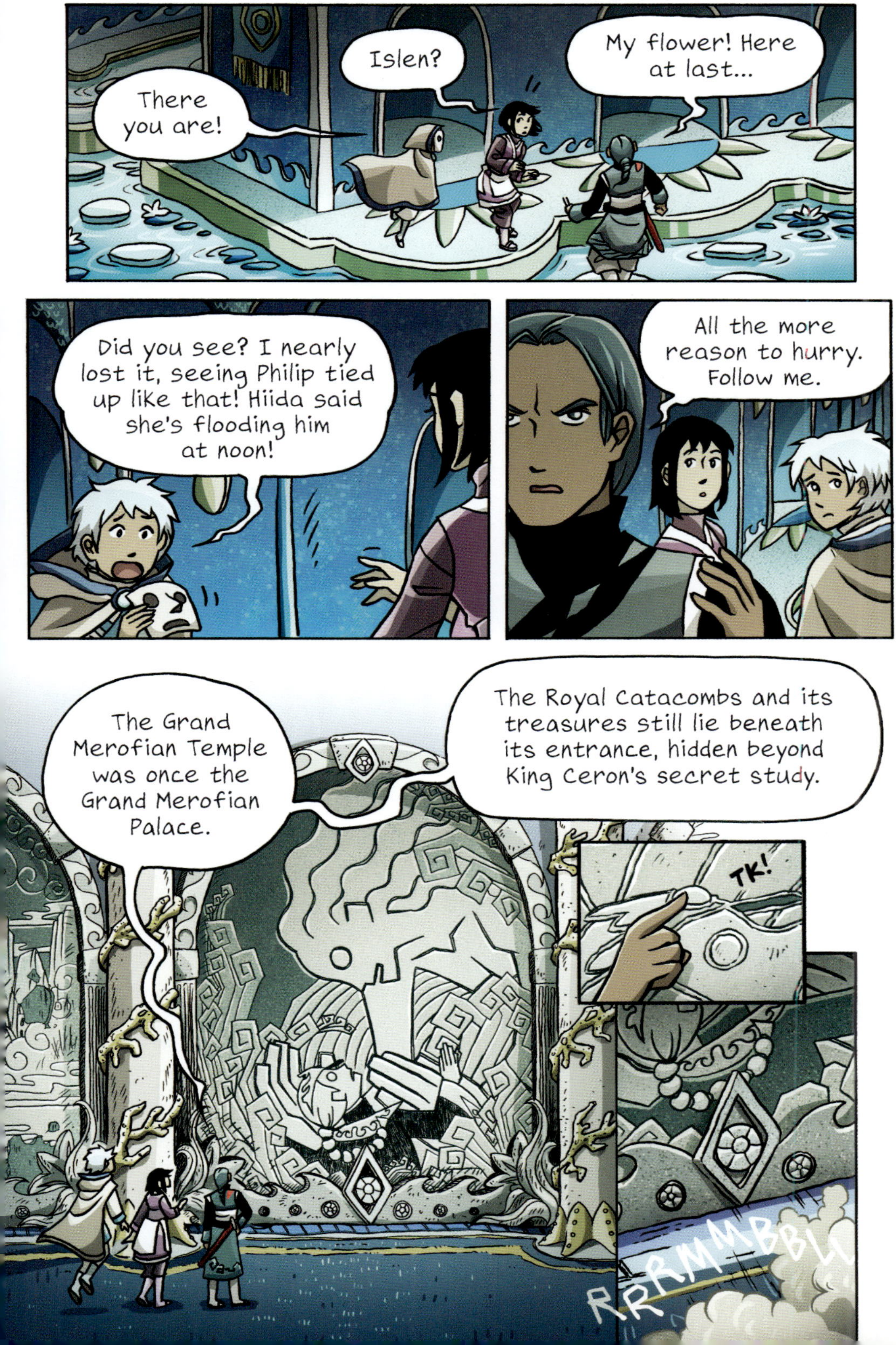
There you are!
Islen?
My flower! Here at last...
Did you see? I nearly lost it, seeing Philip tied up like that! Hiida said she's flooding him at noon!
All the more reason to hurry. Follow me.
The Grand Merofian Temple was once the Grand Merofian Palace.
The Royal Catacombs and its treasures still lie beneath its entrance, hidden beyond King Ceron's secret study.
TK!
RRRMMBBL

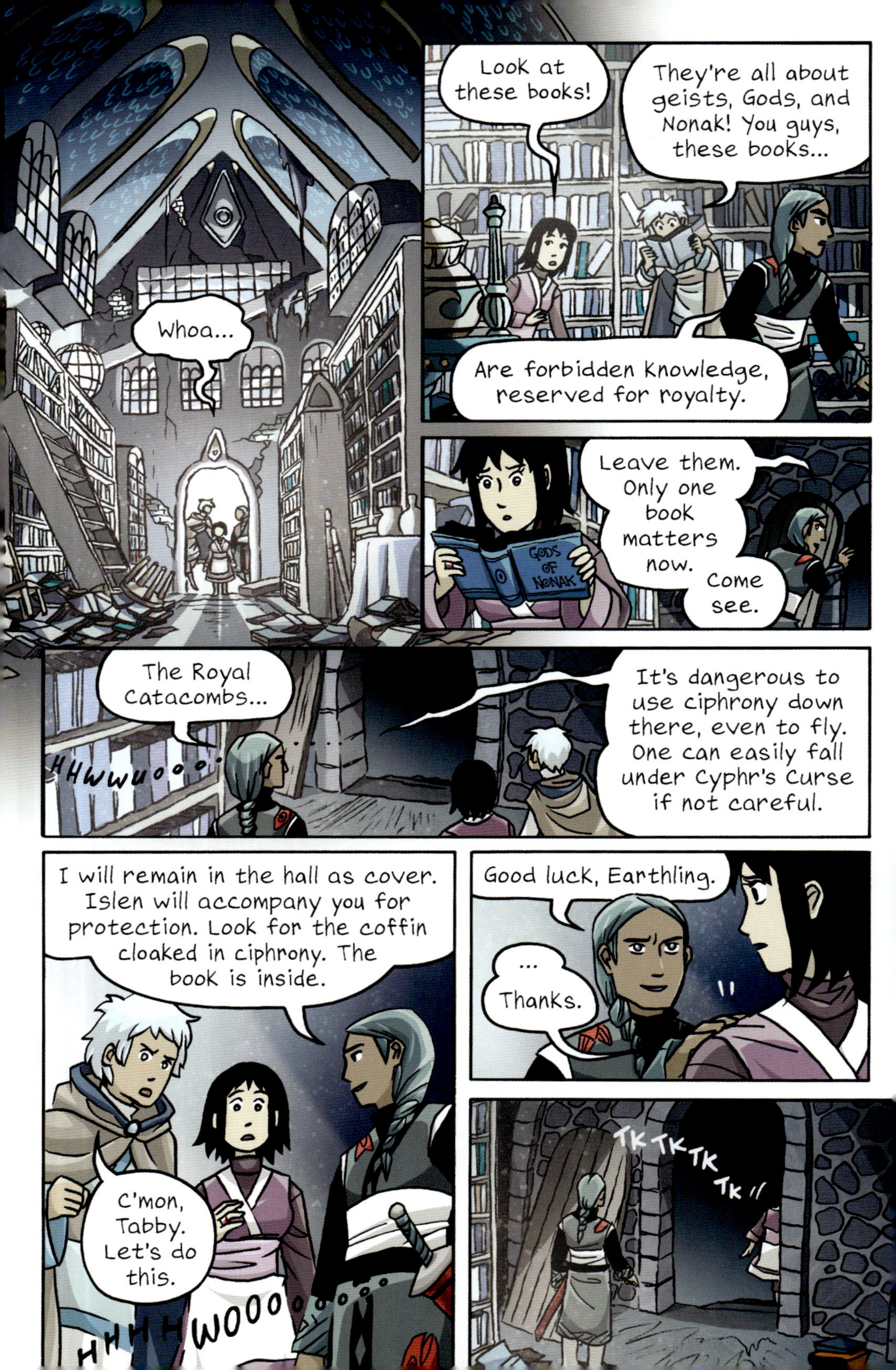
Whoa...
Look at these books!
They're all about geists, Gods, and Nonak! You guys, these books...
Are forbidden knowledge, reserved for royalty.
GODS OF NONAK
Leave them. Only one book matters now.
Come see.
The Royal Catacombs...
HHWWUOOO
It's dangerous to use ciphrony down there, even to fly. One can easily fall under Cyphr's Curse if not careful.
I will remain in the hall as cover. Islen will accompany you for protection. Look for the coffin cloaked in ciphrony. The book is inside.
C'mon, Tabby. Let's do this.
HHHHWOOOO
Good luck, Earthling.
... Thanks.
TKTKTKTK

PART III
THE GEIST PRINCE

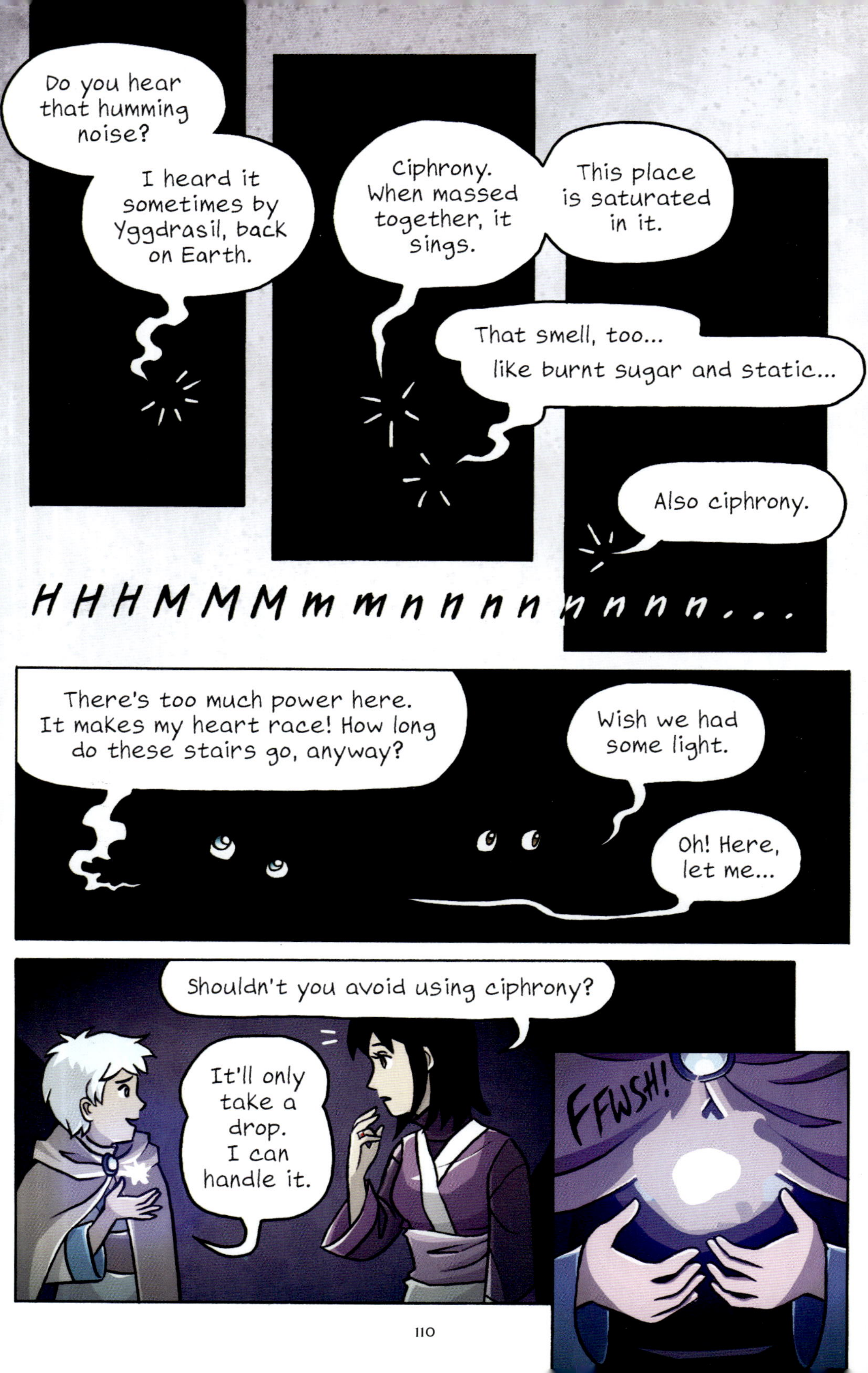

Do you hear that humming noise?
I heard it sometimes by Yggdrasil, back on Earth.
Ciphrony. When massed together, it sings.
This place is saturated in it.
That smell, too... like burnt sugar and static...
Also ciphrony.
HHHMMMmmnnnnnnnn...
There's too much power here. It makes my heart race! How long do these stairs go, anyway?
Wish we had some light.
Oh! Here, let me...
Shouldn't you avoid using ciphrony?
It'll only take a drop. I can handle it.
FFWSH!

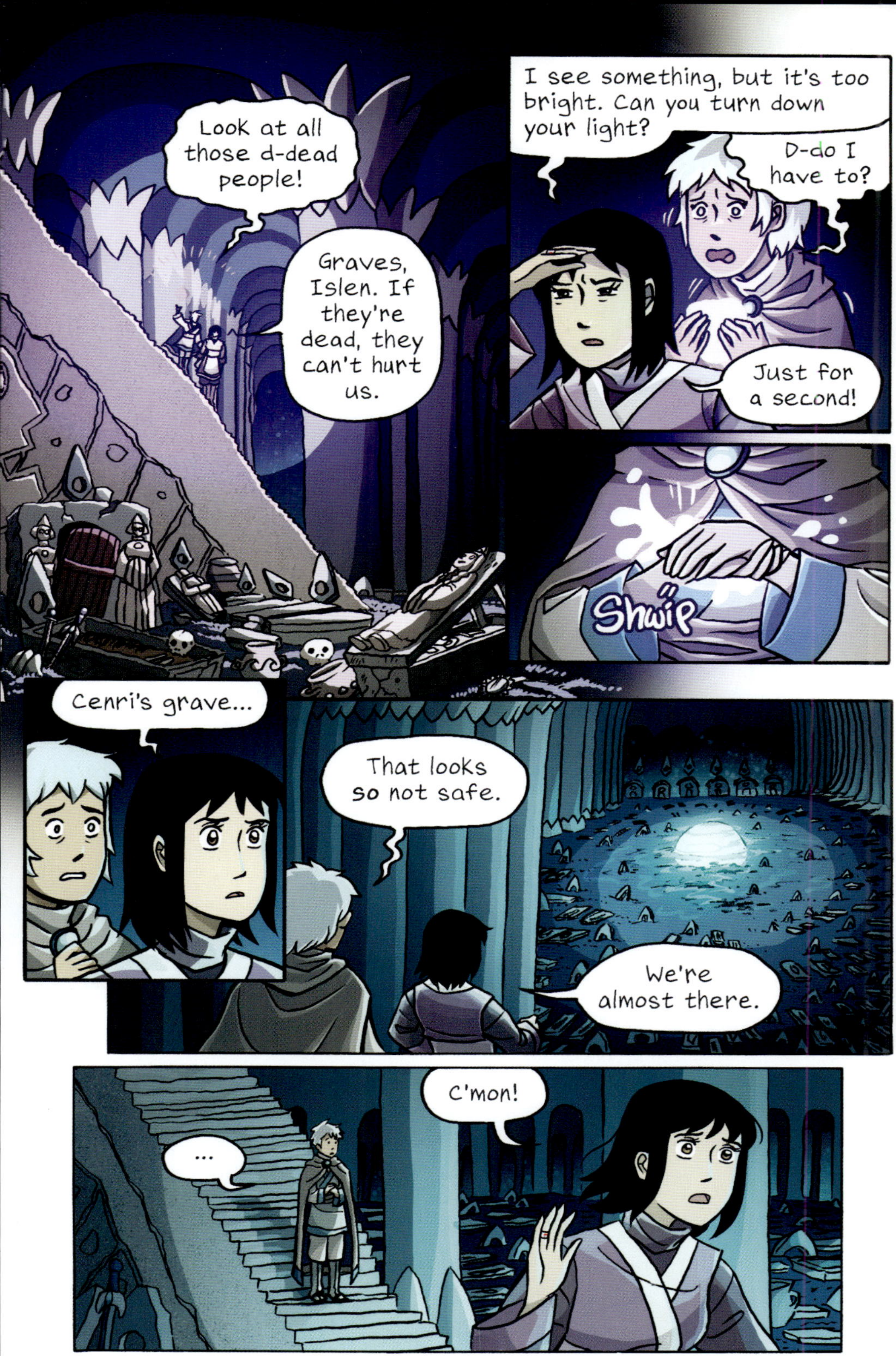

Look at all those d-dead people!
Graves, Islen. If they're dead, they can't hurt us.
I see something, but it's too bright. Can you turn down your light?
D-do I have to?
Just for a second!
Shwip
Cenri's grave...
That looks so not safe.
We're almost there.
C'mon!
...

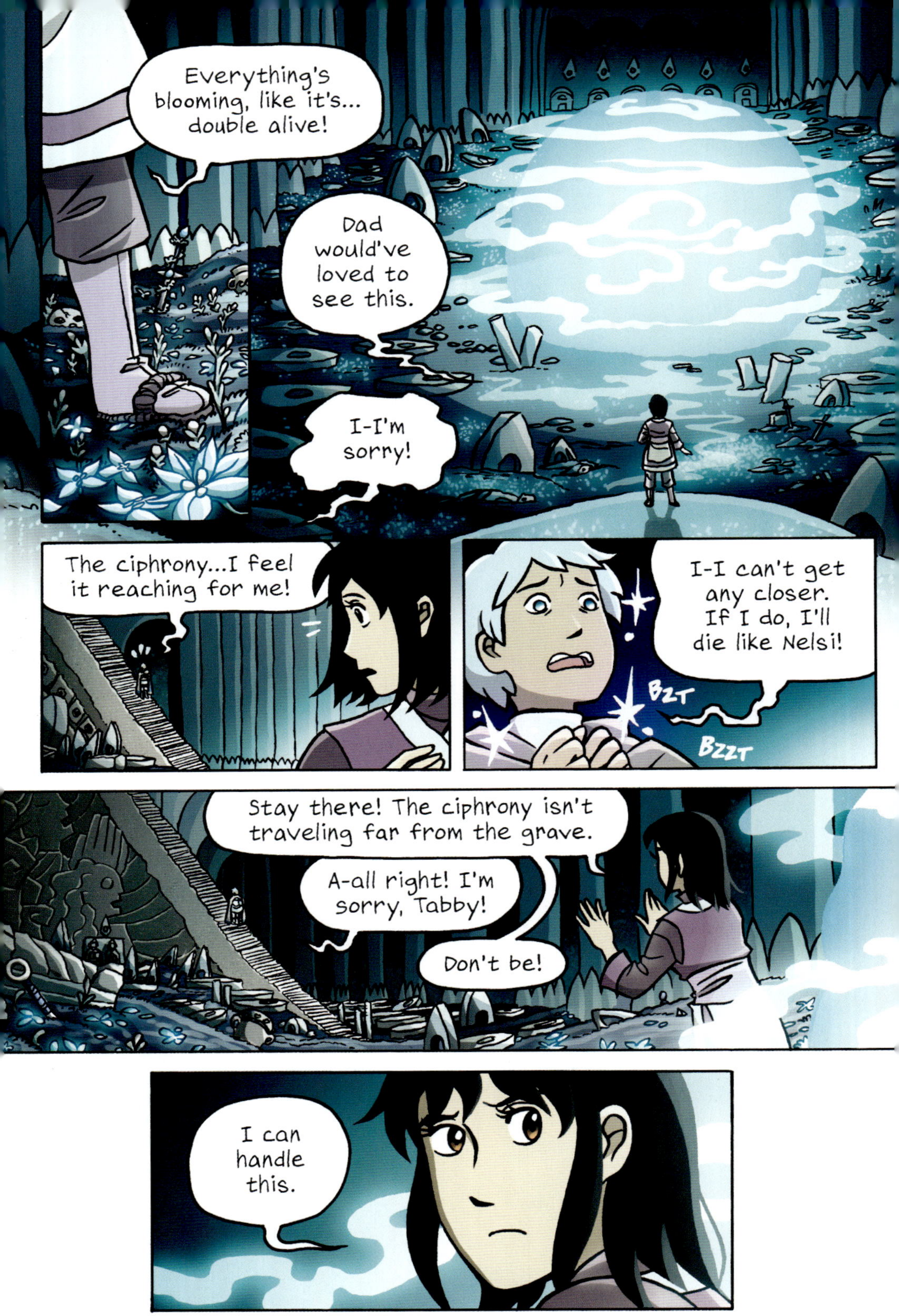
Everything's blooming, like it's... double alive!
Dad would've loved to see this.
I-I'm sorry!
The ciphrony...I feel it reaching for me!
I-I can't get any closer. If I do, I'll die like Nelsi!
BZZT
BZZZT
Stay there! The ciphrony isn't traveling far from the grave.
A-all right! I'm sorry, Tabby!
Don't be!
I can handle this.

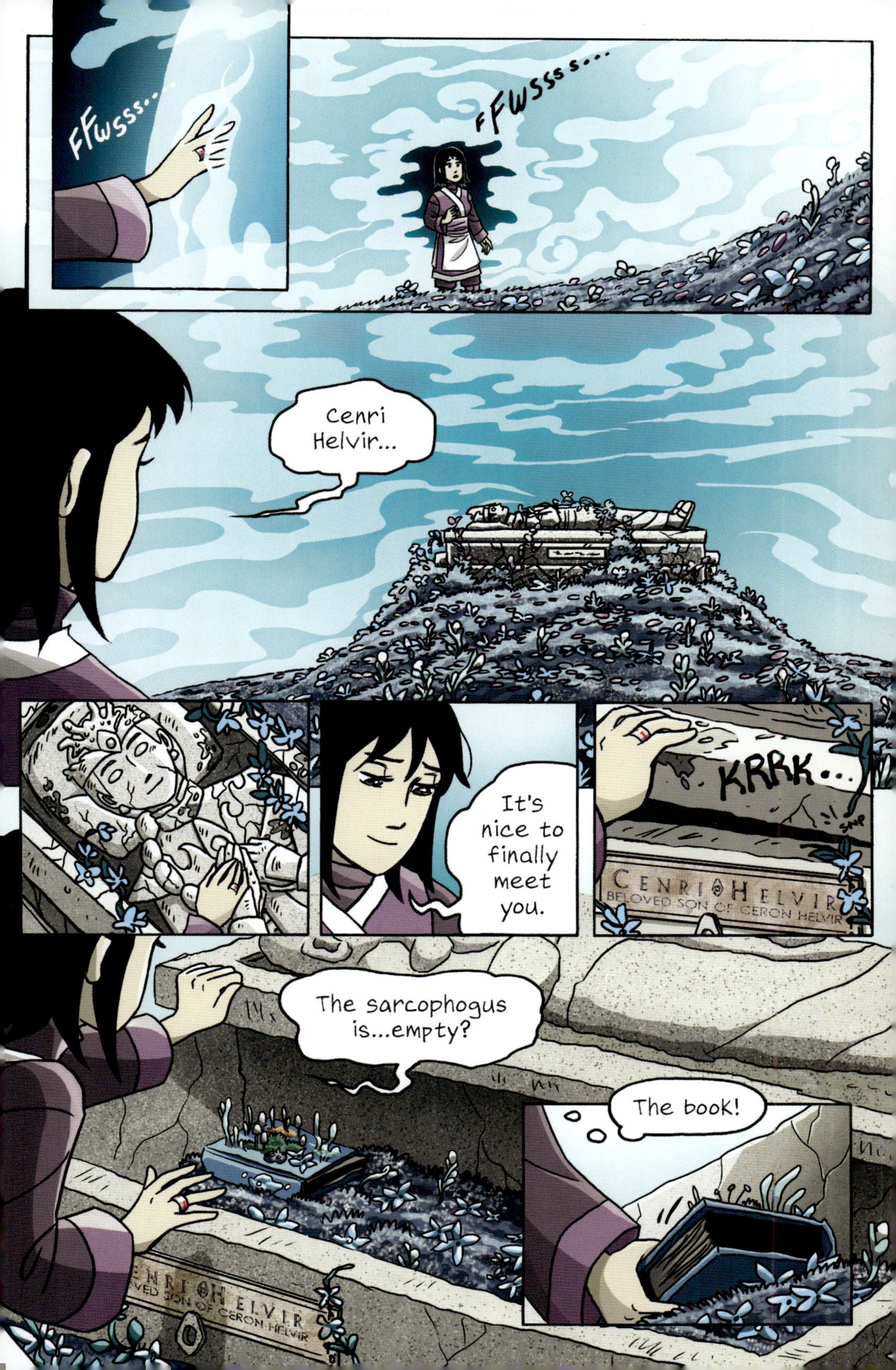
FFWSSS...
FFWSSSS...
Cenri Helvir...
It's nice to finally meet you.
KRRK...
CENRI HELVIR
BELOVED SON OF CERON HELVIR
The sarcophogus is...empty?
The book!

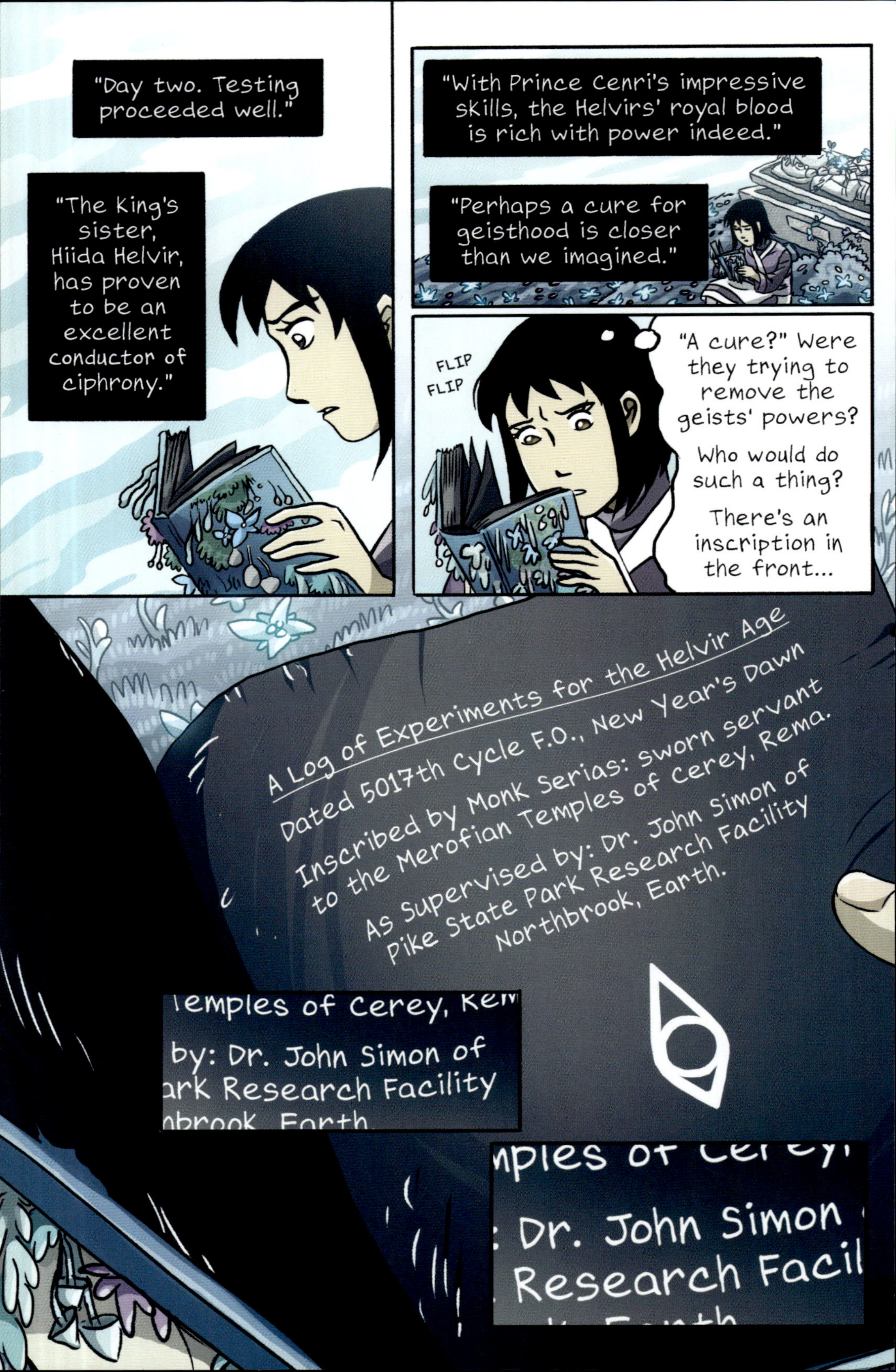
"Day two. Testing proceeded well."
"The King's sister, Hiida Helvir, has proven to be an excellent conductor of ciphrony."
"With Prince Cenri's impressive skills, the Helvirs' royal blood is rich with power indeed."
"Perhaps a cure for geisthood is closer than we imagined."
FLIP FLIP
"A cure?" Were they trying to remove the geists' powers?
Who would do such a thing?
There's an inscription in the front...
A Log of Experiments for the Helvir Age
Dated 5017th Cycle F.O., New Year's Dawn
Inscribed by Monk Serias: Sworn servant to the Merofian Temples of Cerey, Rema.
As Supervised by: Dr. John Simon of Pike State Park Research Facility Northbrook, Earth.
by: Dr. John Simon of
ark Research Facility
Dr. John Simon
Research Facil

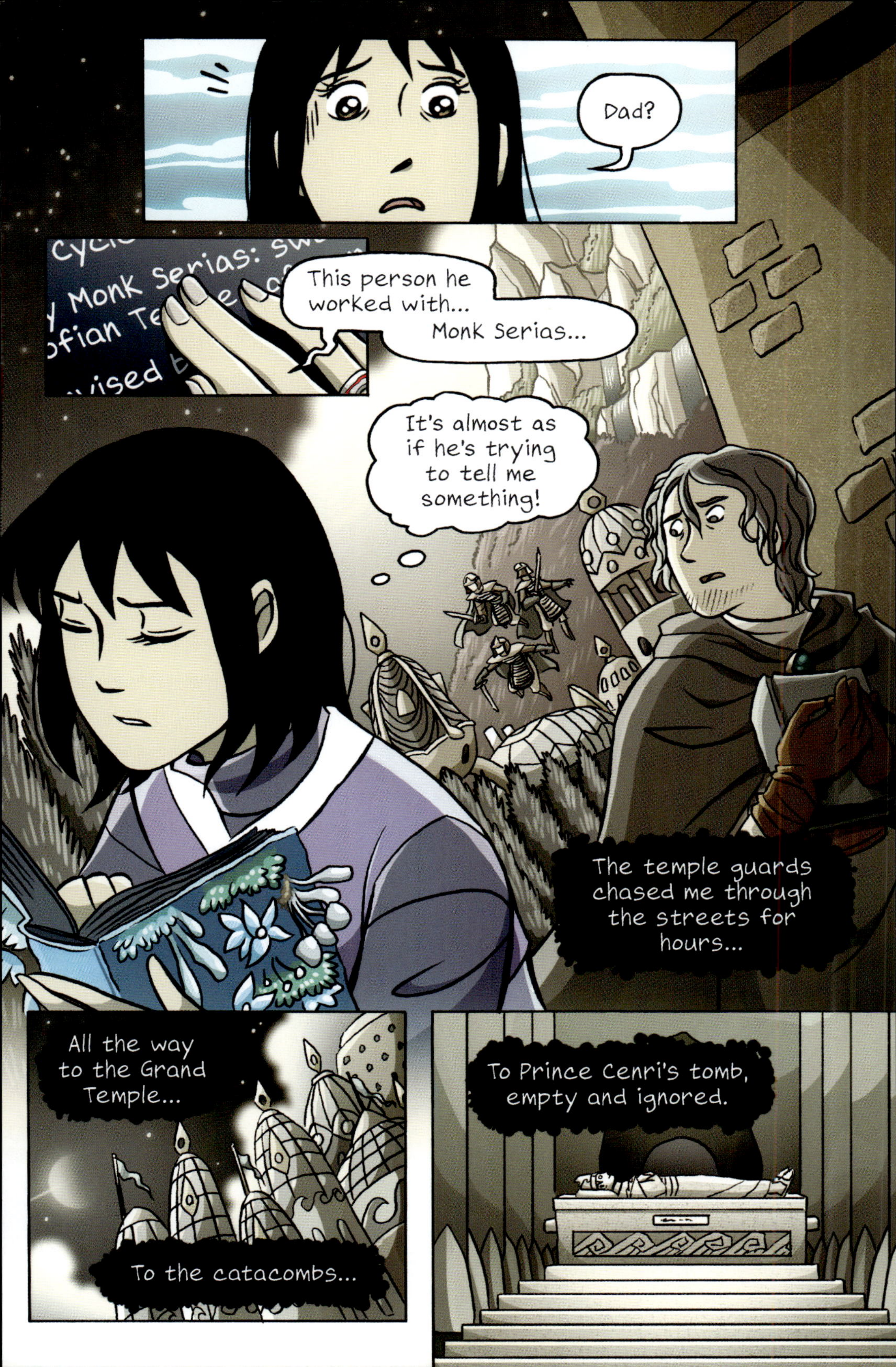
Dad?
This person he worked with... Monk Serias...
It's almost as if he's trying to tell me something!
The temple guards chased me through the streets for hours...
All the way to the Grand Temple...
To the catacombs...
To Prince Cenri's tomb, empty and ignored.

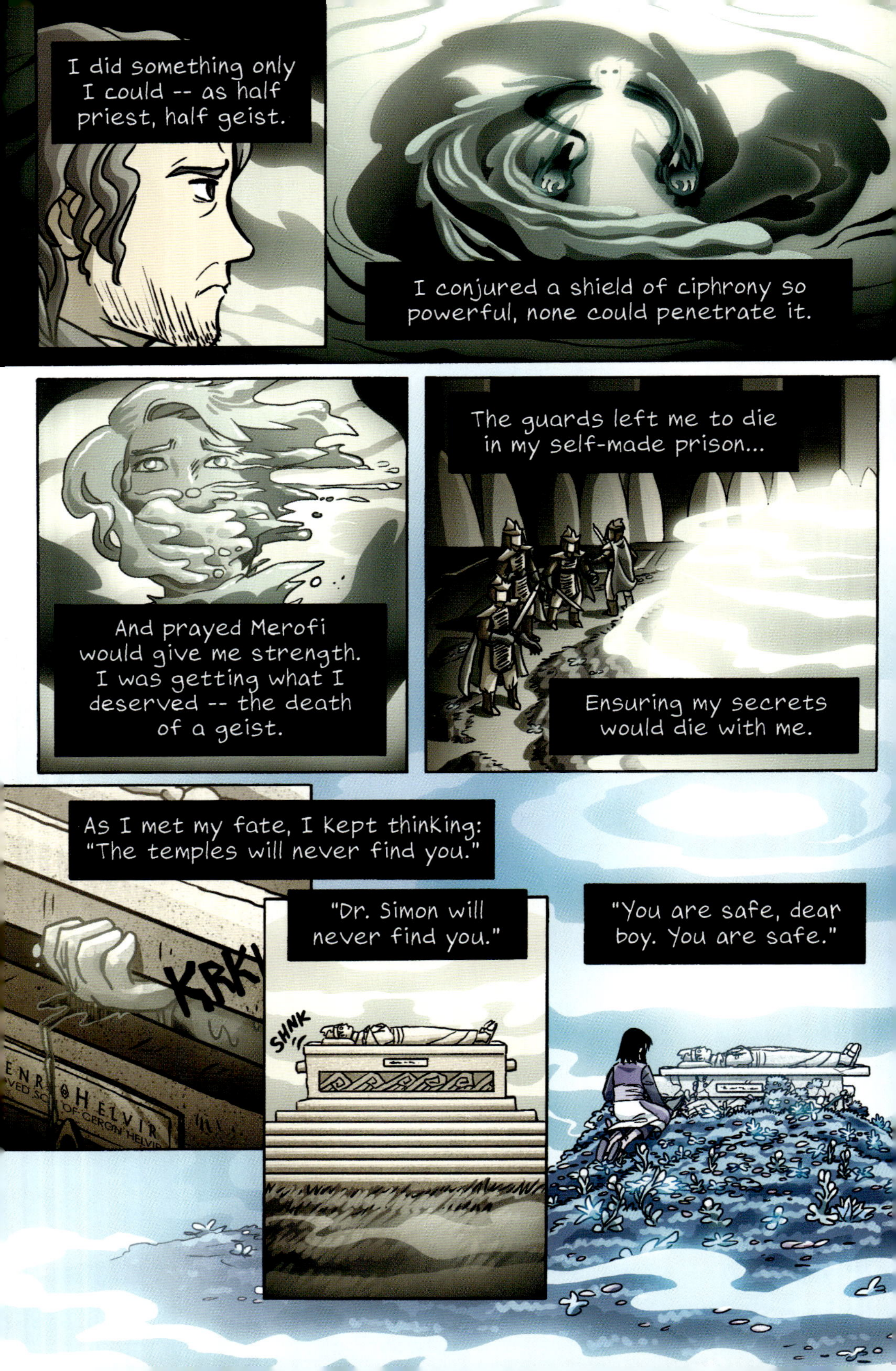

I did something only I could -- as half priest, half geist.
I conjured a shield of ciphrony so powerful, none could penetrate it.
And prayed Merofi would give me strength. I was getting what I deserved -- the death of a geist.
The guards left me to die in my self-made prison...
Ensuring my secrets would die with me.
As I met my fate, I kept thinking: "The temples will never find you."
KRK
"Dr. Simon will never find you."
SHNK
"You are safe, dear boy. You are safe."

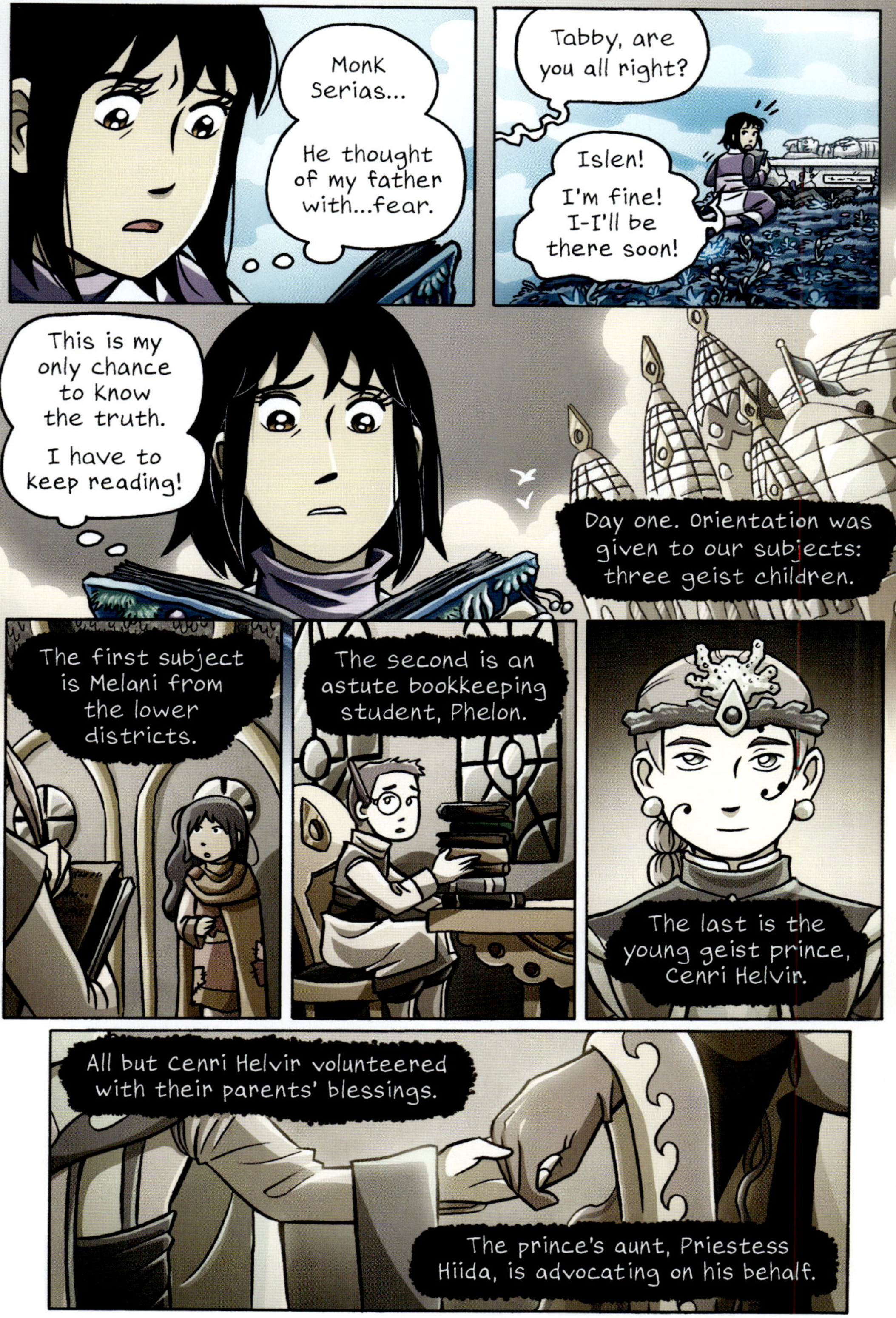
Monk Serias...
He thought of my father with...fear.
Tabby, are you all right?
Islen!
I'm fine! I-I'll be there soon!
This is my only chance to know the truth.
I have to keep reading!
Day one. Orientation was given to our subjects: three geist children.
The first subject is Melani from the lower districts.
The second is an astute bookkeeping student, Phelon.
The last is the young geist prince, Cenri Helvir.
All but Cenri Helvir volunteered with their parents' blessings.
The prince's aunt, Priestess Hiida, is advocating on his behalf.

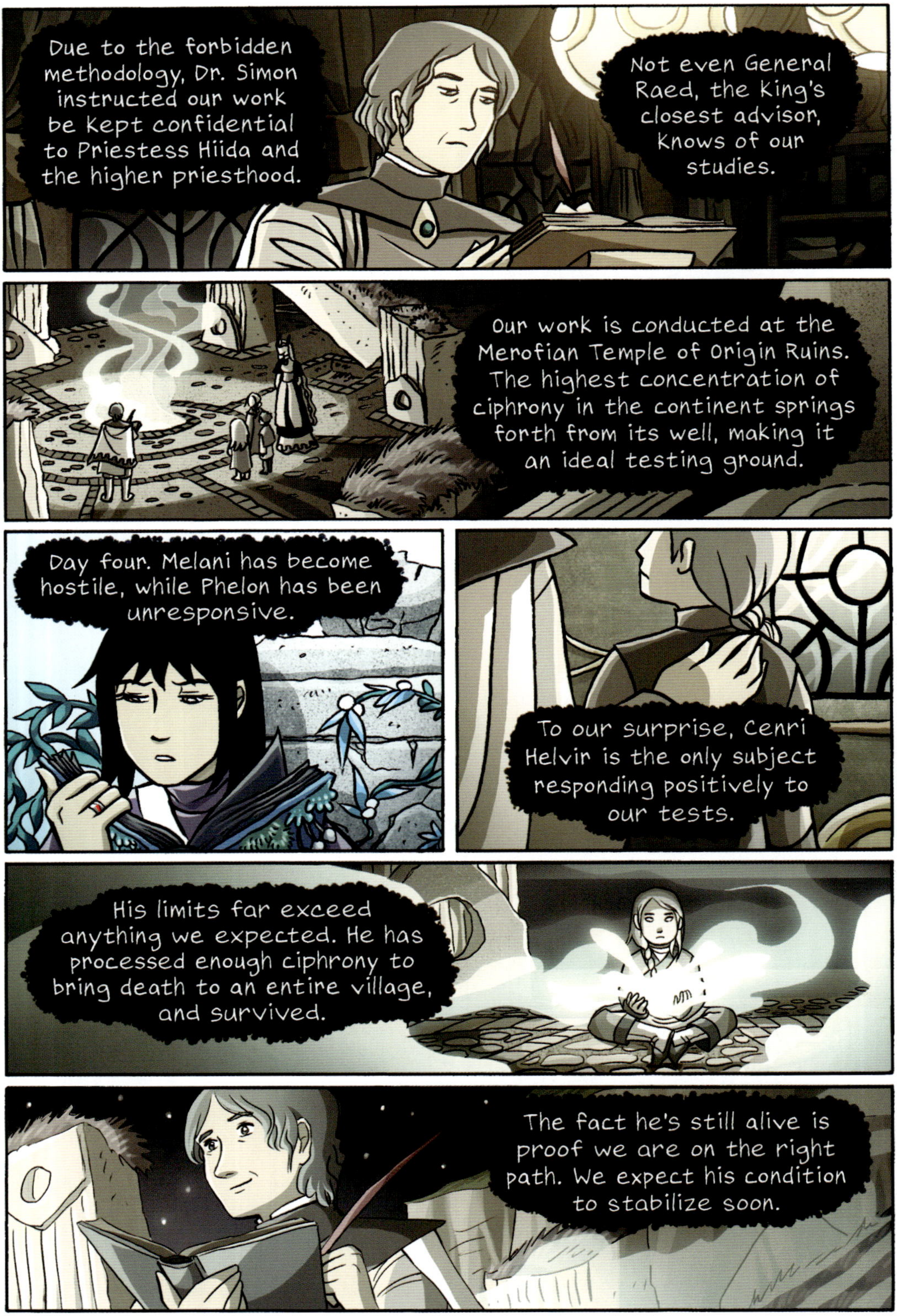
Due to the forbidden methodology, Dr. Simon instructed our work be kept confidential to Priestess Hiida and the higher priesthood.
Not even General Raed, the king's closest advisor, knows of our studies.
Our work is conducted at the Merofian Temple of Origin Ruins. The highest concentration of ciphrony in the continent springs forth from its well, making it an ideal testing ground.
Day four. Melani has become hostile, while Phelon has been unresponsive.
To our surprise, Cenri Helvir is the only subject responding positively to our tests.
His limits far exceed anything we expected. He has processed enough ciphrony to bring death to an entire village, and survived.
The fact he's still alive is proof we are on the right path. We expect his condition to stabilize soon.

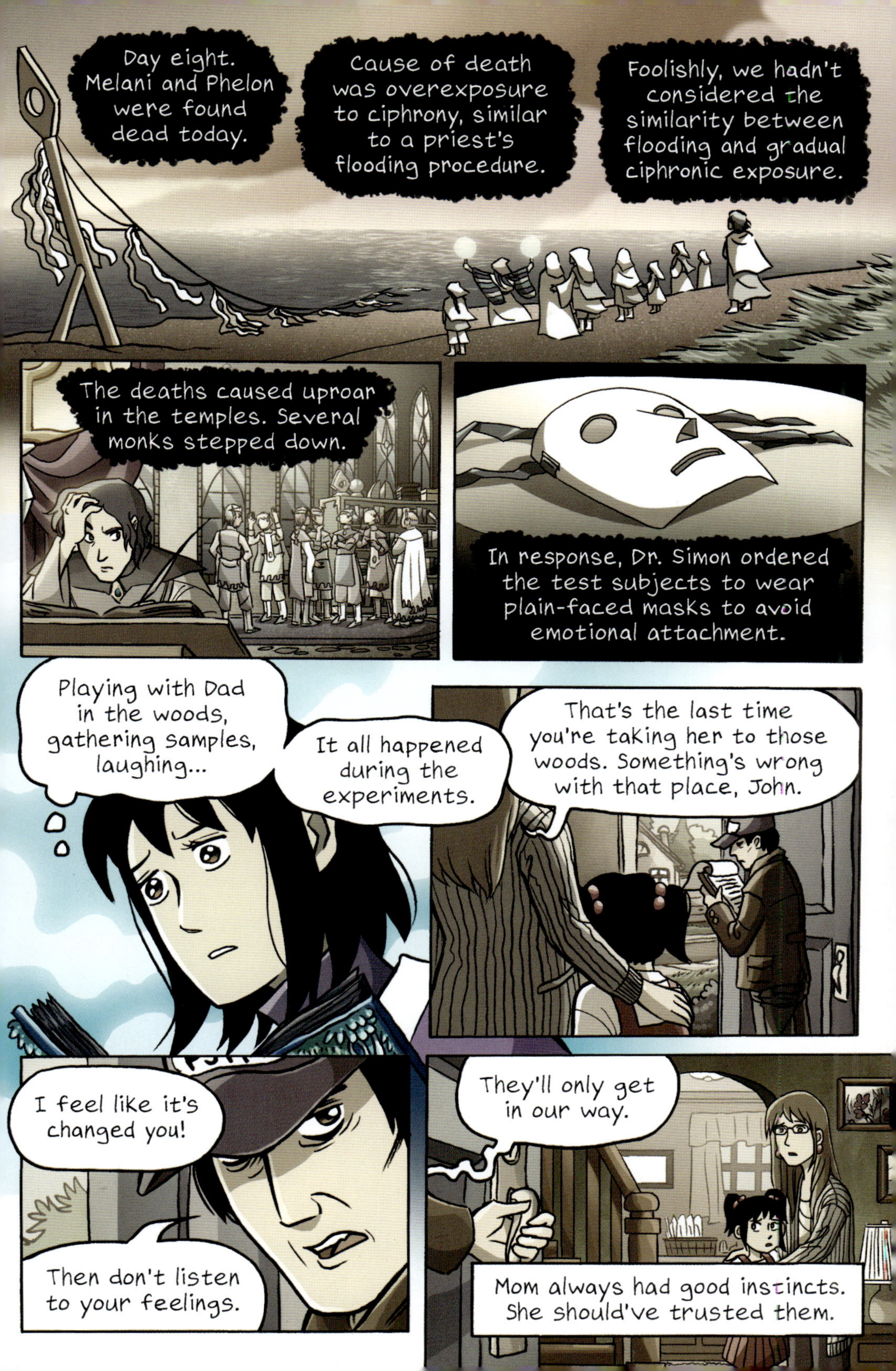
Day eight. Melani and Phelon were found dead today.
Cause of death was overexposure to ciphrony, similar to a priest's flooding procedure.
Foolishly, we hadn't considered the similarity between flooding and gradual ciphronic exposure.
The deaths caused uproar in the temples. Several monks stepped down.
In response, Dr. Simon ordered the test subjects to wear plain-faced masks to avoid emotional attachment.
Playing with Dad in the woods, gathering samples, laughing...
It all happened during the experiments.
That's the last time you're taking her to those woods. Something's wrong with that place, John.
I feel like it's changed you!
Then don't listen to your feelings.
They'll only get in our way.
Mom always had good instincts. She should've trusted them.

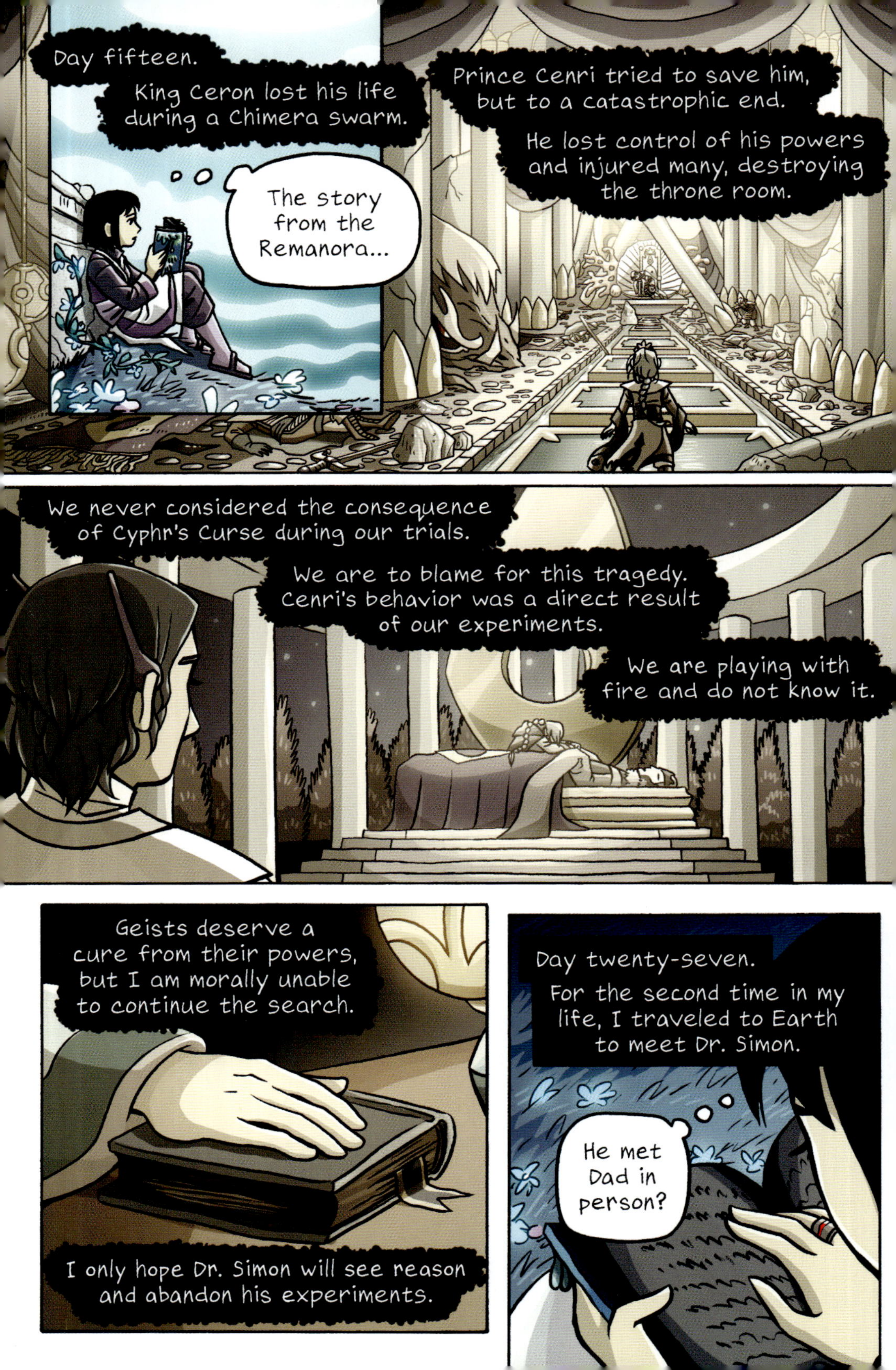
Day fifteen.
King Ceron lost his life during a Chimera swarm.
The story from the Remanora...
Prince Cenri tried to save him, but to a catastrophic end.
He lost control of his powers and injured many, destroying the throne room.
We never considered the consequence of Cyphr's Curse during our trials.
We are to blame for this tragedy. Cenri's behavior was a direct result of our experiments.
We are playing with fire and do not know it.
Geists deserve a cure from their powers, but I am morally unable to continue the search.
I only hope Dr. Simon will see reason and abandon his experiments.
Day twenty-seven.
For the second time in my life, I traveled to Earth to meet Dr. Simon.
He met Dad in person?

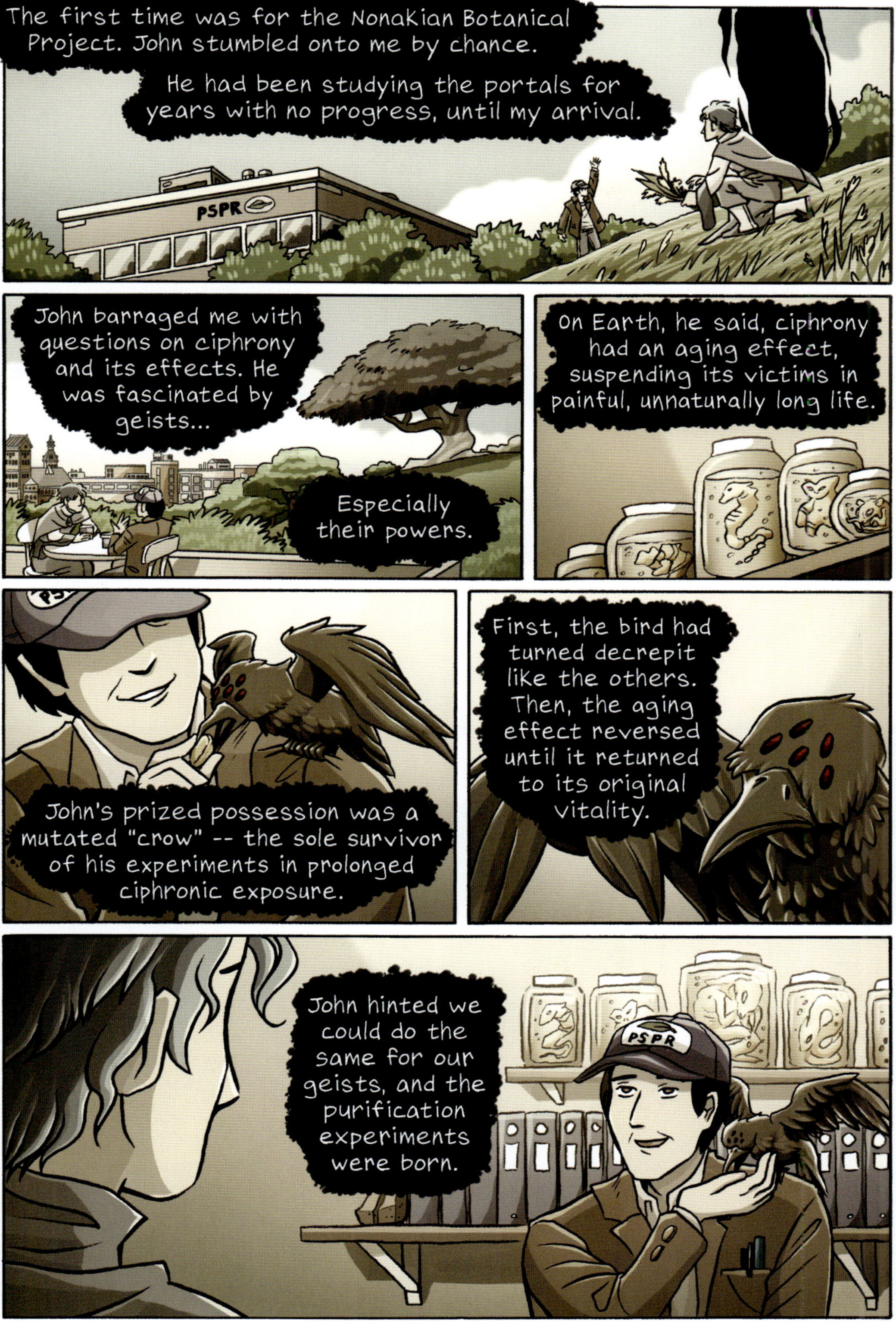

The first time was for the Nonakian Botanical Project. John stumbled onto me by chance.
He had been studying the portals for years with no progress, until my arrival.
PSPR
John barraged me with questions on ciphrony and its effects. He was fascinated by geists...
Especially their powers.
On Earth, he said, ciphrony had an aging effect, suspending its victims in painful, unnaturally long life.
John's prized possession was a mutated "crow" -- the sole survivor of his experiments in prolonged ciphronic exposure.
First, the bird had turned decrepit like the others. Then, the aging effect reversed until it returned to its original vitality.
John hinted we could do the same for our geists, and the purification experiments were born.
PSPR

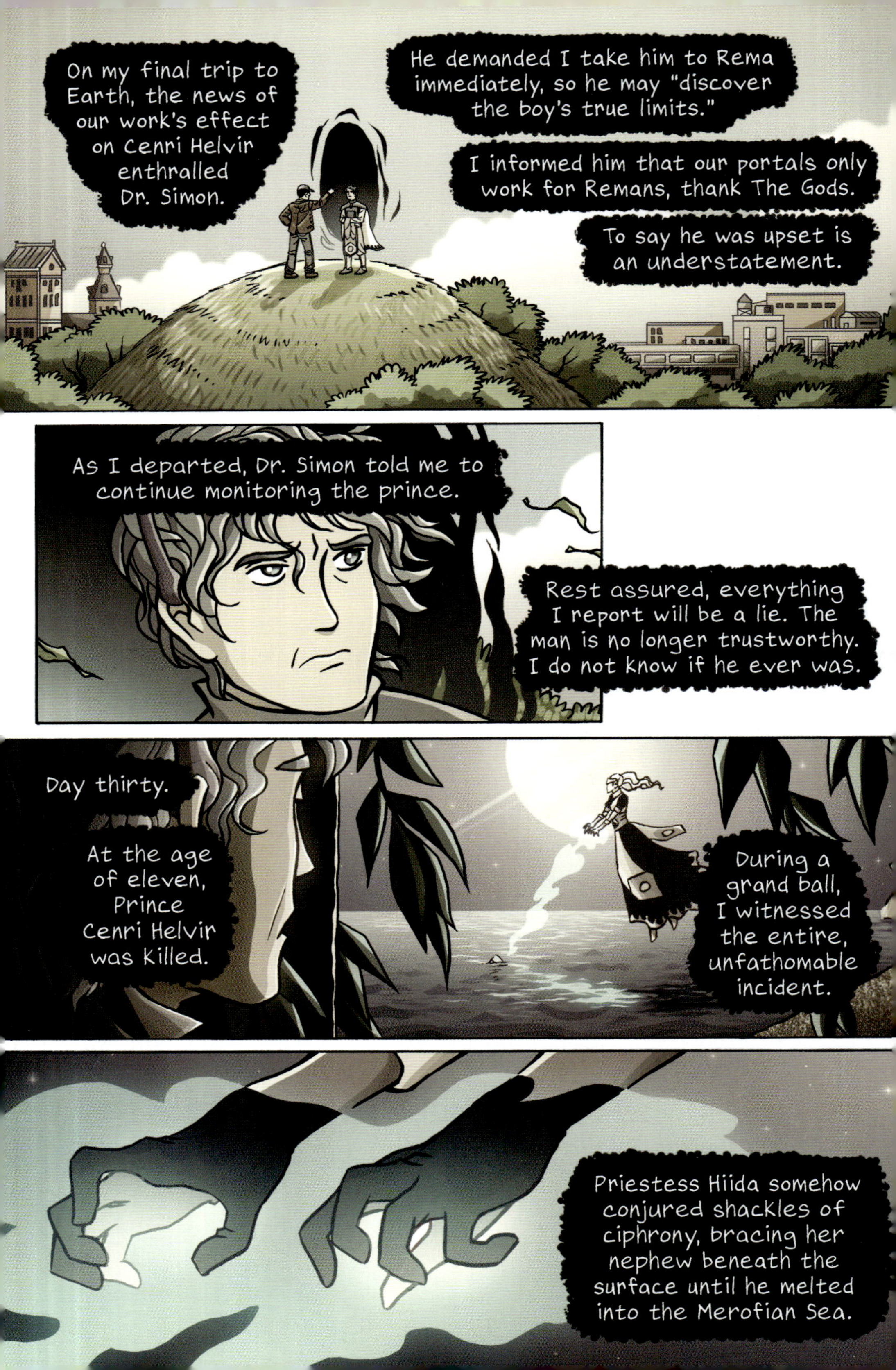
On my final trip to Earth, the news of our work's effect on Cenri Helvir enthralled Dr. Simon.
He demanded I take him to Rema immediately, so he may "discover the boy's true limits."
I informed him that our portals only work for Remans, thank The Gods.
To say he was upset is an understatement.
As I departed, Dr. Simon told me to continue monitoring the prince.
Rest assured, everything I report will be a lie. The man is no longer trustworthy. I do not know if he ever was.
Day thirty.
At the age of eleven, Prince Cenri Helvir was killed.
During a grand ball, I witnessed the entire, unfathomable incident.
Priestess Hiida somehow conjured shackles of ciphrony, bracing her nephew beneath the surface until he melted into the Merofian Sea.

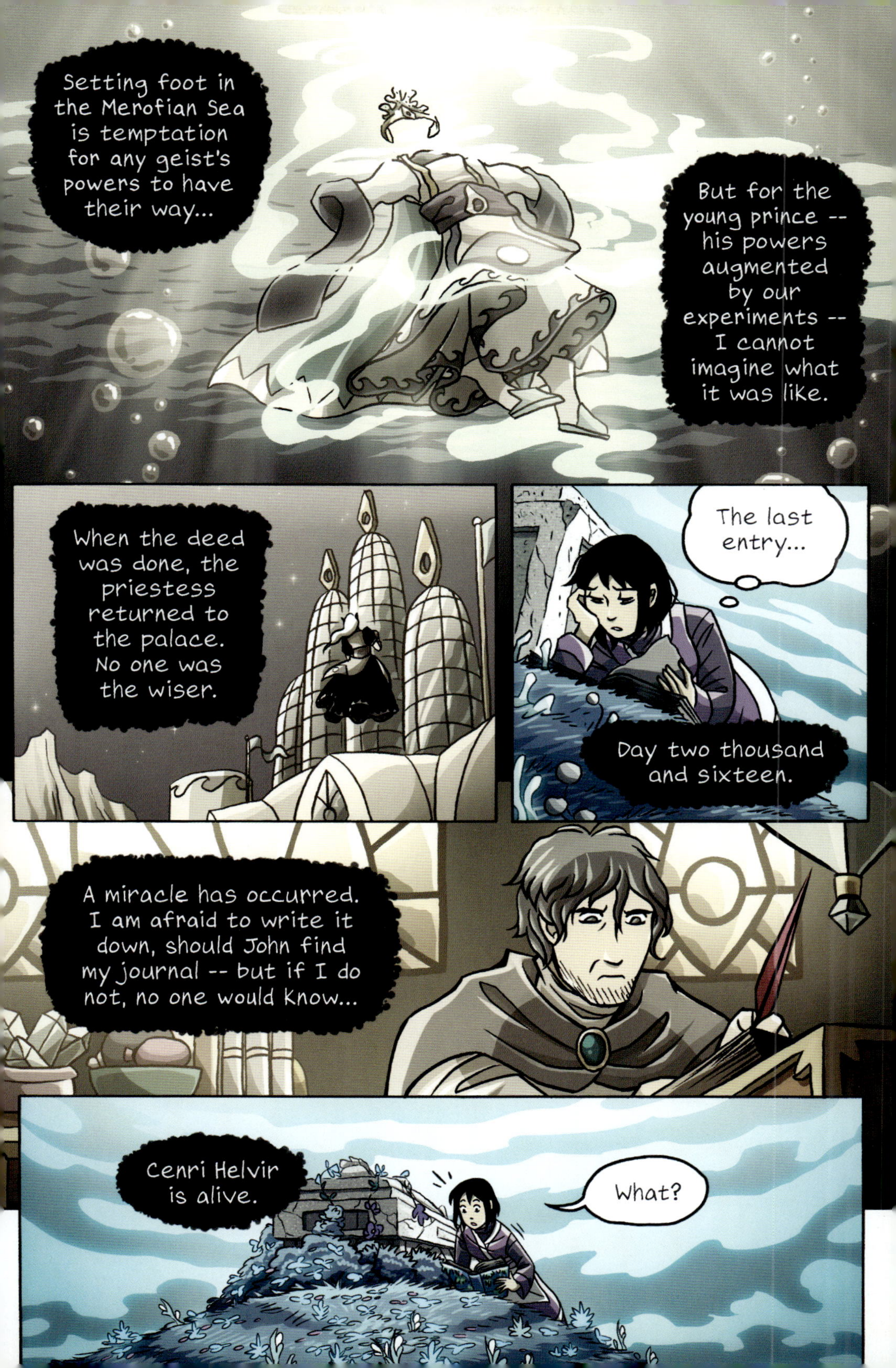
Setting foot in the Merofian Sea is temptation for any geist's powers to have their way...
But for the young prince -- his powers augmented by our experiments -- I cannot imagine what it was like.
When the deed was done, the priestess returned to the palace. No one was the wiser.
The last entry...
Day two thousand and sixteen.
A miracle has occurred. I am afraid to write it down, should John find my journal -- but if I do not, no one would know...
Cenri Helvir is alive.
What?

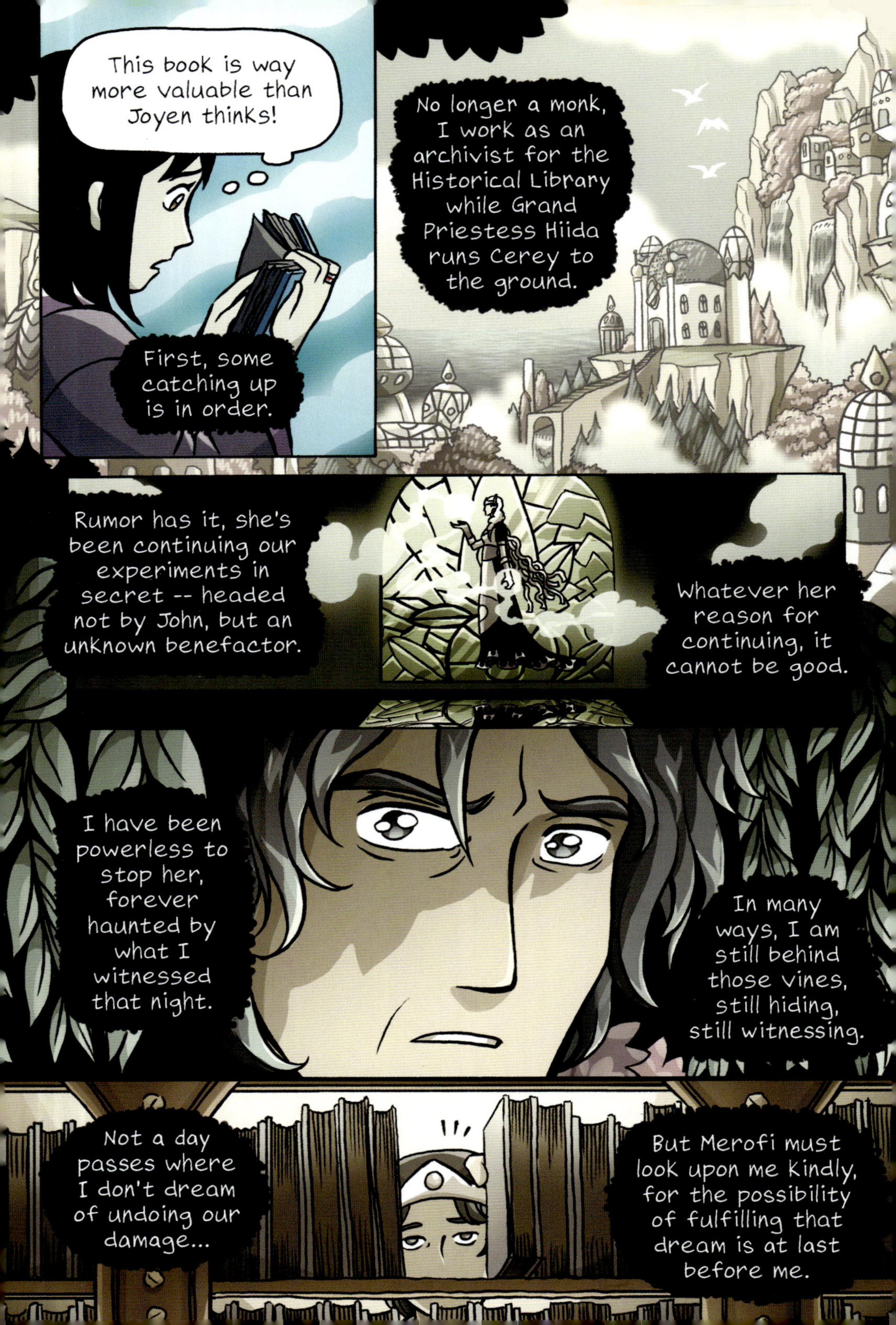
This book is way more valuable than Joyen thinks!
First, some catching up is in order.
No longer a monk, I work as an archivist for the Historical Library while Grand Priestess Hiida runs Cerey to the ground.
Rumor has it, she's been continuing our experiments in secret -- headed not by John, but an unknown benefactor.
Whatever her reason for continuing, it cannot be good.
I have been powerless to stop her, forever haunted by what I witnessed that night.
In many ways, I am still behind those vines, still hiding, still witnessing.
Not a day passes where I don't dream of undoing our damage...
But Merofi must look upon me kindly, for the possibility of fulfilling that dream is at last before me.

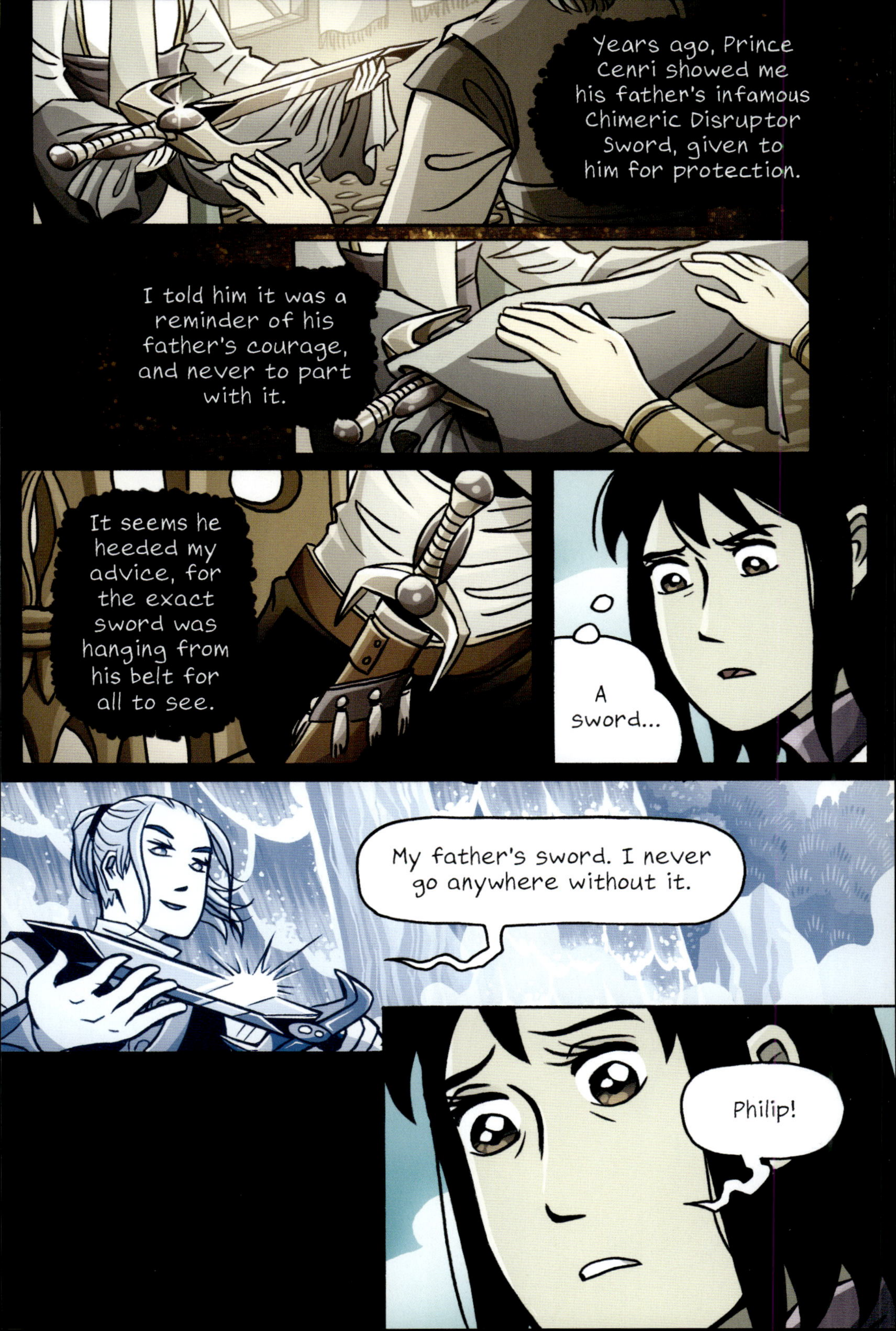
Years ago, Prince Cenri showed me his father's infamous Chimeric Disruptor Sword, given to him for protection.
I told him it was a reminder of his father's courage, and never to part with it.
It seems he heeded my advice, for the exact sword was hanging from his belt for all to see.
A sword...
My father's sword. I never go anywhere without it.
Philip!

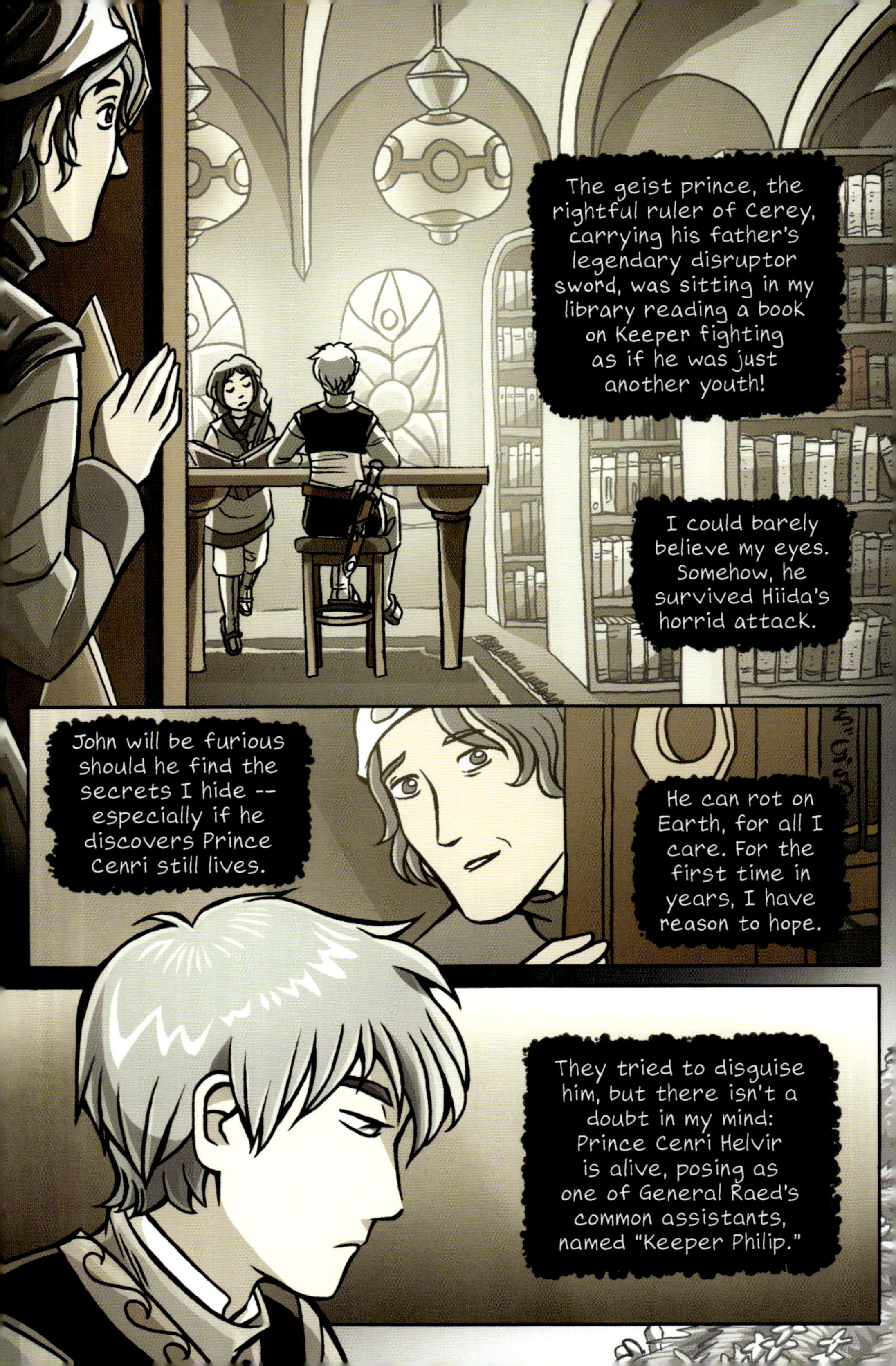

The geist prince, the rightful ruler of Cerey, carrying his father's legendary disruptor sword, was sitting in my library reading a book on Keeper fighting as if he was just another youth!
I could barely believe my eyes. Somehow, he survived Hiida's horrid attack.
John will be furious should he find the secrets I hide -- especially if he discovers Prince Cenri still lives.
He can rot on Earth, for all I care. For the first time in years, I have reason to hope.
They tried to disguise him, but there isn't a doubt in my mind: Prince Cenri Helvir is alive, posing as one of General Raed's common assistants, named "Keeper Philip."

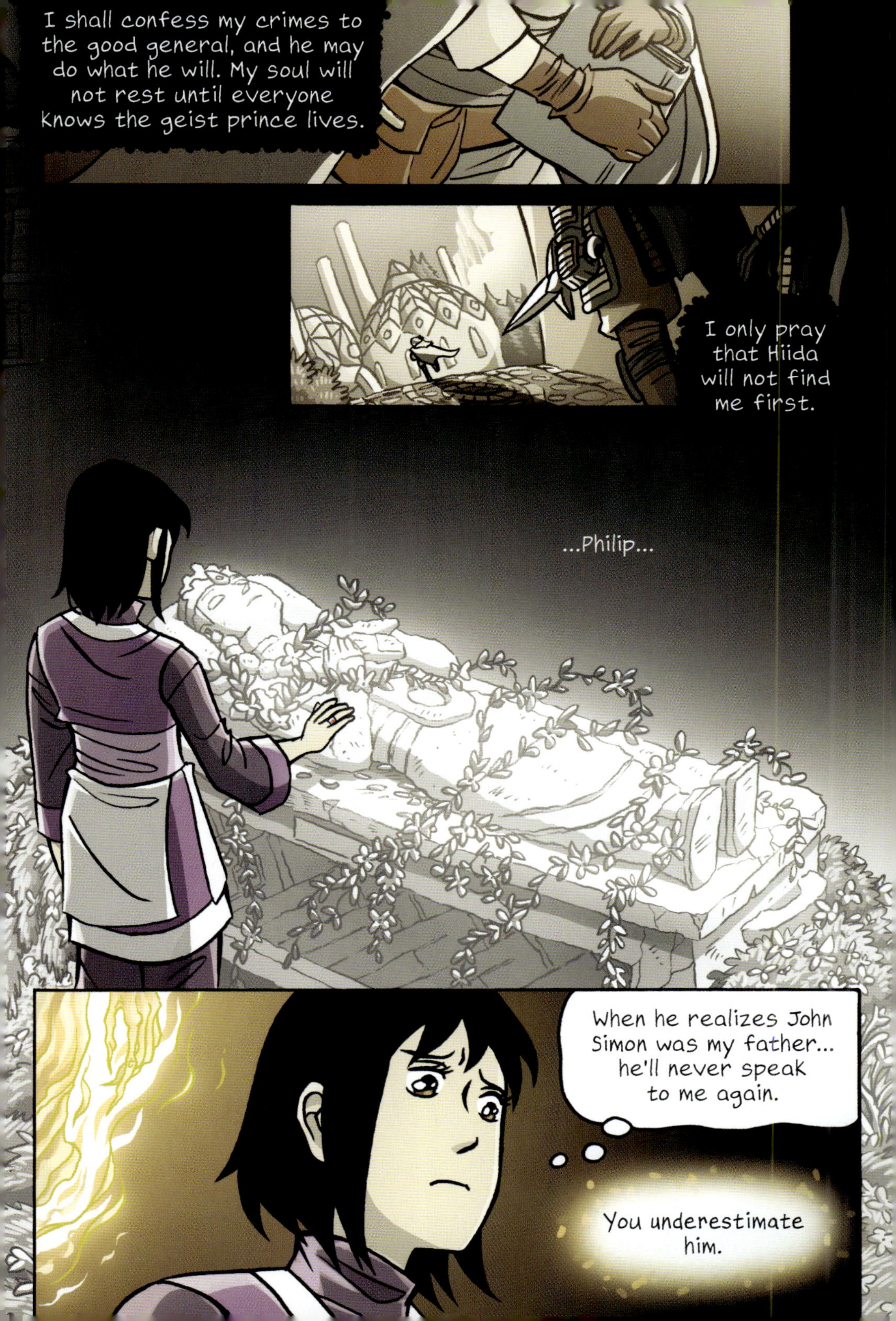
I shall confess my crimes to the good general, and he may do what he will. My soul will not rest until everyone knows the geist prince lives.
I only pray that Hiida will not find me first.
...Philip...
When he realizes John Simon was my father... he'll never speak to me again.
You underestimate him.

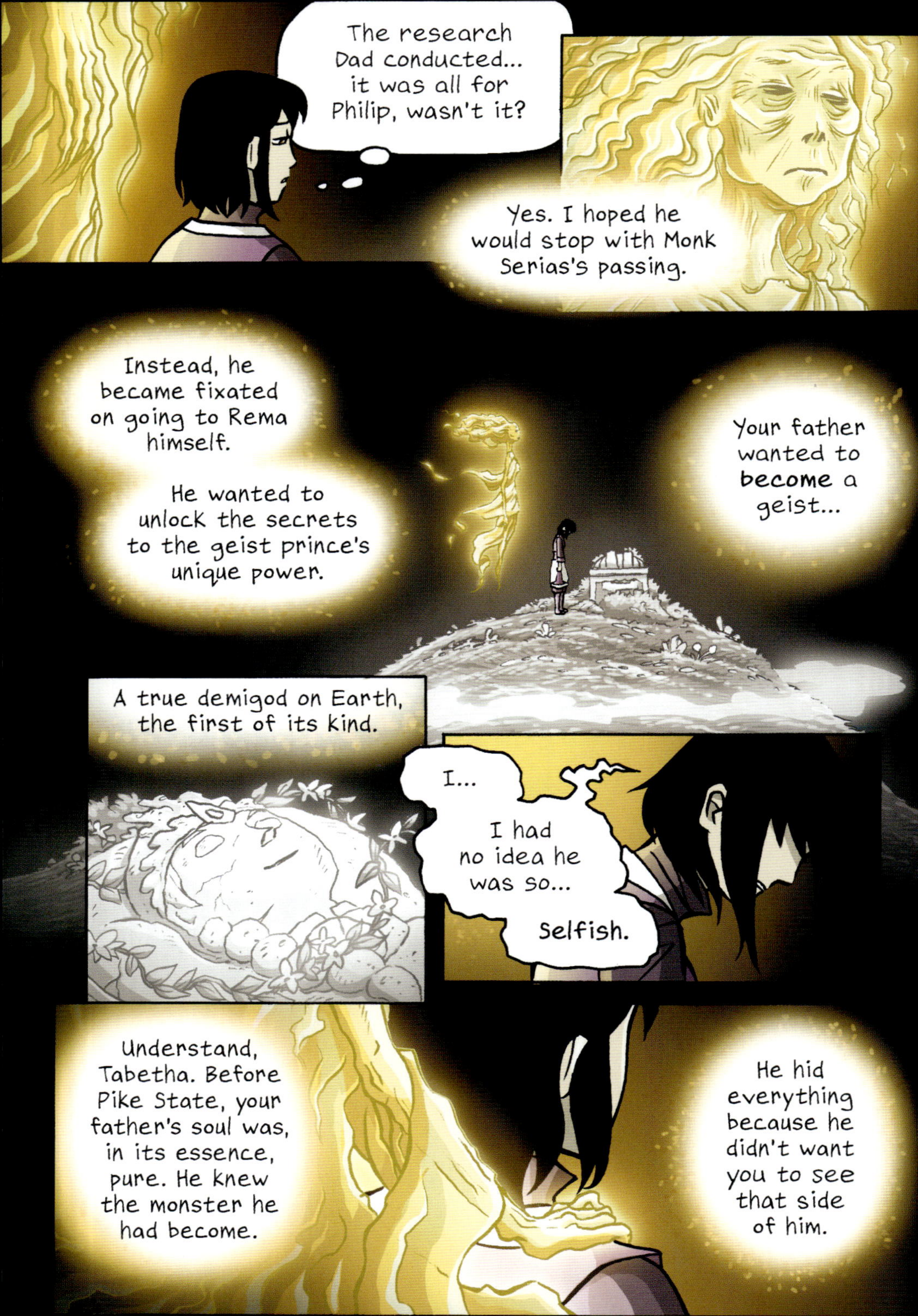

The research Dad conducted... it was all for Philip, wasn't it?
Yes. I hoped he would stop with Monk Serias's passing.
Instead, he became fixated on going to Rema himself.
He wanted to unlock the secrets to the geist prince's unique power.
Your father wanted to **become** a geist...
A true demigod on Earth, the first of its kind.
I...
I had no idea he was so...
Selfish.
Understand, Tabetha. Before Pike State, your father's soul was, in its essence, pure. He knew the monster he had become.
He hid everything because he didn't want you to see that side of him.

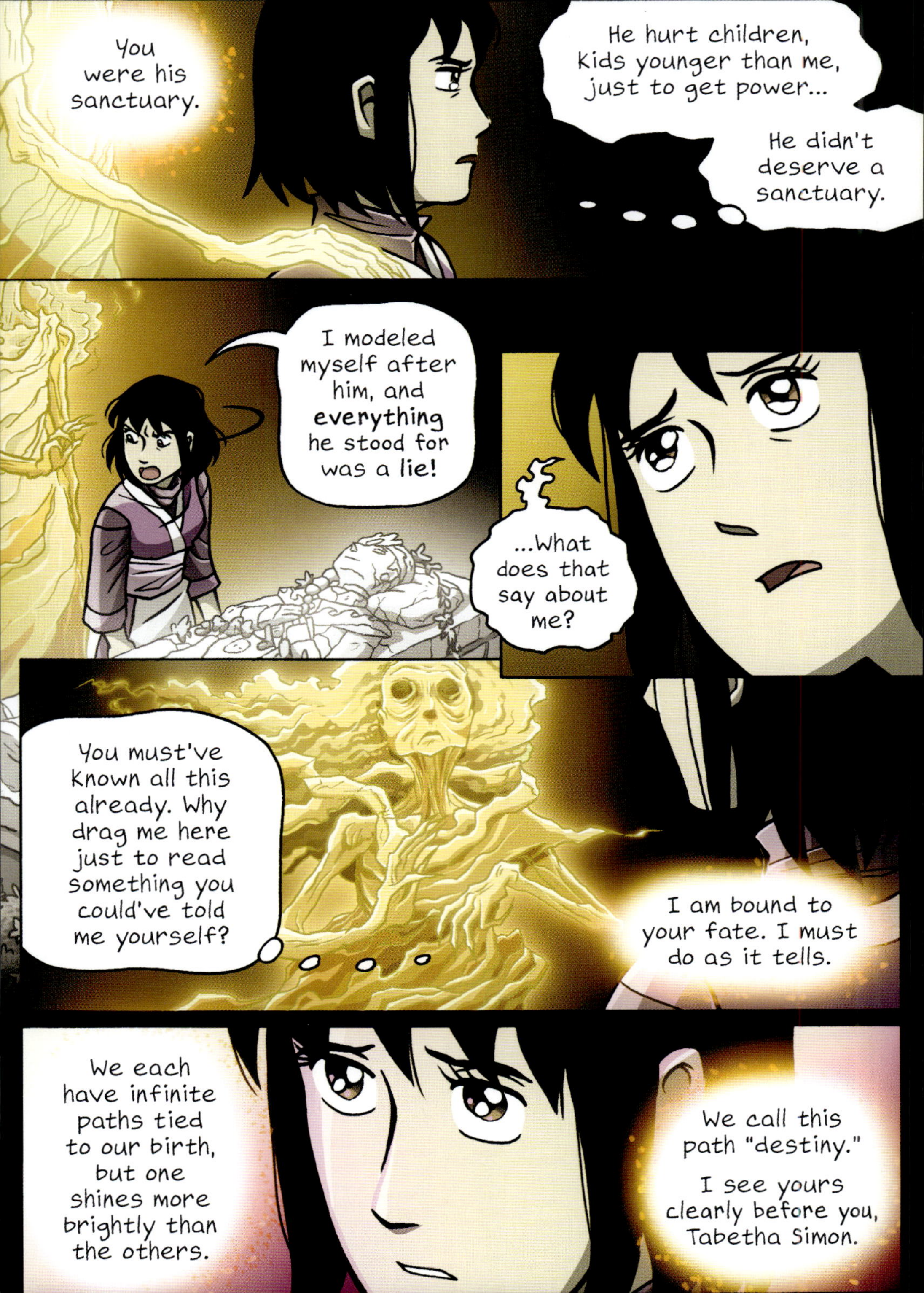

You were his sanctuary.
He hurt children, Kids younger than me, just to get power...
He didn't deserve a sanctuary.
I modeled myself after him, and **everything** he stood for was a **lie**!
...What does that say about me?
You must've Known all this already. Why drag me here just to read something you could've told me yourself?
I am bound to your fate. I must do as it tells.
We each have infinite paths tied to our birth, but one shines more brightly than the others.
We call this path "destiny."
I see yours clearly before you, Tabetha Simon.

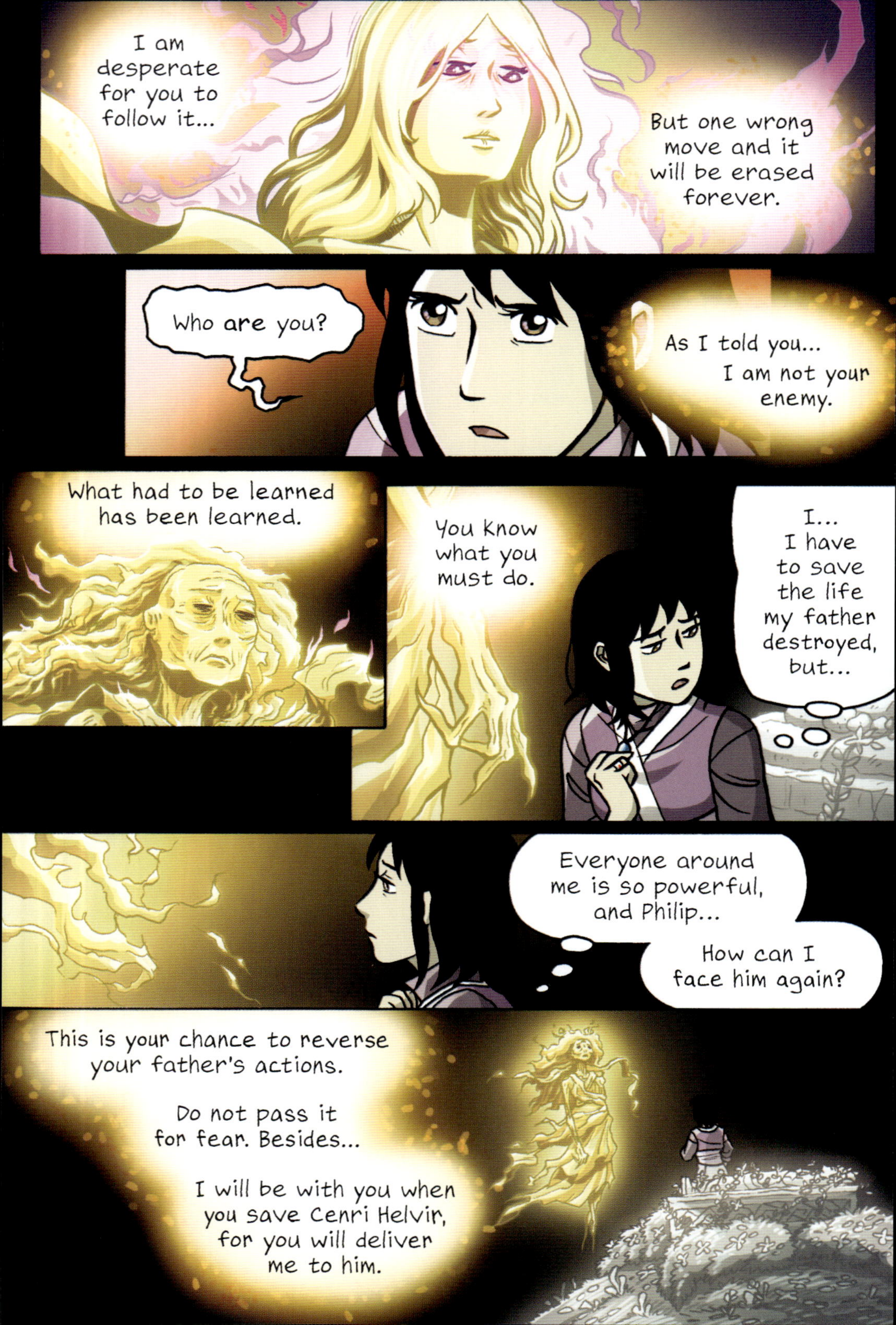
I am desperate for you to follow it...
But one wrong move and it will be erased forever.
Who are you?
As I told you... I am not your enemy.
What had to be learned has been learned.
You know what you must do.
I... I have to save the life my father destroyed, but...
Everyone around me is so powerful, and Philip...
How can I face him again?
This is your chance to reverse your father's actions.
Do not pass it for fear. Besides...
I will be with you when you save Cenri Helvir, for you will deliver me to him.

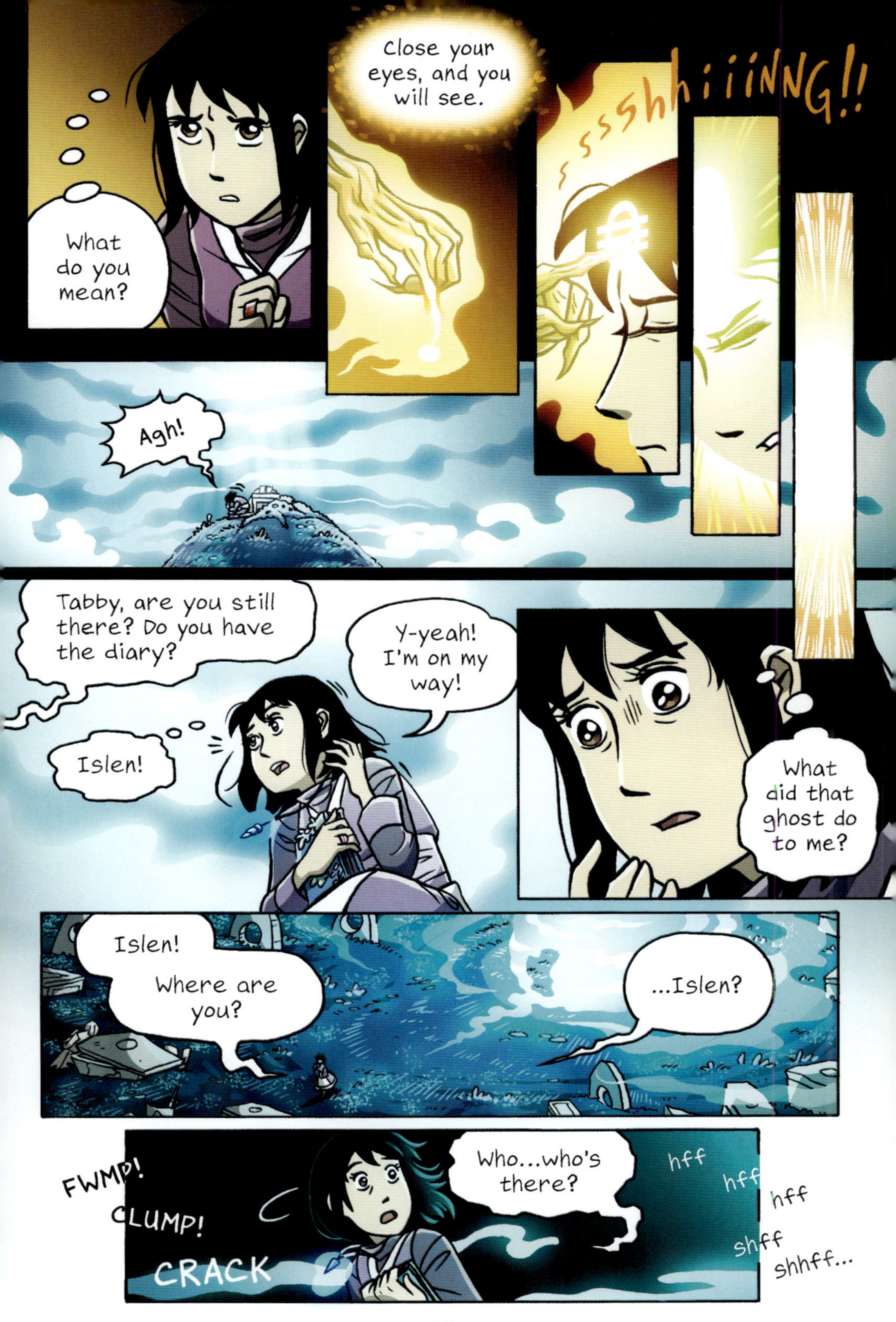
What do you mean?
Close your eyes, and you will see.
sssshhiiiNNG!!
Agh!
Tabby, are you still there? Do you have the diary?
Y-yeah! I'm on my way!
Islen!
What did that ghost do to me?
Islen!
Where are you?
...Islen?
FWMP!
CLUMP!
CRACK
Who...who's there?
hff
hff
hff
shff
shhff...

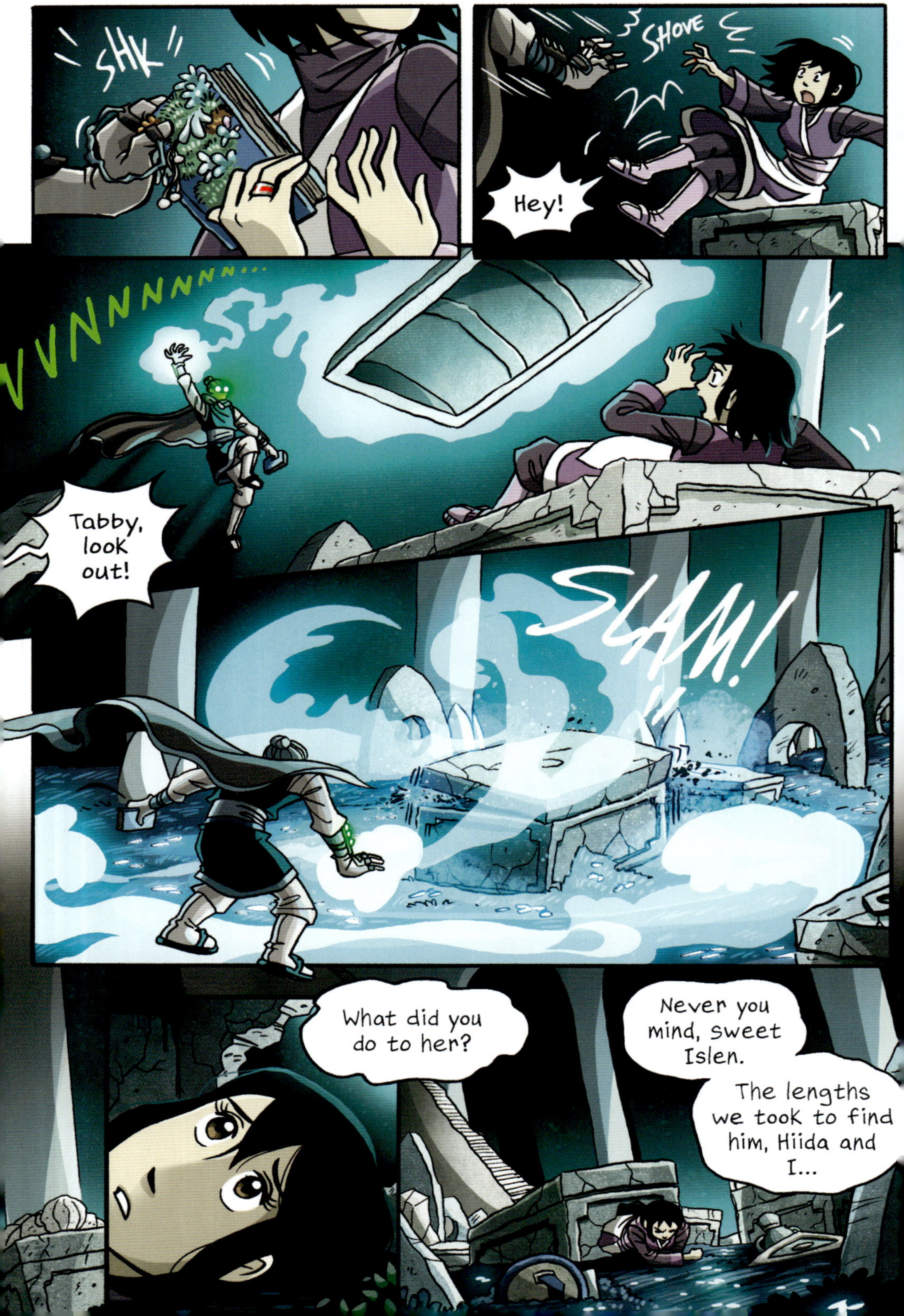
SHK
SHOVE
Hey!
VVNNNNNNN...
Tabby, look out!
SLAM!
What did you do to her?
Never you mind, sweet Islen.
The lengths we took to find him, Hiida and I...

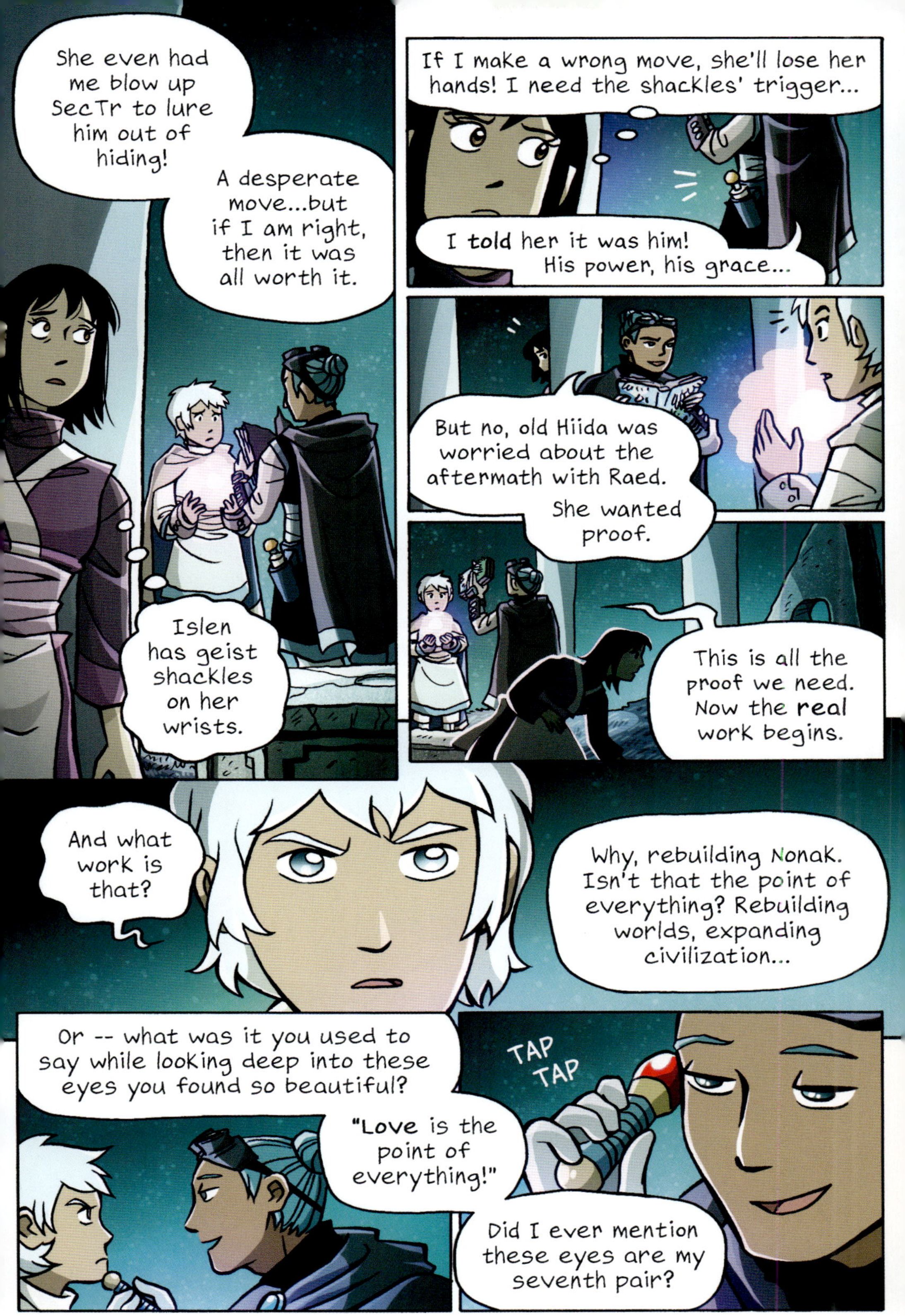
She even had me blow up SecTr to lure him out of hiding!
A desperate move...but if I am right, then it was all worth it.
Islen has geist shackles on her wrists.
If I make a wrong move, she'll lose her hands! I need the shackles' trigger...
I **told** her it was him! His power, his grace...
But no, old Hiida was worried about the aftermath with Raed.
She wanted proof.
This is all the proof we need. Now the **real** work begins.
And what work is that?
Why, rebuilding Nonak. Isn't that the point of everything? Rebuilding worlds, expanding civilization...
Or -- what was it you used to say while looking deep into these eyes you found so beautiful?
"**Love** is the point of everything!"
TAP TAP
Did I ever mention these eyes are my seventh pair?

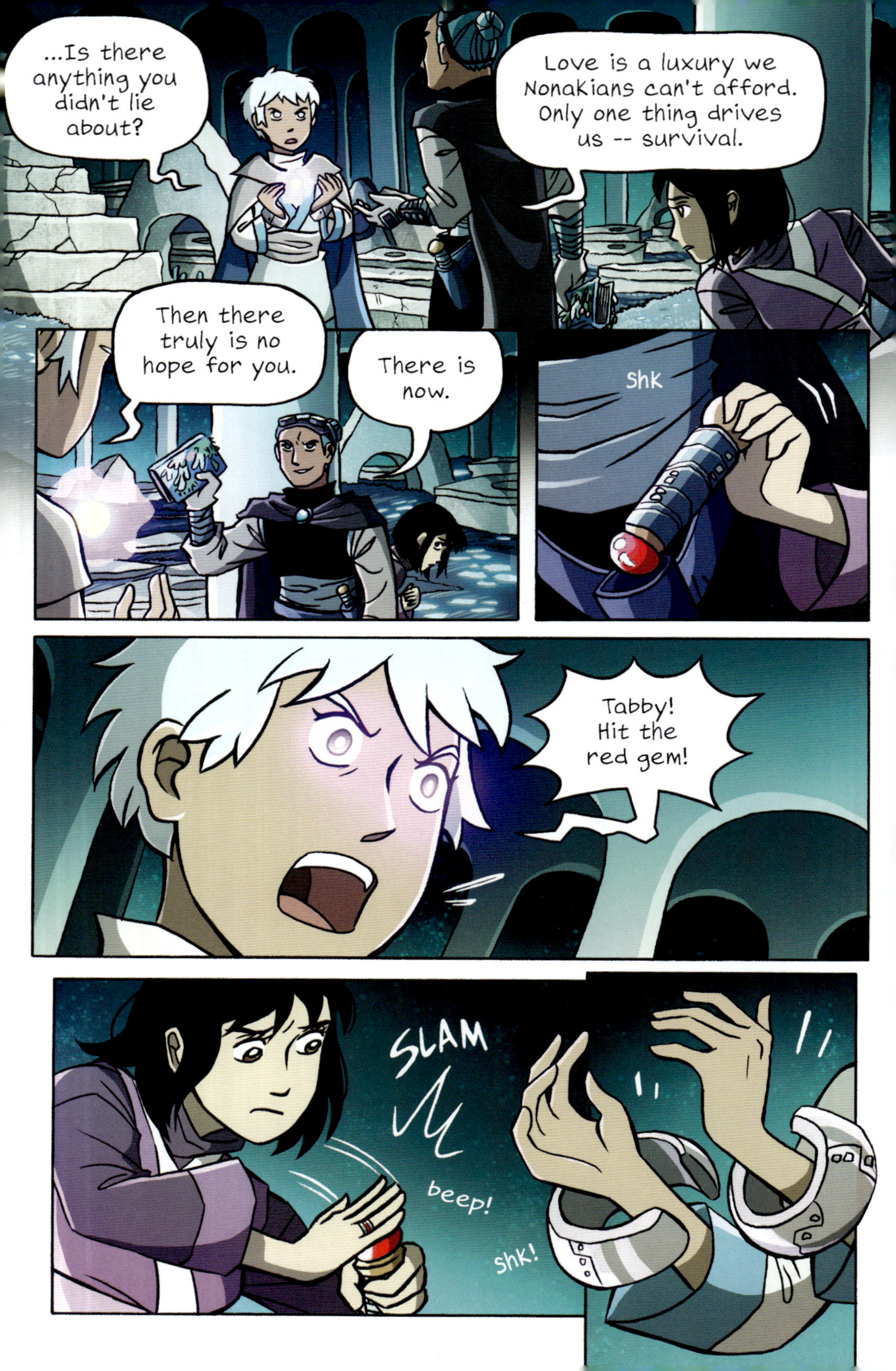

...Is there anything you didn't lie about?
Love is a luxury we Nonakians can't afford. Only one thing drives us -- survival.
Then there truly is no hope for you.
There is now.
Shk
Tabby! Hit the red gem!
SLAM
beep!
shk!

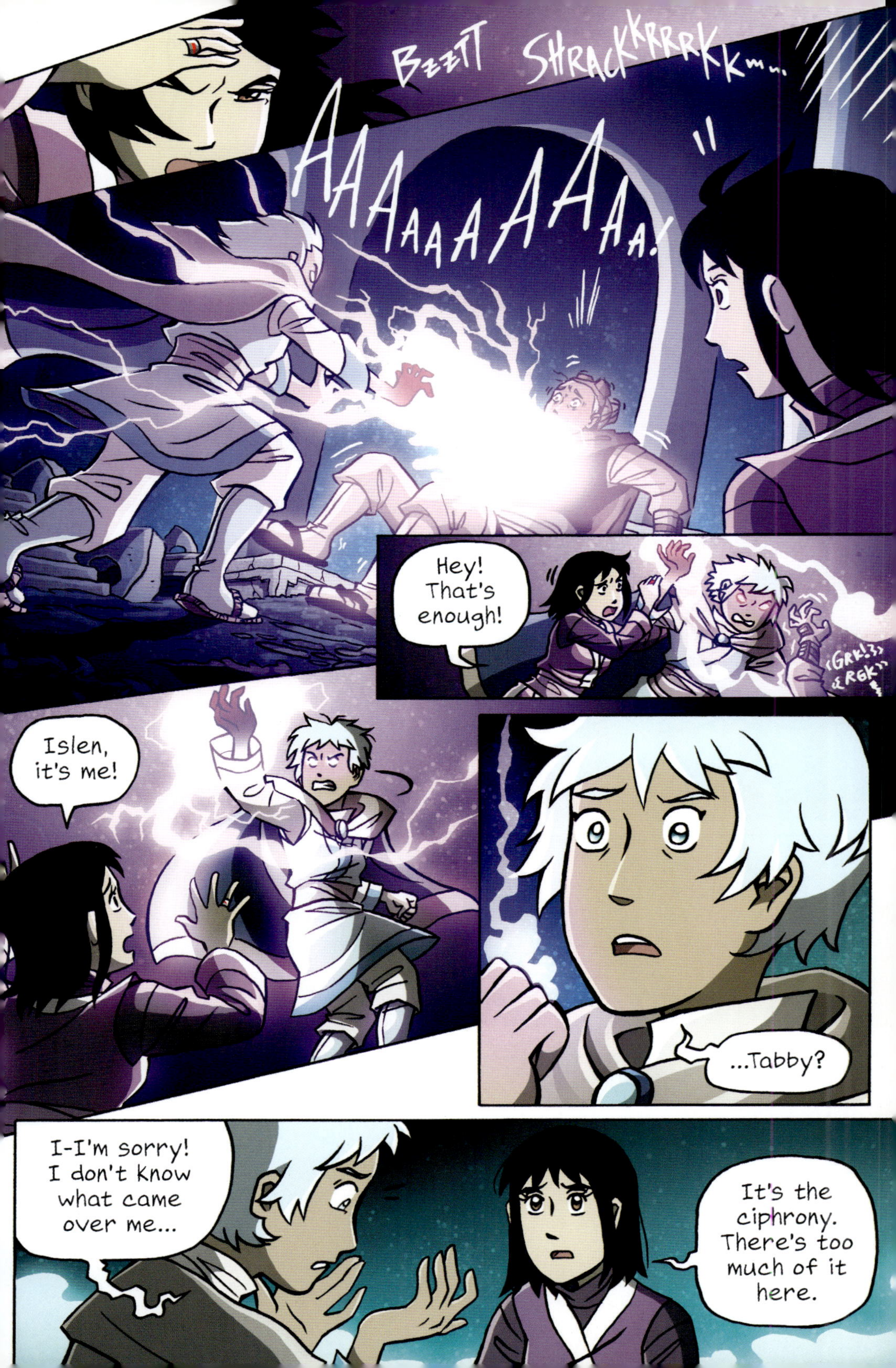
BZZTT SHRACKKRRRKKm...
AAAAAAAAAAAA!
Hey! That's enough!
GRK! RGK
Islen, it's me!
...Tabby?
I-I'm sorry! I don't know what came over me...
It's the ciphrony. There's too much of it here.

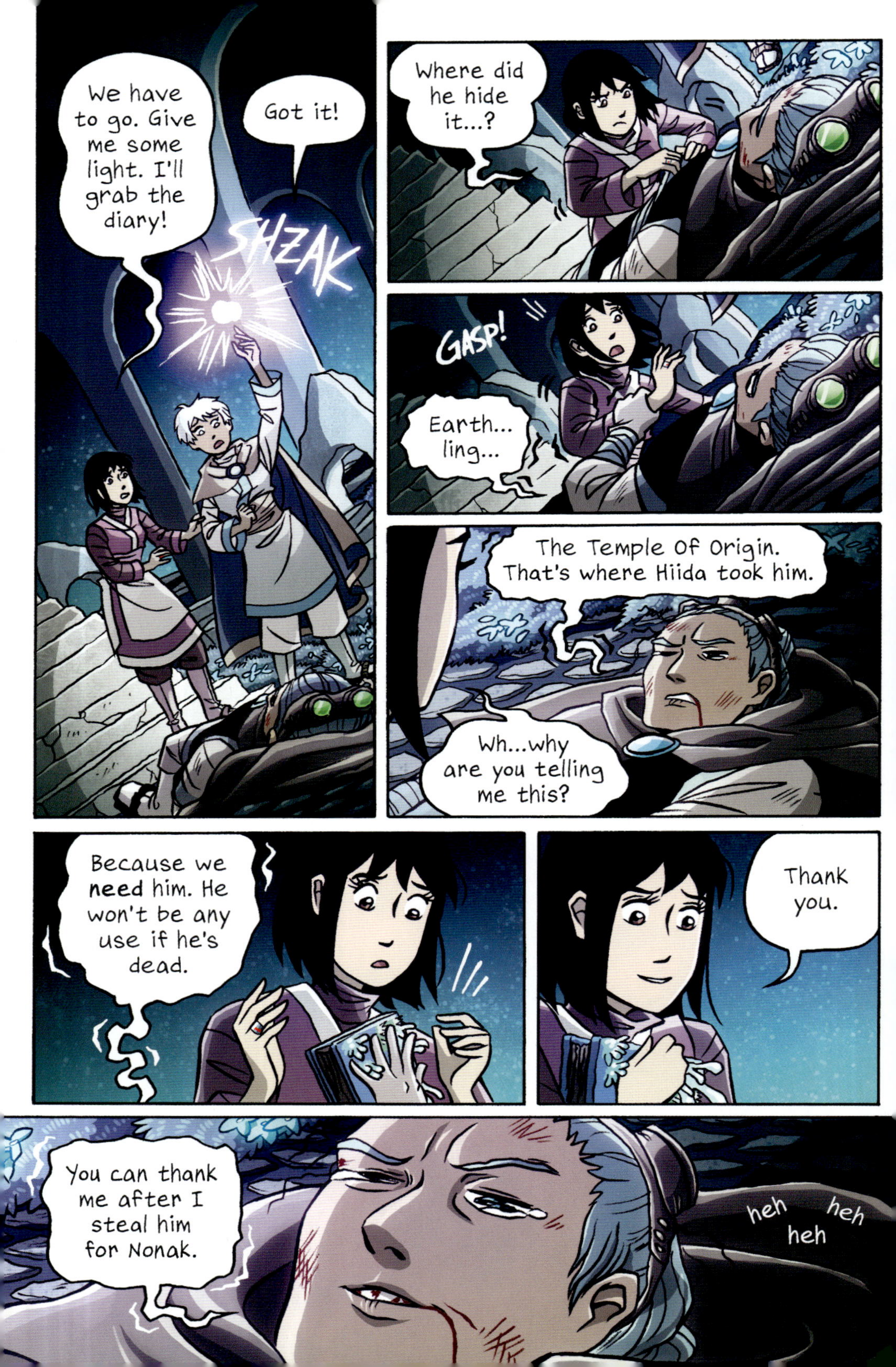

We have to go. Give me some light. I'll grab the diary!
Got it!
SHZAK
Where did he hide it...?
GASP!
Earth... ling...
The Temple Of Origin. That's where Hiida took him.
Wh...why are you telling me this?
Because we **need** him. He won't be any use if he's dead.
Thank you.
You can thank me after I steal him for Nonak.
heh heh heh

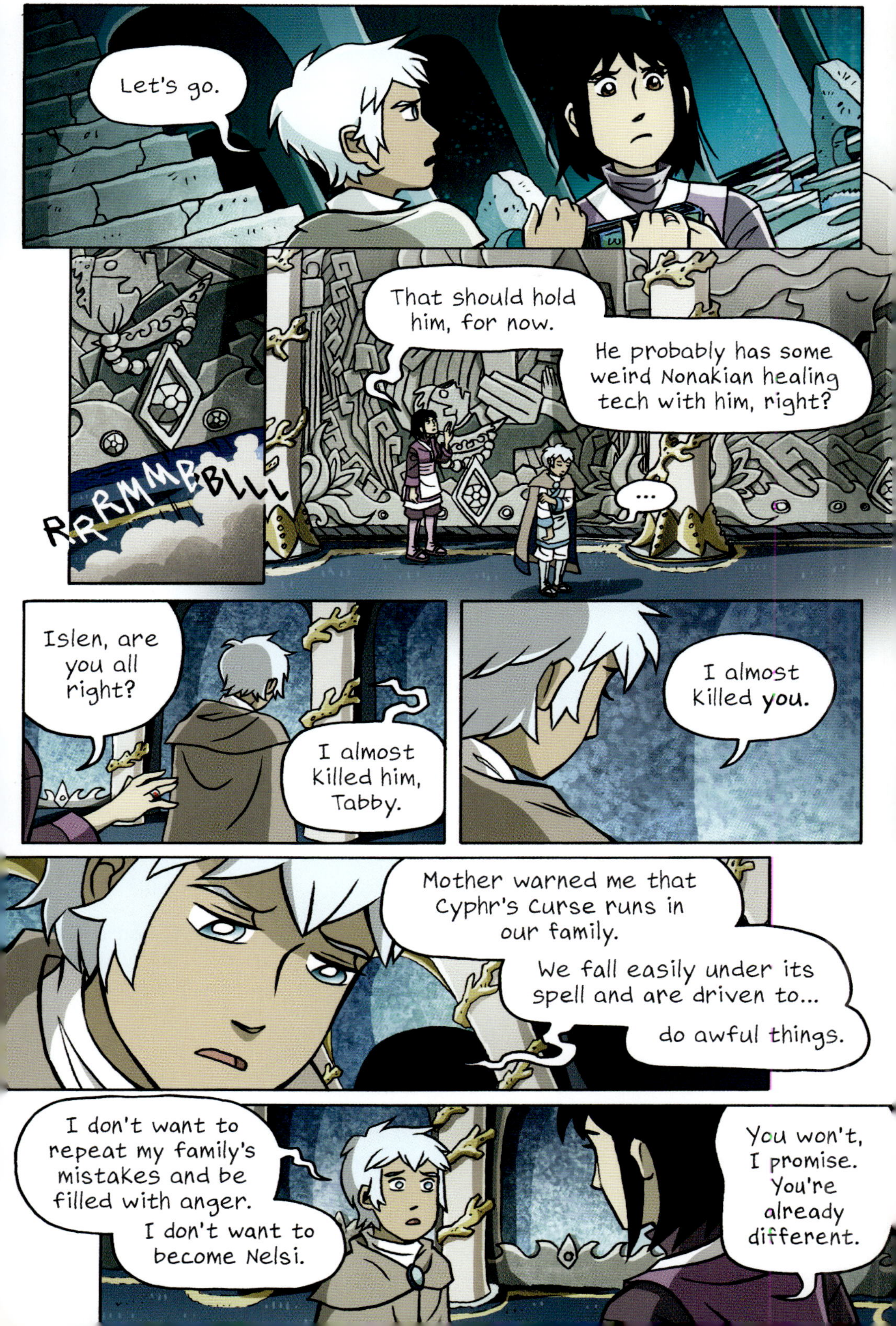
Let's go.
That should hold him, for now.
He probably has some weird Nonakian healing tech with him, right?
RRRMMBBLLL
...
Islen, are you all right?
I almost killed him, Tabby.
I almost killed you.
Mother warned me that Cyphr's Curse runs in our family.
We fall easily under its spell and are driven to...
do awful things.
I don't want to repeat my family's mistakes and be filled with anger.
I don't want to become Nelsi.
You won't, I promise. You're already different.

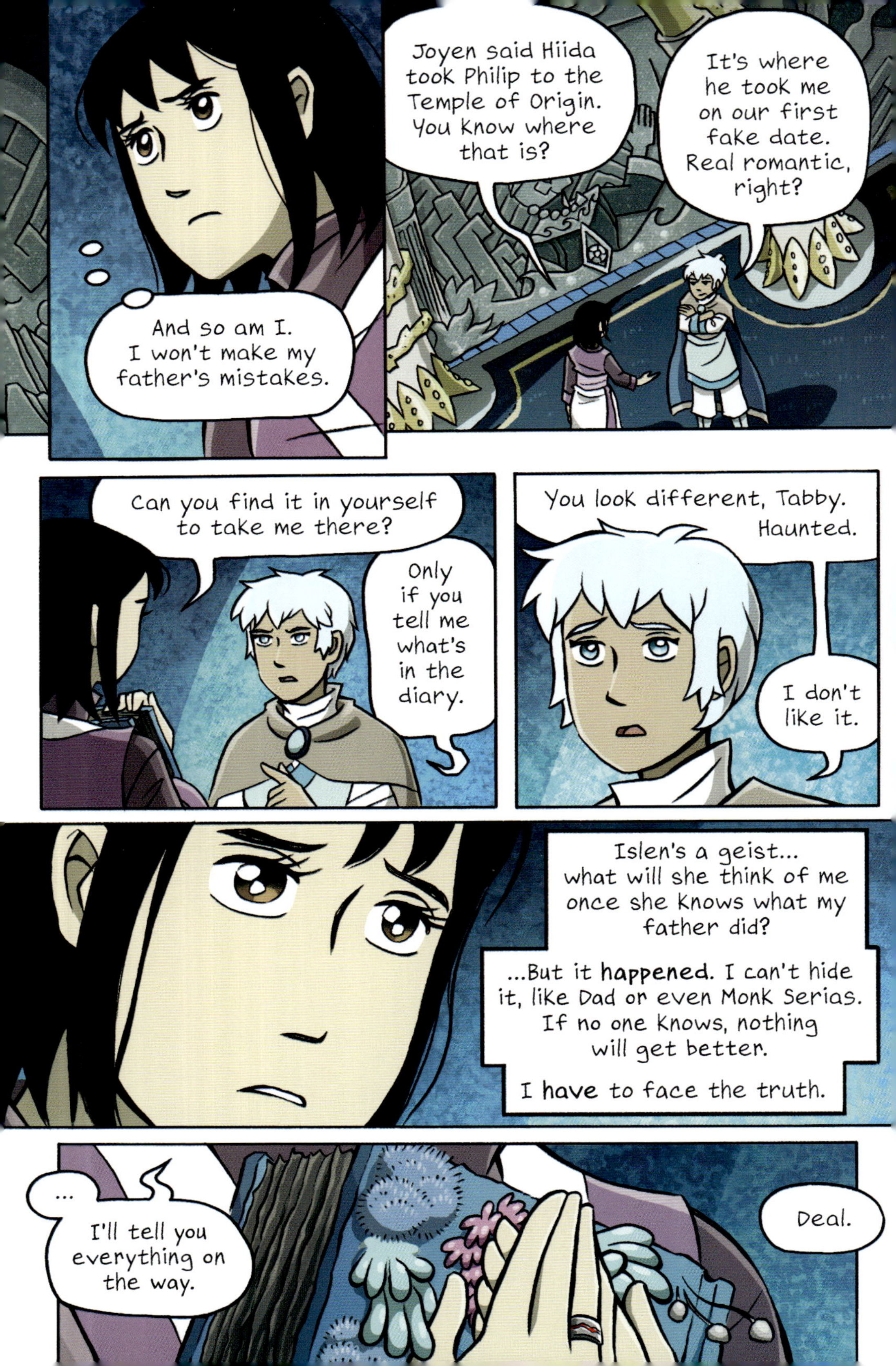
Joyen said Hiida took Philip to the Temple of Origin. You know where that is?
It's where he took me on our first fake date. Real romantic, right?
And so am I. I won't make my father's mistakes.
Can you find it in yourself to take me there?
Only if you tell me what's in the diary.
You look different, Tabby. Haunted.
I don't like it.
Islen's a geist... what will she think of me once she knows what my father did?
...But it **happened**. I can't hide it, like Dad or even Monk Serias. If no one knows, nothing will get better.
I **have** to face the truth.
...
I'll tell you everything on the way.
Deal.

PART IV
THE WATER GODDESS

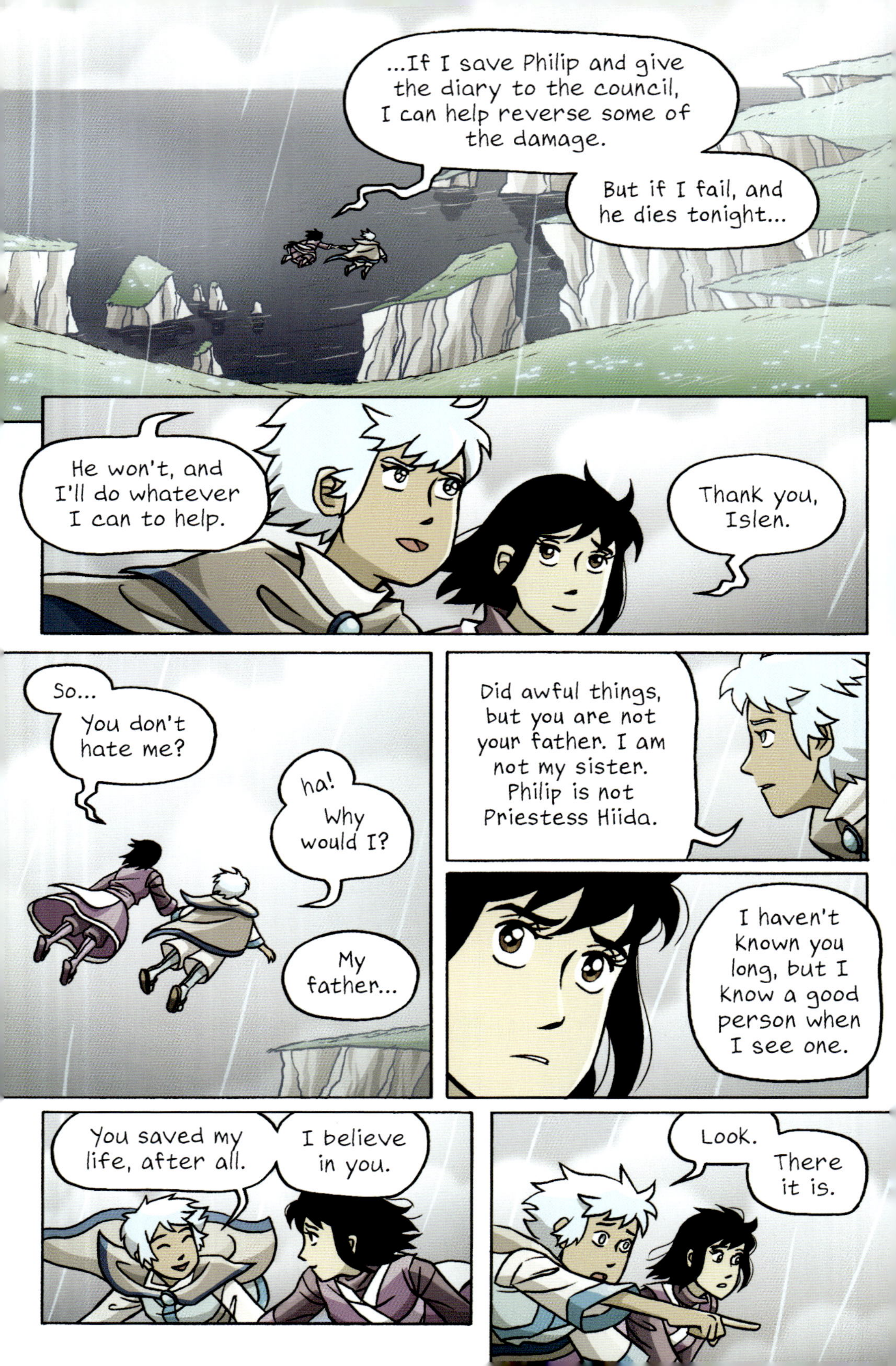
...If I save Philip and give the diary to the council, I can help reverse some of the damage.
But if I fail, and he dies tonight...
He won't, and I'll do whatever I can to help.
Thank you, Islen.
So... You don't hate me?
ha! Why would I?
My father...
Did awful things, but you are not your father. I am not my sister. Philip is not Priestess Hiida.
I haven't known you long, but I know a good person when I see one.
I believe in you.
You saved my life, after all.
Look. There it is.

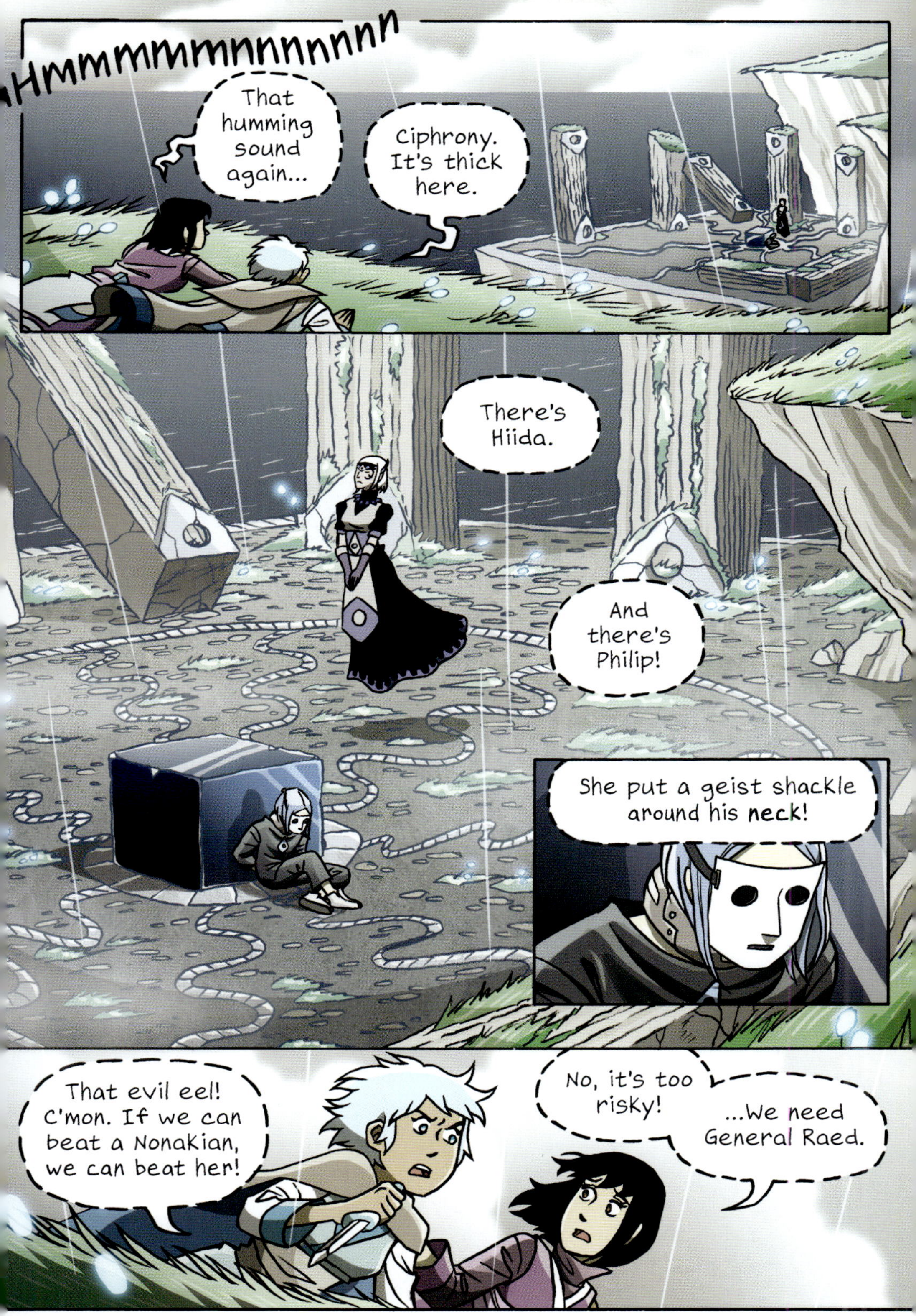
HMMMMMMNNNNNNN
That humming sound again...
Ciphrony. It's thick here.
There's Hiida.
And there's Philip!
She put a geist shackle around his **neck**!
That evil eel! C'mon. If we can beat a Nonakian, we can beat her!
No, it's too risky!
...We need General Raed.

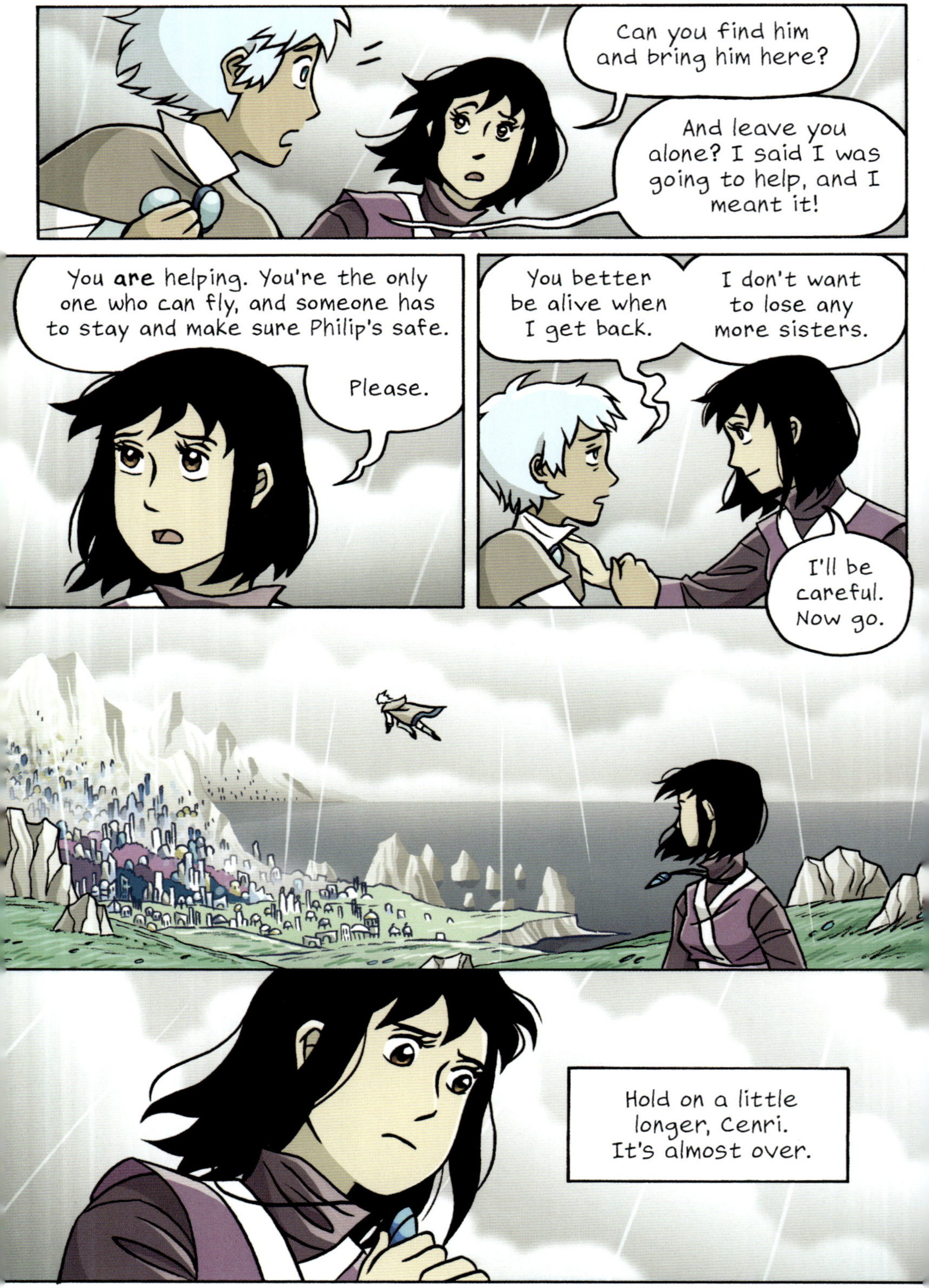
Can you find him and bring him here?
And leave you alone? I said I was going to help, and I meant it!
You **are** helping. You're the only one who can fly, and someone has to stay and make sure Philip's safe.
Please.
You better be alive when I get back.
I don't want to lose any more sisters.
I'll be careful. Now go.
Hold on a little longer, Cenri. It's almost over.

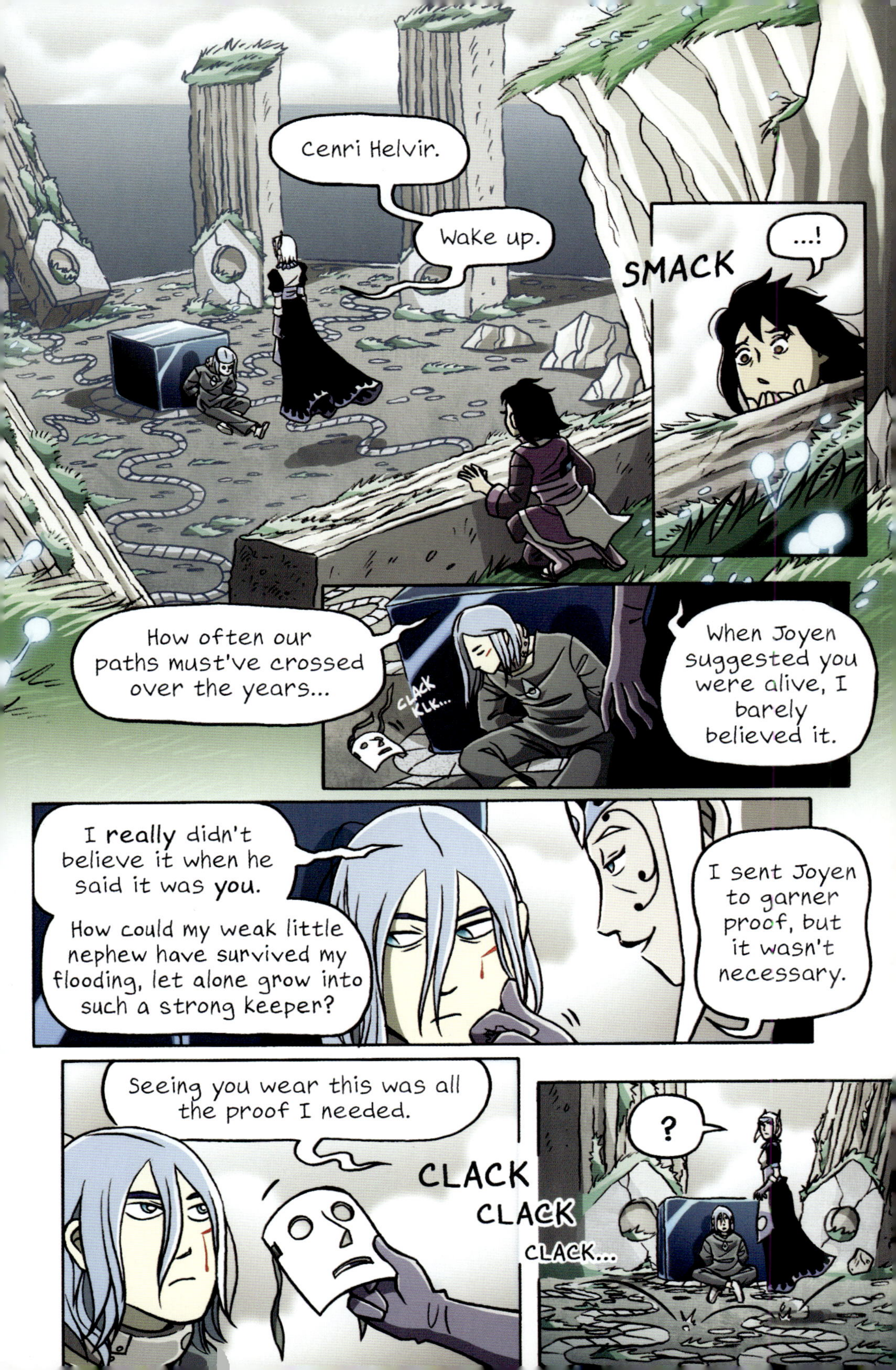
Cenri Helvir.
Wake up.
SMACK
...!
How often our paths must've crossed over the years...
CLACK KLK...
When Joyen suggested you were alive, I barely believed it.
I **really** didn't believe it when he said it was **you**.
How could my weak little nephew have survived my flooding, let alone grow into such a strong keeper?
I sent Joyen to garner proof, but it wasn't necessary.
Seeing you wear this was all the proof I needed.
CLACK
CLACK
CLACK...
?

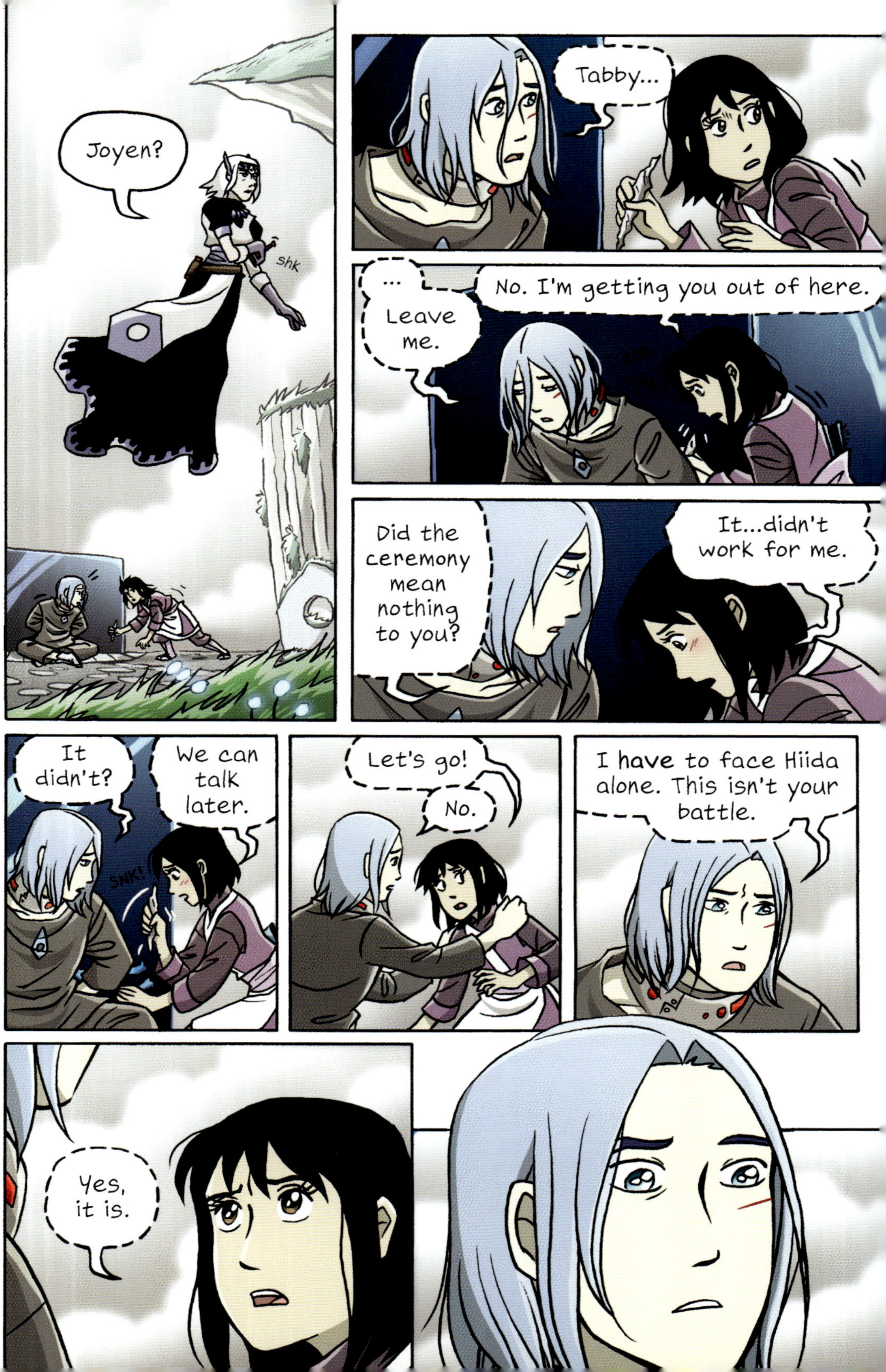
Joyen?
shk
Tabby...
...
Leave me.
No. I'm getting you out of here.
Did the ceremony mean nothing to you?
It...didn't work for me.
It didn't?
We can talk later.
SNK!
Let's go!
No.
I have to face Hiida alone. This isn't your battle.
Yes, it is.

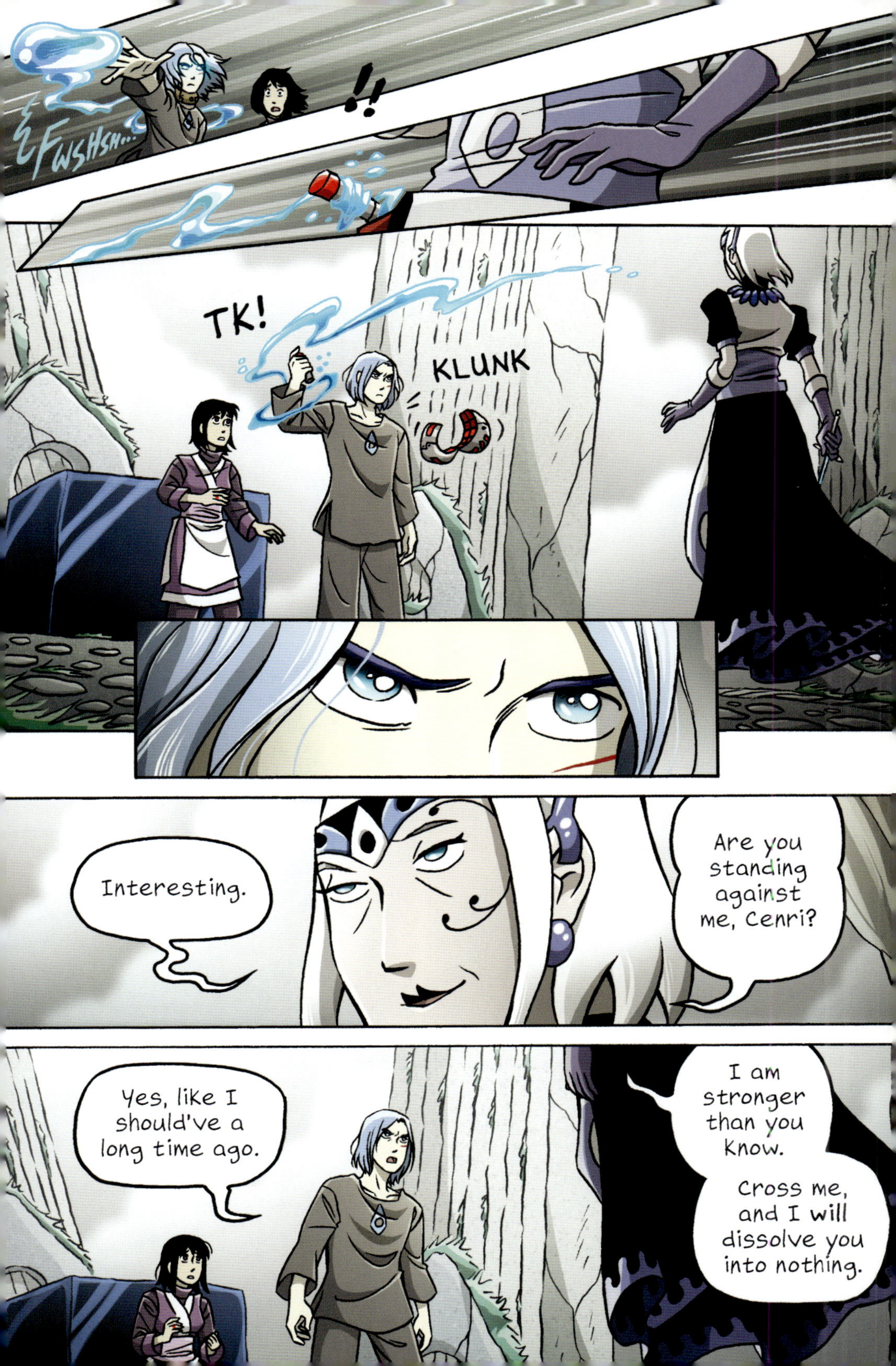
FWSHSH...
!!
TK!
KLUNK
Interesting.
Are you standing against me, Cenri?
Yes, like I should've a long time ago.
I am stronger than you know.
Cross me, and I will dissolve you into nothing.

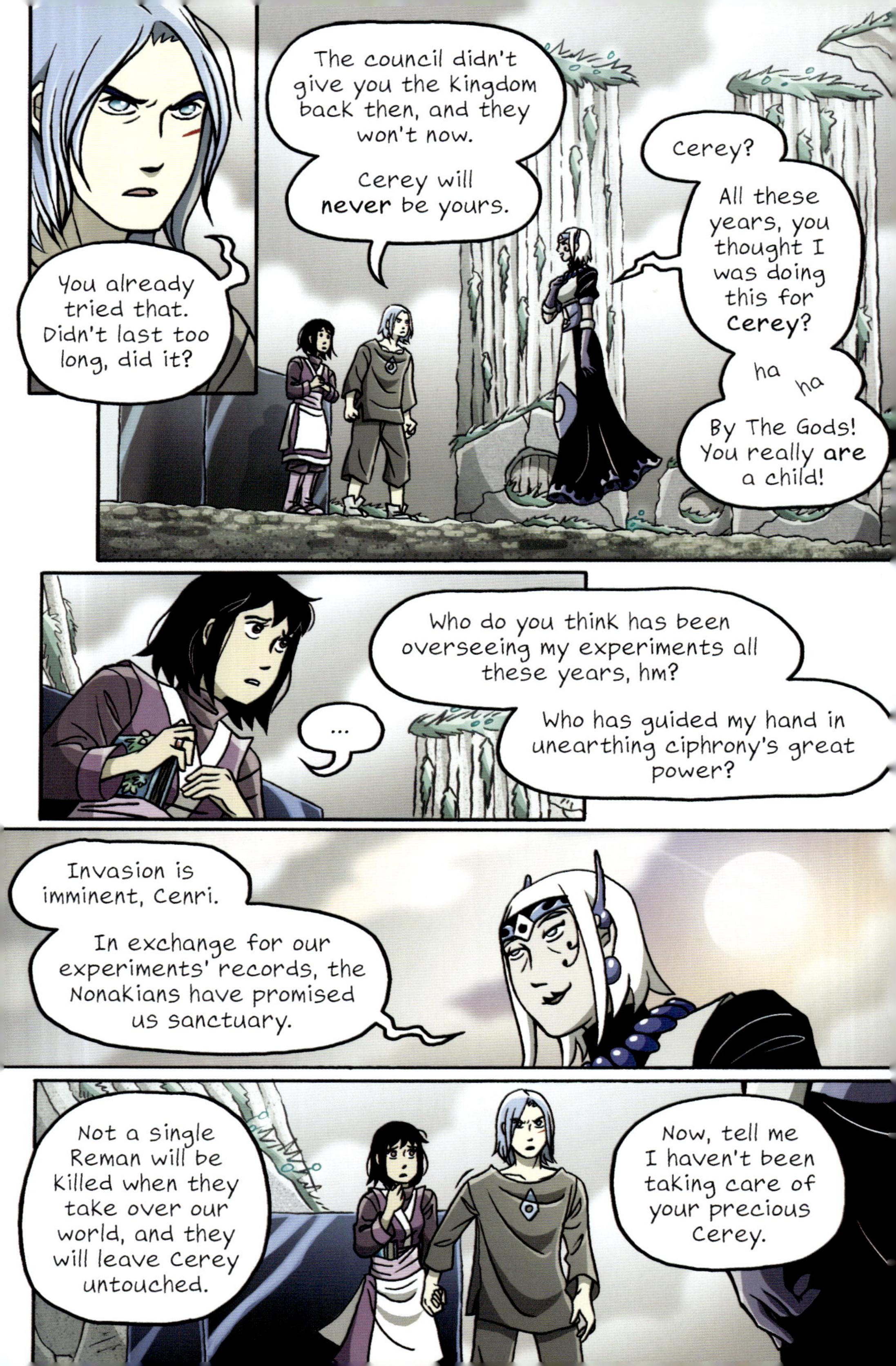
You already tried that. Didn't last too long, did it?
The council didn't give you the Kingdom back then, and they won't now.
Cerey will never be yours.
Cerey?
All these years, you thought I was doing this for Cerey?
ha ha
By The Gods! You really are a child!
...
Who do you think has been overseeing my experiments all these years, hm?
Who has guided my hand in unearthing ciphrony's great power?
Invasion is imminent, Cenri.
In exchange for our experiments' records, the Nonakians have promised us sanctuary.
Not a single Reman will be killed when they take over our world, and they will leave Cerey untouched.
Now, tell me I haven't been taking care of your precious Cerey.

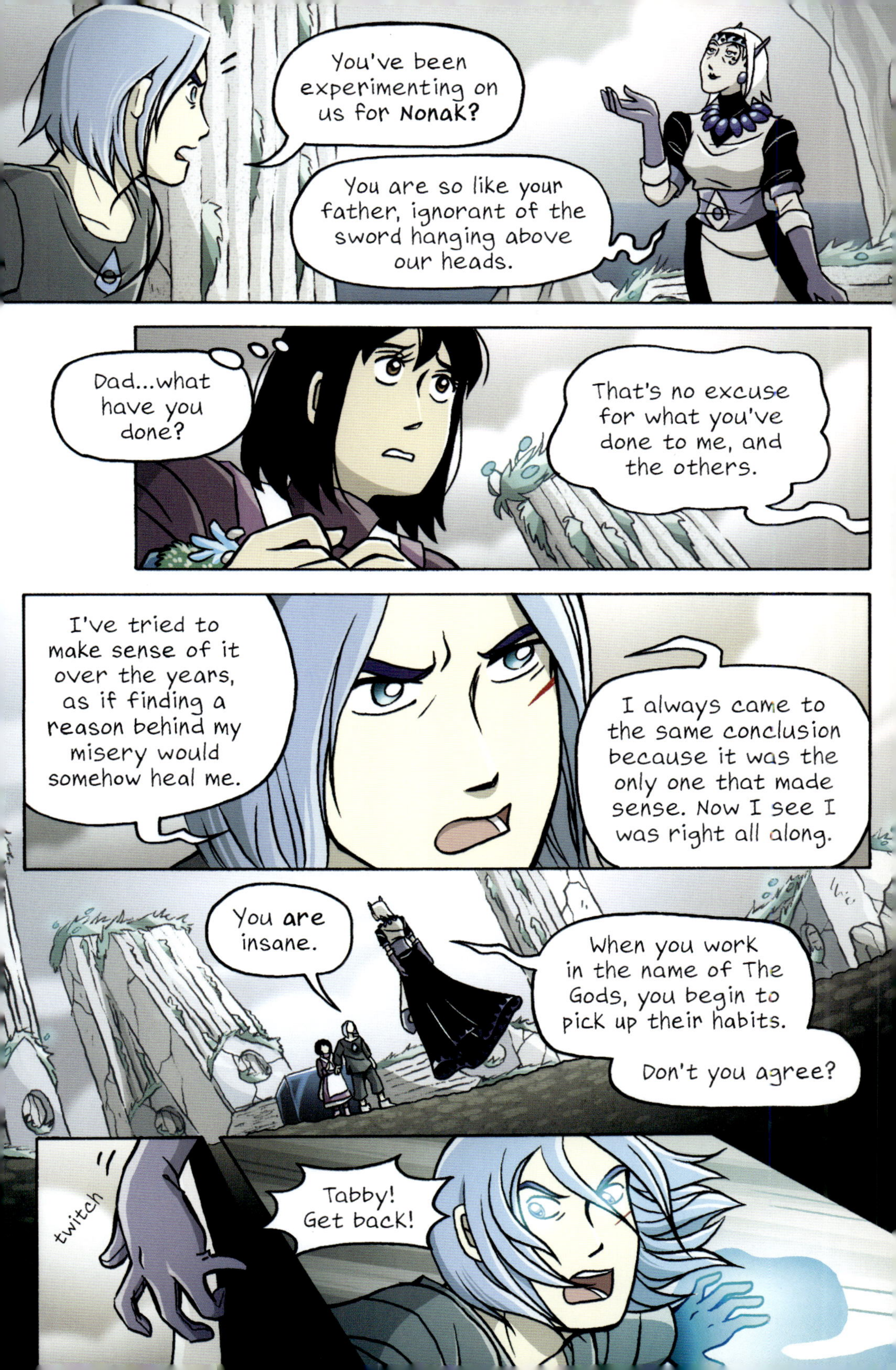
You've been experimenting on us for **Nonak?**
You are so like your father, ignorant of the sword hanging above our heads.
Dad...what have you done?
That's no excuse for what you've done to me, and the others.
I've tried to make sense of it over the years, as if finding a reason behind my misery would somehow heal me.
I always came to the same conclusion because it was the only one that made sense. Now I see I was right all along.
You **are** insane.
When you work in the name of The Gods, you begin to pick up their habits.
Don't you agree?
twitch
Tabby! Get back!

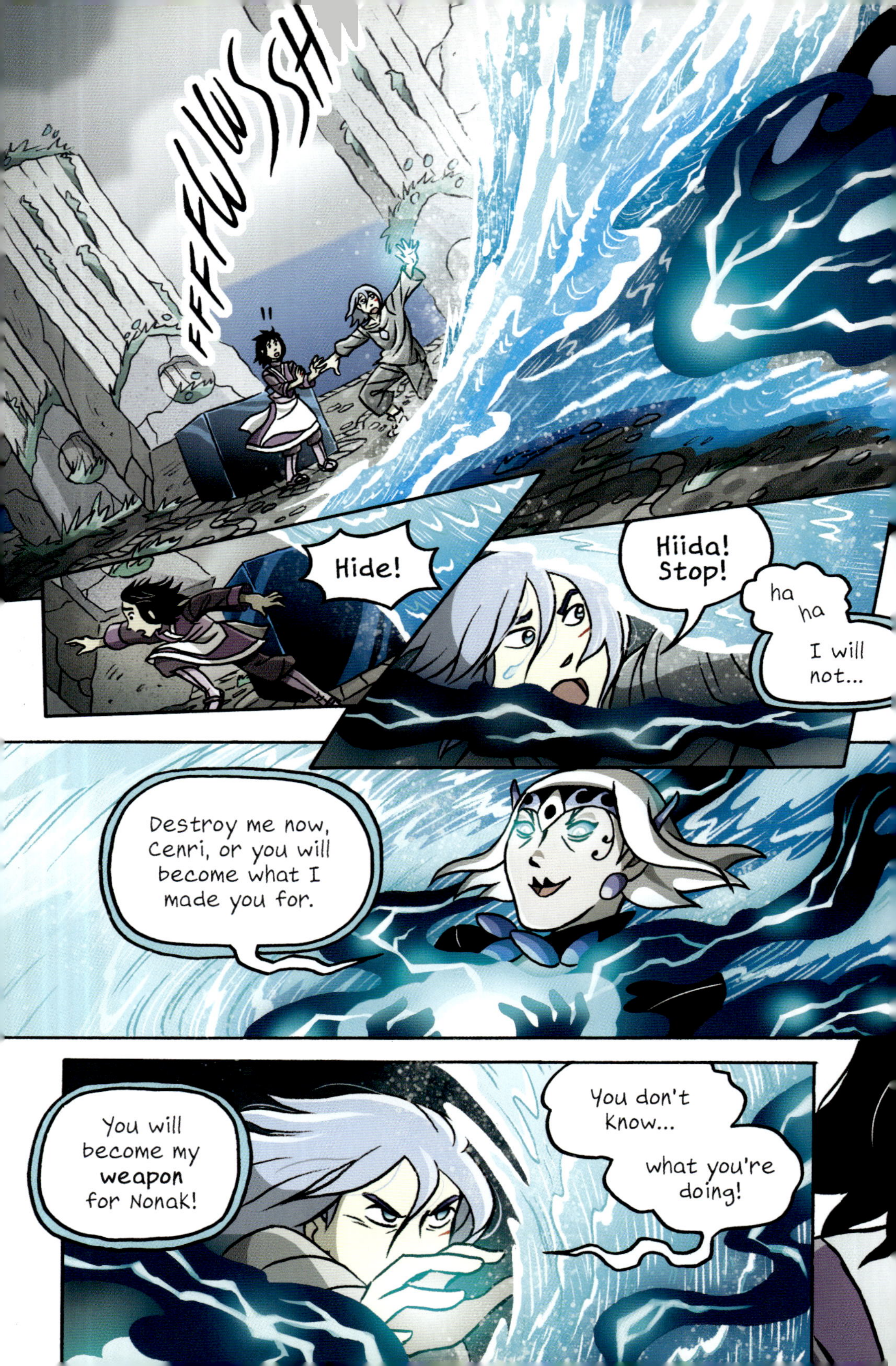
FFFWUSSH
!!
Hide!
Hiida! Stop!
ha ha
I will not...
Destroy me now, Cenri, or you will become what I made you for.
You will become my **weapon** for Nonak!
You don't know...
what you're doing!

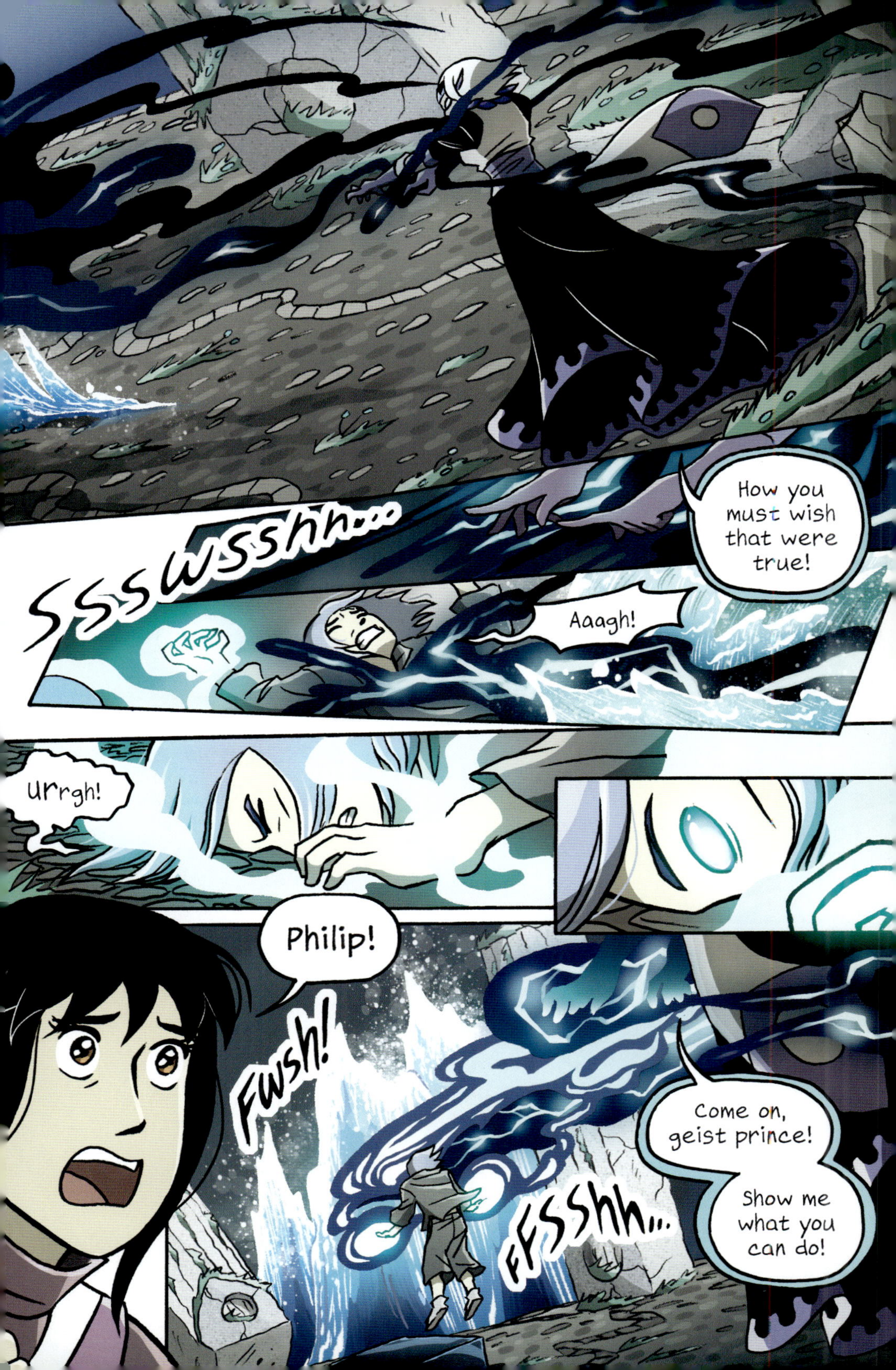
How you must wish that were true!
SSSWSSHH...
Aaagh!
Urrgh!
Philip!
Fwsh!
Come on, geist prince!
Show me what you can do!
FFSShh..

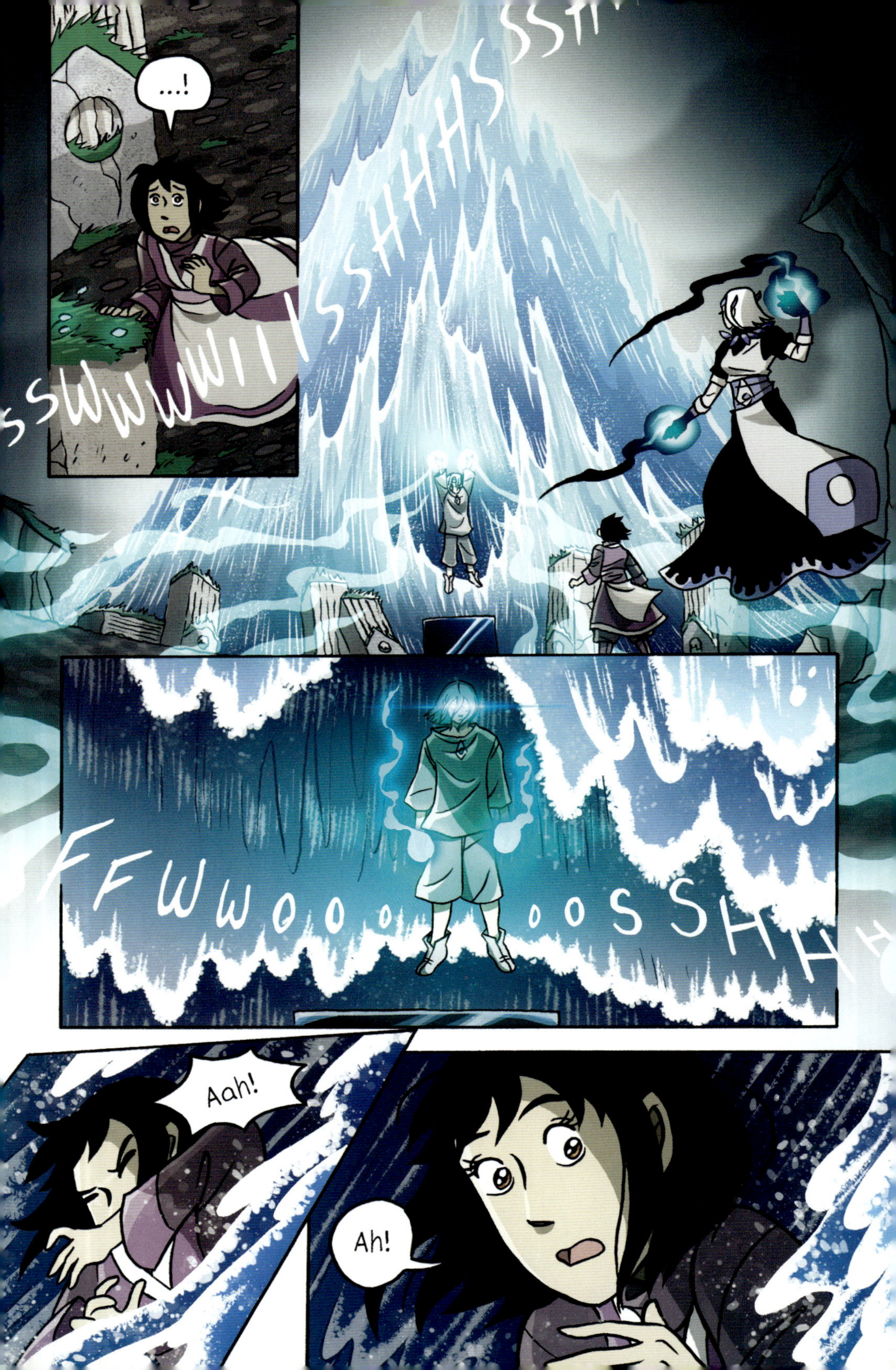
...!
SSWWWWIIISSSHHHSSSH
FFWWOOOOOOSSHHH
Aah!
Ah!

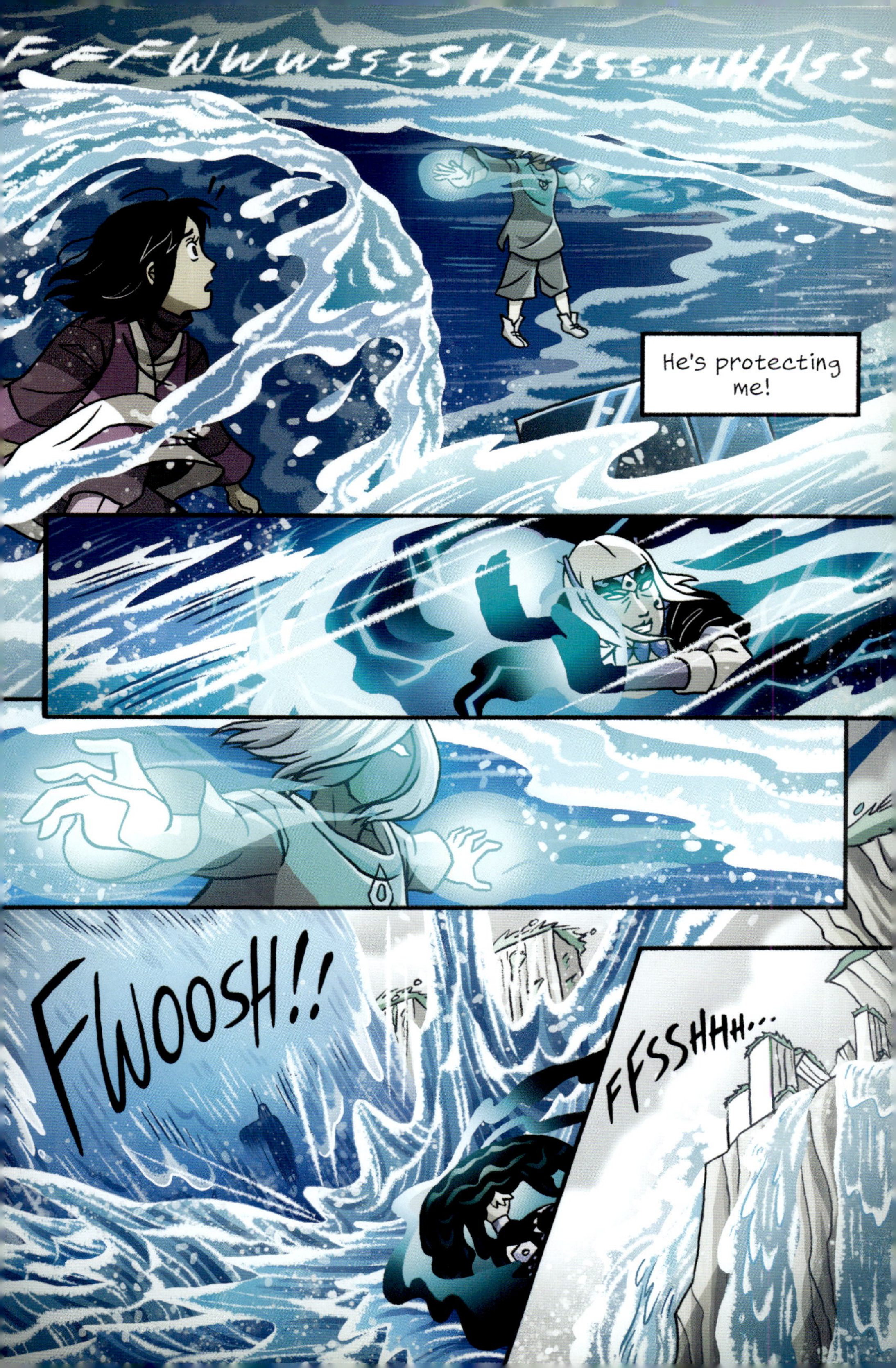
FFFWWWWSSSSSHHSSS.HHHSSS
He's protecting me!
FWOOSH!!
FFSSHHH...

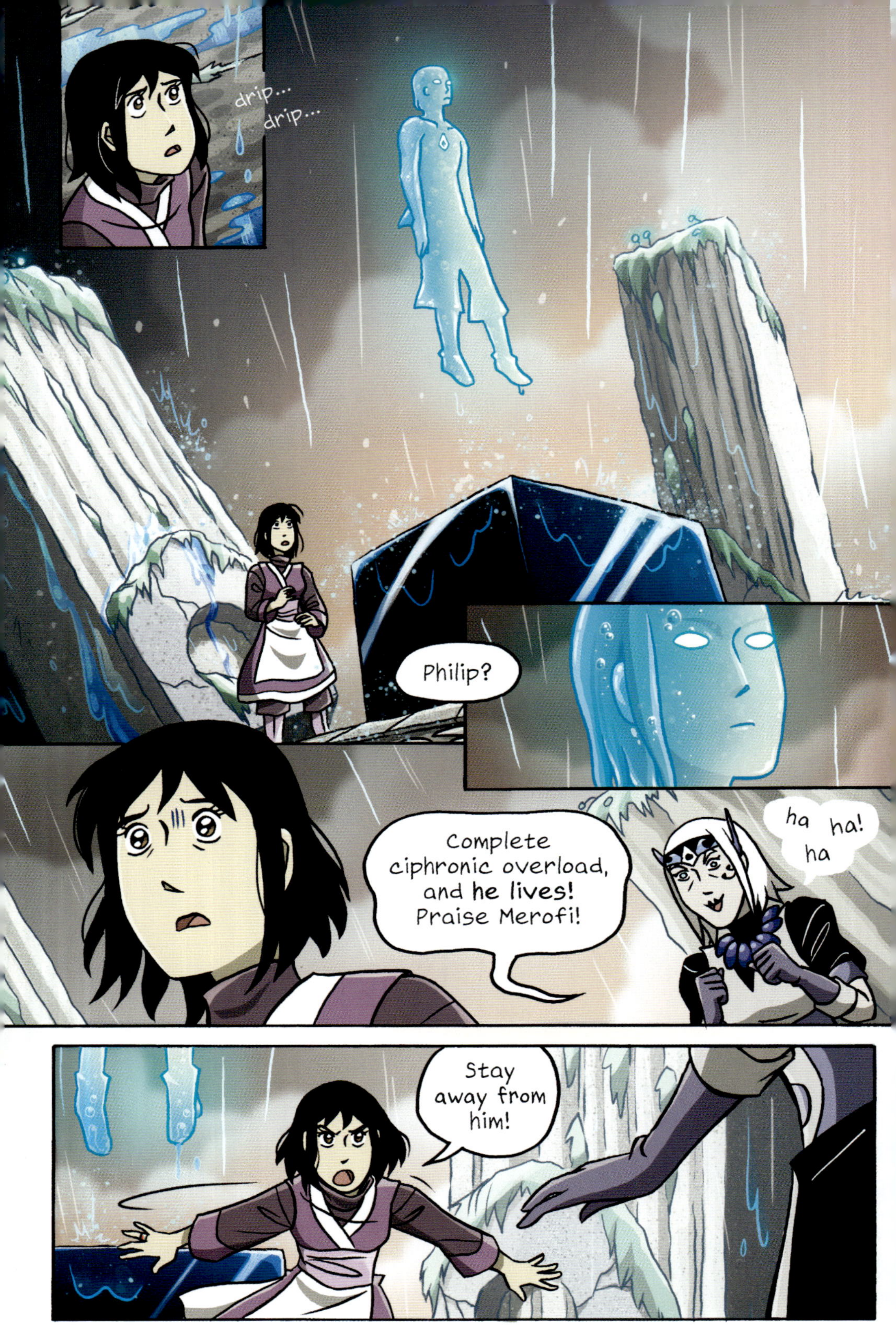
drip...
drip...
Philip?
Complete ciphronic overload, and **he lives!** Praise Merofi!
ha ha! ha
Stay away from him!

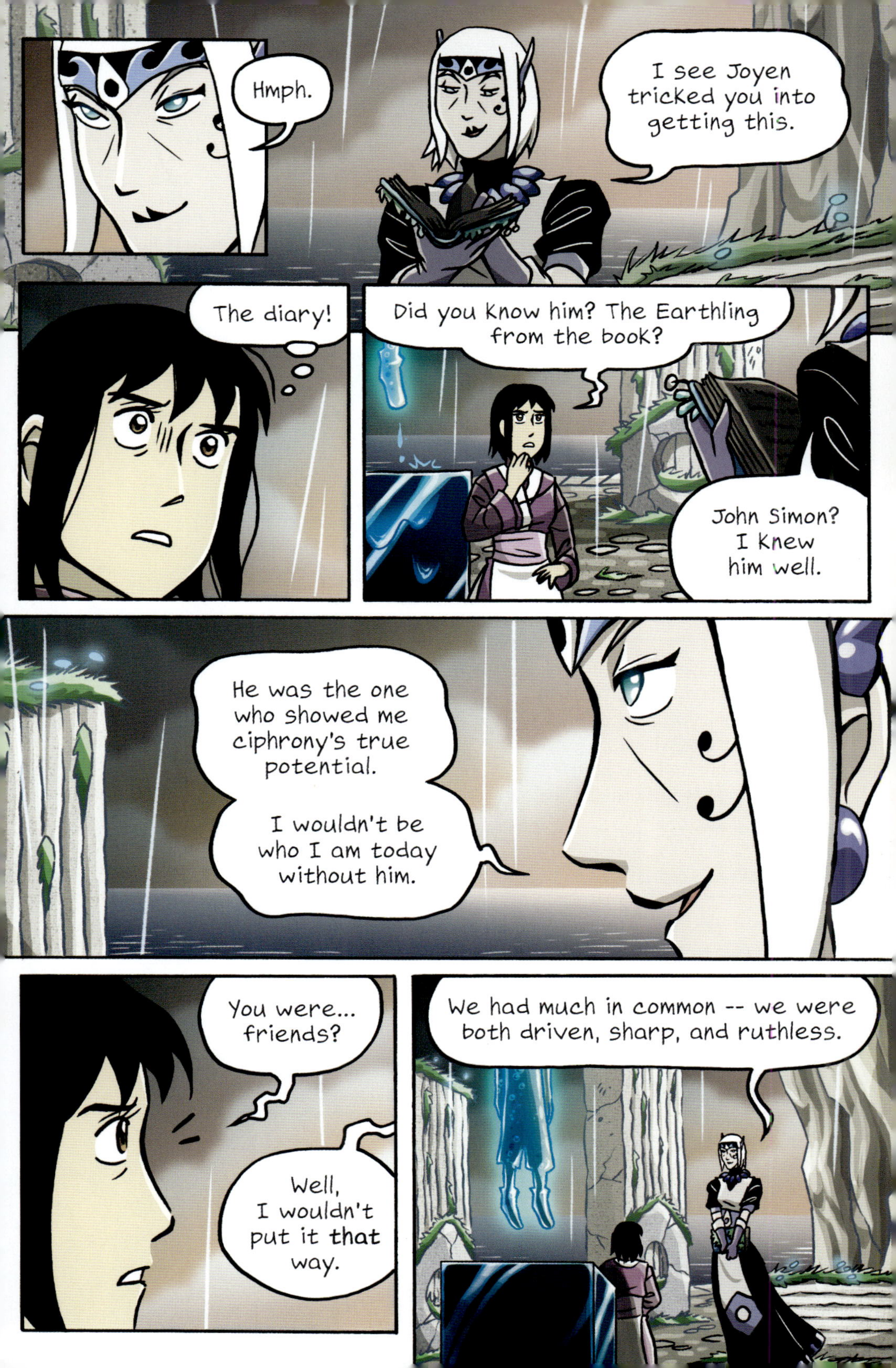
Hmph.
I see Joyen tricked you into getting this.
The diary!
Did you know him? The Earthling from the book?
John Simon? I knew him well.
He was the one who showed me ciphrony's true potential.
I wouldn't be who I am today without him.
You were... friends?
Well, I wouldn't put it that way.
We had much in common -- we were both driven, sharp, and ruthless.

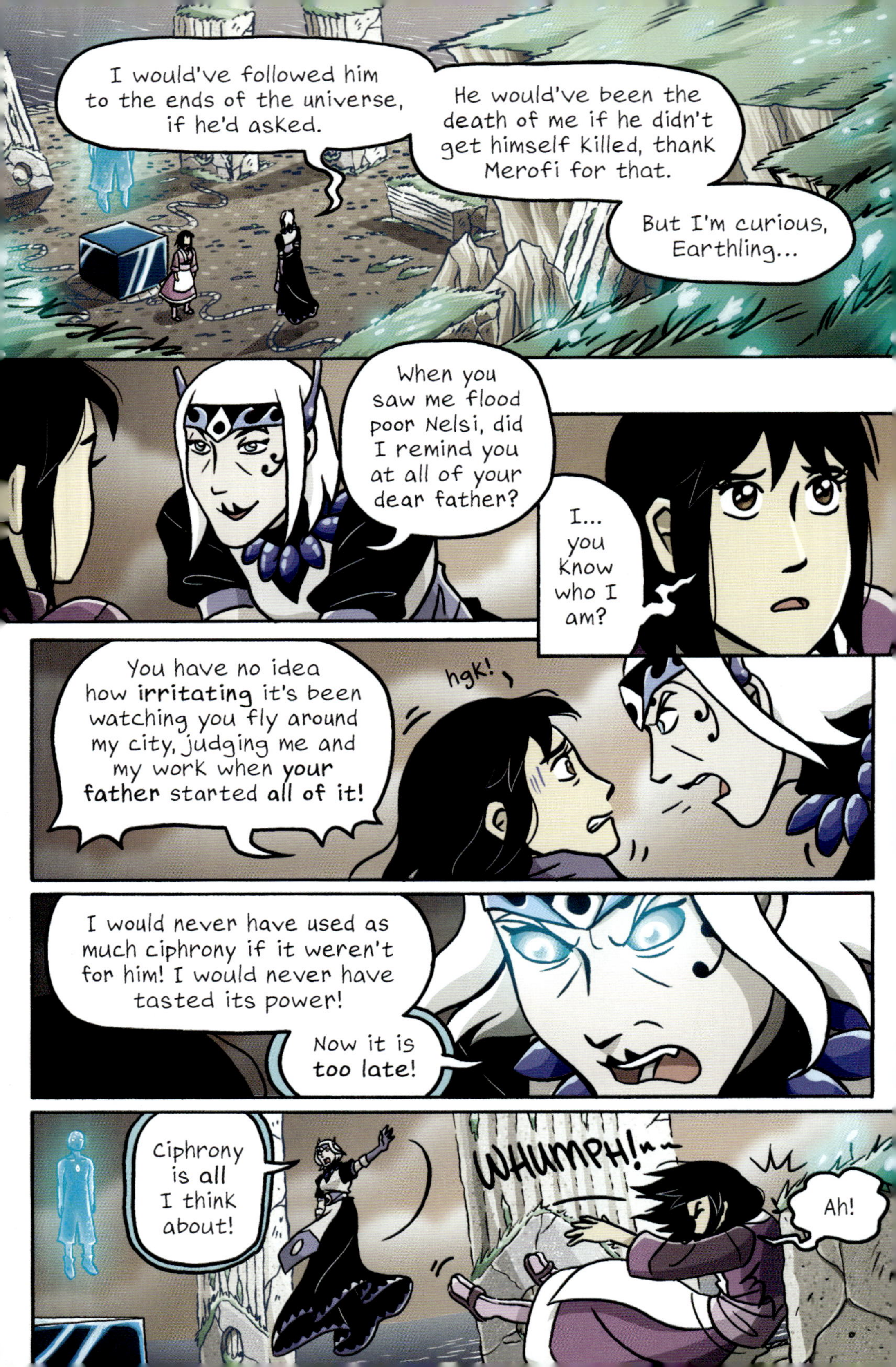
I would've followed him to the ends of the universe, if he'd asked.
He would've been the death of me if he didn't get himself killed, thank Merofi for that.
But I'm curious, Earthling...
When you saw me flood poor Nelsi, did I remind you at all of your dear father?
I... you know who I am?
You have no idea how **irritating** it's been watching you fly around my city, judging me and my work when **your father** started **all of it!**
hgk!
I would never have used as much ciphrony if it weren't for him! I would never have tasted its power!
Now it is **too late!**
Ciphrony is **all** I think about!
WHUMPH!
Ah!

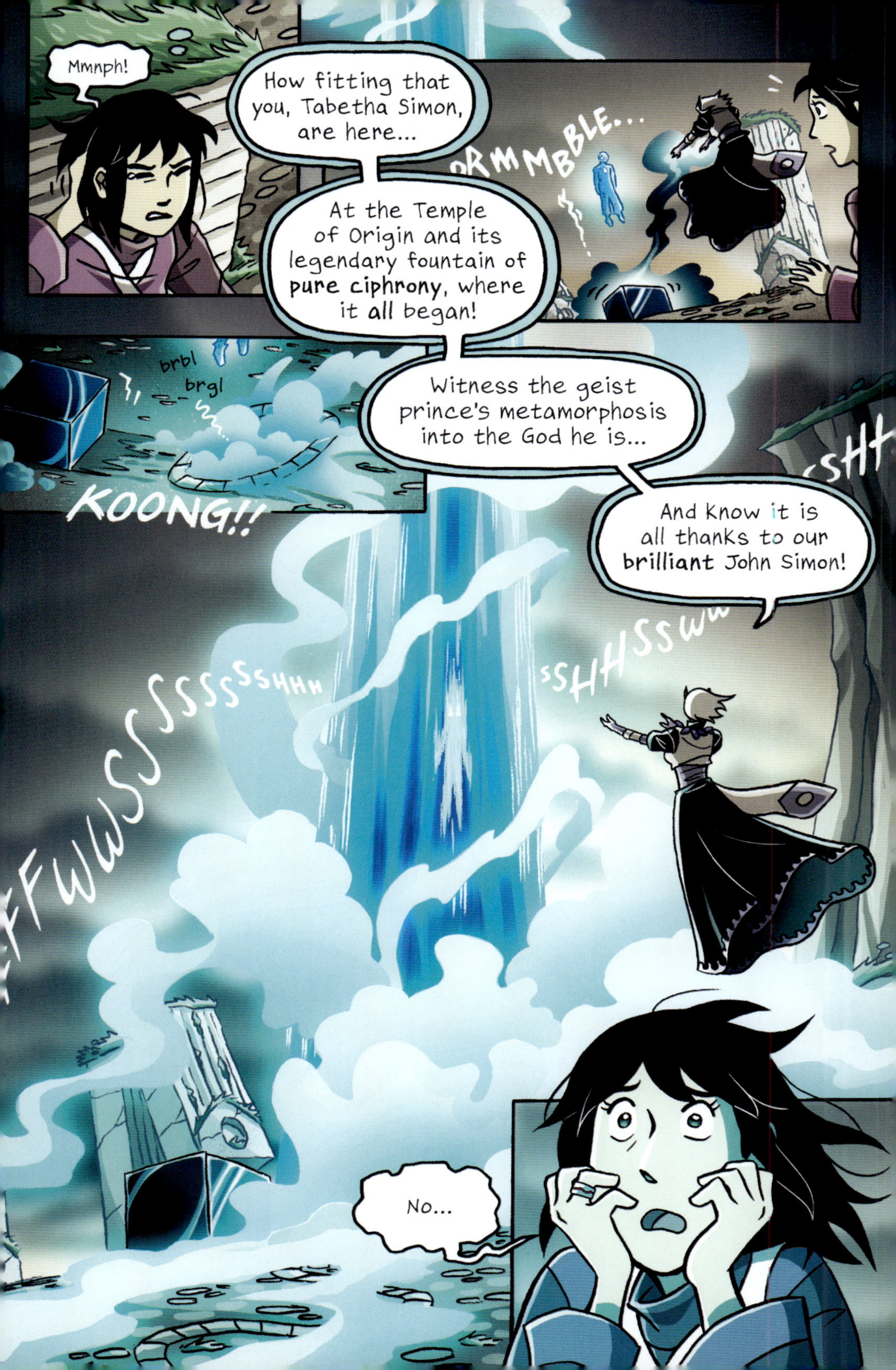
Mmnph!
How fitting that you, Tabetha Simon, are here...
At the Temple of Origin and its legendary fountain of **pure ciphrony**, where it **all** began!
DRMMBBLE...
brbl
brgl
KOONG!!
Witness the geist prince's metamorphosis into the God he is...
And know it is all thanks to our **brilliant** John Simon!
SHHSSWW
FFWWSSSSSSSSHHH
No...

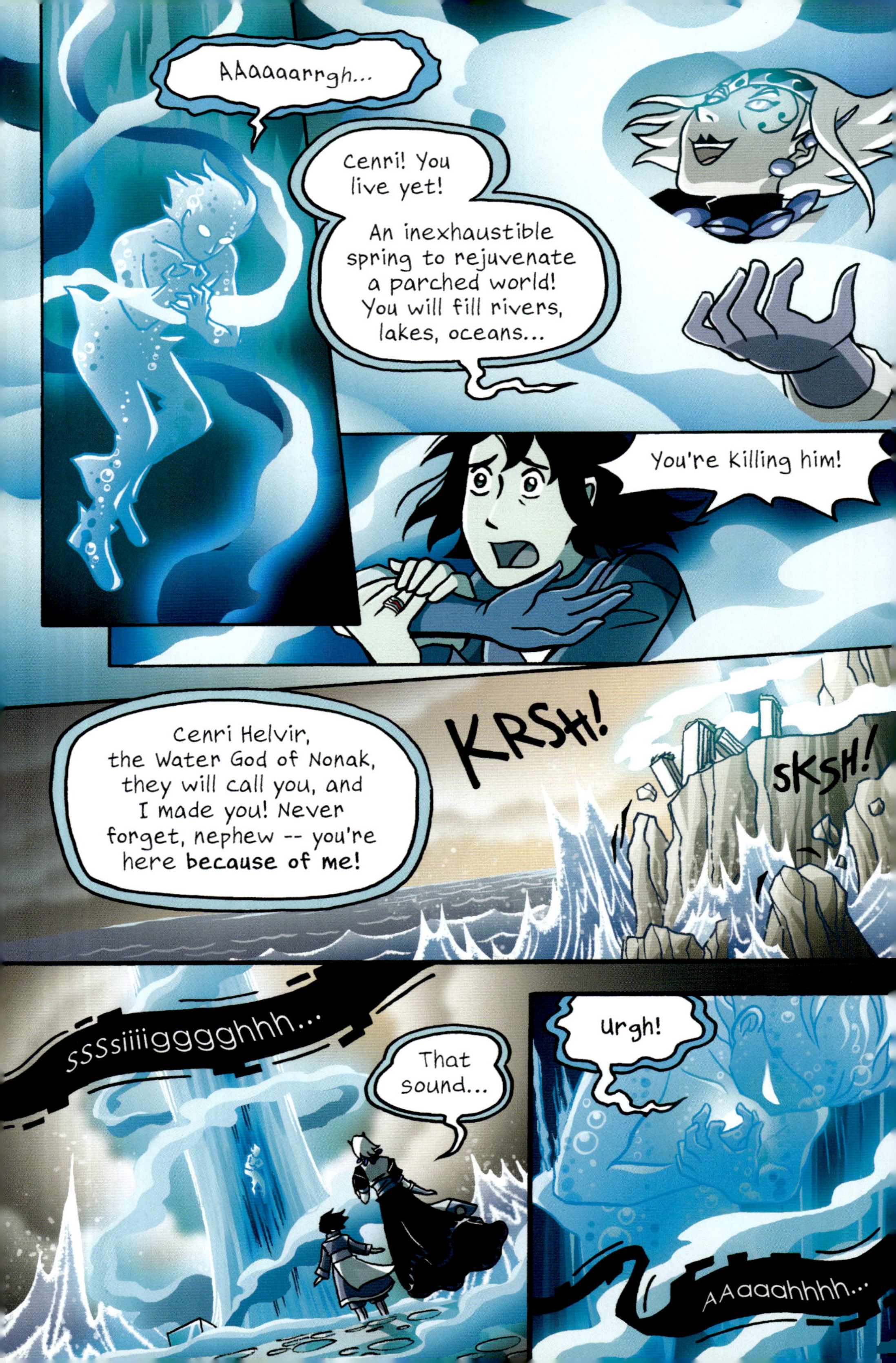

AAaaaarrgh...
Cenri! You live yet!
An inexhaustible spring to rejuvenate a parched world! You will fill rivers, lakes, oceans...
You're killing him!
Cenri Helvir, the Water God of Nonak, they will call you, and I made you! Never forget, nephew -- you're here **because of me!**
KRSH!
SKSH!
SSSiiiigggghhh...
That sound...
Urgh!
AAaaahhhh...

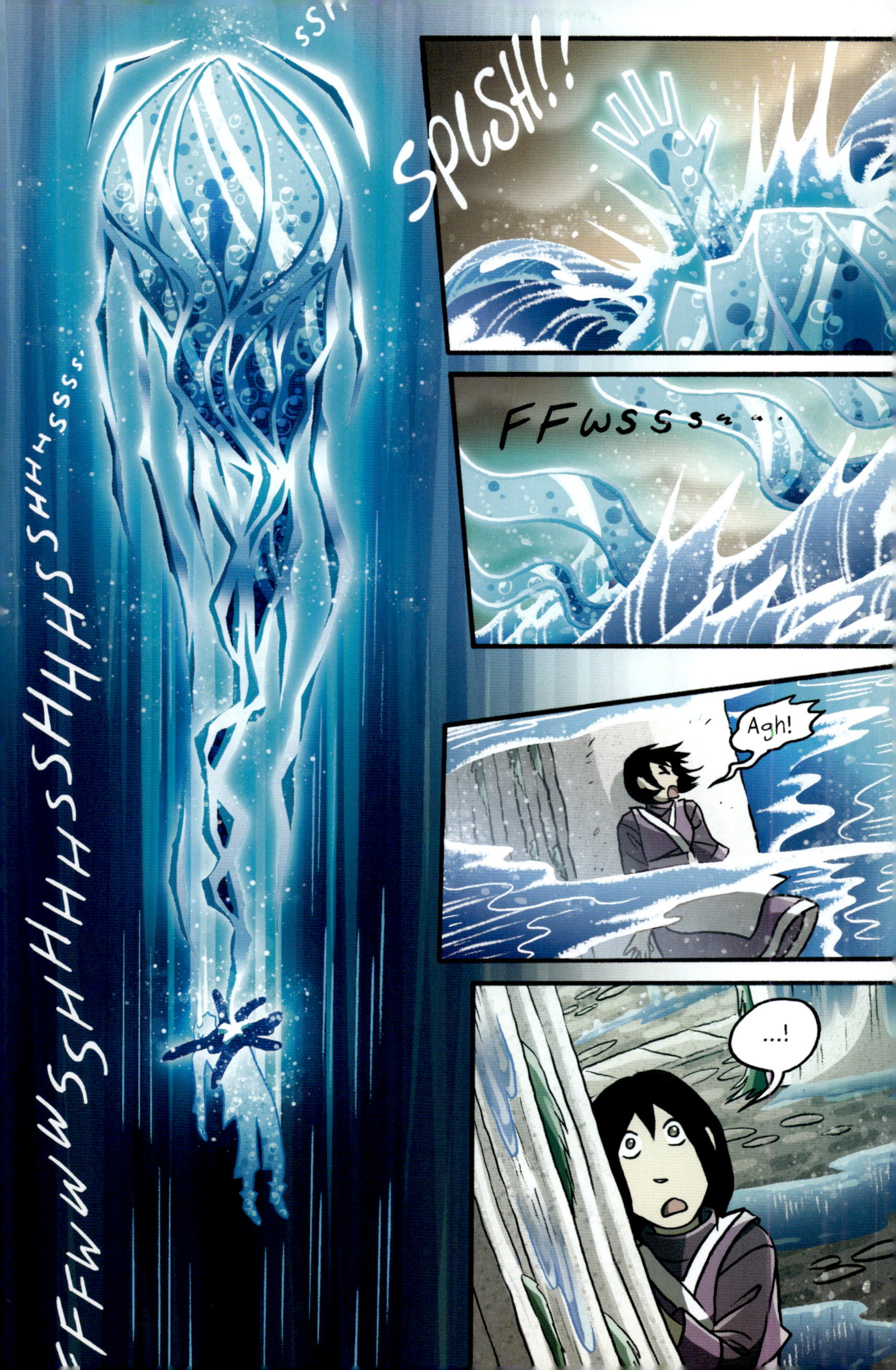
FFWWWSSHHHHSSHHHSSSS...
SPLSH!!
FFWSSSs...
Agh!
...!

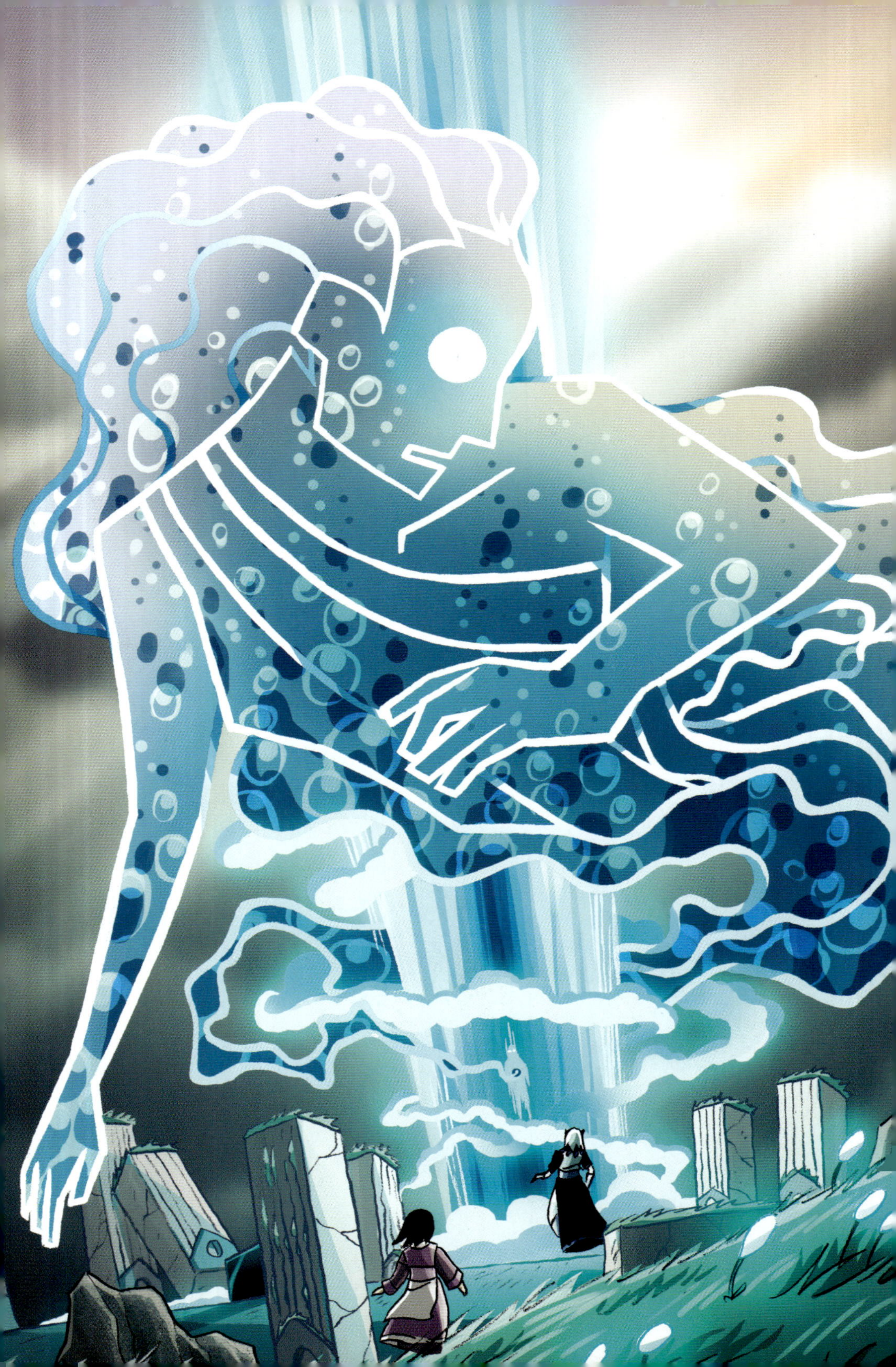

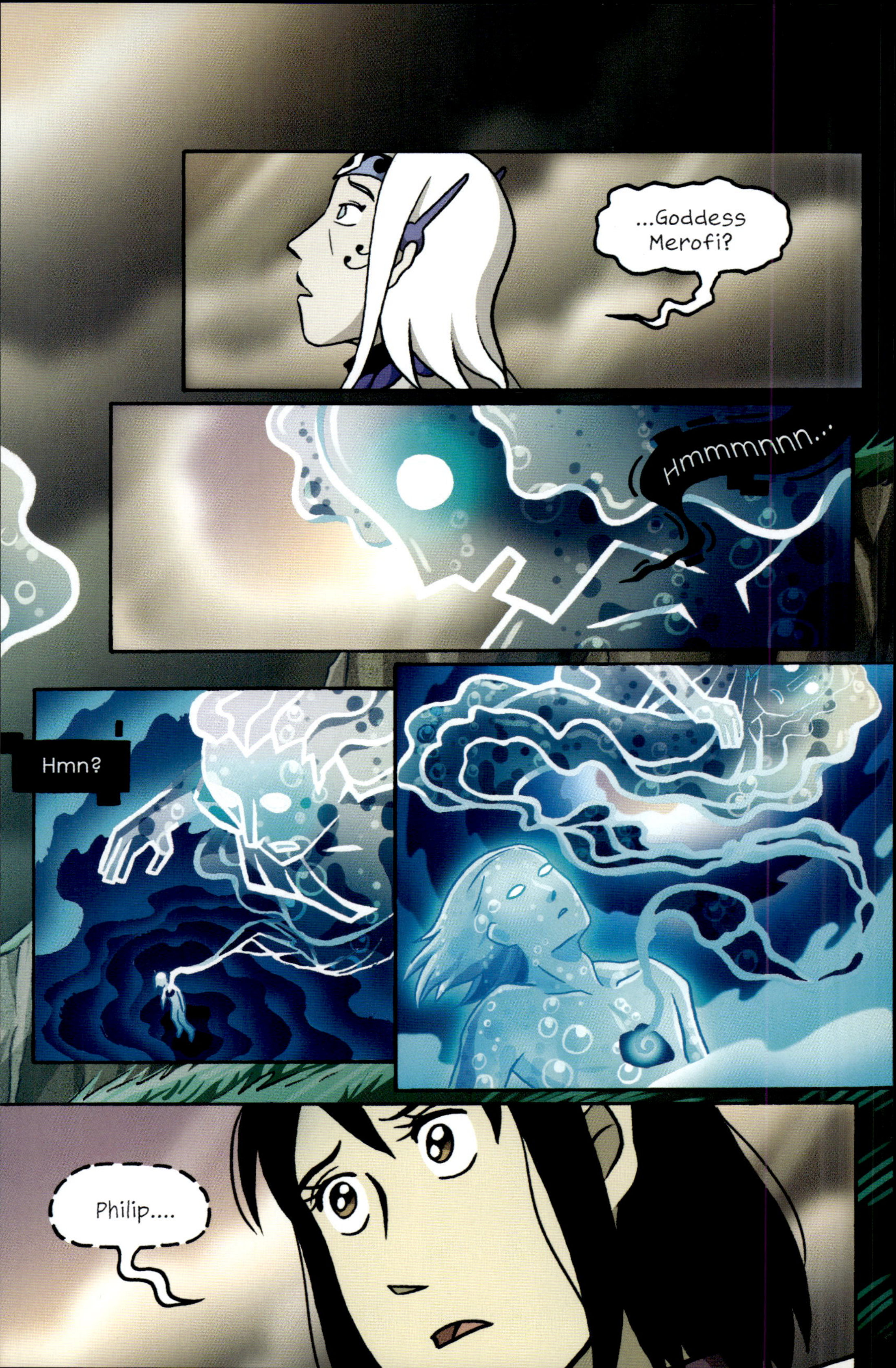
...Goddess Merofi?
Hmmmnnn...
Hmn?
Philip....

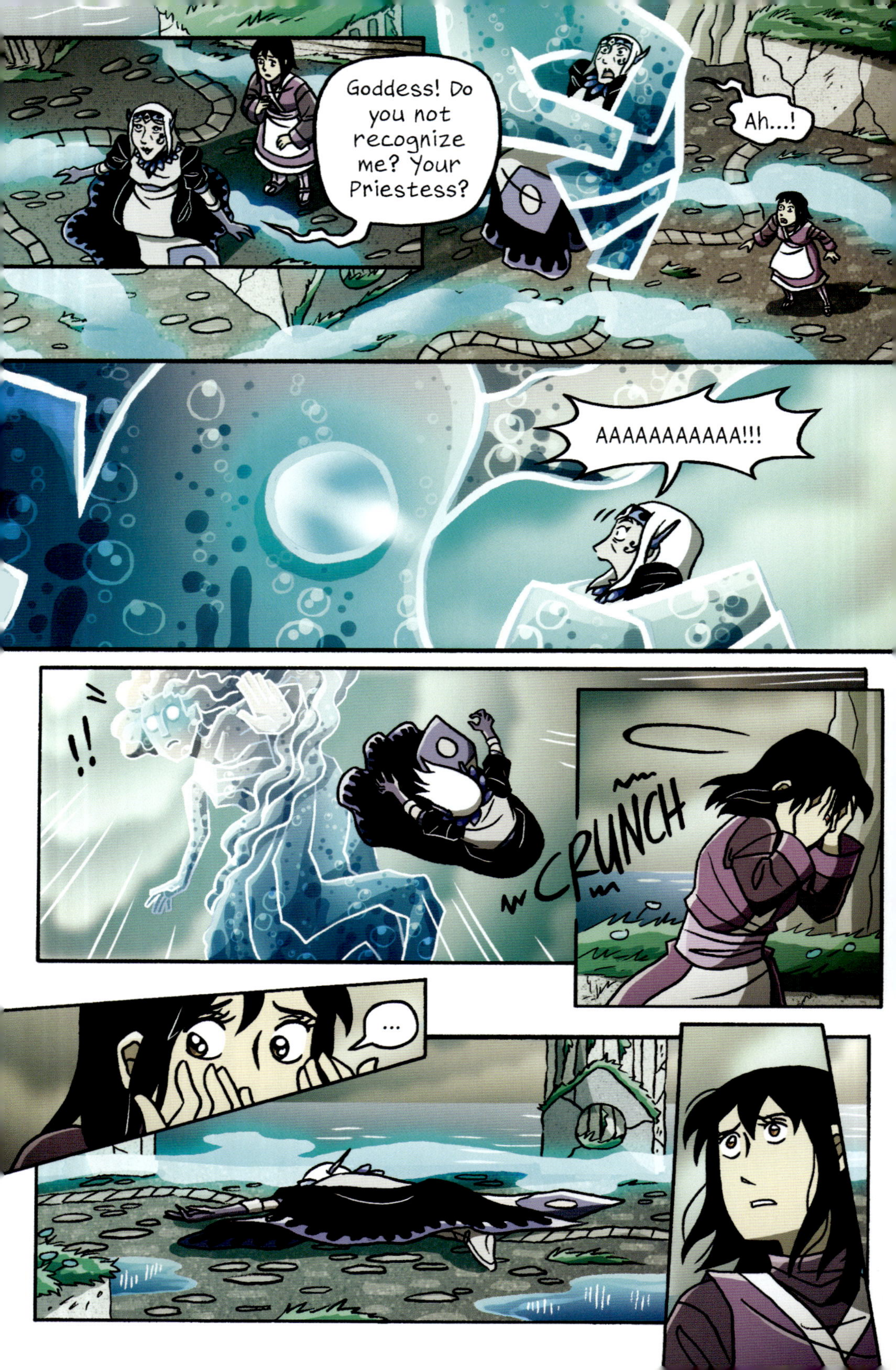
Goddess! Do you not recognize me? Your Priestess?
Ah...!
AAAAAAAAAAA!!!
!!
CRUNCH
...

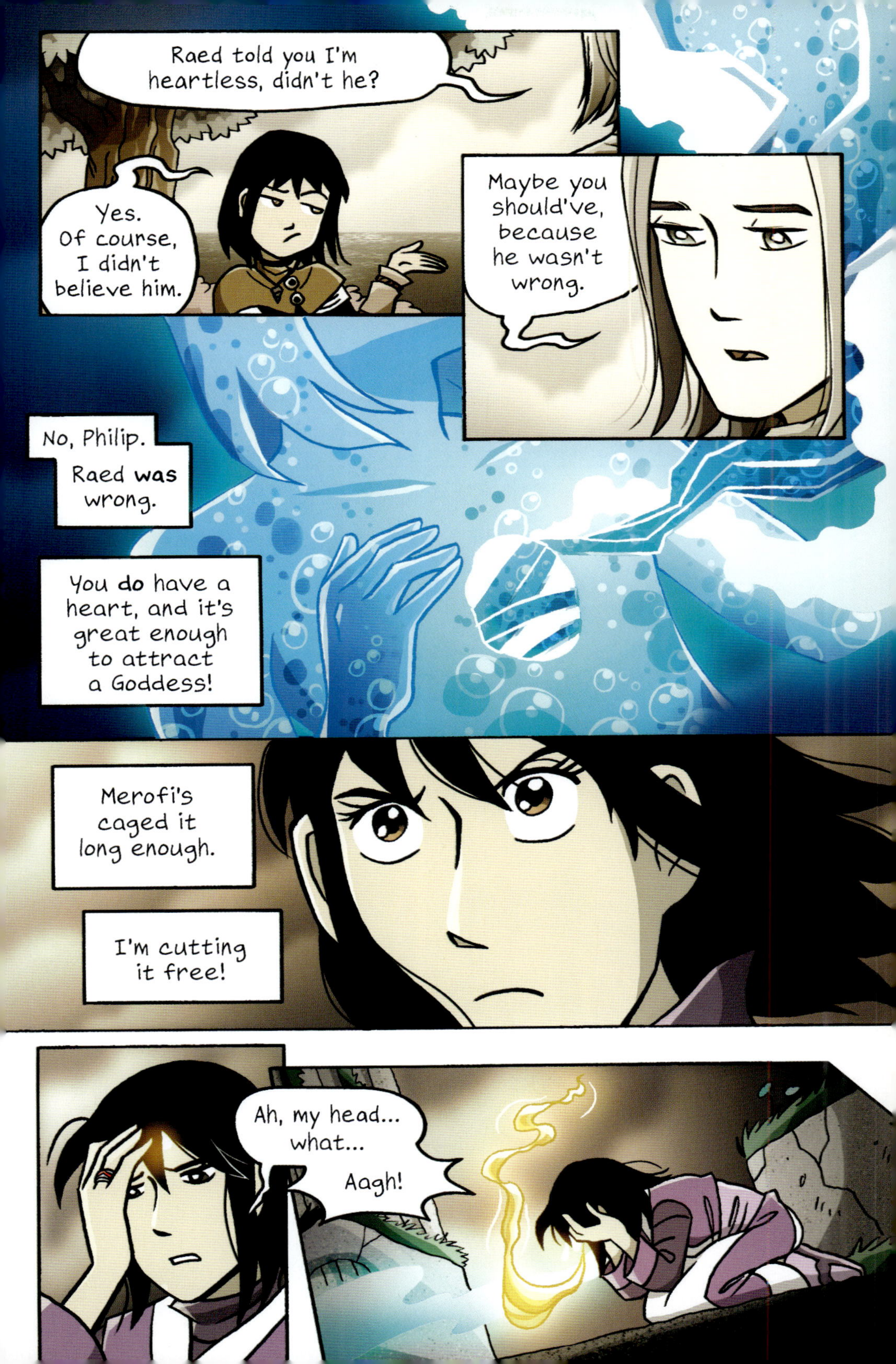
Raed told you I'm heartless, didn't he?
Yes. Of course, I didn't believe him.
Maybe you should've, because he wasn't wrong.
No, Philip.
Raed **was** wrong.
You **do** have a heart, and it's great enough to attract a Goddess!
Merofi's caged it long enough.
I'm cutting it free!
Ah, my head... what...
Aagh!

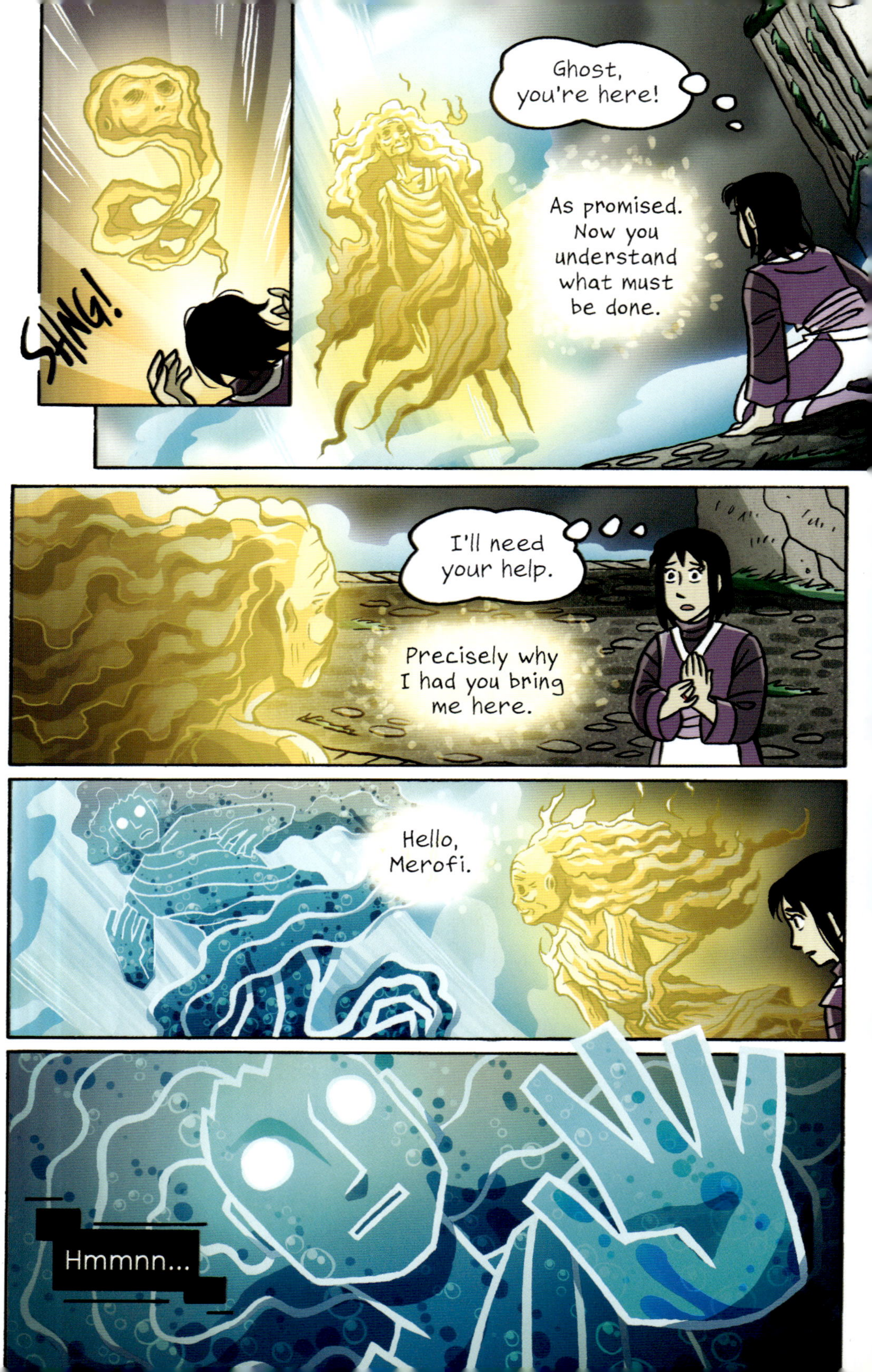
SHNG!
Ghost, you're here!
As promised. Now you understand what must be done.
I'll need your help.
Precisely why I had you bring me here.
Hello, Merofi.
Hmmnn...

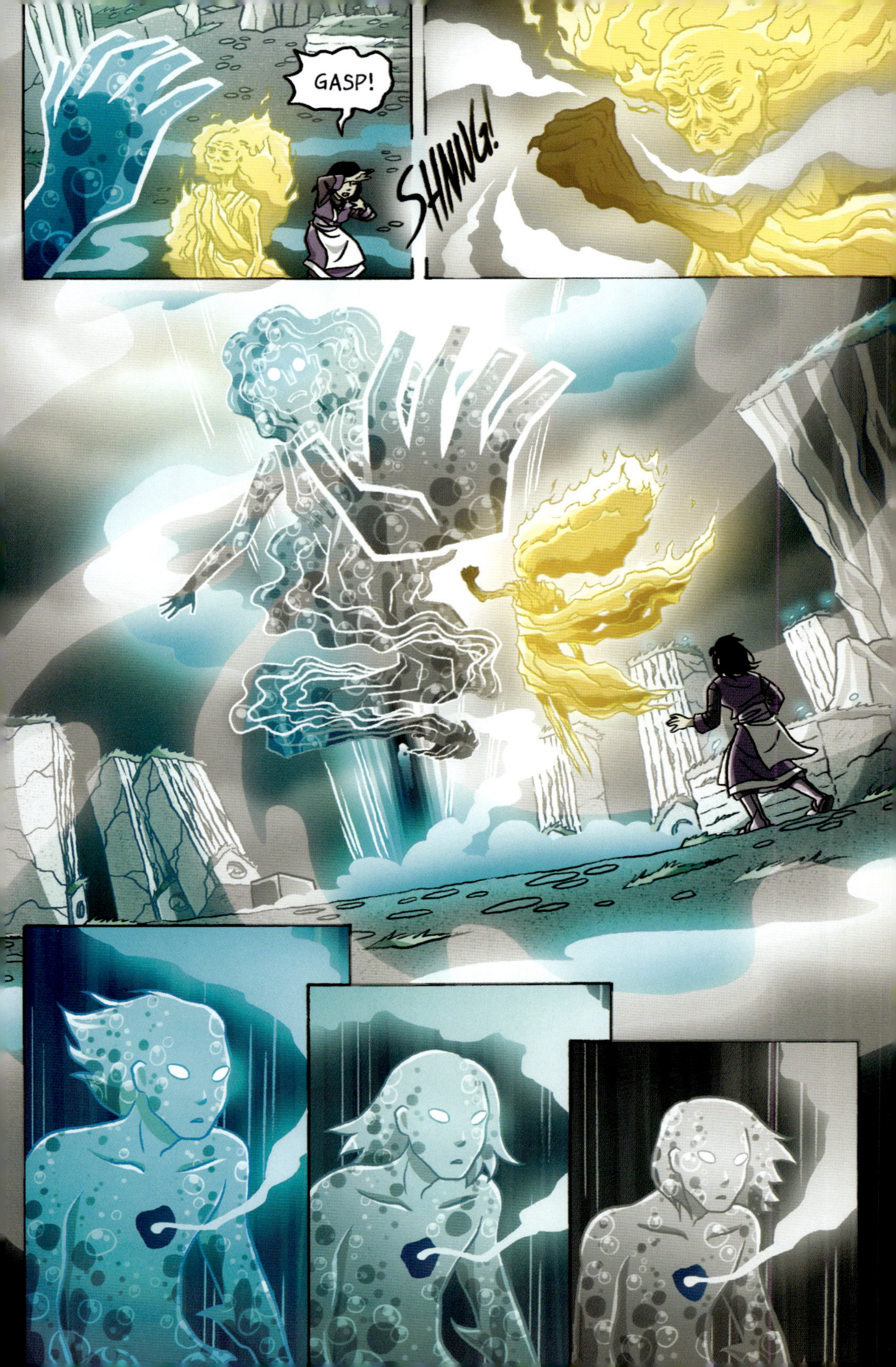
GASP!
SHNNG!

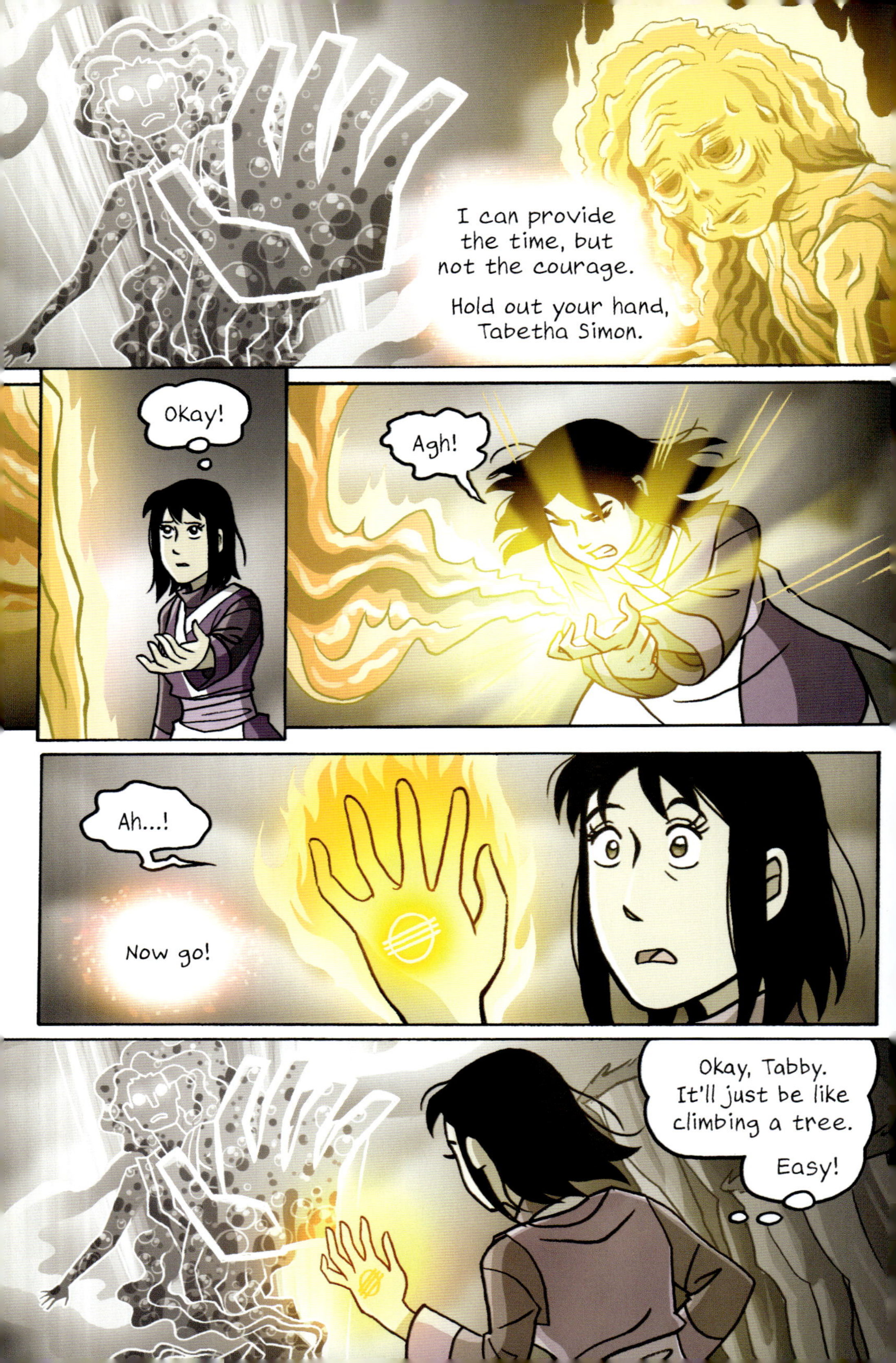
I can provide the time, but not the courage.
Hold out your hand, Tabetha Simon.
Okay!
Agh!
Ah...!
Now go!
Okay, Tabby. It'll just be like climbing a tree.
Easy!

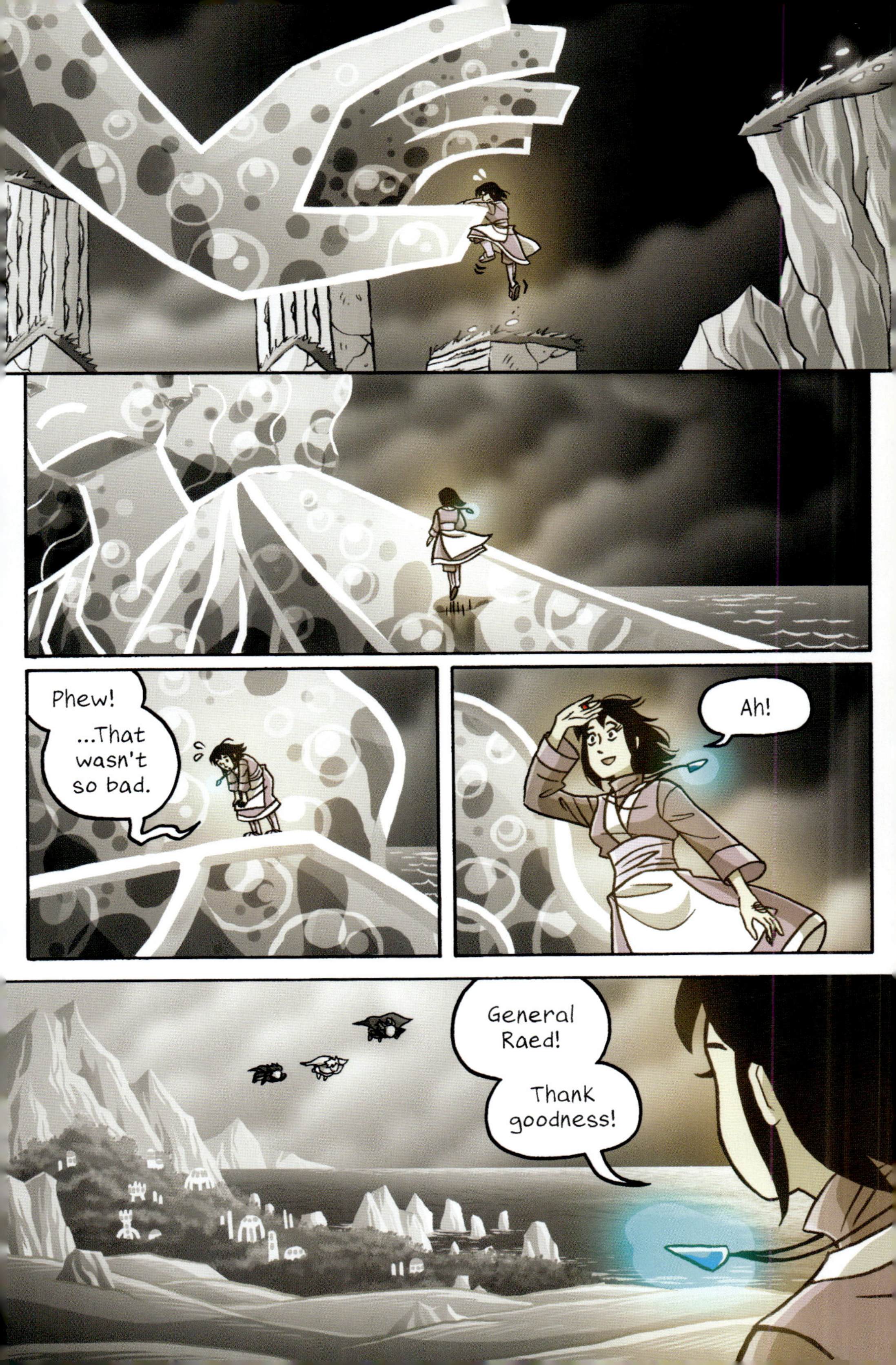
Phew! ...That wasn't so bad.
Ah!
General Raed!
Thank goodness!

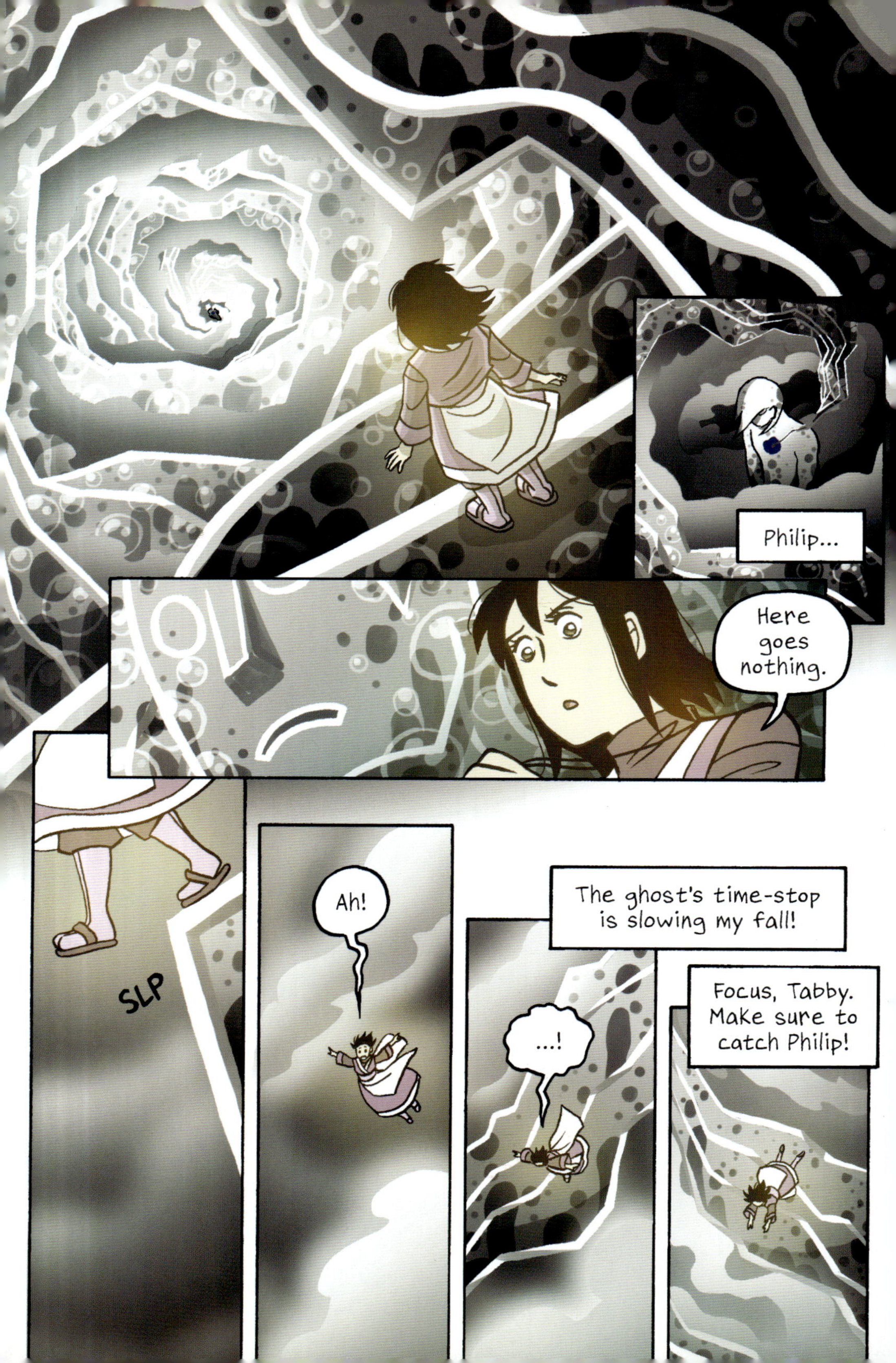
Philip...
Here goes nothing.
SLP
Ah!
The ghost's time-stop is slowing my fall!
...!
Focus, Tabby. Make sure to catch Philip!

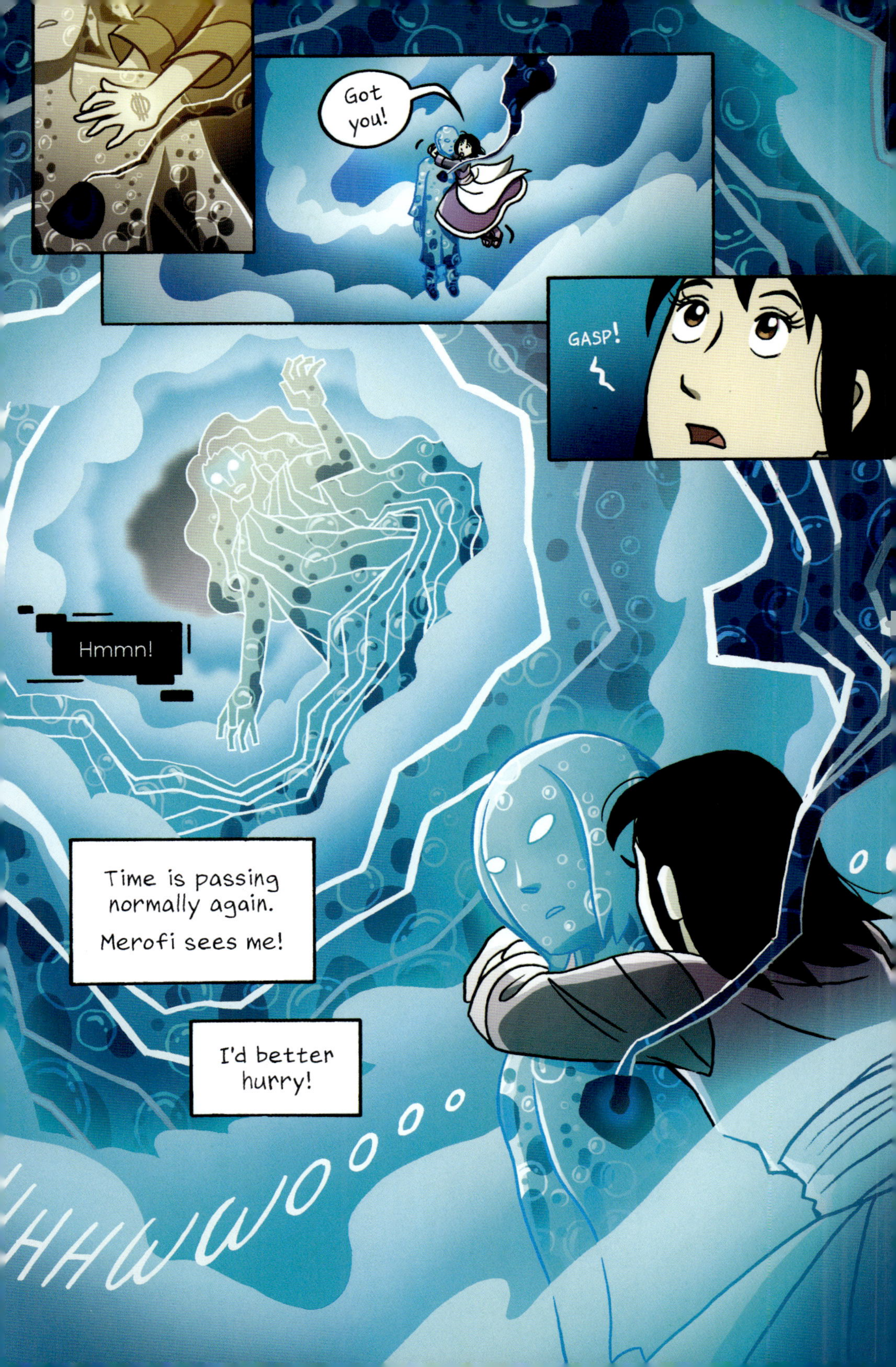

Got you!
GASP!
Hmmn!
Time is passing normally again.
Merofi sees me!
I'd better hurry!
HHWOOOOOO

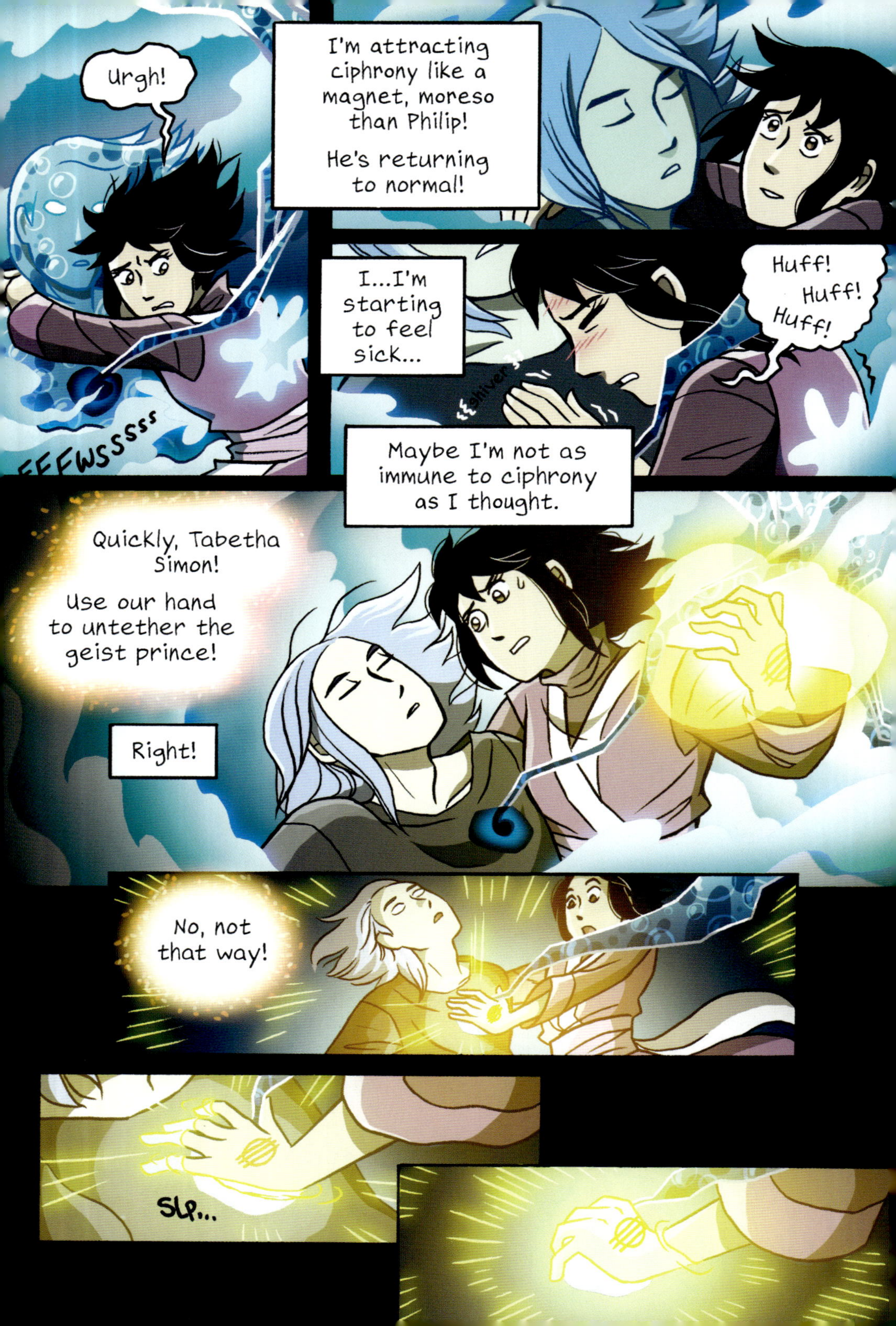
Urgh!
I'm attracting ciphrony like a magnet, moreso than Philip!
He's returning to normal!
I...I'm starting to feel sick...
shiver
Huff! Huff! Huff!
Maybe I'm not as immune to ciphrony as I thought.
Quickly, Tabetha Simon!
Use our hand to untether the geist prince!
Right!
No, not that way!
SLP...

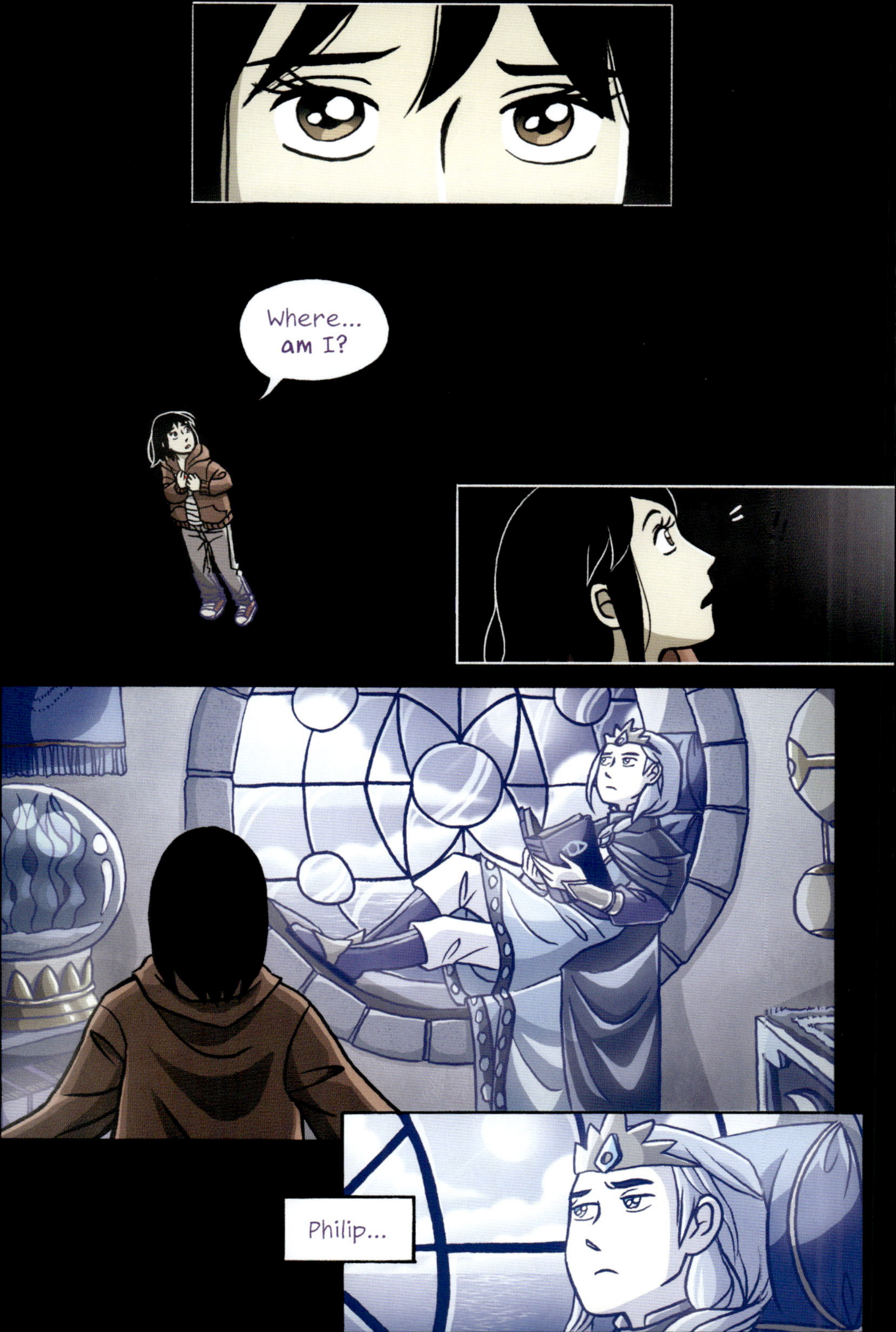
Where... am I?
Philip...

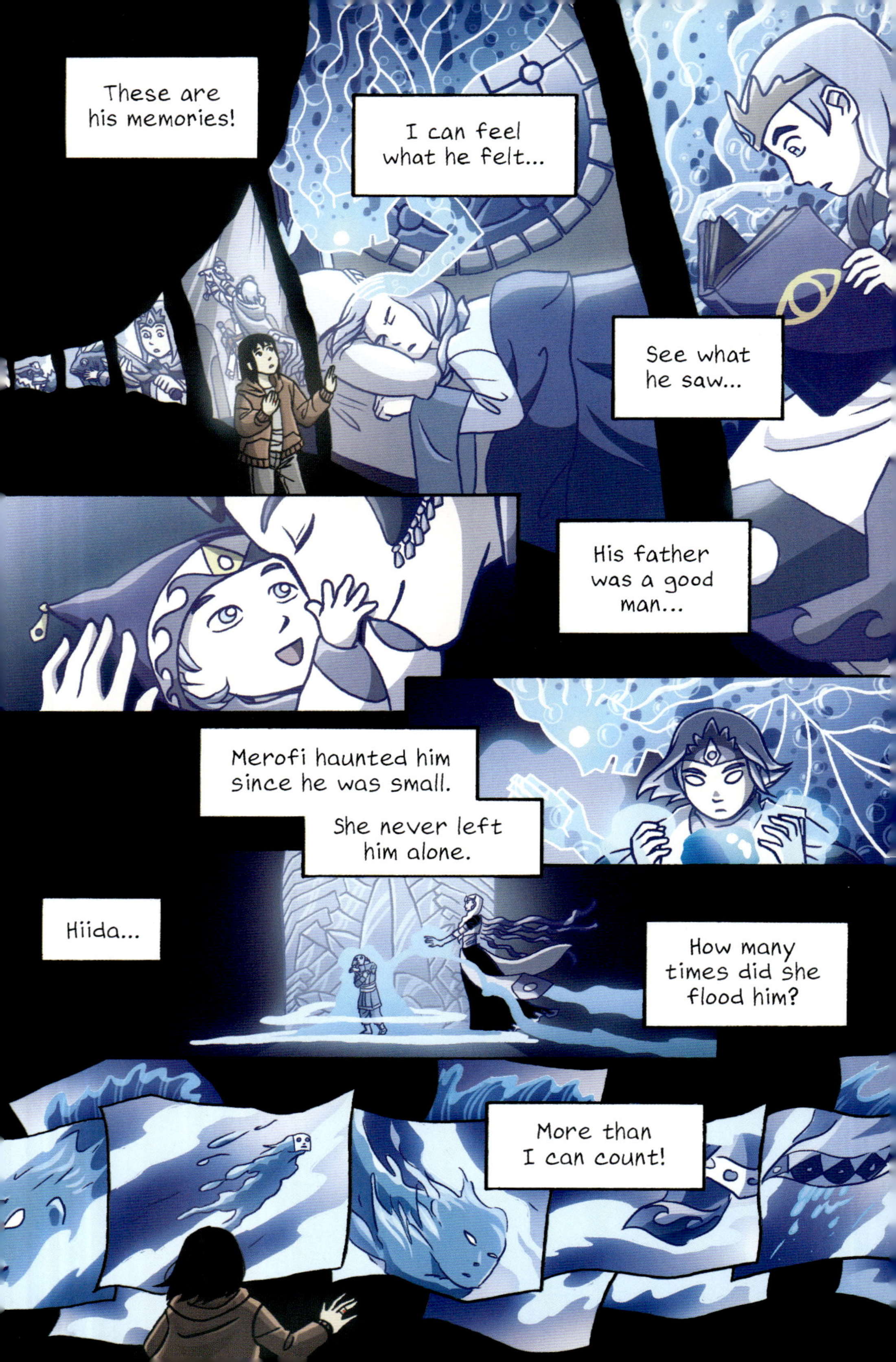
These are his memories!
I can feel what he felt...
See what he saw...
His father was a good man...
Merofi haunted him since he was small.
She never left him alone.
Hiida...
How many times did she flood him?
More than I can count!

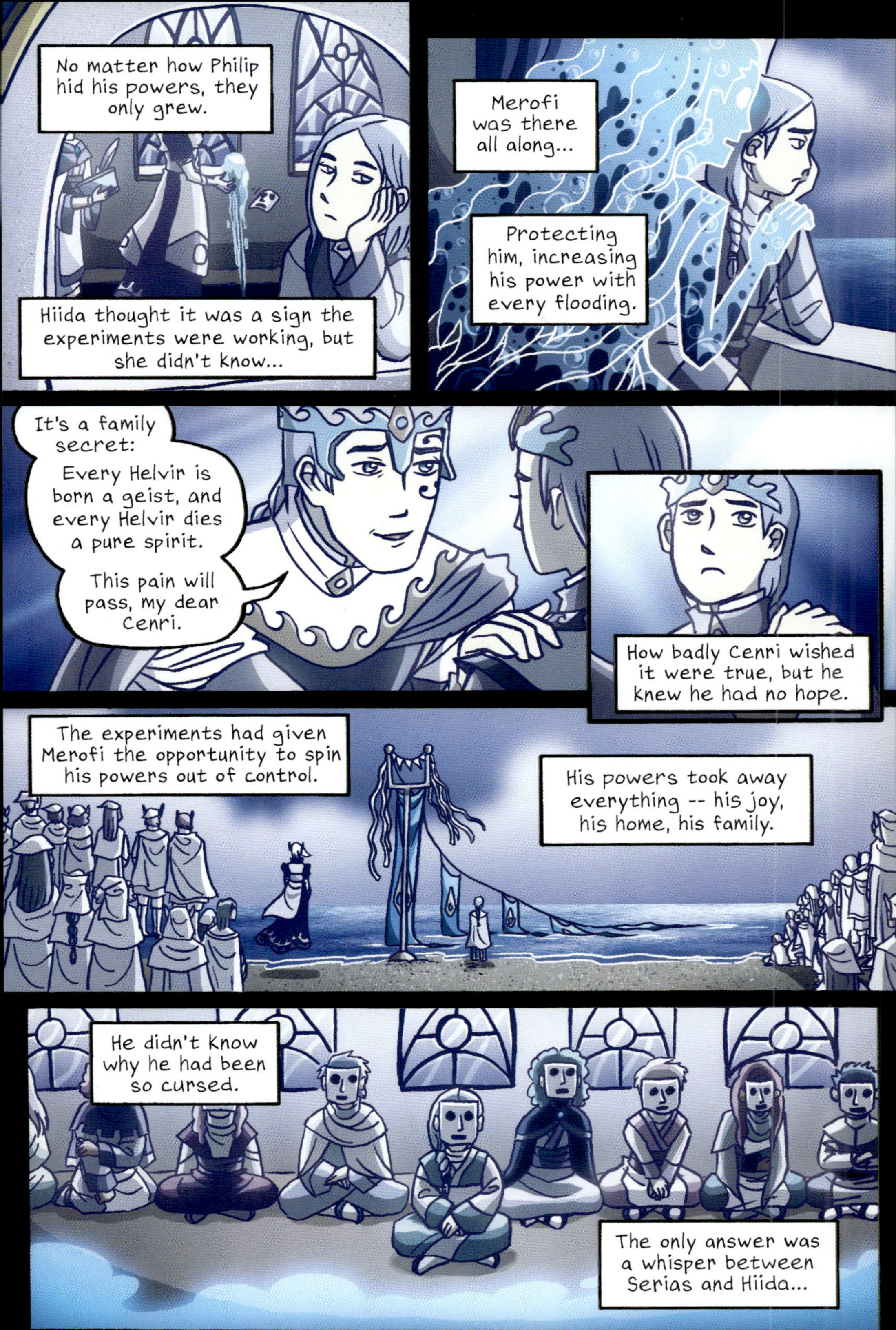
No matter how Philip hid his powers, they only grew.
Hiida thought it was a sign the experiments were working, but she didn't know...
Merofi was there all along...
Protecting him, increasing his power with every flooding.
It's a family secret:
Every Helvir is born a geist, and every Helvir dies a pure spirit.
This pain will pass, my dear Cenri.
How badly Cenri wished it were true, but he knew he had no hope.
The experiments had given Merofi the opportunity to spin his powers out of control.
His powers took away everything -- his joy, his home, his family.
He didn't know why he had been so cursed.
The only answer was a whisper between Serias and Hiida...

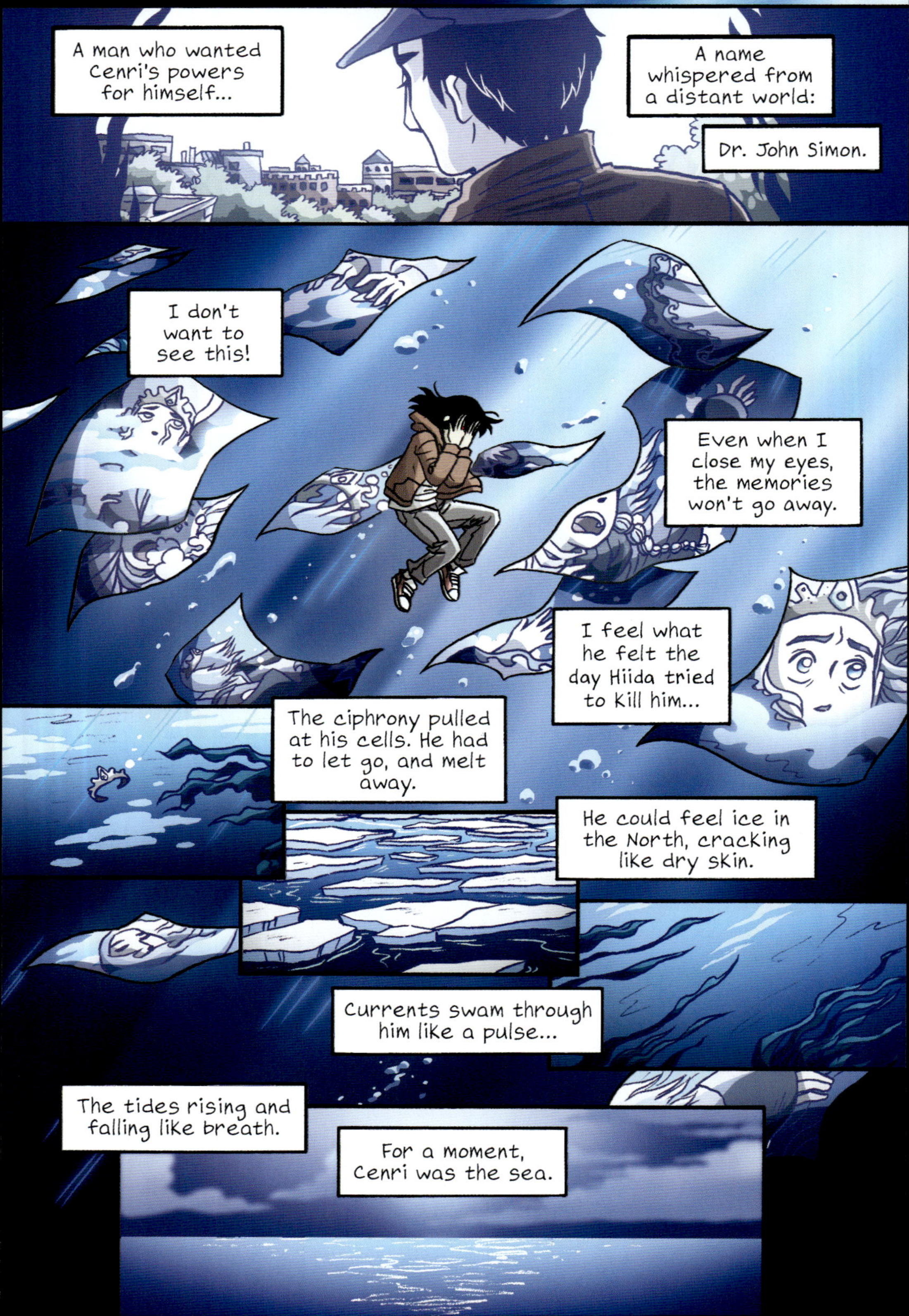
A man who wanted Cenri's powers for himself...
A name whispered from a distant world:
Dr. John Simon.
I don't want to see this!
Even when I close my eyes, the memories won't go away.
I feel what he felt the day Hiida tried to kill him...
The ciphrony pulled at his cells. He had to let go, and melt away.
He could feel ice in the North, cracking like dry skin.
Currents swam through him like a pulse...
The tides rising and falling like breath.
For a moment, Cenri was the sea.

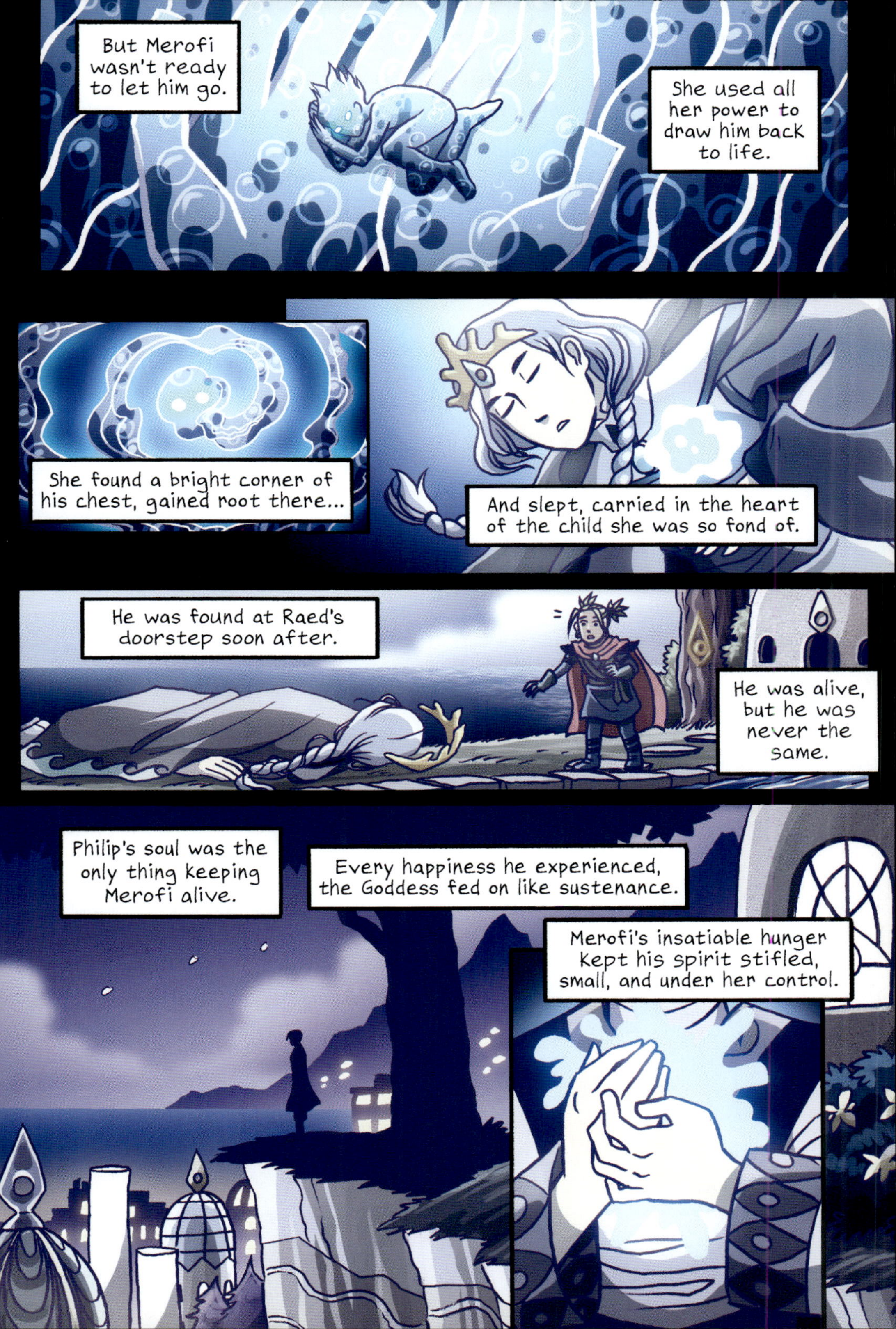
But Merofi wasn't ready to let him go.
She used all her power to draw him back to life.
She found a bright corner of his chest, gained root there...
And slept, carried in the heart of the child she was so fond of.
He was found at Raed's doorstep soon after.
He was alive, but he was never the same.
Philip's soul was the only thing keeping Merofi alive.
Every happiness he experienced, the Goddess fed on like sustenance.
Merofi's insatiable hunger kept his spirit stifled, small, and under her control.

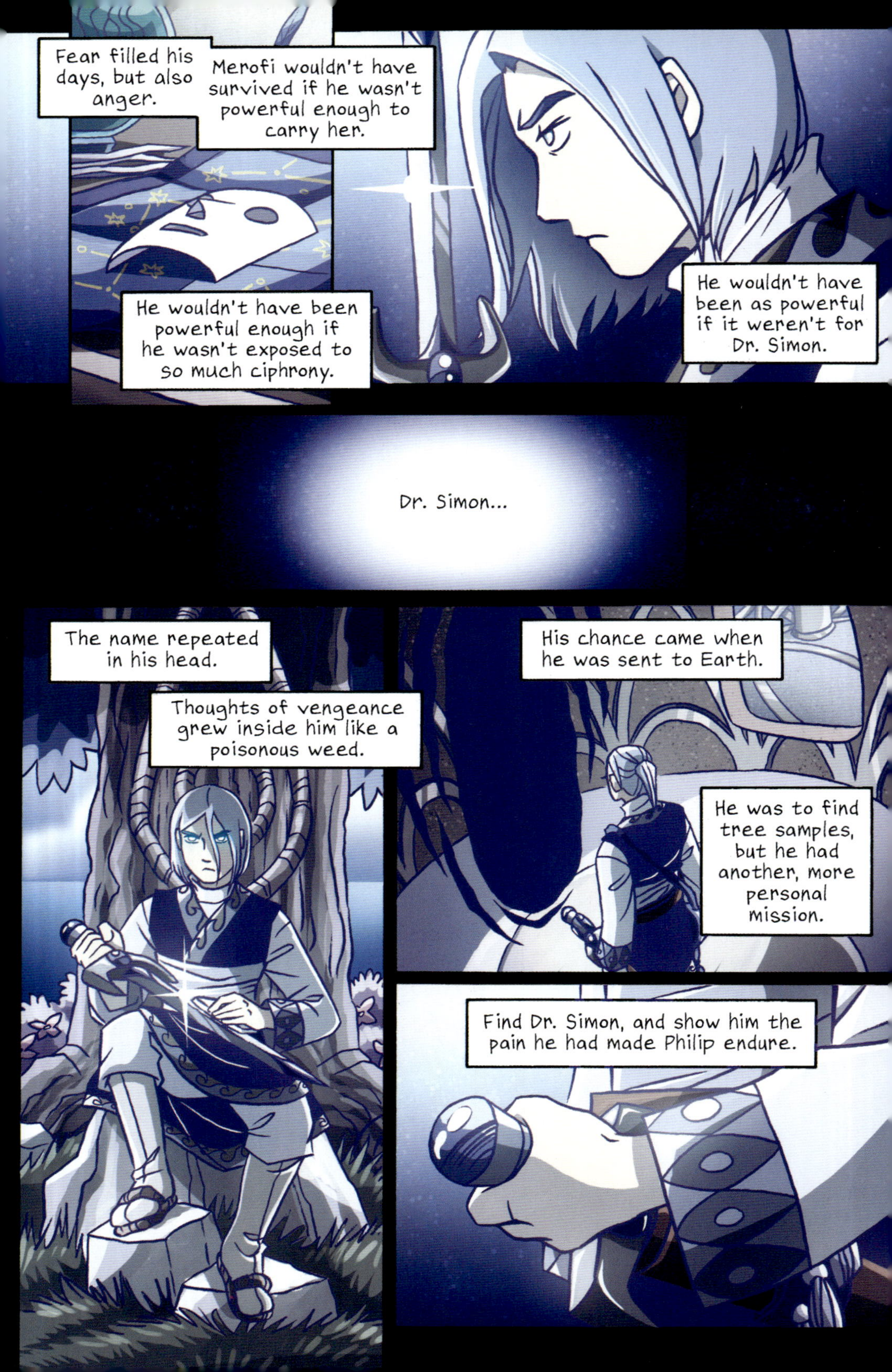
Fear filled his days, but also anger.
Merofi wouldn't have survived if he wasn't powerful enough to carry her.
He wouldn't have been powerful enough if he wasn't exposed to so much ciphrony.
He wouldn't have been as powerful if it weren't for Dr. Simon.
Dr. Simon...
The name repeated in his head.
Thoughts of vengeance grew inside him like a poisonous weed.
His chance came when he was sent to Earth.
He was to find tree samples, but he had another, more personal mission.
Find Dr. Simon, and show him the pain he had made Philip endure.

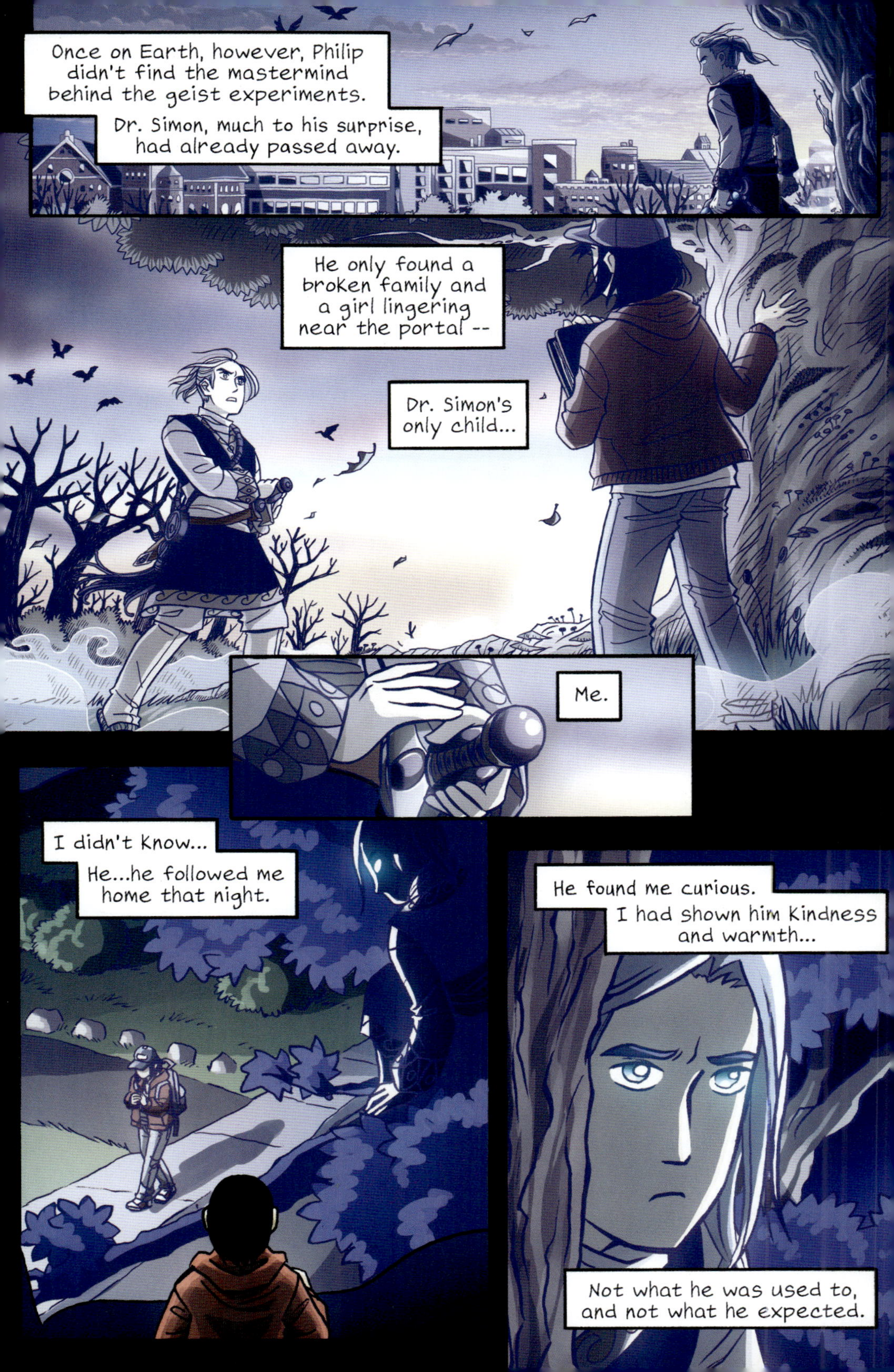
Once on Earth, however, Philip didn't find the mastermind behind the geist experiments.
Dr. Simon, much to his surprise, had already passed away.
He only found a broken family and a girl lingering near the portal --
Dr. Simon's only child...
Me.
I didn't know...
He...he followed me home that night.
He found me curious.
I had shown him kindness and warmth...
Not what he was used to, and not what he expected.

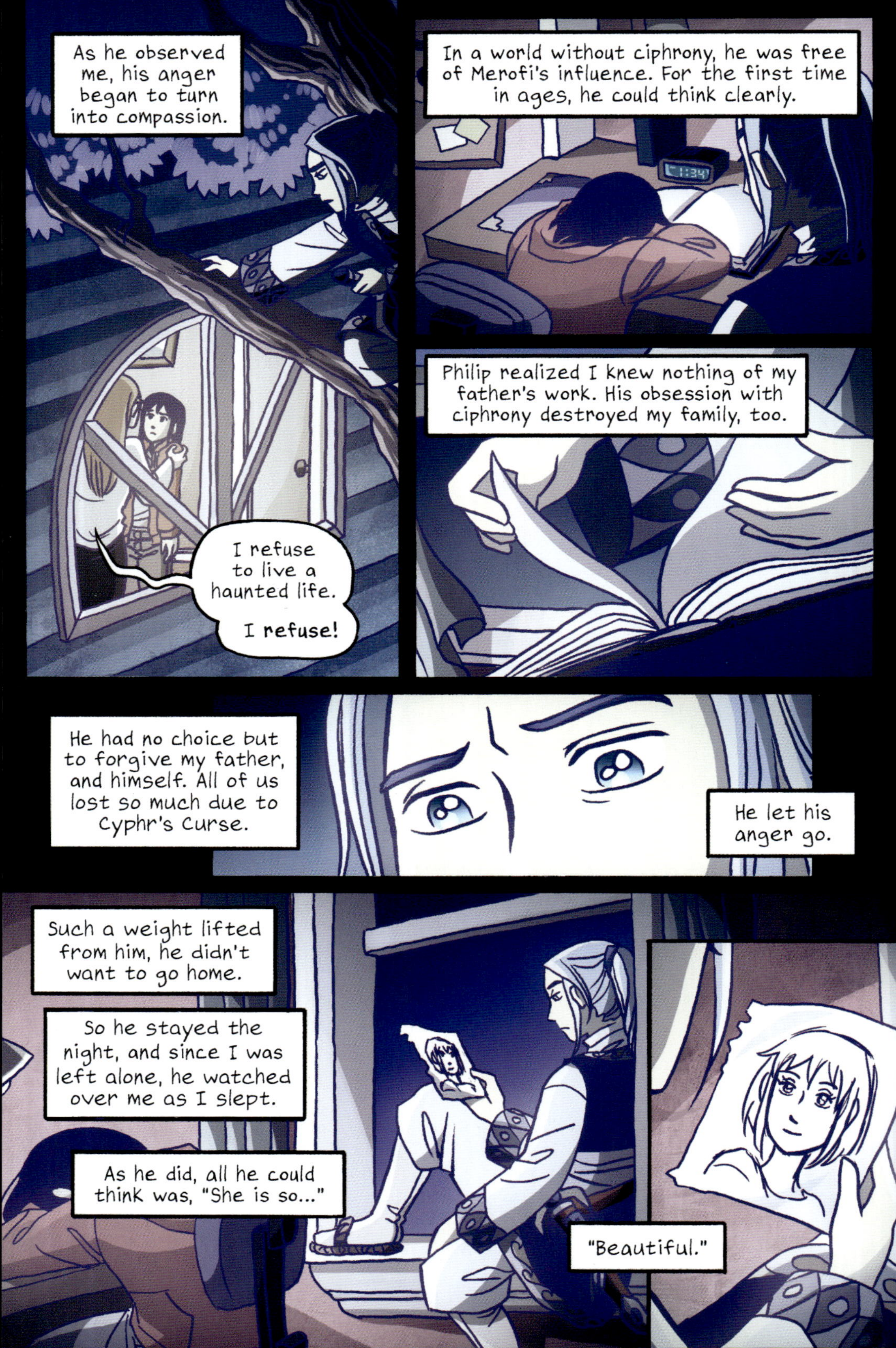
As he observed me, his anger began to turn into compassion.
I refuse to live a haunted life.
I refuse!
In a world without ciphrony, he was free of Merofi's influence. For the first time in ages, he could think clearly.
1:34
Philip realized I knew nothing of my father's work. His obsession with ciphrony destroyed my family, too.
He had no choice but to forgive my father, and himself. All of us lost so much due to Cyphr's Curse.
He let his anger go.
Such a weight lifted from him, he didn't want to go home.
So he stayed the night, and since I was left alone, he watched over me as I slept.
As he did, all he could think was, "She is so..."
"Beautiful."

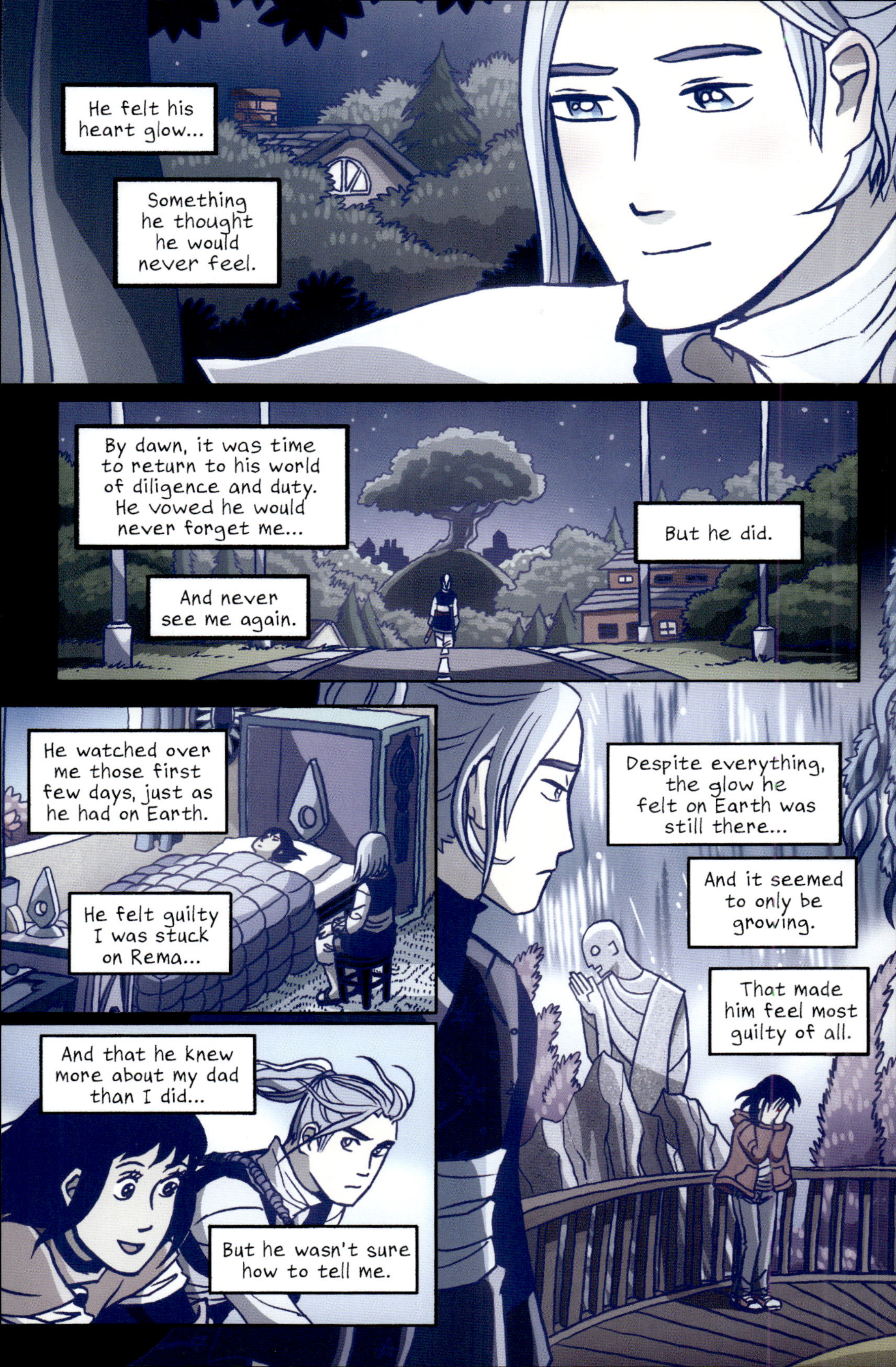
He felt his heart glow...
Something he thought he would never feel.
By dawn, it was time to return to his world of diligence and duty. He vowed he would never forget me...
And never see me again.
But he did.
He watched over me those first few days, just as he had on Earth.
He felt guilty I was stuck on Rema...
And that he knew more about my dad than I did...
But he wasn't sure how to tell me.
Despite everything, the glow he felt on Earth was still there...
And it seemed to only be growing.
That made him feel most guilty of all.

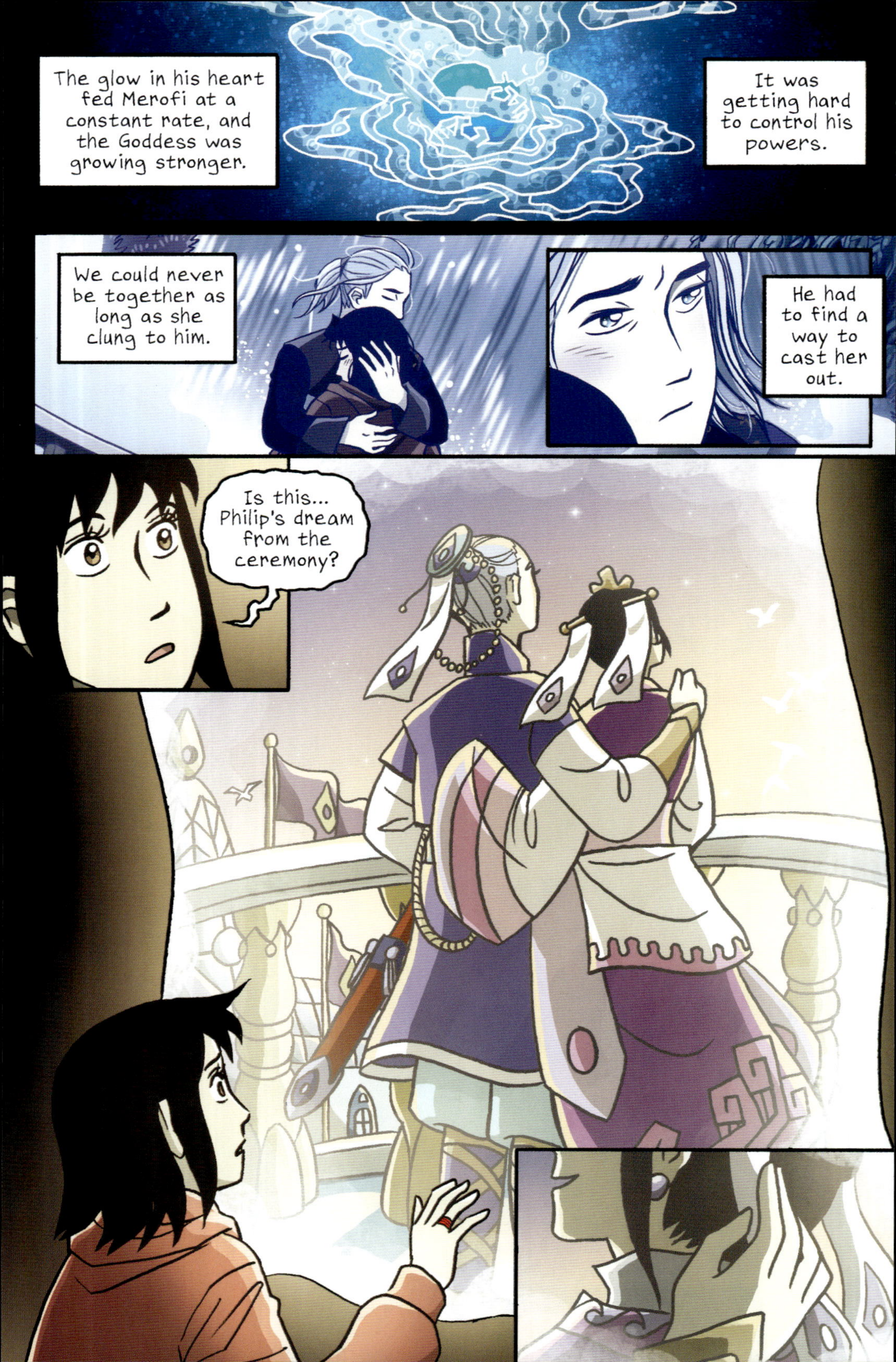

The glow in his heart fed Merofi at a constant rate, and the Goddess was growing stronger.
It was getting hard to control his powers.
We could never be together as long as she clung to him.
He had to find a way to cast her out.
Is this... Philip's dream from the ceremony?

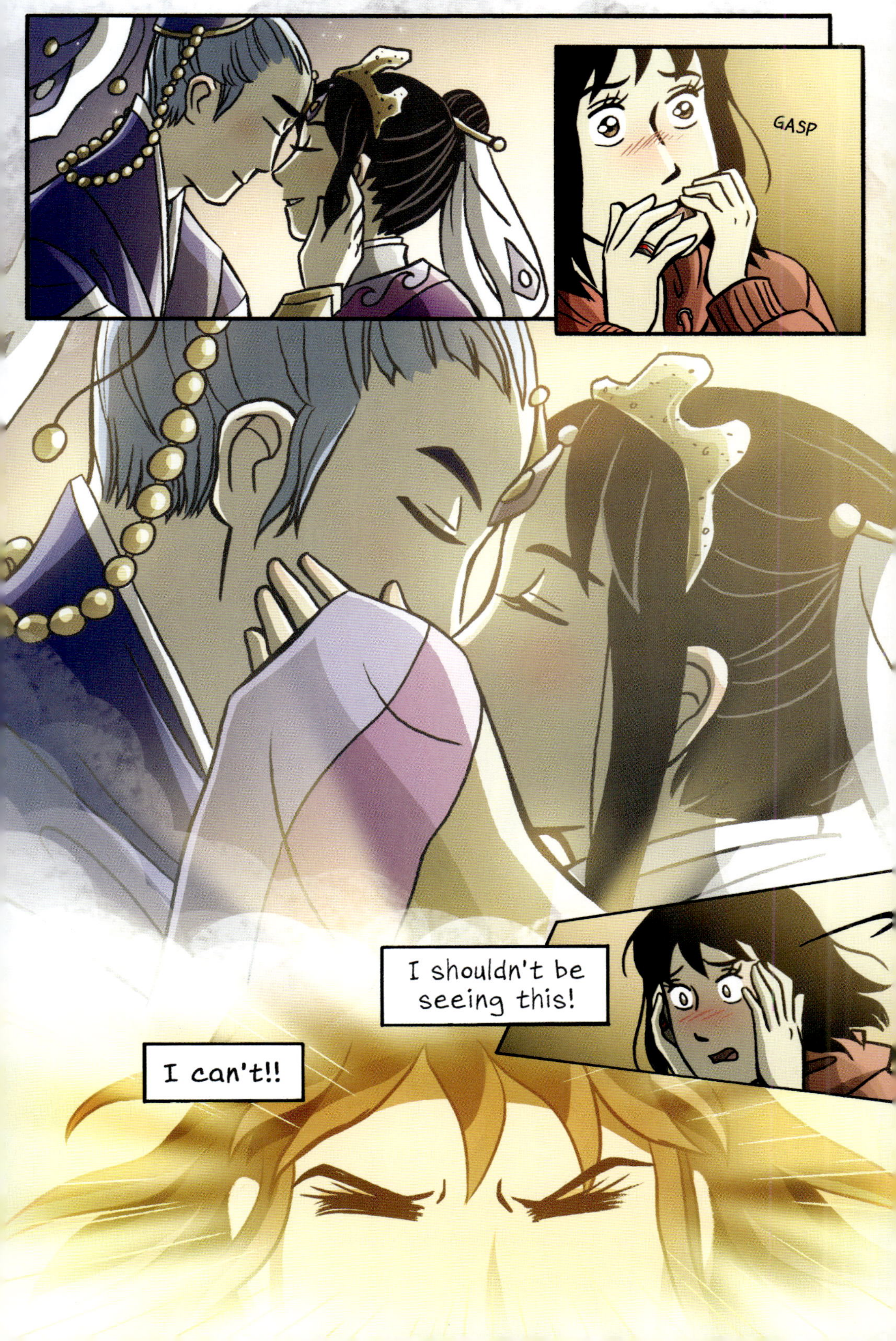
GASP
I shouldn't be seeing this!
I can't!!

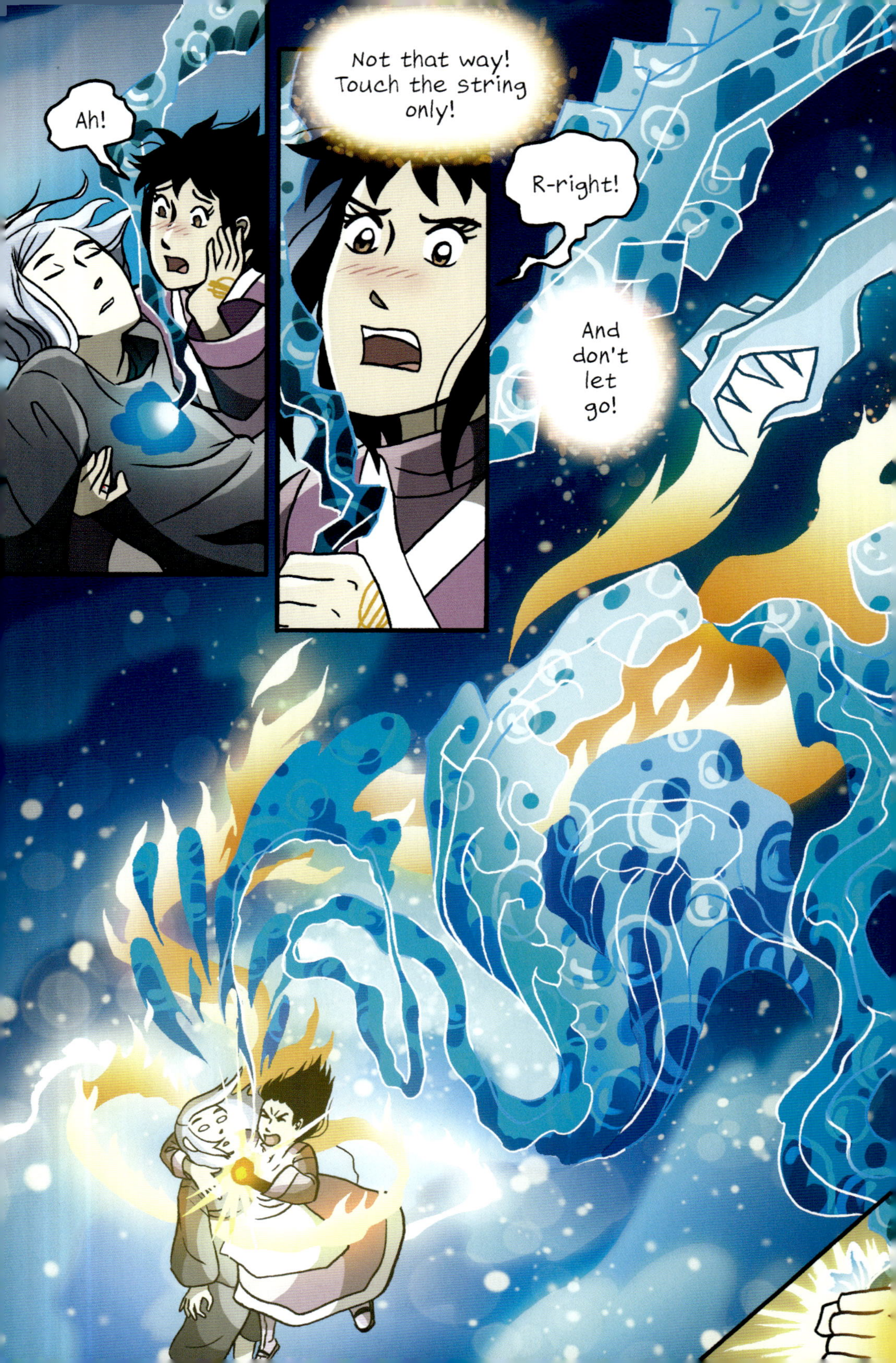
Ah!
Not that way! Touch the string only!
R-right!
And don't let go!

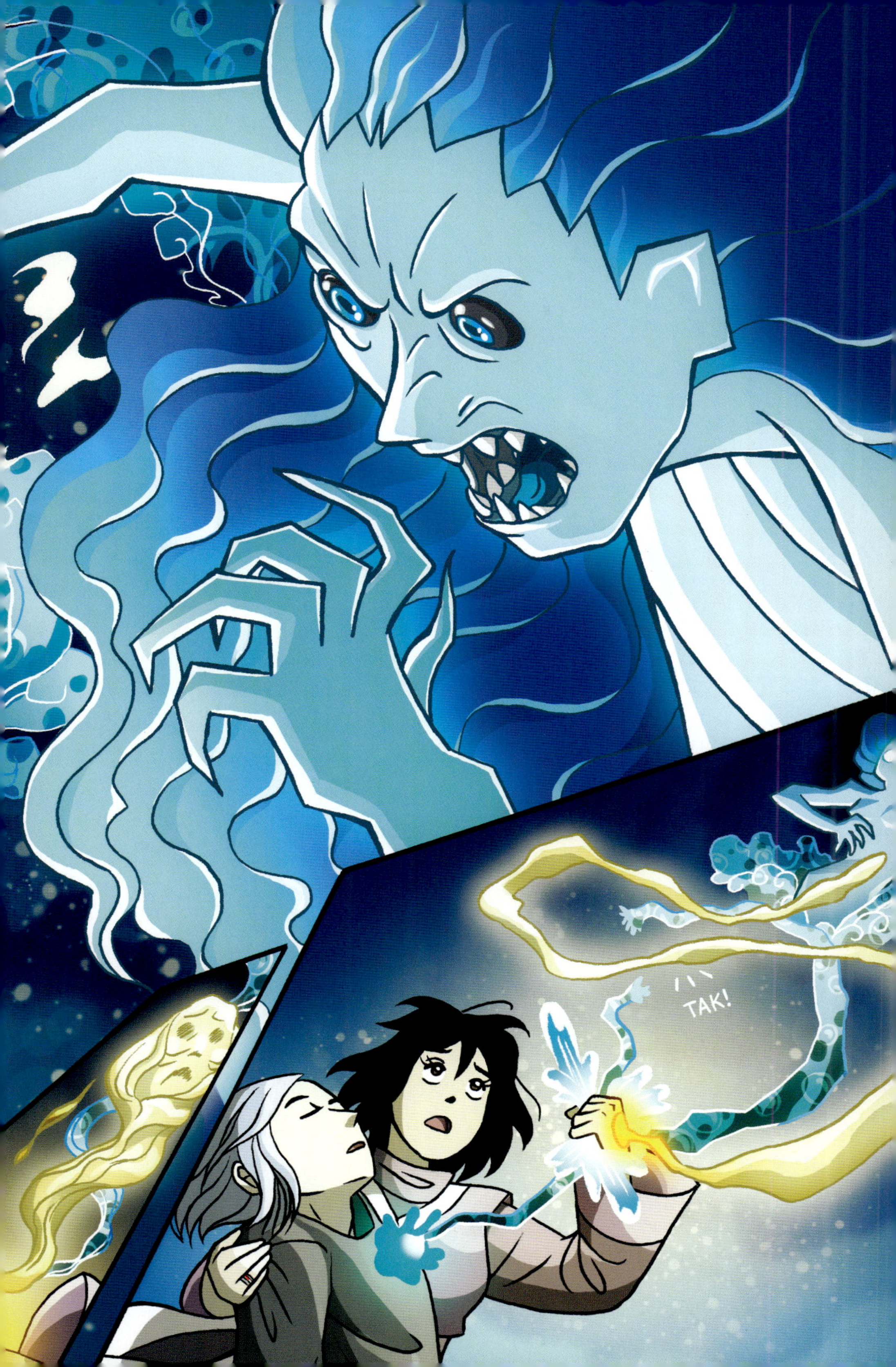
TAK!

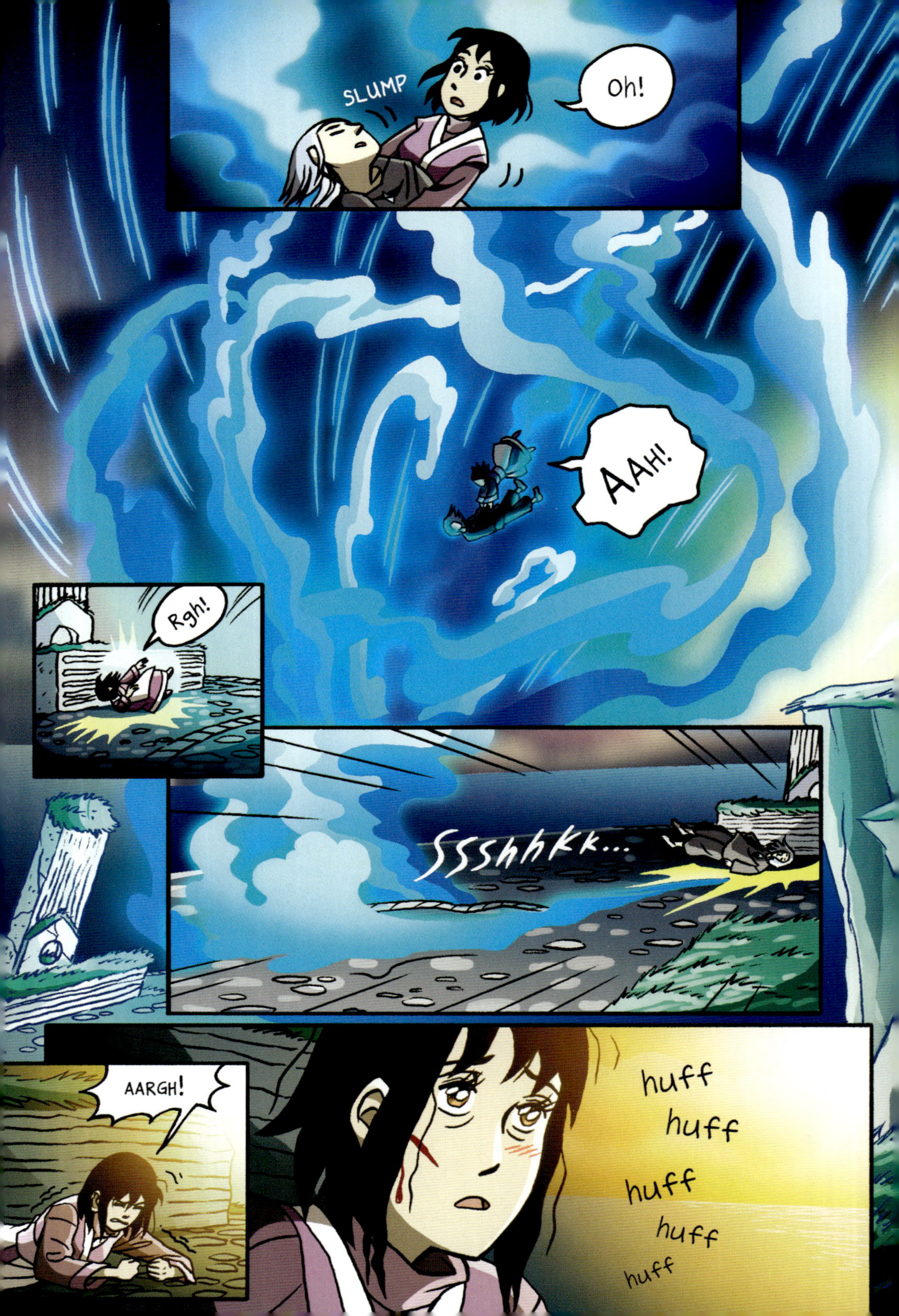
SLUMP
Oh!
AAH!
Rgh!
SSSHHKK...
AARGH!
huff
huff
huff
huff
huff

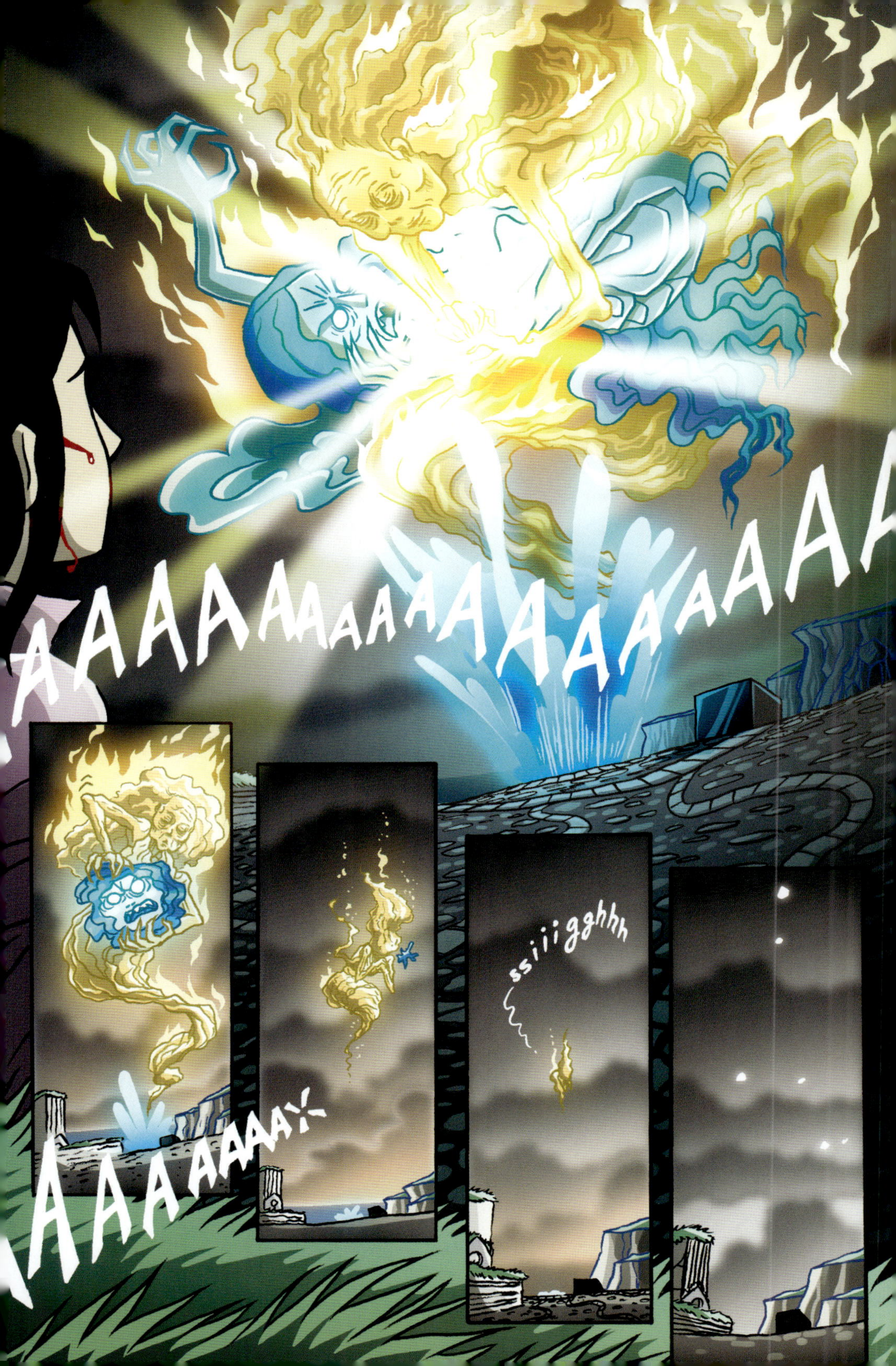
AAAAAAAAAAAAAAAAAAA
AAAAAAA
ssiiigghhh

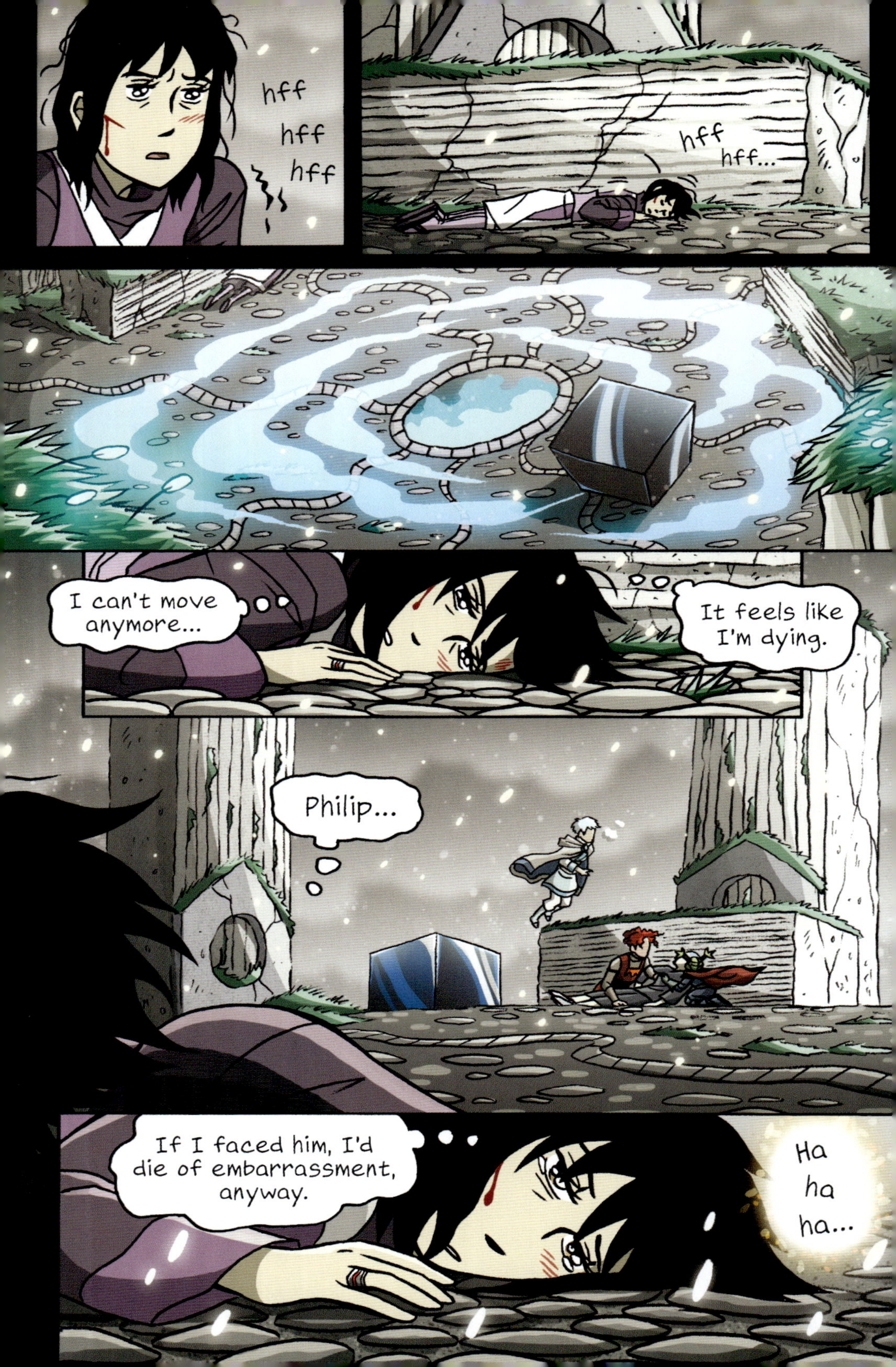
hff
hff
hff
hff
hff...
I can't move anymore...
It feels like I'm dying.
Philip...
If I faced him, I'd die of embarrassment, anyway.
Ha ha ha...

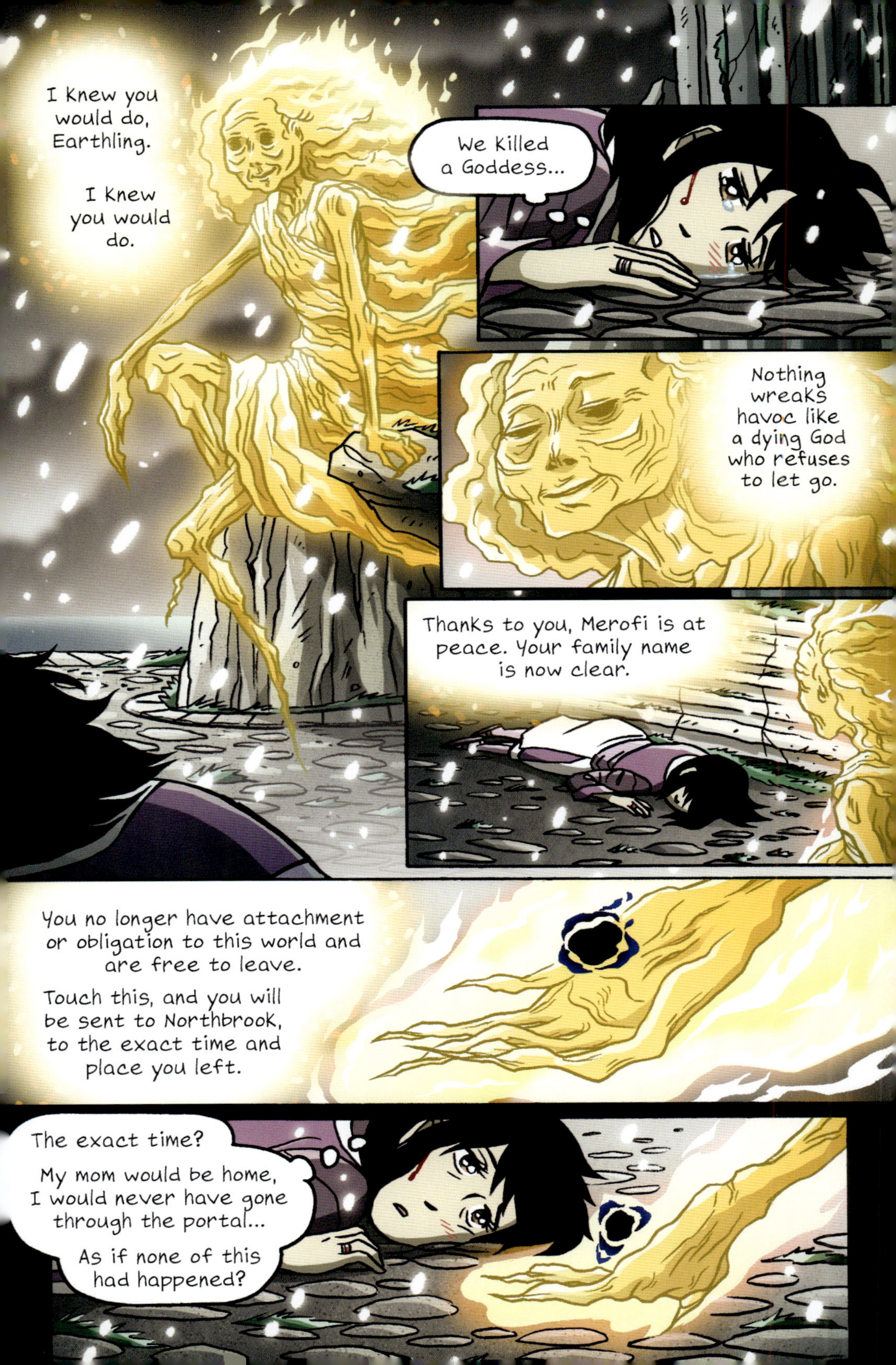
I Knew you would do, Earthling.
I Knew you would do.
We Killed a Goddess...
Nothing wreaks havoc like a dying God who refuses to let go.
Thanks to you, Merofi is at peace. Your family name is now clear.
You no longer have attachment or obligation to this world and are free to leave.
Touch this, and you will be sent to Northbrook, to the exact time and place you left.
The exact time?
My mom would be home, I would never have gone through the portal...
As if none of this had happened?

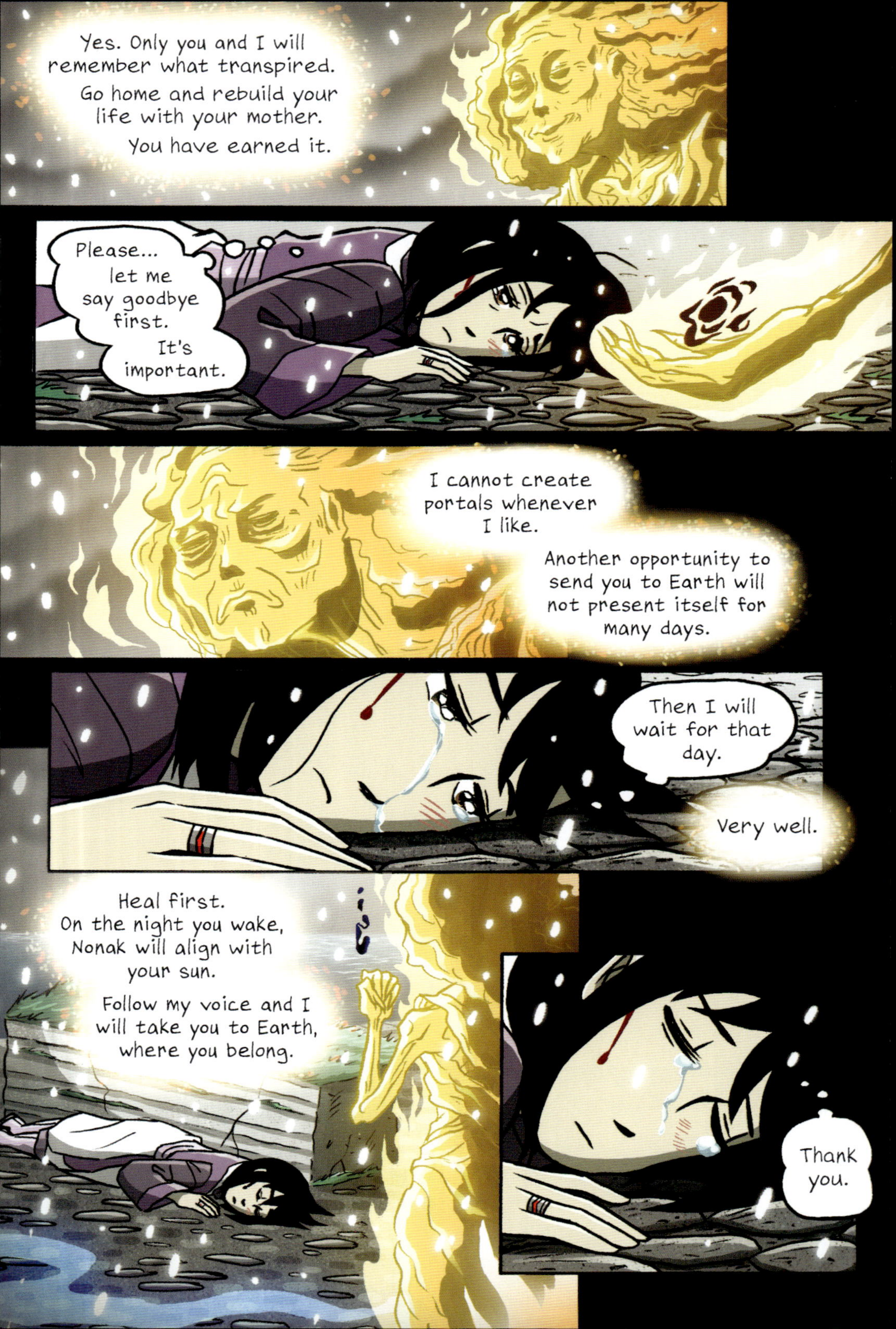

Yes. Only you and I will remember what transpired.
Go home and rebuild your life with your mother.
You have earned it.
Please... let me say goodbye first.
It's important.
I cannot create portals whenever I like.
Another opportunity to send you to Earth will not present itself for many days.
Then I will wait for that day.
Very well.
Heal first. On the night you wake, Nonak will align with your sun.
Follow my voice and I will take you to Earth, where you belong.
Thank you.

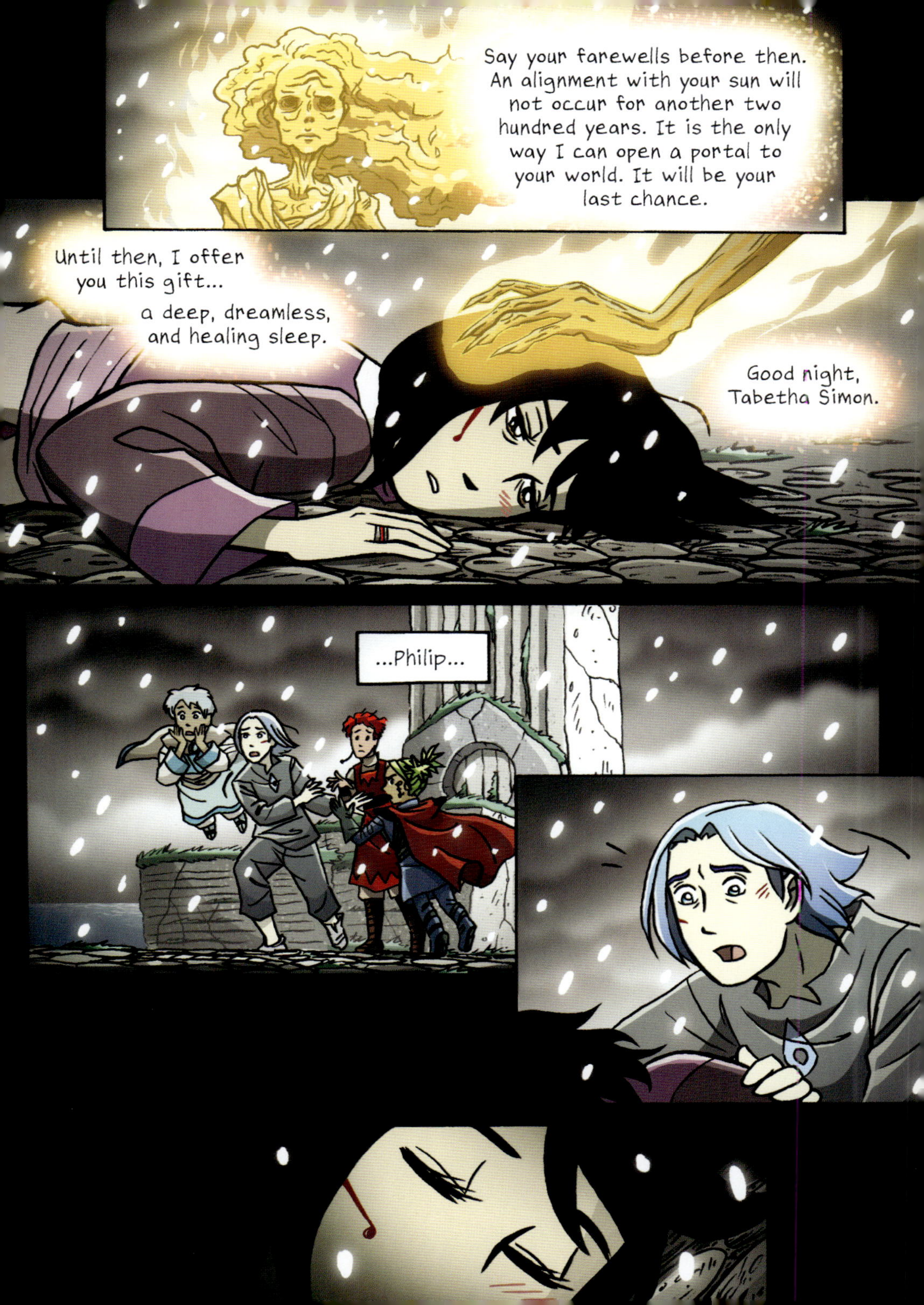
Say your farewells before then. An alignment with your sun will not occur for another two hundred years. It is the only way I can open a portal to your world. It will be your last chance.
Until then, I offer you this gift...
a deep, dreamless, and healing sleep.
Good night, Tabetha Simon.
...Philip...

PART V
THE KINGDOM OF CEREY

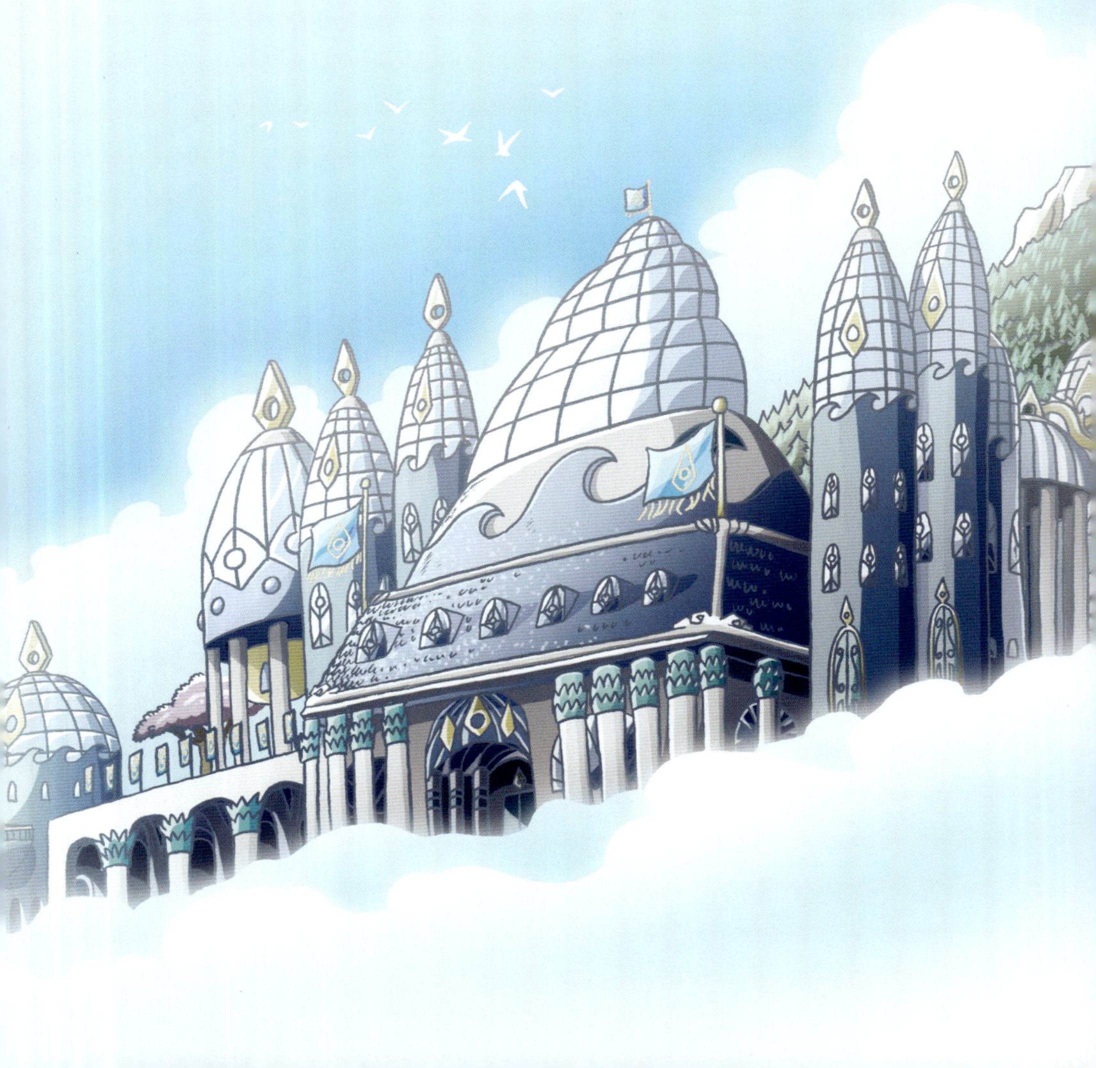

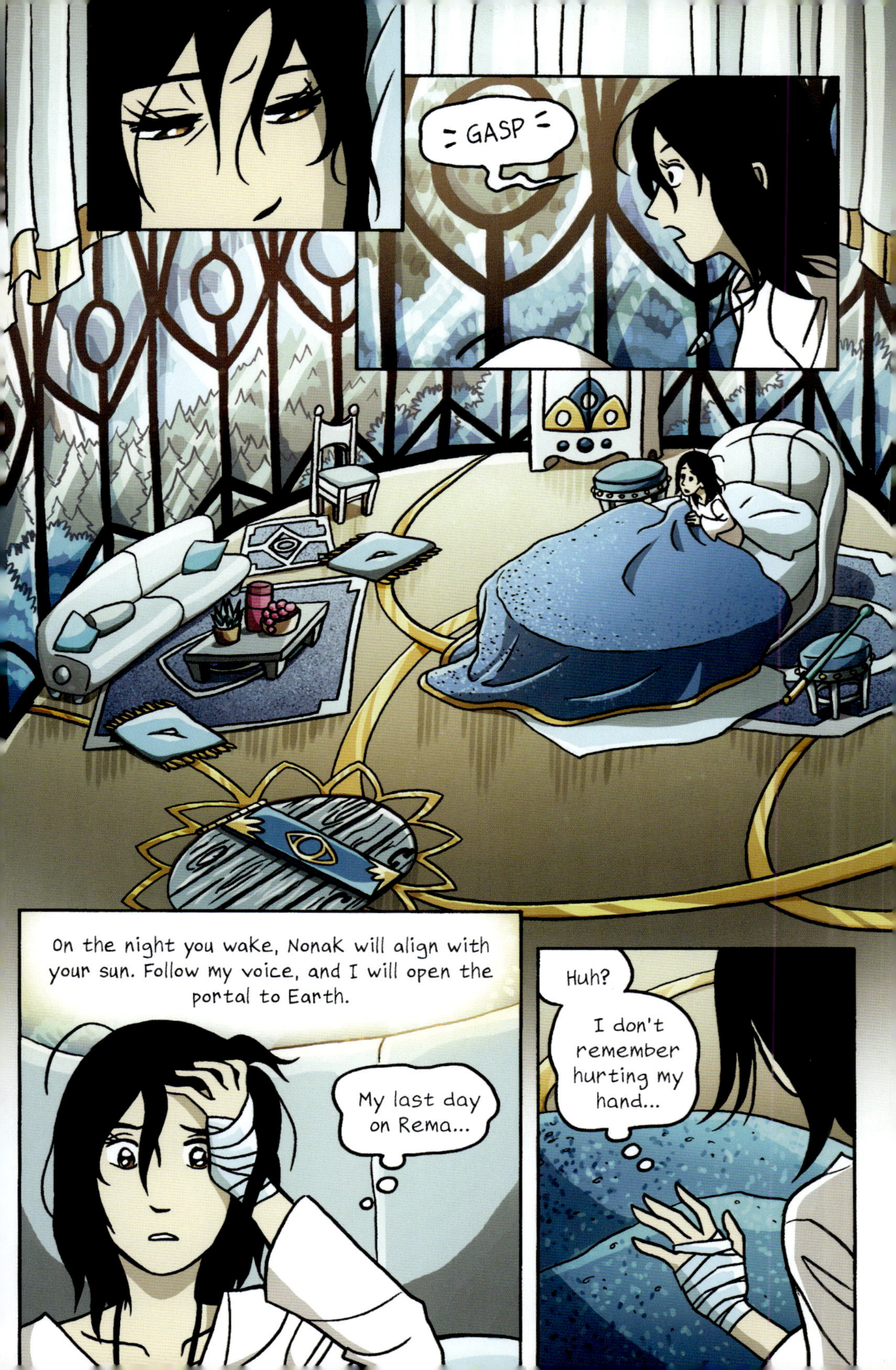

GASP
On the night you wake, Nonak will align with your sun. Follow my voice, and I will open the portal to Earth.
My last day on Rema...
Huh?
I don't remember hurting my hand...

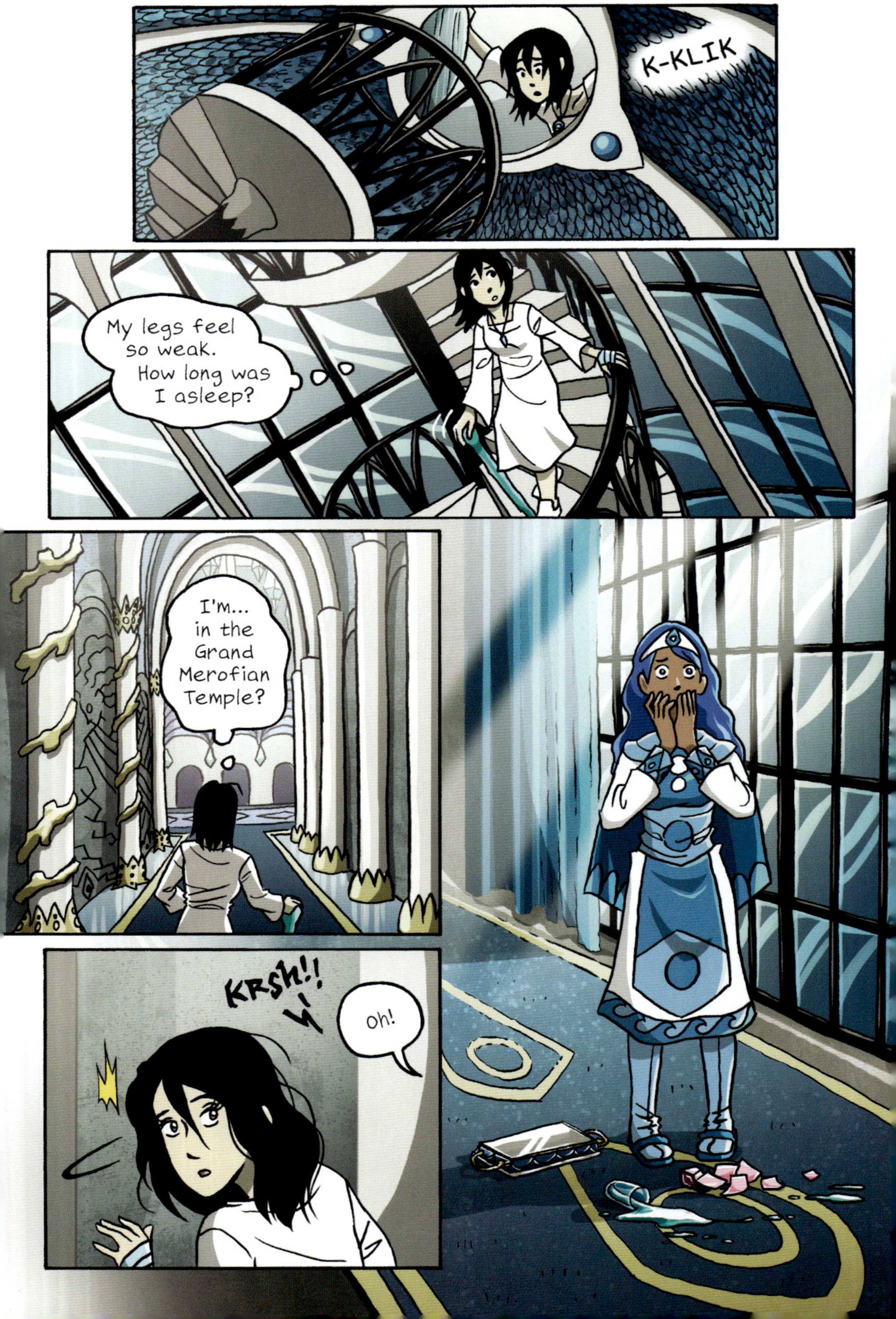
K-KLIK
My legs feel so weak. How long was I asleep?
I'm... in the Grand Merofian Temple?
KRSH!!
Oh!

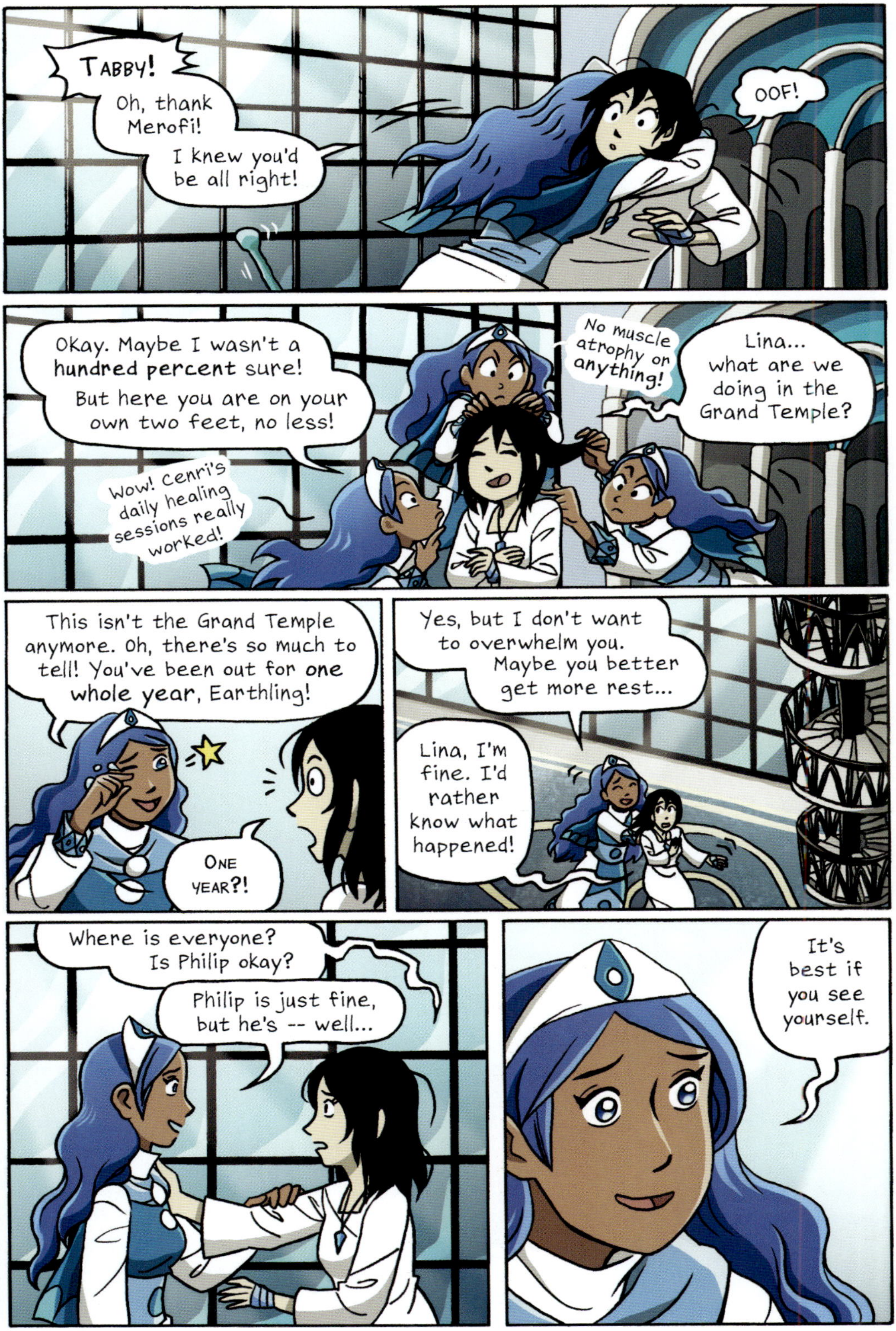
TABBY!
Oh, thank Merofi!
I knew you'd be all right!
OOF!
Okay. Maybe I wasn't a hundred percent sure!
But here you are on your own two feet, no less!
No muscle atrophy on anything!
Lina... what are we doing in the Grand Temple?
Wow! Cenri's daily healing sessions really worked!
This isn't the Grand Temple anymore. Oh, there's so much to tell! You've been out for one whole year, Earthling!
ONE YEAR?!
Yes, but I don't want to overwhelm you.
Maybe you better get more rest...
Lina, I'm fine. I'd rather know what happened!
Where is everyone? Is Philip okay?
Philip is just fine, but he's -- well...
It's best if you see yourself.

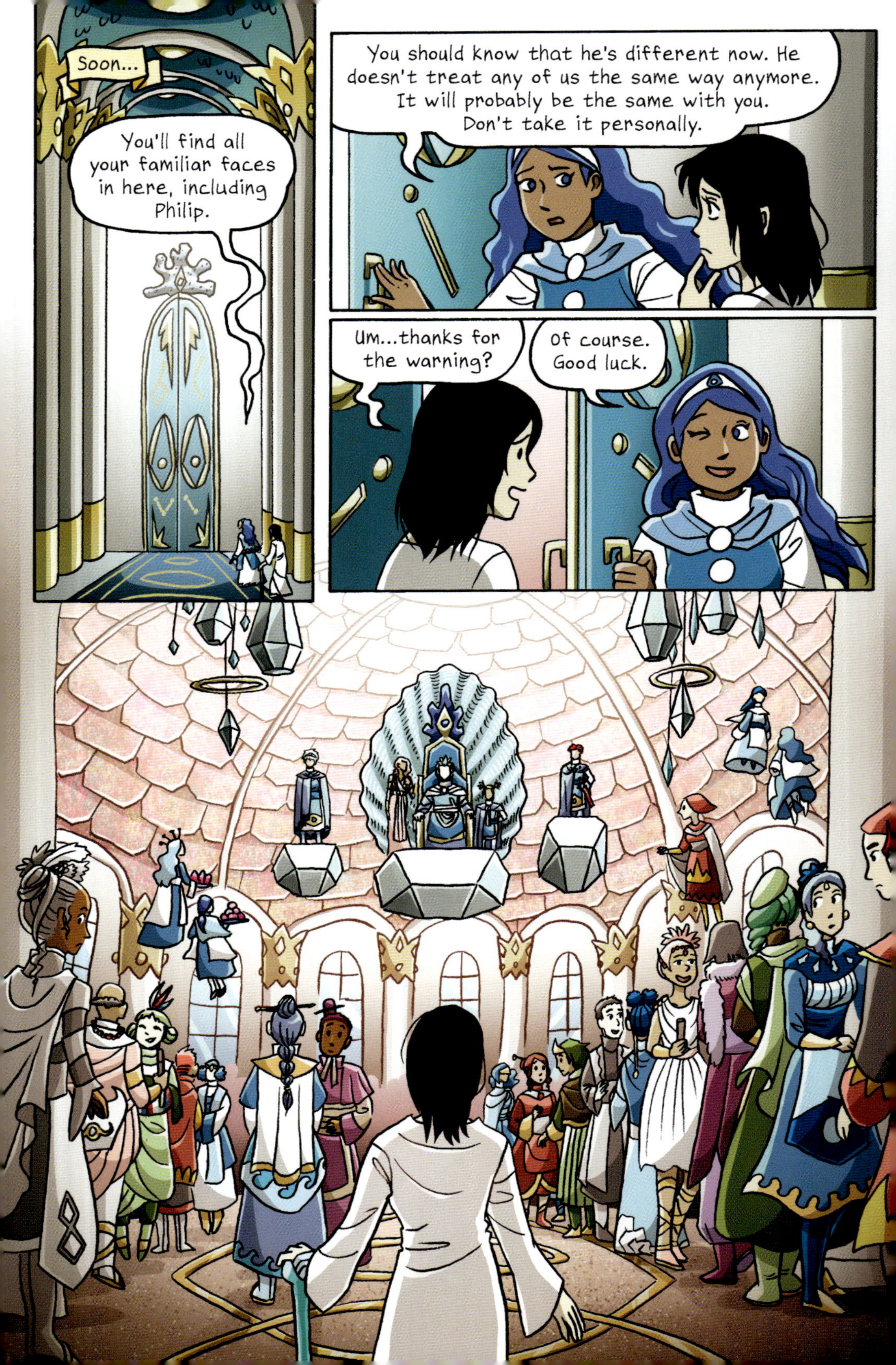
Soon...
You'll find all your familiar faces in here, including Philip.
You should know that he's different now. He doesn't treat any of us the same way anymore. It will probably be the same with you. Don't take it personally.
Um...thanks for the warning?
Of course. Good luck.

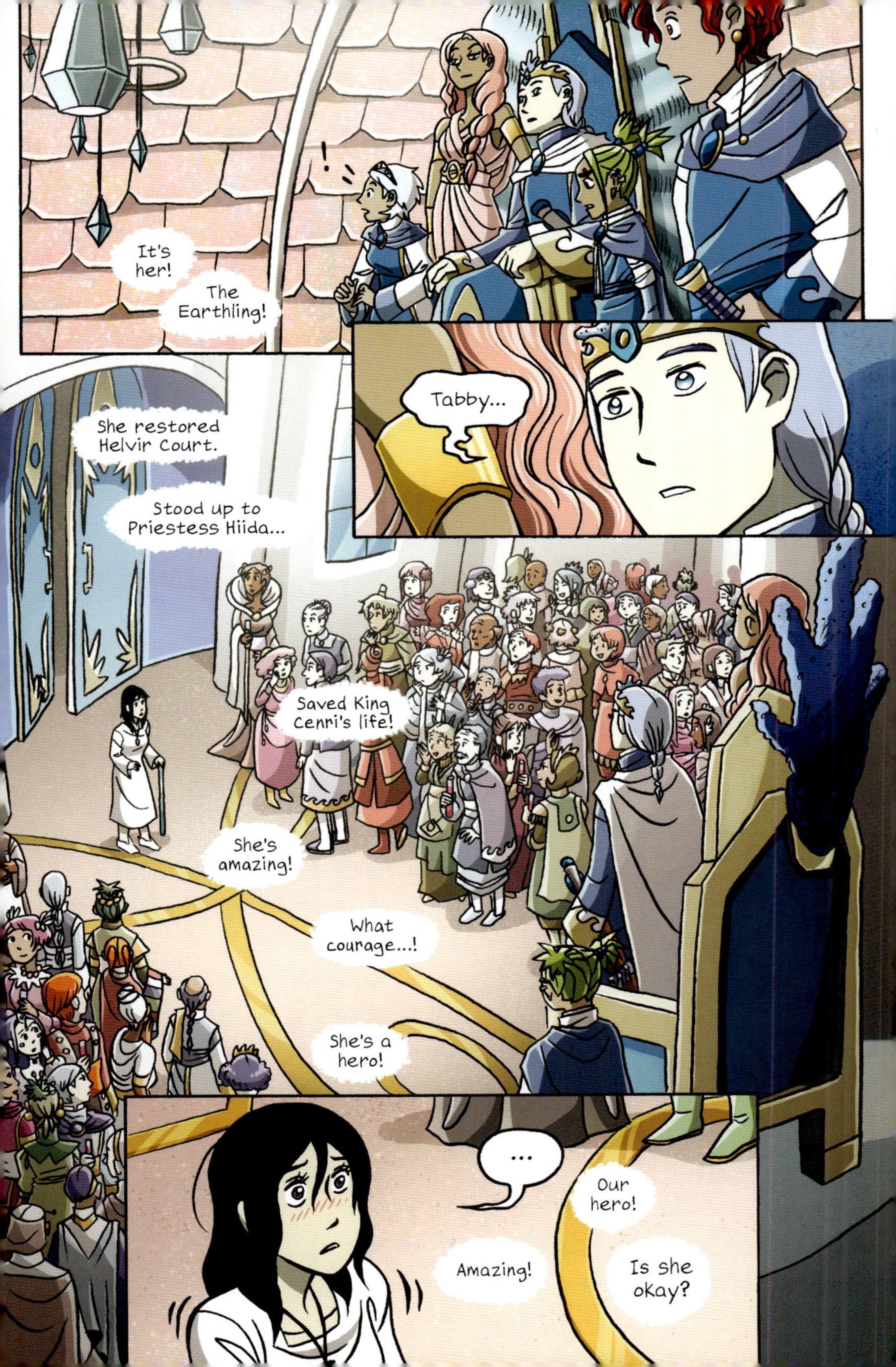
It's her!
The Earthling!
Tabby...
She restored Helvir Court.
Stood up to Priestess Hiida...
Saved King Cenri's life!
She's amazing!
What courage...!
She's a hero!
...
Our hero!
Amazing!
Is she okay?

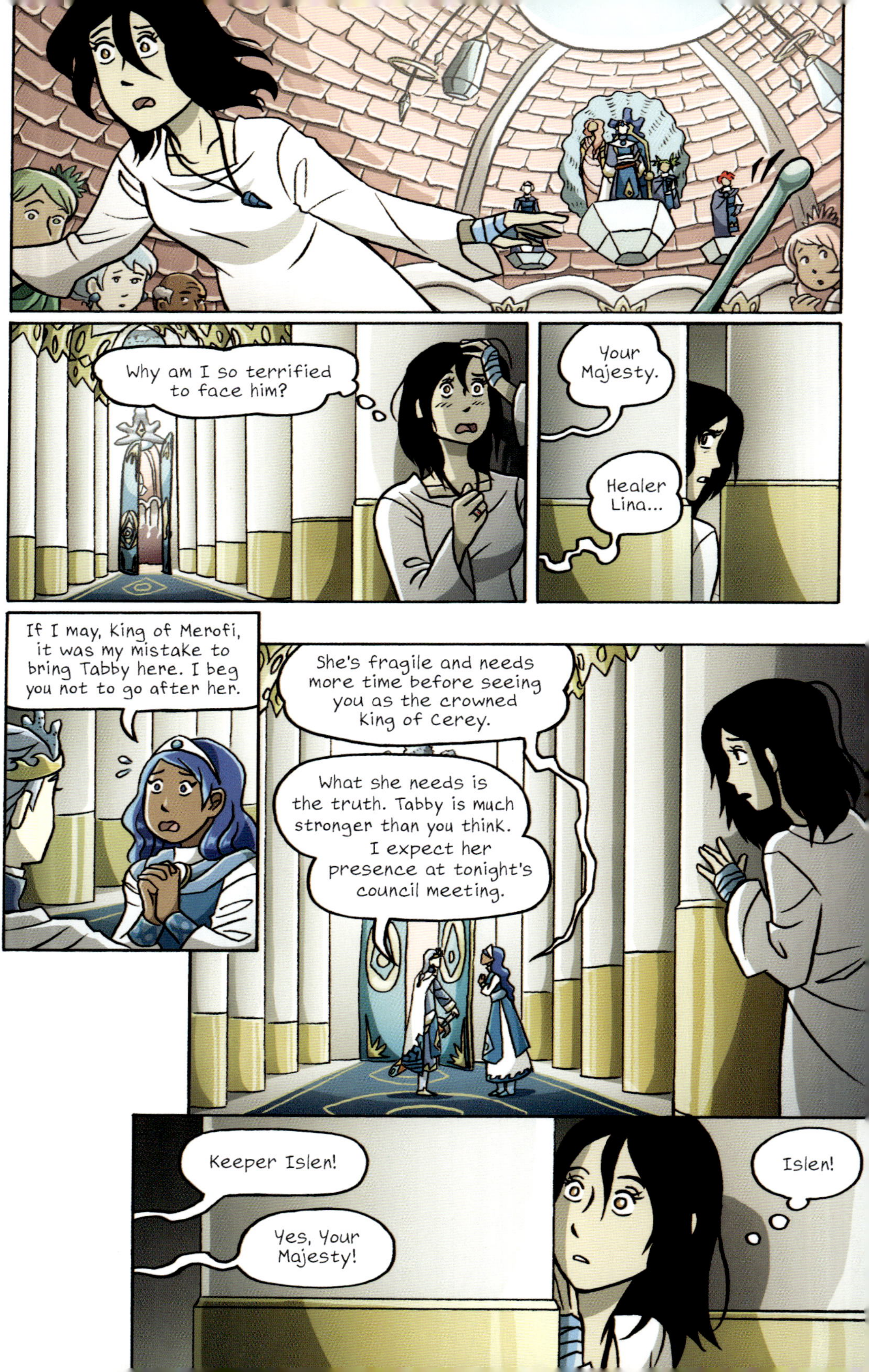
Why am I so terrified to face him?
Your Majesty.
Healer Lina...
If I may, King of Merofi, it was my mistake to bring Tabby here. I beg you not to go after her.
She's fragile and needs more time before seeing you as the crowned king of Cerey.
What she needs is the truth. Tabby is much stronger than you think. I expect her presence at tonight's council meeting.
Keeper Islen!
Yes, Your Majesty!
Islen!

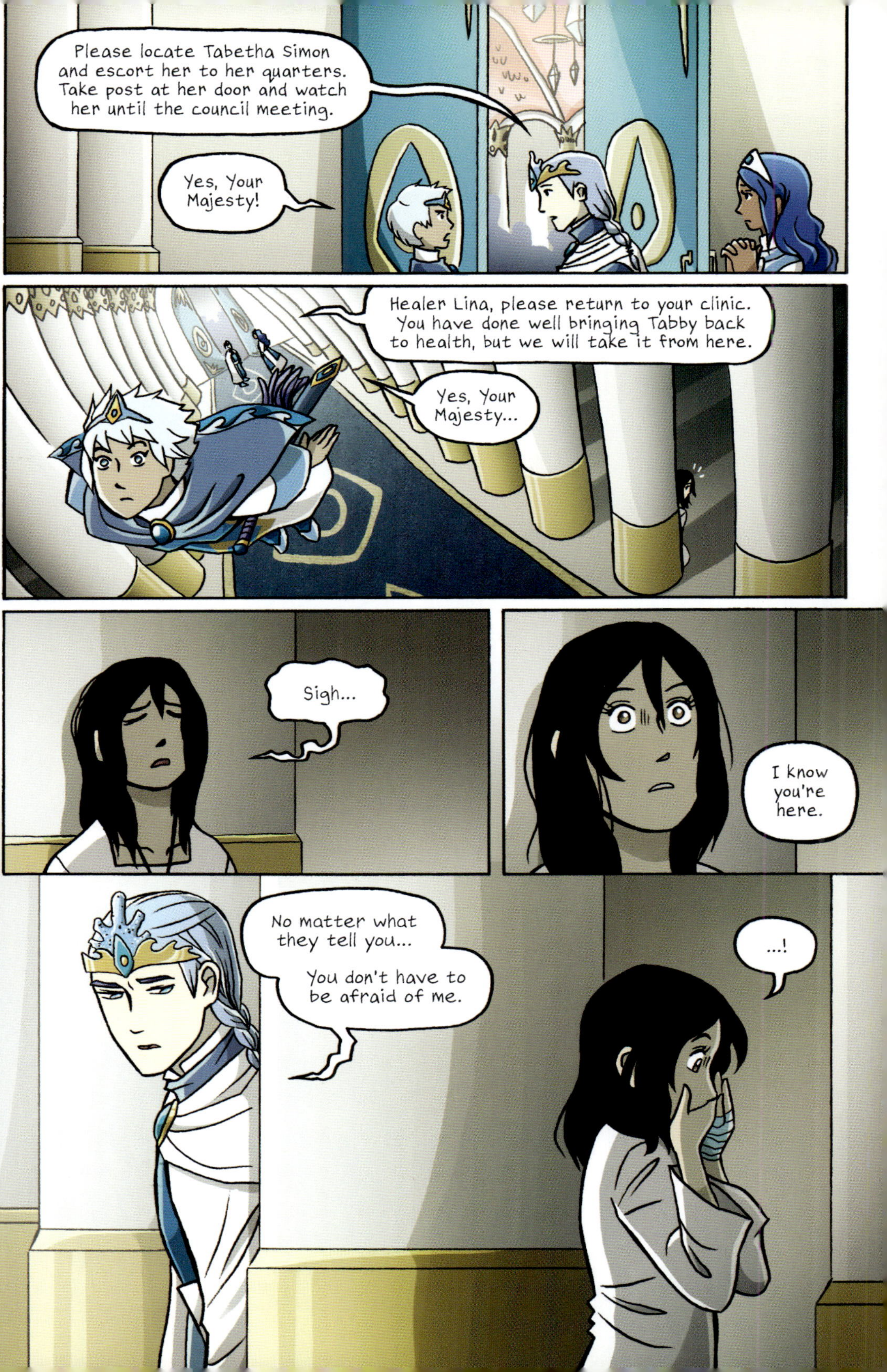
Please locate Tabetha Simon and escort her to her quarters. Take post at her door and watch her until the council meeting.
Yes, Your Majesty!
Healer Lina, please return to your clinic. You have done well bringing Tabby back to health, but we will take it from here.
Yes, Your Majesty...
Sigh...
I know you're here.
No matter what they tell you...
You don't have to be afraid of me.
...!

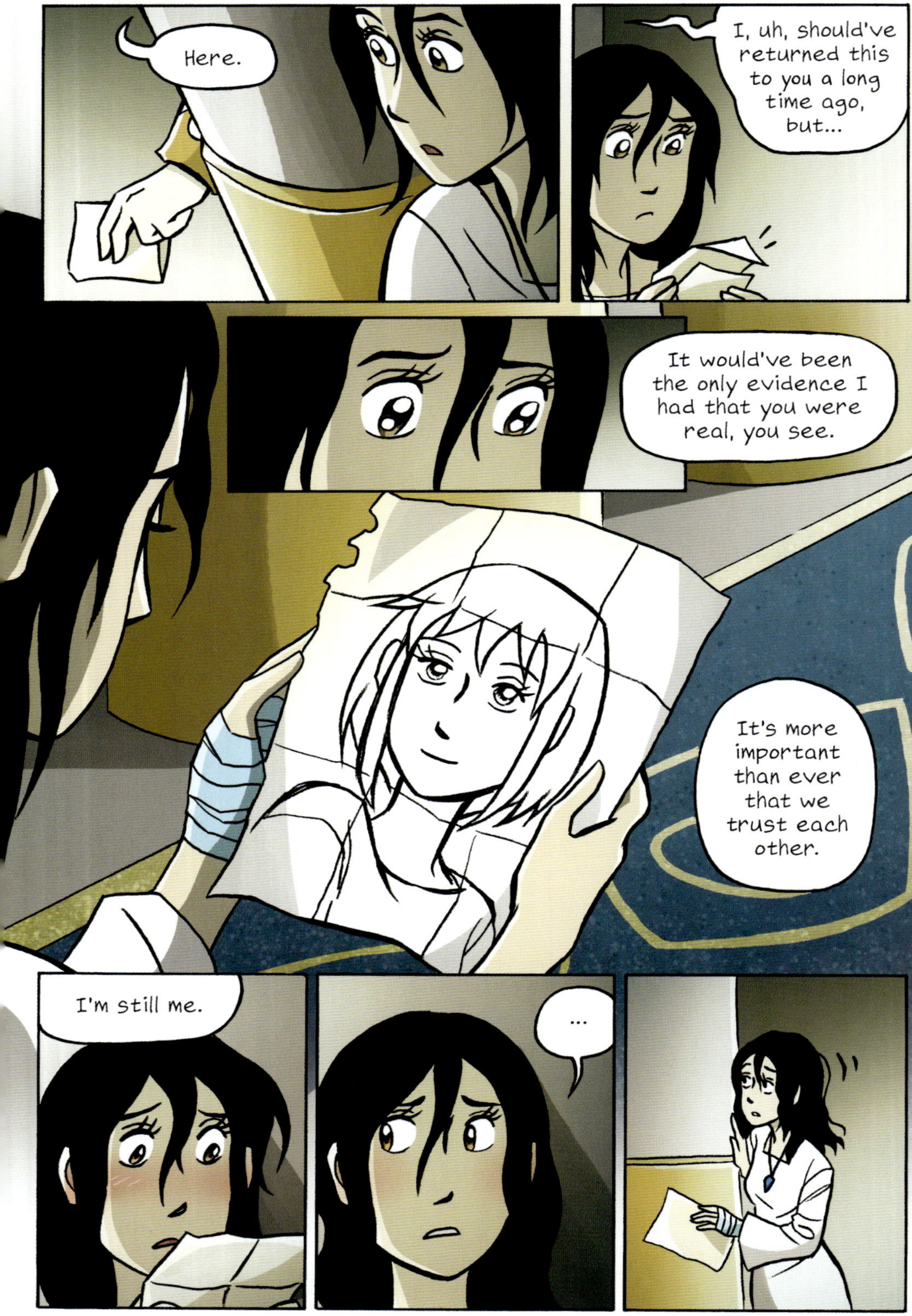
Here.
I, uh, should've returned this to you a long time ago, but...
It would've been the only evidence I had that you were real, you see.
It's more important than ever that we trust each other.
I'm still me.
...

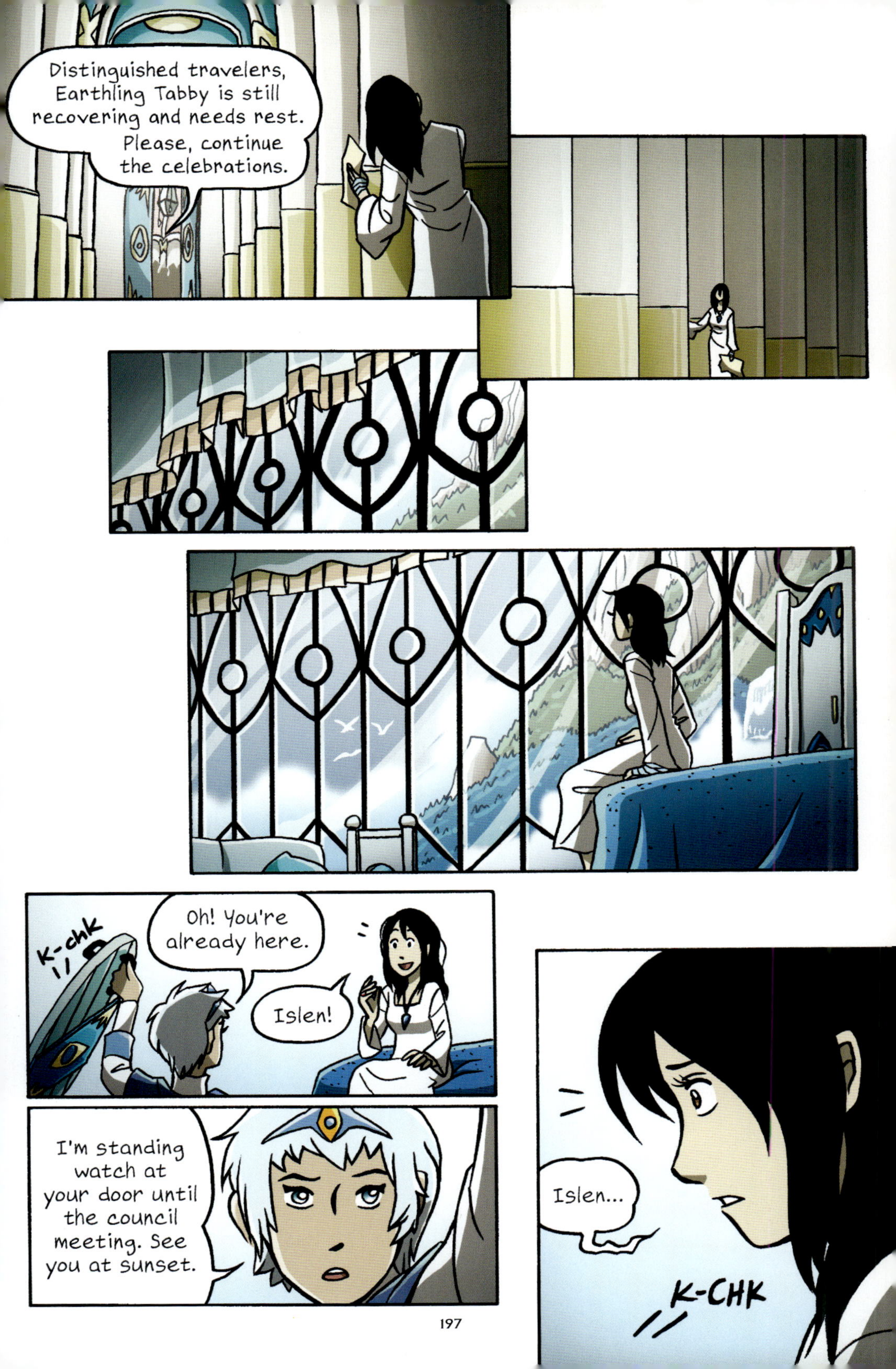

Distinguished travelers, Earthling Tabby is still recovering and needs rest. Please, continue the celebrations.
K-CHK
Oh! You're already here.
Islen!
I'm standing watch at your door until the council meeting. See you at sunset.
Islen...
K-CHK

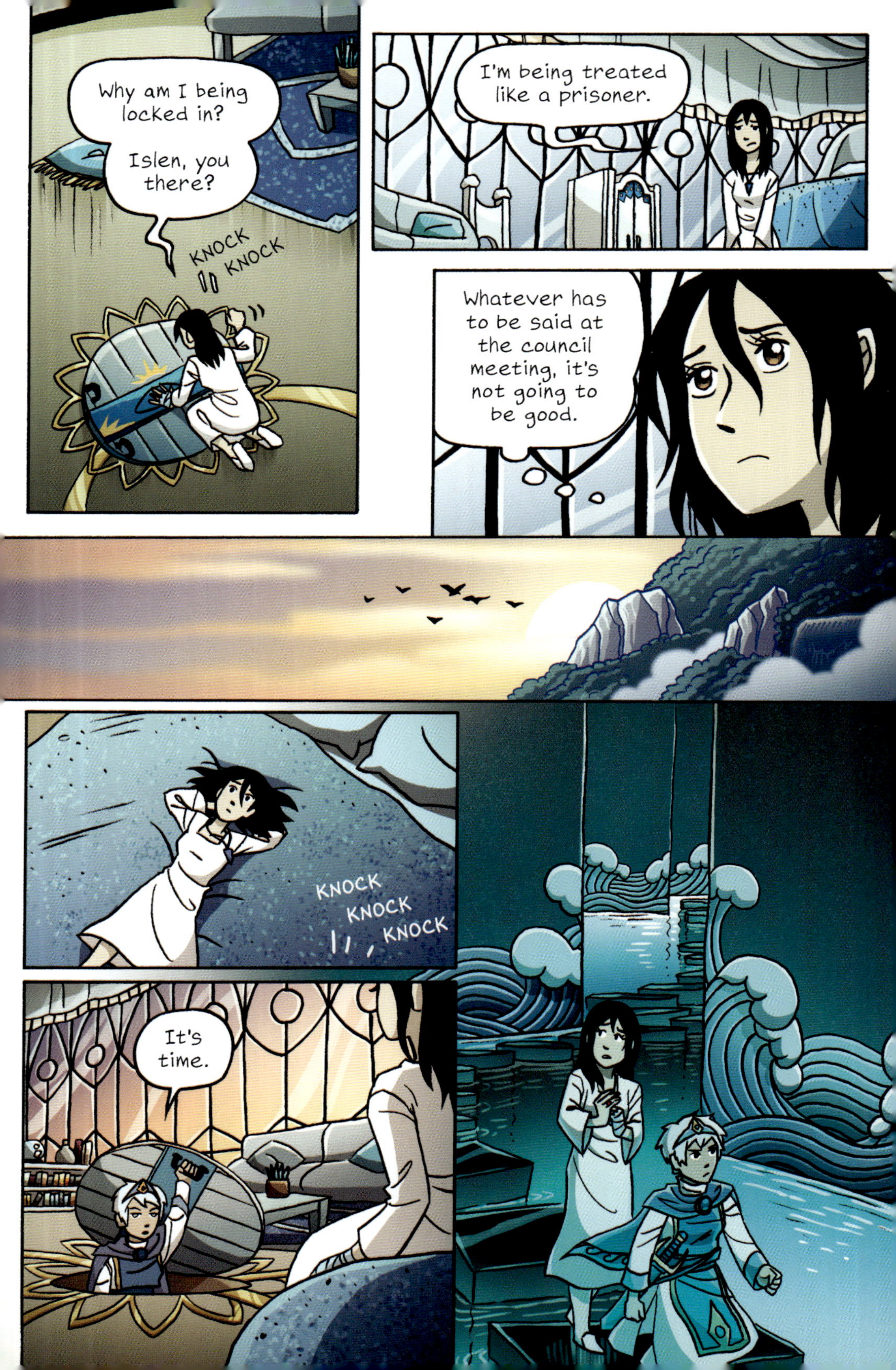
Why am I being locked in?
Islen, you there?
KNOCK KNOCK
I'm being treated like a prisoner.
Whatever has to be said at the council meeting, it's not going to be good.
KNOCK KNOCK KNOCK
It's time.

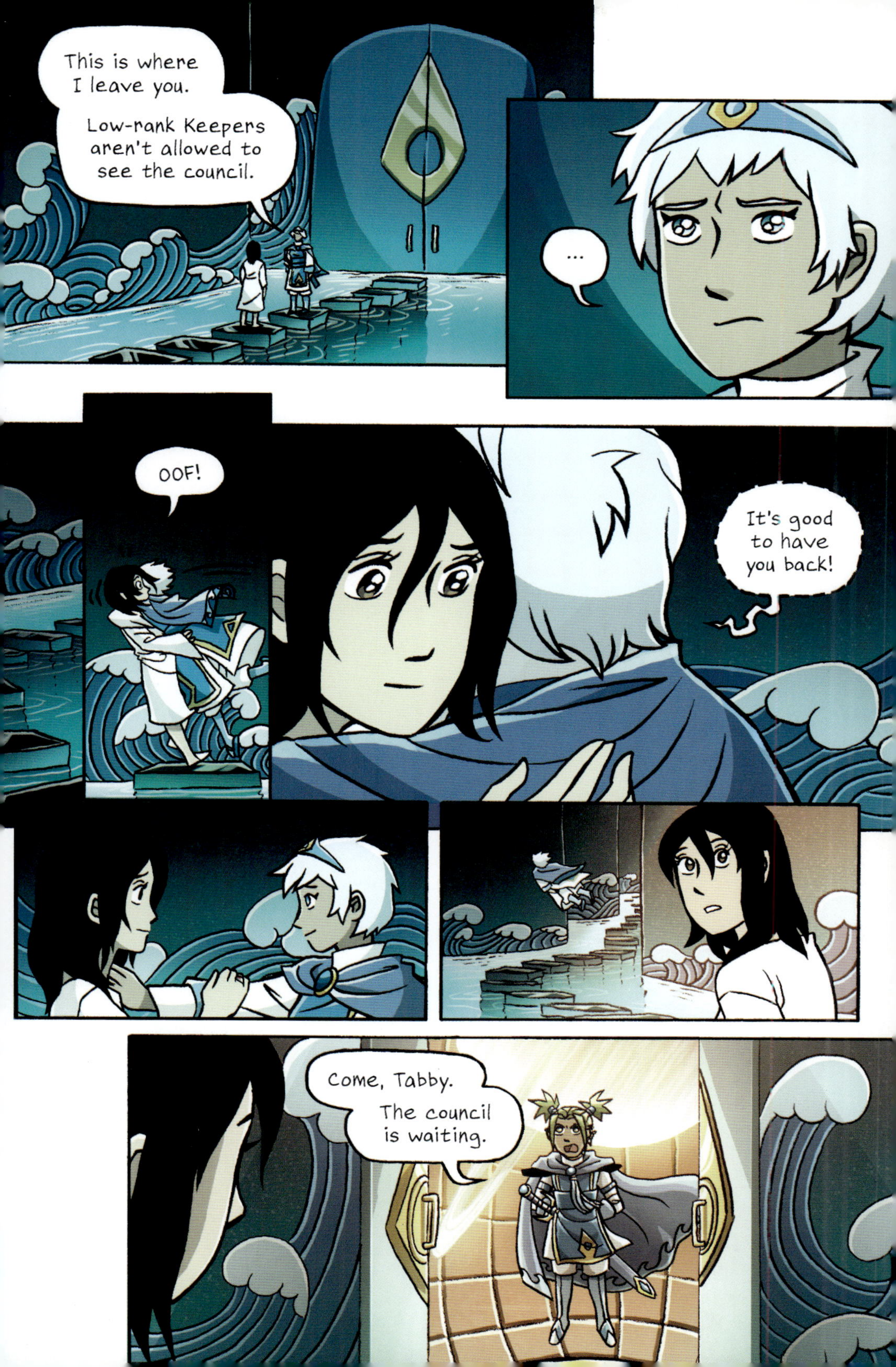
This is where I leave you.
Low-rank Keepers aren't allowed to see the council.
...
OOF!
It's good to have you back!
Come, Tabby.
The council is waiting.

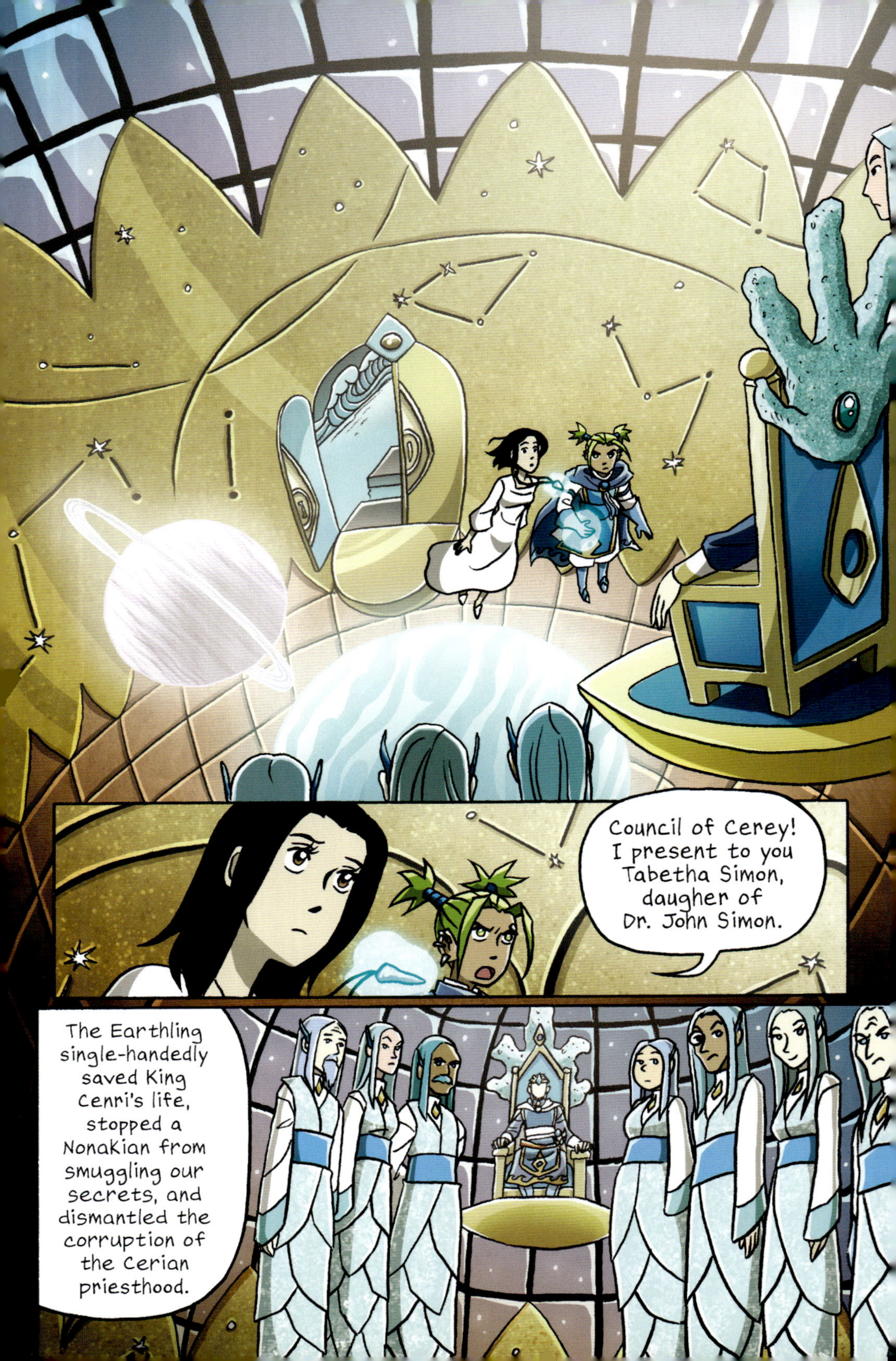
Council of Cerey! I present to you Tabetha Simon, daugher of Dr. John Simon.
The Earthling single-handedly saved King Cenri's life, stopped a Nonakian from smuggling our secrets, and dismantled the corruption of the Cerian priesthood.

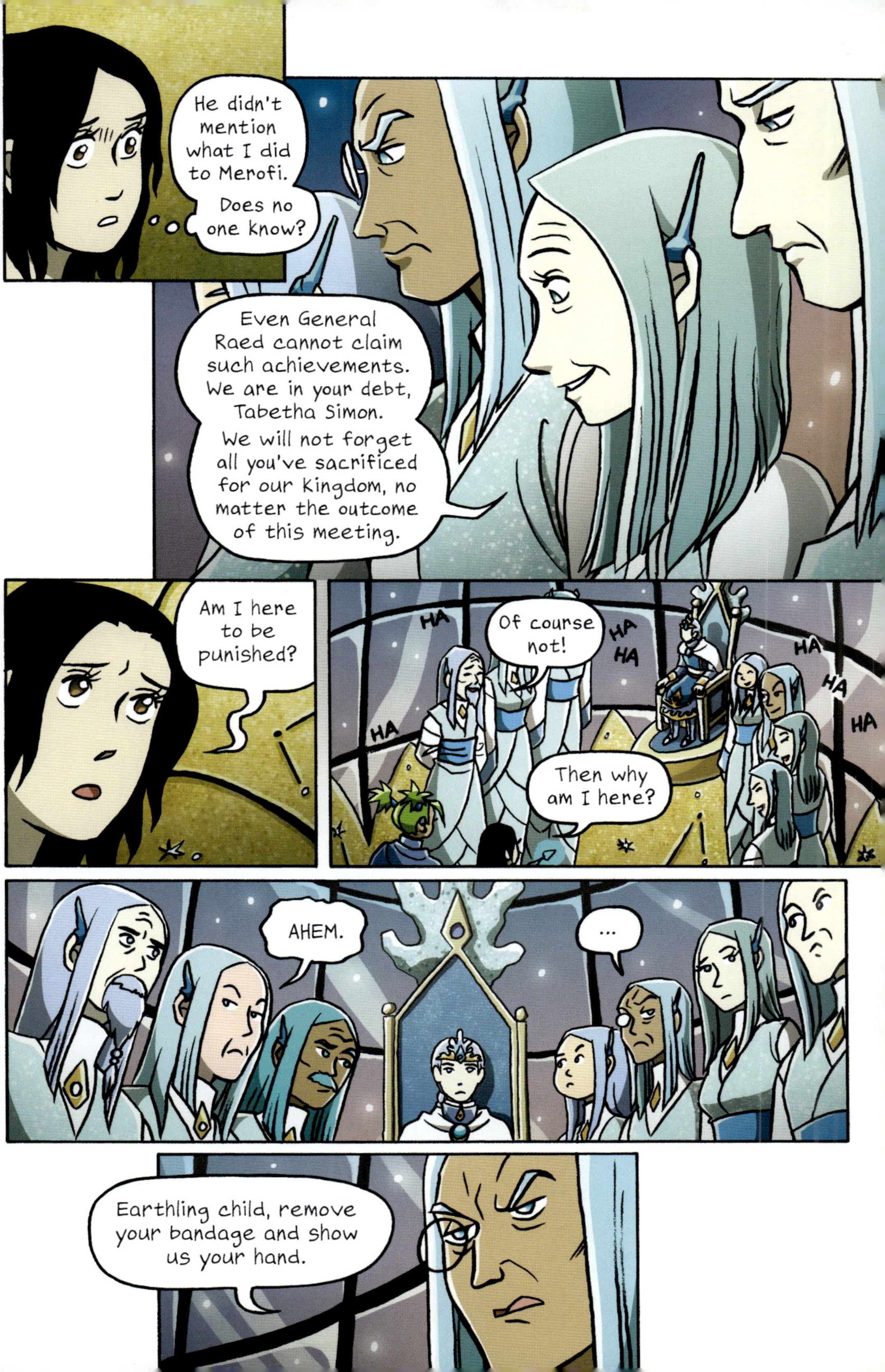

He didn't mention what I did to Merofi.
Does no one know?
Even General Raed cannot claim such achievements. We are in your debt, Tabetha Simon.
We will not forget all you've sacrificed for our Kingdom, no matter the outcome of this meeting.
Am I here to be punished?
HA
Of course not!
HA HA
HA
HA
HA
HA
Then why am I here?
AHEM.
...
Earthling child, remove your bandage and show us your hand.

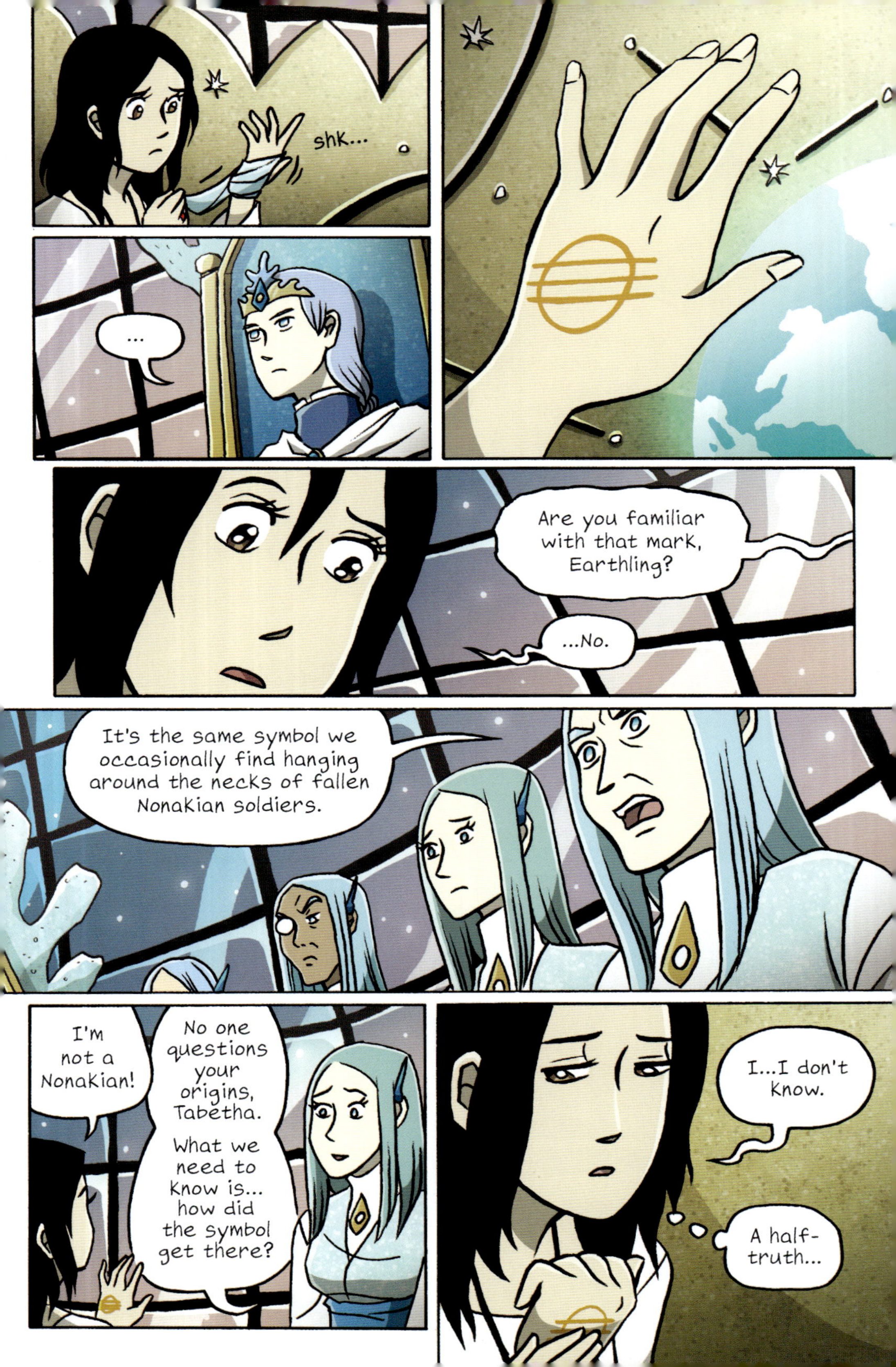
shk...
...
Are you familiar with that mark, Earthling?
...No.
It's the same symbol we occasionally find hanging around the necks of fallen Nonakian soldiers.
I'm not a Nonakian!
No one questions your origins, Tabetha.
What we need to know is... how did the symbol get there?
I...I don't know.
A half-truth...

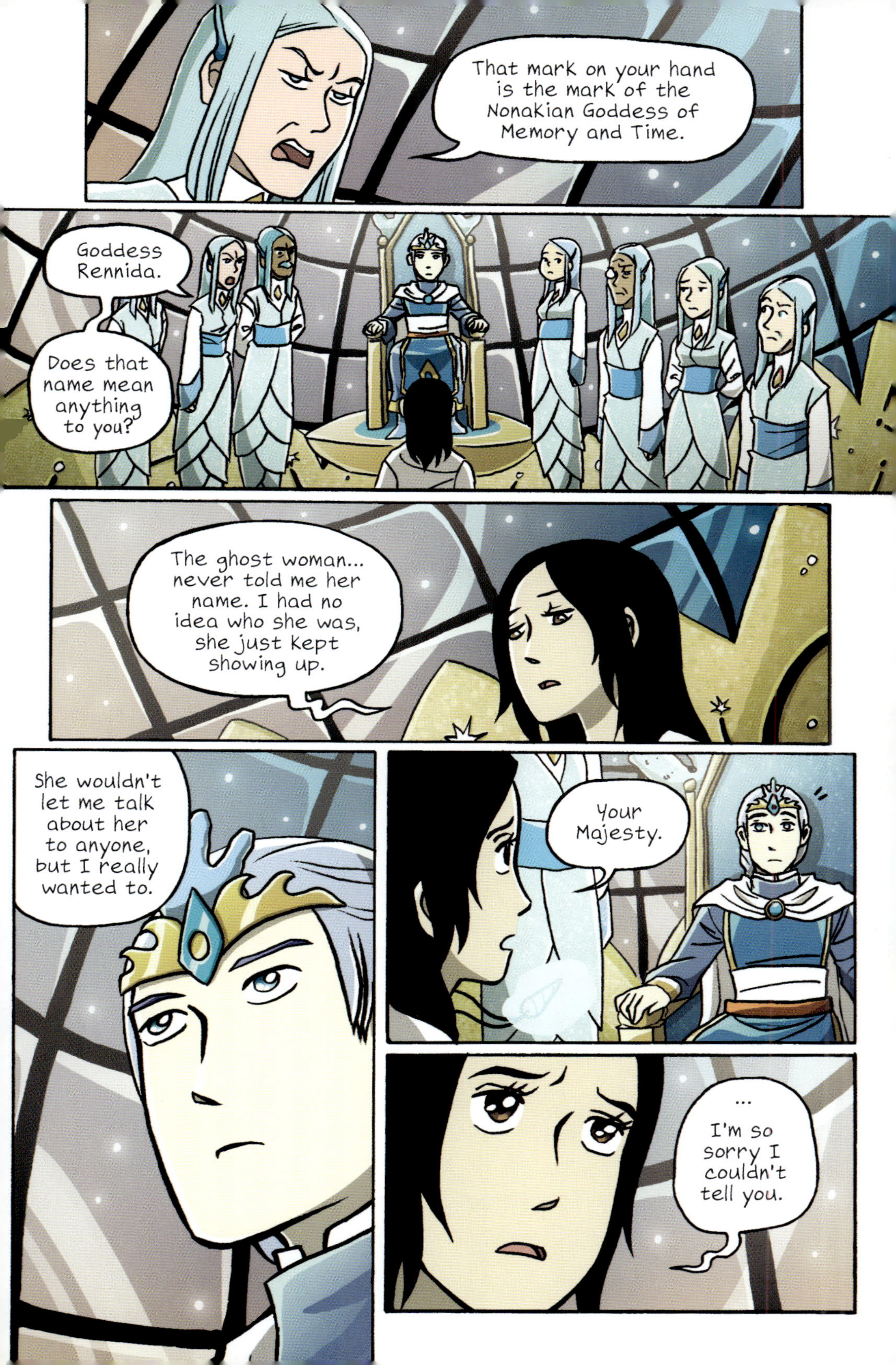
That mark on your hand is the mark of the Nonakian Goddess of Memory and Time.
Goddess Rennida.
Does that name mean anything to you?
The ghost woman... never told me her name. I had no idea who she was, she just kept showing up.
She wouldn't let me talk about her to anyone, but I really wanted to.
Your Majesty.
...
I'm so sorry I couldn't tell you.

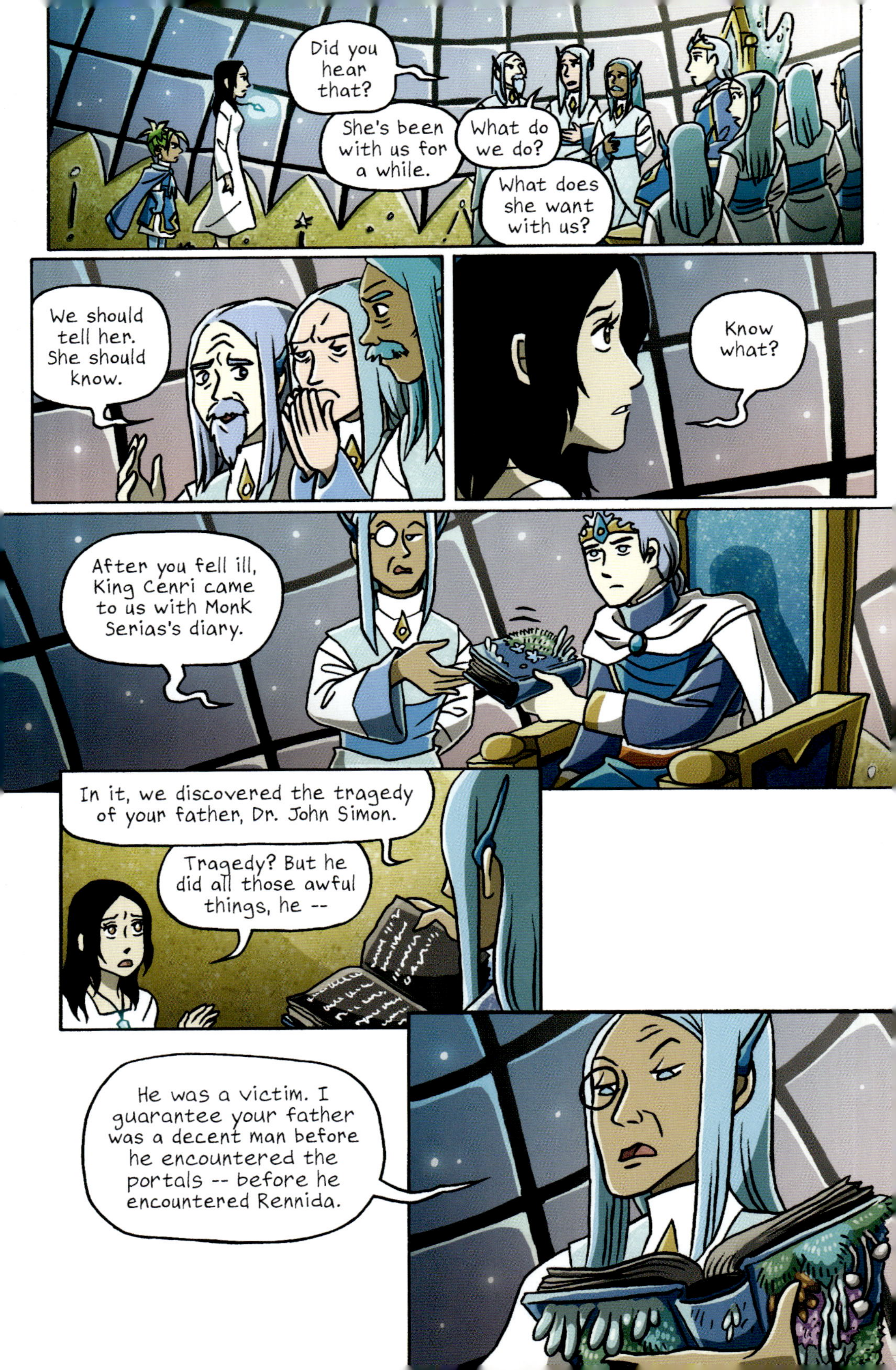
Did you hear that?
She's been with us for a while.
What do we do?
What does she want with us?
We should tell her. She should know.
Know what?
After you fell ill, King Cenri came to us with Monk Serias's diary.
In it, we discovered the tragedy of your father, Dr. John Simon.
Tragedy? But he did all those awful things, he --
He was a victim. I guarantee your father was a decent man before he encountered the portals -- before he encountered Rennida.

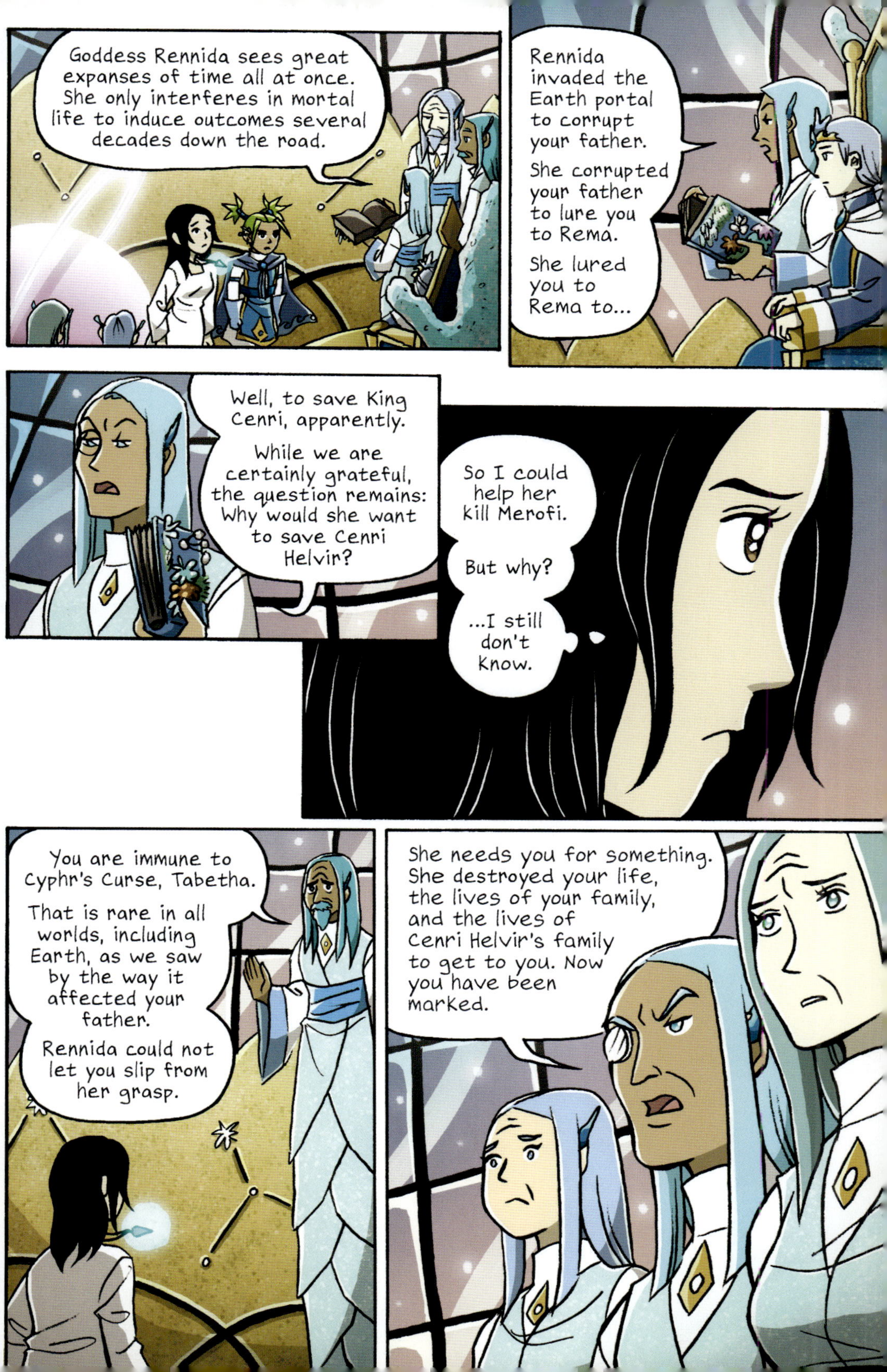
Goddess Rennida sees great expanses of time all at once. She only interferes in mortal life to induce outcomes several decades down the road.
Rennida invaded the Earth portal to corrupt your father.
She corrupted your father to lure you to Rema.
She lured you to Rema to...
Well, to save King Cenri, apparently.
While we are certainly grateful, the question remains: Why would she want to save Cenri Helvir?
So I could help her kill Merofi.
But why?
...I still don't know.
You are immune to Cyphr's Curse, Tabetha.
That is rare in all worlds, including Earth, as we saw by the way it affected your father.
Rennida could not let you slip from her grasp.
She needs you for something. She destroyed your life, the lives of your family, and the lives of Cenri Helvir's family to get to you. Now you have been marked.

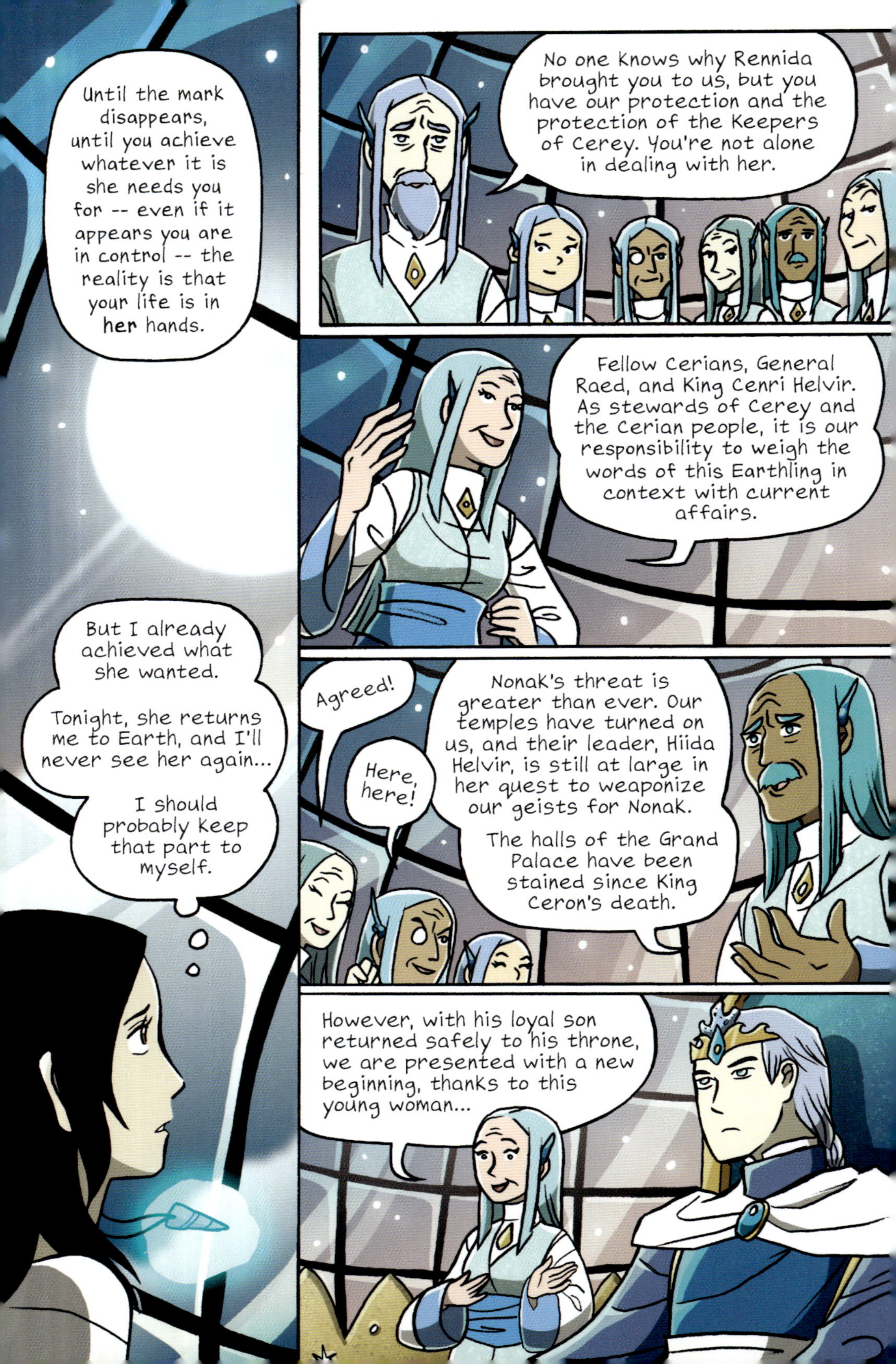
Until the mark disappears, until you achieve whatever it is she needs you for -- even if it appears you are in control -- the reality is that your life is in **her** hands.
No one knows why Rennida brought you to us, but you have our protection and the protection of the Keepers of Cerey. You're not alone in dealing with her.
Fellow Cerians, General Raed, and King Cenri Helvir. As stewards of Cerey and the Cerian people, it is our responsibility to weigh the words of this Earthling in context with current affairs.
But I already achieved what she wanted.
Tonight, she returns me to Earth, and I'll never see her again...
I should probably keep that part to myself.
Agreed!
Here, here!
Nonak's threat is greater than ever. Our temples have turned on us, and their leader, Hiida Helvir, is still at large in her quest to weaponize our geists for Nonak.
The halls of the Grand Palace have been stained since King Ceron's death.
However, with his loyal son returned safely to his throne, we are presented with a new beginning, thanks to this young woman...

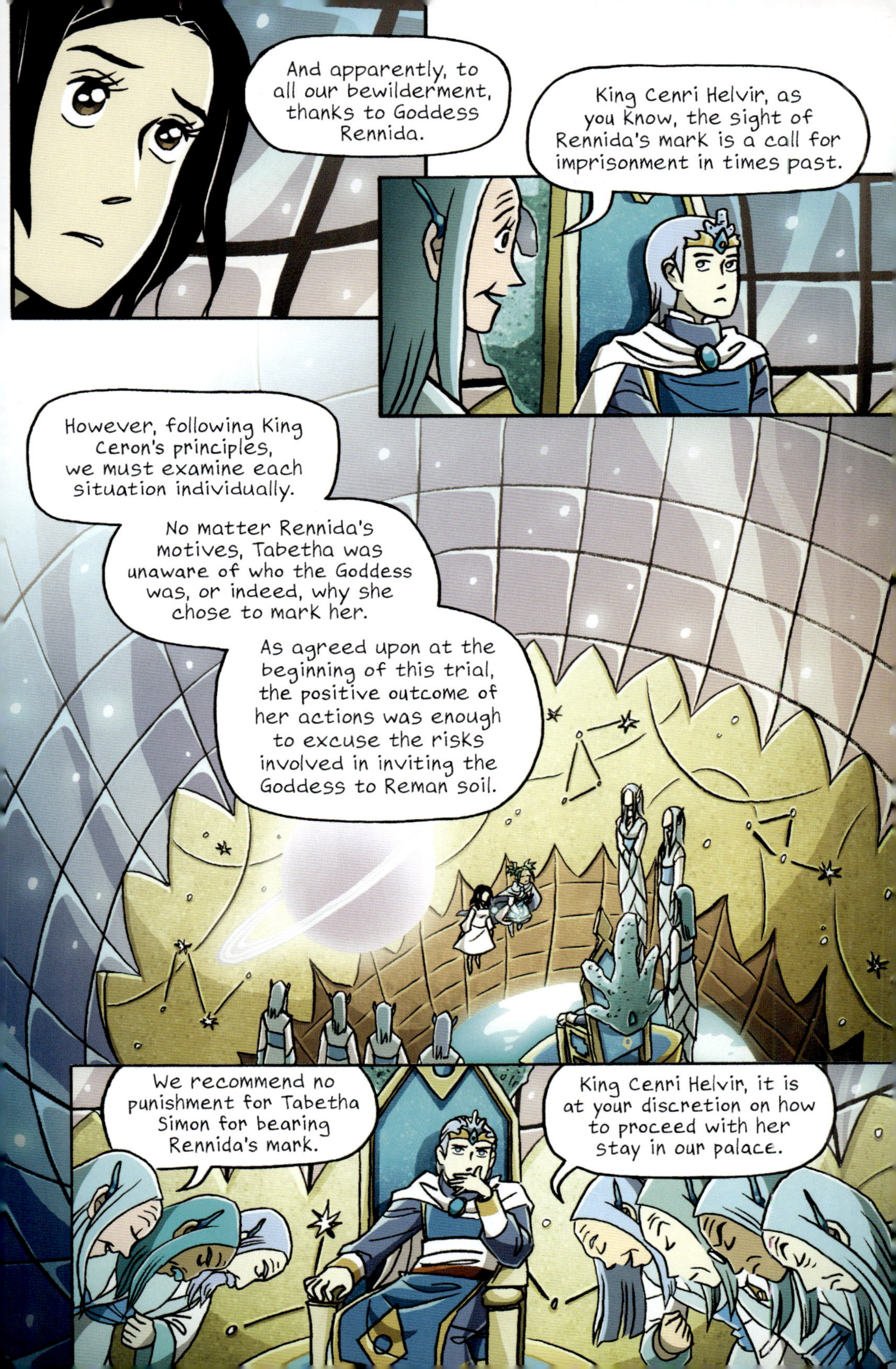
And apparently, to all our bewilderment, thanks to Goddess Rennida.
King Cenri Helvir, as you know, the sight of Rennida's mark is a call for imprisonment in times past.
However, following King Ceron's principles, we must examine each situation individually.
No matter Rennida's motives, Tabetha was unaware of who the Goddess was, or indeed, why she chose to mark her.
As agreed upon at the beginning of this trial, the positive outcome of her actions was enough to excuse the risks involved in inviting the Goddess to Reman soil.
We recommend no punishment for Tabetha Simon for bearing Rennida's mark.
King Cenri Helvir, it is at your discretion on how to proceed with her stay in our palace.

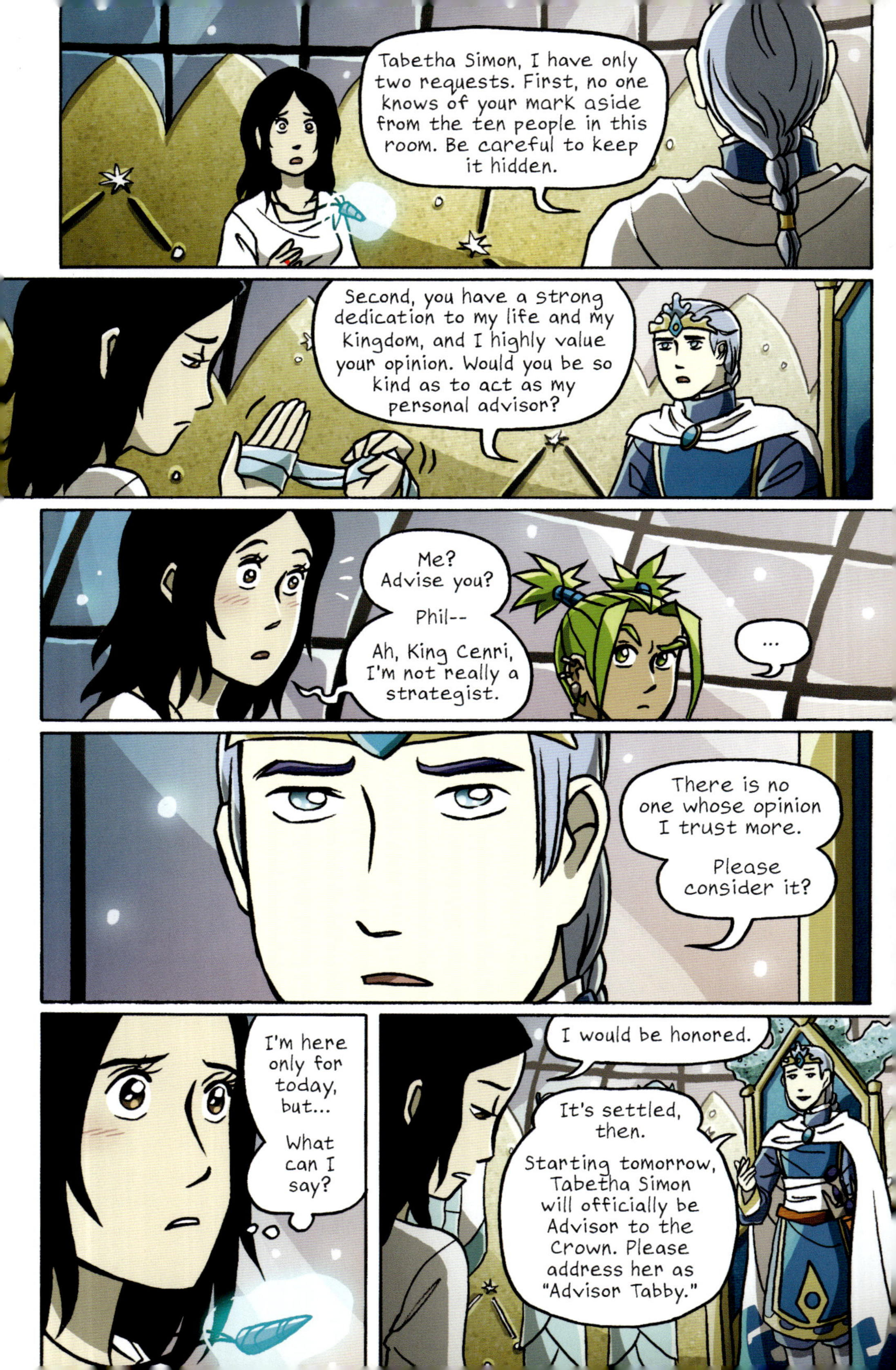

Tabetha Simon, I have only two requests. First, no one knows of your mark aside from the ten people in this room. Be careful to keep it hidden.
Second, you have a strong dedication to my life and my Kingdom, and I highly value your opinion. Would you be so kind as to act as my personal advisor?
Me? Advise you?
Phil--
Ah, King Cenri, I'm not really a strategist.
...
There is no one whose opinion I trust more.
Please consider it?
I'm here only for today, but...
What can I say?
I would be honored.
It's settled, then.
Starting tomorrow, Tabetha Simon will officially be Advisor to the Crown. Please address her as "Advisor Tabby."

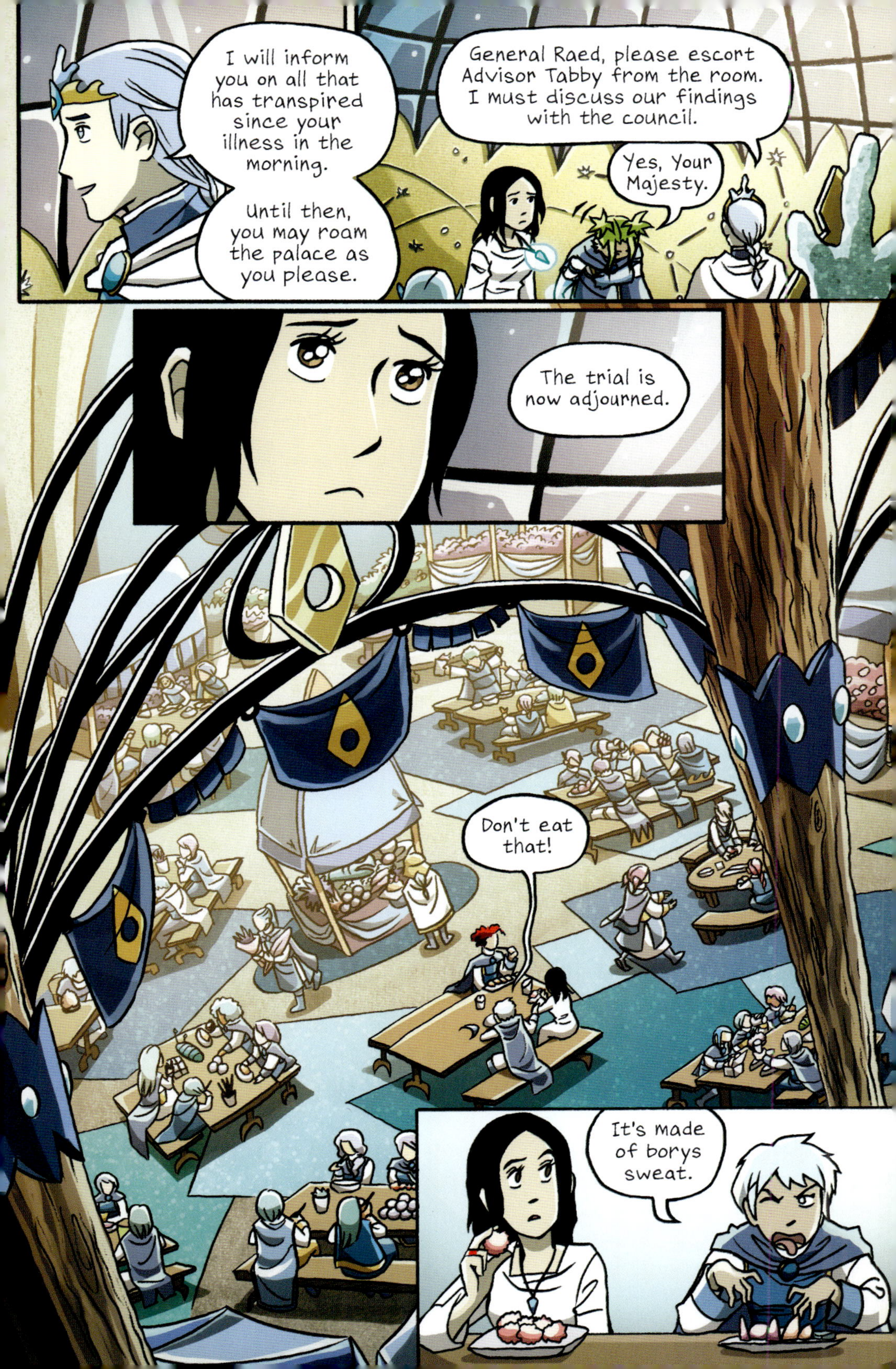
I will inform you on all that has transpired since your illness in the morning.
Until then, you may roam the palace as you please.
General Raed, please escort Advisor Tabby from the room. I must discuss our findings with the council.
Yes, Your Majesty.
The trial is now adjourned.
Don't eat that!
It's made of borys sweat.

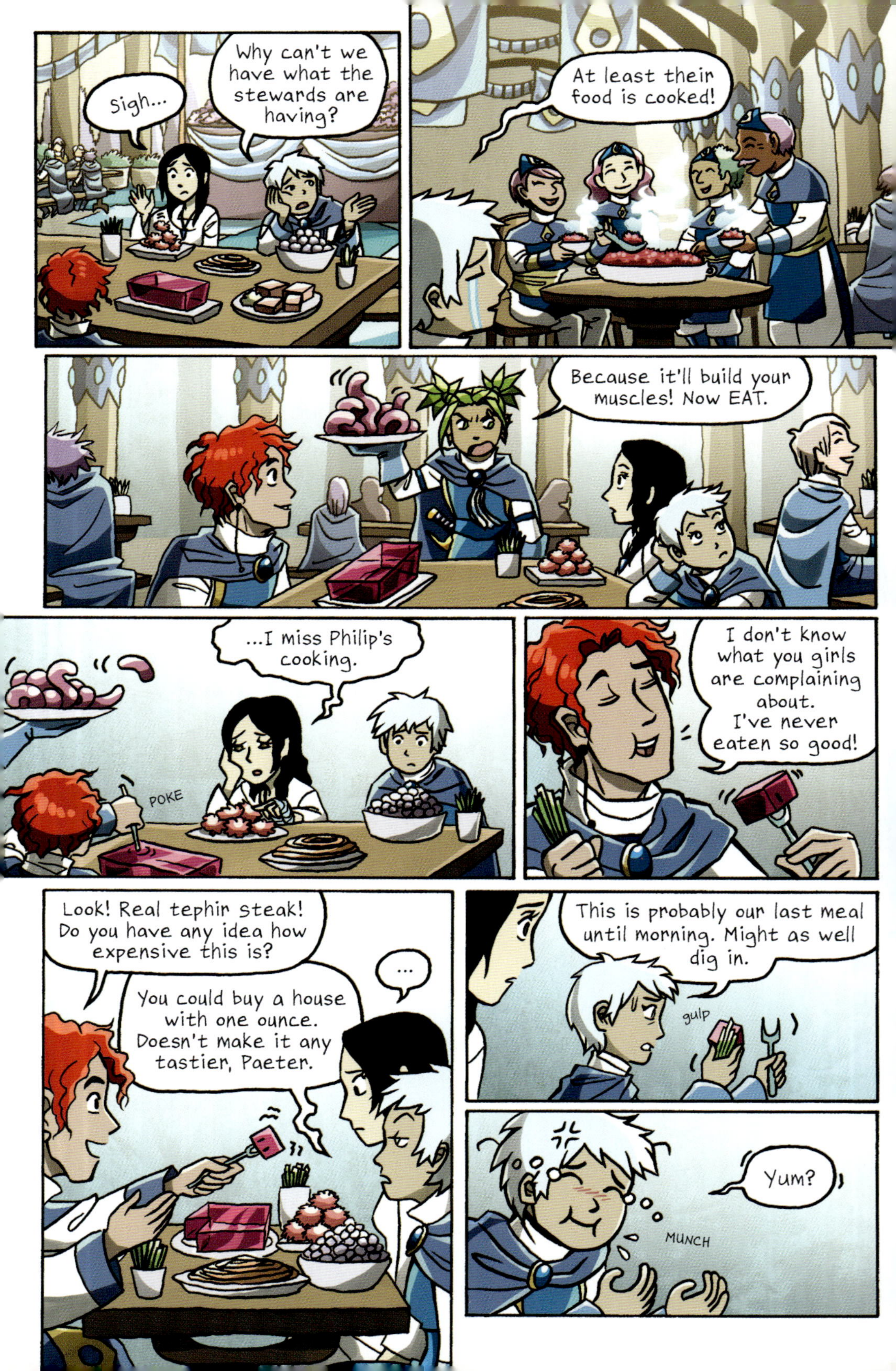
Sigh...
Why can't we have what the stewards are having?
At least their food is cooked!
Because it'll build your muscles! Now EAT.
...I miss Philip's cooking.
POKE
I don't know what you girls are complaining about. I've never eaten so good!
Look! Real tephir steak! Do you have any idea how expensive this is?
You could buy a house with one ounce. Doesn't make it any tastier, Paeter.
...
This is probably our last meal until morning. Might as well dig in.
gulp
Yum?
MUNCH

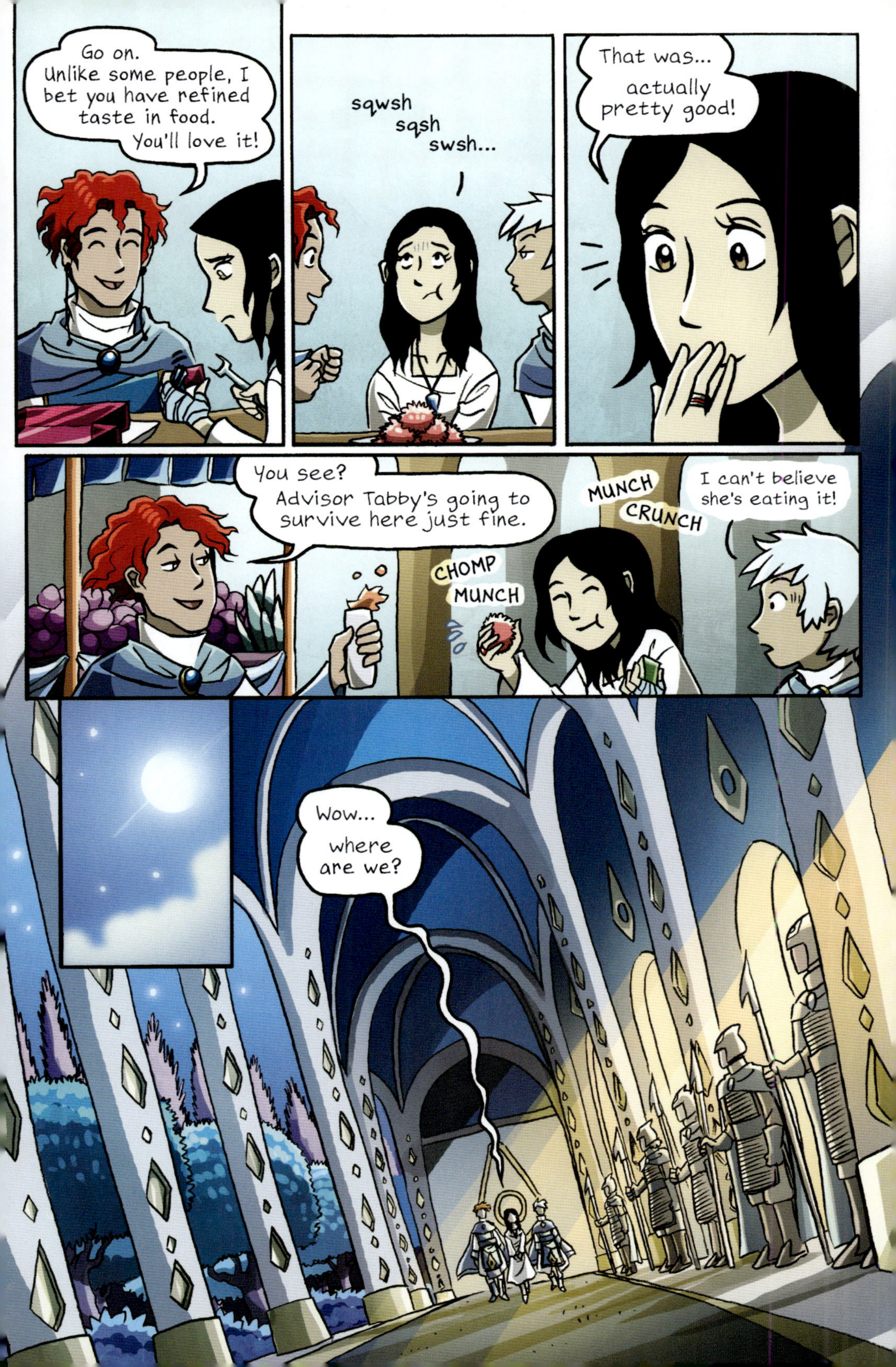
Go on. Unlike some people, I bet you have refined taste in food. You'll love it!
sqwsh sqsh swsh...
That was... actually pretty good!
You see? Advisor Tabby's going to survive here just fine.
CHOMP
MUNCH
MUNCH
CRUNCH
I can't believe she's eating it!
Wow... where are we?

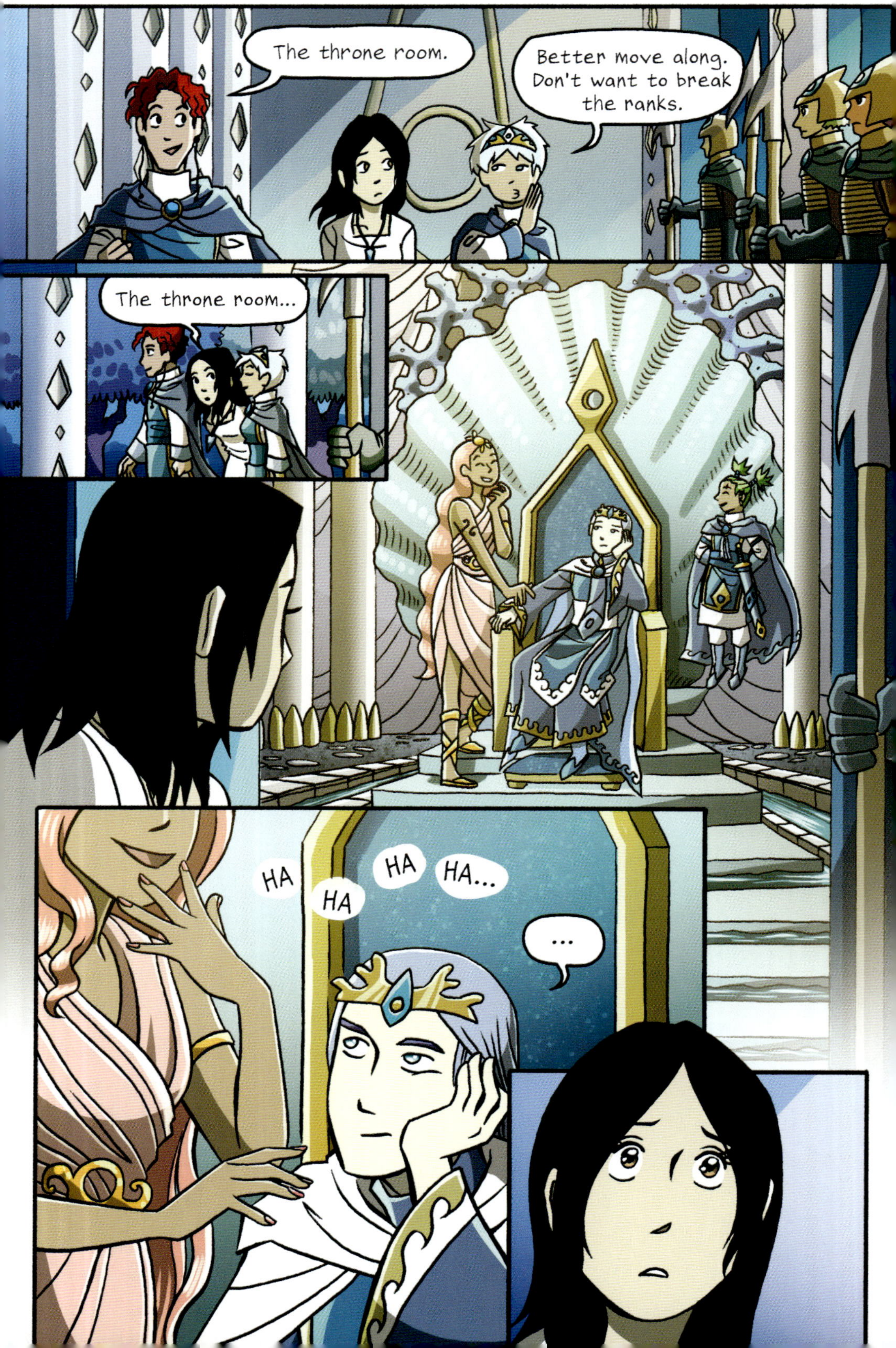
The throne room.
Better move along. Don't want to break the ranks.
The throne room...
HA
HA
HA
HA...
...

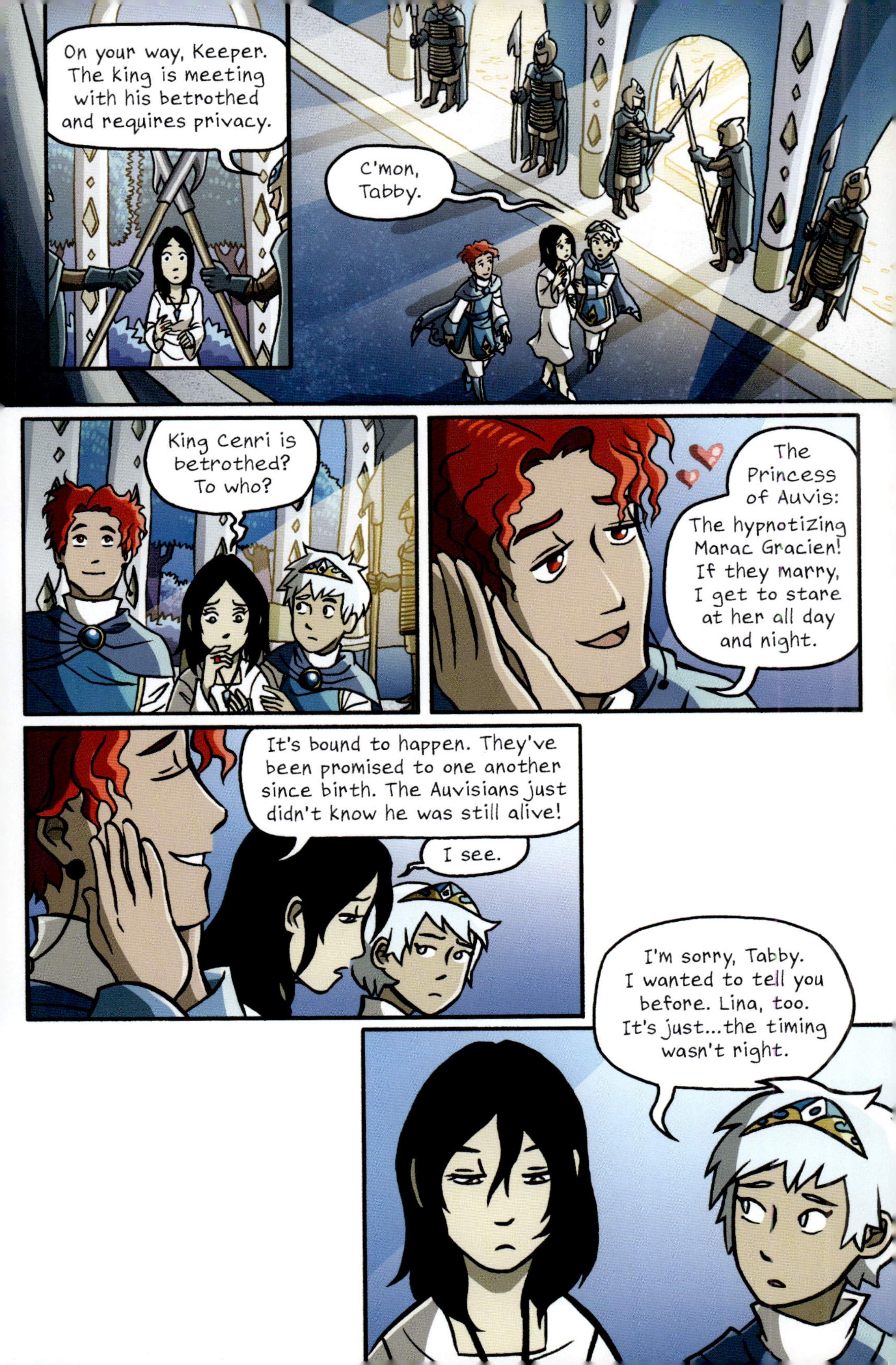
On your way, Keeper. The king is meeting with his betrothed and requires privacy.
C'mon, Tabby.
King Cenri is betrothed? To who?
The Princess of Auvis: The hypnotizing Marac Gracien! If they marry, I get to stare at her all day and night.
It's bound to happen. They've been promised to one another since birth. The Auvisians just didn't know he was still alive!
I see.
I'm sorry, Tabby. I wanted to tell you before. Lina, too. It's just...the timing wasn't right.

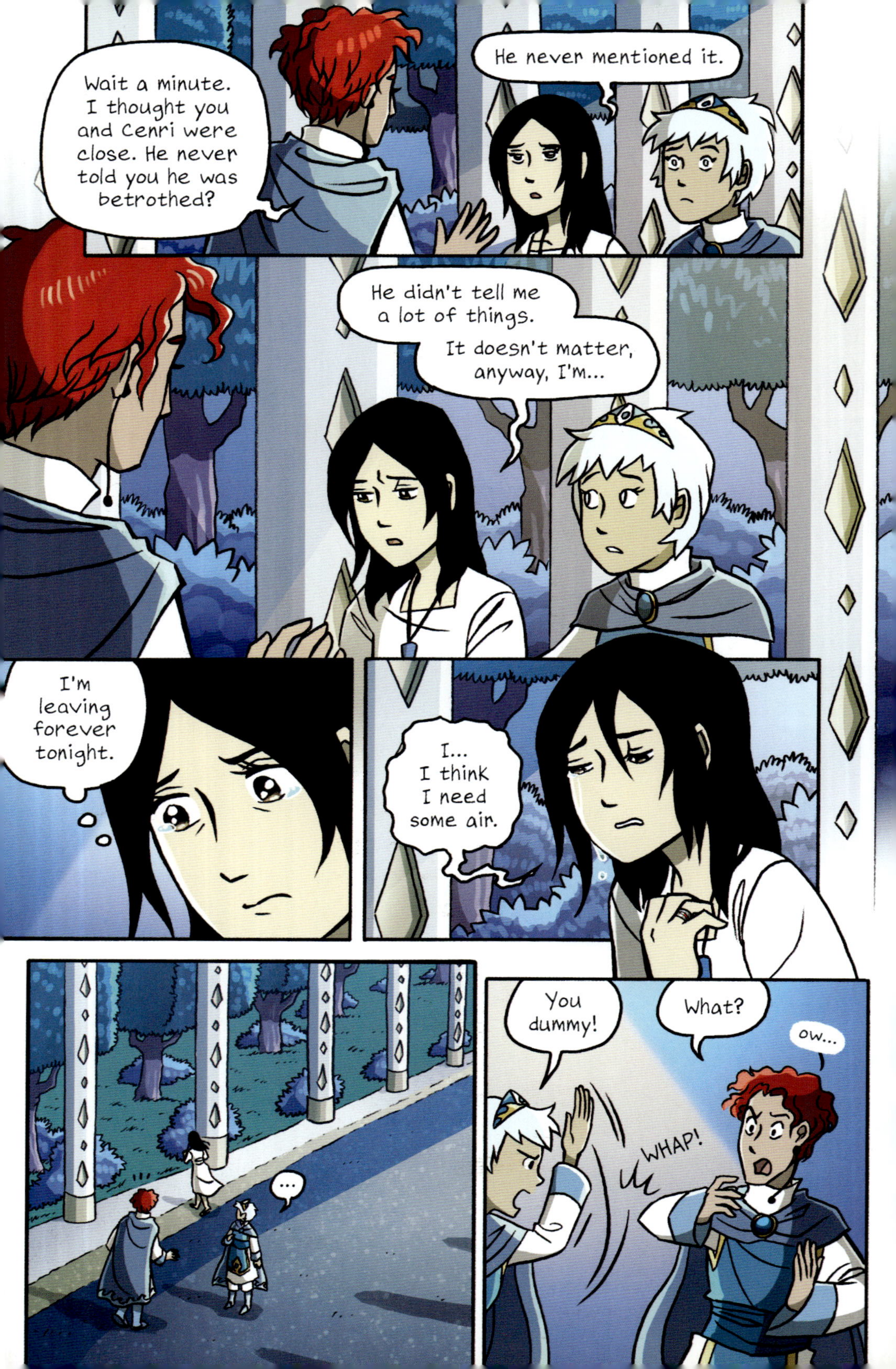
Wait a minute. I thought you and Cenri were close. He never told you he was betrothed?
He never mentioned it.
He didn't tell me a lot of things.
It doesn't matter, anyway, I'm...
I'm leaving forever tonight.
I... I think I need some air.
...
You dummy!
WHAP!
What?
ow...

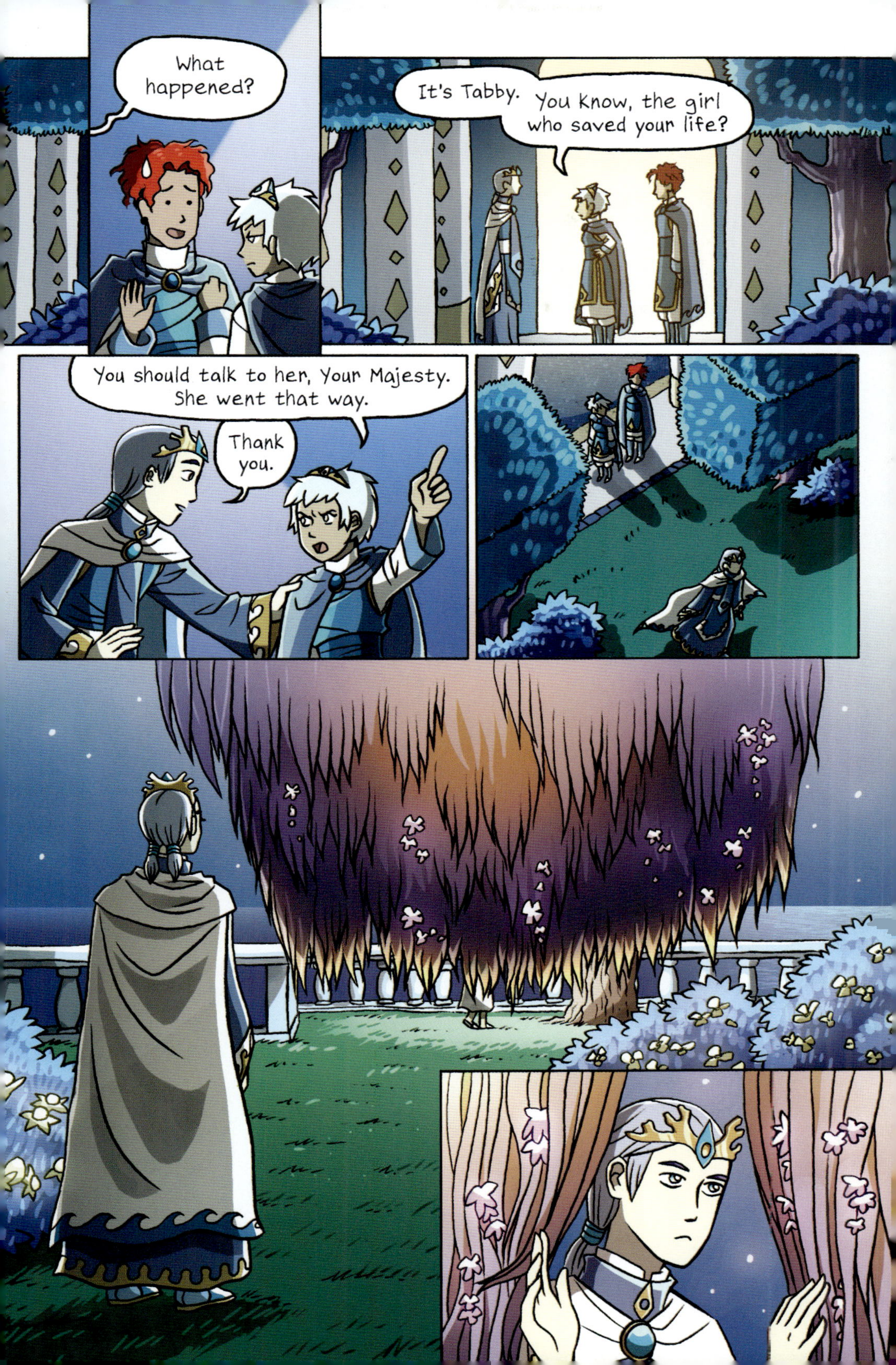
What happened?
It's Tabby.
You know, the girl who saved your life?
You should talk to her, Your Majesty. She went that way.
Thank you.

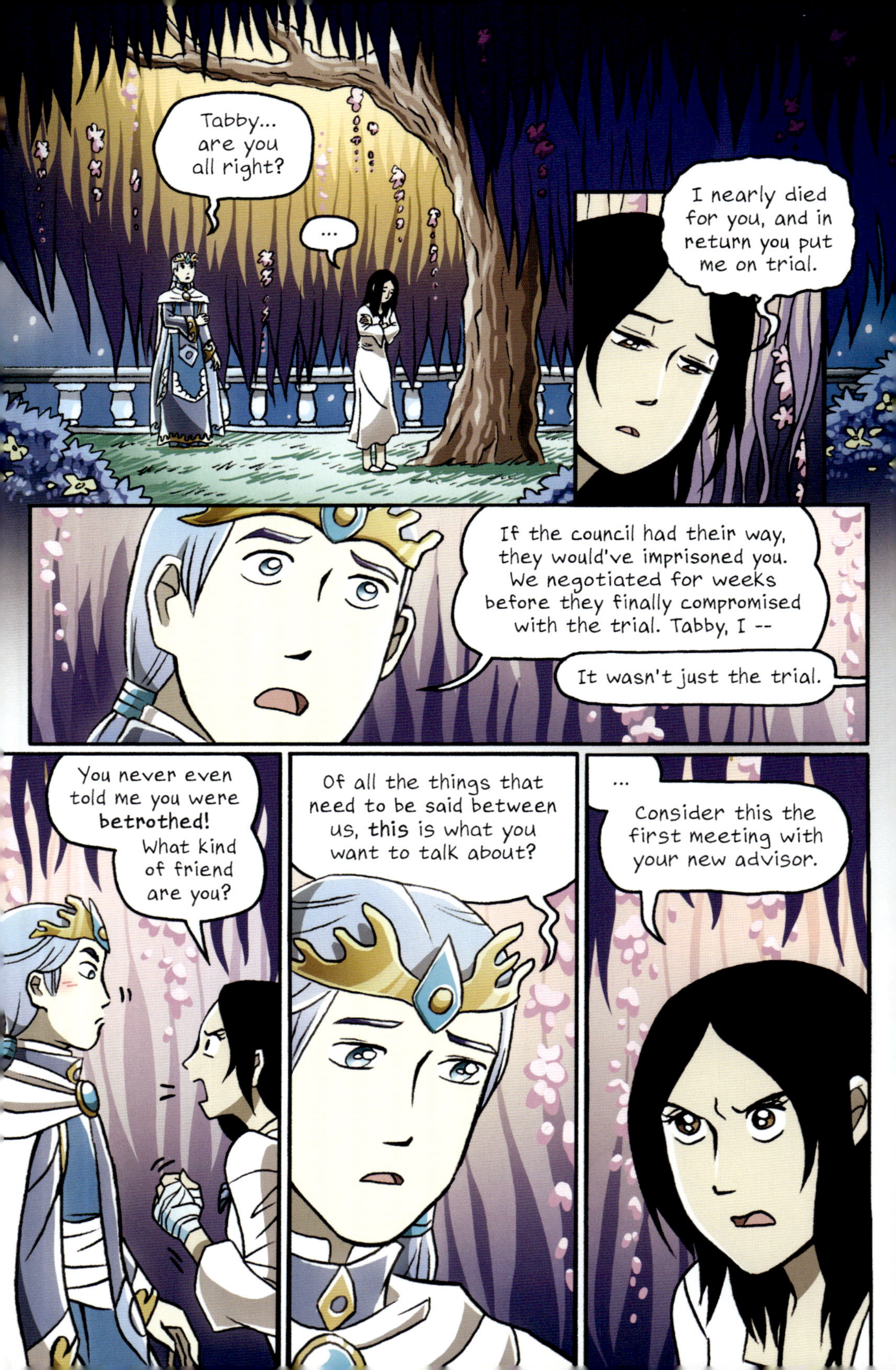
Tabby... are you all right?
...
I nearly died for you, and in return you put me on trial.
If the council had their way, they would've imprisoned you. We negotiated for weeks before they finally compromised with the trial. Tabby, I --
It wasn't just the trial.
You never even told me you were **betrothed!**
What kind of friend are you?
Of all the things that need to be said between us, **this** is what you want to talk about?
...
Consider this the first meeting with your new advisor.

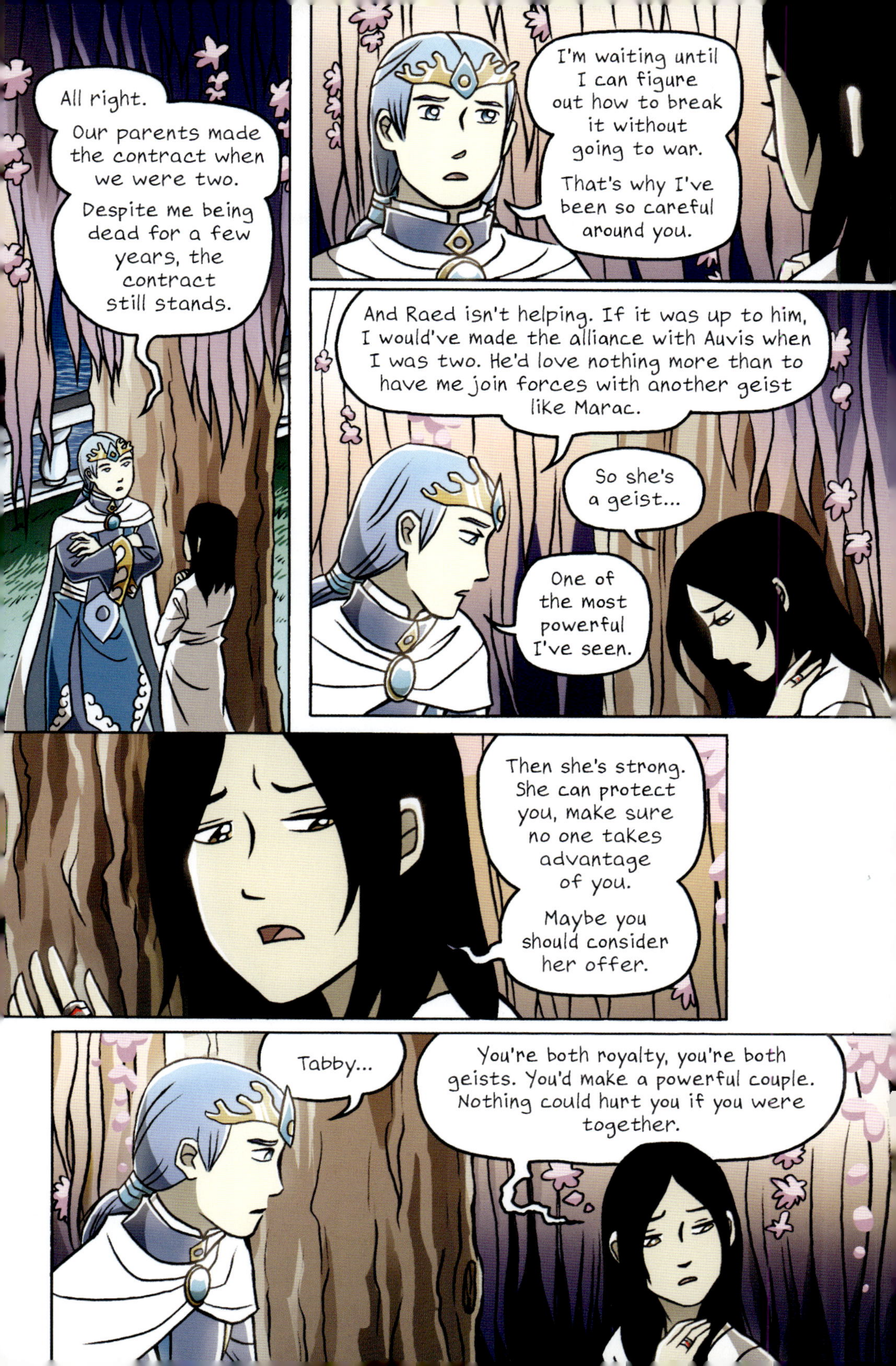
All right.
Our parents made the contract when we were two.
Despite me being dead for a few years, the contract still stands.
I'm waiting until I can figure out how to break it without going to war.
That's why I've been so careful around you.
And Raed isn't helping. If it was up to him, I would've made the alliance with Auvis when I was two. He'd love nothing more than to have me join forces with another geist like Marac.
So she's a geist...
One of the most powerful I've seen.
Then she's strong. She can protect you, make sure no one takes advantage of you.
Maybe you should consider her offer.
Tabby...
You're both royalty, you're both geists. You'd make a powerful couple. Nothing could hurt you if you were together.

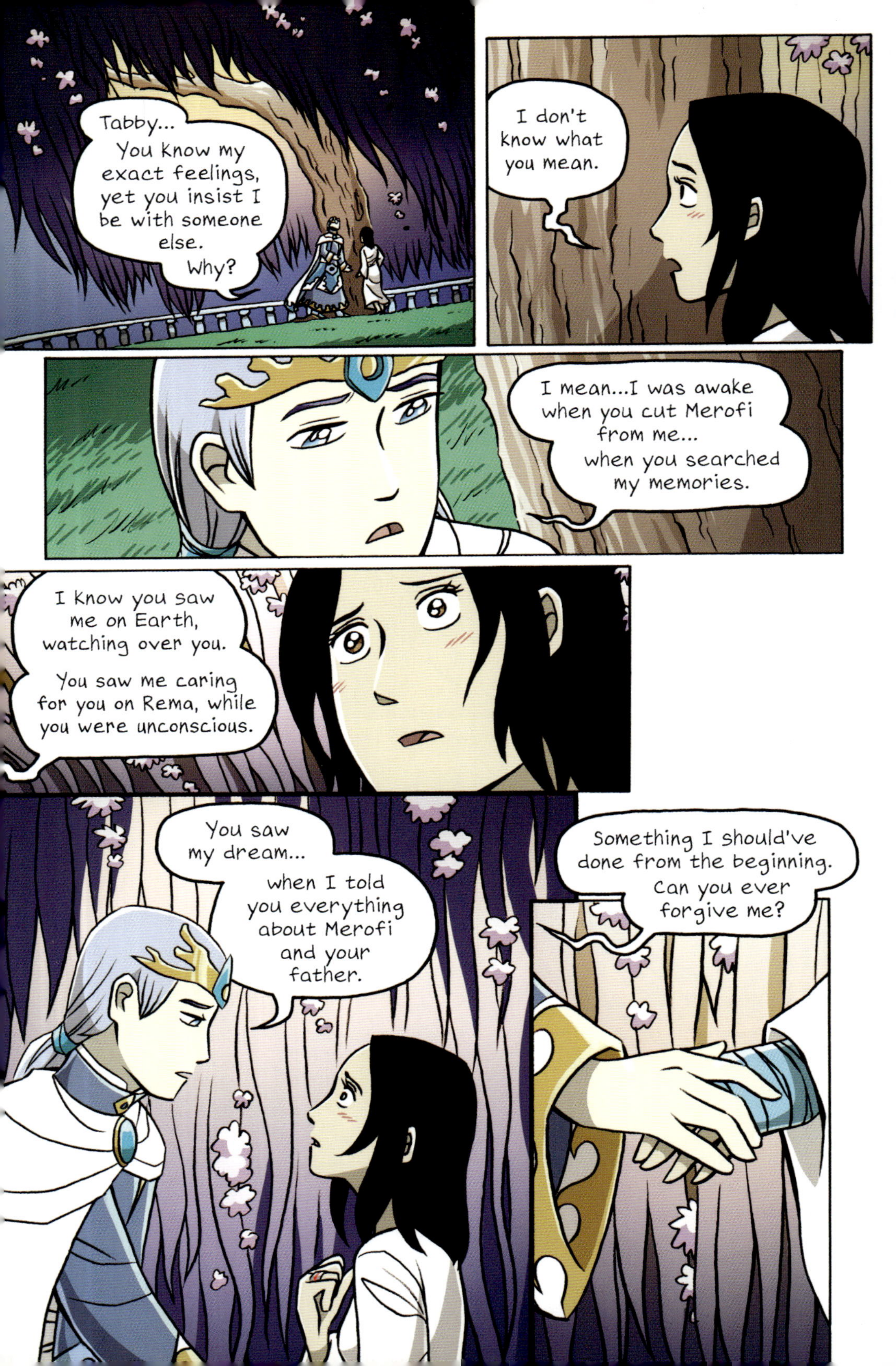
Tabby... You know my exact feelings, yet you insist I be with someone else. Why?
I don't know what you mean.
I mean...I was awake when you cut Merofi from me... when you searched my memories.
I know you saw me on Earth, watching over you.
You saw me caring for you on Rema, while you were unconscious.
You saw my dream... when I told you everything about Merofi and your father.
Something I should've done from the beginning. Can you ever forgive me?

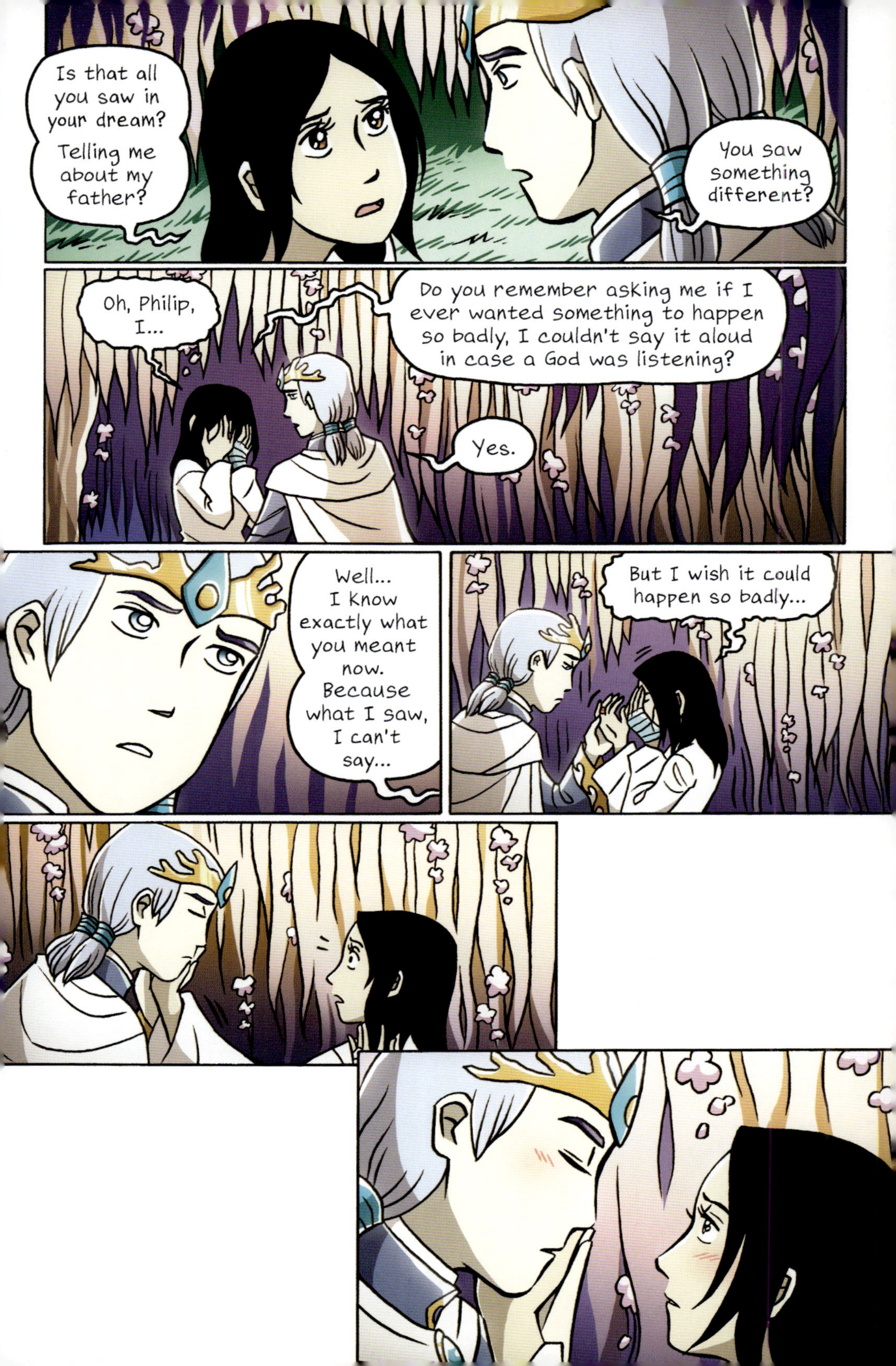
Is that all you saw in your dream? Telling me about my father?
You saw something different?
Oh, Philip, I...
Do you remember asking me if I ever wanted something to happen so badly, I couldn't say it aloud in case a God was listening?
Yes.
Well... I know exactly what you meant now. Because what I saw, I can't say...
But I wish it could happen so badly...

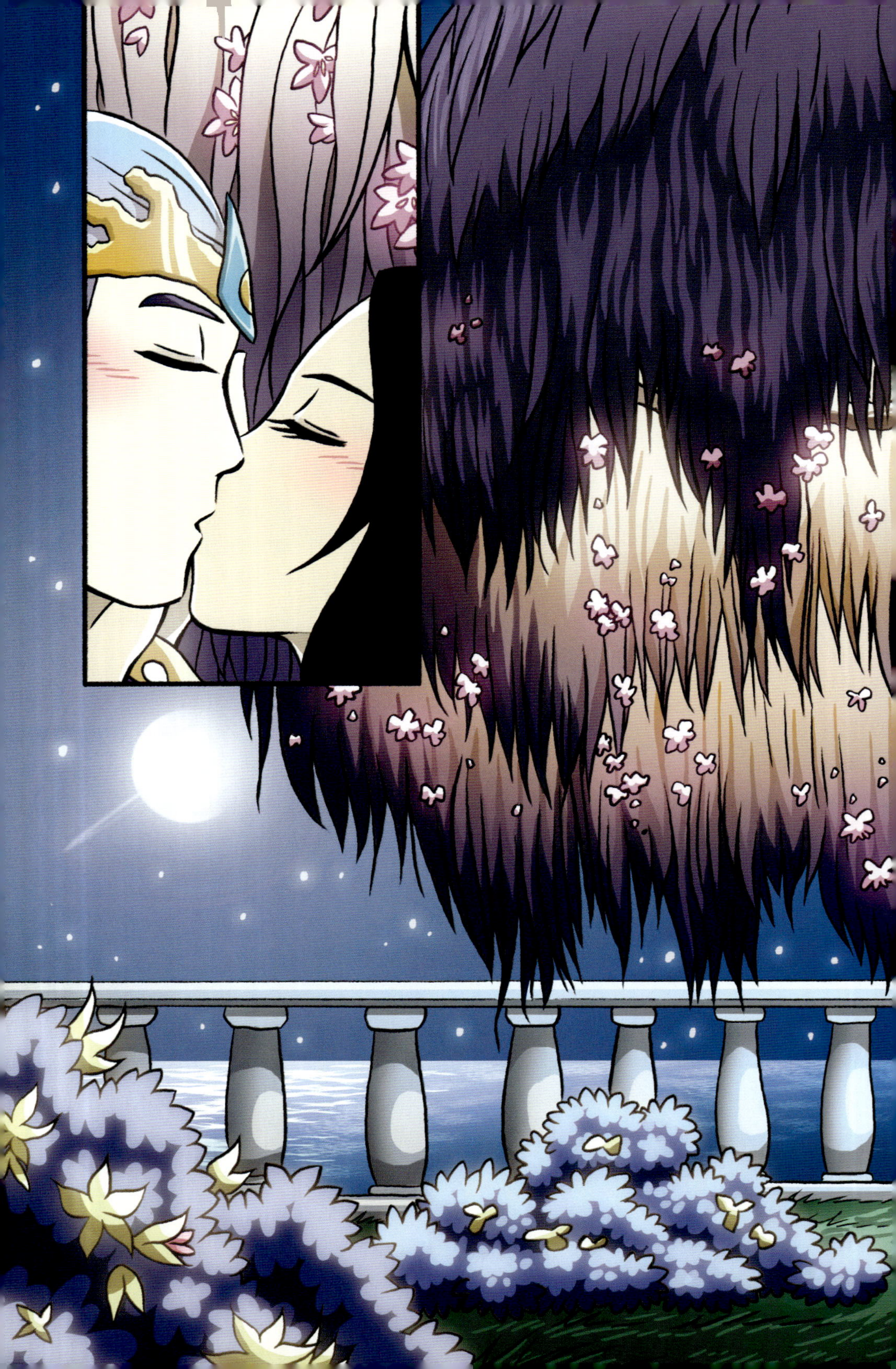

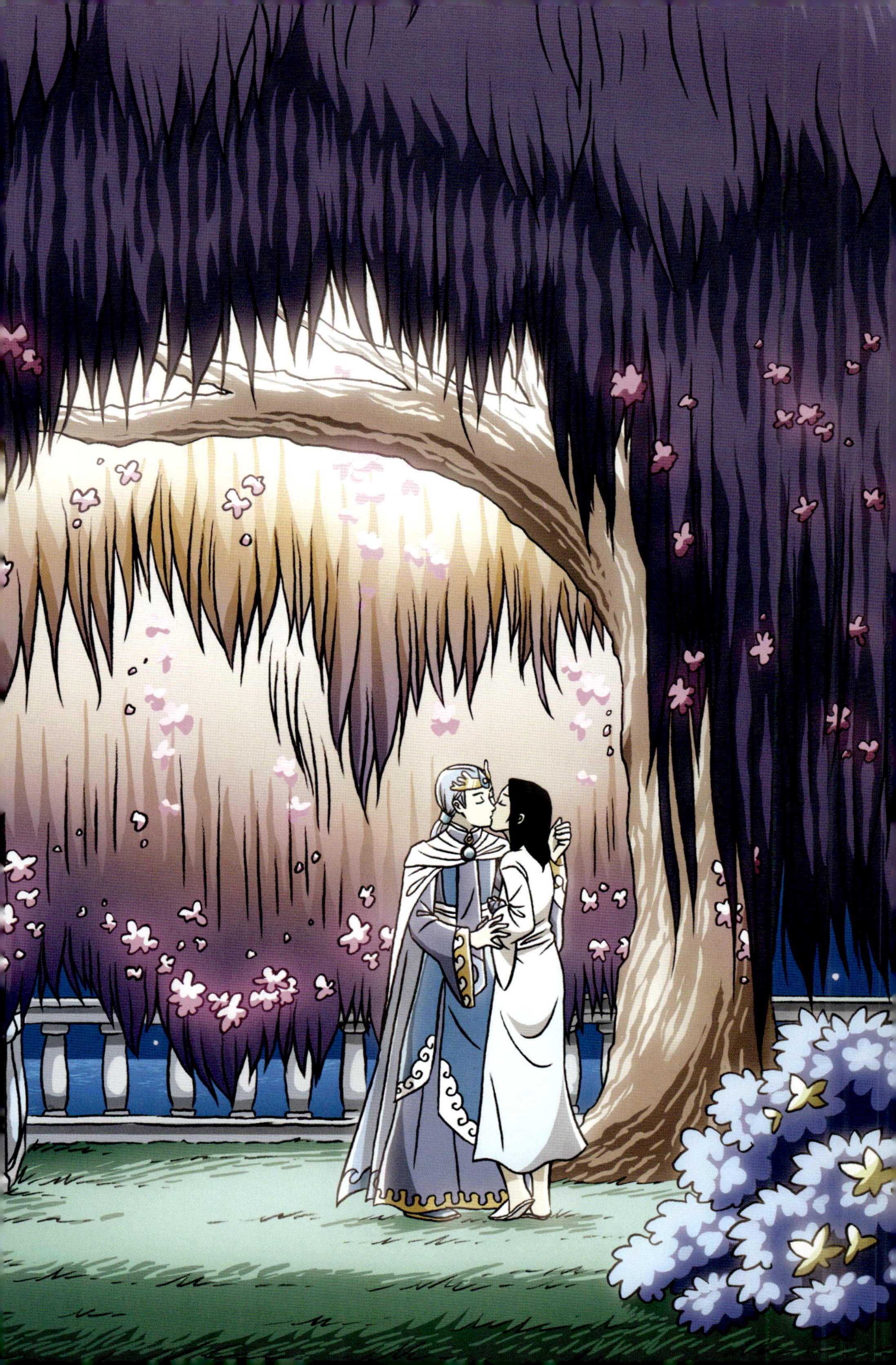

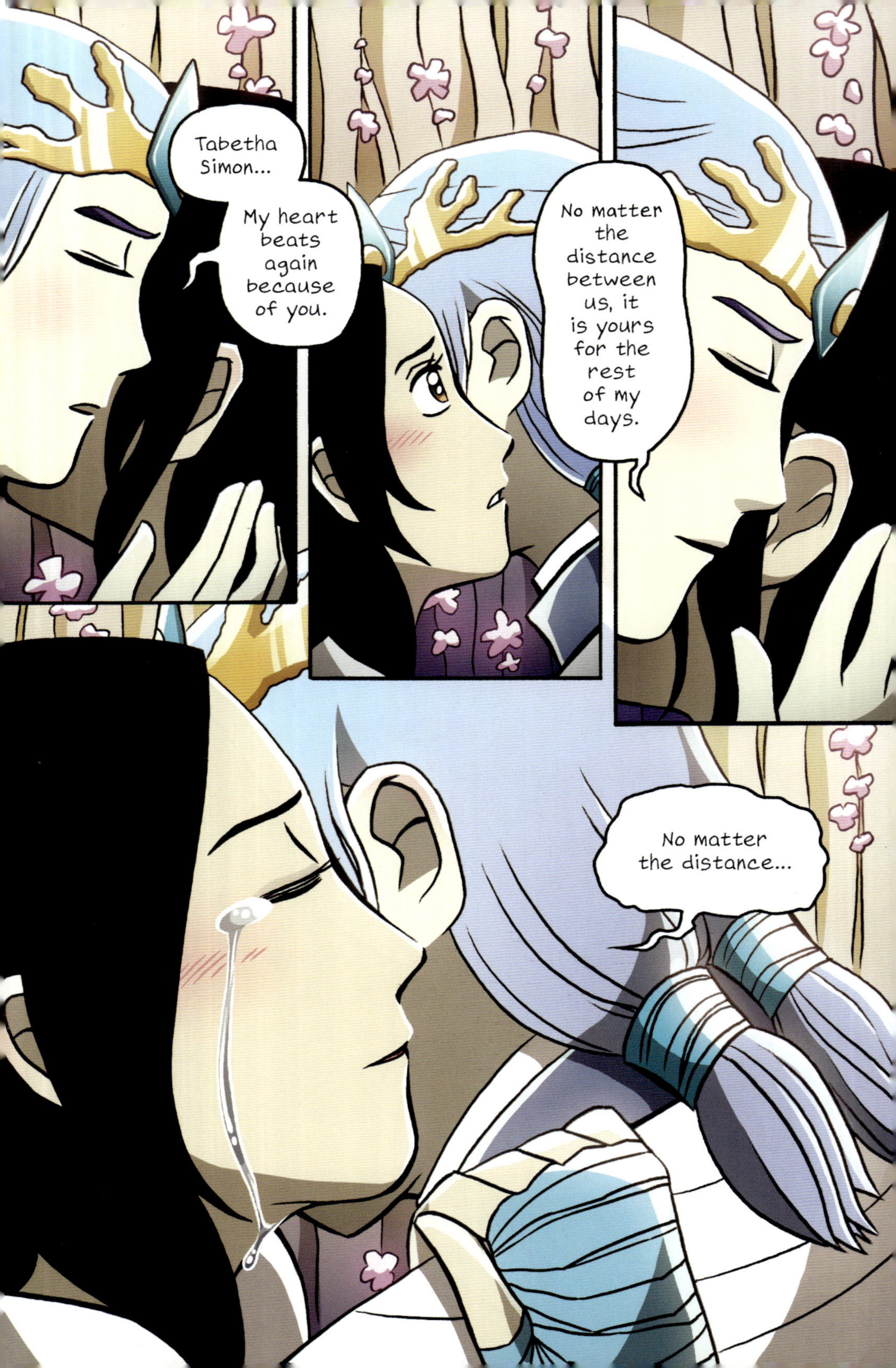
Tabetha Simon...
My heart beats again because of you.
No matter the distance between us, it is yours for the rest of my days.
No matter the distance...

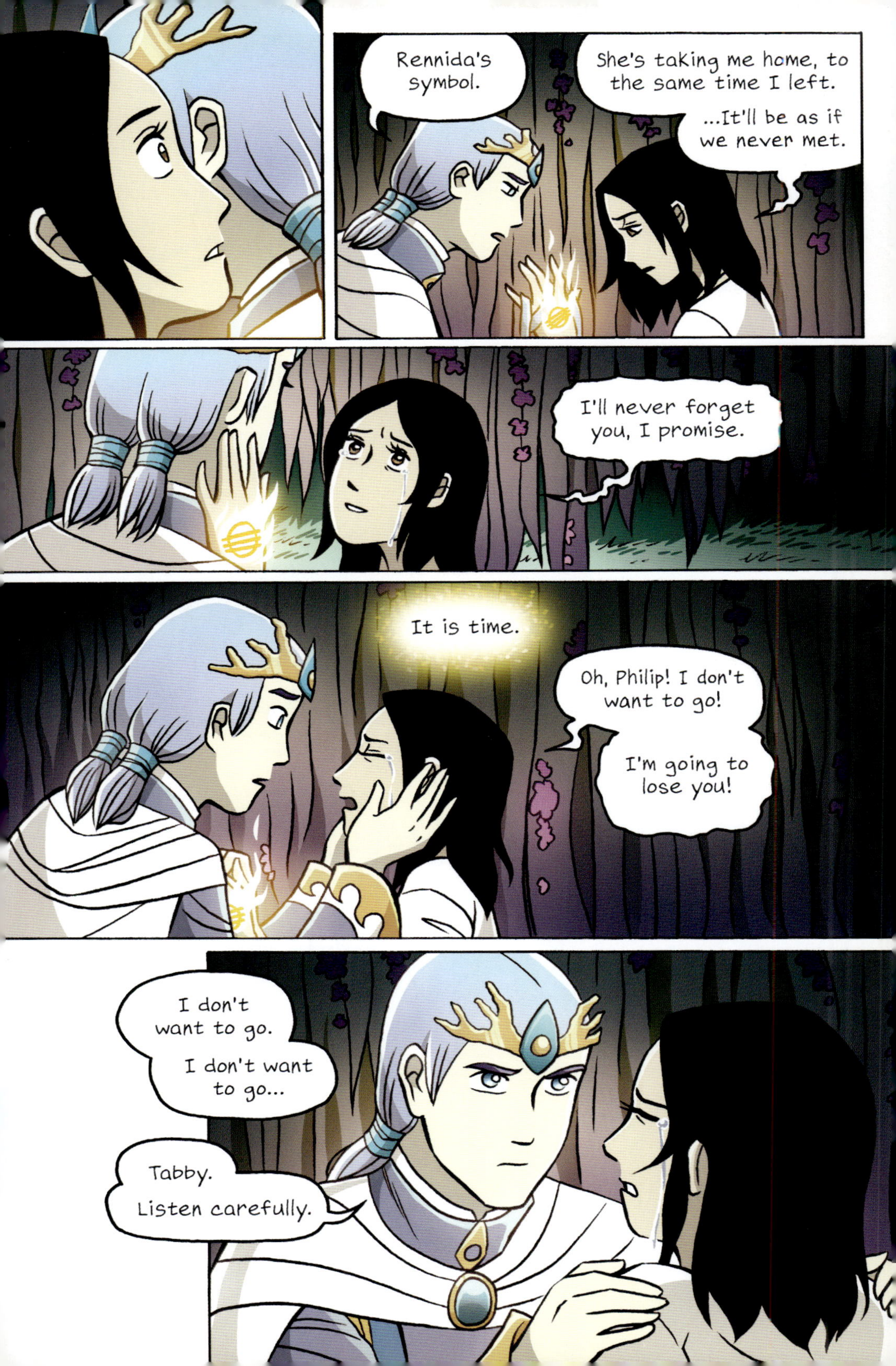
Rennida's symbol.
She's taking me home, to the same time I left.
...It'll be as if we never met.
I'll never forget you, I promise.
It is time.
Oh, Philip! I don't want to go!
I'm going to lose you!
I don't want to go.
I don't want to go...
Tabby.
Listen carefully.

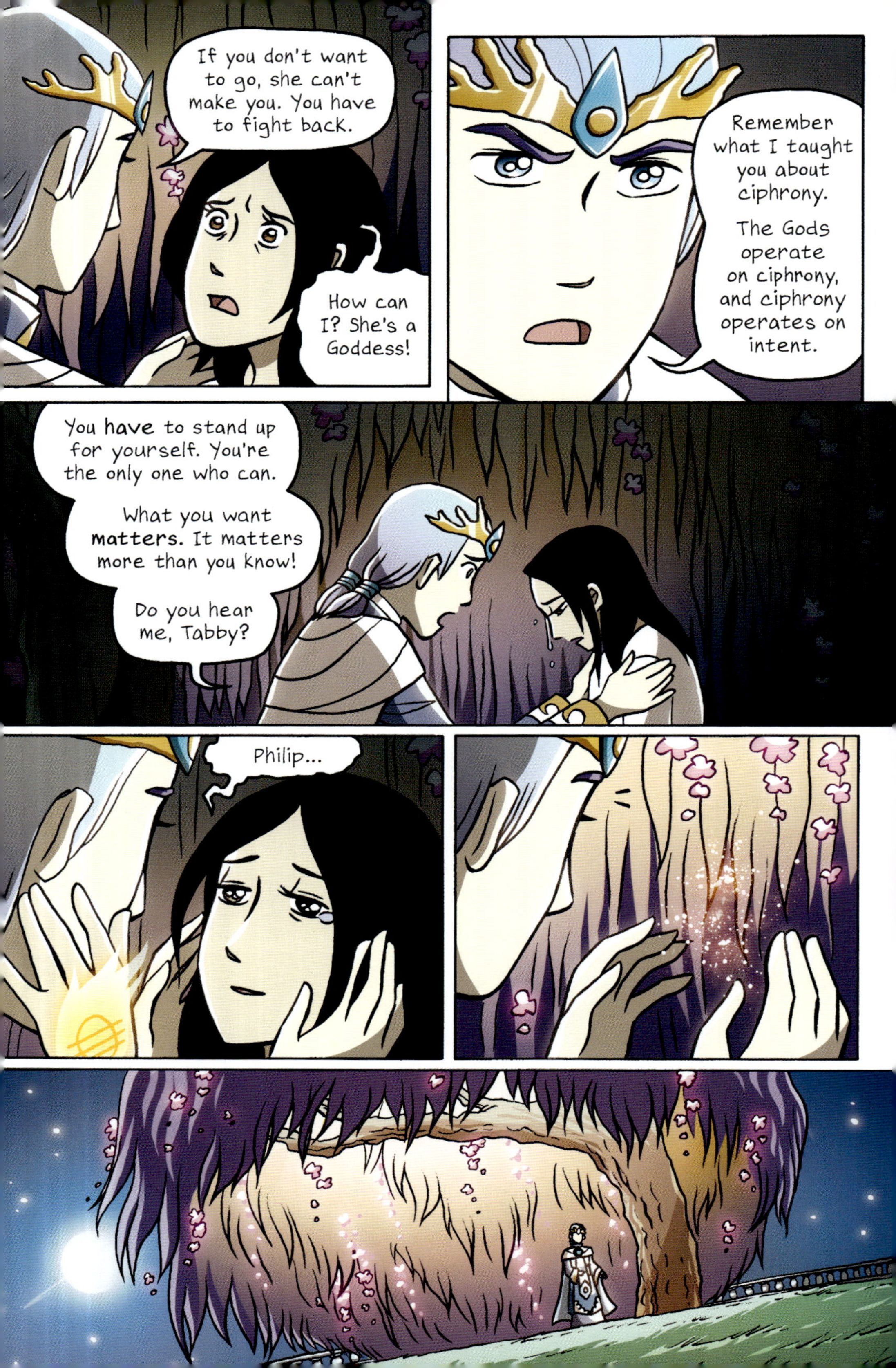
If you don't want to go, she can't make you. You have to fight back.
How can I? She's a Goddess!
Remember what I taught you about ciphrony.
The Gods operate on ciphrony, and ciphrony operates on intent.
You **have** to stand up for yourself. You're the only one who can.
What you want **matters.** It matters more than you know!
Do you hear me, Tabby?
Philip...

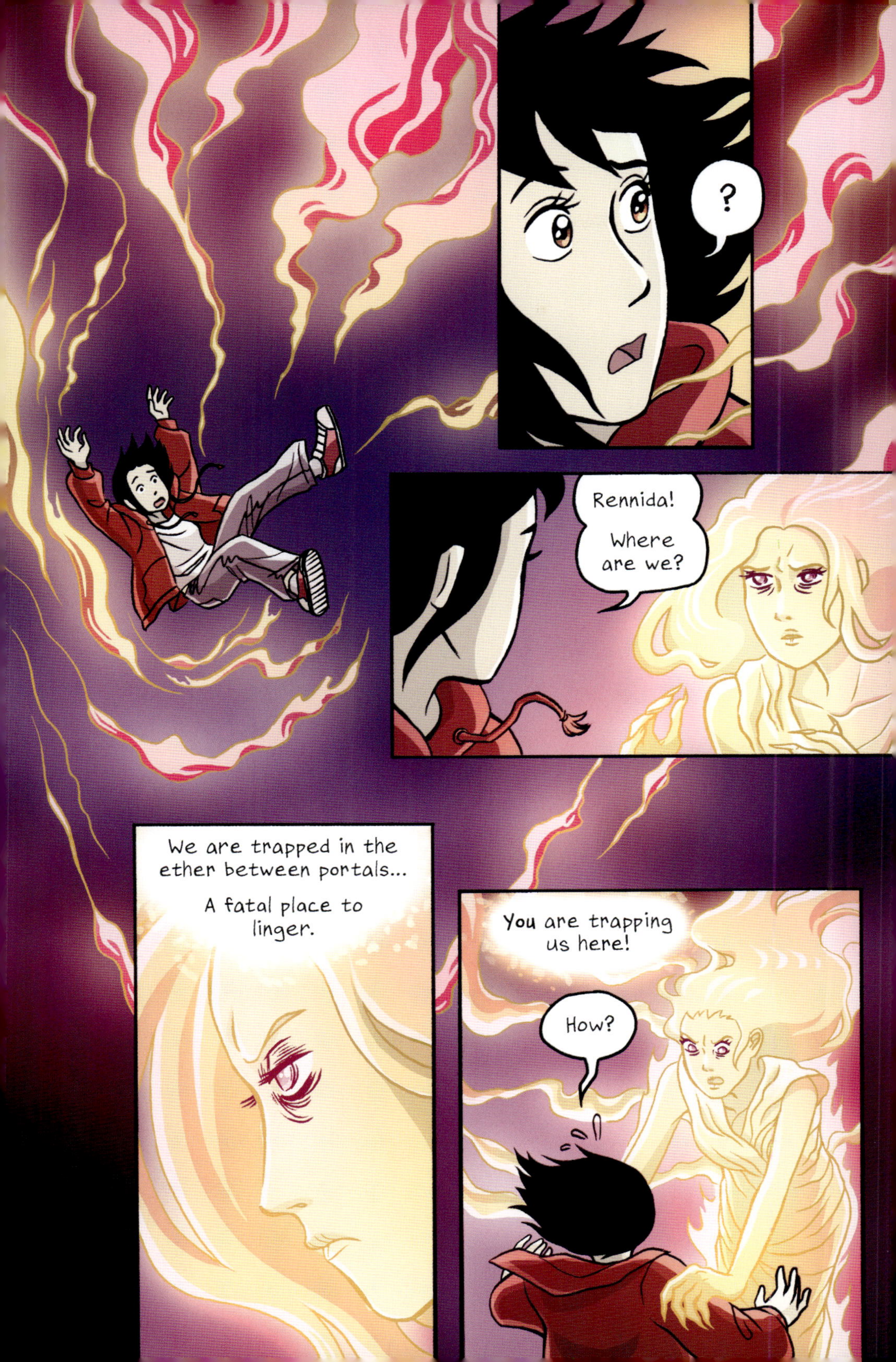
?
Rennida!
Where are we?
We are trapped in the ether between portals...
A fatal place to linger.
You are trapping us here!
How?

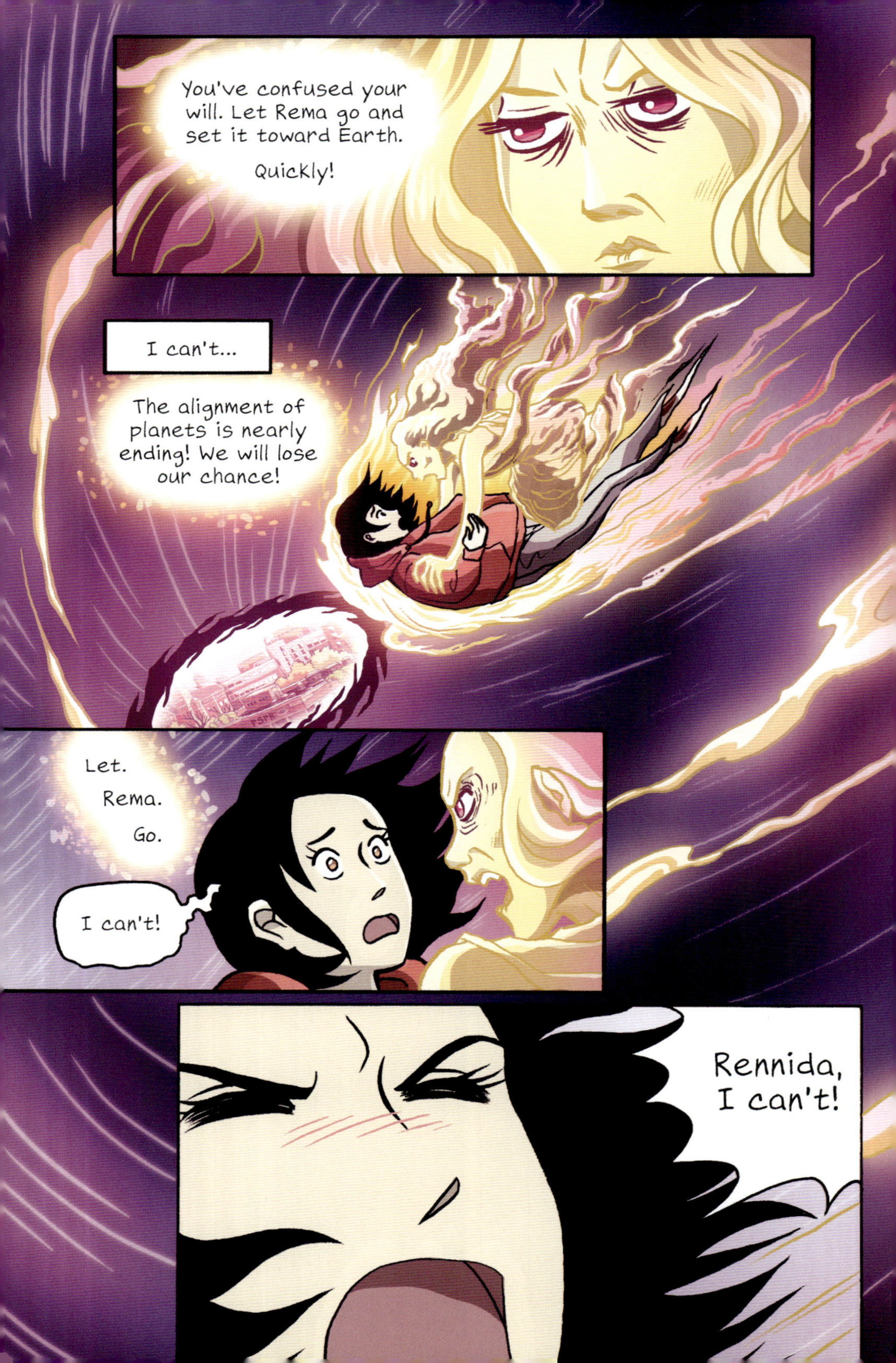
You've confused your will. Let Rema go and set it toward Earth.
Quickly!
I can't...
The alignment of planets is nearly ending! We will lose our chance!
Let.
Rema.
Go.
I can't!
Rennida, I can't!

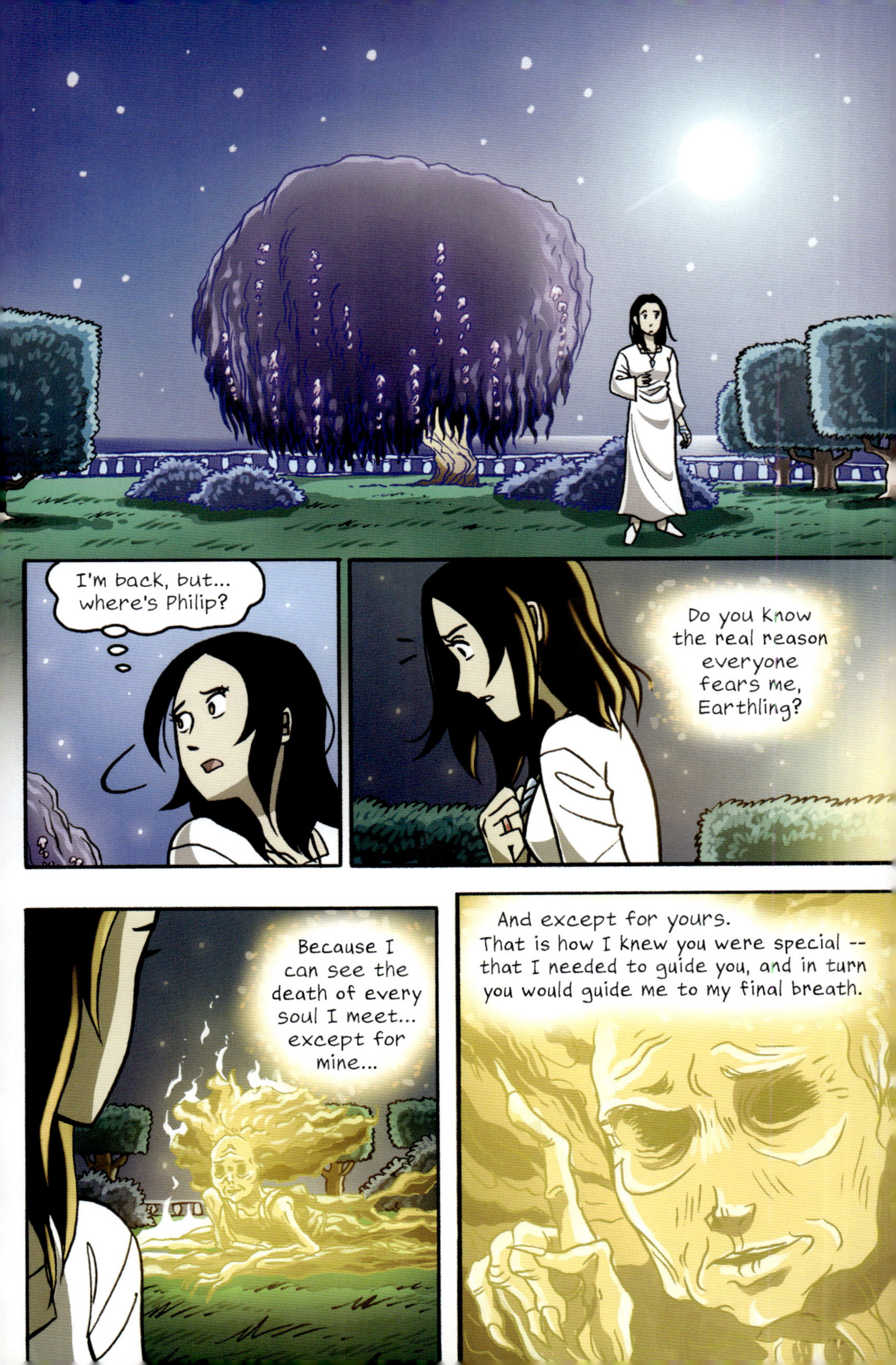
I'm back, but... where's Philip?
Do you know the real reason everyone fears me, Earthling?
Because I can see the death of every soul I meet... except for mine...
And except for yours.
That is how I knew you were special -- that I needed to guide you, and in turn you would guide me to my final breath.

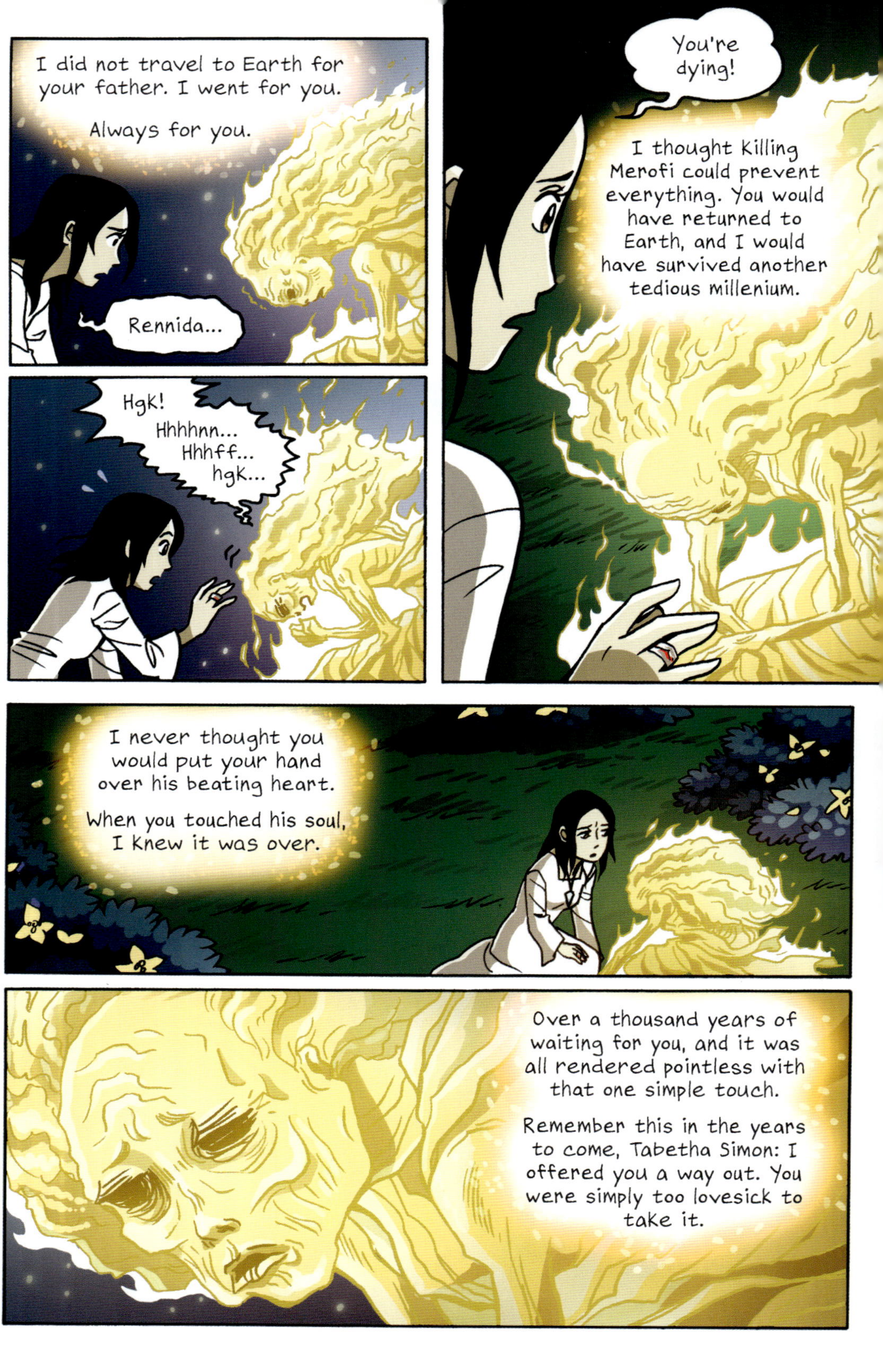
I did not travel to Earth for your father. I went for you.
Always for you.
Rennida...
Hgk!
Hhhhnn... Hhhff... hgk...
You're dying!
I thought Killing Merofi could prevent everything. You would have returned to Earth, and I would have survived another tedious millenium.
I never thought you would put your hand over his beating heart.
When you touched his soul, I Knew it was over.
Over a thousand years of waiting for you, and it was all rendered pointless with that one simple touch.
Remember this in the years to come, Tabetha Simon: I offered you a way out. You were simply too lovesick to take it.

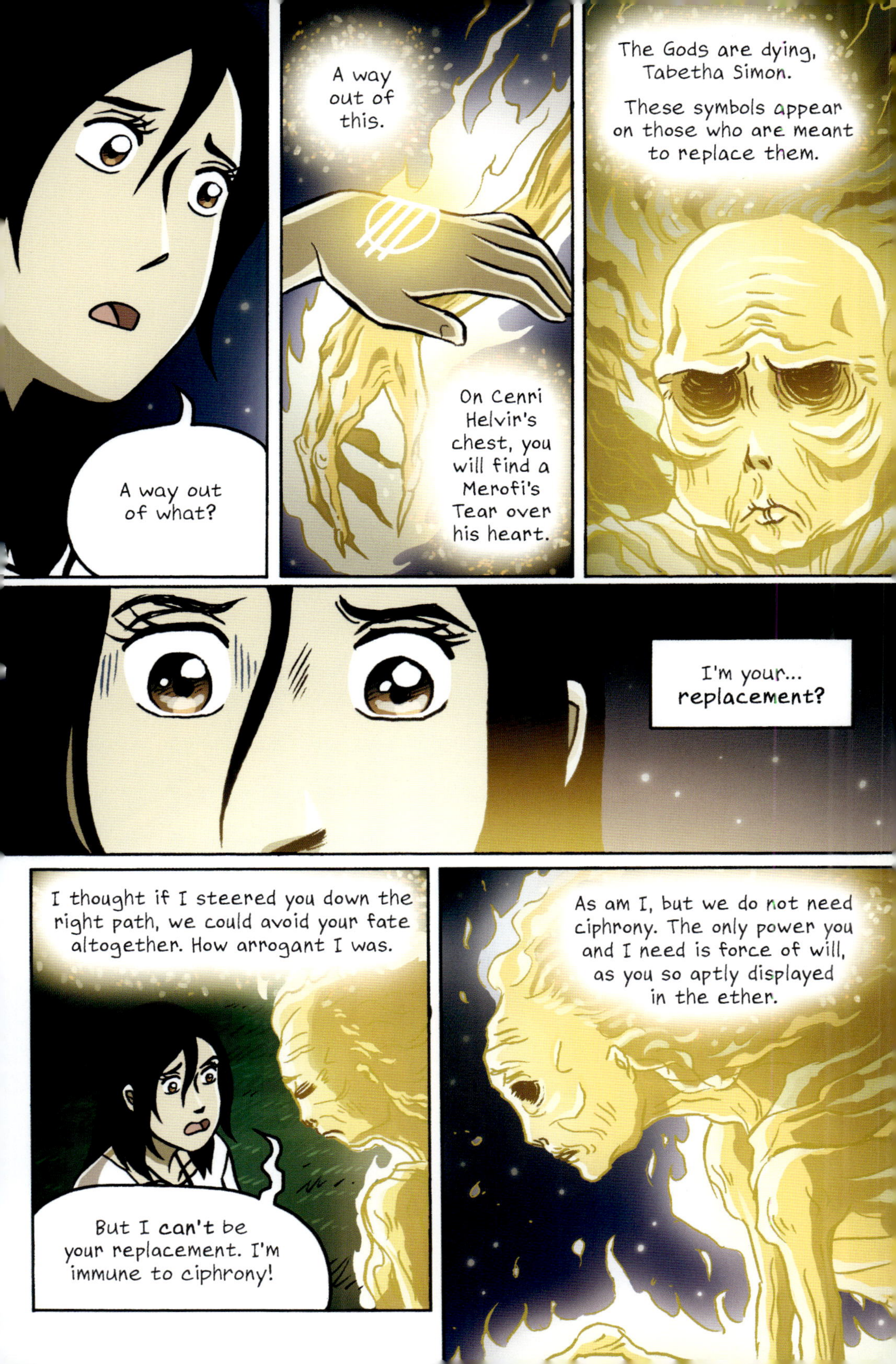
A way out of what?
A way out of this.
On Cenri Helvir's chest, you will find a Merofi's Tear over his heart.
The Gods are dying, Tabetha Simon.
These symbols appear on those who are meant to replace them.
I'm your... **replacement?**
I thought if I steered you down the right path, we could avoid your fate altogether. How arrogant I was.
But I **can't** be your replacement. I'm immune to ciphrony!
As am I, but we do not need ciphrony. The only power you and I need is force of will, as you so aptly displayed in the ether.

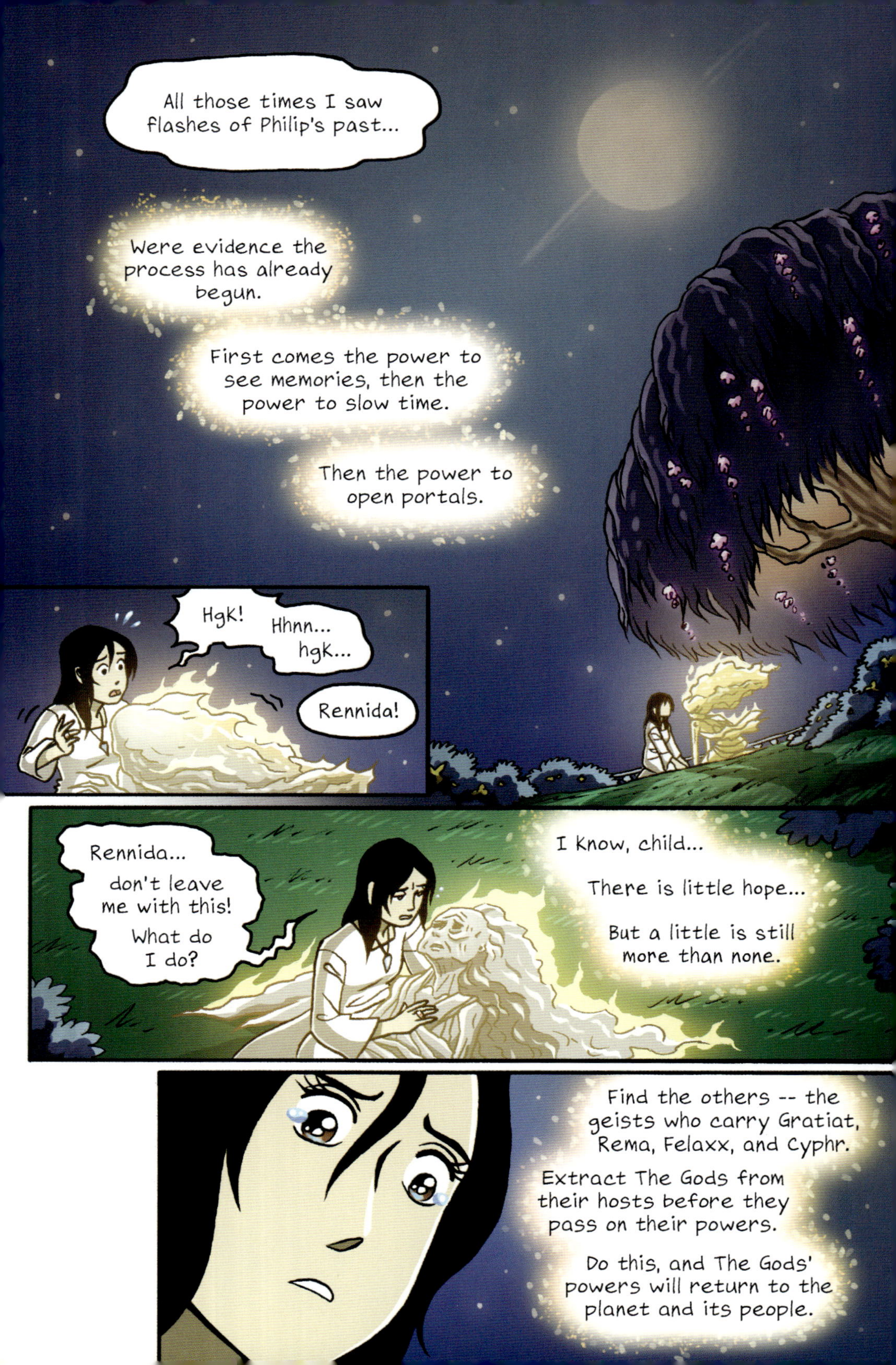
All those times I saw flashes of Philip's past...
Were evidence the process has already begun.
First comes the power to see memories, then the power to slow time.
Then the power to open portals.
Hgk!
Hhnn... hgk...
Rennida!
Rennida... don't leave me with this! What do I do?
I know, child...
There is little hope...
But a little is still more than none.
Find the others -- the geists who carry Gratiat, Rema, Felaxx, and Cyphr.
Extract The Gods from their hosts before they pass on their powers.
Do this, and The Gods' powers will return to the planet and its people.

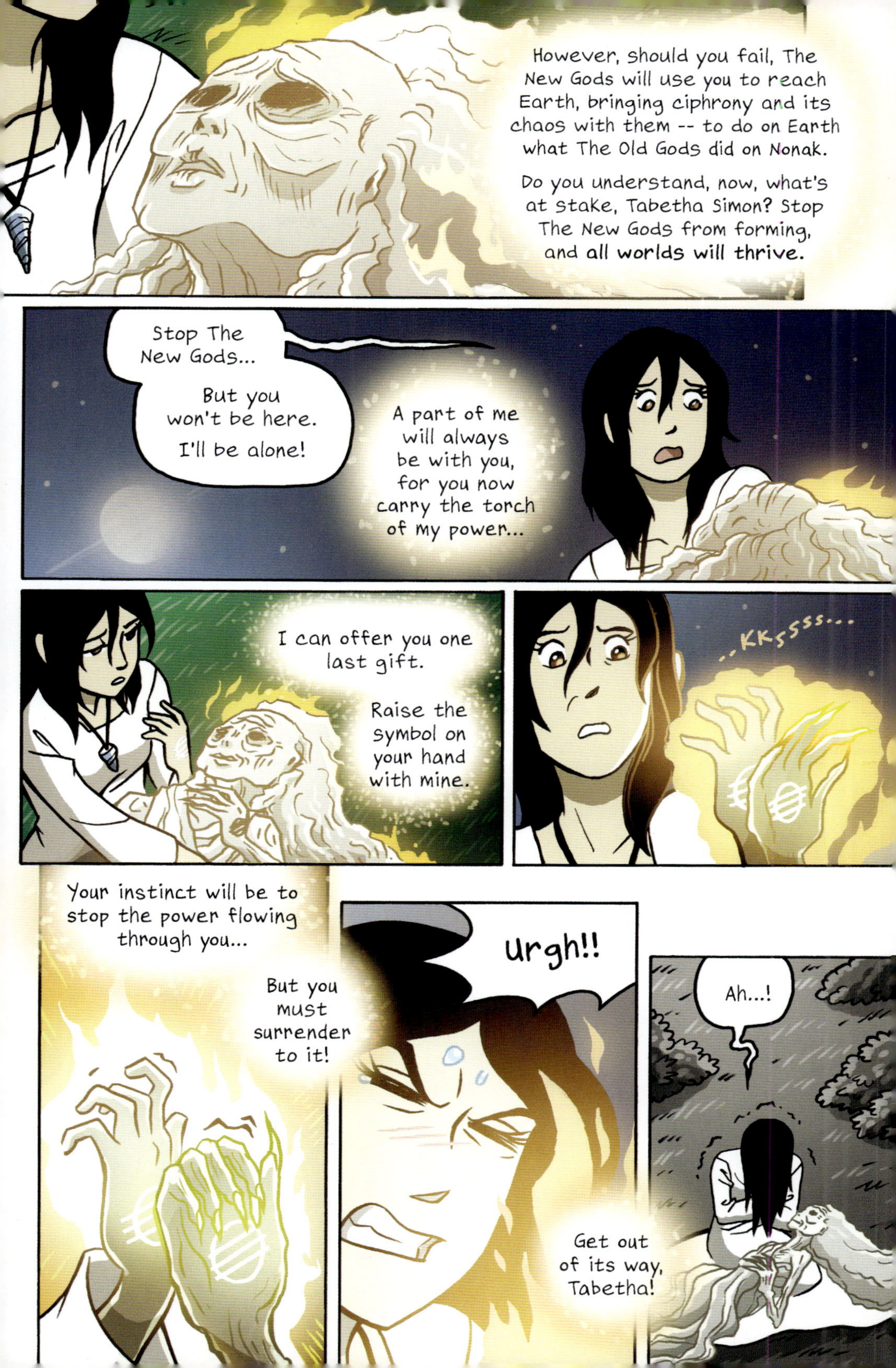
However, should you fail, The New Gods will use you to reach Earth, bringing ciphrony and its chaos with them -- to do on Earth what The Old Gods did on Nonak.
Do you understand, now, what's at stake, Tabetha Simon? Stop The New Gods from forming, and **all worlds will thrive.**
Stop The New Gods...
But you won't be here.
I'll be alone!
A part of me will always be with you, for you now carry the torch of my power...
I can offer you one last gift.
Raise the symbol on your hand with mine.
..KKSSSS...
Your instinct will be to stop the power flowing through you...
But you must surrender to it!
Urgh!!
Ah...!
Get out of its way, Tabetha!

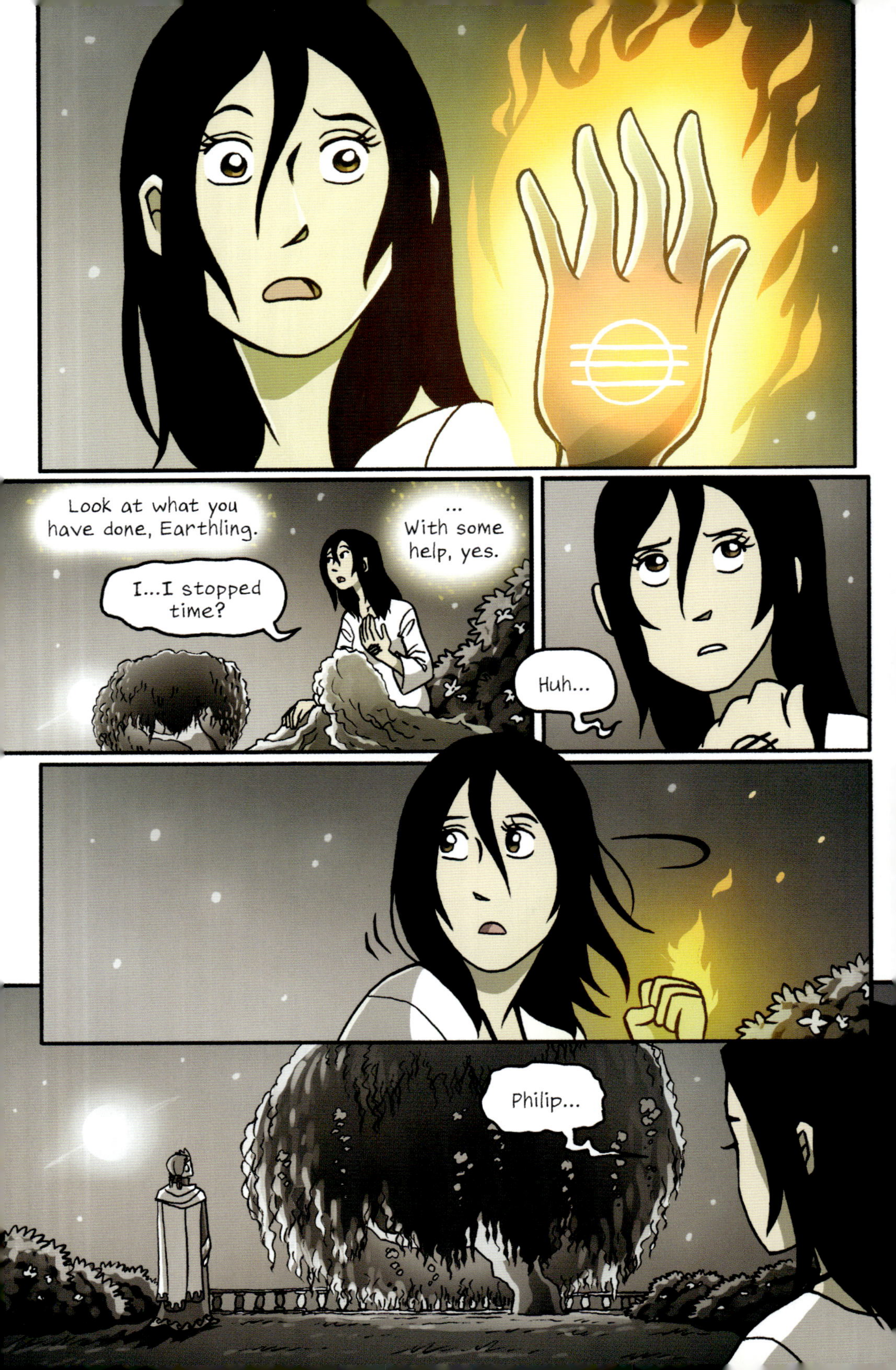

Look at what you have done, Earthling.
I...I stopped time?
... With some help, yes.
Huh...
Philip...

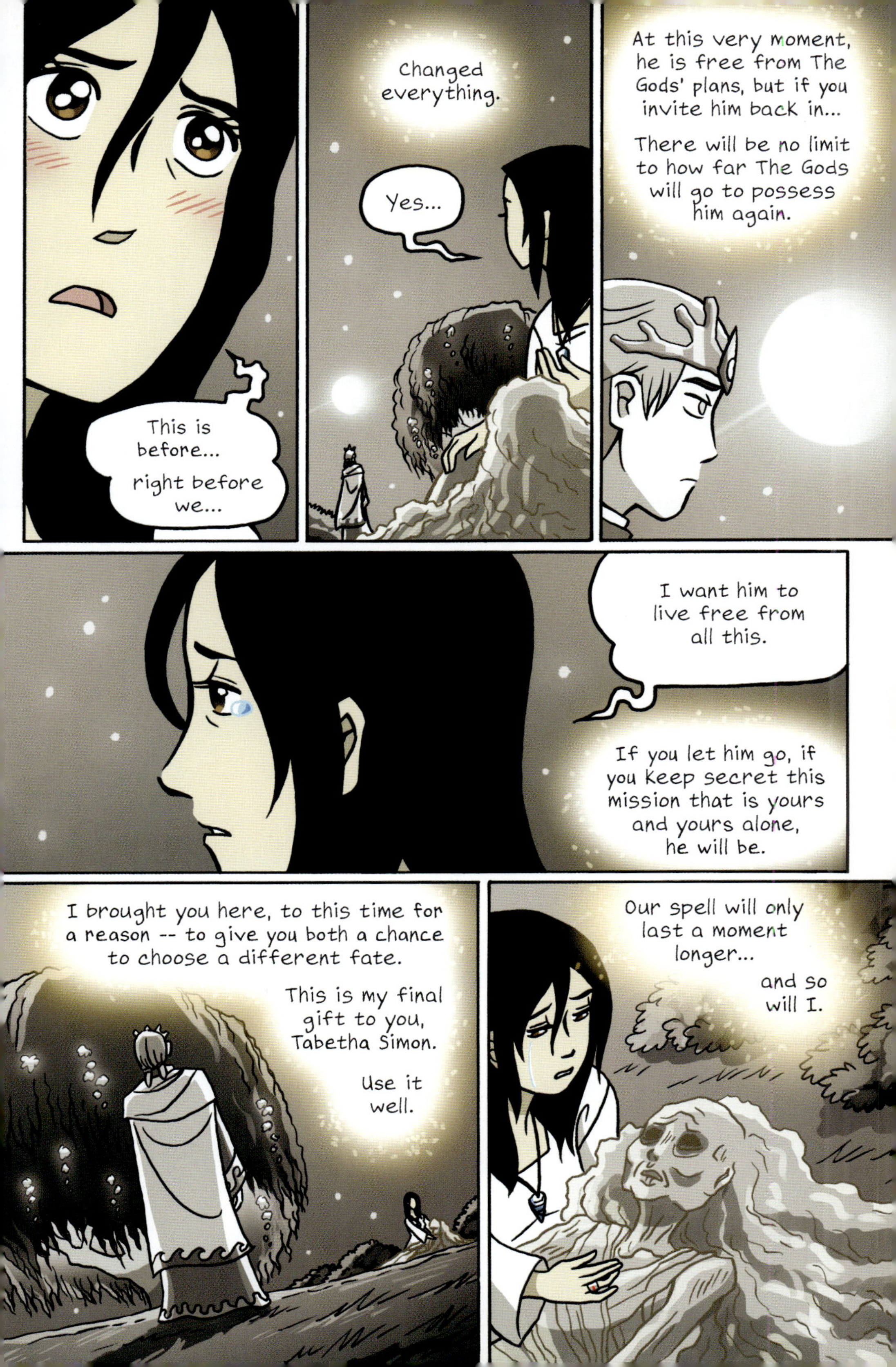
This is before... right before we...
Changed everything.
Yes...
At this very moment, he is free from The Gods' plans, but if you invite him back in...
There will be no limit to how far The Gods will go to possess him again.
I want him to live free from all this.
If you let him go, if you keep secret this mission that is yours and yours alone, he will be.
I brought you here, to this time for a reason -- to give you both a chance to choose a different fate.
This is my final gift to you, Tabetha Simon.
Use it well.
Our spell will only last a moment longer...
and so will I.

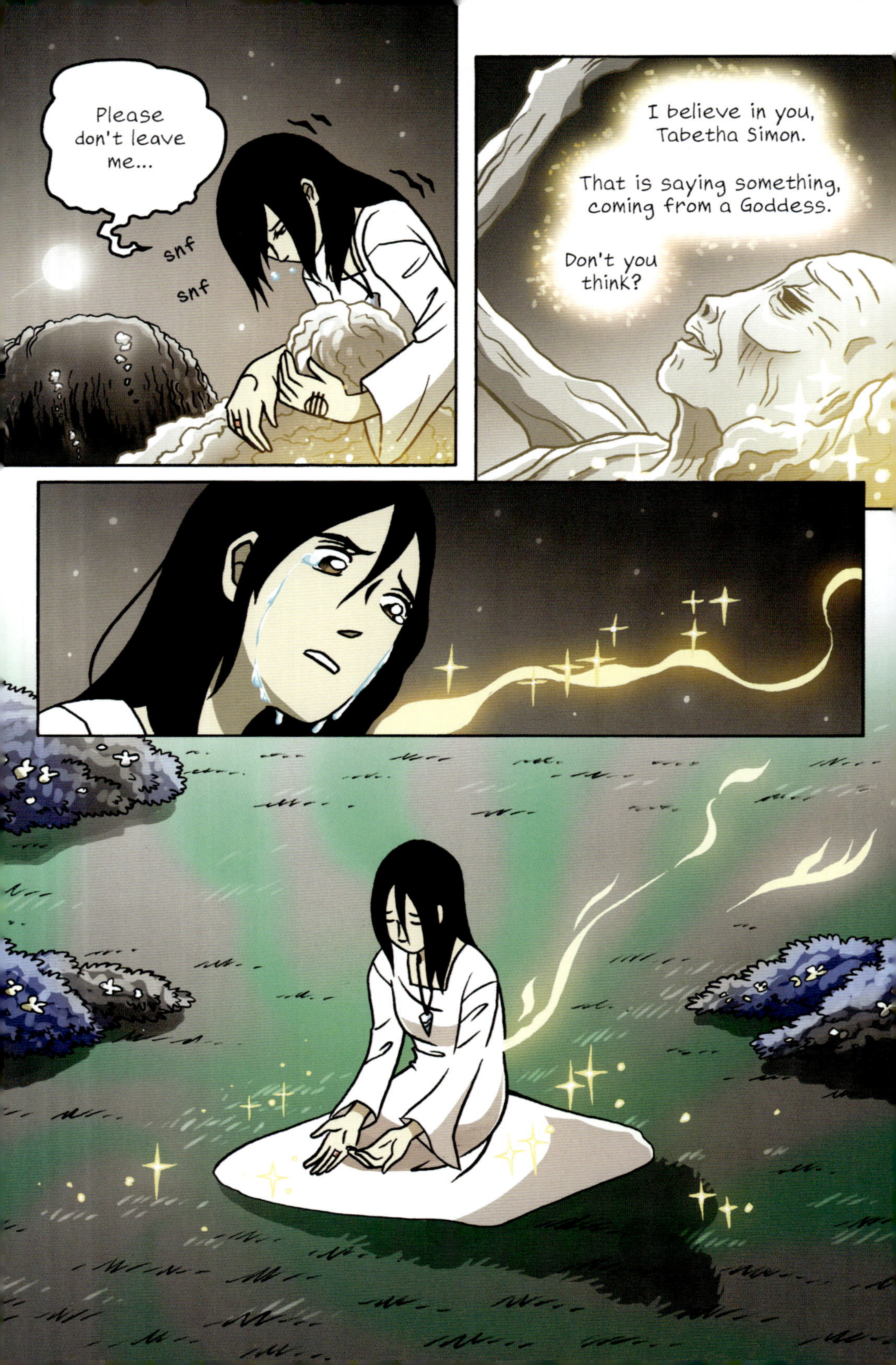
Please don't leave me...
snf
snf
I believe in you, Tabetha Simon.
That is saying something, coming from a Goddess.
Don't you think?

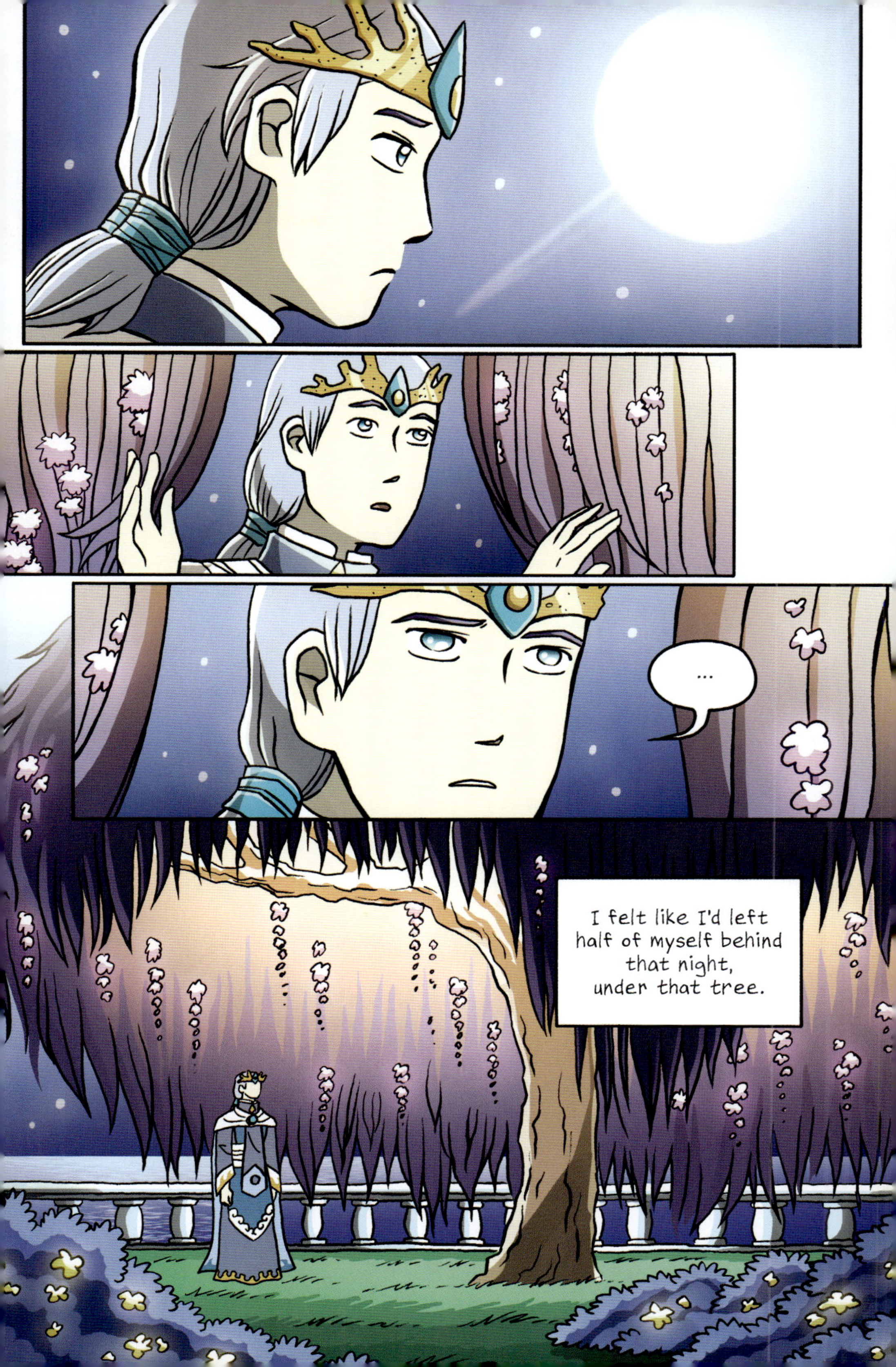
...
I felt like I'd left half of myself behind that night, under that tree.

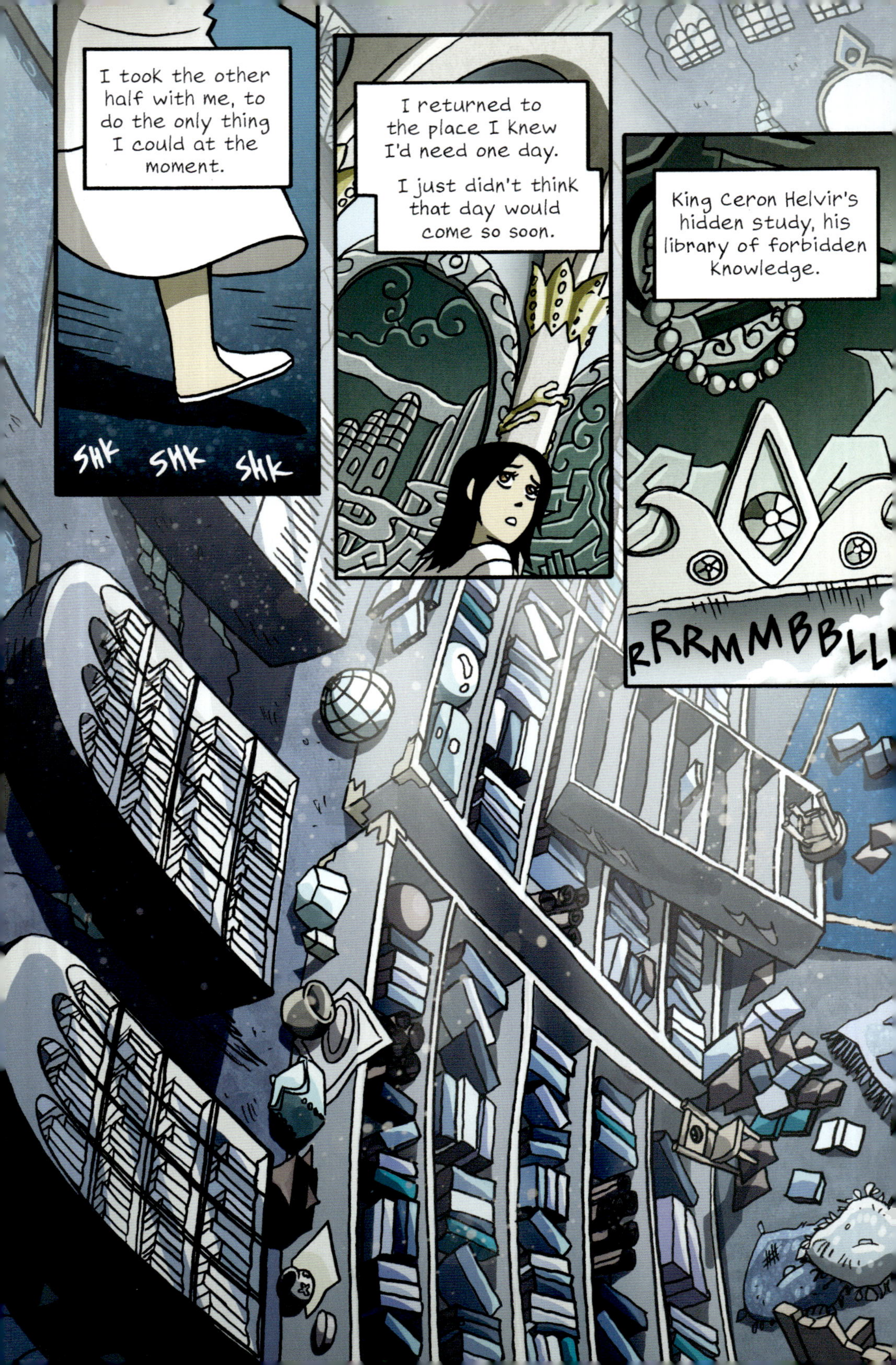
I took the other half with me, to do the only thing I could at the moment.
SHK SHK SHK
I returned to the place I knew I'd need one day.
I just didn't think that day would come so soon.
King Ceron Helvir's hidden study, his library of forbidden knowledge.
RRRMMBBLL

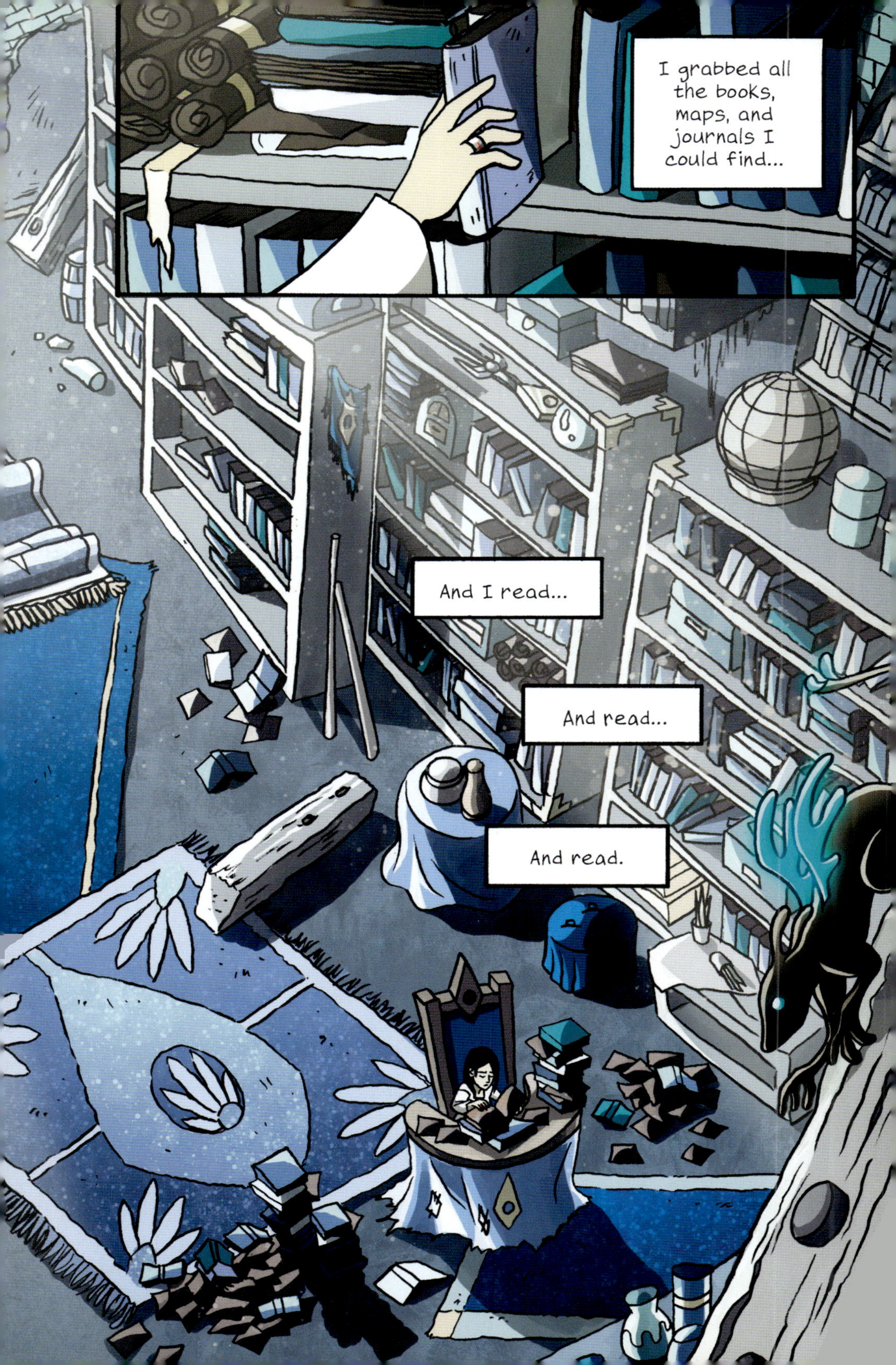
I grabbed all the books, maps, and journals I could find...
And I read...
And read...
And read.

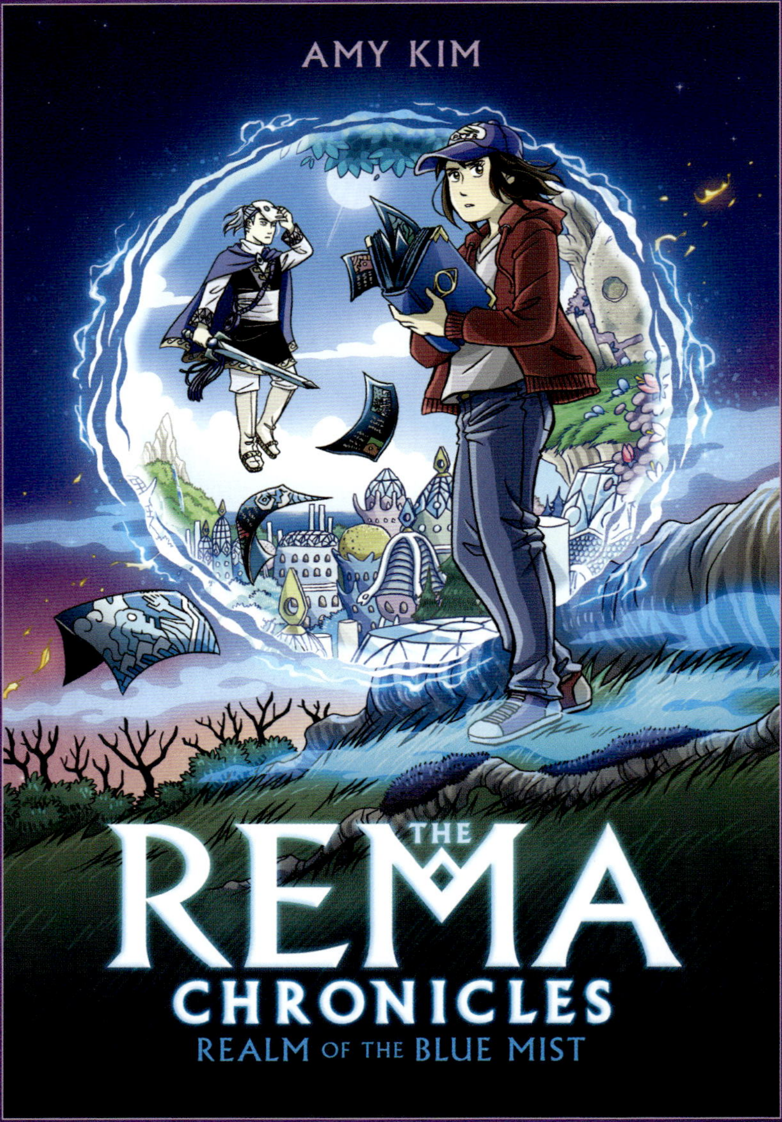
AMY KIM
THE REMA CHRONICLES
REALM OF THE BLUE MIST